SCOTT M. SWAINE

FORGOTTEN MASTERS VIII

IRONY OF FATE

Primix Publishing
East Brunswick Office Evolution
1 Tower Center Boulevard, Ste 1510
East Brunswick, NJ 08816
www.primixpublishing.com
Phone: 1-800-538-5788

This is a work of fiction. Names, characters, places, and incidents either are the product of the author's imagination or are used fictitiously, and any resemblance to any persons, living or dead, is entirely coincidental.

Published by Primix Publishing: 12/20/2024

ISBN: 979-8-89194-172-4(sc)
ISBN: 979-8-89194-260-8(hc)
ISBN: 979-8-89194-173-1(e)

Library of Congress Control Number: 2024907950

Because of the dynamic nature of the Internet, any web addresses or links contained in this book may have changed since publication and may no longer be valid. The views expressed in this work are solely those of the author and do not necessarily reflect the views of the publisher, and the publisher hereby disclaims any responsibility for them.

CONTENTS

We are the Mind of the Enlightened.
We are the Thunder of the Stampede.
The Arm of Justice, the Voice of Virtue,
The Wardens of the Righteous,
And the Stewards of the Undaunted.
We are the Stormhooves!

Mantra of the Stormhooves

Chapter 1

ESTABLISHMENT

It was the beginning of a new business day on Azgarén, when a neatly attired young woman was making a visit to the downtown office of C.P. Security in the city of Capitol Prime. She was dressed in a formal suit, which included a white shirt and dark blue pants, a matching jacket, and black ankle socks. The style was typical of a professional Suuden'kai businesswoman in a high-level office position, but the color selection and prim arrangement signified someone in a serious line of work.

Ayene knew this office well. She used to work here when she was serving her old administrative position as a security and law enforcement officer. This was before she transferred to her military role, but she still held several relations with the other officers here, especially her former boss, and so she was well-respected amongst her peers. This was good, as she would need this in order to pull a few strings.

She entered the double doors into the lobby and marched up to the registration desk. The girl behind the counter looked up at her and offered the standard greeting.

"Welcome to C.P. Security," she announces in the classic monotone. "How can I help you?"

"You must be new here," Ayene submits casually. "I don't remember you from the last time I visited. I used to work here before I signed up for Central Command. I'm here to speak with Captain Bein'talan. Is he still working here?"

"Yes, he is. Do you have an appointment?"

"Actually, no, but this is an important occasion. I have an urgent need to speak with him in relation to my current duties."

"I see, and this relates to Central Command?"

"Indirectly, yes. I'm currently assigned to a new top-secret government department. We have a need to interface ourselves with the local security offices as part of our operations. I'm starting here since I held a previous relationship with the Captain."

"A new top-secret department?" she muses. "This is interesting. I do not recall hearing anything about that."

"I suppose that's why it's described as top-secret," Ayene smirks discreetly. "It's not intended to be openly publicized. So far, we're conducting a number of highly sensitive investigations, some of them at the government level. This is not the sort of thing you want to have broadcast to the world at this point in time."

"Government investigations of government officials..." she frowns faintly. "That sounds serious. May I ask who it is you are investigating?"

"Unfortunately, the nature of our investigation demands us to keep this under wraps until we can find our conclusions...you know, to protect those who might otherwise be innocent. Also, this same activity might invoke one or more scandalous sensations. Those individuals who might be guilty need to be caught, not given a chance for escape or take any form of retaliation."

"Retaliation! Just a moment, how would they possibly retaliate? This sounds like it is more than a simple investigation."

"It is, and thus the formation of our new department. We are a new security agency given high-level authority that supersedes the traditional law enforcement and government policymaking. We serve the letter of the law, regardless of who is on the other side, and this includes the Council itself."

The secretary drew back in her chair at the statement. She glanced around the lobby briefly, but the area was currently clear of any other officers passing through.

"Does this investigation concern any of the councilmembers we have now?" she asks.

"Yes, but it is not limited to them. We also have our eyes on certain top-ranking military officers, and a number of others who are apparently working for the Council illegally. We are also watching the Marshal and his activities."

"The Marshal?" she gasps. "In all the nether-space, what has he done?"

"You don't want to know, and this is the reason I need to speak with the Captain. We need his cooperation, and that of the other law enforcement agencies, to bring them into the loop in order to consolidate our position and take action when the time is right."

"You do not have your own service for this?"

"Ours is mostly investigational at this time. We would still make use of the traditional courts, and we feel it is simply natural to apply the existing security forces, as they already have a functioning service in operation."

"Oh. Well, yes, I see."

"Of course! This, along with their associated facilities to detain and prosecute these people. Therefore, once we pinpoint them, we will call the regular security services to do the work for us, since they have an established portfolio of facilities and procedures for the physical side of law enforcement. We will provide the evidence, and the standard practice of law will handle the rest."

"Naturally, and this does make sense. Well, I believe the Captain is in his office. Do you know where that is?"

"Yes, I do. Thank you."

Ayene turns and strolls out of the lobby along one of the corridors, passing several offices until she comes to the one for the station Captain. She knocks gently before entering. Once inside, she finds a middle-aged man sitting behind his desk reviewing several status reports on his data terminal. He looks up to meet his visitor and instantly recognizes her face.

"Lieutenant Ti'van! I have not seen you for a long time. How have you been? Did that special assignment work out well for you?"

Ayene stepped forward, closing the door behind her. She approaches one of the chairs by the desk and leans on it as she makes her greeting.

"I am quite well, Captain, thank you. And I suppose you could say that assignment had its ups and downs, but ultimately, I'm in a good place now. What about you? Is the city security still in good hands, or have you fallen asleep on the job again?"

"Again?" he raises his brow at the curious attempt at humor. "You seem rather perky today. What is the special occasion for the visit?"

"Well, Captain, other than simply to say hello, which I am certainly happy to do, my department has a need for your service, but it has to be discreet, and it has to be kept under a tight security profile."

"Really. What is it Central has for us this time?"

Ayene pulls the chair out and takes a seat, drawing it up close to the desk so she could lean in for a private chat. The Captain took notice of this odd behavior, so he pulled in as well.

"Captain," she begins. "Listen carefully. I'm not working for Central at this time. Instead, I'm part of a classified operation. Technically speaking, I was never here."

"Never here...as if to say, this new project of yours is highly sensitive?"

"Well, yes. But more importantly, as if to say, Central Command believes me to be dead."

The Captain instantly jerks back as he glares at her for the audacious statement.

"Then how do we explain the fact that you are clearly alive and sitting in my office?"

"We explain it as a cover-up for my true job description. Captain, I am currently working as part of a new top-secret government security department being developed, and we need to interface ourselves with the other law enforcement agencies, like this one, to consolidate and reassert our legal procedures at all levels."

"Reassert? I thought we already had that."

"No, we don't. Your biggest excitement for the day is pulling someone over for a speeding ticket, or failing to yield at a traffic light. I'm talking about conspiracies and top-level government intrigue. Our service is designed to uncover espionage, terrorism, and corruption by those people who think they are above the law, and this includes the Council, perhaps certain members of our military, and also the Marshal, who has apparently taken more than his share of authority in OUR world."

The Captain frowned sternly at the suggestion.

"All right, Lieutenant, wait. Before we go any further with this, I need to know what you are talking about. When you involve such as the Council, the military, or even the Marshal…my own feelings on him notwithstanding…I need details, especially if you are fishing for support. First of all, for whom are you working? And how does this relate to that special assignment you took once?"

"That special assignment…" she huffs. "Again, technically speaking, that assignment is not directly related to where I am now. Indirectly, perhaps. It was at a mining base the Marshal was operating illegally on a world in a completely different universe he directed our military at to pull up a mineral substance our science knew nothing about, and he didn't bother to teach us. He then made us deliver this to a processor facility to produce a highly volatile explosive material of massive destructive potential…and I'm speaking of destruction on a stellar scale…but again, he didn't bother to inform us as to what it was or why he needed it."

"A stellar scale?" he winces. "In all the nether-space, yes, I think I would at least want to know why he would ask for this, to say nothing about the rest of it."

"It goes deeper. Our industrial capacity was inadequate to mine this mineral, so we had to use local labor. The world was fully inhabited when we first found it. But the Marshal didn't bother to make any sort of negotiation for the mineral. He simply brought in our military and ordered them to blast it to oblivion, down to one surviving city, and then to enslave what remained to perform our work for us."

"What?!" he shouts, and then flinches as he grabs the neural interface on the side of his head.

"We were told to use a strange narcotic substance he found once to drug the mining crews from the city. This substance was apparently toxic and lethal after a while, so we constantly had to call up new crews to replace the old ones."

"Why?!"

"The reasoning is multifold here. But primarily because the city we were managing didn't know we existed behind their backs. The Marshal installed someone to manage them using deception and falsehood, creating a scenario of war outside their doors, and the minerals were being sent out as part of a support effort for friendly forces, when in fact it was us essentially stealing their resources from them. The drug was to ensure they did the work without any opposition. He doesn't like 'little things' arguing the point."

"Ayene!" he blasts. "Why would you be a party to any of this? Surely, for all your law degrees and prior security work, you would know the difference between right and wrong."

"Oh, I do," she croons. "As did the full staff at our base, including our Commander. But unknown to you and the rest of our public, the Marshal had a secret mandate he pushed through the Council once, along with the An'gamu Seeds and the Tav'ageen Suppressor chip. This one was called a military authority override chip, and it was mandated for all our military personnel. It sits alongside the other chip, and when placed into active mode, it turns a person into a tool to do whatever he orders us to do. We don't have any free will after that. After all, the Marshal doesn't like 'little things' that argue the point. Get it?" she raises her brow.

"You must be joking!" he grimaces and clutches at his interface harder for the feedback he was now receiving. "And on each of those points!"

"Unfortunately, I'm not. Those of us at the base didn't actually have it turned on, but the threat was enough, especially for what his agent was imposing on us. He was also forcing our female members to service his sexual fantasies, and his manners were violent and abusive, even murderous. But the Marshal wanted his minerals, and we were expendable. And once again, if we argued too boldly, bam, here goes the active mode of that chip."

"I cannot believe what I am hearing, Ayene. I never really liked him to begin with, but this only makes matters worse. What was this you said about being registered as dead?"

"The Marshal has long described us to be fighting what he calls insurgents, right? Well, they aren't insurgents, but old rivals Sargeras and his kind once got into a fight with and lost. This was much more of a law enforcement action for what his kind once did to so many… little things. The Marshal was apparently in that other universe on a plan of revenge, hoping to make a secret advance on them, and presumably to use this weapon as a terrorist device. Unfortunately for him, he was discovered and chased away. But in the process, he opened a door to his old enemies, and now they are following him… all the way back here."

"Uh oh… So, what we are saying is he lied on several critical points, not the least of which were these insurgents he spoke of so often, and now they are actually aware of him and making an advance? What does this mean for us, and how do you fit into it?"

"I'm working for them now. They found us at that mining base. They captured the base and took us prisoner. But they also realized we were just as much victims of the Marshal and his agent as all the rest. So they explained who they were and what they are doing. Our full base crew is now supporting them. But to excuse ourselves from the Marshal's service, we had to put on a show that he lost his precious mining activity, along with his weapon, due to…" she coughs subtly, "…circumstances outside his control, and these circumstances involve his agent turning rogue as part of the cover-up."

"This is starting to sound very complex."

"And it's just the beginning. Our base commander was Fleet Commander Lajivi Kriv'tik, a well-respected member of Central

Command. He tells us he was sent on multiple of these cleansing missions to blast whole worlds for nothing more than to purge the Marshal's insurgents from existence, when in fact those worlds never saw it coming, and probably held no relation to anything other than to serve as target practice for our young military."

"That in itself would represent a criminal act beyond anything I might otherwise be able to define."

"Indeed! The Marshal is a murderer and a criminal on so many levels, it goes beyond our laws to define them. But at the same time, he is a godlike being in relation to us, so we need to dismantle his conspiracy machine quietly in order to weaken him before we make our final move."

"A conspiracy machine... All right, wait. Explain this part to me."

"Our forces recently made their arrival here on Azgarén, but covertly so far. As part of this effort, we are establishing several operations to discover the extent of his actions here. He came here and lied to us about everything, just to gain our support for his cause. Our Council bowed down and started kissing his tail as soon as he mentioned this promise of great wisdom. Then he started interacting with us on several of his early projects, such as the Tav'ageen Anomaly, and therefore his solutions and the associated mandates we now suffer, meaning the seeds and the chips."

"Right, I recall this, and personally, I did not care for any of it."

"When our base crew was captured, our chips were disabled and removed. This on my head here..." she points at her interface, "... is fake, just for appearances. His solutions for the Anomaly were false to cover for something he was hiding from us, and the seeds were another false play he made. He wanted us to have them for ulterior motives."

"What ulterior motives?" he inquires warily.

"We can't demonstrate this yet, as we're still collecting the scientific study, but we believe they are genetically engineered to serve a role where Sargeras is concerned. I think that's as much as I should say for now. Since that time, the Council has been said to be in private deliberation within their chambers, and no one has seen them since. This causes some of us to wonder what actually happened to them."

"Yes, and it is also starting to sound like a dangerous situation. And you? Who do you work for now?"

"I'm working for someone who is part of the real enemy to Sargeras and Darumon, but I'm limited in how much I can actually reveal at this time. The Marshal is a powerful being, and he wants us as his playthings to do as he commands. The military has these chips for a reason…to serve him without question. It's the same as with that drug we were using on those miners…to do as you're told and not talk back. He doesn't like his minions questioning him. They become expendable after that."

"Oh, how nice of him. And he is the one we so often describe as our benefactor."

"Yeah, it's a bit ironic when you think of it, but it goes even deeper than that, and at this moment, I should keep the rest to myself. Each of our associates needs to be kept to a certain level of involvement for security reasons. If he should discover any part of it, he might go looking for the rest, and we can't afford this."

"Right, I get it. But then, where do I come in? You came in here fishing for support, remember?"

"Yes, and here's what I need from you. We are setting up a new top-level security agency called Azgarén Central Intelligence. My old Commander is managing it on behalf of our friends. This will be a type of secret service to monitor and expose corruption and intrigue behind the scenes and at all levels, including the Council, wherever they are…assuming they even exist by now. One of our first objectives is the media. My Commander once told me it is known within certain military circles that the Council has imposed regulators within the media stream to censor, and even to falsify our news broadcasts to only what the Marshal wants us to know."

"Censorship? This is one law I am familiar with, and they should not be there. What do you have on them so far?"

"I have yet to go in there personally, but when I do, I'll call on you to provide your support. I also need to investigate the Council proper to see where they are and what they're doing. But we do not have the resources to actually haul people away and drop them in a prison cell. We still need the standard law enforcement services to carry this part. We will conduct our investigations and provide the evidence. We will contribute to the court procedures, but you must provide the physical means to drag them away and incarcerate them."

"The sort of thing we are supposed to be doing anyway, assuming we had any real work to do around here."

"Right, but considering who our enemy is, we need to be quiet about it. No doubt, he'll be watching, and he probably won't like us dismantling his work. He might try to retaliate by performing his own cleansing operation right here at home. And with our military under his control using those chips, that's bad."

"In all the nether-space, Ayene, do you think he would actually do that right here on Azgarén?"

"At this point, anything is possible, and we're not taking any chances. So, our work has to be conducted in ways he won't take immediate notice of."

"What about these people you are working with...these old enemies of his."

"They need to make a careful approach, or else he might try running away, as he did the first time, and we can't afford him to simply disappear on us. If you think he did a lot of damage the first time, we don't want to see the next one."

✦ ✦ ◆ ✦ ✦

"Lieutenant Girhani, how is your research progressing?"

Petrith was in his disguise as a military officer working undercover inside Central Command to access their data terminals. He was working alongside Ayene as a spy to tap into the military networks in order to obtain any relevant information they could use against Marshal Darumon and his operations. Along the way, he was investigating their security protocols and operational procedures.

He turns to the address as the base captain approaches. He rises and offers a customary salute.

"Captain," he replies confidently. "As a matter of fact, I have been noticing a few discrepancies which I thought might be noteworthy to report to you."

"Oh? By the way, where is your Captain? I thought I saw her here earlier, but then I heard she had to leave on an errand."

"Yes, she has a tendency to do that as part of her duties. We need to coordinate between several of our offices in order to ensure the compatibility of our system integration."

"Naturally, and your work here, what have you found so far?"

"As you know, my specialty is network security protocols. Part of my training involves the design and integrity checking of network security, and as I was reviewing the existing configuration we use here, I took notice of the age of these protocols. It would seem we have not revised the algorithms for a very long time, and this concerns me."

"In what way? They seem to have served us during this time. Are you suggesting it might be time for a revamp?"

"In actuality, I would say it is past due. Some of these have been in service for centuries and a few for even longer than that. I would consider this not only a security risk, but a danger to our networks should anyone ever try hacking into them."

"Hacking into our networks?" he muses. "But who would you suggest in this case? Our networks are secure against any civilian attacks, as it is an isolated circuit. And even at that, you would need a security clearance just to gain access to a terminal, let alone any of the data files."

"Yes, but if you consider all those insurgents and what they might be capable of, I am concerned for the potential of a loophole being exploited."

"The insurgents? Lieutenant, to my knowledge, in all the time we have been fighting them, I have never once heard of them attempting to break into our networks."

"Never once heard of... Is this to say they would openly come to you and say, 'Hello, I'm an insurgent, and I want to thank you for NOT changing your protocols for so long that I was able to tap into them during this time?' This is precisely my point, and I feel this is our discrepancy. The Marshal came to us representing a society of a higher form of sophistication than our own, and this naturally implies a higher form of technology and its potential to override our system integrity. Now, as I understand it, our military has served admirably in our offensive against their incursions into our space. But Captain, in all of your experience, how can you explain a society of a higher level of technological esteem allowing themselves to fail each and every time they make a run at us? There is a serious error here. In the nearly ten millennia they have been making these attempts, they did not succeed one time."

"Yes, you have a point. And as for your implication, I can also see your direction. But is this to say they might have an alternate plan? If their purpose is to target Sargeras..."

"This is true, of course. One thing I would point out is their apparent lack of capacity to improve upon themselves, as we have done in the past to meet the challenge to oppose them. Are we therefore saying there is a cap to what a technological society is capable of, and they have already met that cap? I think this would represent a rather foolish statement on our part. Instead, I think we should address the apparent failure on their side to succeed in a military offensive. After all, they were presumably successful in ousting Sargeras in the first place. Surely, if he is all he claims to be, he had to have a potent military force to keep him in power. One might suggest, if he did not, and an opposing force rose up to overthrow him, he basically had it coming. What do you think?"

"Yes, I suppose you do hold a valid point. He would want to protect his position."

"Naturally. But where is it, this opposing force? And how can a military power WE can so easily defeat overwhelm whatever HE surely had. This alone represents a serious shortfall. Maybe not simply a shortfall in their apparent lack of proficiency, but maybe also a lack of our military prowess to think in such terms to begin with. After all, we didn't start out a militaristic society…and in many ways we still are not."

"Well, yes, I may need to agree, as we did not start out that way."

"Did not start out, and most of us simply do not follow this sort of predatory instinct to begin with. Therefore, as a society of a higher potential, they should have won at least one battle in all this time, but according to our historical records, they did not. Why, then, do they continue to try, unless they are misdirecting us in some way. Maybe also realizing our LACK of proficiency to think in such terms that we take so much for granted, and never question these discrepancies, even after they drag our horns so low that we no longer even recognize them right in front of our faces."

The Captain glares at the young man for the intrepid statement.

"A misdirection…" he ponders. "Yes, I see your perspective now. If they are seemingly unable to oppose us in battle, or perhaps are simply making it appear that way, they must have another motive. In all the nether-space, young man, and if they should attempt to use any of this superior technology of theirs…but of course! The misdirection! We won so many battles because they misdirected us to easy targets, and perhaps by infiltrating our own networks to drop clues. Blast it! And we fell for it during all this time. We need to close this hole immediately. Do you have any suggestions?"

"Indeed I do. I have been testing a number of new protocols using extended hashing algorithms and dynamic keys. This should make things significantly harder to crack. But to employ this new system would require a revamp of the old protocols and a global software upgrade."

"All right, we should pass this through the High Commander for his approval. I would also like to review these changes with your Captain when she returns."

"Of course, I will pass the word as soon as she reports in."

The Captain nods and turns to leave the room. Petrith watches as the man passes through the door, and then he returns to his seat. The room was empty, except for him, as he was given his own office to conduct his work in peace.

"That's right, Captain," he mumbles quietly with a demure grin. "We'll fix things nice and neat. You won't have to worry about those nasty insurgents again…at least not THOSE insurgents. But the other ones…" he chuckles mischievously. "Well, you'll learn about them soon enough when Ytani shows his face again."

He returns to his terminal and begins programming a new set of subroutines with his own flavor of security.

"And we'll see what the Marshal has to say about it when he can't log into his own terminal again. We already dropped that hint that he was conducting something illegal with Morndindor, so this will simply build on it."

◆◆◆◆◆

"So, what we have now is an office, which in itself is a very curious aspect of this war, and Kaliya, you're also employing some local labor to serve the secretary positions?"

"Yes, Kailen… First of all, Kriv'tik is working on his projection skills, but he still needs a little more practice. We also have a number of officers from the Ghan'aju joining our ranks, and we're assigning them under his command, so they're also in training. Meanwhile, we need a reliable full-time staff in physical form, rather than our projections, some of which may come and go as they still have their academy classes to attend."

"I never would've thought to see the day," he shakes his head. "Managing a rebellion on our old home soil, and by remote access as projected bodies."

High Commander Kailen Nazég and his younger sister, Kaliya, who was recently promoted to Captain, sat in discussion of the recent plans they were pursuing on Azgarén. They were attending a meeting in the Watchmen Intelligence Center in the city of Rolsklinde on Therinë, along with Lord Thaelyn and General Gabarleine.

"This will provide us with a useful venue," Thaelyn offers. "The more people we have working the problem, the more efficient we become. And even if our operatives are not present, we can still take messages. Then, once someone returns to their post, we can relay them back here."

"This should work well enough in the beginning," Kaliya notes. "It wouldn't be any different from someone working a regular business shift and simply being out of the office during off hours. But once we get deeper into our operations, I will want to have someone working around the clock just in case we see any trouble coming our way."

"Indeed, and hopefully by that time some of your operatives will be coming close to finishing their classes and have more time to invest into it."

"I have Ayene working on her contacts today. I sent her out to check on her old boss at C.P. Security. She seemed confident she could persuade him to come over to our side. Once she's done with that, I'll have her investigate the local broadcast station and the Council chamber. I want to know what's inside the Grand Hall."

"The Council Grand Hall..." Kailen muses affectionately. "That term is almost a legend to us here. It's something passed down to us from better days, when our father once held his position on the Council. He told us of the elaborate ornamentation, the sculpted architecture, the domed ceiling with its mosaic tiles and gold leaf inlays, and the majestic benches and tables of noble wood and polished granite," he sighs. "I almost dread to hear what she'll find in there if the Council is actually vacant now."

"I know, Kailen. But she has instructions to photograph everything and bring it back to us as evidence. My biggest concern is if the Council really is missing in action, what do we do about it...or do we do anything at all? Maybe we'll have to cover it up, at least for now, until we're ready to spring our own trap on Darumon."

"This is my only suggestion," Thaelyn mentions. "If no one currently knows about it, then we should keep it this way, as it would cause too much of a sensation otherwise. The people seem to depend on the Council acting as their government, but if they are discovered missing from the equation, this leaves a very large gap in their expectations of who is actually running their society."

"And there won't be anyone to fill that gap, unless you factor in the Marshal, who is not supposed to be running anything to begin with."

"Indeed, and since Darumon has been playing his game so carefully, we must play ours the same."

"But we still need to bring a few people into the loop, like C.P. Security, as we'll need their support to contain the situation... whatever situation might eventually come out of it."

"This is true, so we should wait for Ayene to return with her word on their participation."

"We also have those regulators inside the news media. If we're going to take control of their media with our own brand of propaganda, we need those people out."

"And again, this will need to involve the local law enforcement."

"I find it curious," the General interjects. "Those regulators are described as serving the Council, but if there is in truth no Council to serve, how do we explain their association, unless the Council is simply being used as a figurehead in this affair."

"A figurehead...exactly," Kaliya affirms. "And this would defer the blame from Darumon, as they're clearly serving him, rather than anyone else. But this does bring up an interesting point. Anyone or anything that might serve the Council needs a contact of some kind. Who or what is serving as that contact? Are they simply working by proxy, one subordinate department to another without any direct interaction to a Council at all? Or is Darumon impersonating someone from time to time to give instructions."

"This would surely make life interesting for him, I suppose, and it also adds one more facet we must be aware of in case we should come across anything."

"That's right, so we should see about those regulators and whoever they answer to. Then, who that one answers to, and on up the ladder, removing each rung as we move forward. I'm also reminded of his research institutes and all the death toys they made for him along the way."

"Like those we found being used here in this world, yes. We

already know of one called the ARC, which is so conveniently located in Capitol Prime, so we should have someone look into that for us."

"I'm thinking of Ayene again. She knows the place. She was also hoping to carry out that mission to pick up the seed specimens for Ankhia to research her solution to that horrid little parasite of theirs."

"We should have her make that errand for us soon," Thaelyn asserts. "Surely, the Med-tech will require enough time to conduct her studies, and if this seed entity is indeed instrumental in feeding into Sargeras, we will want to remove it, or at least some portion of it, with all due haste to weaken him."

◆

A young intern strolls along the halls of an elaborate medical research facility on the rim of the bustling metropolis of Capitol Prime. This was a hallway she had passed on countless occasions during the course of her residency, and today was no different. She was making her way along to the office of the facility's executive officer. As she arrives at the door, she first presses an announcement button before entering.

The office was neatly presented with an elegant desk and chair, several bookcases filled with medical journals and reference sets, which were largely for show rather than actual use, as well as plaques and frames holding certificates and commendations hanging on the walls. There were small potted plants near the windowsill, and a pair of taller ones set in the corners. The setting represented a warm atmosphere of professional comfort, but it also seemed a contradiction in terms, as it was again on the Suuden-Aryku home world of Azgarén, and the contradiction revolved around their application of what they called Suppressor chips, which effectively muted their emotional output.

The office belonged to Director Ghantil Bak'vayn, Chief Administrator for the Ark'ravan Research Center, or ARC in short form. As the intern enters the room, the Director glances up to meet her.

"Intern Nur'ten, I've been expecting you. Do you have anything to report this time?"

"Nothing of special interest," she relents distantly. "Here is my quarterly review," she hands over a holo-chip with her report filed on it. "The highlight of this period is only the recurrence of a few mood swings, as I continue to reflect on some of the odd research we did for Central, but where nothing ever came back on what it was for."

"Azina, I'm sure we went through this on many occasions. Central keeps their secrets very close. Each of those projects was probably classified, like everything else they tend to do, so we shouldn't dwell on it as something we'll ever learn about."

"But Ghantil," she urges. "They're out there doing…something. Aren't we supposed to be a society of intellectuals who want to learn something on occasion? I know I am! And I'm fairly sure you are as well. That's why we're conducting our research in the Project. No one is allowed to continue the study, so you're doing it anyway, but as a secret effort to unlock that age-old mystery of what actually happened all those millennia ago."

"Yes Azina, I'll admit, I'm just as curious as you are on what Central is doing. But my experience with them tells me we're not going to get anything out of them short of someone coming forward and spilling all their little secrets right in our lap. And do you know the chances of something like that happening? I think they're just as likely as any of us living up to the promise of moving off-planet and colonizing new worlds, as we were once encouraged to do before all this began."

He glances down at himself briefly to reflect on the seed entity that clung to his back and permeated his body at various intervals. Azina knew immediately what he meant by the statement, and she followed by reviewing her own body.

"I hate this thing. Why do I need it if I'm not going anywhere?"

"Unfortunately, we both need it in the modern day due to all the pollution we created as part of the Marshal's plan to fight his insurgents. We had to build up that large military to defend ourselves. There was apparently no other way."

"And so, instead of moving off-planet to other inhospitable worlds, we created our own. I remember the stories you shared with me, Ghantil…"

Azina strolls over to the window to look outside. She studies the hazy sky above which was gray with smog.

"The world was once clean," she reminisces. "The air was fresh, and the flowers and trees would bloom, scenting the breezes with all their fragrances. And we had animals running free out there, living in accordance with their natural instincts. Now, everything is either dead or dying, and those animals are mostly in artificial habitats struggling to survive."

"I know, Azina. I feel it, just like you. But it's out of our hands."

"Yeah, out of our hands, just like that long-standing promise of great wisdom. Ten millennia, and it's still out of our hands. When do we see something come back for all we had to sacrifice? He came here asking for our help. You might think, at the very least, he would give something back for all he asked of us. We very nearly destroyed our world for him. Aren't we deserving of a little compensation for that?"

"I would tend to agree, but again, I'm not the one making the rules. It's been said often enough that the Council is in their deep deliberation, so maybe we did receive something back, and they're simply trying to understand how to approach it."

"That deliberation is another paradox. It's been ongoing for a long time now. Even when I was a girl, they were deliberating, and it still hasn't delivered anything."

"Once again, I would have to agree. And it's been ongoing for much longer than your lifetime. My only suggestion is that they must have delivered something to some other research institute that we aren't aware of, and maybe the application is still too complex for any of us to make efficient use of yet."

"All right, I suppose I could accept that. I just hope we do see something come out of it before I die. But as for those research projects we made for Central, some of them were just too weird to be any kind of casual application. Like that Belvik Spore to destroy some kind of alien neural tissue. I loved that one," she smirks satirically. "It lasted four centuries. What were they fighting that they couldn't just hit with a big stick? Then, my all-time favorite, the modified An'gamu seed loaded into a rifle-propelled missile projectile. That was a masterpiece of engineering, both from the genetic side as well as the technological design work. I wonder what they were shooting at. Could it be that same thing they were hitting with the Belvik Spores?" she giggles.

"I don't know, Azina," he smiles tenderly. "But those certainly were a couple of unique applications of our research department."

"And what about that rush order for the Kajik'tav Serum? Ten millennia of no reported cases, and suddenly we need enough for a small army."

"My thoughts once circled around the idea that they sent someone to one of those inhospitable worlds and needed the Serum as a counteragent to the local effects."

"Due to some kind of breathing difficulties? Maybe, but the seed is supposed to do that for us, therefore the Serum was made obsolete."

"Yes, and this is the only impediment to the theory, which is also exemplified here at home with our native pollution issue."

"But this again suggests they are...out there..." she waves a hand to the sky through the window. "And here we are down here with no word on anything new and interesting we're supposed to be discovering."

"Azina, you're young, and clearly very ambitious to learn something new. I don't blame you. You've been a part of the Project for about a century now. If it were not for that, well, maybe you would not feel so many emotions driving you to such high expectations."

"Maybe...maybe not..." she frowns. "I think I would still have some expectations, even with the chip turned on," she taps a finger on her interface. "I just wouldn't be able to express them as freely. We're a society that loves to explore and learn, but in my lifetime, I haven't seen anything new except for Central ordering up their weird projects with no explanation as to why they need them."

"I would tend to blame this in part on the application of the military control chips. That would certainly put a damper on revealing just about anything they get their hands into."

"But only if they're in active mode. Are we then saying the full military is on active, with no one conducting any kind of exploration that would filter down to us?"

"I don't have the answer to that. This was one of the Marshal's inventions, and again it revolved around those insurgents making so many attempts at us."

"Well then, what about any civilian exploration? Surely, there must be normal people going out there and discovering the universe."

"Unfortunately, Azina, the only time I ever heard of anyone going out there and doing anything at all was in the beginning when the Tav'ageen Anomaly was causing so much panic. You recall the history of it, right? Those first children who were discovered and then mysteriously died, and then more cases involving adults, and apparently hitting at random throughout the population."

"Yeah, and the people were losing their horns over it, as our medical science couldn't figure out what it was or where it came from. Then the Marshal shows up at just the right moment to help us find the answer. But YOU…" she waves a finger at him teasingly. "You and that old research faction… What was it called? Metaphysics… Paranormal science…as if something like that could ever be described as a science…"

"Carefully, Azina… There were those who truly believed in it, even though the Council downplayed it so often. Some of us within our faction were discovering clues to something that rose above us, and it didn't fit with the more traditional sciences."

"All right, but it doesn't help that it's outlawed now and rejected by everyone else."

"I know, and this is the reason for our Project. We have to conduct these studies in secret now, hoping one day to understand what it was, so that maybe we can come forward with the evidence to prove the others wrong."

"And even though I volunteered to be a part of the Project, it still scares me a little that I might wake up one day and see some kind of ghost thing in my bedroom."

"This is why we have the monitor installed in there, so if anything should happen, we can catch it before it becomes critical or life-threatening."

"And using me as bait…"

"Would you prefer not to be a part of the Project? I can always relieve you of the service if it bothers you so much."

"I know," she sighs. "But if to choose between being used as bait for some alien organism to mimic my body, or to be put back under the effect of that chip, I think I would choose the organism, and hope it's intelligent and we can try communicating with it, or at least try to identify it…finally."

"I agree. The trouble is we have a large number of people out there already, and none of them have reported anything so far. This is our other problem, trying to understand if it's still rooted in our environment to be a continued threat to our people."

"Yeah, I remember the briefings. In these past ten millennia, we're asking if it could still be out there, or did it die off by now. This is one of the reasons for the Project, to test if the Suppressor chips are still needed, or if we can finally discontinue them."

"I'm sure a lot of people would be happy for that, but until we can get a definitive answer, we can't make any movements."

"So, by turning them off, we're essentially conducting an illegal research project to find out if something we could never positively identify is still present in our environment to be a threat to us. Ghantil, this Project seems to carry its own paradox. How and when do we know if we have an answer of any kind? We don't know what we're looking for, and trying to test to see if it's still out there."

"I realize this, and I've tried to rationalize a solution. In a way, I'm hoping we can find evidence of it still being present, rather than nothing at all. But in the total absence of anything, I must consider how to justify discontinuing the chips in the face of the Council mandates that still demand them."

"Wouldn't the evidence of no activity be sufficient cause to justify the decision?"

"You might think so, but they are said to be very finicky. They want evidence of existence, not the lack of evidence suggesting nonexistence."

"And that simply brings us to yet another paradox…how to prove something does not exist, especially something our science could never prove existed in the first place, but the Marshal says it does."

"Yes, Azina, this is one that stumps even me. He claims this is so, but even HE did not provide any evidence, to my knowledge. And yet, the Council still accepted it."

"Ghantil, is this to say the Council took someone's word without that famous evidence, but they wouldn't take OUR word to say otherwise? Who are they supposed to be serving here, an alien being or our own people?"

"Yes," he chuckles. "That would be a good one to ask."

"Maybe we should just go up to the Marshal and ask him why he says it does, and to give us the evidence we need to decide for ourselves."

"This would surely provide a solution, but if you recall what I once said about my mentor…"

"Oh no, not that one again…" she throws up her hands. "Beware the Marshal, for he may not be entirely truthful to us. Well, considering everything else he's done, or NOT done, after we did so much for him, maybe I should start listening to it by now. Then, what does this ultimately mean for us? Are we saying he gave us an excuse for something that actually seemed to work, if you look at the final results, but some of us weren't happy with it, so we're looking for other ways around it?"

"Basically, yes. The chip was a solution to halt the death syndrome caused by the Anomaly, presumably by disabling the focus center in the brain that this alien…whatever…zeroes in on. Once these were applied in our population, we stopped seeing those odd deaths. But after such a long time, we're asking if it's still out there and if the chips are still needed. So, until we can find our answer, we still need to play along, which means you and the others who are part of the Project need to remember to act like all the rest."

"No emotions…right," she sighs. "But for how much longer, Ghantil? It really comes down to that. How many are in the Project now?"

"You know I can't answer that directly. You already know you are part of the third generation, a group of around twenty thousand, but that's as much as I dare say about it."

"Right, and just to keep us safe in case any of us are discovered. This simply exemplifies the illegal aspect of it. And no one has reported anything since those early days."

"I haven't heard of any reports since the application of the chips, and that includes within the Project."

"There's something wrong with that. What about children? It originally developed in young children. Do we have any of those in the Project?"

"No, and unfortunately, to involve such would need to bring the parents into it."

"Well, what about those who are already involved? Don't they have any children?"

"I'm sure many of them do, but also with someone who is not otherwise in the Project. And we can't allow this to get out, even under such conditions. I don't know, maybe I'm being a little paranoid on the matter."

"A little?" she smirks. "What about the general public. Are there any reported cases of the symptoms coming into any of the clinics? I know we have a privacy policy, but this would be an important issue to reveal at least the statistical numbers. It could also answer the question of whether this thing is still out there."

"Yes, it could, but unfortunately, the Council mandate demands the immediate application of the chip if any of those symptoms arise. There is also a clause of nondisclosure in those cases."

"Ghantil, there is something wrong with that statement. We're trying to understand if something we can't identify is still out there, but the only evidence…and I use the term loosely…is hidden behind a layer of bureaucracy. That sounds like something other than an alien infestation at work."

"It does…" he reflects softly. "And it's that same paranoia that caused the people to go into a panic in those early years. The nondisclosure statement is to prevent any more of that, but at the same time, it prevents our statistical reporting as well."

"And therefore our ability to determine if it's still out there, thus forcing us to take the chips whether we like it or not…whether we NEED it or not."

The Director leans back in his chair to ponder the situation. Azina stood there watching him, placing her hands on her hips, and feeling weak for the futility of the conversation.

"What about this," he suggests. "Maybe I can contact some of the local clinics and see if anything came up in recent times, possibly to work an arrangement with them to report in, very discreetly of course, if any new symptoms are discovered. This might provide us with at least enough evidence to see if it's still out there."

"All right, this is a start. And then we would know if all this work is actually worth the effort. I just wish I knew someone else around here…besides you, that is…who had emotions so I could carry a meaningful conversation with them."

"I understand, Azina. All I can say is to keep your spirits up. One day, I hope we'll learn the truth."

"But then what, Ghantil?" she retorts. "What do we do with it? Do we take it to the Council? Will they actually listen to us conducting this illegal research and reverse some of their old decisions, or simply throw us in prison for it. We'll need a really strong case, plus a lot of people backing us up to demonstrate it in the face of all that."

"I know, but for now, that's another matter, and one we can't do anything about at this time. Let's just get our evidence and see where it takes us."

"Right. So, if I see any ghosts that look like me, you'll be the first to know," she smiles timidly.

The young intern offers a gentle wave as she turns to leave the room. The Director watches as she closes the door behind her, and then turns to look out the window.

"Yes..." he muses silently. "He showed up at just the right moment to give us his answer...one we could never verify, but the Council sure liked it. 'I will promise you the secrets of the universe...' he said. 'But first, you need to pollute your bodies, and then your home to prove your trust in my overwhelming wisdom...' And so we did," he huffs.

He continues to gaze out the window at the hazy sky above.

"Now we're stuck here in this polluted world, and no closer to the secrets of the universe today as we were before he arrived. But that Anomaly sure stirred things up for him. He was so eager for us to vacate our home before he found himself forced to deliver this other solution of the chip. What was the reason for it? If the answer was in the chip, why didn't he offer this to begin with?"

✦✦✦✦✦

Ayene had just finished her visit to C.P. Security, after securing a new relationship with her former Captain. He would begin communicating with the other precincts to draw in additional support, but his instructions so far were to keep it discreet until a later time when the situation stabilized. Ayene's new objective was to visit the local media hub, known as Capitol Prime Communications. Otherwise known as CPComm, it was a global distributor, and a highly recognized provider of news and information, entertainment programs for young and old, and served billions of people around the world. To secure a connection there would provide a valuable outlet for the propaganda campaign Thaelyn had in mind to turn the people away from Darumon's rhetoric.

Ayene was projected in her bird form at this time, flying high above the city as she transited across to her new destination. She gazed down at the people and traffic on the ground as she passed over the streets and other city structures.

"This sure beats driving," she muses quietly. "I remember when

I was working my old job, and how I had to fight some of that down there. Now, I just fly right over their heads and bam, there I am. In fact, I don't even need to do that much. I could just fold my way over to it, but that would probably turn a few too many heads to see someone go poof like that," she giggles softly.

She soon spies the target building and surveys the local area for a place to land and reshape herself to her natural form. As a projection, which was essentially an unknown entity in this world, she didn't dare do this in open sight, so she found a convenient nook behind the building where she landed and recomposed herself before stepping out onto the sidewalk. From there, she made her way up to the front door.

As she entered inside, she saw a reception desk with a young lady managing the flow of visitors. She approaches to make her greeting.

"Welcome to CPComm," the girl offers politely. "How may I help you?"

"I have an urgent need to speak with the Administrator of this facility. Who is that?"

"The Administrator? That would be Mister Kan'tarru. But he does not normally take meetings with visitors off the street…"

"I understand, but I'm not a common visitor, young lady. I'm on official business with Azgarén Central Intelligence. We have a report of illegitimate activities taking place, and I'm here to investigate. Therefore, I will ask you to call his attention immediately, or else show me to his office."

"Um, wait, please," she hesitates. "Who do you work for? I do not recognize that name."

"Azgarén Central Intelligence…"

Ayene now takes out her trans-com from a pocket and pulls up an app with an electronic security ID badge for display. She then flashes it at the girl, who studies it tensely.

"We're a new government security agency," Ayene continues. "And right now, I'm investigating a report we received from a reliable military informant of an act of conspiratorial intrigue occurring here that violates Article Nine, Section Fourteen of the Charter of Laws.

Therefore, please inform the Administrator that I wish to speak with him immediately."

"In all the nether-space… Yes Ma'am."

The girl at the desk reeled back from the strong assertion, and even with her inhibitor chip, she was clearly showing emotional stress. She quickly responded by reaching for her vid-com terminal to relay the message.

"Mister Kan'tarru, this is Teela at the front desk. I have a security officer here that needs to speak to you about something, and it sounds serious… No, I do not know what it is, but she is quoting legal infractions at me… Uh-uh, she is with some new government security agency… Yes! She flashed a very official ID badge at me, and by the look in her eyes right now, I think we are both splashing our hooves in a very bad puddle here. Please come down here and deal with it."

The girl hangs up and nervously returns back to Ayene.

"He will be right down. Please wait a moment."

Ayene nods casually and turns away from the desk to slowly pace around the lobby. She felt a hidden sense of contentment that she was finally serving a role that would ultimately change the order of the world around her, and it felt good. The sense of affirmative purpose, the backing of her support connections, and the confidence in her direction as part of Thaelyn's military activities gave her a sense of authority. She would unravel Darumon's plans one thread at a time, beginning with this one.

From somewhere down the corridor, a neatly dressed businessman made a hurried pace in her direction. His hastened hoof steps echoed into the room, drawing Ayene's attention to his arrival. He paused briefly at the desk, where the girl timidly pointed at the professional young officer. He then turned to meet her.

"Uh…" he clears his throat. "Are you the security agent sent here as part of some sort of investigation?"

"I am," Ayene states casually. "Are you the Administrator of this facility?"

"Yes, I am. My name is Tyram Kan'tarru. What is going on here? And who exactly are you, by the way? Are you with C.P. Security?"

"Not specifically..." she pulls out her ID badge again. "But we are affiliated with them as part of our law enforcement operations. I'm with a new government division called Azgarén Central Intelligence. We're a new security agency that has recently been installed to investigate and counter any and all security threats to our people, our world, and our way of life, whether internal or external in their point of origin. This includes corruption, conspiracies, and abuse of authority at all levels, even up to the Council itself."

"The Council..." he flashes a glance at the girl behind the desk. "And what would bring you here? Are we accused of something?"

"I have a report from a reliable military source that there is an infraction occurring within our media streams that violates Article Nine, Section Fourteen of the Charter of Laws. This translates as the Truth in Reporting Act of 3752 CTD. The report further implicates Council involvement as the perpetrators of this action, and this suggestion alone elevates the situation as a conspiratorial movement to censor our media streams, thereby limiting the freedom of information to the public by unknown persons and for unknown reasons. My investigation currently involves your facility and what we might find here to verify this claim."

"Verify? But...if the Council mandated this..."

"The Council is not above the law, Administrator," Ayene asserts firmly. "Regardless of any war protocols, as I understand this may have been a prompting factor at one time, the Charter of Laws must apply to everyone equally. They created these laws to govern us, but they are also citizens that should be bound to those same laws they created. They should not think themselves to be immune, even though it would seem some of them do believe in this. My department was established by a new authority that intends to crack down on these matters and bring those who are responsible to justice...even if I have to drag them out of their chamber myself."

"And what sort of authority do you actually have, if you're a new security department?"

"The sort of authority that doesn't take no for an answer, or wait for some alien creature to one day, maybe, if all the stars and planets align the right way, teach us the nature of existence. There are those of us who have finally…and I say this with such regret that it took ten millennia to actually take notice of it…but finally realized there are errors occurring here, and we need to take back control of our lives from those authorities that stole it away from us. And to demonstrate this, would you like for me to call Captain Bein'talan of the East City Center Precinct of C.P. Security, and have him make a visit? I could call for your entire staff to be dragged out of this building for interrogation."

"Um…wait…" he hesitates. "I do not wish to seem uncooperative. I am simply very surprised at this sudden announcement. It also sounds like you are creating a type of revolution here."

"So be it if you do not wish to argue the point, but a revolution it is, if only to teach the people why we are infested with these bugs and chips no one ever wanted, and were always promised to be a temporary solution to a problem to be resolved…any day now," she smirks conspicuously.

The Administrator glared at her, at least as much for the statement as also her apparent display of emotion.

"Administrator," Ayene continues. "It is all around us, but that statement of 'any day now' has dragged our horns so low that we forgot how to count the millennia since it all began. And none of it, Administrator, was ever truly necessary. And yet, we were made to believe it was."

"But as for this allegation…" he inquires cautiously.

"Right. The allegation refers to the Council regulators said to be monitoring and restricting, perhaps even falsifying your news broadcasts, Administrator. Where are they?"

"What?!" Teela shrieks. "We have regulators in here?"

Both Ayene and the Administrator turn to gaze at the girl as she jumps out of her chair to join the conversation.

"What do you mean by regulators?" she asks urgently.

"How interesting," Ayene muses ironically. "You work here, and not even YOU know of it? This is almost funny...almost."

"Her position does not afford her this level of internal review," the Administrator explains.

"All right, then to inform her of what sort of work she is performing for this most prestigious establishment, I am speaking of the ones who are said to be limiting what your news reporters put on the airwaves. They are said to be owned by the Council and supplied by military information sources. What this tells us is the military is regulating your flow of information, and with compliance of the Council, even though Article Nine, Section Fourteen says they should NOT hold this level of capacity. Now, I can certainly understand how they might have their security restraints, but this flow is also said to be feeding false information into the public media stream. This is where the violation comes into play. If all they wanted was to NOT feed us sensitive details, it is as simple as not providing it in the first place. But to intentionally falsify our news broadcasts is to feed us stories that are not even real, but they claim them to be such. And according to my office, this now invalidates any and all authority by those parties responsible."

"I do not believe this..." Teela gasps.

"One moment," the Administrator interjects. "The Council put them there, and this would suggest they are required to serve a purpose. After all, this is the Council we are speaking of here."

"Administrator," Ayene declares. "Your loyalty to our government authority is admirable, but misplaced in this case. You are blindly following an authority figure that is clearly breaking its own laws. Once again, if their purpose is to restrict sensitive information, or perhaps dangerous details that could cause public discord, it is as simple as NOT to provide it in the first place...although I might also suggest the people still have a need to know, especially if it holds relevance to public safety."

"Well, yes, I would need to agree on that point."

"But to provide something entirely false...this is unacceptable and unjustifiable. Therefore, who is it that should govern the government, if they do not hold themselves accountable for their own actions? By this definition, we, as citizens, are expected to take their word for whatever they tell us we should believe in, regardless of the factual nature of it. Is this right? No. It is entirely authoritarian and oppressive of the truth. And yet, no one was ever given the authority to question THEM, or to hold THEM accountable for the very laws they force upon the rest of us. This is where WE come in. We were created for the purpose of bringing to justice anyone who might break those laws we hold so high, including a Council body that seems to like to play god with our lives."

"Playing god, is it..." he muses quietly. "But this sounds like you are positioning yourselves above the government."

"The law, Administrator, IS above the government. Either that, or the government is above what we think it to be, as we are made to think it IS a god entity, and can do no wrong. A properly functioning form of government must have a system of checks and balances, to keep everyone's tails straight. But it would seem everyone THINKS the Council's tails are inherently straight, simply because they ARE the Council. Therefore, the Council is past due for a review. And I have heard from others, who were closely related to Council positions in the past, tell tales of how they are so often drunk on their perceived positions of power and authority. This speaks to me."

"All right, but allow me to ask you this. What will happen once you find whoever is responsible for all this? These regulators have been stationed in our offices for a very long time. One question that comes to mind is why it took so long for anyone to take notice, and then do something about it. Another is what will come after...to us, to the Council..."

"First, we need to remove these people from your backs. But I suspect this conspiracy runs deep, so I am going to make an arrangement with you that we should keep this highly confidential for now. Whoever is at the top, I want them to stay complacent and not get any wild ideas of escape. My investigation still has a way to go, as I climb this ladder of intrigue until I learn who started it. If it involves anyone on the Council, I want them. But since the informant was military in nature, and he told us there are other forms of military interaction, I want to know their involvement, as well. This reeks of a change of attitude in our government policy to one of authoritarianism, and I can only imagine where that came from."

"What do you mean? The Council is transforming into something else?"

"If their tails are not as straight as they make us think them to be..." she muses indignantly. "This investigation is only one of several my department is pursuing right now. But the direction implies a transition of some form, and it seems to date back quite some distance into our history. Unfortunately, as you said, it took us this long to figure it out. It's shameful, really, that our society of intellectuals might take so long to ask those questions we were supposed to ask so many millennia ago. Much like you, no one seems interested in questioning the Almighty Council and their mandates. Well, now we are. At the very least, because we have grown tired of all these promises, and now we want results. Furthermore, because we are noticing a series of clues presenting themselves, and SOME of us are taking notice of a message written between the lines. And horns will fly once the answers are revealed."

"I see. Well, at least now we will have some real news to report... that is, once you clear the security status."

"Yes, but for now, just remember, I do not want any of them to know I'm coming, which means you cannot reveal our work until after we are ready to go public with it. This will surely create a sensation in the public eye, and while I will not argue that they need to be told at some moment, I want those who are responsible in our custody first. Therefore, until further notice, you must follow our direction to maintain an image of all being as they expect it to be, and until such time as the situation is stable. Understood?"

"Yes Ma'am. But now, where do we go from here?"

"I'm going to call Captain Bein'talan and have him send a few of his officers over here to assist in gathering up those responsible, since it seems our suspicions were correct. I would also like to conduct a number of interviews with some of your people, especially your news reporters, for their experiences and interactions along the way. Do we have a room available where we can find some privacy?"

"Yes Ma'am, we have a conference room we could use for this purpose. I'll show you where it is."

It was a new day in Rolsklinde, and Thaelyn was holding his ritual meeting in the WIC building. Ayene was in attendance and reporting on her recent investigation.

"And so," she relates. "The two regulators they had in there are now in custody with Captain Bein'talan. He tells me he will be working in cooperation with Administrator Kan'tarru, as well as the other district security offices, and the heads of the other network stations, to continue the investigation until everyone is accounted for."

"But they will keep this confidential," Thaelyn notes, "until we are ready for our public release, correct?"

"Yes, this much I made clear. The situation would represent a public sensation, to say the least, and until we have the full chain of corruption in our custody, we don't want anyone getting any funny ideas."

"Anyone, meaning to say Darumon," Kaliya snickers. "But he's not one you can simply put behind bars."

"No, he is not," Thaelyn affirms. "And I find it highly unlikely that simple bars would hold him, anyway. But for as long as we can continue to break apart his propaganda machine, we will do so, and further to bring those people out of their intellectual hibernation."

"I also had an opportunity to speak with several of their reporters," Ayene continues, "including Ileani Ur'paran, as she is one of their main anchors. She seems to be a reasonable enough person, and she confided in me that ever since her first days, she felt stifled by those regulators always editing her reports. I think she was almost ready to bow down and kiss my hooves for the favor of removing them."

"That would be a curious sight," Kailen grins impishly. "If only she knew she was kissing the hooves of an insurgent, I wonder what her reaction would be."

"Not just her," Kaliya adds. "But the Administrator and all the rest."

"My next objective is the Council building itself," Ayene resumes. "One thing I learned from those two regulators during my interrogation is that they receive their information through a contact at the Council Grand Hall…a public relations office."

"And according to what you said before, they seemed to believe themselves perfectly within their rights to do this work. This makes me a little curious as to what you'll find inside that building. If their Council has become some all-powerful godlike force that no one questions, we might have to bring everyone in."

"That could be problematic," Kailen notes. "Technically speaking, your Azgarén Central Intelligence isn't a fully legitimate government program…it's OUR program trying to usurp their government. If their Council should question it as something they never instigated as part of their own operations, we would be the ones going to prison… assuming they could even find us out here."

"C.P. Security is on our side," Ayene asserts. "This much we can be sure of. They now know about these regulators, so this is a point against the Council's credibility. Furthermore, the apparent extent of their infiltration simply compounds the guilt factor. And the fact that these people admitted to their operation as a Council mandate, including the fabrication of at least half of the reports that went out on the airwaves, and how everything came out of an office in the Council building, won't help the Council's position at all. Also, Petrith and I made sure work during these past couple of months to register all the proper documents to make it seem our office is legit, regardless of who in the Council might…or might not…remember commissioning it. After all, we're on the government payroll," she giggles.

"Your Lordship," Kailen wonders. "How many of those marks does she have on that list of yours?"

"She has a couple, that I recall thus far," he smiles. "But I think she is not finished yet."

"She'll never get as many as me," Kaliya smirks. "She's too straitlaced for that."

"Excuse me," Ayene retorts pertly. "Is that a challenge?"

"Nevertheless," Kailen offers. "It still comes back to this. If there is no Council at all, we have only one other direction to point our fingers, and he IS an all-powerful godlike force."

"Maybe not quite all-powerful," Kaliya reflects. "But powerful enough for our purpose…and dangerous. We just need to keep things under control and use his own methods against him."

"I've been trying to consider how to approach the Council building," Ayene submits. "If we have people in there that need to be pulled out, whoever they answer to will eventually learn about it. This might bring us back to the military side, or even Darumon himself. How do we cover ourselves for this? Install a fake?"

"If we are speaking of yet another agent," Thaelyn considers. "We may need to locate and remove that one as well. But ultimately, Darumon is surely behind it somewhere. I would say to investigate who this next one is and where he links up to. I suspect we will need to install a substitute at some point, but I would prefer it not to be directly under Darumon, to offer a buffer space. Our observations of him within Central Command make it appear as though he does not interact with a great many individuals outside his office. For instance, he seems content to govern the actions of the military largely through the High Commander, with minimal interaction through anyone of a lesser rank."

"So, to replace someone a step below that interface level would allow him to give his orders to a predictable agent, but after that, he simply assumes all his underlings will carry it through the chain on their own. So trusting…" she chuckles ironically. "I guess we really are the trained animals he wanted us to be."

"If this is his weakness, we will exploit it. But those trained animals, Ayene, will be learning a few new tricks," he winks.

"All right, I'm fine with that. Personally, I'm tired of lifting my tail to that creep."

"We must also remind ourselves of your requested mission to the ARC about those seed specimens."

"Ah yes! I nearly forgot about that. I'll plan on that sometime after my trip to the Council chambers. I suspect, if we're right about the Council, I'll need to report back to the Captain to inform him so we can take some sort of action and secure ourselves from yet another scandal. Then we can see about those people inside the ARC."

"Don't forget to take pictures," Kaliya mentions.

"Yes, I have my trans-com ready. Fortunately, these things seem to work even in the phased condition of our projected mode."

"Yeah, but we look a little silly as birds flying around with a utility belt strapped around us."

"Hey, it's a modern world. Can't we enjoy a little luxury?"

The group shares a brief laugh together.

"Well then," Ayene relents. "If there's nothing else, I should be on with the next mission."

She gets up from the table and offers the traditional bow and salute, then retires to an adjacent conference room to conduct her projection. She sits in one of the chairs and relaxes into it, allowing herself to enter a form of meditation, where she imagines her physical body falling away and her spirit emerging independently. The ghostlike image of her conscious projection rises up from the chair and coalesces into a tangible shape resembling her natural self.

Ayene checks her image and reimagines it into her special agent costume, including her dark blue suit and prim appearance. When she was satisfied, she flashed away from the room in a puff.

She reappeared on a rooftop in the north central area of Capitol Prime, just across from the feature known as the Council Plaza. The district resembled a parklike setting with decorative walkways, planters, benches, and several prominent displays of sculpted artwork. It was circled by a variety of office buildings, but the centerpiece was the large Grand Hall, representing the focal point of the Azgarén world government body.

Ayene considered her prospects on where to begin her investigation. She crouched low on the rooftop so as not to be especially noticeable up there. She had at least two primary objectives to fulfill here, one being to investigate the public relations office, and the other to find a way inside the Council chambers, where the Council spent all of its time in deliberation of the many sensitive details they were supposed to be making decisions on.

She studied the plaza from her rooftop perch and the flow of people moving around at ground level. Trying to fold her way to the ground in that clutter would be difficult if she hoped not to be seen. Instead, she looked for an alley or an alcove she could use, and spotted a small utility area for trash disposal. She placed her focus within that zone and folded her image to the ground, reappearing in a secluded nook. From there, she casually strolled out onto the main plaza, where she paused to survey the area, taking note of the variety of shops and cafés lining the circumference.

"If the regulators are receiving their reports from an agent inside," she muses. "I wonder about any other form of press releases. I recall the Council has a home page on the DataNet. I wonder what that has to say. Maybe I could check into it briefly before I make the big plunge."

She turns to find the nearest café and strolls across the plaza to make a visit. She peers inside the busy establishment. There were people sitting at tables sipping tea and other refreshments, some enjoying a small snack, and most of them engaged in one or another conversation. On one side, along the back wall, was a series of public data terminals which were often available to patrons as a recreational service. These were connected to a worldwide information network where people could research news and recent events, or anything else of interest.

Ayene realized these terminals were intended for patrons of the establishment, but in her projected form, she couldn't actually eat or drink anything, and it might appear improper for her to simply walk in and sit at a terminal without otherwise buying something. So she had to fake it.

She glanced around to see if anyone was paying attention, and then quickly folded herself across the room near a restroom door, making it appear as if she had just come out. From there, she created a drinking cup in her hand and casually strolled across the room to the terminals, where she sat down and discreetly surveyed the scene for anyone who might have noticed her arrival.

The cup she was holding wasn't real, just another projected image, and she had to keep it in her hand as part of her projection. This left her with only one hand to work with, but it was enough to engage the terminal. The rest of it used a voice interface.

As she engaged the terminal, she pulled up the Council home page, with the Council logo and a selection of default imagery representing the various government services displayed on the screen. Then, a pleasant female voice announced itself on the speaker.

"Welcome, Citizen, to the Council Public Information Center. How can I help you?"

The voice wasn't a real person, but rather an interactive AI as part of the DataNet interface. But still, it gave a subtle feeling of a social interaction.

"My name is Ayene Ti'van, and I am conducting some research for a university review. I have several questions I would like to ask."

"We are very happy to answer your questions. Please state your first inquiry."

Ayene now begins inventing some questions to see if there is anything to be learned from the service.

"First, I would like to know if the Council has released any new and important research grants relating to…um…the exobiology studies."

"I am sorry, but there is no new information to be released relating to…new and important research grants relating to the exobiology studies."

Ayene stared at the terminal with the graphic logo still emblazoned on the screen, and the remarkably inane response that seemed almost mechanical.

"Well," she mumbles quietly. "I have to admit, I never really used this thing before. So I guess I shouldn't hold out too many expectations."

She tried again with a new inquiry.

"Very well," she continues. "Does the Council have any new information relating to astrophysics and the surveys of other star systems?"

"I am sorry, but there is no new information to be released relating to…new information relating to astrophysics and the surveys of other star systems."

"Well, isn't that efficient. Do you just repeat everything I say? Let me ask you this… Are we still investigating other star systems for habitable worlds?"

"I am sorry, but there is no new information to be released relating to…investigating other star systems for habitable worlds."

"What in all the nether-space…" Ayene whispers urgently. "Is the Council investigating ANY new sciences for future study?"

"The Council is unable to comment at this time. But the Public Information Center will provide our citizens with new developments as they become available."

"Really! Is that anything like what you're doing now?"

"I am sorry, but your question was not properly formulated. Please try again."

"What is the meaning of life?"

"I am sorry, but this service does not contain any references to… the meaning of life."

"Does Azgarén go around the sun?"

"I am sorry, but this service does not contain any references to… Azgarén going around the sun."

"I swear! My old Tuka doll was smarter than this thing."

"I am sorry, but your question was not properly formulated. Please try again."

"Are you programmed with anything useful?"

"This service contains all the latest developments released by the Council relating to new scientific investigations and their associated discoveries, proposals of new theories, and the assignment of research grants to further our technological advancement. The service also provides departmental reports, budget summaries, political overviews, recent legislative proposals, and a roster of the current Council members and their factional reports and objectives. Please select from the menu which service you would wish to inquire on."

"Interesting. All right, let's try this. Do we have any significant new legislative proposals currently in debate?"

"There are no new legislative proposals currently in debate. For a list of previous legislation and its resulting impact to the existing Articles of Law, please reference the section on the Charter of Laws."

"What was the result of the last political election?"

"The results of the previous political election are summarized in this report..."

The screen now changes to display a listing of the most recently elected Council members. Ayene studies it carefully.

"This looks to be in order..." she murmurs, "...as far as I can tell. When was the last election held?"

"The last election was held four years ago during the election period 9862.4 CTD."

"Can you compare the results of that election to the previous one?"

"A comparison of the results of the election period 9862.4 CTD, and election period 9862.3 CTD are summarized in the following table..."

The display now alters to show a side-by-side review of the results of the Council elections from the previous two periods, which occurred a decade apart. The calendar references were based on a Centennial Time Delineation, with the numbers represented in centuries. Ayene studies the report, and again it seems to match her personal experience.

"These are the same people in the same positions. All right, let me ask you this. I want to research the last time we had a change to any position within the Council in the past...oh, centennial period."

The computer pauses briefly as it researches the inquiry. In a moment, it returns a result.

"The results of the inquiry are displayed in the following table… There are no matching results."

"No matching results?" she ponders. "But this still represents a result, in a way. Show me the last change in any Council seat during the past millennium."

Again, the computer pauses to research the historical files before returning a result.

"The results of the inquiry are displayed in the following table… There are no matching results."

"Nothing in a full millennium? Surely, there ought to be someone changing a seat. Show me the last change in a Council seat during the last two millennia."

Once again, the computer processes the request, with the AI voice returning the result.

"The results of the inquiry are displayed in the following table… There are no matching results."

"Wow, either these people are diehards, or this isn't looking good for our government. Show me the last recorded occurrence of a change in any Council seat."

The computer processed this new request, seemingly taking an extended moment to find the results, until a new display popped up, and the AI responded with her answer.

"The results of the inquiry are displayed in the following table… The last recorded change of occupancy within the Council occurred during the non-election period 9764.53 CTD with the removal of Council Elder Velen Nazég and the associated factional representation."

Ayene gawked at the report. If she had been physical, she would be turning pale by now.

"In all the nether-space…" she wheezes. "But that takes us all the way back to the beginning. Show me the last time any active Council member was quoted in a public report or seen in a public function."

The computer now processed this new request, once more taking several moments to research the extensive array of historical files, news reports, science journals, and other public records. Then a new display came forward.

"The results of the inquiry are displayed in the following table... The last recorded public report involving an active Council member occurred on Actana 32, 9765.31 CTD during a public news announcement. Do you wish to review the video?"

"Actana 32..." she mumbles softly. "Early in the year 9765.31... almost eight decades later... A news announcement? Yes, let me see the video."

Ayene watches as the display now changes to play an old archival news broadcast. It shows several people standing in front of the Council building on a podium often used for giving presentations to the news media.

"We are pleased to announce to the people the development of a preventative solution to this awful blight that has become known to us as the Tav'ageen Anomaly. As you all know, this terrible plague has taken many lives, and our medical professions have struggled during these past decades to find the cause, but to no avail. Fortunately, with the aid of our new benefactor, Marshal Darumon, and his enlightened teachings, we have developed this treatment to sustain ourselves until we can finally be rid of this terror by following his direction to depart from our home, and thereby leaving this alien menace behind us.

As part of this plan, the hurried application of the new An'gamu Seed has prepared our people for their departure, and although we find ourselves delayed in our exodus due to these new incursions of insurgent forces into our space, the Marshal assures us that his efforts at redeveloping our military service will pave the way for us to spread our seeds to distant worlds and at last conquer the stars as we were meant to do from the dawning of our modern age..."

"Oh, how lovely..." Ayene huffs. "And so inspirational! It almost makes me think we were accomplishing something. This must've occurred after our people were infected with the seeds, but just before the Suppressor chips were installed. This would also account for the development of the military chips. So, we have all his little tricks now fully mandated through the Council, and I suppose this is the last time they served any useful purpose. No wonder they disappeared so fast. He had no further need of them, and instead started managing things himself through all his proxies."

She leaned back in the chair to ponder this revelation.

"If they've been missing during this full length of time…" she muses distantly. "What is actually inside that chamber of theirs? Computer, where is the Council right now?"

"The Council is currently in deep deliberation of a series of highly sensitive topics relating to newly proposed research materials."

"How long have they been deliberating these topics?"

"This information is not available."

"All right, when will they have something available for release?"

"The Council is unable to comment at this time. But the Public Information Center will provide our citizens with new developments as they become available."

"Oh no, not that line again," she sighs. "What are these topics the Council is deliberating?"

"This information is not available."

"Of course, that much I'm sure of. So, we don't know what they're deliberating or how long it might take. This sounds just like Darumon's rhetoric. All right, let's approach it this way. Surely, if people go missing, someone ought to take notice, like family members. Computer, search for any references to a Council member reported dead or missing since CTD 9765.31."

The computer complies with the request and the voice soon returns the response.

"There are no results to this inquiry."

"So, no one is reported dead or missing, which might make sense if we're all supposed to believe they're in their chamber deliberating something. But this also smells of a cover-up. How does a person lock themselves away in a room without someone, not even a family member, taking notice of them…unless…uh oh…"

Ayene felt a sudden cold spike hit her, at least in a psychological sense, as she wasn't physical to feel the actual sensation. She leans in to formulate a new inquiry.

"Computer, choose a random Council member active since CTD 9765.31, and cross-reference with any known immediate family members. Then report on the condition of that family member, either deceased, or missing."

The computer now processes this new request, again churning away at archival news reports and public records, until another summary comes out.

"This inquiry has resulted in multiple records of a classified nature. This terminal is not authorized to process this request. A military rank of Captain or higher with Class 3 security clearance is required to review these records."

"Oh really! Then maybe I should have my alter ego at Central look into it. But why would something like this be classified? Computer, modify the search to include all active Council members. Search for any immediate family members reported as deceased or missing, and filter as not requiring a military security clearance."

The computer now conducts an extensive search, referencing all the Council members and their families, and filtering the results to meet the criteria.

"This inquiry has resulted in multiple records of a classified nature. There are no matching results to meet the filter requirements."

"Let me see if I can fool you…" she mumbles softly. "Computer, remove the filter and modify the search to include the following criteria…" she pauses to clear her throat. "Referencing the currently active Council members, selecting any and all immediate family members, such as spouses and children, who are currently known to be living, as might be evidenced by such legal documentation or public sightings to demonstrate their active condition. Examples might include tax returns, active licensing documents, owned real estate, education records, and public social activities."

"The prescribed search criteria in this inquiry references sensitive government information. A government security clearance code is required to unlock the results."

Ayene makes a quick glance around the room to make sure no one was paying any special attention to her interaction before responding.

"Try Azgarén Central Intelligence code Ti'van-97225. Unlock."

The computer applies the code through a secure interface window, and then processes this final request. Ayene waits as the data is collected. After a few moments, the voice comes back on.

"There are no results to this inquiry."

"And that's as good as a result in itself, despite your restrictions. I doubt there would be a security issue just to know if someone is alive, maybe to say going out shopping, paying taxes, kids going to school, and so on. This simply leaves us to conclude that they're all gone. The only people who might take notice of a Council gone missing are themselves missing. And if Darumon is involved, this is probably classified under some military protocol to cover it up, and therefore to confound anyone from realizing what's really going on out there."

She again glances around the shop to see if anyone had been paying attention to her private musings, but the rest of the patrons were apparently too busy with their own affairs, so she decides to close out this session.

"That is all. Goodbye."

"Thank you, Citizen, for using the Council Public Information Center. Have a pleasant day."

She glared at the terminal for the perky tribute, and reflexively tried lifting her cup to her lips, only to realize there was nothing inside, nor could she drink it if there was. She stared at it quizzically before shaking her head with a concealed smirk, then got up and left the building.

"The deeper I dig into this dung heap," she whispers privately. "The more it stinks. So, what's next...the Council building? Do I dare peek into that place that probably hasn't seen the light of day for nearly ten millennia? I'm going to have to if I want my answers. Maybe they're all just asleep. Or maybe they're all skeletons."

Across the plaza from her was the Council Grand Hall. It was the centerpiece of the plaza, being a large circular building capped with a tall domed roof rising out of the center. It was a brilliant white marble structure with columns lining the outer rim, and large doors leading into an ornate lobby. Ayene reflected on the imagery, and how once, when she was a young girl, her parents made a visit to see the sights and explore the history of their native culture.

She paused to examine the scenery before making her move. It was a sunny day, as much as it could be for the pollution levels, and there were many people moving through the area. Some were political officials, while others were legal advisors, and there were a number of tourists and local citizens visiting the area simply to enjoy the sights. As Ayene studied the building, she discreetly examined the nearby pedestrian traffic to ensure no one was watching before banishing the image of the drinking cup in her hand. She then began strolling forward as a professional woman on official business.

She arrived at the front entrance and passed through the doors into the large lobby. A short distance ahead was a reception desk with a lone secretary attending to her duties. Ayene steps forward to give her greeting. As she does, the receptionist looks up at her expectantly.

"Welcome to the Council Grand Hall. How can I help you today?"

"My name is Lieutenant Ti'van, and I work for Azgarén Central Intelligence…" she pulls out her trans-com again to flash her ID badge. "I am investigating a report of fraud being conducted by certain individuals said to be located in our government offices. Can you direct me to the public relations office?"

"Fraud? And who do you work for?" she glances at the badge briefly. "I do not recognize that name."

"Ours is a new service recently established to provide internal security of our government operations, as well as to investigate wrongful actions by other government departments and their assigns.

Right now, I have a need to pursue a lead that points to the public relations office."

"What lead, and why there?"

"I am limited in what I can reveal, as our investigation needs to maintain a certain level of confidentiality in order to avoid a public scandal that could then interfere with our future actions. Suffice it to say that the lead was the perpetrator of a criminal act who confessed to us about a contact he associated with here in this building."

"But…this is the Council Grand Hall. You do not simply go around and start asking…"

"Young lady," Ayene interrupts. "I've already been through this conversation a few times. The Council is not a god entity, although they seem to be behaving this way, along with everyone else who seems so complacent to simply trust that they can do no wrong. Well, Miss, WE are questioning what they are actually doing, wrong or otherwise, as we are tired of the perpetual rhetoric that they cannot be questioned for their acts. Do you understand?"

"I understand your statement, yes," she retorts. "But I will say again, I do not recognize your department. And I have worked here long enough that I feel I should know."

"All right, I will grant you this much. But I will also repeat my statement that we are NEW, and we do not WANT you to know anything until WE say otherwise. If the Council likes to play god, so will we, and precisely to uncover why they like playing god. Therefore, I will go around and ask questions, wherever and whenever I must, including here in this building. They are no more above the law than the rest of us, regardless of the fact that they are the Council, and no one cares to question their integrity. As I said, we have a confessed criminal who pointed his finger at an agent here in this building, AND under Council instruction to violate a very clearly defined Article in the Charter of Laws. Now, what do you think the LAW should do about it, if not to investigate why THEY are violating what WE are all expected to obey?"

The receptionist was clearly affected by Ayene's formidable stance, but her reaction was not entirely one of submission to Ayene's authority. Instead, she was at least partially offended to have someone come in off the street, claiming to serve some otherwise unknown security service, and making accusations about the Council. But for the lack of any other recourse, all she could do was glare at Ayene and huff.

Ayene continues, "Now, where is the public relations office? I need to see who works there and what relation he has to this other person before I proceed further."

"All right, you will need to travel down the hall here to my right, about a quarter turn around the building, and the office is on the right. You will see the sign for it as you approach. But I would ask you not to disturb any of the other offices unless it becomes necessary as part of your investigation. This building is managed by a lot of top-level officials, and is not a tourist attraction to stick your horns into any room you please."

"I understand it is not a tourist center, but if my investigation demands it, it is not simply the rooms where I will stick my horns."

Ayene offers a slight nod before turning down the corridor, leaving the receptionist to study her dubiously as she departed from the lobby.

She directs herself along a hallway that leads between a long series of offices that circle the outer perimeter of the building. She studies each door and an associated nameplate for the officer that works there. Along the way, she recalled the briefing at the WIC building.

"If this guy is directly under the Marshal," she considers. "We probably shouldn't do anything to him, as Darumon might take notice. But if he answers up to someone else, and this represents a bottleneck to the propaganda chain...hmm."

As she strolled along the hallway, she came upon the door marked for Public Relations. She paused outside to study it.

"Here he is. Now, how to approach this... Do I go hard or soft? I don't want him reporting anything to a higher authority, but if he's an underling, I want to take him out."

She mulled her thoughts for a moment before getting an idea. Then she pulled out her trans-com.

"If I can get him to talk about anything, I'll record it and file it with the Captain. I'll let him deal with it afterwards, assuming I get what I want."

She places the trans-com into record mode and sticks it back into her pocket. She then steps forward to press the announcement button before peeking in the door.

"Yes?" ushers a mature male voice from within the room. "Come in."

Ayene enters the office, which seemed rather frugal in design with a basic desk and a couple of chairs, a bookcase filled with several rows of reference libraries, and a number of plaques hanging on the wall behind the man. He looked up to see the professionally attired young woman waiting patiently for his attention. He studied her briefly, as if trying to judge who she might represent.

"Who are you?" he inquires flatly.

"I'm here in reference to the two regulators that were working inside CPComm. They said I should speak to you."

"About what?"

"About the information they were receiving from you and passing through the media stream. They said you should be able to provide me with more detail relating to the nature of that information."

"And just who are you to be asking these questions? This is a Council-mandated operation, not a junior school homework project."

"Well, aren't we polite today. I guess the Public Relations office isn't high on the congeniality of public relations."

"This is not my job description. I do not take visitors in here for casual conversation."

"Of course. Then let me get onto business. My name is Ayene Ti'van. I'm a special agent working in a classified security project. At one time, I was working for Central Command, at least until I was transferred to this other department. Now we are attempting to verify the flow of this information said to be passing through here, and that it meets with the intended interests."

"A new security department? Is the Marshal changing his

regulation policy now? And why would he send someone like you here? What happened to his secretary?"

"Oh, my apologies, I thought you knew. Ours is a new department we recently developed to consolidate and ensure the integrity of the policies we are supposed to be maintaining. Naturally, as you are an integral part of his management network, you would need to be included in our overview process, correct?"

"Well, yes, I suppose. Is this to say he intends to apply a new policy to our operational procedures now?"

"For the moment, we need to make a series of reviews of the existing operations, and yours is currently on the list. It is my understanding you receive reports, which must then be relayed to the regulators in their offices at the media stations, is this correct?"

"Yes, it is. I receive them from the Secretary of External Affairs in the Marshal's office at Central Command. They pass through here, where I make a review of the official signatures, and then they go to our regulators in their offices to be blended into the outgoing media broadcasts."

"Do you interact with these reports in any way? What I mean is, do you alter or modify their content before sending them forward?"

"No, I leave that to the regulators. They usually contain informational elements and instructions on how to regulate the outgoing news reports so to keep the public image stable."

"I see, and this comes prepackaged from the Marshal's office. Then your role here is largely a store and forward link, and you interact with such as CPComm and other broadcast stations."

"Yes, when the reports come in, I send them out as a mass-mailing to all our regulators."

"Very good, and this helps me to understand your office and the role it plays. I will record this in our journals and let you know about these changes once they are put into action."

"How long before I might receive this notice?"

"Oh, I think it should not be too much longer. This particular chain doesn't seem too complex, overall. We have the Marshal and his immediate secretary, then this office, where you are best described as a type of interface between that and the broadcast networks. And of course, we have the regulators themselves. I think we should be able to tidy up these operations quite easily. But now, if you will excuse me, I need to report back to my office."

"Of course, and good day to you."

Ayene offers a polite nod and leaves the office. As she returns back down the hall, she mumbles to herself.

"Yes, very neat. Take him out and we have our break in the Marshal's chain. Then we just replace him with a fake, and start broadcasting our own news reports."

She continues back to the lobby with her mind now turning towards her next objective. She again arrives at the receptionist's desk. The girl looks up at her hesitantly.

"Yes Ma'am, is there anything else I can help you with?"

"Anything else? With respect, young miss, you don't seem especially willing to help with anything to begin with, other than directing traffic for those people you believe are supposed to be travelling through here."

"Look, I am just a girl trying to do a job. It pays the bills, and that is all."

"All right, fair enough. I was once one of those, although I was a law enforcement officer, and directing traffic, in my case, might also involve arresting people."

"Uh huh…"

Ayene turned her gaze in the direction of the ornate double doors deeper inside that led to the Grand Hall itself. The receptionist takes notice of her direction and instinctively follows her gaze.

"Wait a minute!" she interjects. "I have instructions. No one is to disturb the Council while those doors are closed. They are also locked, to ensure the Council has its privacy while in deliberation."

"All right, well said," Ayene relents calmly. "But when was the last time you saw anyone come out of there for any reason?"

"Me? I have never actually seen them come out during my work shift."

"Not during your work shift. How long is that? And is there anyone else who works this desk?"

"My shift runs six hours, and then a replacement comes in. I think there are several of us, all six hours each, and we rotate our schedules."

"Very well, I can accept this. But it would seem to me the Council should also take an occasional break, right?"

"Well, I suppose they might, but it was never during my shift."

"Do you ever speak to any of the others who work this desk to see when that actually occurs?"

"I only know a couple of the girls who work here, the one I replace at the end of her shift, and the one who replaces me at the end of mine. After that, I am at home, or maybe out shopping or something. But in answer to your question, we do not generally talk much about what the Council is doing in there. It is always the same story."

"Yes, it is, the same story, day after day, year after year, century after century."

"Huh? What are you talking about?"

"Oh, surely you know the story. The Council is in deep deliberation of something, and it goes on forever. I did a little research on the DataNet before coming in here. It was rather educational. Do you know the last time any Council member was ever seen in public?"

"Um, no..."

"It was almost eight decades after the arrival of Darumon and Sargeras, during a press conference relating to the new development of the Suppressor chips."

"Eight decades...but wait a minute, that was...um..."

"Roughly ninety-seven centuries ago. And I'm fairly sure some of those people were past middle age at the time. Then I learned there hasn't been a change in the Council seating during that entire time, even after all those election periods we should've had along the way."

"But that is... That seems strange, to say the least. Ninety-seven centuries and not one new election?"

"The search results only showed one change in the Council, and that was the expulsion of Former Elder Velen Nazég. Now, let me ask you a simple question, Miss. How old are you?"

"Me? Why me?"

"Humor me a moment."

"All right, I am eight and a half."

"Let's say you were one of the Council Elders, and like I said, some of them had to be old-timers…a hundred plus. In all this time, do you think they would still be alive if they've been serving the same seats without change? Our people still have natural lifespans, last I heard. We have not unlocked the secret of immortality just yet. And what about all those who might have been campaigning for those seats, but failed? Where did those votes go? Surely, in these ten millennia, someone ought to have earned enough votes to replace someone by now."

"Ma'am, I would not have the answer to that. I just work here to direct the flow of people through the building."

"I see, so I guess you don't pay much attention to what happens behind those doors, unless someone actually opens one."

"Right, and I will caution you again, in case you are getting any ideas. The Council is not to be disturbed, and those doors are locked. And I will call security if you try to go past me."

"Do I have to remind you who I work for?"

"No, but I will also remind you, and I stand by this, regardless of your earlier statement. I do not know YOUR department. As far as I am concerned, you could be anyone walking in off the street with a very cleverly designed fake ID badge."

"All right, since you seem to be so experienced…" Ayene relents politely. "Unless I get angry and call that same security to demonstrate just what level of authority I do actually have. The Council plays god, no one questions it, and no one ever opens those doors to ask why they are breaking their own laws. Then, when someone finally develops the horns to actually do the impossible, people like you question why we don't tell YOU about it, if our enemies are the ones you place so much unquestioned trust into."

"Ma'am, while I can see the point you are trying to make, I must still stick to my position. It is my job."

"Very well then, and I suppose I must admit, you do your job well," she nods. "You are a feisty young one. By the way, where is the nearest restroom? I have a sudden urge coming on."

"Oh, it is just down the hall and on the left."

The receptionist points down the other corridor to a sign on the wall indicating the local facility.

Ayene nods and strolls away to the restroom door. She peers around casually to see if anyone was looking, but there was currently no one except the receptionist in view, and she wasn't paying any attention by this time. So she ducks inside.

Once out of view from the hallway, she reimagines her shape to a small insect. But this leaves her trans-com falling to the floor, as she was now too small to carry it.

"Hmm," she ponders in her thoughts. "This isn't good. I need this with me."

She now tries to think of an alternative. She reshapes her body to that of a squirrel, which was at least large enough to wear a utility belt and a holster for the device. She places the unit in the slot and recalls the image of the lobby and the ornate Grand Hall doors. She would fold her image directly to a location behind the receptionist and carefully proceed from there.

She disappears from the room in a puff and reappears in front of the large doors. The receptionist is clueless to her arrival as she was too busy with her other duties. Ayene pulls out the trans-com and gently sets it in the corner, then turns to examine the door, looking for a convenient way inside.

The doors seemed to fit seamlessly within the framework, but in her projected form, Ayene was not limited by size or shape. She tried imagining herself as thin as a sheet of paper, and narrow like a ribbon, then sliding through the tiny gap under the door. When she emerged on the other side, she found the room was pitch-black.

She couldn't see anything around her. There were no windows or other light sources, and the place seemed deathly quiet. She reshaped her image to her natural form, even though she couldn't see herself to confirm the result, and then she tried something new by holding up a hand and creating a bright orb of light shining out from it.

The effect illuminated the immediate area well enough to allow her to locate herself near the door and to search for a light switch on the wall. After a few moments of fumbling, she finally found one. She hit the switch and turned around to see what the rest of the room looked like. But as soon as the switch flipped on, she took notice of a muted electrical crackling, followed by several showers of sparks raining down from above. Some of the fixtures had apparently shorted out on activation and the bulbs burst.

"That's not a good sign," she muses softly.

Some of the lights were apparently still in an operable condition, if only barely, and she could hear a faint buzzing, as if more shorts could occur at any moment. She stepped forward to examine the room, but as her eyes came into focus, she couldn't believe what she saw.

"In all the nether-space!" she wheezes. "Look at this place!"

In the dim lighting, she could see the remains of the Council Grand Hall. The floor was littered with debris that was clearly the result of long-term decay. She bent down to pick up a piece and examined it closely, then looked up at the ceiling.

"This is old plaster that chipped off. Look at it up there! That ceiling looks like it's falling apart."

She stepped forward into the room, glancing around at the walls. All around her, the plasterwork had chipped away and now lay on the floor. It gave the appearance of nearly an eternity of decay in a closed environment. The walls and ceiling were eroding down to the metal framework, and even that appeared to be barely holding up. She studied the rows of audience chairs, where she saw the heavily lacquered varnish peeling away from rotted wood, along with crumbling seats and their disintegrating leather cushions, and everything buried under thick layers of dust. She continued forward to the Council Bench in the middle of the room.

The Bench was a large semicircular table arcing around on one side of a raised platform at the head of the room. In the center was the Speaker's chair positioned to oversee the rest. But everything was empty. The chairs appeared to be neatly tucked away, and a heavy layer of dust, plus debris from above, obscured what remained of the natural luster of the stone tabletop. Ayene gazed at it and sighed, then hung her head in despair.

"All my life," she mourns. "I've heard of the Grand Hall, the center of our government, with all its glamour and heritage, the prestige of our society to govern and direct us to pursue greater knowledge and wisdom. And here, these unbelievably incompetent dull-horns can't even check the light bulbs on occasion, to say nothing of the rest of it."

She makes a quick survey of the rest of the room, now diverting herself to walk along the outer rim to check for any other doors. But the room was a closed environment with only the main door leading in.

"I would imagine that ceiling will come down one of these days," she muses. "I'm surprised it hasn't already, for the amount of damage I'm looking at up there. With that door closed, and no one ever coming in here, this room must have been isolated from the outer environment, including most of the moisture content. But not for much longer, I think. And then I'll bet someone will take notice when a huge crashing noise takes place. Wouldn't that be a surprise…and on multiple levels. How can a society be so inept as to let something like this go by without checking on it once in a while? You would think a building manager would call for occasional inspections, at the very least."

Having seen enough, she now returns to the door, silently debating over what to do about this.

"Damage like this should be noticeable at some moment," she grumbles privately. "Holes in the roof, sounds of falling debris…and SOMEONE getting a thought to check on things, regardless of the fact the Council is supposedly deliberating something and doesn't want to be disturbed. The building safety codes should override some part of that."

She ponders her choices and inspects the door. She finds the locking bolt, which was turned to lock the door from the inside. She knew if she should open the door, she would probably draw the immediate attention of the receptionist outside. But at this moment, she had the answers she needed as far as this building was concerned, and to go the next step would need to involve outside help anyway. So, she turns the bolt to unlock the door, and opens it to let herself out.

The door slowly creaks open as the half-rusted hinges grind through layers of corrosion. The sound echoes through the room and the lobby outside.

The receptionist perks up at the sudden announcement and turns to peer over her shoulder. There she sees Ayene standing near the double doors to the Grand Hall, and instantly her ire renews at the continued persistence of this young officer poking her nose into places she otherwise should not be.

"You!" she shouts and jumps out of her seat. "This is a restricted area!"

Ayene turns to see the young female rushing towards her, so she steps up to meet her.

"I warned you," the girl shouts. "But this is final! I want you out of here, and then I am calling…"

Ayene lurched forward and cut the girl off in midsentence by grabbing one of her horns.

"Hey!" she gripes. "Ow! What are you doing! Let go of me! I am calling security for sure now and have you arrested!"

"Miss," Ayene states calmly. "I AM security! And no one tells ME what to do. I have C.P. Security in my back pocket, so you go ahead and call them, and we'll see whose tail gets thrown behind bars. Now, if you want a little education for your eight and a half centuries, let me tell you something. My research on the DataNet told me no one has seen the Council for almost ten millennia. I also tried researching why no one saw them. For instance, surely the family members might tend to notice their loved ones gone missing. But do you know what I found? Those same family members are also missing, and the reasons are apparently hidden behind a Class 3 military security cover-up. Now isn't that interesting?"

"I have no idea what you are talking about, but let go of my horn!"

"Sure... But first, I want you to see what that six-hour job of yours is protecting. Do you recall the phrase to drag someone by the horns? Well, I'm going to apply it in literal context and show you what the Council is deliberating."

Ayene now turns and begins dragging the younger woman by her horn, forcing the girl to follow along to the door, where Ayene pulls her inside.

"Miss, I present to you the Council of Elders. But wait, where are they? And just look at this place. You know, if I were a Council member, the first thing I might want to deliberate would be a repair bill."

The receptionist gaped at the scene. The musty air tingled her nose, and the outlandish disarray of debris and decayed furnishings stifled her. She simply stood there, motionless, as well as speechless. She gazed all around the room, stepping forward to inspect some of the seating, and further to examine the Council benches.

"What happened here?" she whispers timidly. "Where is everyone, and what happened to this room?"

"I don't know if I could answer the part of where the Council actually is, but it's not in here deliberating anything. And if you recall what I was trying to tell you earlier, half of them should have died of old age by now, and our elections haven't chosen any replacements since those early days. And this room is a clear indication that no one, not even a maintenance crew, has been inside here. How do you explain THAT, Miss Guardian of the Grand Hall?"

"All right, you have my attention...finally. Please do not rub it in any further."

"Don't rub it in..." Ayene chuckles ironically.

The girl took quick notice of Ayene's emotional display. Even though it was small, it stood out as unnatural in their emotionally restricted society.

Ayene paused to examine the young woman for her obvious reaction.

"You question my integrity as someone who has had a horn-full of this nonsense?" she pans her gaze at the scene in front of her. "Our office isn't listening to those tail-yankers anymore. Therefore, my chip is disabled. We don't actually need that torture device. The whole reason behind it was fake."

"Fake?"

"Yeah, and you can thank our All-Powerful Council that can do no wrong in the eyes of the people. That, and these 'temporary' seeds we're forced to take."

"The seeds...but what about the pollution up there?"

"Let me build a little picture for you. First, the Council, at the request of the Marshal, enacted these war protocols due to his insurgents making threats against us. As a result, we have this sudden need to build up a heavy military to defend ourselves. As a consequence, we also need a lot of heavy industry to build that military. The result of THAT is pollution...lots of it. But hey, we were told to evacuate our home planet due to this awful Tav'ageen Anomaly, which frightened the horns off our planetary population to the point where they forgot we have all sorts of advanced tech to do the job. Instead, our illustrious Council, with all their unquestioned wisdom, and again at the request of the Marshal, told us to use the one thing no one ever wanted to use, the An'gamu seed. It was a matter of 'any means necessary', where the term 'any means' doesn't seem to involve any of the normal tech we would prefer to use. Are you with me so far?"

"Yes ma'am. But..."

"And then," Ayene interrupts. "Even though we were told this is all temporary, AND our heavy military should have the problem under control...any day now...we allowed this heavy industry, with all of its pollution, to continue to destroy our home, when in fact we had more than enough time, as a society of thinking people, to realize we actually DO have cleaner industrial tech to replace the emergency stuff, despite the fact that...any day now...we might be leaving. Therefore, we had the luxury of time to REMEMBER all the other tech, to CORRECT the pollution, and thereby to STOP using the seeds as our 'any means necessary' to solve our issues, if not for the continued rhetoric by our unquestionable Council AND our most beloved benefactor, the Marshal, claiming, once again, how… any day now…it'll all be over. Are you STILL with me? Or do I have to…rub it in…even further, Miss eight and a half centuries?"

"All right! Look, for all my eight and a half centuries, I am just a young girl trying to make a living. It is hard enough to pay my bills and get by. I do not play with politics. I see your point. The Council clearly slipped the tip on all these obvious failures of reasoning and corrective procedures. But this all occurred long before I was born. I am simply trying to survive in whatever is left of it."

"I would say this is worse than simply slipping the tip. This is a deliberate effort to distract us. Especially with people like you blocking access to those answers the rest of us should be pushing to learn about."

"Yes, I suppose you are right."

"Very well," Ayene relents gently. "I understand your perspective for this much. I was there once, myself. But it stings, nevertheless, to realize you are born into a society that holds itself so high, and yet forgot what it means to actually live up to that standard. Here is where we have people like you who refuse to question the Almighty Council and their unquestionable wisdom, leaving this situation STILL out there, and us STILL with all this garbage no one actually wants."

"Right. So, you are blaming them for a lot of errors that brought us to where we are now, and none of it justified. It should have been realized and corrected long ago when it became clear we were NOT leaving…any day now…and probably when those days turned into decades and centuries, and finally millennia, with our pollution levels steadily increasing, until we find ourselves where we are now," she pauses to examine the room again. "And the Council is not even where they are supposed to be, or doing what they said they were doing."

"Exactly."

"But listen, I am sorry, but my orders were very simple. While those doors were closed, the area was forbidden. This is all I know for my job description."

"Of course, and surely to keep the secret. I have heard of similar 'orders' made by others, and for similar reasons, and those reasons are often to cover something up that they who give those orders don't want us to know about. By the way, who is it that gave you those orders?"

"My boss, the Internal Secretary."

"Then I may need to add him to my list, because if the Internal Secretary doesn't even open that door to check the light bulbs on occasion, no one would know about this until the roof caved in."

"Yes, I would have to agree. But what does all this actually mean? Who are you really? Because I do not recognize that department name you gave me."

"Of course... But there is also a reason for that. And that reason is a countermeasure to all this," she waves her hand at the room.

Ayene stepped outside the door briefly to retrieve her trans-com, and then returned to flash her ID badge again for reference.

"Azgarén Central Intelligence... We are essentially those people who should've been asking the questions the rest of you neglected to ask when all this got started. We're a new secret service agency people like you aren't supposed to know about beyond a name and a general sense of dread for the level of authority we carry. If the Council likes playing god, we will match them at this game. We do not stop at locked doors or security blocks, because those blocks are apparently there to keep people like you from realizing the greater truth, and that truth is essentially threatening our civilization."

"Threatening our civilization? Is it really that serious? I mean, well, yes, the pollution, and then..." she pauses to examine her body.

"The pollution is simply a symptom, not the cause," Ayene nods. "It runs deeper than that, to those who demanded it, and then covered up their reasoning. And the reasoning involves that perpetual story of...any day now...blah blah. It involves the reason why we were made to take the seeds when we have tons of other tech to do the same job. But oops…we all forgot about that, due to that old Tav'ageen Scare."

"That's not nice. I didn't like having my body deformed by this thing if it was actually preventable."

"You and me both. And assuming they were actually present in this room, even the Council should be afraid of us. We are the security force that monitors the security forces, as well as the government and anyone else who thinks they can play god with our people. The Council is breaking their own laws, which is beside the point of them not playing the role we hired them to play as our world government. And the rest of us are expected to obey them without question."

"Uh huh…" she relents. "Then you must be very new. Like I said, I have worked here for a while, and thought I was well-versed in all the departments. But then, who ordered this new department, if not them," she glances at the empty room.

"Yes, this might open a controversy. Why would THEY hire someone like US, who might then turn on them if they aren't doing their job. Well, in answer to this, we ARE new, as well as discreet. But THEY didn't hire us. We were installed by those other authority bodies who got tired of listening to that 'any day now' nonsense, and the Marshal's perpetual promises, as well as suffering all this 'temporary' garbage they pushed at us for half an eternity. We are now questioning why we're still here, why all this is still hovering over our heads, and why he is STILL making his promises, along with our Council, but without any demonstrable results. And we're not buying this eternal deliberation business anymore. It shouldn't take ten millennia to review the secrets of the universe without a simple press release that they ARE reviewing the secrets of the universe, rather than sleeping their years away at their desks."

"Um, alright."

"Therefore, we are keeping a low profile precisely for this reason," she again waves a hand at the scattered remains of the room. "Granted, it would normally be the Council to authorize and establish a department like ours. But we represent a type of checks and balances office to ensure THEY are keeping to their legal demands as our government body, and according to the…spirit of the words…of our Charter of Laws."

"Why did you just now put emphasis on that term?"

"Because the spirit is how we are made to believe in something they seem to be toying with for their personal needs. Therefore, we are this separate agency NOT established by the Council, but rather another responsible authority, and for the purpose to actually question the Council and their…needs. As such, we are not subject to them, their mandates, or their god complex pushing all their rules onto people like you. We will push THEM instead."

"But this sounds like you intend to overthrow them."

"Overthrow? This?" she points at the empty room. "If we choose to follow that 'spirit' of our laws, THAT should be the governing authority, and they should be following the same. However, we began to suspect something a while back. Let me ask you this. Why would someone want to overthrow a government authority? I can think of a few reasons right off the top. One might be a hostile body that wants to take power for themselves. Another is to bring down a corrupt body that is abusing the people. You need look no further than that bug on your back, and that chip in your head for the abuse, and the reasoning behind how and why they are pushed at you. Now ask yourself. Would you want to overthrow that, or continue infesting our people with these parasites and chips no one wants, and a polluted world which is our natural home we apparently are NOT leaving?"

"All right, but then, what about the Anomaly that caused it?"

"The whole thing is being brought into question as for its validity. We have real colonization tech, so why not use that? We can certainly mobilize ourselves, if need be, to leave home in the time it takes to actually find another world to colonize. And yet, they pushed a piece of old, and generally unwanted tech at us for our solution. Why? Then, in the time it took for us to realize we're not going anywhere, we thoroughly polluted our world with this dirty tech, so we needed it right here at home. This represents an ulterior motive that was preventable if our Council was actually providing a proper service to the people."

"Yes, I see it. But this naturally leads us to ask why the seeds. And then the chip."

"Yes, it does. And THIS naturally leads us to question the unquestionable wisdom of that government body we all placed our unwavering faith in that they can do no wrong in the eyes of the people…according to the spirit of the thing. We are made to believe in something on faith…like a religion. And yet, we are not permitted to actually hold a religious belief. It's tragically ironic, and it's kicking us in the tail, and we don't even realize it."

"Of course, I can see that now."

"Unfortunately, my department is tasked with a rather disturbing objective. We believe there is a conspiracy at work here, and the Council was originally implicated as holding a role in it. But if the Council doesn't actually exist, this raises it to an even higher level…one that we feared from the beginning, and this would be our evidence," she glances once more at the room.

"And what is that?"

"That an alien creature came to our world and took over, and we were all told to look the other way."

"An alien creature? Wait, do you mean…"

"The Tav'ageen Anomaly was purported to be an alien infestation killing our people. Well, it was, but not the one we were made to believe in."

Ayene now dials up a number on her trans-com and waits for an answer.

"This is Captain Bein'talan of C.P. Security, how can I help you?"

The receptionist glared at Ayene for the casual manner of calling up such a high-ranking security official. New department or otherwise, it hinted at a relationship that was establishing itself rather deeply, and in secret.

"Captain, this is Ayene, we have a situation here at the Council Grand Hall. You are going to need to see this personally. And I'll also ask you to bring a large posse of troops. We need to secure the full building and interrogate everyone. I already know of one person we need to arrest in connection with Article Nine, Section Fourteen, and I suspect the Internal Secretary may hold some relation, if for no other reason than his simple negligence for the building maintenance."

"All right, one thing at a time. What sort of situation do we have, Lieutenant?"

"The Council is missing, and I suspect it dates back to the last time Darumon wanted them for any of their mandates."

"In all the nether-space!" he shouts. "When you say missing, what do you mean?"

"I am currently standing inside the Grand Hall, the inner chamber where they have long been said to be deliberating something. The place looks like it's ready to collapse on me for ten millennia of abandonment and neglect. In fact, I'm surprised the roof is still holding up, but I think only because the doors were locked, thereby keeping the interior environment relatively isolated. There are no bodies. Instead, it appears as though they left and never returned. But this isn't the end of it."

"All right, what else do you have?"

"I did a little research on the DataNet a short while ago. The last known sighting of a Council member was on 9765.31 for the press release of the then-new Tav'ageen Suppressor chips. Since then, they apparently went into hiding and no one has seen them since. Also, I suspect our elections were rigged to reelect the same people consistently during this full length of time. And finally, their immediate family members, those who might be the only ones to take serious notice of missing people, are also apparently missing. But the reasons are classified behind an executive-level military grade security clearance, so I'll need to investigate that separately the next time I visit Central Command."

"Do you have access to that grade sof security?"

"I'll manage. Meanwhile, this leaves us without any form of official government, even though we were told they're in some kind of important deliberation. This brings me back to our earlier discussion of the seeds and the chips. Darumon only needed them for this much, and the rest is being managed through his proxies, like with the news media."

"All right, I will gather up some of my men and meet you there. But what do you propose we do about this? You were talking about scandals and sensations with the regulators inside the media, but this will take things through the roof."

"I know, but if Darumon is behind it, we need to keep it extremely quiet until our counterforce is ready to move. He still controls our military with their chips, and this is a dangerous situation for the rest of us."

"I just hope those people can make their move before he does."

"We have some solid support behind us, and we're developing a number of very elaborate plans. Meanwhile, I need to take a series of photos of this place for our own records. I'll wait for your arrival, Captain."

"Good, see you soon."

They end the link and Ayene glances at the young receptionist. The girl was clearly showing worry now, and clutched gently at her interface.

"What's your name?" Ayene asks tenderly.

"Lena..."

"All right, Lena, you will do exactly as I say and ignore your boss from this moment. You speak of an overthrow? Maybe you're right, but THEY..." she points into the room, "...are not the government body we're trying to overthrow. They probably don't even exist anymore. Meanwhile, none of this happened. We need to cover this up. Our enemy is that one we've been calling a benefactor for so long. He came here with a bag full of lies, and our dull-horned Council, to say nothing of the rest of us, all listened to it. Now, it's a matter of survival, because that military he worked so hard to build, presumably to fight his so-called insurgents, could just as easily turn their guns at us down here."

"What do you mean? Aren't they our own people?"

"Yes, but unfortunately, they're controlled by a classified chip he mandated once through the Council to override their minds.

I should know…I had one of my own, although I was fortunate enough never to have it turned on. But he has a history of blasting whole worlds apart using programmable soldiers, so let's not give him another target."

A group of Suuden'kai soldiers were trudging their way through the darkened corridors of a dank subsurface maze. The bright lighting produced by their helmet lamps illuminated the surrounding walls to reveal countless ages of accumulated sludge and waste materials, and the seepage of water trickling along trenches and drains.

The stench of decay was absent to them through their environment suits, which involved the internal regulation and recycling of a sealed air supply. The suits were armored and had numerous sensors embedded into the chest plate and helmet, producing a tactical readout on a HUD inside their visor.

"These passageways do not seem to follow logically," notes one soldier through his com-link.

"Agreed," answers another one. "My interpretation is they must have been constructed and reconstructed without any prior organization. But there must be a connecting chamber to another segment."

"I think we have passed through this tunnel once before," a third one pauses briefly. "See there…" he points at a pile of rubbish. "I recall that mound from a previous sighting."

"They all look the same to me by now."

"There is a corridor approaching at the next intersection," the first one directs. "We will try that one."

They arrived at an intersection, where they ventured earlier by branching off to one side, but now they try the other direction. They now travelled through a new tunnel leading off into the darkness.

The catacombs they were following were an ancient maze of old sewers and forgotten chambers below the streets of the city of Sigil…a large, enclosed construct in the shape of a torus, located somewhere among the Outer Planes, although its exact location sometimes came into debate.

The internal surface of the hollow space housed a bustling cityscape, where the city wrapped fully around the circular form. Beneath its street level were sewers and other passageways descending down through the layers until it came upon the outer hull of the construct, where these Suuden-Aryku had earlier cut a hole to gain access from outside.

They continued through the soggy halls filled with piles of refuse that had collected over time, whether as the result of debris amassing into clumps, or by some local denizen forming up a nest. In the distance, their HUD monitors detected motion.

"Another one," calls the group leader. "Prepare for combat."

They raised their plasma rifles to target the object on their scanners, while continuing to move forward undaunted as to their own mission and ready to blast anything that got in their way. In the distance, they noticed a small creature approaching. They studied it, making ready to fire if it made any aggressive moves.

The creature appeared to be some manner of rodent, and it was clearly intimidated by the group of four tall Suuden'kai soldiers. It noticed the onset of their bright lights and scurried away through a small opening in the wall. The soldiers did not pause to examine this feature, but instead marched forward slowly.

Another intersection came into view. They halted and brought out portable scanners in an attempt to detect what might lie beyond the shadows.

"To the right," the leader suggests. "I am detecting an incline."

They follow the new path and up a gentle ramp, leading into a new chamber. The room was a large cathedral-like setting, with several alcoves lining the walls and an altar at one end. There were also many shapes looming at the edge of their lanterns.

"Beware, this room is active," the leader cautions.

"These lifeforms do not register on my HUD," advises another member.

"They are mobile, that is sufficient. Prepare yourselves."

Several of the shapes take notice of the new arrivals. They turn and begin advancing on the group, sounding out morbid moans and wails. They staggered along mindlessly but purposefully, with more following behind from deeper in the room.

"They appear hostile," the leader observes. "Ready your weapons… And fire…"

The soldiers opened fire with plasma bolts flying out in a wide spray ahead of them, striking the bodies of the advancing force and obliterating them in flaming detonations. The mass continued to move on them, and the Suuden-Aryku methodically plowed through with more plasma fire. As the assembly made its steady motion into the light of the helmet lamps, the Suuden-Aryku were better able to see the details of their attackers.

"These creatures do not appear as living entities," observes one soldier as he picks a new target. "It is irrational that they have the power of movement."

"This entire universe appears that way, continue your attack."

The bodies of the undead creatures exploded from the intense firepower of the Suuden'kai weapons, keeping the front line well enough away that the soldiers could eliminate the horde before it made contact. The floor of the room was now littered with fragments. Those that were still connected with an upper torso and skull twitched and attempted to claw their way forward.

"How can a creature continue to persist with such damage?" asks one soldier.

"My HUD does not show a valid lifeform present," answers another one. "These are not natural entities."

"We should move forward," the leader asserts. "They are not a threat at this time."

The soldiers followed another corridor out of the room, through a series of interchanges and up another incline. They soon found themselves in what seemed to be a more active environment, with the sounds of running water echoing through the halls.

"We may be nearing an exit soon. Stay alert."

They moved along a tunnel with a stream of water flowing

along a channel in the floor. Drain exits on the walls poured out a continual flow, and once again, their HUDs detected movement.

They pressed forward cautiously. The readouts were showing life signs this time. First, one, and then several gathered together as a group. They could hear the sounds of thrashing and grunting. An open space came into view in the distance. They were approaching another room.

"Prepare yourselves," warns the leader.

They emerge around the next corner and are confronted by a trio of large burly creatures standing upright on two legs and sparsely covered in course hair. They stood on hoofed feet, their hands terminated with sturdy claws, and their heads were covered in a shaggy mane and bore a set of curved tusks. The first of them turned and rushed the intruders, intent on making a meal of the bulky Suuden'kai form.

The soldiers took up a defensive posture and blocked the charging beasts with their weapons. The leader twisted and slammed the butt of his rifle into the sternum of one creature to knock it back, while another soldier jammed his rifle into the next one's gut. A third soldier thrust his shoulder into the last one, sending it reeling backward. He then brought his weapon around and blasted it.

The other two creatures squealed and lurched back at the sudden flash from the rifle and the decimation of their fellow. They jumped away and ran off through an adjacent tunnel.

"We will not pursue," the leader commands. "They will not likely make another attempt."

"What if they return in greater numbers?"

"Then we will destroy them. But for now, we must continue our mission."

They keep moving through the tunnels, following another incline, and now they can hear the common noises of activity echoing through a gated opening. They approach and peer through the gate onto a street outside. The leader studies the gate to find a latch held by a chain lock. He motions the others to stand back while he blasts it with the rifle, bursting the doors open and allowing passage. They peered outside to examine the scene.

"Our orders are to locate the rift aperture, but not to interact with the local population, if at all possible."

"Understood," responds another one. "We should inform the ship of our progress."

"Agreed."

The leader activates his com-link to their ship to give his report.

"This is Lieutenant Ki'sav to the Tul'ryk. We have arrived inside the city."

"Tul'ryk to Lieutenant Ki'sav," responds a voice through the link. "Acknowledged, we have been charting your passage through the structure. We will continue to monitor your movements. You will report when you have discovered any anomalies."

"Affirmative."

They strolled out onto the street, taking notice of the unusual architecture lining the curved interior surface of the immense structure. The roadways and buildings stretched out in all directions, up the side, over their heads, and back down behind them, while at the same time following around the circular curve of the torus shape. The spectacle would have been an impressive sight, were it not for their lack of emotion due to their Suppressor chips dampening all sensations.

"This aspect of the assignment will be time-consuming," remarks one soldier. "There are no specific parameters on what to search for."

"Our instructions are to seek any bound space," the leader recalls, "bordered on four sides to create a frame."

"Is that to describe a door or a window?"

"The instructions describe any two-dimensional space bounded on all sides, including furniture, floors, walls, alcoves, gaps, and holes."

"With respect, Lieutenant, that statement is irrational. How can a rift persist under an item of moveable furniture or a random hole in a wall?"

"I would agree, but I must also remind you of the abnormal nature of this space. Therefore, I cannot give a viable answer. These are the instructions given by the Marshal, so he must know what he is talking about. Spread out and observe if there are any reactions in the surrounding environment. It is described to present itself if we pass within close proximity."

"My HUD is registering a viable atmosphere outside," comments the third soldier. "Shall we remove our helmets? We may draw too much attention if we continue like this."

"You may be right, but at the same time, be alert."

The squad engages an environmental cycling release before unlatching their helmets to remove them. They then tuck the helmets under their arms, keeping a watchful eye on the local populace for their reactions.

Many of the people passing by on the street glanced curiously at the tall strangers, noticing the pale blue skin and spiral curved horns, along with the armored suits. But they simply turned away and resumed their travel. The city was well-known for the visitation of odd beings, so the sight, while not generally familiar, was also not especially significant.

The soldiers began moving out in different directions, investigating the various objects and areas in the local neighborhood, watching to see if anything changed as they passed by. One of them stepped inside a local shop while another found a small alley. A third one was inspecting several boxes and a wagon sitting next to a building. The leader simply walked slowly along studying the surrounding features.

There were many pedestrians moving through the avenue, some on their way to the markets, while others were in conversation with fellow citizens. As the soldiers worked their way along, several passersby took notice of the odd behavior, but chose not to interact due to the imposing stature of the visitors.

They continued their inspection of the nearby buildings and associated furnishings, working their way along the street in the direction of a small plaza. On the other side of the plaza were a group of beings hovering above the ground and apparently conducting maintenance on one of the buildings. They were tall and dressed in flowing robes. They stood stiffly erect, with a shock of white hair and horns protruding in a narrow corkscrew jutting forward from either side of their foreheads. They were intently focused on their work, until one of them noticed movement out of the corner of his eye.

Normally, he would not concern himself with the comings and goings of the common people on the street, but this image represented one to take special notice of, as he had instructions to watch for such strange visitors lurking about, and with such features as these. He angled his view around rigidly, rolling his eyes over to examine the arrival of the tall, blue-skinned foreigners in their clearly militaristic technological battle suits.

He returns to gain the attention of the others, displaying a form of symbolic language floating over his head to communicate his sighting, and the group follows with a similarly aloof motion to study the newcomers. Another member of the group displays a series of symbols as a directed order, and the first one turns and briskly floats away over the buildings and into the distance.

The Suuden'kai soldiers continued their survey of anything they could find in the local area to satisfy the requisites of their mission, but so far nothing presented itself with any indication of a response to their passing. They worked their way slowly around the plaza, taking care not to invoke any interaction with the local inhabitants, or the odd floating beings working on the building overhead. They were just coming full circle around the plaza and preparing to return to the main avenue when the sounds of shrieks and screams resounded from the other direction.

The squad turned abruptly to follow the cries. They saw people running through the streets and taking up shelter inside buildings and alleys.

"Something is occurring," the leader observes.

"There…" points another soldier, "…hovering above the buildings. And it is moving this direction."

In the distance they could see a roughly feminine figure in an ornate robe and elaborate mask floating over the cityscape and moving determinedly in the direction of the plaza, followed closely by one of the laborers. The leader glanced quickly at the other two beings still working the building, but now oriented in the direction of the new arrival.

"Those creatures must have reported us," the leader surmises. "That one appears as a governing official."

"We were warned to beware of that one," suggests the second soldier.

"We did nothing to draw attention. It is irrational to suggest we invoked this response."

"That being departed as soon as we entered the precinct. It was waiting for us."

"Waiting for us? Impossible."

The leader quickly pulls up his com-link to make a report.

"Tul'ryk, this is Lieutenant Ki'sav. Urgent! We are being approached by an entity hovering above the landscape. It appears as a governing official. We believe it may have been called by another being we observed in the local precinct portraying a civil maintenance worker..."

In the air above, the ornately clad figure descends on the plaza. Her focus was directed at the squad as they tried reporting in. An instant later, a volley of razor-sharp blades flies out from around her mask, circling once, and then shooting out at the invaders. The flurry of action lacerated and flayed the soldiers to the bone.

On the com-link in the ship, the Captain listened as the message was cut short by screams and gurgling sounds, and then silence. The officer at the security station studied his crewmember status readouts, observing the bio-monitors of the soldiers now altering and displaying alert signals. Their life signs had gone flat, and the data links faded.

In the plaza, the mutilated bodies of the Suuden'kai soldiers lay in a heap on the roadway. The eyes of many wary citizens peered out of windows and doorways around the plaza to observe what happened, clueless as to the meaning of this event. The ornate figure loomed over the corpses to examine them.

"Commencement... Infiltration..." her voice reverberates around the district.

She then sensed something very old, very familiar, and very unsettling. She moved closer for a better look, and then let out a resonant wail.

"Infestation...! Intolerance...!" she moans harshly.

She turns back towards the being floating at a distance behind her, reeling in her blades as she pulls back from the carnage.

"Notification... Encroachment... Amalgamation..."

The being nods and displays a series of symbols as a response, and then moves away.

The female turned back to the scene of the slaughter and extends a hand over it. The bodies suddenly burst into a brilliant flash of blueish fire, incinerating them down to ash, fully destroying the corpses such that no part could ever pose a threat to the city's security. When she was satisfied, she circled around and lazily returned home.

Chapter 2

AMBITIOUS MINDS

"Why is it staring at me like I'm next on the menu?" Sulíma mumbles hesitantly.

"Try not to look it straight in the eyes," Túfula suggests. "It might be regarded as a challenge."

"But if I turn away, it might charge at me."

"I honestly don't think either of you is in danger," Petrith consoles. "It's just another of Relissa's class projects."

"Aye," Relissa offers. "But I'm still getting used to him. I just got the assignment this week, you know."

"At least it's not a hawk," Haran quips. "Like your last project. I came away from that one completely drenched."

Relissa and Haran were sitting in their usual spot in the guildhall courtyard with their Daanen'kai friends Sulíma, Túfula, and Petrith. It was after class, and they were going over their daily lessons and other gossip.

"Well, if you recall," Relissa teases. "I didn't tell you to start a water fight. Just do something wacky so I could send my little spy in to check up on you and report back."

"And a water fight isn't wacky?" Sulíma wonders.

"Aye, well, it was a lot of fun in the long of it. I think even the supervising Master had a few good rounds."

"So, how does this one work?" Túfula asks. "How do you use a wolf as a spy?"

"This one won't serve only as a spy. He can also be a survival companion. These are pack animals, so I could have a bunch of them follow me around, a bit like a family where they all watch each other's backs. They can work as spies like most others, peeking around bushes and trees, but also hunt and protect."

"That could be very useful, I suppose," Petrith considers. "If you're out in the wilderness by yourself, it might be nice to have a few bodyguards."

"And you said there are different varieties of them?" Túfula inquires.

"Aye," Relissa replies. "This is one of the bigger ones, called a gray wolf. They can be very loyal if you teach them right. But like with most animals, you need to know how to pull the right strings, which is what I'm studying right now."

"But is it actually safe for you to have this one outside a cage?"

"This one is already tame. We keep him and a bunch of others in a habitat for trainees like me to practice with."

"But is it normal for him to look so hungry?" Sulíma winces.

"Nah, he's not really hungry. I think you're just imagining things. Come over and pet him. He likes it."

Relissa coaxes her new wolf companion to her side while Sulíma reluctantly bends forward to reach out a hand. The wolf extends his snout gingerly to sniff her hand, and then begins licking it.

"Ew!" she jerks back tentatively at the contact. "He's tasting me!"

"Suli, he's not tasting you. This is a show of affection, by licking your hand, and even your face, if you get close enough. See his tail?" she points. "When it's wagging like that, it's a sign of friendship."

"Uh huh…and what would he do if he sees my tail wagging," she giggles.

"Let's not test that theory, shall we?" Petrith cautions impishly.

In an open area near the front of the courtyard, a large upright circular plane takes shape. The rippling surface denotes a planar fold being created as a form of interdimensional transport, though it is not certain as yet by whom. Nevertheless, such apparitions as these are not used by common people.

"Jiggers!" Relissa shouts. "Look at that!"

The group turns to face the spectacle, as the sight draws the attention of the rest of the visitors in the courtyard. The surface emanates a concentric rippling pattern, and then a form emerges into view. It hovered above the ground, a tall robed being of rigid composure, a shock of white hair, and with horns protruding from its forehead.

"Buggers! It's one of them!"

"What in the names of the gods," Haran mutters. "Relissa, what is that?"

"That's a dabus from Sigil. I remember seeing those when Thaelyn took us up there that day to meet Aelwyn, and also, um… the Lady."

"Ah, so that's what they look like. But what's he doing down here? This would be a bit like slumming if I understand it right for those people."

"Aye, but I can only think of one thing right now."

The dabus moved slowly over the grounds, surveying the lowly Prime lifeforms staring at him from all sides.

Relissa jumped to her feet and approached reverently. He gazed down at her with lofty disdain, projecting a series of symbols over his head.

"I'm sorry," she replies politely. "I don't know your language, but I can call Lady Aerlie. She should be able to tend to you well enough, I think."

He nods haughtily.

Relissa calls her newest companion and ushers up an assemblage of low whines and howls, mixed with a few keywords as instruction.

Sulíma, Túfula, and Petrith all stare at the outrageous presentation of animal communication, while the dabus glares down his nose at the primitive interaction, rolling his eyes and wondering silently if he should've ever attempted such an exchange.

The wolf barks and howls a reply, and then takes off in a hurried dash out the front gate. He races down the road to the intersection, then turns off to the left towards the Temple of the Planes, where Aerlie spent most of her time.

It ran along the avenue, drawing the attention of people walking by on the street, and then sharply ducked through the open double doors of the temple. It charged up the aisle towards the dais and began sniffing its way around the altar, and further to the rear of the room to an office.

Aerlie was attending a series of administrative duties at her desk when the oversized animal poked his nose through the door. The unexpected intrusion caught her attention almost immediately.

"Well now," she coos. "Is Relissa playing one of her little tricks on me this time? How quaint," she giggles softly.

Aerlie whistles gently to draw the animal in further, and he starts howling and prancing with body language suggesting he desired her attention.

"Relissa needs me up in the courtyard? All right, little fellow, lead the way..."

Although Aerlie didn't actually speak like a wolf, her Celestial skill at telepathy allowed her to see the imagery within the wolf's mind, and communicate back in the same primitive form to convey her acknowledgement of the message, and together they dashed out of the room.

They emerged outside and the wolf takes off in the direction of the guildhall, halting briefly to ensure Aerlie was still following. Aerlie spreads her wings and charges forward, flapping briskly to lift off the ground and glide along the avenue behind the wolf. Together, they rush along the road and up to the gates, where they reconvene in the guildhall courtyard.

Aerlie sets down on the ground near Relissa. She takes immediate notice of the dabus waiting anxiously amongst these curious, if also unsophisticated beings.

"Relissa, when did he arrive, just now?"

"Aye, and he doesn't look too happy, assuming they ever look happy."

Aerlie turns to their visitor and makes her approach, offering a polite bow as she makes her greeting.

"Companion dabus," she begins respectfully. "Do you have a message?"

The dabus reveals several lines of symbols over his head, relaying the missive from the Lady, the governor of Sigil. Aerlie studies his wording, as does the rest of the group in the courtyard.

"Cu'Nar's grace," Sulíma moans quietly. "How does he do that? Is that some form of writing? Don't they speak?"

"As far as I understand it," Haran mentions softly. "This is how they communicate. They also tend to be very snooty, so it's best to treat them with a lot of tolerance."

The dabus finishes his statement and Aerlie considers the message briefly.

"Very well, and thank you. Tell her I will pass this to Thaelyn. I cannot be sure how we will approach this in the immediate term, but we will consider our options carefully and see about a solution as quickly as possible."

He nods and turns, forming a new planar fold, and then passing through it, thereby departing from the local space.

"My Lady," Relissa inquires. "What is it? Did something happen up in Sigil?"

"Yes, apparently the Suuden-Aryku have discovered the city. A squad of soldiers was seen in the streets and dispatched. We are safe so far, but there was something else."

"What else? When it calls one of them to come all the way down here for it, I get the wiggles crawling up my back."

"The Suuden-Aryku were said to be found with the essence of what the Powers often refer to as the Ancient Ones on their bodies, as if it was a part of them. I'm not completely sure how to interpret this at the moment, but it is disturbing to think that each one might be a potential threat, if any should find the portal gate."

✦✦✦✦✦

Thaelyn and his officers were engaged in the latest of their daily meetings in the WIC building. Ayene was reporting on the final outcome of her investigation of the Council Grand Hall on Azgarén.

"He's thorough, that's all I can say. He covered for himself by removing the immediate family members of the Council, and with a clever excuse for it as well."

"What sort of excuse?" Kailen wonders.

"When I did my research on the DataNet, I originally tried to search for any that were listed as dead or missing, thinking he was trying to remove any witnesses or potential threats that might take notice of the missing Council members. The results initially came up requiring a Class 3 military security rating, which is one of the upper levels in terms of command rank."

"Excuse me, please," the General interjects. "But how do these ratings measure out?"

"Oh, I'm sorry, yes. The lower-numbered ratings are actually higher security levels for the upper echelons of rank. For instance, Class 1 would be the HC. Someone like Commander Kriv'tik might have a Class 2 or 3, depending on his service record. If we look at someone like Captain Ta'yeen, who oversees the control booth in Central, he might have a Class 4 most often, although again depending on his service record, he might carry a special allowance for a Class 3. And so on. In C.P. Security, we use a similar system, and I started at Class 12, which is entry-level, then moved up to a Class 7 by the time I enrolled in the Marshal's special assignment on Morndindor. This was enough to qualify me as a junior officer in that position."

"Most interesting, and thank you. Please continue."

"Anyway, I used my Captain disguise in Central, and along with Petrith and his recent work at, um…" she coughs subtly, "…

reconfiguring their security protocols," she grins innocently. "We were able to tap into that file to see what it had to say."

"I love how she describes it as reconfiguring the protocols," Kaliya muses affectionately. "It carries such a promising overtone, don't you think?"

"Indeed," the General smiles.

"You kids..." Kailen muses and shakes his head. "I recall when it was once called hacking."

"Nevertheless," Ayene continues. "The results we found were not so pleasant. According to the history, the Council and their immediate family members were secretly sequestered away as part of a type of quarantine procedure to protect our government body from the Tav'ageen Anomaly, treating it as a form of plague."

"This would actually make sense to me," Thaelyn suggests. "It would not be uncommon for a collection of prominent officials to be hidden away in a secure facility to prevent their loss from contamination or some other disaster in a world that is stricken by calamity."

"I can't personally recall any historical example of this, but then our history dates back so far that any historical event involving a large-scale contagion would be largely forgotten by now, except to those who specialize in ancient history."

"And for us," Kailen adds. "That easily dates back to our medieval period, which is at least a thousand millennia ago."

"Good gracious," the General relents. "Such dates."

"Maybe so, General..." Ayene grins cautiously. "But this is who we are. So, the stories of them occupying the Council Grand Hall were mostly fabricated from the beginning, with the doors kept closed and locked to prevent anyone from discovering their government was actually hiding elsewhere. This also accounted for anyone who knew anything about this being kept silent with security protocols, saying those people were absent from public view with justifiable cause. This might include family friends and the more distant relations."

"Indeed," Thaelyn admits. "Leaving only those who are very close to the source as the weak link in the equation."

"The whole assembly, meaning the Council members and their immediate families, were presumably relocated to a place they called Site One-Alpha. Naturally, this made no sense, as we've never heard of a place called Site One-Alpha. So, I had Petrith do a little more digging. Site One-Alpha was a codename for an old Sentinels' frontier outpost we had in the early days, before Darumon started tinkering with things. It was apparently repurposed as this quarantine site, and the Council would be returned to Azgarén only on those occasions when a public showing was necessary to give press reports and announcements, like the one I told you about in that video I found."

"How convenient," Kaliya moans.

"But here is where it gets flaky. Sometime shortly after that one broadcast in 9765.31 CTD, with the announcement of the new Tav'ageen Suppressor chip, we have a reference suggesting the Council was repatriated due to the stabilization of the situation of the Anomaly."

"Essentially to say, the crisis is over, they can come home now."

"Right, and this is where they go into their new deliberation of something big and important without end. But the condition of the Grand Hall tells a different story. According to Lena, that receptionist, her orders are to keep people out. The area is off-limits, forbidden, a no-go zone under any circumstances, and this is apparently backed up by her boss, the Internal Secretary."

"Do we know if he is serving Darumon in any form?" Thaelyn asks. "Either directly or perhaps as a proxy?"

"He tells us he received his instruction from his predecessor, who received it handed down by the previous one, and so on. Apparently, his story goes that the Council was given high-level topics to discuss as part of the Marshal's promises, and these were described as very delicate matters. As such, they had to sequester themselves away to ensure their maximum security. The press wasn't allowed inside, no tourists, no visitors, and no family members until further notice. When asked about such simple things as food and rest, he said they were supplied with accommodations inside the chamber to serve their needs, as they had to remain entirely isolated from everyone else due to the highly critical nature of this superior wisdom they were researching which could alter the fundamental way of life for our people."

"Are these the actual words he used?" Kaliya inquires.

"Yes, and I was taking note of these along the way. It makes the whole thing sound like we really did receive the secrets of the universe out of Darumon, but no one is allowed to know about it until someone on the Council can figure out what to do with them."

"Wow, so how do we explain the poor condition of the Grand Hall if we have all these secrets given to us that could change what we thought we knew about life, the universe, and everything?" she smirks.

"Yeah, it kind of deflates the whole image, doesn't it?"

"And how do we explain those election results," Kailen inquires. "If the Council is in this dedicated deliberation, with no visitors and no alterations to their membership due to these secrets they were given, is everything else simply a front to excuse it as business as usual?"

"I asked him about this. He said yes. This one Council was tasked with the highly extraordinary opportunity to unravel these remarkable secrets granted to us by the Marshal, and no one else was permitted to examine them until this one, and ONLY one Council had finished their deciphering of those secrets into something our population could finally make use of."

"Was this before or after you dragged HIM into the Grand Hall to rub his nose in his own excrement?"

"Before, naturally," she snickers. "I wanted to see the look on his face, as well as hear the screech he made from his feedback, when he saw the truth."

"Something tells me you have a little bit of a mean streak in you," he grins. "Where is he now?"

"Captain Bein'talan has him, and will keep him incarcerated for now until we can figure out what to do with him. I don't necessarily consider him a bad person, just highly disillusioned, like a lot of people, probably."

"And his job position? Someone will need to fill in as a replacement, much like that public relations officer you took out."

"Right. We may need to call in one or more replacements from the Stormhooves, at least for now, but maybe we can eventually hire someone from the local workforce who would qualify as a permanent replacement, only under our authority."

"Did I say you had a mean streak?" he chuckles. "I think you're actually enjoying this."

"Well, as Lena said during this time, it's an overthrow. Our ultimate purpose is to usurp and replace the existing government, isn't it?"

"Yes, I suppose, but I never heard of it being done like this before."

"But now, as for the Council and their family members, here is where it gets dark. Site One-Alpha no longer exists. It was apparently an early casualty of the insurgent attacks. However, on the bright side, according to the security report, it was unoccupied at the time," she shrugs.

"Uh huh…" Kaliya muses. "And so, where did everyone go if they're not showing up as alive and well, but instead listed as security protocol Class 3 dead or missing."

"That's a good question, but it's one we're not likely to find the answer to at this point. This was nearly ten millennia ago, so if it was destroyed, the debris is probably long gone by now. If we make an assumption, it was either blasted as one of Darumon's early target practice sessions, or maybe it was emptied and the people dropped somewhere out of sight and out of mind, and probably on a dead world."

"Or maybe it's still out there, abandoned in the cold of space."

"And filled with a lot of skeletons? Maybe. But it's a forgotten piece of space trash as far as Central is concerned."

"And so," Thaelyn reflects. "The Council was removed from power once they served no more functional value to Darumon, leaving the Grand Hall empty and neglected with the excuse of them being sequestered away for this exceptionally high-level study. There are no mentionable witnesses remaining to speak on anyone's behalf, and Darumon is essentially in full control of their government authority, in one form or another, through his traditional means of misinformation and proxy servants."

"This reminisces so much like his plays here in Rolsklinde," the General relents.

"And it also reinforces some of our assumptions about him, that he needs these plays to maintain any level of control, as the operation is otherwise very complex with too many loose ends."

"But some of these loose ends are now coming under our control," Ayene offers.

"Indeed, and this is good. Now, from this moment, we must make our plans against him using our own propaganda campaign. I would first desire to conduct a few studies, one being that journalist, Miss Ur'paran. Let us see how much we can depend on her by dropping a few enticing leads in her lap. But we must take care in how we formulate this, as it must simulate the Marshal's censorship practices, while at the same time offering suggestive clues as to the true nature of the world around them."

"Oh, that'll be fun," Kaliya winces.

"We must also try to disarm his capacity to produce his death toys. Without this, he loses one of his offensive capabilities, although the most sinister is still the military."

"Yeah, that's the one I'm waiting for. We left a deep impression with the crew of that control booth, including High Commander Geilv, when we blew up the mining base on the com-link."

"I still feel sorry for him about losing Commander Kriv'tik," Ayene mourns. "I had no idea the two of them might be friends, but Lajivi tells me they shared a close bond for their long term in the service."

"I feel for this situation as well, Ayene," Thaelyn nods. "But in the end, we can repair this by reuniting them. The only obstacle here is Darumon. And based on our spy video of the occasion, I am asking myself if this play we made might actually offer us a potential weakness we could exploit later, with the only uncertainty being to find the right moment for it."

"We'll keep our eyes open, my Lord," Kaliya affirms. "Although it's difficult to predict what and when. This also reminds me of that video clip of him in the processor facility. Did you have time to review that, and if so, what is your impression of it?"

"Ah yes, where he seems lost in his personal thoughts where the mining was concerned, as well as the output product. 'To teach them how to do this on their own…' This is what he pondered. That, along with some manner of justification NOT to share this wisdom, and concluding with that curious mention where 'he' could learn of it."

"My Lord," the General offers. "The term 'he' must clearly refer to Sargeras, but why should Darumon care as much if he holds an opinion over the Suuden'kai harvesting the metal themselves, and therefore processing it into this weapon?"

"My opinion, based on the wording, might not relate directly to the processing of the metal, but Darumon's mention of the technology ladder he would need to carry them through simply to understand the nature of adamantium in order to harvest it at all. This would correlate to teaching them the one thing he seems averted to, meaning the dynamistic flows, and therefore Master Velen's science faction. And those teachings could ultimately identify HIM."

"Oh dear! But of course."

"He would need to help them learn…finally…what all this so-called 'abnormal energy' is, and what it is good for. But this would open up a rather vast amount of subject matter for study. At the same time, it would likely break most of their existing science. And for a society that is already, as he said, very mature, this would simply exacerbate the situation."

"Teaching us those secrets he never wanted to teach us," Ayene nods. "This could truly uplift us as a civilization."

"Indeed. And this, in itself, speaks to me, based on some of our earlier spy recordings, like that of the Governor here in Rolsklinde. They are overseers, and did not apparently care for competition. If the Suuden-Aryku are already regarded as very mature for their standard sciences, to finish it by teaching them the arcanic versions would tip the scales such that Sargeras might not like what he sees. My only conclusion, therefore, is Darumon is protecting his investment for all his previous work at developing them, such that he can finish what he started without his master intervening and tossing away a valuable asset, due to his own prejudices."

"Well, I suppose I might actually feel somewhat heartened by that statement…somewhat. But this also suggests he is walking a fine line to achieve his goal, while trying not to offend his master at what he created to achieve that goal."

"Yes, I would agree," he chuckles faintly. "But if their purpose is this revenge attack, combined with releasing the remainder of the Primordials, I would have to regard this as a tolerable means to an end."

"Maybe so. But it also means we need to walk a similarly fine line to achieve our goal. We need to stop him at Sigil, we need to reverse his games on Azgarén, and we still have Ytani's image to use somewhere along the way."

"And speaking of him, have they taken any new actions where Ytani is concerned?"

"We already saw them beef up their security around Azgarén local space," Kaliya asserts. "And so far, this is stable. And they're continuing this campaign of dropping jump-space listening buoys everywhere. They're creating such a thick web in their detection grid that Ytani won't have a chance of getting close without someone noticing."

"I'm not surprised," Ayene muses. "With over seventeen hundred units of star-destroying bombs in his pocket, I'd be a little nervous, too."

"Yeah, but it seems a bit futile, from my perspective. If each of them can create a blast radius of two and a half lightyears, what good does a countermeasure do? You just need to jump one sacrificial ship into the local area and boom, no more local area."

"Still…" Thaelyn asserts. "We will need to bring his image back into play at some moment. But rather than play the terrorist bomber, this young man holds much closer desires. If we recall his delusions of godhood, as expressed on Morndindor, he desired to rule a world with a slave population and his own private army. Furthermore, he would not wish to play this game on a world with such inferior lifeforms as those. He will instead wish to take this home, where he can find more interesting lifeforms to play with, especially if you factor in his primal lust for female attention."

"So, he'll want to do the same as he was with our base staff," Ayene accedes. "He was demanding female sex partners, and using his threats of the chips or his private army to enforce his authority."

"Now, the way I see it, at first, he must make a presentation, and his arrival has to be public. After all, he wants to present himself to his new subjects. Then, he will make one or another demand, and he will likely expect results."

"Meaning tribute, like more girls… But if he's expecting results, how does Azgarén deliver on this?"

"This is looking nasty," Kaliya smirks. "I wonder how Darumon would respond to it. Would he actually give in to a terrorist wielding his own weapon?"

"Clearly," Thaelyn resumes. "We cannot make this move until after we have some form of space fleet to make a physical presence in Azgarén space. This would reinforce the notion that Ytani has returned with his unknown friends, and they have access to Azgarén, despite their counterefforts. But at the same time, I would suggest we measure ourselves carefully. It is Darumon who is our enemy. The Azgarén military needs to be brought under some level of containment. We do not wish to invoke a panic, and therefore injury. This is where our opportunity might come into play, assuming we can find our opening."

"Right, but this sounds so ironic. He spends half an eternity to develop us as a minion species, and one of them turns on him with his own bomb and starts ransoming the rest."

"And this eventually brings us to our beachhead. We need to set down a local base of operations so we can make our official approach to dispose of Darumon and Sargeras, and rid Creation of the last of their kind."

"This is the hard part," Kaliya remarks. "I have my people

scouting all sorts of areas, but it would help if we had some idea of what to look for and how we plan to approach it. We're checking hills, valleys, canyons, as well as looking for any kind of caves, in case we want to go underground. So far, I'm assuming we don't want to be too far away from Capitol Prime, so we can keep a close eye on Sargeras, but not knowing how this will play out is raising a lot of mystery for us."

"I understand, and I agree we must decide on our methods. Personally, I am hoping those last few quatrains in Adalon's book hold some special clue, but we have yet to discover the keys to unlock them. She has been leading us on a very careful course of action thus far, and if those last pieces are being held in reserve as containing details on how this will ultimately reveal itself, I feel we must watch for whatever critical events are forthcoming to unlock those passages so they can explain to us how to proceed."

"That sounds tricky, my Lord, and it places a lot of faith on something we can't be entirely certain of. But on the other hand, Adalon does seem to hold some inside knowledge, so I guess we don't have any choice. Between her and Maker Kuroku, it would seem our entire journey up to this point has been engineered."

"It does, and so we may have no other recourse but to follow our direction as it is laid out for us. Therefore, my suggestion for now is to catalog everything we can, and hope time is on our side."

✦✦✦✦✦

"Marshal, I have a report."

The head of the Suuden-Aryku military, High Commander Geilv, is making a special report from his office on the vid-com to Marshal Darumon. He announces himself in his traditional cool monotone voice, which was the combined result of his emotion inhibitor chip and the military authority chip he and all the rest were mandated to possess, but in his case, it was turned on, therefore restricting his manners even further.

"Yes, Commander," the Marshal responds with his typical gravelly tone. "What is it?"

"We just received a report from the Tul'ryk on their investigation of the city structure."

"Good, and what do they have for us this time?"

"They advised that the most recent expedition into the structure managed to infiltrate the street level and began conducting an investigation of the local area for the rift aperture. Unfortunately, the expedition was lost."

"Lost?" he barks. "Is this to say they misplaced their directions, Commander, or do you mean to suggest the squad no longer exists?"

"It was terminated."

"Did I not say, Commander, to be careful when moving through that city?"

"Affirmative. The Captain of the Tul'ryk reports there was a final communication before losing contact. The message described the sighting of a being of formal appointment was seen approaching, possibly called to attention by another being serving a municipal function."

"Called to attention? How, in all Creation, would any local inhabitant know enough about us to suggest this, unless that squad made some inane blunder to bring down the law on them!"

"Unknown, but the Captain is sending another team to continue the search, with instructions to avoid more of the same as seen on the previous occurrence."

"Good. Perhaps this is simply the result of your troops representing a foreign body in that space, and they're very easily agitated. We should keep a low profile whenever possible. Keep in mind we are dealing with some very strange beings as compared to anything you may have encountered before. We don't know what sort of capabilities they might have, but we shouldn't take anything for granted."

"Understood."

"Did we receive an adequate description of these creatures to know what to look for next time?"

"The description was incomplete, but future expeditions will study the native inhabitants more closely to determine the most likely candidates."

"Excellent..." he pauses a moment in thought. "Ultimately, however, trying to make a thorough search of that place will likely be problematic, especially if they are so jittery. I'll need to think on this a while to see if we can, eh, optimize our efforts...yes. Let me know as soon as they have anything new to report."

The Marshal ends the link, leaving the Commander gazing into the room as he pondered his instructions. Suddenly, a minor tick erupted in his right cheek. His expression didn't change for the odd disturbance, as he continued to stare blankly into the distance. Then another tick flinched from the corner of his mouth.

"Containment procedures..." he mutters softly.

He stands up and begins a slow march out the door of his office and down the hall towards the control center. This was the nerve center of their main military headquarters located just outside Capitol Prime, called Central Command. As he arrives in the room, he is greeted by the resident staff members, including the officer who most often oversaw their local operations, Captain Ta'yeen.

"Captain," Geilv states flatly. "I require your assistance."

"Yes, Commander, what do you need?"

"The Marshal wishes to relay instructions to the Tul'ryk that their future expeditions must be made as discreetly as possible to avoid any further contact with the local population."

"Yes Sir, this much I think is well understood. But Sir, this incident suggests they might have been expecting us. The response was much too rapid and decisive to be coincidental."

"Agreed, and this reminds me of our operation on Therinë. The Marshal was discovered by his opponents there and had to withdraw. Could those same opponents be operating this facility as well?"

"Um, Sir. I seem to recall a news bulletin relating to that, suggesting it was actually something completely innocent that required rethinking the approach."

"Yes, Captain, you are correct. That report was given to the media to keep our situation stable for the implications of the discovery. If it was contained on that other world, it might not spill over to us here. And for all our history here, we do not need any more public disturbances in our streets."

"So, we fabricate the news announcement, in this case, to keep the situation calm. How nice. Very well, do you have any thoughts on this new development?"

Geilv stared vacantly into the Captain's eyes, which was not unusual for a person under the influence of the military chip. Then another tick erupted on his cheek. The Captain took immediate notice of this.

"Commander," he cautions. "It is happening again. What else did he say?"

"He suggested devising methods to optimize our efforts."

"And what is your impression of this suggestion?"

"Containment procedures..."

"Oh no, not more of those," he shakes his head. "Sir, with respect, this could backfire on us. Especially, as you say, if this facility belongs to those opponents you spoke of. If they should make any efforts at retaliation, we could find ourselves losing more than just a single expedition. You said he was discovered once, and it should have been contained somewhere. If this response is something related, I might say, it may NOT be contained at all."

"Agreed, at least in theory. The Marshal suggests we be aware of the abnormal nature of the local population. I want a full assessment of this nature and how it compares to our own example. We are going to perform what the Marshal never apparently allowed anyone to perform before...an analysis of the target. Relay an order to the Captain of the Tul'ryk to compile a survey report."

"Yes Sir. Is this in addition to their primary mission objective, or are we altering it?"

Geilv gazed into the distance as he mulled the idea.

"Make this objective the priority for now. Perhaps they were attacked because they were armed and represented a public threat potential. Perhaps there are gun laws in effect."

"That is a very interesting thought. It might also explain why they were attacked so quickly. Although I might also suggest an alternate idea."

"And what is that, Captain?"

"If they went in as fully armed soldiers ready for a fight, this might suggest a hostile approach. This is effectively foreign ground we are walking into. Someone must clearly own it, and might not like us behaving as if WE own it."

"Good point."

"So, what if we try sending a few expeditions in there appearing more like...tourists, perhaps?"

"It offers a new approach, but apply caution, nonetheless."

✦✦✦✦✦

Aerlie was reporting to Thaelyn and the other officers in the WIC building after her meeting with the dabus in the guildhall. They were now considering what manner of response they might have. They knew the purpose of the Suuden-Aryku infiltrating Sigil was to locate the ancient portal rift where the Estelar once incarcerated the surviving Primordials during their campaign of the Celestial Wars, and Darumon was apparently hoping to release them.

"We knew this moment would come eventually," Thaelyn admits.

"So far," Aerlie advises. "It would seem they only now arrived, and this was their first attempt to infiltrate the city...or at least that is to say in open view of anyone."

"There are no external entrances to the city, as far as I know, so the only way for them would be to literally cut a hole in the outer shell and work their way in, most likely from the lower sewers, as unpleasant as that may seem."

"Welcome to Sigil!" Kaliya heralds. "And over here we have a pile of refuse," she giggles.

"Indeed!" he laughs. "And this would not make for a desirable first impression. My worry is if they begin to realize there is a potentially hostile force inside, they will alter their methods, either to send in heavier forces to counter it, or take evasive action to avoid it."

"Heavier action would not be the wisest course," Aerlie suggests. "If they're trying to sneak in, they wouldn't want to draw so much attention. After all, they will eventually want to deliver the components of a conveyor into the portal, and you can't do that as easily while fighting your way through the streets. More likely they would choose covert measures, trying to avoid detection altogether."

"I would agree," the General muses. "But at the same time, I wonder how long it will take for them to understand the hierarchy of authority in the city. If it were me, I would attempt to pass a word back to my superior if I came under any form of attack, so the next team would be better informed to know what to watch for."

"This is reasonable," Thaelyn affirms. "But it also leads us to ask how many of these teams the Suuden-Aryku are willing to sacrifice before they make this realization, and then to consider their tactics to be futile."

"Personally," Kailen notes. "I'm trying to understand the underlying motivations at this point. Darumon's weapon is gone, so he can't move forward on that side of it, hoping to do away with the Estelar so he and the others can take control again. Therefore, unless he's simply hoping to locate and identify this portal for future reference, he couldn't expect to do anything with it while the Estelar are still out there. He should feel a bit stifled by now."

"Perhaps, therefore if he should wish to try again, he would need to start over with the development of a new weapon, and this would buy us a considerable amount of time if to consider the quantity he was amassing the first time."

"But for that," Kaliya offers. "He needs to find someone capable of harvesting it, as he already seems avoidant of teaching the Suuden-Aryku the means."

"While this may be true, I think we should not take too much for granted. I would tend to err on the side of caution for this much. His statements in that video at the Madzurki base might suggest his concerns, but this could also change. Our actions, beginning here on Therinë, then at Morndindor, should see him losing his edge by now. Time may be on his side, if he thinks he can afford it, but let us also consider that same statement of the Suuden-Aryku already appearing very mature. There may be an upper limit on Sargeras's tolerance for such sophisticated examples. So, this might come down to a simple act of desperation to reach his final goal before that occurs."

"Oh great! Thank you very much," she huffs. "Just one more thing to watch out for. Well, we have our spy cameras inside Central, so if he gives any kind of order, we can watch and maybe try to intercept something."

"A better solution would reflect more on the Commander's idea," Aerlie glances at Kailen. "Deterrence, to stifle his motives... This one patrol was unfortunate enough to pass by a group of dabuses. But now that we know they are present, if we had more eyes out there watching, maybe to send out more alarms, we could possibly prevent them from moving around at all, keeping them away, or at the very least, to stifle their ability to make any real progress."

"More eyes..." Thaelyn wonders. "Perhaps in the form of a civilian watch?"

"Yes. As the General said, they will eventually become wise to the dabuses being a kind of early warning system. But if we put out something like a public notice...or wait! I know! A wanted poster! Ooh, I like it."

"My Lord," Kaliya eyes Aerlie suspiciously. "Did she ever get any marks on your list?"

"Indeed, she did qualify for one or another. Fortunately, I married her, so I can keep a close eye on her," he grins. "But this is a curious mention. A wanted poster, which might include a picture, or perhaps a drawing, and a brief description of the suspect. These could then be spread throughout the city for the average citizen to take note of, and therefore report any sightings. Yes, and this would surely invoke a rapid retreat of any new incursions. It could buy us some time, but I think we should still consider what might ultimately follow as they find themselves so completely stifled. Much like the Commander said, if he is out there at all, even without his weapon, this might already suggest a form of desperation, or at least reckless daring."

"We'll need to locate where they're coming from," Aerlie considers. "We could use our borrowed time to see about a countermeasure… maybe a little of Kaliya's famous love and kisses approach," she smiles sweetly.

"Oh dear cu'Nar," Kaliya moans. "What have I done?"

"Hey, it worked on the other occasions, so maybe we could invoke another mutiny. But we can't let it filter back up to their headquarters unless we can contain the reaction in some way. So, my first suggestion is to find their ship, get inside, and do a little reconnoitering to see what we have to work with."

"All right, I can do this. And once inside, I'll look for openings, maybe to see if they're working with their military chips on or off, and how reactive they are to a little conspiratorial gossip."

"My next concern is this, however… With these wanted posters out and about, the Suuden-Aryku will quickly realize they are known offenders of some sort. This, in itself, could serve as a deterrent, but it could also invoke a reaction by Darumon, again depending on how desperate…or daring…he is to get inside there. I see maybe two possible outcomes to this. The first is simply to pull out and sulk over his latest failure to achieve his objectives."

"Aw, so sad…" Kaliya frowns.

"Yes, if he is without his weapon, it stands to reason this objective might not hold as high a priority, as he would not be able to sustain himself in the face of the Estelar, who would surely take some form of action for this offence."

"So, he goes into hiding again," Kailen relents. "But for how long? Eventually, he'll want to try again. But if he feels his enemies are getting wise to him, would he simply wait another billion years before coming out again?"

"Somehow I think that would not work," Thaelyn notes. "My impression is that Maker Kuroku would have something to say about that, for the path she has been leading us on thus far. She wants him…now!"

"All right, so this backs him into a corner, even if he doesn't know it yet."

"Furthermore," Aerlie continues. "My impression of him is one who doesn't take kindly to these constant failures. Therefore, my second, and personally, my most worrisome concern, is that he steps things up a notch."

"Uh oh…" Kaliya intones warily.

"How do you envision this?" Thaelyn wonders.

"He is known to us from multiple accounts to be vindictive and destructive," Aerlie recalls. "The academy students here in Rolsklinde, for instance, when they were complaining about that conjuring."

"Also his statement at Morndindor," Kaliya muses. "When the base supposedly blew up, and the dwarves…how did he say it…got a taste of their own."

"Exactly. This is an example of his nature, given his own devices and his confidence in his position. Now, consider if he is so desperate, or else daring, to enter Sigil and find the portal. Those people will not represent an obstacle to him…he'll just push them aside."

"And this becomes problematic," Thaelyn nods. "We still have the Lady, who will not be at all pleased for the offence. And although the other Estelar are generally forbidden to enter the city, this does not prevent them from taking action on the outside."

"And if he's actually so desperate," Kailen offers. "Maybe he would simply go to war with them? What would his chances be?"

"Not good," Thaelyn muses. "But then we do not know the full capacity of his military might. He could perhaps do some damage, and the Estelar might choose not to make their own incursion into Azgarén space if there are no flows to support them. But they could send others with more conventional technologies, and this is bad enough. Whatever the case, this is not a favorable situation. We should try to avoid it, or disable it with all due diligence if it should come up."

"I agree. Then, Kaliya, you need to find your way into that ship and make an inspection."

"I'll need to locate it first," she admits. "I'll have to go to Sigil, and wander around those same sewers until I find the hole they made, and see where it takes me from there."

"And once we have a result there," Aerlie concludes. "We need to consider the repercussions with Central Command. If we are able to turn them away from Sigil, we need to dissuade Darumon from ever returning."

"For this point, I think we could play something like what you used here on Therinë, the threat of the Estelar discovering his operations. If it worked once, it might work again, if he really is trying to hide from them. After all, he is operating right under their noses. How could they possibly miss that?"

"All right, this is a possibility, but it will require us to feel around for it, first. He might find himself confined to Azgarén after this, and then all we have left is his local military. If we can take that away from him, he'll have nowhere left to run."

"But to take that away from him, we'll need to contact someone, and for this, the only one to contact has to be Commander Geilv. He's the top man, and according to our observations on the spy-cams, Darumon seems to limit his interactions to only a select few to do his proxy work, with Geilv being one of those."

"And this would bring us back to that opportunity we spoke of," the General reflects. "Somewhere along the way, we need to push him over the edge. If he reacted so badly to the loss of the mining base, how would he react to anything we might play with Sigil?"

"The loss of something," Kaliya ponders. "Wait a minute, I've watched some of these videos with Kailen. Geilv has been mumbling about something he calls containment procedures, which is likely the excuse Darumon uses for his cleansing tactics on all those worlds he blasted, including Morndindor and maybe also this one."

"I do recall some sort of mention of this," Thaelyn accedes. "It was during that brief conversation we shared on the trans-com just as they were pulling out. He mentioned this world had to be contained during their local operations."

"All right then, there you have it. This is how he describes it."

"Then, what is your suggestion, Kaliya?" the General asks. "Are you saying our play should involve destroying something new?"

"I think it largely depends on how things play out. But if Aerlie is right, and Darumon gets antsy about his goals, it could very easily result in the loss of those ships."

"And that would surely carry an affect," he admits.

"And if Geilv takes the message, he is facing the Estelar on one side, Ytani and his doomsday weapon on the other, and only one person to point a finger at for imperiling his world."

"Gods above, that poor man," he chuckles. "I would not want to be in his shoes at that moment. Or perhaps I might have to say this for Darumon, once Geilv turns his military around the other direction."

"All right," Aerlie asserts. "In the meantime, we should at least put up these posters as a way to inform the people of Sigil what to watch for. This is our starting point. It will slow the Suuden-Aryku and give us time for these other options, and it shouldn't cause too much suspicion with Central if they think there is a public warrant out for them. Perhaps I could recruit Aelwyn to spread the word amongst some of her friends to assist. And then we have this issue of what the dabus mentioned about the Suuden-Aryku carrying this essence."

"Yes, this is rather disturbing," Thaelyn considers. "How did he describe it again, as something combined into their being?"

"It certainly sounded that way. But are we speaking of something within their native tissues, or implanted?"

"I would suggest we are speaking of the seeds again," Kaliya notes. "If our earlier suspicion is right that they are engineered to serve as a type of funnel into Sargeras, this might require some element of his essence, and the Lady's suggestion of this recognition could be a form of proof. It might relate to Ankhia's mention of that really weird alien genetic code."

"Very well," Aerlie nods. "This sounds reasonable. But let us not forget your own origins, if to say Darumon engineered you using his own seed."

"Yes, but I doubt he would represent as much a threat as Sargeras and the other Primordials, as they were the focal point of the original offence that started the war."

"Good point."

"I might also suggest one other thought. If you were to custom engineer something to serve as an energy feed into such a being as a Primordial, or any other form of divine entity, wouldn't it be more efficient if you could somehow key it to his personal needs?"

"How interesting! Yes, it might. And nicely done, Kaliya."

"Wait a minute…" she retorts playfully. "Are YOU testing me now?"

"Why not?" she grins. "You seem to expect it from Thaelyn by now, so I need to throw a curve at you to see how you respond."

"Cu'Nar's pity… Kailen, it never ends around here!" she chuckles.

<hr>

Intern Azina Nur'ten was making a quarterly inventory at the ARC as part of her routine duty roster. The center's cataloging system was entirely computerized, but her job was to verify the database logs with the actual stored volume of products in their refrigerated storerooms and cryo-chambers. There was rarely ever an error, but still it was a mandatory process to maintain accurate records.

The process was monotonous, and she could almost recite the numbers from memory by this time, they were so predictable. She had become intimately familiar with virtually every item on record, by name, age, quantity, last production run, and the last time it was called to order.

She ran through the list and compared it to the amount on-hand as she cycled the motorized shelving rack within the automated delivery conveyor inside the refrigeration compartment. A rack of shelving would rotate into view through the window where she could visually tally up the stored containers and compare that with the accounting on the screen. She would then move to the next rack and repeat the process.

As she worked her way through the Center's stock, she came upon a familiar sight.

"And here we are again," she notes quietly. "Nothing new on this since it was discontinued. Four centuries of regular production, annual deliveries of fairly consistent quantities, and then it quits without explanation. I guess they finally killed it…whatever it was. There must've been a lot of them, though. What did they do, exterminate a full species of something? I still wish I knew why we had to research a Belvik Spore to destroy some odd alien neural tissue. That seems like an extreme amount of effort when a simple plasma rifle would be more effective."

She moves to the next item on the list, now only partially attentive to her work as her mind drifts to the early research on the project.

"Was it a local lifeform, maybe a parasite of some kind?" she wonders half-mindedly. "But why would they need four centuries of it delivered inside a dispenser node? That's a medical implant, so if you can get close enough to implant a medical device, why not just hit it with a big stick instead?"

Her curiosity invokes her to halt her recordkeeping and return to her desk briefly. She engages the terminal to look up the original requisition order.

"This is dated about four centuries ago, when it all started. Yes, I remember this now. We had to subcontract this part to an engineering firm. What is that thing? It almost looks like something you would wear around the neck, like a collar. This was the implantation unit. So, whatever it was they were doing, they had to put this around something, probably hold it there long enough for the unit to implant the dispenser node, and then what? Sit and wait for it to tick off? These things had a configurable release timer built in. That just doesn't make sense to me."

She gets up from the desk and returns to her work.

"And worst of all, using Belvik Spores!" she growls softly. "In all the nether-space! What a way to conduct pest control!"

She halts her outbreak to look around the room. She was alone in the lab on this occasion, which was good, so that no one would notice her brief emotional display.

"And even if it was a parasite, maybe something attached to the body, after four centuries you might think they would find a more conventional way to deal with it, or leave that world altogether if it was so bad," she sighs heavily. "The military…who ever said they had the mind to think for themselves. Not with those authority chips, that's for sure!"

She continues her work, moving on to take account of the seed implant stores.

"Oh yes, and then there's these little beauties," she proclaims sarcastically. "The charm of Azgarén! Every citizen of adult age must present themselves for implantation, by mandate of the Almighty Council! This is what Ghantil and I were talking about not so long ago. 'We need this in order to spread out to other worlds, even if they're not friendly to our lifeforms…all because ours is contaminated by some alien bug no one can identify.' Yeah, and after almost ten millennia, we're still here."

She continues counting up the store as she muses over the public rhetoric of the seeds.

"We're still here…and only NOW do we actually need the things because in all those inhospitable worlds we were supposed to be colonizing, ours became the first and only."

Once again, she pauses to glance around the room to ensure she was alone during her little tirade. When she finishes this set, she moves to the next item on the list, still under the category of seed implants. She stares at it thoughtfully. It registered only a small quantity in stock, and had only one occasion of manufacture. It had not been called for since.

"And what were you about?" she wonders silently. "Three and a half centuries ago, we get orders to modify the seed. And even crazier than that, we had to package it in a delivery system resembling a gas-propelled rocket! And oh, let's not forget how advanced that rocket was! Yes, a nanotech image recognition guidance system, cryo-stasis inside a vessel of super-cooled hydrogen-based fuel, and if memory serves, it was designed to be deployed from…a rifle!" she giggles senselessly. "A rifle firing a rocket with a biotech seed, what'll they think of next?"

She turns to make the inventory assessment and continues on down the list, now entering the section of pharmaceuticals. This section was lengthy, as the Center held a broad array of medicinal treatments, anesthetics, antibiotics, and other products for the treatment of common ailments. She methodically courses her way through it, now placing more focus into her assignment to make up for lost time, until she comes to another line entry with a surplus volume of a rare medication. She pauses and sighs feebly.

"And then we have you, the good old Kajik'tav Serum. I remember researching you, a treatment for an ultra-rare lung disorder, one that hasn't been seen since all this began and we got these lovely little seeds stuck to our backs, which effectively oppresses the cause of the disorder. No one even remembered what it was until I looked it up in the old archives."

She turns to check the stores. The rack showed a single neatly sealed crate on the shelf.

"Why, in all the nether-space, would they call for you?" she continues. "This illness hasn't been reported for ten millennia, and suddenly we get a one-time rush order for a substantial quantity to be delivered to some remote outpost somewhere. What was that about! Did the whole outpost suddenly come down with this illness?"

She returns to confirm the notation on the terminal, checking the dates as she reviewed the record.

"This came in that same year they stopped ordering the Belvik Spore. Hmm, maybe they finally killed the little creep, and it gave them all lung disease," she chuckles amusedly.

She proceeded through the rest of her work detail until she finally wrapped up and marked the job complete for another period. She then moved off to find her next assignment, but the memories of those odd occurrences dwelt within her. She reminisced mutedly over her final thoughts.

"They are…out there…" she reflects dreamily. "Somewhere

travelling across the stars and discovering stuff we'll never know about...so it seems. All because they keep their secrets so tight, we couldn't pry them open with a hydraulic spreader. But they sure seem to be calling for some fascinating toys. Cures for rare illnesses, brain-eating Belvik Spores, rocket-propelled seeds," she giggles quietly. "Explore the galaxy! Discover new worlds and new lifeforms! But do I get to hear any of it? No. They just order me to stick a genetically engineered bug on my back, and a chip in my brain, and tell me life is good."

◆◆◆◆◆

"Ankhia wants to be a part of the research, as you know," Likha reports. "But since she's still a little burdened with her newborn, she'll be taking it slowly. Nevertheless, I can do some of the preliminary work, based on our previous testing to sequence the genetic structure and apply a tentative programming to the Spore. We can have her check my results when she gets time for it, and assist during the testing phase."

"Will you be employing that replicant again?" Thaelyn asks warily.

Likha was visiting the WIC building for a conference regarding Ayene's upcoming mission to visit the ARC and procure a seed specimen for testing at the Naarg uy'Sodrad medical ward. This was part of a project to determine a solution to kill it, and thus remove it from the body. Not only would this benefit Ayene, but all the Suuden-Aryku, whether the refugees on Ruuki uy'Daan, or those back home on Azgarén.

"But of course!" she chirps. "Poor little Banni has been sitting in that lonely cryo-chamber for such a long time now."

"Powers help us... Have you not found a more eligible companion yet?"

"Unfortunately, no, Your Lordship. You know how things are with the severe imbalance of gender ratios. Ankhia has been trying to encourage me to get out and meet a few of those servicemen we, um, acquired from the base and that ship we hijacked," she titters. "But so far, I don't feel entirely comfortable with the idea of pairing up just yet. Besides, it's fun to pretend Banni is my boyfriend. He's such a good listener."

"Indeed, and I would imagine he does not argue the discussion topics. Very well, but I would still encourage your interaction with other, eh...living...bodies that might offer a positive return. And I would think those servicemen we acquired could use the social interaction as well."

"Of course, you're right. But at the same time, we can't bring them in to our little village by the Naarg uy'Sodrad because the Elder Council doesn't know we have them yet."

"This is true, as they need to remain outside the loop for the security issue with Darumon."

"But I suppose one good thing about it is I'm still young, so I can wait. Maybe this war will be over soon, and I'll have a whole world full of choices, if only to find one who knows how to appreciate my feelings."

"Have faith, Likha. In the meantime, Ayene, we must now prepare you for your mission."

"Yes, Your Lordship," Ayene replies. "I've been waiting anxiously for this, and I'm eager to see it through."

"I am sure of that. But let us proceed with all due diligence and careful planning. This is the ARC we are now approaching. The seed specimens are not the only item of concern here, as we know they are responsible for at least one or more of Darumon's death toys."

"Yes, I recall the briefings... The Kajik'tav Serum, at the very least, also the seeds, maybe those Belvik Spores, and who knows what else. I'll see if I can poke around, but carefully. It depends a little on who they give me to assist with this thing. Maybe I can try a little of Kaliya's love and kisses approach to pry open a few lips."

"I swear," Kaliya moans. "I'm never going to live that one down, am I."

"But it is such a valuable new tactic," Thaelyn teases. "And surely, it has proven itself."

"Yes, I suppose I can't argue that point. But this is becoming as much my own bane as Petrith and his soap."

"And Ayene," Thaelyn continues. "Do you have your requisition from your Commander?"

"Yes, I do…" she pulls out a holo-chip from a pocket and holds it up for display. "My story is this: I'm requesting this for field testing on a newly discovered world where we have an especially difficult environment. And rather than risk any of our own people, we are going to apply this to a replicant platform…borrowing from Likha's boyfriend on this occasion," she grins, "to see how the entity performs as part of a new colony survey mission."

"Wow," Likha muses. "That almost sounds like Banni has a life of some kind. He's exploring new worlds now."

"I figure this might go well if we play on the old stories of how we were supposed to be moving out and colonizing new worlds once. That way, if anyone asks questions, I have a viable answer."

"Nicely done," Thaelyn nods.

"Commander Kriv'tik also marked it with a mention of the Marshal ordering the study, although we can't simulate his signature directly. But the order should still pass."

"Ayene," Kaliya considers. "Just a small note here. Do you think there might be any difficulty in presenting that chip due to the little detail that your full base staff is very likely listed as dead by now?"

"I doubt the ARC would have access to the classified personnel files at Central Command. The data systems are designated as confidential and official use only. What usually happens is I bring this in, they pull it up on their local monitor, review the signatures and security codes, to make sure everything is in order, and that should be all. They have their military contracts, but they shouldn't necessarily be cross-checking the living or deceased status of the person who wrote it. But if they do give me any trouble, I'll just make up an excuse, like we did for our base staff, and that of the Ghan'aju, with our secret assignments."

"And thus those private vid-mails you sent out. I still wonder how well those were received, but I guess there's no way to know until later when everything blows over."

"Right, although I hope one day to visit my home and speak to my parents. I'd like to get a few things off my chest where the Prodigy Gift is concerned."

"Perhaps we can attend to that at a later time," Thaelyn affirms. "For now, I believe we have covered as much as we can. I will send you forward, Lieutenant. Keep alert, maintain a clear mind, and bring us back our samples, and whatever other curious results you may find."

"As you wish," she smiles.

Ayene nods as she stands up from the table. She turns and leaves the room to find the conference room they often used for their projection exercise. She takes up a seat and settles into her meditation. Not long after, her conscious projection lifts up from her body. She checked herself to ensure a complete presentation, in this case assuming the image of her original military uniform. From here, she placed her focus of mind on a familiar location in Capitol Prime, and vanished in a puff.

✦✦✦✦✦

Azina was returning to her usual workstation in the research center after a short break between shifts. Her duties mostly kept her in the medical lab, sometimes at the prescriptions counter, and other times filling orders to be sent to other medical wards and clinics. The work was repetitive, but it kept her busy.

The ARC was the main provider for the city's medical needs, producing a wide range of pharmaceuticals, implantation devices, and delivery systems, not only for local consumption, but also for distribution to smaller clinics around the city, as well as to other cities around the world. It was a large high-tech firm incorporating several research departments and an array of automated manufacturing facilities to produce goods onsite, along with an integrated medical ward serving the immediate vicinity.

She took up seating at her desk to review the latest work orders, processing them one at a time by calling up the order, sending a data request to a computerized delivery system within the refrigerated stores, where a robotic sorting and packaging operation would prepare the item and deliver it on a tray via a conveyor belt to her station. She would then compare and verify the item by its tag number before forwarding it to the next destination, often using a parcel delivery route for shipping to another office.

Ayene had arrived in the city, having chosen on this occasion to arrive on the rooftop of one of the taller skyscrapers in the downtown section. This location was mostly out of view by other nearby buildings, and hardly a cause for drawing the attention of anyone who might have line-of-sight to it. Still, she made her arrival in a corner near a roof access doorway, where she would not stand out as much. She stepped out into view to survey the surrounding sights.

The city of Capitol Prime was a bustling metropolis of roughly five million residents. The downtown district was dominated by skyscrapers and busy traffic, not only on the street level, but also with elevated roadways of levitating vehicles. It was nighttime, by Azgarén circadian standards, which were remarkably elongated due to a slow rotational spin. Everywhere Ayene looked, the city lights glowed, filling the night sky with their illumination. The roads on the surface were lined with lighted tracks and markers for the traffic to follow. Many of the buildings were well-lit from offices working through the dark hours, as well as signs and billboards outside and along the avenues.

She studied the nearby buildings, making sure there was no one in the immediate area looking out in her direction, and then she changed her form into that of a hawk, lifting off the ground and taking flight above the city skyline.

She soared well above the ground, turning to find her bearings within the city and finally to orient herself in the direction of the large research center. The building stood out well against the surrounding structures, especially as viewed from above. She glided gracefully through the air, watching the traffic below and thinking quietly to herself of the people in the city. None of them could possibly know of the presence of one such as her. She could be anything, a small animal, a potted plant, even a beverage cup, so innocently stationed in full view and spying on them, and they would never know the difference.

This projection skill was a potent ability, often described as godlike. Such beings as hers should not be in possession of it, but she was, as was Kaliya and so many others discovered to hold this power. But she had to remind herself, this power demanded great respect if she were to use it properly. A lot was riding on her to see the job done and earn the appreciation of her peers. This was very important to her. For the first time in her life, she had real friends, and this is a precious commodity to one who comes from a society where emotion is absent due to their Suppressor chips. This, along with many other relationship cravings such people like hers would normally desire.

The research center was coming into view below her now. She needed to find a way down to it, while also reshaping herself to her natural form outside of view by anyone in the area. The city was densely packed with buildings, but she managed to spy a small alley behind a row of offices, used for utility and refuse storage. She descended down to it, landing on the ground behind one of the buildings. The area was clear, so she reimagined her shape back to her natural military officer image, then cautiously but professionally strolled out onto the sidewalk.

The street traffic passed by, and there were several pedestrians walking along, but no one paid any special mind to her appearance. She walked towards the nearby intersection, where the roads made a T-crossing in front of the research center. She waited for the light to change, and then crossed the street, reaching the other side and angling towards the stylish front entrance. She opens the door and steps inside.

The lobby was an elegant scene of architectural design, with granite floors, seating areas, and a broad front desk to welcome and direct visitors and clients. She walks up to it to make her first presentation. A young woman behind the counter looks up at the smartly dressed officer.

"Welcome to the ARC. May I assist you?" she announces in a disconnected tone.

"I am here to requisition a sample from the biotech division," Ayene responds calmly.

"Do you have a requisition order?"

"Affirmative."

Ayene brings out her holo-chip and sets it on the counter. The clerk picks it up and plugs it into her terminal to read the order. She studies the request, along with the authorizing security codes, and pulls up a cross-reference for verification against the institution's military contracts. The codes matched the Center's records to an authority under the directive of Central Command. She pulls the chip out and hands it back.

"You will need to present your order to the bio-lab directly for this requisition," she instructs. "Follow this corridor to the lift and proceed to Level Three, then approach the administrative desk."

Ayene nods and turns down the corridor leading deeper into the building. She walks along until she reaches the lift, presses the call button and waits. Several interns pass by in the hall on their way to or from their assignments, none of whom paid any special attention to the young officer. The lift door opens and Ayene steps inside, then selects the button for the third floor.

As she arrives, she finds the desk for the lab department. She recognized this place. This is where she once visited during her assignment at Morndindor when Commander Kriv'tik was preparing his insurrection against Ytani and the Marshal for the working conditions they had to suffer. Ayene was sent here to requisition three diagnostic probes to disable their chips, so they could find freedom from their effect. Now she was here again for this new order. She approached the desk and presented her holo-chip again.

"Greetings," she announces. "I am here to process a requisition."

The intern behind the desk glances at Ayene and nods. She

takes the chip, plugs it in, and examines the request order, the same as the girl downstairs.

"How do you require these to be packaged?" she asks.

"In cryo-stasis tubes."

"Very well then. This order will require secure processing. I will call someone to assist you."

The intern activates a local intercom.

"Intern Nur'ten, report to the front."

While Ayene waited for the assistant to arrive, she scanned the activity around her. No one had a clue that she was only a metaphysical projection. As far as they could tell, she was as real as any of them. It was the same as with anyone else she had been interacting with since her return to service.

People passed by in the hall, approaching the desk next to her to place their own orders, and then moved on. Not one of them looked at her with any suspicion as to the reason why she was here. To them, she was just another military officer on assignment to pick up a special request, which likely occurred on many occasions.

A moment later, and another young woman came to the desk. She stared at Ayene for a brief period before responding.

"I remember you from a previous visit. It was Lieutenant…um, something. My apologies for the lapse."

"It is quite alright. Ayene Ti'van. Yes, I recall you when I came in for those probes. I am actually pleased to see you again."

"You are?"

"Well, for the familiarity of the occasion. It is pleasing to work with someone on a repeating basis."

"I see. Well, thank you. What do you need on this occasion?"

The desk intern responds, "This officer has a request for two An'gamu Seeds."

"Two seeds? This is interesting. All right, we need to take this to the lab. Please follow me."

Azina turns and leads Ayene down another corridor, past several order processing desks and workstations, a few offices, and finally to a large laboratory at the end. They enter inside and she directs Ayene to a chair while she takes up behind a desk and a local terminal. As she settles herself into her seat, she decides to try some small talk to set the mood.

"How did those D-probes work for you? I recall something about working conditions."

"Ah, yes," Ayene reflects. "They came in very handy along the way, and we were finally able to correct for that unfortunate situation."

"What sort of working conditions, by the way?"

"We were stationed in a very dry and dusty landscape…hot, uncomfortable…not very pleasant."

"I see."

She pulls up the lab inventory.

"May I see your requisition order, please?"

Ayene places it on the table for the girl to plug into her terminal reader.

"It shows here you only require these to be packaged in standard cryo-tubes?"

"Yes, please."

Azina begins filling in the form on her terminal to order up the robotic delivery of two seed specimens. As she does, she unconsciously begins mumbling to herself.

"No rocket launchers today, I guess…"

Ayene noticed the display. It was a curious response.

"Excuse me? Did you say something?"

Azina realized she spoke aloud and tried covering for it.

"Oh, I was recalling an old order. It is not often the military comes in with a special request for these seeds."

"I suppose so. After all, what could they possibly use them for? Everybody has one already," she shrugs. "But an old order? Was it anything like this? And did I hear you say something about rockets?"

"Um, well, yes, there was this one time… But you know Central, everything is classified with them."

"Yes, they do this often. My goodness, it might make a person wonder what it is they are doing over there."

"Yes, it does!" Azina's voice unconsciously rises. "And I've seen a lot of these orders pass through here."

Ayene took brisk notice of this reaction in the young intern. It resembled a hidden ambition, a bit like the captain of the Ghan'aju and his desire to understand the secretive nature of the Morndindor mining operation. She found herself suddenly curious to see where this could lead, thinking it might be one of those special opportunities she was supposed to watch out for. So, she tried playing into it.

"Well, personally, I would be just as curious, so I doubt I could blame you for it. But a rocket? How do you mean? Are they sending them into orbit now?"

"Orbit?" Azina muses humorously.

The statement was clearly an attempt at humor, but Azina knew enough to catch herself before she let out any unintentional giggles. She discreetly laid a pair of fingers over her mouth to suppress her response, and then tried coughing the sensation away.

The gesture caught Ayene's attention, as she was studying the young woman by now, and this was an obvious attempt to stifle an emotional reaction, but not necessarily unexpected due to the threat of a feedback response from the chip.

Azina continues, "I, uh…well, it's a classified project, so we're not really supposed to talk about it openly…you know, due to the security restrictions."

"Did you happen to take notice of my uniform? I'm military, so if it involves a military security protocol, I might already know about it."

"You might?" her voice trails off as she studies the uniform and ponders the possibilities. "Well, um, yes…I mean, sure, you might. But let's face it, if you're military, you would be restricted under the same protocols that keep everyone else in the dark."

At this time, Ayene was now paying closer attention to this girl's manner of speech. Not simply the rise and fall of her vocal tones, but another aspect she didn't originally expect to find. It was a mode of speech not normally practiced by anyone using the chip. This made her want to dig deeper, and her mischievous manners were starting to kick in.

"Yes, I suppose you have a point, including most of us on the other side…"

Azina suddenly halted her work on the terminal and jerked up to glare at the woman sitting across from her. She gazed with a look of surprise directly into Ayene's eyes.

"Huh?" she blurts. "Like most of you?"

"Oh, Intern," Ayene raises her brow and turns away nonchalantly. "If you could only hear some of the recent scuttlebutt going around Central right now…"

"Like what? Or wait…well, this is probably none of my business, right?"

"You know, that's what a lot of our officers are saying lately. Everything is so heavily classified, you might think NONE of it is ANYONE'S business, including those of us who are supposed to be doing the work. It's enough to unravel your horns after a while."

"Then how do you get anything done if no one knows what anyone else is doing?"

"It goes a little like this…" Ayene prepares to illustrate with her hands. "Person A is given an order to do something, but then it's classified so no one knows what he did. Then, Person B is given another order, and again it's classified. So, no one is allowed to know what, where, how, or why he did anything. In the end, something is apparently being done, but no one knows what it was, or even IF anything was done at all."

"But again, how do you even know if you're doing any work, or what kind of work it is you are doing?"

"It's been said most of this is controlled by the Marshal, and he has been described on at least a few occasions to be very secretive, possibly due to his advanced knowledge and what he needs people to do in order for us to effectively pursue his insurgent opponents."

"Oh, that!" she huffs and seems to relax her posture somewhat.

Ayene continues, "Which naturally leads many of us to wonder what we're actually doing to pursue those insurgents that none of us are made aware of to know what we are pursuing."

Azina glares at the woman perplexedly. She frowns deeply, as well as unconsciously, which gave a clear, if also unwitting, indication of an emotional response…and without a feedback hit from her chip. Ayene watched, and took a mental note of it.

"Therefore," Ayene continues unabated. "We might have such as those rocket-propelled seeds you mentioned."

"Yeah, and suddenly I'm afraid to ask about them now."

"Yes, surely someone should know what they were, but probably not the ones who ordered them, OR used them."

"In all the nether-space!" she shouts. "Then who would know anything, out of that bunch of dull-horns, to actually ask questions of?"

"Granted, a few of us might know something, but you really need to know the right people. For instance, what was this about a rocket-propelled seed, at least from your side of it? Maybe I know a little bit, as someone who MAY be so privileged to have crossed paths with something. But surely, I could never…officially…say anything. You know; because those security restrictions can be a real horn-puller."

Azina gawks at the woman, with her mouth slowly dropping open.

"Lieutenant, are you saying you might actually tell me something about what Central has been keeping secret all this time from everybody?"

"Officially?"

"Oh, of course! NEVER officially…"

"Excellent. You understand. Especially as how the recent scuttlebutt over in Central is beginning to realize the level of intrigue is keeping these details away from any kind of scrutiny that SHOULD be analyzing it."

"Should be? Does this mean someone should be aware of what's happening, but all those classified restrictions are keeping it away from you?"

"It would appear this way. But we should also consider some of those security restrictions may actually be legitimate."

"Wait. Some of them…ACTUALLY legitimate," Azina wonders. "As if to say, there are others that may be…"

"…Someone's idea of hiding things from anyone they think doesn't have a need to know."

"A need to know. I suppose that may say something."

"Yeah…anyone who did not otherwise order it, use it, or simply isn't permitted to know about it."

"Not permitted? That sounds rather restrictive."

"I suppose it may also be subjective if you consider what the Marshal keeps secret and why. After all, he does come from a much higher-grade society, so he might have his reasons. I just wish he would explain some of it to us so we would understand what we're supposed to be doing out there."

"Oh great! Is that how it goes? Well, all right. I suppose I'm game enough. This could be the chance of a lifetime to answer a few old questions. Let me see, those seeds… First, this was a masterpiece of engineering…" her voice begins to surge with a subtle note of passion. "Truly unique! Gas-propelled, nanotech IR guidance, and of all things, launched from a rifle! Who would need such a thing as that?"

"From a rifle? I hope they aren't planning on taking aim at any of us!"

"Oh please! Not that!"

Ayene was becoming very amused by this girl's obvious display. Her naughty sense of intrigue wondered if she could invoke even more out of her. Along the way, she had been slowly relaxing her own presentation to see if the girl would take notice. But so far, the intern did not seem to be paying as much attention to such details as the language usage, or the subtle hints at emotion. Ayene might need to step it up a little.

"So, it was nothing like what we're ordering today. This would be considered rather dull in comparison, right?"

"Oh, yes…just a plain old seed in a cryo-tube. Perish the thought that we would put such a mundane design in this masterpiece of technological curiosity. The order also demanded we make a special modification to it, for some odd reason."

"Let me guess… Whereas ours is supposed to enhance, this one was to debilitate, or some such, right?"

Azina glared at Ayene for the obvious association.

"Then you know about it?"

"Who, me? Officially, I don't know anything," she shrugs and turns away casually.

"Uh huh…officially. So, what about unofficially? You don't sound like one of those same dull-horns who is told to look the other way when someone does something no one else is supposed to know about."

"Now you're catching on. See, I knew you were a clever one."

Azina suddenly felt a warm cozy feeling come over her, and she impulsively formed a tiny smile as she returned to finish typing out her order. But the continued display of emotion, and still without any feedbacks, made its impression on Ayene. She decided to try one more time to test it.

"Tell me, did you ever produce anything else that caught your attention? Maybe something like, oh, rare pharmaceuticals or strange applications of stuff inside dispenser nodes?"

Azina halted her typing and froze at the mention of these two depictions. She rolled her eyes around to Ayene in apprehension.

"Rare pharmaceuticals, you say? And a dispenser node with something inside…like what, for instance?"

"Well, naturally, we couldn't be speaking of anything as nether-wild as Belvik Spores. After all, they are a popular medical treatment for delicate and unusual procedures."

"Are you playing with me?!" she balks coyly. "Yes, they are, but what would YOU know about a dispenser node filled with the Spores?"

"Maybe the same as I know about that Kajik'tav Serum you had an order for once."

Now Azina dropped her jaw and pulled completely away from the terminal.

"In all the nether-space, the planets must've just aligned for us. What do you know about that? I've been sitting here ever since the day we got the rush order for that Serum, struggling to figure out who ordered it and why. Do you know what it's used for?"

"Under normal circumstances? From what I've heard, it's supposed to be for a rare lung disorder."

"Yeah!" Azina affirms avidly. "But it's obsolete ever since the seeds were put into service. The Serum itself was shelved way back in the beginning since it was no longer needed. So WHY, of all things, did Central order two crates of the stuff?"

"Two crates? How many were in each crate?"

"As I recall, each one held a hundred vials, and they represented several doses each. That's enough for a small army."

"Wow, and how rare is this illness?"

"Very… And like I said, not since the time the seeds were put into service."

"And that represents nearly ten millennia ago, I suppose. Why not for the seeds?"

"The seeds effectively negate the original illness for their enhancing effect."

"Ah, I see," she nods. "And the Spores?"

"Yeah, now get this," she continues enthusiastically. "Four centuries of consistent orders for supply. The dispenser nodes carried a reservoir to hold the Spores, and a programmable nanotech timing circuit to release them into the body. But this was just crazy, because they were designed with a cytoplasmic decomposition agent and programmed to attack some kind of alien neural tissue. So, my question is, if this is being used to attack something, like some alien entity or maybe a parasite, why would you go to the trouble of using the Spores, and why put them in a medical implant with a timer on it?"

"Yes, I think I can certainly appreciate the inanity of that one."

"And these orders stopped at roughly the same time they ordered that Serum. So, I'm thinking the two might have been related, or something."

"Related," Ayene wonders. "As if to say they finally killed the parasite and got sick with a rare lung illness along the way?" she raises her brow.

"That's exactly what I was asking!" she urges sharply and returns to her terminal. "I mean, in all the nether-space, if you can get close enough to stick an implant in the thing, why can't you stick a knife in it instead?"

"That would certainly make more sense if your purpose was to kill it...or maybe to kill it immediately. But you said it had a timer on it. Maybe this is the answer, a delayed response."

"Delayed...right..." she huffs. "And for four centuries? What were you people doing over there that you couldn't find some other, maybe simpler solution. Or maybe you just like spending money."

"Well, I'll admit, Central does have a hefty budget. I'm not the one who manages the books, but you might wonder sometimes about all these elaborate expenditures."

"So, do you have anything you can say about this? Or were you just yanking my tail?"

"Me? Oh no. I would not wish to yank your tail about any of this. Some of it gets very serious, and not something to yank a tail over...unless you're one of those people told to do something by someone, and without any explanation as to why."

Azina halts her work again to glare at Ayene briefly.

"Uh huh...but this sounds exactly like what we were just talking about."

"Yes, and most likely by that same source that does it to us."

"What?" she shouts. "The same source? You mentioned the Marshal a moment ago, with all his secrets where his insurgents are concerned."

"Yes, I did, to which so many of US don't even know who or what they actually are, unless he points a finger at them and tells us to open fire."

"But...but...don't you people even have a description of what to look for?"

"Not unless HE chooses to tell us...and allows us to actually record that description on anything less than the active mode of our chips."

"Wait a minute here!" she screeches. "Active mode? He tells you to open fire only on the active mode?"

"I once heard my CO say it's to make sure we get the job done. As if to say we are too incompetent to do it if you simply ask us."

"In all the nether-space...again! Did I say dull-horns earlier? This goes beyond dull-horns, and you're not the ones with the dull horns here."

"Exactly. And some of us are getting tired of it."

"I don't doubt it!"

The conversation pauses as Azina returns to finish the order. Ayene reflected on this rather extraordinary dialog, and the young intern's clearly emotional display, which could only mean one thing by now.

"By the way, what was your name again?"

"Azina Nur'ten, or am I getting myself in trouble now."

"Oh, hardly that!" she waves it off. "In fact, I'm actually enjoying this little chat. We don't often get to do that over there, you know. The military has this nasty habit, it would seem."

"Oh dear. Which one is that?"

"No one talks to anyone to share details of any kind."

"Oh great! More of those security restrictions?"

"Yeah, it would seem that way. In this case, applied as the simple lack of common gossip."

"I swear..."

"But, as for this, remember, none of it is...official," she flutters her fingers. "So, we can't say you're getting in trouble for anything. Well, not unless you consider your use of linguistic contractions during this time."

"Huh?"

"Contractions, you know, words like I'm, you're, can't, won't..."

"Yeah, but this is part of our language, last I heard, or did someone change that rule?"

"It was changed on the day you people invented the Suppressor chips. So, why do you seem to have this, along with your rather boisterous emotional display during our conversation?"

"Uh oh..."

Azina freezes, suddenly realizing her reactions and unconscious outbursts, which were a leftover from her earlier inventory-taking and her old thoughts and frustrations of unfulfilled desires for answers. Now she felt a cold shiver run through her. She had been discovered; the one thing she was not supposed to let happen. She quickly fumbled for a response, one of several she had previously formulated if this should ever occur.

"Um, wait," she flusters. "I can explain that easily enough. You see, I'm undergoing a special maintenance period right now where my chip is temporarily disabled for an extended diagnostic. You just happened to catch me in the middle of it."

"Hey! That's a good one, almost as good as my excuse for these seeds."

"It... Your... Huh? What do you mean an excuse?"

"Azina, you're clever and ambitious, but you need to bump up your observational skills a little."

"I do? Um, wait..." she frowns. "Hold on! Did you just say you're? That's a contraction too."

"Yeah, along with that initial explanation I gave of the words we are NOT supposed to be able to say with the chip turned on."

"Oh, drat!" she slaps her forehead. "That was simply devious, Lieutenant."

"Yes, you might say I've been developing a habit of testing people lately," she grins.

Azina now glares at Ayene for HER obvious emotional display. This turned the tables a bit for the implications.

Ayene continues, "So, how do we explain this...really?"

"Um, I'm not allowed to say."

"And you speak of Central and their secrets..." Ayene rolls her eyes.

"Well..." Azina flusters.

Ayene leans in privately and lowers her voice.

"I suspect you have one of your own, so let's go off-the-record here a moment, yours and mine. How did your chip get turned off?"

Azina felt compelled to answer, since it was clear by this time that Ayene also had emotions, which meant her chip was also disabled.

"Maybe I should ask you the same thing?"

"All right, then let's make a little deal together. I already spilled a bunch of stuff for you, so maybe it's time for you to give a little back. I'll keep your secret if you keep mine."

"Um… But we're not supposed to talk about this, not even to each other."

"So, does this mean…what? Maybe we're related in some way?"

"Well, unless yours just magically quit on you, I can't imagine anything else right now. It relates to the Project. And the rules say we're not supposed to know about each other, to say nothing of talking about it."

"Oh… That…" she rolls her eyes away. "Yes, that might tend to stand out."

Ayene knew nothing of this thing Azina was talking about, but it clearly represented something important, as well as secretive. Now she knew there was something occurring, and she felt it could prove useful to learn more about it. She decided to probe around for more information.

"So, this is the reason for your chip?" she asks subtly.

"Yeah, and you? But you're military, so how did you get involved?"

"Oh, I'm sure I'm a special case. And it goes along, at least in an indirect manner, with what I said about some of us getting tired of all the rhetoric. How long have you been inside? By your appearance, I suspect you have been in there for a while now."

"Yeah, about a century… I'm part of the third generation of volunteers. And you?"

"I'm fairly new to all this. Some might say I still suffer from the computerized mind I developed over so much of my lifetime."

"I'm sorry to hear that. But then, if you're military, I suppose the training they put you through can take its toll."

"Yes, it does, and that doesn't help matters on top of everything else."

"Wow, but at the same time, I have to admit, I'm actually happy to finally meet someone else around here that has emotions. Do you know how difficult it is to live in a world like ours when you have to bottle up everything inside?"

"I had my troubles ever since my fourth decade, and it started with my family."

"Oh no…"

"So, you don't know of anyone else?"

"No, everyone is supposed to remain anonymous. I think only the Director knows all of them, as he's the one who manages the list."

"Yeah," she chuckles. "And I wouldn't want to be in his hooves for that point. What about the results, though? We're talking about the third generation here. What have you found in the time you spent with it?"

"Nothing at all. All my reports are simple mood swings so far."

"Mood swings?" she raises her brow. "Anything like what we just saw?"

"Yes, but fortunately they were in private. But YOU…you little troublemaker… I think you did that on purpose."

"Maybe a little…" she grins. "I got curious when I started to notice your manner of speech. Sorry, but it goes with the job. They train us to be very attentive. But just mood swings? There's got to be more to it than that."

"Well, if the Project is to study the Tav'ageen Anomaly, then I haven't had any of my own results…"

Ayene fell silent at the mention of that term. If she were physical, she would have turned pale by now. This defied everything she thought she knew about the research on the subject. But this was apparently a secret operation, so who authorized it, if not the Council.

"…And according to the Director," Azina continues. "Even though he has his own restrictions on what he can talk about, he says no one else has had anything come up, either."

"Fascinating…" she croons. "And considering the circumstances we have to work under, I have to ask how likely it might be to actually learn something."

"Why? Do you think this alien…thing…might no longer exist

by now? This is one of the theories we're toying with, that it's been so long since we saw any attacks, we don't know if it could still be out there."

"This is certainly a viable theory, if you consider it was something infesting our world at one time. Then again, when you have a world full of people who get this chip at four decades, what is left of their psychology by the time you have someone at our age? By the way, how old are you?"

"Eleven, and you?"

"Thirteen and two, and this is certainly long enough for us to lose a considerable part of ourselves that might otherwise allow us to make an easy discovery."

"You think so? I was speaking to Ghantil…the Director…about this thing showing up in those early children, and if we should be looking more at them for an answer."

"While this is reasonable, it is also problematic. First, you need to disable that Council mandate that plugs a chip in their brain at the first sighting of the symptoms."

"Right, and Ghantil is currently trying to negotiate with a few clinics to see if he can gain any statistical data on whether there were any reported symptoms recently."

"You don't get any as a standard procedure?"

"No. There's a nondisclosure clause to prevent any more of that public panic we once had. But this also denies us to maintain any statistics on the progress, or lack thereof."

"Oh how convenient!" Ayene snaps suddenly. "So, not only does he cover it up with the promise of these chips, he also covers his tail with the denial of any feedback."

"A cover-up?" Azina pulls back. "What do you mean?"

Ayene glanced out the door and the row of windows that opened to the hallway outside, checking for anyone who might be observing before returning back to the conversation.

"All right, listen," she whispers determinedly. "Briefly, as I need to get back to my office. I'll only say this much for now. The chips were his solution to the Anomaly, and if the mandate denies you feedback for any form of review, it's likely to keep you from realizing you do or do not actually need the chips. He WANTS us to have them. Recall what I said about all his little secrets he never teaches us about. No doubt, this is one of them, and with the convenience of that nondisclosure thing to keep people from asking questions…a little like that authority chip, to prevent people from analyzing the truth."

"Analyzing the truth!" she blasts.

"Beyond that, it gets complicated, as well as dangerous, and once again, as a hint to you, to put people on active to get the job done… without analyzing the truth…get it? He doesn't like people asking a lot of questions relating to all his private little details."

"Uh oh…"

"So, I'll tell you what… I made a promise to you, and I want to hold up to it, but this visit is taking a little longer than expected, and I need to report in. Let's make a deal together. I honestly enjoyed our little talk, and I would like to see more of it. But we might have to arrange our meetings at some time when I have more opportunity."

"Right, so I guess they work you hard over there."

"The military service doesn't give us a lot of free time, and I have a lot of duties in front of me that demand my attention right now. So, let's finish our business and make a date to meet again. We can continue this then, alright?"

"Well, all right," she frowns and turns back to the terminal.

Ayene reaches out to pat the girl on the shoulder. She offers a gentle smile to soften the deal, and this smooths Azina's hesitation out as she returns the pleasure.

"Maybe we could also be friends," Ayene offers. "Would you like that? I'm always open to find a new friend."

Azina smiles gently and nods, then picks up the delivery that was waiting on the tray near her station. She checks it off through her terminal and hands it over.

"By the way, what was that excuse of yours for these things?"

"Oh, I had a good one in mind for this. Officially…" she raises her brow conspicuously. "We're conducting a test of the seed's effectiveness in a new and especially difficult environment to see how well it performs. But we're not using any of our people…it's too risky. So, we're preparing a replicant platform and we'll monitor it from there."

"Really! I should take lessons from you for your ability to make up stories."

"Yeah, I learned from a crew of professionals, Azina. This is premium quality here."

The two of them share a soft giggle.

"And the real story?" she asks.

"The real one is darker and more sinister. We're actually going to conduct an experiment on the seeds themselves to see if there's a way to kill them without killing the host."

"What?" she yips. "That's impossible! How do you plan on doing that?"

"The impossible part is likely because none of YOU ever tried doing it."

"Oops…yeah."

"As for doing it, we have a clever idea, but this is the part we need to test, to see if it works. And in the end, we might have something interesting to deliver back to you. But I probably shouldn't say anything more than that for now, because this part really is classified, and needs to be kept especially quiet. There are those out there we simply don't want to become aware of what we're doing, and it's not people like you."

"Uh oh…who then?"

"The ones that don't otherwise allow this sort of research."

"Someone doesn't allow it? Who doesn't allow it?"

"Azina, did you people, who invented this thing, ever receive instructions to UN-invent it?"

"Um…"

Azina paused to consider this inquiry, as it would naturally follow with her own ambitions to find answers to the same dilemma.

Ayene continues, "Since the beginning, it was said only to be temporary, on the condition we will one day leave home due to that same Tav'ageen Anomaly we're all supposed to be so afraid of. Well, Azina, in your eleven centuries, did anyone tell you we're finally leaving home? And what about in the many millennia before you were born? We're still here in case you missed it. And we're still using the seeds."

"Well yes, but…"

"Yeah, before you say it, the pollution came later, as we poisoned our native environment waiting to be told we're leaving home, which we never did. So, why didn't anyone pay attention to any of this to correct the pollution before it became so critical that we needed these things right here…the LAST place we needed them at all."

"Oops. That's bad."

"Yeah, and on multiple levels for our society of thinkers who forgot how to think. And so far, this has nothing to do with the fact that we never needed them in the first place. Not for all our other…preexisting…colonization tech we would normally use to spread out to other worlds. What are we expected to do, colonize a world tail-naked as Stone Age hunter-gatherers? If we can build a space station in the vacuum of space, we can surely build anything we want on a foreign world. Why do we need the seeds for it?"

"And that's another oops."

"And then you tell me it's impossible to remove them. It's impossible, Azina, because the people that told you to invent them never told you to un-invent them. So, here we are, using something we never needed to begin with, and living in a world we polluted intentionally, if only because of the fear factor for that old panic, and the resulting drive to evacuate, but never did. Further, we are told… any day now…we are leaving, so don't bother thinking of anything else. And on top of things, along the way, we also forgot all the eco-friendly tech we have to replace the other stuff, even after millennia of waiting for that any day now."

"And that's a massive oops!" she yelps. "It sounds like someone isn't thinking with both horns!"

"I think this goes a little beyond not thinking with both horns.

Someone fed us a lot of stories to keep us bottled up behind such things as these mandates and their associated nondisclosures."

"Uh oh…" she intones solemnly. "So, did someone finally tell you to un-invent this thing?"

"Someone, yes, but not those people who are supposed to be giving out these instructions. As far as they're concerned, it's business as usual. As for the rest, I need to save that for later. Think on this a bit, and see if that ambitious eleven-century mind of yours can come to a few of its own conclusions."

Ayene smiles tenderly as she takes her package. She then offers a gentle wave as she leaves the room. She finds her way back outside and across the street to the alley where she first arrived. She passes a careful glance around the scene to ensure it was clear, and then folds away in a puff.

The meeting left Azina with a flurry of new feelings. On one side, she felt a warm and cozy feeling that she finally found a friend who also feels emotion. On another, the bombshells Ayene left behind had her mind swimming in a sea of new controversies. Ultimately, she could only return to her workstation looking forward to a chance to share more conversations about what was happening in the world. But she never would've expected it to come in the form of a military officer…who was apparently willing to drop so many of their secrets right in her lap.

◆◆◆◆◆

Ayene arrived back in the strategy room at the WIC building, and promptly set down her package on the table.

"Here you are, Your Lordship," she asserts proudly. "As promised, two specimens of what we call the An'gamu Seed, direct from the ARC in Capitol Prime."

"An'gamu…" Kailen relents sarcastically. "Is that supposed to represent the name of the person who invented it? Well, I suppose even atrocities need names."

"Yes, so it seems."

Likha was sitting next to Kailen. She picked up the package, which was neatly sealed in a biological specimen container.

"So professional," she muses. "I wish we had an industry like that."

"Their labs involve a lot of automation, so once you submit the order, it goes through a sterile robotic process to package and deliver the result."

"Really! Well, I suppose that's good, actually. From the technical standpoint, it sounds very efficient."

"Ayene," Thaelyn submits. "Did you have any difficulty in obtaining this sample?"

"No," she shakes her head. "Just like I expected, it followed through very cleanly. I went in, gave them the order, they directed me to the appropriate department, and there I met with a very nice young intern who processed it. In fact, I recall her from my last visit when I ordered those probes."

"Indeed, then perhaps this is to our benefit if you shared a previous experience."

"Yes, it was, and in fact, I learned a few things from her along the way. We had a nice little chat about a number of things, including all those other inventions they made for the Marshal."

"Oh, you did? Hmm, and could this be the reason you appear so perky at this time?" he eyes her suspiciously.

"Perky? Do I look perky?" she smiles innocently. "No, I'm sure you must be mistaken. After all, I didn't uncover a secret and probably illegal research project her Director was conducting. No, nothing like that..." she grins.

"Ugh... General..." he moans delicately.

"Oh dear," the General shakes his head. "Here we go again."

"Very well, Ayene, so what is this about a research project?"

"The girl had emotion," she asserts. "Which means her chip was disabled. We were discussing a few random topics when I decided to dig a little about those inventions. I noticed some of her responses, so I carried a clever dialog to invoke a reaction out of her to test a theory. And with her being rather young, probably also inexperienced at such as intrigue and espionage…"

"Uh huh…so you no doubt pulled rank on her for your prior experience."

"Well, it yielded a result, so what can you argue about?"

"Indeed! General, please apply a mark for this peculiar talent role."

"Very good, my Lord," he smiles.

Ayene continues, "The conversation began with her displaying discontent over so many secrets within the military, and these special orders they had from time to time. And I certainly can't argue with this from my own experience."

"Naturally," Thaelyn nods.

"I carried the dialog as if I was innocently admitting that she's not the only one, and even we get it with such anomalies as being told to do things without explanation, and one hand not knowing what the other hand is up to."

"Oh dear."

"And this naturally leads up to the Marshal for all his private little secrets relating to his insurgents, which he must surely know how to oppose, but unfortunately he doesn't teach any of us, or allow us to analyze what we do for his use of the active mode of the chip."

"And another oh dear."

"So innocent…" Kailen shakes his head. "You might almost think it should be common knowledge around there."

"Yes, well…" Ayene shrugs. "You can probably imagine she was a little surprised, and it showed not only in her face, but also her comebacks…and without any feedback hits."

"I see…" Thaelyn muses. "Very clever, as well as harmless. It also suggests she has been this way for long enough to become accustomed to the sensation that she can let it pass so casually."

"A century or so, but yes. She apparently is supposed to cover it up, but she must not be very good at it…or else I'm simply better at playing it from my side," she smirks mischievously.

"Very likely," he smiles.

"She told me along the way she experiences mood swings, so this might say something. And of course, all of this had to be prefaced as unofficial conversation, which she understood from the start."

"Most interesting. And did we learn anything about all these little secrets?"

"For one thing, she was surprised that I would even bring it up, being military and knowing their reputation for keeping everything hidden. It began with the rocket-propelled seeds, and progressed from there. She must've been trying to invent her own ideas for what they were for, as much as a medical intern might do without someone actually telling her the Marshal is a murderous fiend. She was marveled by the technological proficiency, as well as the budget expense Central must be going through, on all these little gadgets. But unfortunately, these people had no idea what the Marshal was doing out there, so she was speculating we were fighting some horrible parasite using medical implants and Belvik Spores to kill it."

"A parasite?" Likha winces. "What sort of parasite would you need to use medical implants on to kill it?"

"This is what she was asking, and why use the Spores if a simple knife would do the same job. Then the Kajik'tav Serum, where the timing occurred roughly the same as the Spores being discontinued. According to her, this is for a very rare lung disorder that hasn't been seen since the application of the seeds, so the Serum was discontinued way back in the beginning. And yet, here we have a sudden rush order for enough to feed a small army. What happened to cause this? And then we have those other seeds they used on Ruuki uy'Daan."

"So, all of them were researched at the same place?"

"Yes, it would seem the Marshal is playing favorites with this one lab, maybe because it's so conveniently located in C.P. Maybe also for its popular brand name and high-end research capacity. This could make things easy for us if we want to take it away from him. And since they're already involved in this secret research project, we might have a very interesting opportunity in front of us."

"This is curious," Thaelyn wonders. "And how do you envision this?"

"They apparently reopened the research of the Tav'ageen Anomaly. This girl, her name is Azina, she's part of a third generation of volunteers who are apparently turning off their Suppressor chips hoping to discover if this alien infestation is still present after so long without any apparent new cases. But here we seem to have a few complications. The Council, when they first mandated these chips, also included a nondisclosure clause to prevent any feedback for statistical recording of the infestation's progress. This was apparently to prevent any more word leaking out and causing additional panic. But it also prevents them to monitor their medical results."

"And this would serve as a very convenient excuse to continue the application of those chips. The threat alone would perpetuate the response."

"This is exactly what we were talking about. Her Director is currently hoping to gain a little insight to see about this progress, but my discussion with Azina led us to another idea. She said, for all the people in this Project, there have been no useful results returned, which means no one is discovering anything. This would equate to no one experiencing the Gift, even by accident."

"Indeed, and this could offer us a form of empirical result that the chip not only denies the initial discovery, but it could also create a lingering effect even after it is disabled. As I recall, you had a difficult time rediscovering the Gift for all the procedural training you received that left you rather restricted in your perceptual creativity."

"Yes, and she might be suffering the same. She was about the same age as me, so by this point in our lives, it might be hard to reassociate with our early childhood and that first chance we get at finding it. But the fact that it was so carefully covered up to prevent feedback is probably just another of Darumon's games."

"And how do you think we can use this?"

"First, I think I should mention, I had one of my own reactions, so I had to cover for it with a few careful words."

"Uh oh…what sort?"

"It reflected on our conversation…the Marshal doesn't like people questioning or analyzing things, therefore, boom, active mode for us in the military. The mandate, along with the associated nondisclosure clause, is just another example. He wants this, and he does NOT want people questioning his superior alien wisdom. So don't go out making noise."

"Ah, very good."

"She understood this rather quickly. So I think we can trust her for this much. But if they're already questioning the Council over their old mandates, I figured I might test a potential scenario. I had to give a little to get a little in this situation, but if to reflect on Kaliya's tactics, I figured it was a worthy cause. I left a conspiracy theory in her lap about how and why our world is such a mess and no one ever did anything to fix it…meaning to say, those authority figures who are supposed to be doing all the thinking, aren't doing any thinking, and neither is anyone else."

"Indeed, this would certainly raise a few questions."

"I then made a promise to meet with her again and discuss more of these dirty little secrets. If our intention is to take over the place, we need a road to the inside, and this might be a good starting point. She said her Director is apparently the one coordinating this Project of theirs, and that represents a strong position to win to our side."

"Yes, it would be, at that."

"I explained our story about these seeds, but I also secretly revealed to her that our true intention is to conduct a secret research project to find a way to kill them, with the reason being the Council never permitted THEM to do this, and they invented the thing. Furthermore, is to say we intentionally destroyed our home, forcing us to use these seeds, even though we have no justifiable need, for ANY reason, and this includes all our eco-friendly tech our government so conveniently forgot about. And the motivation behind all this is that old panic, and our fear and aversion to run away from this alien thing, then repeating the message that…any day now…blah blah, and around it goes. So, it's our own fault, first to allow it to happen, and second for not thinking of the corrective actions, and now it's too late."

"And her response?"

"Like with everyone else, her response was one of surprise, as she apparently didn't piece this together on her own," she shrugs.

"And this represents a form of complacency," Kaliya considers. "Much like we've seen in so many other places. Darumon did a real good job at turning down their horns in that world."

"But not completely, Kaliya," Ayene affirms. "We do still seem to have a few who are asking questions, even if they don't have access to enough information to provide positive answers. I think this might indicate some who are getting tired of listening to the same old story. And in fact, I even used this suggestion as part of my 'innocent' release of our military getting tired of OUR orders."

"All right, then this is good, but it also means one more element to contain when we go out and start broadcasting our own propaganda. We don't want HIM getting anxious about the people asking so many questions. So, I suppose, given this new development, we should probably…"

"My Lord!" shouts a voice rushing through the halls.

At this moment, a mature High Elf pops into view in the doorway of the strategy room. She leans against the frame panting from a hot run.

"Gods above," she wheezes. "I'm getting too old for this."

Everyone at the table turns to see the figure trying to catch her breath as she stumbles into the room.

"Vonafel!" Thaelyn calls. "Powers pay witness, did you run all this way? Perhaps you should hire a mage with a direct rune transit if you are to make such impromptu visits."

"I'm sorry, my Lord, but another quatrain just opened up for us. I swear, the closer we get to the end of that book, the more excitable I get."

"Another one?" he wonders curiously and glances around the table.

"Yes, it came up a short while ago. I glanced over it briefly with my assistants, and we all agreed to bring it to your attention right away. What just happened over here?"

Thaelyn rolls his eyes up to Ayene, who was standing at the end of the table, before turning back and replying.

"The most noteworthy event is we just had an interesting new form of interaction with the Lieutenant here and the ARC, that medical research center on Azgarén. She just now returned to us with her report. Does this help any?"

"Maybe."

Vonafel approaches the table and plops down a heavy book before taking up a seat at the end. She opens it to the last set of pages.

"This one follows in sequence to the last one," she announces. "Where Kaliya made her initial arrival on Azgarén. This doesn't leave much more for us on this last page. We seem to have one more vacant spot before that one where Kaliya made her meeting with Adalon in her chambers."

"The one that spoke of the silver wings?" Kaliya asks.

"Right, and then we have a large open area on that last page before the very end with that one final quatrain that doesn't make any sense to me."

"Very well," Thaelyn accedes. "What do we have on this occasion?"

Vonafel refers to her book and begins to read.

"Ambitious minds with muted voice, a minor song is played; a careful chase will turn His eyes, in the Forgotten One's parade."

"Powers above, Ayene, you must have found us an important piece."

"Nicely done, Ayene!" Kaliya smiles. "I knew I made a good choice when I selected you."

"But does this mean I'm now revealing these things?" she wonders.

"It must be, at least on this one occasion. But now, my Lord, how do you suppose we interpret this?"

"I can already suggest one thing," Ayene reflects. "That girl was ambitious, asking all her questions."

"Indeed," Thaelyn agrees. "And her Director with his secret project... These are people who are dissatisfied with the current situation and want to move forward with new studies and revised findings. But if we suggest this project must be kept hidden, this could represent the muted voice. They cannot reveal it openly."

"Good, so they're keeping secrets already, and this simply opens a door for us to expand the conspiracy."

"Yes, a conspiracy, a minor song, kept hidden behind these muted voices. They are essentially opposing the ruling of their Council here. I think it also goes without saying the mention of the Forgotten One's parade is Darumon again and all his games to twist their lives around."

"And that careful chase," Kaliya muses. "That has to be us and our counteractions, turning his eyes somewhere else. Ooh, I'm starting to like this."

Chapter 3

INCITING CONSPIRACIES

"It's amazing," Marelle ponders. "I never would've thought one day I would be learning all this, but here I am, in class doing exactly that."

"Which part are you talking about?" Relissa asks.

"I'm currently studying how to use those rune stones to open portals. Here in the Sixth Circle, we start getting into that. I can't mark them yet, that's Seventh Circle, but I can at least use them."

"Aye, I was there last year. Now I'm Seventh, so I'm learning how to mark them. Maybe we could team up on the practice field. I can mark them, and you can play with them," she chuckles.

"That would actually be a great idea. It'd be nice joining you on the practice field again, but these days you're working the upper field while I'm still on the lower one."

"Nah, don't worry about that. You lost a year while having your twins, but you'll catch up."

"Yeah, but by the time I catch up, you'll be finished with your classes. This is your last year, right?"

"Aye, Seventh is my goal. My ranger training will be finishing up this year, also."

Relissa, Marelle, and their friends were again meeting in the courtyard for their afternoon chat. It was a pleasant summer day, and they felt invigorated by the steady progress they were making through their coursework.

Marelle had fallen behind the others by a year to give birth to her twins, and now she was working to catch up. The first several months were slow-going until she could recover from childbirth and the pressures of early motherhood, but now she was picking up a more robust schedule, calling a nanny to care for the twins at home while she was away at the academy. They were filling up her schedule, and she found herself putting in extra time on the weekends to make up for the loss. She was eager to get back into the rhythm, but the work at the academy wasn't the only thing on her mind.

"I hear they're waiting for me to push through this so I can start testing some of their newest prototypes out at the BRC."

"Which ones do they have waiting for you this time?" Sulíma asks.

"So far, they tell me they made a successful prototype test of the arcanic jump drive, which wasn't too much of a stretch when you consider how often we use rune stones to open portals. Making a technological version was a fairly easy step forward, but putting it into a fighter craft was another thing."

"And they want you to test it now?"

"The first test was using a prototype configuration that was largely automated based on principles they borrowed from elsewhere, like with the gateway nodes, and combined as a new hybrid technology with your Daanen'kai science. Then, a drone was launched with some custom engineering to invoke a marking action, using this new process they created to identify a perception characteristic to mark an exit point. The drone was then moved to a new location, which in this case was further downfield, where it engaged another custom function to call on this, opening a portal back to the previous location. They say this action to mark destination endpoints results in a data object which can then be shared with other units on the field, maybe a whole fleet of them, allowing them to move around."

"Just like calculating a nav point in a ship to jump to a new location."

"Exactly, and this is part of our new hybrid technology. So far, the tech only allows us to mark destinations where we can physically locate a ship to call on this process, but they hope to develop it further one day to allow us more flexibility. In the meantime, they're waiting for someone with sufficient mage skills in marking and conjuring portals for the next phase," she finishes with a thumb point at herself.

"And what's the next phase going to be about?"

"We need to establish a series of waypoints for future travel. So far, the easiest way to do this is by actually marking destination endpoints using a ship physically located at that destination, much the same as how we use normal rune stones. And so, they need me to pilot those ships."

"But to pilot them, you first need to know where you're going, and if you need to jump there…but we're in different universes! So, how will you find where you're going if you can't get there without first using a jump drive before you can actually mark it to jump… Marelle! You've got me all twisted around, you little fiend!" she teases.

The group shares a laugh at Sulíma's confusion before Marelle offers up the answer.

"This is a nice little paradox, I'll admit," Marelle responds. "But we have a convenient hidden card we can play here. We already have access to these other worlds by other means. If it were not for that, we'd have to do it the hard way, like your people once did while exploring the stars. This war gave us a shortcut to all that."

"This war seems to have given a shortcut to a lot of things," Túfula concedes.

"Yes, it did," Marelle reflects on the notion. "Thaelyn mentioned on a few occasions how we weren't meant to come so far, so fast. Tae'Eladar is still in its Early Industrial age, and those of us on Therinë were even more backward for what little we had before he arrived. We used horses and other beasts of burden to haul wagons and carriages from place to place, and a lot of manual labor in our industry. Tae'Eladar is using electricity now, as well as some mechanical vehicles. And I don't even dare try to compare the magical side of it."

"And now look at you. You might still be using horses and wagons, but now you're flying aircraft, and soon spaceships."

"And the people don't have a clue what all this is about yet, since most of it is classified as military secrets. Only a very few pieces are filtering out right now. Those of us in this group might be privileged to know about it, but most others have to take the longer route. And the craziest part of it…I'm on the leading edge. If my mom and dad could only see me now, a mother of twin Celestial babies, something we never heard of before Thaelyn showed up, and then all this. He says we shouldn't normally expect to be at this level for at least a couple of centuries for the types of technologies we're currently developing, and more after that for access to other worlds."

"And to think of how long it took us to develop this much," Petrith muses. "Hundreds of millennia…"

"But remember, Petrith," Túfula considers. "Everything tends to run much slower for us, probably because we develop so much slower, so we take our leisurely time with it."

"Not in this school!" Sulíma yips. "We've been here barely more than a year and a half, and they've rushed us through two language courses, early mage training for the first two Circles, introductions to history, culture, their own form of science and mathematics, some of which we're actually flying through based on our previous studies back home…"

"Yeah, but that part was mostly just to fill in the blanks we missed as our own education was cut short due to the attack."

"True, so we can expect that much. And later, we get to look forward to double-duty on our scheduling, as some of it will be based on the academy here, and other parts at our new university on Therinë to pick up our native studies."

"I think it's mostly because of this elixir of theirs," Petrith notes, "and how quickly the local races need to push ahead for their short longevity. We'll be learning what might normally take us several decades to a century back home, in just as many years here."

"More than that," Túfula adds. "When you consider what we're learning at the academy, much of which wouldn't otherwise be on the agenda back home, like mage studies and the associated technologies you can create from it. This is something we never had before."

"But it's not just your people learning what we have," Haran asserts. "We're also learning a great deal of what you have, though perhaps more slowly due to the nature of it, and the fact we need to evolve into it a bit."

"Yes, but Haran, your people will probably learn as much as we have before I'm ready for my first child. That's a little disconcerting for someone like me," she chuckles.

"Maybe so, but in that time, you'll be talking about this to my great grandchildren," he grins as he shares the humorous moment.

✦✦✦✦✦

"What's this here, young cutter?" asks a local shop merchant.

"It's a flyer from the Sensate's Guild," the boy urges anxiously. "There's trouble afoot in the city! Read up on it, quick like. We're bein' called to put out spyin' for the likes of a clueless bunch of berks who are tryin' to get inside the city to steal somethin' grand. Even the Lady is on the watch for them, and she needs to know if yeh see 'em, promptly."

"Wait now, I don't go talkin' to the Lady…"

"It don't matter who yeh talk to, she needs to know of it. These blighters are cuttin' holes in the place to get inside. That's enough right there! Pass the word to a dabus, if yeh got nothin' else, but get it out. There's a war out there, and these berks are tryin' to get at a door no one is supposed to know about. If they get inside, it's the pike for the rest of us. Now post this up on that wall there!"

A young boy dashes off through the streets of Sigil passing out flyers and posting notes on local billboards. He was one of a small army recruited to spread the word around the city, warning the citizens of outsiders trying to gain access to places even the Lady didn't want revealed. Every street corner and tavern, every inn and marketplace was being notified.

Most of the people were reluctant at first, not wanting to get involved, especially with mention of the Lady on the notice. But when they began reading through the wanted poster, they started to realize these invaders were villainous, apparently cutting holes from outside the city, which was already a violation, and further by sending soldiers marching through the streets, either to sneak in, or potentially to use force, if necessary, to find some hidden portal door. These were more than just wild ravings. This was a hostile invasion, something the city had never technically seen before, as no one was supposed to be able to infiltrate the city in this manner from the outside.

The city of Sigil was a floating construct located somewhere in the Outer Planes, and certainly nowhere near any other formation that could be used as a launching point for an attack. There were no openings to enter or leave the enclosed space, which is why the city was often nicknamed The Cage.

No race native to the Outer Planes would dare assault the city, for fear of bringing down the wrath of the Lady. Whoever this was, they were clearly not local, but invaders from somewhere outside the multiverse, and unconcerned for the local politics. They were apparently invading for a reason, and this reason was said to be very dangerous. If the Lady was keeping a secret, and these outsiders wanted it, it couldn't be a good thing.

Messengers, both young and old, rushed through the streets tacking up posters and giving out warnings and instructions to seek out the nearest dabus, the city's municipal workers and close servants to the Lady, if they make any sightings. The posters included a hand-drawn portrait, based on one of the Suuden'kai refugees on Ruuki uy'Daan as a model, for visual identification. They were instructed not to interact directly, instead to seek the nearest official to pass the word along. Even the local guardsmen were told to keep at a distance, allowing the Lady to deal with these most unusual trespassers, due to the fact that they were said to be in possession of weapons powerful enough to blast away buildings, and also of something dangerous to the city security that could only be dealt with by the Lady herself.

In the Clerk's Ward, just outside the Guild of Sensations, a young lady was working to coordinate the army of runners. She was a close friend of Aelwyn, from her time as a Cardinal Sensate attending the local guild. This was before she relocated to Tae'Eladar for her service there. This woman held a similar composure, but of a slightly different variety, with long platinum hair and pointed ears, pale gray skin with several tattoo markings, and with violet eyes... crystalline, like shards of amethyst.

"Cardinal Nemelle," shouts a boy as he dashes into the plaza. "We've got signs up all 'round the Ward. A bunch of us are workin' our way down through the Hive, and another crew's just comin' 'round to the Market Ward, last to my knowin'."

"She asks herself," Nemelle remarks serenely in her unusual third-person manner of speech. "How many will listen to these words? Perhaps enough, in the beginning, and then more after that..."

"Aye, I'll bet once a few glimpses go 'round, people will spread it by themselves. There's already talk in the Market Ward of one time the Lady flamed a crew of berks, and a host of local people got the shimmies for it."

"She admits this is a beginning, and there may be more after, but she wonders how many in total will come through, and if any may find what they seek."

"What do you think they'll do if any more come in after we get the word out?"

"She considers the prospect, and asks herself if they might see it with their own eyes, and then turn back. But she silently wonders if they will ignore it and press forward, and more imperatively if they will call upon others, and how vigorously they will search."

"It doesn't sound like a happy end, if that be the one."

The boy takes up another stack of posters and runs off again, with his youthful energy carrying him down the avenue to another district of the city.

Nemelle watches him leave, still concerned over the prospect of these invaders eventually locating the hidden portal. The plaza was a busy center of commerce and entertainment, but to the far end was a locked grate, a door leading into the tunnels below the street. Her gaze drifted off to it.

"And finally, she ponders," she murmurs quietly. "What lurks below even now?"

Somewhere in the tunnels beneath the street, another squad of Suuden-Aryku was navigating their way through the labyrinth of sewers and catacombs. Several teams had been sent by this time, some of them lost as they penetrated the street level and were discovered by the local authorities. A few managed to escape back into the tunnels hoping to lose their pursuers in the underground maze. At this moment, they were spending more time charting the complex array of corridors and locating exit points, to gain a better understanding of where to find easy access to make short appearances.

They arrived at another grate which, like all the others, was locked with a chain. But rather than blasting it, as the first squad did, they brought with them a mini plasma torch to cut the chain neatly and quietly. They opened the gate and peeked outside. The street was not as busy here as it was elsewhere, so they stepped out cautiously, peering around for any dabuses in the area. By this time, they knew what to look for. The coast was clear, with only a few local citizens walking by, most of whom appeared intent on their personal affairs.

The soldiers spread out to the local buildings and alleys checking for any disturbances to arise as they passed by. At this time, they were still looking for a portal rift to open when they came within close proximity to it. The newer procedure of appearing as tourists was not fully in effect yet.

A local citizen was emerging from a shop when he noticed the odd group of four tall visitors dressed in strange attire, seemingly searching for something. Their peculiar behavior caused the man to pause and stare at them. Their features were unique, not reminiscent of any of the local races. They wore what appeared to be a form of armoring, but not of any common design known in the city. And they had a strange device slung over one shoulder, displaying several soft lights, some of which were steady and others flashing. He had never seen anything like it before, but it was clearly powered and vaguely resembled a ranged weapon.

"That's a funny sight," he asks another patron just coming out behind him. "What do yeh think that is over there?"

The woman turns to follow his direction to see the squad members moving slowly through the street. She turns back towards the shop to examine a wall with a billboard on it, where a wanted poster was hanging. She glances back at the soldiers, and then returns to study the poster carefully for comparison. She feels a rush of fear wash over her.

"It's them!" she screeches. "Find a dabus, quick like, they're here!"

The woman dashes away down the road, leaving the man standing there in a near state of panic.

The shop owner hurries outside to see what the commotion was about. He takes immediate notice of the soldiers and begins shouting.

"Everyone, they've gotten through to the Ward. Take shelter or clear the area. And get a dabus in here!"

The people on the street began screaming and running in confusion, now taking greater notice of the intruders. The shopkeeper ducks back inside his store, chasing through to a back room and a rear exit, and then leaving through the alleys.

The Suuden-Aryku quickly became aware of the disruption, but uncertain as to the cause since the language was foreign to them. They observed the people running and screaming, and a lone man still standing by the shop entrance across the street from them.

"Lieutenant," calls one of the members urgently. "This disturbance could bring unwanted attention to us."

"Agreed, but do you see any of those floating creatures?"

"Negative. It began with a female, and then a male from that structure there," he points at the shop.

"That male, he is staring at us," notes another soldier of the man standing by the shop. "We may be the cause of this."

"The previous incursions may be alerting the general populace by now."

"We have not entered this segment before," the Lieutenant considers. "And these people do not present the impression of such connectivity."

"Maybe not, Sir, but it is all one big city, so a person could potentially walk to this side and tell someone."

"Yes, you are correct."

The man near the shop stood frozen, waiting to see what the strangers will do next. He noticed they turned their attention in his direction, but couldn't believe they were actually an invading force. He turned to find that poster the woman was studying a moment ago, glancing back at the soldiers to associate the likeness with the image on the paper.

"The announcement came from that building," the Lieutenant states. "Go investigate what that male is reading, quickly, before those creatures arrive. Then we must take cover."

A soldier moves across to the shop while the others pull back in the direction of the sewer gate. The man at the door saw the tall alien form making haste in his direction. He yelps and runs deeper into the shop, hiding behind the counter. The soldier halts at the door and briskly surveys the billboard, spotting the wanted poster.

"There is a notice of some kind on this wall," he reports on his com-link. "It has an image of us on it."

"Collect it and return to the tunnels."

The soldier pulls the notice off the wall, and then hurries back to the sewer to join the others, where they make their way back below ground.

"This is good work, so far, Likha." Ankhia admits as she studies a data-pad and one of the medical station monitors.

"This part was fairly simple, considering our previous study of the Ruuki uy'Daan specimen."

"But the coding here differs with those alien strains we tried to study once. What was that name you gave?"

"Ayene calls it the An'gamu Seed, as it is known on Azgarén."

"Well, I suppose all things need a name, no matter how disgusting they are," Ankhia winces. "The sequencing looks good, and I see you have the programming for the Spore, also. We look ready for our test."

"Poor little Banni," Likha mourns. "He's about to get hit a second time."

"Better him than a living subject."

"True. The applicator is ready when you are."

Ankhia and Likha were in the final preparation stages of testing their solution to the seed entity in their cloning lab. The replicant they once used during the trials on the seed specimen taken from the orcs on Ruuki uy'Daan, which was used to find their answer to the mutation victims, was being brought into service yet again for this example.

The clone substitute represented the major portions of a torso, complete with internal organs, but minus any limbs or even a head. It had been placed inside a suspension tank where a robotic arm was being lowered into place with an applicator containing the seed core.

Ankhia manipulated the controls to bring the applicator into contact with the torso and injecting the core into it. The two of them watched as the entity came to life, spreading out over the surface of the body and penetrating through the tissues as it searched for key organs and other principal body components.

Ankhia studied the bio-monitors on the screen which displayed the biorhythmic readings for the various organs and other tissues. The status indicators were jumping from their natural rhythms into a new and seemingly artificially controlled rhythm. The results were very similar to their earlier experience.

"Well," Likha relents. "It wasn't quite as shocking on this occasion as it was that first time."

"Still, I shudder to think of it being applied to any living being, and worse, an entire world society."

"And then to think of how to remove it from that world society."

"One thing at a time, Likha. Let's get the Spore ready."

Ankhia retracts the first arm from the tank and brings the next one in with a hypo-spray attachment. It had already been prepared with a sample of the reprogrammed Spore. She lowers it into place alongside the entity on the torso skin, presses it against the body and injects the contents. When she was finished, she removed it and closed the tank lid to keep the experiment contained.

"Now, we wait," she announces. "Our previous study took about a month, and we're calibrating this to work the same. Keep your eyes on those monitors and let me know if anything unusual pops up. I won't be able to spend quite as much time watching it on this occasion, but I'll check in from time to time."

"All right, Ankhia. How's the little one coming today?"

"He's keeping us busy. Kailen and I are taking turns at home, but Kailen needs to spend most of his time at the WIC to coordinate our war efforts. Meanwhile, Tyanna has been like a mother to me, so I think we're in good hands."

"I'm so happy for you. After all, she is little Sani's grandmother. He's very fortunate to have that. Maybe, when my turn comes, she would offer the same support."

◆◆◆

"My mother and I, as I'm sure you can relate, share a very tepid relationship. It's just the sort of thing you get when you can't share emotions."

"Azina, I wish I could even admit to that much where my mother is concerned. She and I never held this level of bonding."

"What? Ayene, why is that? Surely, even with the Suppressor chip, you must feel some level of familial bond."

"I don't know, but quite often I feel as if she treats me like a stranger that she would rather not have visit even during my rest periods."

"No, I can't accept that. Why would she behave this way? She's your mother!"

"For a long time, I asked myself this same question. My final answer was there must've been a moment in my life when something dire happened. I can only guess what thoughts go through her mind when we meet, but I know one of these days I need to confront her with it. As I move forward, I've been thinking about this. I agree it can't go on, for a number of reasons, but how to solve it may be a bit problematic right now."

"When do you think you will take care of this? You shouldn't let it go for too long."

"I know, but I doubt it'll change much before I'm ready. I'm just not ready for it right now. Maybe later when a few other details of my life come around."

Ayene and Azina were having a friendly chat in a private room in the research center during a recess in Azina's work shift. This was one of the follow-up sessions to the first meeting when they discovered each other to share something in common, and Ayene was working hard to develop the relationship into something meaningful.

Azina was happy to find a new friend. Ayene was also happy, but feeling a little guilty for playing this game about who she was. She enjoyed the friendship, but she also had very serious work to do, and the survival of a species was at stake. And so far, Azina knew nothing about this.

"What kinds of details are those?" Azina asks.

"It has to do with my work, which is a little bit complicated to explain right now."

"I remember you promised to tell me something about all those inventions."

"That's right. I wasn't personally present with those things...I was stationed elsewhere at the time. But I learned about them later, at least as far as someone was ordering and applying them."

"But wait a minute... I recall you once said something about one hand not knowing what the other hand was doing, and this included those people who ordered and used these things."

"Well, all right, you do have a point. It was NOT by them. This is mostly secondhand information by those who observed the result afterwards."

"And not the ones who ordered or used it? That sounds almost like a double-blind testing procedure."

"Curiously, I suppose you could call it that. Although the testing aspect is not accurate, as they were simply aiming for an end result, not a test."

"But secondhand by who, if not the ones who ordered or used it?"

"The best way to describe it would have to be someone ordered it, but like so many other things, without any reasoning to it, and neither with anyone truly knowing what was inside the box. Then it being delivered to someone who was not affiliated with the ones ordering it, and they were the ones using it. And THEN, the result, if you can call it that, being later observed by yet another party, also not affiliated with anyone else."

"Ugh! That sounds worse than a double-blind test. How do you get any kind of result out of that?"

"Oh, there was most certainly a result recorded," she chuckles ironically. "And I suppose, you can guess the products did behave as advertised."

"And you?"

"I received a briefing once, and by those final people. But this was actually after I had been reassigned into a new service."

"A new service… So, is this to say you're no longer serving Central Command? I still can't believe you can be a part of the Project and also the military. I mean, what we're doing here might be regarded by some as illegal."

"Actually, I don't think having the chip fully disabled would be technically described as illegal. The Council mandate says to install it at four decades, and to maintain it for the duration of the threat of the Tav'ageen Anomaly. Unfortunately, that nondisclosure statement you mentioned doesn't give us a way to resolve that threat through a continued study to see if it still exists."

"Yes! Exactly! This is what Ghantil and I were discussing once. This makes for a cute little loophole, doesn't it? You said something about a cover-up, and how it seems intended this way, and basically not to argue the point, which I'm not too happy about, because it suggests something bad, and not necessarily the Anomaly itself. And then all that other stuff about us forgetting to think of what we're doing, which brings us to where we are with the seeds, the pollution, and so on. But this begs me to ask what all that was about. You know, you seem to be dropping a lot of little clues to something, but you're not finishing the statements."

"I know, Azina, but it's not an easy life out there. You may not like having so many secrets passing around, but some of them are necessary, because knowing everything up front can actually be dangerous in the wrong circles. If only I could give you the full history of the world. It would send those horns of yours flying through the walls. I used to be a law enforcement officer; did you know that?"

"Uh oh…that's even worse than the military where the Project goes. So much for my freedom!" she chuckles.

"Yeah, we've got you tail-tagged here, so you may as well give it up!" Ayene smirks. "But I studied law over at CPU, and I hold a degree in it now."

"Really? Then why do you work in the military and not a law office?"

"The military was something special that came up once. In the beginning, I was hoping to get involved in law, and maybe politics, as this was another interest I held. But sitting behind a desk didn't seem as appealing to me after a while as compared to going out and getting physical."

"I see. So, what did you get physical with?"

"To start off, I worked in administration over at C.P. Security, at least until I could build myself a little. I ran some patrols around the city, and during my initial training for my military career, I logged some time in sector security, where I was a helmsman in one of our cruisers."

"That sounds interesting, even if it is only sector security. How long did this last?"

"Until about four centuries ago."

Azina glares at Ayene for this curious number.

"Four centuries is also the length of time we were shipping out those Spores, do you remember that?"

"Yes, but my assignment was elsewhere, like I said. I think it was probably coincidental…or maybe not, depending on how you look at it."

"Ayene, either it's coincidental, or it's not coincidental. I don't think the way you look at it could be a deciding factor."

"Well, all right. The Marshal was conducting some exercises on a world he found once. At the same time, we were assigned to an outpost performing some other functions which were not directly related to his immediate exercises, but we were working on a secondary project he hoped to use somewhere along the way."

"Um…yeah, and this is why you say it might depend on how you look at it. Well, maybe you're right, after all," she chuckles. "What was this project of yours?"

"A mining operation…"

"Oh wow, Ayene. That sounds so exciting, I'm almost ready to flip over backwards. Almost…" she grins. "And this is what you call getting physical?"

"Yeah," she chuckles ironically. "I know what you mean, but for me, at the time, it was a chance to get out and hopefully do something useful."

"A mining operation is useful? Well, I mean, sure it is, but, um…"

"What I mean is, even though it wasn't great, it was stated to be important, and related to the Marshal and his crusade against his insurgents. Like all things, it was highly classified, and we didn't actually know it was a mining operation until after we arrived. That's how he does things."

"Uh huh…more of that need-to-know business," she shrugs.

"Yeah. My duties weren't very exciting, just monitoring a control panel to regulate a reactor and a conveyor, and the supply and work crew assignment of a processor facility. But it kept me busy."

"Another desk job, by the sound of it. All right, but what were you mining?"

"It was a local mineral we found with some rather peculiar

properties to it. Our technology didn't hold the appropriate capacity to mine it directly, so we were using local labor for this purpose."

"The local labor had better technology?"

"I think the term technology is subjective. They held native knowledge and understood the methods necessary to provide the service. Technology, in the manner we would define it, doesn't apply. It's more about technique."

"Oh, I see, like a local tradition or something? Interesting. And then you sent it to a processor. What was it used for?"

"The Marshal demanded it for a project of his. We didn't actually know much more about it, only that it was something he wanted."

"Incredible, so another case of one hand versus the other, and none of it explained to you. The Marshal simply tells you to do something, and you just do it without asking questions?"

"Don't forget those chips. We didn't have them turned on, but the threat was there."

"But wait a minute. That's actually suggesting he's taking advantage of those chips in some way."

"Yes, and some might even say this is their sole purpose."

Azina went silent as this concept began to sink in. She gazed at Ayene as she tried to come to terms with this suggestive and controversial statement.

"Then who is it that actually controls Central?" she wonders. "I thought the High Commander was the head of the military."

"Officially, yes, at least in the eyes of anyone who pays attention. But he also has the chip, just like the rest. And my Commander once told me he was on active quite often."

"On active!" she shouts. "But that means...um... On active means he's placed into a condition to follow instruction from a higher authority. So, who is the higher authority in this case? It would have to be the Council, I think, wouldn't it?"

"Ordinarily, the HC would answer to the Council as our traditional chain of command, assuming the Council had any special need to give such orders, which isn't very often, as it turns out. But we also need to consider they've been lost inside their chambers deliberating that big important…thing…they've spent all their time on since who-knows-when, and not talking to anyone else along the way."

"Um, hold on a second. I know the Council has been said to be deliberating something big, and I know our labs haven't heard much from them for who-knows-how-long to start any new research projects, or even to refresh any old ones. But if they're not actually doing anything at all outside their chambers, who is the HC taking orders from?"

"The same one who built our military in those early years after we started having all these troubles with insurgents, the Marshal. He's the one who actually runs the military these days. We have to reflect on our history for this point. This is when we used to have a Sentinels' service, rather than a full military."

"That goes way back, but yes, I think I recall this from my history lessons."

"The Marshal reinvented the Sentinels into a true military. Of course, he's also the one who invented these chips, and so many other things, or at least he aided in their development, and then had the Council mandate them on each and every one of us."

Azina stared at Ayene in awe for the suggestive statement.

"I was speaking to Ghantil once about some of this…the seeds, to be precise. I never once had an opportunity to go off-planet, but I'm still mandated to have this horrible little bug on my back. Why, simply for the pollution over our heads?"

"The story goes like this in the modern day, but like I said earlier, we polluted our world intentionally, and here we are."

"Wait a moment. Help me to understand the internal reasoning here. I remember what you said before, but why do you say it was intentional?"

"Step One, we have the emergency of the insurgents. Step Two, we have an urgent life-or-death demand for a heavy military to defend us. Step Three, this also demands a heavy, and subsequently very polluting industry to provide for it. We apparently didn't have time or opportunity to use any of our clean tech. Step Four, who cares if we use clean tech anyway, as we're all being pushed, using any means necessary, to leave home due to the Tav'ageen Anomaly. Therefore, we intentionally destroyed our world."

"And here we are, still ON our world," she moans. "And again, STILL with all that polluting industry no one remembered to clean up. I swear, Ayene."

"And the seeds were that 'any means necessary' aspect of things."

"Yeah, as opposed to all our OTHER tech to do the same job. Wow, I wonder where all the horns went to give us THAT answer."

"The panic must've caused a lot of people to simply forget things. Maybe also because no one ever used it to begin with."

"No one ever used it? But I thought…well, with outposts and such…"

"But no colonies, Azina. An outpost is not a colony. It's barely an office space with living quarters. And not a civilian thing, so they're not even involved to realize it."

"Oh, really!" she huffs.

"Anyway, the history continues with the panic of the Tav'ageen Scare, which came from our lack of ability to understand the actual Anomaly, and our only real solution was to evacuate to other worlds, leaving this one behind. But then these insurgents got in the way. So, the Marshal eventually came up with these chips as a way to hold it back until he could build up our military to fight the insurgents and clear the way for us to move forward."

"Yes, and this matches what I know of our history."

"Good. So, the real question is why are we still here?"

"Um, could it be because the insurgents are still out there?"

"Well, that's certainly the story, isn't it? So, let's look at a few things and see how they fit together. The Marshal comes in, tells us his story, and we give our aid, like the good people we are. He offers his promise of great wisdom as payment, and the Council goes tail-crazy over the idea, but before we can really accomplish anything, we have this trouble with the Tav'ageen Anomaly. He does his bit to help us solve it, but the solutions are incomplete to meet up with his grand promises."

"How do you mean incomplete? The chip seems to offer a solution for it…at least insofar as we don't see the symptoms anymore."

"Yes, you have that much right, but it wasn't his FIRST solution. His FIRST solution was to run away. If he's such a fantastically brilliant mind, why wasn't the first solution to use the chips, instead of telling us to run away?"

"Uh oh… And I recall Ghantil speaking of these ideas a few times, too. He wanted us off this planet for some reason, at least until those insurgents got in the way."

"I suppose that could impose a problem. Meanwhile, the Council is apparently in deep deliberation over something, and we might actually suggest it relates to this great wisdom. But…" she emphasizes with a finger. "Have you ever researched anything on the DataNet relating to them?"

"Not really. I don't spend much time on that thing. It just runs you around in circles, from what I hear."

"You're right about that!" Ayene smirks. "I tried it not long ago. My old Tuka doll was more intelligent than that thing."

The two of them share a laugh over the idea.

"Apparently," she continues. "The Council is busy with something entirely unknown, and no one knows if or when they'll be ready with it. That's not a very satisfying answer to someone who's been waiting a lifetime for it."

"No, it's not."

"Furthermore, there's no one you can ask about it. If you try going into the Grand Hall, the people inside will just tell you to stay out, it's private and they're not to be disturbed."

"Wow, so I guess it must be really sensitive."

"It certainly seems that way, and all the more reason to ask who is running our government if the Council locked themselves away so tightly, they don't even come out for a breath of fresh air on occasion, or even the polluted stuff."

"Huh? Wait a minute, are you speaking figuratively, or literally."

"Literally…"

"You're kidding!" Azina intones alarmingly. "But don't they at least come out for a break, or to go home once in a while…or simply to eat?"

"According to the Internal Secretary, no they don't. I had a chance to speak with him recently. He tells me they had provisions delivered inside the inner chamber to supply their needs, and the doors are kept locked to maintain their privacy."

"Unbelievable! I didn't know that. What about their families, don't they ever get a chance to see them?"

"That largely depends on who you talk to. No one has apparently seen the Council outside since the last public interview, which was recorded on the DataNet in 9765.31 CTD at the announcement of the new Tav'ageen Suppressor chip."

Azina turned pale at this statement. She gaped at Ayene for the incredible measure of time in the calendar date as compared to the modern day.

"Since that time," Ayene adds. "You have a curious story that begins like this: Prior to this date, probably towards the beginning of this crisis, they were relocated out of the Grand Hall due to the Tav'ageen Anomaly posing a potential threat to their safety. So, the military carried them away to a top-secret facility codenamed Site One-Alpha as a type of quarantine procedure to protect them. This also included their immediate families."

"Wow, Ayene, was it really that bad?"

"Someone must've thought so. They were only delivered back here for their press releases. But people like you were never intended to know about this as it was sealed behind a Class 3 military security rating, which means you need a Fleet Commander or higher authority to unlock the file."

"In all the nether-space…" she wheezes.

"However, after the chips were released, and things settled, the Council was brought back, and they locked themselves away ever since. But if you search on the DataNet, you'll get a strange little reference. You should try it sometime. The families are still hiding behind a Class 3 security rating."

"Why?"

"That's a really good question, but if you conduct a search on the last time anyone saw one of them, it dates to before any of this ever occurred. Search for this AFTER that date, and its Class 3. Ask if they are listed as alive and well, and you get no results. This includes casual observation if they simply go out shopping, kids going to school, owning a home, or paying taxes, whatever you might have access to, as some of this might also require a security code simply for the privacy laws."

"Uh huh..."

"And by the way, Site One-Alpha, according to our records in Central, is gone."

"Uh oh... Why?"

"The listed reason is an early casualty of the insurgent attacks."

"Oh no, so they blasted the station, or whatever it was, and maybe these families were still inside?"

"It certainly does give that impression. But we still have the question of the Class 3 rating. Even if they died, someone might still issue a death report. Why hide it in the first place?"

"Oops, yeah, that doesn't make a lot of sense."

"Unless there's more to it than that..."

"More to it, like what, do you know?"

"You would be shocked to know what I know. It would have to involve one or another of those secrets we are prevented from learning about. That one hand versus the other. The Marshal essentially controls our military with his Council-granted authority to protect our world from these insurgents, and hopefully one day to carry us through this process of returning Sargeras home. He also ordered these chips to be put inside their heads for some reason, and I'm sure you, as a medical intern, know what they can do. They were probably researched in this lab, like all his other toys."

"Toys..." she muses. "That's an interesting word to use. Yes, actually, that work was done here, I believe."

"Also, the Council is effectively absent from any of their normal governmental duties, and the elections we've had during this entire period of time have been rigged to reelect the same people."

"Just a moment!" she shouts. "I'm no law student, but wouldn't that be described as election fraud?"

"As a university law degree holder, I can solidly say yes. Furthermore, it was confirmed by the Internal Secretary after I arrested and interrogated him for these allegations."

"Whoa!" Azina's eyes bulge. "Arrested?"

"Yeah, part of that 'getting physical' aspect of my recent work," she smirks. "He confessed to knowing and covering up this fallacy. He claimed the Council held a special privilege, granted by the Marshal, to deliberate these…things…they were supposed to be deliberating. This special privilege overrode our traditional political process such that this one and only one Council should remain intact to continue deliberating for as long as it takes to figure out what it is they're supposed to be looking at…ten millennia of it, so far. And no one told us about it. Azina, do you know how old some of them were before all this began? Many of them were old-timers."

Azina grew cold at the notion, as the term held a special meaning in their culture.

"Do we know how many could still be alive by now, especially if no one has seen them in this time?"

"You're a medical intern, Azina, and essentially a scientist. Let's see how well your science training helps you to figure this out. How do you prove the existence of a thing?"

"By examining the evidence of its existence. So, if I'm interpreting this correctly, you're saying that without seeing them during this full length of time, we can't be sure if they're alive or dead, especially if someone keeps telling us to stay out and locks the doors."

"We can't even be sure if they were ever in there in the first place. Remember, they were once stationed on Site One-Alpha."

"Oh dear…" her voice trembles. "And it's gone now? But what does this say for our government?"

"We're getting into a scary situation here, Azina. If this is the case, and no one bothered to tell us, it's not a question of what happened, or even why it happened. Rather, it's who did this. Geilv serves the Marshal, so it can't be him, at least not directly. You scream that they're out there doing something, but no one ever tells you what. You talk about weird inventions with no reasonable explanations. And then we have the media streams…the one thing we're supposed to be able to depend on to tell us what's happening out there."

"Oh great, and what are you going to throw at me about that now?"

"As a law student, let me give you a brief education on something that applies here: Article Nine, Section Fourteen of the Charter of Laws. Do you know this one?"

"No, not precisely… What is it?"

"It's a component of our laws that translates as the Truth in Reporting Act of 3752 CTD. This dates back to the early days of our Enlightened Age, a time when we first started seeing ranged forms of communication, like wired or wireless broadcasts. This is where our people were moving forward as a society dedicated to the scientific studies and the assimilation of empirical logic. It basically states that any and all elements of intellectual product based on factual study must be portrayed to the public in a truthful and deliberate manner…to the best of their ability."

"All right, I think I understand. So…what of it?"

"…To…the…best…of…their…ability…" she reiterates slowly.

"Why am I getting chills now?"

"It's a cheat. A loophole someone inserted. There were Council-mandated regulators censoring our media streams, and also falsifying the reports. Their 'ability' was only what someone granted them to actually report."

Again, Azina gawked at the young officer for this newest outrage. She wanted to scream at the offence, but all she could make was wheezing sounds.

"Council… Mandated… Regulators… Censoring stuff?"

"At least until I came along," Ayene states confidently.

"Just who are you working for now? Is this more of that C.P. Security stuff?"

"Partially. My department is working alongside them. We

learned from a military informant that our media streams were being altered, and the feed was coming from a military source. So, if you were complaining about the military doing something, and you never got any explanation for it, this is why. However, we should probably stop a moment to analyze this, as there can be legitimate reasons for this practice."

"Oh really! Like what? And how do we define this with that act of yours."

"Not counting the false reports for a moment, some of it could be due simply to the fact that the military doesn't disclose it for real security reasons. They are military, after all, and the civilian population does NOT actually have the right to know every little detail of their activities. We never had a true military before this, so our society doesn't apparently hold any special clauses in our laws to provide for acts of national security. Not since uniting everything under one flag and with no more concern for international intrigue. Essentially, the Marshal's military doesn't have any special rules governing it outside whatever he installed internally."

"Oh, how nice. So, they can go out and do whatever he tells them to do under the control of these chips of his, and they just do it with impunity?"

"That's the first statement you made today that holds any real substance to it. And if they're the ones feeding our news media, it's only what he wants the people to know. But again, we still need to ask ourselves what this means. After all, like I said, they can have their legitimate needs. So, what is it he's feeding us through these regulators, and what is he holding back?"

"All right, I'm listening."

"If they're conducting any covert moves out there, this already falls under a security heading. And if you consider his fight against his insurgents, I should think there must be at least a few of those. Sometimes war isn't all about who attacked what and which side won. There is often a lot of hidden movement to sneak up on your opponents."

"Yeah, I suppose I can see that."

"Also, this war has been dragging on for ten millennia. That's a long time for anything to take place. Why haven't we won by now? If we were losing, I think we would know about it, but we're still here, so it must be something else. Maybe the military is making movements it needs to keep secret, and therefore the media needs to be controlled for some reason in case anyone is listening."

"Listening…like from outside? In all the nether-space, that's right. Our broadcasts might travel outside the planet, so they could be intercepted by something."

"This could be a problem. But the military might be doing other things besides fighting a war. They're supposed to be discovering new worlds, maybe also conducting some internal research on these discoveries."

"Wouldn't that be the domain of our own research labs? After all, that's what we're here for."

"Azina, while I might agree, the only thing you've been told to research are crazy missile-propelled seeds, and medical implants with Belvik Spores to fight some unknown…thing…for four centuries. If the Council is not doing anything useful, and the Marshal is actually in control of the military, and you had instructions to research anything really important, I doubt he would have you pulling up the old archives of some obsolete pharmaceutical…unless it served HIM for some reason."

"Serving HIM? But what about us?"

"He doesn't apparently care about our needs. He once promised us the secrets of the universe. That was ten millennia ago. In that time, we gave him our military, preprogrammed to serve with the flip of a switch. This may or may not be as much of a concern, if he really is out there fighting insurgents, but then we have his promises. We paid a high price already, with our bodies and with our world. Where is at least a small piece of that compensation? We should be tired of waiting, but apparently many of us don't even bother to ask any more. And neither do we use our own superior minds to see all these disjointed pieces laying around us to put it together, like you on that first day."

"Yes, I see your point, and this doesn't look good for us. We let our horns sag so low, it just rolls right off of us now."

"Let's say he gave something to the Council once upon a time. In the absence of them serving any other proper governmental function, as they should, despite this extraordinarily important deliberation they have in front of them, as well as the simple time offset since the last time anyone actually saw one, we should ask who is in there and what they are actually doing."

"Or if they could still be alive by now, if they were already so old that these ten millennia would've killed them off due to old age."

"Right, so if they DID receive the secrets of the universe, they should at least tell us, so we know WHY we have to wait so long. This could lead us to two possible conclusions. First is we received it, but the Council is hoarding it to themselves, either out of selfishness, or maybe to use for some nefarious purpose. It doesn't sound very realistic, but greed is still greed, even if it is founded in great wisdom."

"I suppose."

"Second is they're gone from the picture, and again, no one bothered to tell us. We're not allowed to go inside and check on them. No one has seen them for almost ten millennia. Their families also seem to be missing, and further to be classified for WHY they're missing."

"And this is extremely suspicious, I think."

"Yes, it is. If it was something innocent, like they got caught in that insurgent strike, we should STILL be notified, AND a new Council elected. But if our only explanation is absent any founding evidence to provide for it, we aren't left with too many options."

"But wait, you said you already arrested that secretary, right? Did you try peeking inside?"

Ayene was now wrapping up her review for the day. She didn't want to give out everything in one bite, and this was already a big one. So, she smiled and stood up from her chair, then turned and glanced casually at Azina one more time.

"Maybe I did," she croons nonchalantly.

"Just a moment!" Azina protests harshly. "You're not walking out on me like this, are you?"

"Azina, I want you to think about these matters for a little while. I suspect you will probably share some of this with the Director, just to hear his opinions. I'll be back, don't you worry. And I'll give you more when I return. But this conspiracy runs deep, and it'll cause so many stirs that it could upset our entire society. The trouble is, we can't be sure who we WANT to know about it…or not."

"Uh oh…meaning we're in trouble. But then, why are you actually telling me? Shouldn't you take this to C.P. Security, or maybe the military…or maybe not if he actually controls them."

"Why you? He likes using this place for his toys. As for the military, not all of them are on active. I think he only uses that when he needs them to behave a certain way, like in battle."

"Toys again…" she frowns. "All right, I'm getting a picture here, and not a nice one. But then what? What are we supposed to do about any of this? Is this department of yours doing anything?"

"We're conducting a number of investigations so far, trying to collect all the data. We have already taken care of those regulators and their immediate contacts. And we'll be watching for anything else."

"But if those regulators were serving a valid purpose, like for security reasons…"

"Yes, but consider… There is a difference between keeping their security and forcefully controlling the flow of information. If you don't want someone to know something, just don't tell them. Don't make the press release in the first place. Why do you need regulators to watch the flow going out if you don't want it to go out at all? Who is leaking this information that the Marshal might want to keep hidden, and what ever happened to his control mechanism, be it simple military discipline or his chips to govern their actions?"

"Wow, now there's a statement. To tell or not to tell, or to have your chip turned on so you don't tell at all."

"Right, and this essentially obviates the need for regulators inside the media stream, unless he has a serious issue of controlling his own creation. This leaves only one other possibility… Authoritarianism.

Those regulators weren't controlling anything, they were fabricating it. As a law enforcer, regardless of anything else, legitimate or otherwise, I would say this invalidates whatever authority they had to be in there, even if it is legitimate to uphold military security. And by the way, this is made worse for the true LACK of communication of anyone in the military, where one hand does NOT know what any other is doing."

"Oops! So, even if they did have a leak, it wouldn't be much of one."

"Yeah. And along with the Internal Secretary, I also arrested the Public Relations officer as a middleman between the media and the Marshal's office. He admitted to me that he received fabricated publications to pass along to the media stations for those regulators to edit into our news broadcasts as our nightly feed on all the wonderful things our military is doing out there, courtesy of the Marshal."

Azina gasped once more at the audacious allegation.

"But Ayene! What does this actually say about him? I mean, for all he promised us, for all we gave him, and are STILL giving him, and everything he says we're doing out there…"

"We should still reflect on the potential for security here. Is he fighting insurgents? Is he NOT fighting insurgents. Could our media be intercepted, and therefore he's feeding false information not to US, but to THEM? Or is he just filling our heads with a lot of children's bedtime stories to cover up for something else? Are there legitimate reasons for all this, or did he come here with ulterior motives."

"Dammit, Ayene, and you're just going to leave me like this until you come back and finish it?"

"Sorry, Azina, but I have to. You can't be told everything all at once. Put those horns of yours to work. Seek out those mysteries your grandmother should've been asking about. See what sorts of reasons could be drawn out of it. Pull together your own research, if you can, and see what comes up for you. It might hold a little more meaning to you if you see it with your own eyes and stop letting your horns sag so low."

"Got it…" she relents feebly. "All right, Ayene, but in the meantime, can I trust anything I see on the news these days?"

"My office is working on a number of covert plans relating to this, so I'll let you know if we come to any conclusions. But for now, I need to go. Take care of yourself, and keep your horns sharp. We'll see each other again soon."

Ayene smiles and strolls away, leaving the room and eventually departing the building, returning once again to her secluded alley where she vanishes back to Therinë.

Azina is left with a volley of lurid questions circling in her mind, some of which she didn't want to ask, but several of them served as pieces to a puzzle, and they were starting to fit together, creating a picture she couldn't ignore.

"The Council is missing…possibly… I can't see how anyone a hundred plus could go almost ten more millennia and still be alive. Our full lifespan isn't that long…well, very nearly. Then the military is basically under the Marshal's control, so regardless of what they're doing out there, HE is the one doing it, and doesn't bother telling us what it is unless he wants us to research something for him. And I don't think I like that to begin with. Toys, all those custom projects… and worse is that SHE knows about them, apparently. And then the media, he tells them what to tell us, whether real or imagined."

She makes her way back to her workstation, still contemplating her discussion with Ayene and running through the different topics they covered.

"Ten millennia…yeah, that's a long time to be doing something, whatever it was. Fighting insurgents? Yeah, but ten millennia of it… I think I would have to agree, someone should've won or lost that fight by now. But they just keep on coming."

She tries pulling herself into her work, only to recall more of her conversation.

"Lies, censorship, a missing government, research institutes that never get to research anything… We're a society of scientists and scholars, but we're not allowed to learn something? Mysteries of the universe or not, there's surely other things closer to home for us, and we don't even get that much. So, what this says is once he got what he wanted out of our Council, the rest didn't matter. Whatever happened to our Council, no one bothered to tell us, and he's out there doing…something…with our military. And the only time we get any excitement is when he has a special request. We've become servants to his personal needs."

She quickly glances around to make sure no one was listening. Her station was positioned off to one side of the room near a conveyor ramp to the automated robotic delivery belt. There were no others in near enough proximity to pay attention to her.

"Ayene," she mumbles quietly. "Who do you actually work for? Because I think it's not the military."

<hr>

"Marshal, I have a report," Commander Geilv announces on the com-link.

"Yes, Commander, I have been eagerly awaiting some news on our progress in that city. Do we have anything special to report this time?"

"The Captain of the Tul'ryk reports increasing difficulty in continuing their search. One of his patrols recently returned with a report that they were identified by common citizens as the result of some manner of public notice being placed around the city. This notice seems to implicate our people as a form of undesired intrusion."

"Blast, that didn't take long, did it. How many patrols have you lost by this time?"

"Two full squads and one partial. Five others returned safe, including this recent one."

"Well, at least this shows a positive progression to preserve our troops. But to see them spreading the word that we're some sort of invader, complete with a wanted poster for our capture or termination…" he ponders briefly. "We cannot allow this to deter us! We must find that rift, do you understand? If our appearance is causing these disturbances, we must make greater efforts at keeping it to a minimum. I do not care if we have to chart every step of that catacomb network of theirs, only to pop into view long enough to make a brief survey of the immediate area. Send in more squads if you must. Distribute them across a broader area. It'll make the effort more efficient. The authorities can't be in all places at once. You will make quick incursions and retreats, too brief for them to track you, understood?"

"Affirmative."

"It is unfortunate, Commander," the Marshal relents. "It is at this moment I wish we still had our precious little Elves. They could infiltrate that city under their invisibility cloaks, or at least not stand out as much as your own kind."

The link ends, leaving the Commander to recall the elves they once controlled on Therinë, before Thaelyn arrived. His orders were to remain at station, not to make any forward movements on Thaelyn's position, thus allowing Darumon to play his little games instead. But then things started turning sour on their operations.

"Elves…" he reflects privately. "I remember them. He wanted to evacuate them, but something happened. The city was abandoned. Where did they go?"

He still struggled against his authority chip, which was set to active mode. It had been like this for centuries, and further toggled on and off throughout most of his professional career. He had come to despise it equally as much as his Suppressor chip that so often fired feedback hits into his neural tissues, every time he felt an emotional response from his duty actions.

"The Priestess," he muses. "She behaved very strangely. Someone came for them…took them away. Yes, those opponents he ran from. They came and reclaimed that world. And him…he spoke to me."

He recalled the brief conversation he shared with Thaelyn on the com-link. Thaelyn essentially scolded him for his attack on an inferior society in their native home. This was a criminal act, and could result in repercussions if he did it again.

"Containment procedures… This is how it was described to us. But they could not pose a threat. Then why was it demanded?"

He allowed his mind to drift further. He now reflected on Morndindor. The memories of that event were painful.

"Lajivi, what are we doing here? You were sent on your missions. What happened there? What happened on Morndindor? It was more containment procedures. Were they necessary?"

He recalled his last conversation with the mining base and the details relayed by Kaliya's false base staff. She was feeding information to him to incite a reaction.

"Ytani… He was errant, abusing his authority, making threats, assaulting the female staff. And he stole that weapon. Yes, the weapon. Marshal, why did you not inform us what it was before it became critical? One unit…two and a half lightyear blast range…"

And then a tick erupted on his right cheek. It was minor at this point, but not an uncommon sight in recent times.

"Containment procedures… What manner of containment requires a weapon of that magnitude?"

His thoughts returned to Therinë, and how the Marshal was operating his localized station within the city of Rolsklinde.

"What was he doing there? Four centuries, he manages that office. Our people analyzed this. They were a different species, but they treated him as a governing official. But that world was stated to belong to his opponents, not to him. Why would they follow his direction…unless he used coercive methods? Yes! Coercive methods, like on Morndindor. He used a narcotic agent to force their compliance. And I recall now he received shipments to that city. Could it be more of the same?"

He recalled how the Marshal imposed the idea of a false war on the city of Rolsklinde.

"He fabricated a scenario. And Ytani also fabricated a scenario. This was to aid in their containment. Containment procedures… Fabrications of scenarios…"

He was now starting to fold a few pieces together, combining the elements of Therinë with Morndindor, and the report received from Kaliya's people.

"Containment procedures!" he growls and flinches sharply from his feedback.

He tentatively reaches for his cranial interface in a vain attempt to offer himself some comfort. Then another thought flashed into his mind.

"The dwarves…in that mine…plasma mortars!"

He felt another sharp twang at his memories of arming and directing the dwarven miners to attack the city.

"Containment…aargh," he clutches at his interface again. "Bah! It was a diversionary tactic during a withdrawal. An unnecessary one. He did not need a distraction to leave his post. He had a conveyor in his basement!"

And finally, he recalled one last image. His eyes bulged suddenly just before another hit shot out from his chip. He flinched again and grunted harshly.

"The reactor! Set to overload…to destroy the city? Murder! Not containment! They came back to reclaim that world. He wanted to destroy what remained of it."

He began to summarize the collected images of the encounters on Therinë.

"Thaelyn… I remember him. We assaulted him. That infiltration mission with the orcs…he simply defended his home. He arrived and continued the same. He joined the others, and aided in their defense. He did not attack us… No, wait."

He pauses as he recollects a late memory from that period.

"I remember. He did attack…that surprise assault of our false line. But it was nonlethal. He said it was intended as nonlethal. He wanted us to leave, nothing more. Opponents? What sort of opponents do not retaliate for a world destroyed? They apparently held the capacity for it."

He ponders this question for a long moment, until a new one finds its way into his thoughts.

"Insurgents… If these are the same, they did not recognize the Marshal on a world they owned. He ran as if they were the same, but they did not give chase, only a warning to me…personally.

What did he say? Be aware, for he is leading us down a dangerous path. Yes, I remember. They are a society of laws, and we violated those laws by attacking that world…a world that could not defend itself. And the Marshal wanted to destroy it further as we departed. Containment procedures!" he scorns. "And now we are making an attempt at another structure, more property that may be owned by those same people. This is dangerous, we cannot fight this. We could lose our own world."

He glances around his office, breathing heavily from his growing ire and the multiple feedback hits. He ponders the array of thoughts and memories and tries to fathom ways in which to approach this paradoxical situation.

"Insurgents…ten millennia…we are sent to fight them. But Lajivi, and those worlds he assaulted… He spoke to me about them. It was the same as with Morndindor…a world destroyed. And the same as Therinë? Another world destroyed? How many?"

Now he feels a cold spike hit him.

"This is dangerous. These beings must be very potent, especially if they frighten the Marshal. But ten millennia of conflict, and Lajivi tells me he hit worlds that could not fight back? Was it more containment procedures? Why so many of them? They could not be the same beings!"

He suddenly perks up as a realization jumps out at him.

"No! They could not be. Thaelyn fought back. His forces appeared inferior to us, but they still fought back, and they were effective. This defies the condition of those other worlds we approached."

He pauses to consider this new thought. There had to be a link, and he struggled against his chips to decide what it could be.

"Yes! I see it. Abnormal energy… He used it against us. This is the key. We do not have this here. Therefore, those worlds could not be related. And Therinë, and Morndindor…they were both lacking this offensive capacity, so they too could not be related. The Marshal behaved as if this discovery was a unique experience. They live in that other universe. There was that invasion he sent, which brought them out, but the Marshal did not expect to see them. But this is strange. What does it mean? He should know his own opponents, but to NOT expect to see them here…even after sending an invasion to that world where they presumably live…"

He pauses to consider this notion.

"We are ordered not to attack immediately, and he uses substandard methods to eliminate them… No, HIM, only him. He wanted to remove him, alone…but why only him, and especially if he did not even know who he was initially, and neither expecting to see him at all. He must have been expecting someone else, or no one at all… Yes, no one at all. More inferior beings to play his containment procedures on. But then, this one shows up, which means he was not expected to be on that other world. And still, the Marshal did not even recognize him when he arrived."

He continues to struggle with his memories, reflecting on several conversations he had at various times with the Marshal as he was stationed in his office in Rolsklinde.

"Associated… He was associated with them. So, whoever these opponents are, this one was associated, and likely not expected to be on a world like that, but in this case he was. This sounds like a case of bad timing. But it also sounds like he wanted to do to them as he did to so many others, and the bad timing simply backfired on him. And then, that conversation. Thaelyn warned us to discontinue our attacks of innocent worlds. His attack was demonstrative, to prove a point."

He impulsively waves a finger in the air as he holds his thoughts to ponder the scenario some more.

"Yes! He warned us. We violated a law, but he only demands we leave the area. He warned me only after he arrived on Therinë and gained control. This was a NEW discovery. Surely, for the ten millennia we were in conflict with someone, they should know us by now…and the Marshal…and Sargeras… Wait…yes! He used this name, but referenced it indirectly. And that argument they had as we were pulling out. They were clearly opposed to each other, but as a new discovery of something unexpected. And wait… The

Marshal used words…terms to describe the others. I remember now. 'You and your over-righteous kin…' This is an indirect reference to someone. Someone ELSE?" he jerks forward in his chair. "Then who were we attacking all this time? Containment procedures, my crinkled tail! Lajivi, I understand now."

He leans back in his chair and tries to find peace from his pain. He lays his hands on his temples, hoping to comfort his mind.

"Those worlds could not have been a threat. Maybe they were more innocent worlds. And even if they were associated, if they could not fight back, they should not have been a target. And if these beings make their home in a completely different universe, why would those in ours be associated with them? How would they even make contact?"

He sighs tenuously and closes his eyes.

"Unless this other side carried the distance. But if they did, I think the loss would stand out much earlier. And he said something about law enforcement. If someone was aware so much earlier, I think we would see them taking action for it already. We did not see this until that one occasion…and it was unexpected. WE found THEM, and they were not expecting to see US. Wonderful," he shakes his head.

He glances around the room trying to distract his thoughts.

"But the Marshal," he continues privately. "He did something. He sent those orcs, and this alerted them. Now they know about him…and us as well. They responded only on that one world. This was a new discovery. Those others did not invoke this. And we are exposing ourselves once again in their space. Thaelyn said they are a governing body…they own everything, and this structure is clearly owned by someone…someone with high potential. Now we are trespassing and causing a local disruption. This is dangerous. We have become criminals. They may not hold back this time."

◆◆◆◆◆

"Remember, Kaliya, you should disguise yourself as something other than Daanen-Aryku, as you might be misinterpreted as one of the invaders, and we do not wish to invoke any difficulties with the natives."

"Yes, my Lord, I'm thinking of taking up a simple human shape, at least until I get inside the sewers. My biggest concern is how to find where the Suuden-Aryku are coming from, if it's such a complex maze down there."

Kaliya was in a meeting with Thaelyn at the WIC building, preparing for her visit to Sigil to investigate the Suuden-Aryku incursions. Her initial objective was to locate the entrance they were using. She was already in projected mode and reviewing a few final instructions.

"My best suggestion," Thaelyn offers, "would be to find a nearby dabus and ask for directions. They would likely know the location of the first incidence, and perhaps you could go from there. I am currently of the opinion that the first appearance on the streets could not be too far from their initial entry point, and this entry point could not be too far from their access."

"Sounds good enough…" she nods. "Wish me luck. It seems I'm going out on another wild hunt, like I did once on Ruuki uy'Daan."

"Yes, but let us hope you do not cause as much a disturbance for your findings," he grins.

Kaliya makes a brief salute, and then vanishes from the room.

She passes through the folds of space on her way directly into the city of Sigil, appearing in a familiar location from a past visit she once made with Thaelyn, Relissa, and Marelle. This was from the time they were visiting to meet with Aelwyn, and when Thaelyn needed to pass his warning to the Lady.

She arrives in a hidden location behind a local building in one of the city's Wards. Initially, she took a small form, arriving as an insect to defray any immediate notice. But as she saw there was no one in the immediate area, she reshaped herself as a female human. From there, she emerged into view and surveyed the area to gain her bearings.

She sees several local citizens strolling through the area, some of them on their way in or out of the local shops, and others just passing through. Nearby was a large structure representing the Guild of Sensations, where Aelwyn once worked, and where Nemelle could still be found. She turns to examine it, taking note of how it resembled a type of temple layout for the architecture. And then, she took notice of a woman in an ornate robe of deep blue, sitting at a table just outside. She seemed a bit lost in thought.

The woman herself appeared young, with pale gray skin and platinum hair peeking out from under her hood. Kaliya recognized the robe as the same design Aelwyn once wore, as it was typical for a Cardinal Sensate from the guild. As for the table itself, she could see several stacks of papers on it, suggesting the woman was handing out fliers or notices. Kaliya decides to walk over and investigate.

As Kaliya approaches the table, the woman perks up from her dreamlike trance to greet her new visitor. She automatically picks up a sheet from the table and offers it to Kaliya as she arrives. And as she leans forward, she speaks in a placid, but unusual third-person form of speech.

"She bids a pleasant greeting, and offers this to her guest, that she will take a moment to read it carefully."

"Uh huh…" Kaliya muses with a gentle smile.

Kaliya takes the paper and glances at it briefly. It was one of the wanted posters Aerlie had ordered through Aelwyn. This meant only one thing as to the identity of this rather odd individual.

"You know," she begins. "You look like a Morier, but ascended as a Celestial. You're an Eladrin, right?"

The woman cocks her head curiously and raises her brow, but remains silent.

"And those eyes give you away," Kaliya continues. "Violet, like the gemstone amethyst. This is another indication."

"She is curious as to the direction of this reference."

"Yeah, and then we have that. You're as bad as Aelwyn on that first day I met her. By the way, did she ever pass my lecture on to you about how to be a Celestial?" she giggles softly.

The woman frowned inquisitively and leaned forward even more.

"She…" she begins, but abruptly halts.

The woman hesitates briefly until she begins to notice something strange about this encounter. She raised her hand to scan the body of the person standing opposite her at the table, but there was no feedback from her telepathic or empathic senses.

"This is curious. You are an associate of Aelwyn?"

"I'm her pride and joy. My name is Kaliya. I'm the result of her recent teachings to create a metaphysical projection."

"Ah!" she rejoices. "Yes! Now I understand. But I thought you were a different Child Race, not a human."

"I am, this is just a disguise, so I don't make any trouble here…" she flashes the poster for emphasis before setting it back down.

"You are another of the same?"

"My people ran away from the main body to find peace, but it didn't work very well for us."

"I am sorry to hear this, for what we have heard of it from this side."

"You're Nemelle, am I right?"

"Yes, and please forgive me of my manners, but it tends to fall into old habits."

"Just like Aelwyn. But you don't need to play that game with me. I work for Thaelyn."

"Yes, I see it now, and such a fascinating presentation. Until I actually applied myself to feel you, I did not even realize you were an apparition. What is it that brings you here?"

"The same as this," she again points at the posters. "I need to find where they're coming from and see if I can, um, tamper with their efforts a bit."

"Tamper…such an interesting word. Very well, but I am not personally familiar with their arrival point."

"Thaelyn says to find a dabus. Maybe you could help? Can you speak their language?"

"Yes, I can, as I think many of the local residents can. And you think they could direct you further? I suppose that does follow procedurally…maybe, at least up to a point."

Nemelle gets up from her chair and leads Kaliya across the Ward to the main avenue outside.

"They have a tendency to move about often from place to place. But I have a trick I can play on our behalf," she smiles gently.

Nemelle raises a hand to her temple and begins projecting a telepathic summons. Kaliya watches and waits. Several long moments pass, and soon they see a figure floating in from above the buildings, making his way across the cityscape from wherever he had been stationed prior to this.

"That must come in handy around here," Kaliya notes.

"From time to time, it does," Nemelle responds. "He and I are familiar with each other from our recent interactions relating to this dilemma."

The dabus settled down at street level and flashed a series of symbols over his head as their native form of communication. Nemelle studied this and prepared to interpret their meaning.

"He is asking if we have any new instructions from the Prime world," she states.

Kaliya turns to the figure in the flowing robe and strange features that simply hovered above the ground.

"My name is Captain Kaliya Nazég, in the service of Lord Thaelyn, King of Tae'Eladar. Good greetings to you," she offers a modest bow.

The dabus nods his head in recognition.

"I am here to investigate the point of origin for these incursions, but I am also curious as to what sort of news you might have for us about the sightings and what actions have been taken thus far."

The dabus turns again to Nemelle and flashes several new lines of symbols as his silent form of response.

"He says there have been numerous sightings," she replies, "and they seem determined to pursue their objectives. So far, two of these have been fully dispatched, one made a partial escape, and the rest have either retreated prematurely before they could be countered, or they were ignored outright."

"Ignored..." Kaliya muses. "Are we speaking of this being due to them taking this new tactic of theirs? We once passed a message that their military command is attempting to understand what they see in here by conducting a type of cultural survey, hoping to interpret the nature of these people in relation to a recognizable standard. We are trying to paint a type of image that we could possibly use later to incite a bit of controversy in their orders and the underlying meaning."

"Yes, I recall that message. It is a most curious approach."

Nemelle looks up into the eyes of the dabus to see if he has anything to say in response. He forms another set of symbols as his reply.

"Yes, he says those who were ignored appeared unarmed and portraying a neutral outward visage. He says they were observed from a distance, and they appeared as if studying the local population and city architecture."

"Trying to assess what they're looking at, and if it could be anything on the scale of what Darumon is claiming as his opponents. Good. If we can play into this, we can maybe turn them against all his stories."

The dabus again forms another series of lines above his head. Nemelle brings her attention to translate them.

"He says there were a couple of occasions where some of the local guilds with their native guardsmen attacked independently."

"Any casualties?"

The dabus responds with a brief display.

"Yes, this is the cause of that partial escape. I believe I heard of this, as well. The guards attacked when the intruders were seen on the streets. There was apparently a fight, and two of the outsiders were killed, while the other two managed to retreat back into the underground tunnels. And this reminds me of other sightings where the outsiders were pursued, but they managed to escape intact."

"Is there any way to prevent this? We want them out, not necessarily dead."

"I know, but unfortunately, this is not as easily governed. These would account as members of some of the other guilds in the city, a few of which tend to be a bit, um…fanatical."

"Really! Well, I guess you can't have everything. Let's just hope they learn to keep away from those areas."

"Indeed."

"Now, as for where they're coming from. My instructions are to see if I can locate the original incursion point, which is suspected to be near to where they made their initial entrance into the city."

"I have heard that was in the Market Ward. I believe he should be able to show you, but it is a fair walk from here."

"Can we fly it instead?" Kaliya smirks.

Nemelle raises her brow at the girl, while the dabus turns to stare at her as if she had lost her mind, thinking she could ever possibly fly.

"Yeah," Kaliya grins. "I don't need to know what you're thinking to catch your meaning, so allow me to demonstrate."

Kaliya now changes her image into her classic hawk form, standing on the ground and looking up at him.

The dabus draws back at the unexpected display, clearly surprised with his voiceless expression of bulging eyes and long face.

"How curious!" Nemelle intones enthusiastically. "And you can fly in this condition?"

"More than just fly," Kaliya squawks. "I can move at unnatural speeds by applying my focus into it."

"And this is Aelwyn's work?"

"The initial studies to develop the projection skills are. But most of it is just me experimenting with it to see where I can take it. You should come down to Tae'Eladar sometime and see for yourself. We'd be happy to have you. You might also want to take time to visit with a friend of mine named Relissa. She's also a Morier, part of a society Thaelyn found on Therinë."

"I have heard of them, and it causes me to wonder how they might differ from my own ancestral clan. Very well, you should be on your way. It was good to meet with you, Kaliya."

Nemelle glances at the dabus, who nods contentedly as he turns and lifts away. He ascends high above the rooftops to float over the city, as Kaliya takes off in her bird form to fly behind him. They course their way around the ring-like interior, and Kaliya looked down at the local people, most of whom did not pay attention to a dabus flying overhead, as it was likely a common sight, but a few did take notice of an alien creature flying along behind him and calling up attention to point at it.

They travelled at least a third of the way around the ring to another market square before settling back to the ground. Kaliya reimagined herself back into her human form for another presentation.

"I suppose it goes without saying," she asserts. "This isn't my natural form. I'm not actually a human."

The dabus gazes at her inquisitively.

"I'm only using this form so as not to cause trouble with the citizens here. My people are part of the same mother race as the Suuden-Aryku entering your city, but we separated ourselves from them once a long time ago."

He nods acceptingly at her.

"Meanwhile, we discovered we had a few very unusual Gifts, like the metaphysical projection skill. Thaelyn thinks our heritage, which carries its own burdens, might actually place us with skills comparable to a Celestial. Things like telepathy, possibly clairvoyance, and even precognition. I'm even able to manifest objects into physical space… within reason."

He raises his brow in admiration of the feats.

"Now, we suspect they came out of a sewer or some kind of underground tunnel system. Where is the nearest exit point?"

The dabus passes his glance around briskly to gain his bearings, and then leads off to a sewer gate just up the road from the square. Kaliya follows.

When they arrive, Kaliya briskly examines the gate, which had been secured again with a new chain. But the charring and blast marks on the doors were a clear indication of what happened before.

"This looks like they blasted their way through the first time."

The dabus points at the chain and displays a line of symbols over his head, peering down at her with a look of question.

"I can't be sure what that says up there, although admittedly, it would make for a fine study. But are you asking if I want you to remove this?"

He nods.

"No need, I can see inside there, which is good enough."

She turns and places her sight on the ground just inside the gate, then folds herself to that location. She turns around to meet him again.

"Metaphysical translocation. What every young girl espionage agent needs," she giggles.

The dabus attempts a soft smile, something he probably had not done throughout most of his lifetime.

Kaliya peers around the scene outside in the street to see if there were any people. The immediate area seemed clear.

"We should be safe enough like this. No one can see me now."

She reimagines herself as her natural Daanen'kai form.

"This is how I really look; in case you were curious. We have a few differences in our appearance from the others. So, if you should see me again, try not to call the guards on me right away."

The dabus examines her tall trim figure and glowing eyes, and dressed in her neatly arranged Order military uniform. His expression hints of satisfaction and he nods again.

"Now," Kaliya continues. "My instructions are to locate the entry point, and begin a series of observations to see what we have to work with and how to bring this under control. Our purpose is to see if we can stop these incursions peacefully, rather than resorting to conflict. I don't know what sort of results we might find, as we have several ideas on the table right now, but I suppose he might send me back to report once we have something in progress."

He nods once again, and then turns to depart. Kaliya also turns and heads down through the tunnels. She knew this would take time, as she had no idea where these passageways led or how many branches she would need to travel.

Chapter 4

BY REFERENCE

"Ghantil?" Azina mutters softly through the door. "Do you have a moment?"

"Yes Azina, come in. Do you have something special to report, or is this a social visit?"

"Actually, I was hoping for a little social visit. I had a few things on my mind recently that I needed to talk about."

"And what sorts of things are these?" he asks cordially.

Azina was making a visit to the Director's office. Her mind was still swirling around her last conversation with Ayene, and she needed another friendly voice to talk to. She reflected on Ayene's suggestion that she might do this, and this was as good as permission to speak, but she still felt a tender sense of responsibility to keep it discreet. So, she stepped inside the office and closed the door, then took up seating across the desk from him.

"Um, Ghantil, I want to talk to you about something I heard recently, and it's very serious, but also, I think it needs to be kept very private so far. Can I count on you?"

"Certainly, Azina, what is this about?"

"First, what do you know about Central and how they operate?"

"That's an odd question, Azina. Why do you ask?"

"I'm trying to piece through a series of controversies that came up recently."

"Controversies?"

"Yeah, bad ones, and each one makes me worry for the implications, because they raise too many questions, and these questions demand attention…by someone."

"All right, where do we begin? And where did you hear about this?"

"A military officer came in a while back with a requisition order for some seeds. We started talking about one thing or another, and she started dropping hints. This makes me think about that discussion we had not too long ago of them finally telling us something about all these secrets. I think someone finally came forward with it."

"This is interesting, but also very curious. Why come forward to us here?"

"I don't know if I could answer that completely, but one part of it relates to what she calls the Marshal's toys, and we are the ones responsible for creating them. This includes those Belvik Spores in the dispenser nodes, that Kajik'tav Serum, and the missile-propelled seeds, to name a few."

The Director instantly frowned and pulled back in his chair, then folded his arms as he clearly seemed interested in this line of discussion.

"Toys. All right, so what did she say about them? Did she tell you what they were used for?"

"Not on this occasion, but I think she knows. She said she was assigned to some other project at the time, a mining base, which coincided with the same timing as the rest, but she didn't learn about this until later, when she was apparently briefed on it by someone who carried a final result."

"That sounds like an afterthought effect. Then, what this tells me is Central doesn't share this knowledge even amongst their own personnel. All right, perhaps these were part of a special assignment, and the other departments simply didn't need to know about it at the time."

"Yeah…need to know…as if ANYONE has a need to know anything that doesn't involve them directly, then to cover it up for the rest."

The Director frowned even more.

"Azina, this is a rather serious accusation."

"Ghantil, it's actually worse than that. According to her, no one knows what anyone else is doing over there, all because the Marshal has a lot of private little secrets he keeps with each person he gives orders to, and sometimes in active mode of those chips to keep them from asking questions about it. Then, the whole thing is covered up so no one ELSE knows what, if anything, ever happened."

"Uh oh…that doesn't sound good. And for multiple reasons. No wonder we never hear anything if no one is allowed to KNOW anything."

"Right, and therefore the Marshal is taking advantage of them, telling them to do things and using the chips to enforce his demands."

"Azina…" he grimaces. "I should think this would represent a violation of some kind, regardless of the military assisting him against these insurgents."

"Not assisting, Ghantil, serving him, and ONLY him. Those chips might be just for this purpose, and nothing else."

"Serving? All right, hold on, we're jumping around too much. What are we actually talking about here?"

"It's complicated, so watch your horns. According to what I've learned so far from this woman, and she promises to come back with more later when she gets time for it, is that he came to us with his promises and his stories of these insurgents. He helped us develop our military and we essentially went to war with these insurgents ever since."

"Right, this much I recall."

"He apparently uses these chips as part of his battle assignments, so maybe they're necessary to aid us in actual conflict, as if to say our people, who were never military to begin with, wouldn't know which direction to point a gun, even if you gave us an instruction manual with pictures in it."

"Ouch!" he winces and chuckles.

"But Ghantil, with the push of a button, they can be made to do whatever he wants, and this could backfire on us."

"But are you suggesting he has ulterior motives here?"

"Listen to the rest and you tell me. This woman is apparently working in some capacity alongside C.P. Security now. She said she once held a position within their ranks, but I guess this is before she went full military, and now my impression is she's part of some new operation, again relating to security and law enforcement, but it doesn't sound like the same people. She also apparently carries a university law degree, because she was quoting legal Articles along the way."

"Uh oh...and what sort of Articles were these?"

"What was it she said..." she ponders. "Article Nine, Section... um, Fourteen."

"Hmm, just a moment..."

The Director pulls himself forward to his desk and calls up a browser app on his terminal. He punches in a search for the Charter of Laws and looks up the associated reference.

"The Truth in Reporting Act of 3752 CTD..."

"Yes! That one... Ghantil, we apparently had people inside our news media censoring and altering our media releases. They were feeding us false information!"

"You're kidding me!"

The Director holds the conversation while he reviews the legal amendment.

"This says that any public release of intellectual creation, which is based on factual account...meaning to say any kind of news report or publication describing something that is happening in the world around us...must be reported in a truthful and deliberate manner. So, what you're saying is these people were violating a very serious law here."

"Keep reading it. Does it also say, 'to the best of their ability'...?"

"Huh? Wait..."

He continues to scan the article until he comes to the end.

"...To the best of their ability. Yes, it does say that."

"All right, so let me ask you a quick question. Just by reading that, how would you interpret it without anything else?"

"Well, this would say to me they should spend whatever ability they have at their disposal to report this information according to its factual content."

"The spirit of the words, right?"

"Yeah, this is how they tend to teach it in our schools."

"And what if someone is governing that ability?"

"Uh oh..."

"Right, suddenly it carries a whole new meaning, and NOT relating to the spirit of those words. We are made to think the spirit of the words means we have a free and open society, with all our personal rights. But that catch in there is a loophole anyone can exploit on a whim, and it's still legal."

"In all the nether-space, you're right, but this would represent a very controversial statement, to say nothing if someone were to actually do this."

"Like the Council itself? Those regulators were mandated by the Council and receiving their information from the military."

"What?!" he shouts. "The Council was violating one of their own laws? Now I see your point for the controversy."

"Violating? They OWN the laws. They made this, and now they're using it. And we're not supposed to know about it because it's hidden behind this spirit of the words. Ghantil, we're not permitted to worship a religion, but we certainly do worship our godlike Council. We follow everything they tell us to do, including polluting our bodies with this nonsense," she directs to her seed entity, "and our world with that horrid industry," she points out the window. "And we apparently stopped asking why a long time ago."

"All right, I think I see your point, although as I look out that window, I wouldn't necessarily say this...nonsense..." he glances at his seed entity, "...is so nonsensical."

"Really!" she smirks. "Then I guess, just like everyone else, you forgot we have all sorts of eco-friendly industrial tech that probably should've been installed in that industry out there, and probably after the first few decades, surely no more than the first century after we realized we're not leaving home. So, our dull-horned Council, to say nothing of our dull-horned population, forgot to complain about the bad air."

"Uh oh…all right, you got me. This might even be exacerbated by the fact of the seed filtering it out. So the people might not even take notice of it…other than for the cloudy skies…and assuming they ever actually paid attention to it."

"Yeah, no one ever looks up. And I'm not finished yet. Apparently, she was part of an investigation that arrested these people, but it goes deeper. We all know the Council has been in these deep deliberations over something since the last time anyone ever saw one publicly. But did you know the last time they were ever seen publicly was at the press release for the development of the Tav'ageen Suppressor chip back in…what was it…9765.31?"

"Azina, that represents a rather extreme measure of time to be absent from public view, to say nothing of being in these deliberations."

"She said you can research it on the DataNet, so I did. In 9765.31, there was a press release for the chip. It was newly developed and ready for release. The Council was seen in the background as the spokesman gave the report. But Ghantil, there's something about the Council we were not told about during that time. They were not occupying the Grand Hall during the hysteria of the Tav'ageen Scare. The military apparently took them away to a quarantine site as part of a plan to protect them from harm."

"Really! And why weren't we told about this?"

"Good question. This officer told me it was codenamed Site One-Alpha, and classified under a high-level Class 3 military security rating. We were never apparently intended to know about it, even after the Council was supposedly returned after the hysteria settled and they locked themselves away inside the Grand Hall. But now, get this. They haven't been seen since, and the doors are kept locked to prevent any interruption to this deliberation they're supposed to be conducting. They don't even come out to eat, sleep, visit their families, or anything else. In fact, one might wonder how a bunch of old-timers could continue to survive this long if kept behind locked doors for almost ten millennia."

"Azina! This doesn't even make sense!"

"Maybe…maybe not…if you now listen to the rest of it. Their families are missing entirely. If you research this on the DataNet, and I had to fiddle with this a little for the privacy rules of personal detail, they're not described as living and taking up residence anywhere recognizable, or participating in any public events, even with kids going to school. If you ask if they're dead, it's Class 3 again. And this officer told me Site One-Alpha, according to military files, is gone, lost to an early insurgent attack."

"In all the nether-space," he turns pale. "This is more than any simple controversy. This sounds more like a conspiracy!"

"The Internal Secretary, the one who apparently manages the operations of the Grand Hall, was recently arrested by this woman and her department as holding back yet another conspiracy. Our elections have apparently been rigged, and I verified this on the DataNet. No new Council members have been elected at all in this time, and this guy confessed it was intended to be this way to allow this one highly privileged body to conduct these deliberations… Something about this being a special gift that only THEY were allowed to have, if you can believe such nonsense."

"And this would violate at least a few additional laws. We now have election fraud, on top of the other one, and I don't even know how to describe the part of them hoarding this to themselves for nearly ten millennia."

"And we were never even told IF they had something real to deliberate, for instance if the Marshal actually did give them something worth deliberating for all this time. In fact, in the absence of anything to prove otherwise, the Council may not even exist right now. They may have been on Site One-Alpha along with the rest of their families when it was lost. This woman apparently peeked inside that chamber, although she didn't say it directly, but I think she did. If it were me arresting people, I certainly would have! And by the tone of her voice and the look in her eyes, my impression is they're missing."

"Missing? But Azina, if they're missing, who is running our government, and especially after all this time since the Anomaly outbreak?"

"The Marshal and his military, along with his regulators in our media feeding us whatever he wants us to know, which apparently isn't much. It's no wonder we never get any normal research projects. If it doesn't serve HIM, he doesn't need it, or want it."

"All right, wait," he flusters. "We need to try to settle ourselves. This is a shocking revelation, but we should also try to rationalize it. What we have is the apparent public absence of the Council, who is supposed to be inside the Grand Hall, but if no one ever sees them coming or going, and if they were once removed to some top-secret quarantine site, maybe they are relocated elsewhere. This could offer one explanation, especially if you consider that military security rating."

"Maybe, but it wouldn't make a lot of sense, and certainly not polite sense, as they ARE our world government, and WE, the people, should know where they are and what they're doing."

"Correct, this much I would agree on."

"Although, if you consider our media is lying to us, I suppose almost anything is possible."

"Including those election results… Maybe someone did get elected, but if the Council is sequestered away in some top-secret location, they might try hiding who is serving on it, as well."

"But Ghantil, don't you think the public should know who is on the Council, whether they're sequestered away in a quarantine site or not? The science factions, at the very least, including ours, should know who is representing them. This still represents fraud if no one is informed as to the true election results."

"Yes, you have a point. And if this was based on the panic of the Anomaly, which has long-since settled, it should no longer be necessary."

"Then we come back to the question of where the Council really is, or if it even still exists at all."

"Yes, but Azina, to say they might be missing completely is to suggest something on the order of a take-over of our government. We still have the military, regardless of what the Marshal is doing with it. I think High Commander Geilv would have something to say about this."

"Oh, yes...him," she smirks. "Yes, I'm sure he would have something to say, if he wasn't on the active mode of his chip most of the time."

The Director gaped at her for the statement.

"What?" he gasps. "He has a chip and it's on active?"

"Yeah, apparently... According to this woman, he has the chip, just like all the rest, and the Marshal keeps it on active most of the time. So Ghantil, who is actually in control of our military, maybe also our government, and then classifying everything behind his security protocols and the censorship of the media?"

The Director stared blankly at her, as he clearly didn't have a proper argument to this.

"All right, Azina, I might have to agree with you on this in principle. But I'm a man who likes to see evidence, and so far, this represents a lot of statements without the evidence in our hands to examine."

"Oh yes, that lovely suggestion of 'evidence of existence' we're all programmed to demand. While I would surely agree, these security restrictions seem designed to deny it to us. Although we do have the DataNet, and it did confirm some of this."

"Fine, but we still have a number of unresolved elements that could be explained by other means...not polite ones, but I would like to hear the rebuttals for them."

"I suppose I also have to admit we have the problem of our general public. No one asks questions anymore. So, regardless of a hostile takeover, no one would take notice of it, and after ten millennia of the same old story, you would think someone would do just that. So, we're all responsible for this, if only for our lack of paying attention."

"Yes, this much I have to agree on. And it's shameful to describe our society this way."

"By the way," Azina adds. "This woman ordered those seeds for her own top-secret project. She explained to me she had an official reason and an unofficial one. How cute…"

"Really! What were they?"

"Officially, let me see, what did she say? It's for some kind of test of a very harsh environment they were encountering and needed to see how effective the seed was against it."

"That sounds like a viable need. And the unofficial one?"

"To do the job we're not allowed to do ourselves…since no one ever gave it to us as a research grant. To find a way to kill it as part of a procedure to remove them. Apparently, our missing Council forgot to tell the rest of us to stop using them after a while. They were only supposed to be a temporary thing to vacate the planet because of the Anomaly, not a permanent feature for the rest of our lives."

"Dammit, Azina!" he curses. "You're right, and this makes me angry now. This has long been one of my arguments. Except for the pollution we have now, it was not supposed to endure this long."

"Yeah, that pollution again, which we brought onto ourselves intentionally, as she describes it. We created this industry using the worst tech available, and never went back to review it. And you can once again thank the Council for that…maybe."

"Maybe? Why maybe now?"

"I've been thinking about this since she gave it to me. She mentioned her project isn't from, 'they who are supposed to be giving these things out', which means the Council. It was the Marshal who gave us instructions to research his toys, and by the way, this was one of them, along with his stories of insurgents and everything else. And since HE never mentioned anything about removing them, because after ten millennia, we're still here, and still using them. And furthermore, this woman had TWO reasons for the seeds, and this is AFTER she removed those regulators, which means she's already fighting against something. Then, who is she hiding it from, if not the Marshal, who's actually in control."

The Director frowns deeply at this mention, as it carried its own implications.

"And who is it you said she works for? It was the military, right?"

"I don't know, Ghantil, she wore a military uniform, but it can't be under the Marshal if she's arresting his agents. She mentioned her research on those family members, checking for such as tax returns and other things that I got hit with a government security block on my own efforts. But if she was able to bypass this, that might suggest something. You need a special passcode for that."

✦

"Such a lovely day for a walk in the sewers," Kaliya muses cheerily as she trudges along. "Come to Sigil, enjoy the sights, sample the local culture, and while you're at it, map the slime-covered underbelly looking for an opening someone made to gain illegal access to a hole in space where you'll find Creation's Most Wanted."

Kaliya has spent the last couple of days in the dank catacombs under Sigil. She alternated off and on with breaks to return home to her body, there to eat and attend to other activities. During this time, she also enlisted the aid of some of her teammates who would make similar visits. They were now branching off in different directions searching for the hole the Suuden-Aryku presumably cut in the side of the city's external shell.

She had managed to descend a few levels by now, having found ramps leading downward to other sections, but the corridors were twisting into loops, and she often found herself going in circles. The passages were also dark, as there were no lights, so she created a simulation of a bioluminescent glow around her to help her see where she was going.

She rounded another corner and approached a wide hallway, with one side appearing as a stairway leading down.

"Ah, another one, how many does this make? I actually can't remember, as I must've backtracked at least a few times by now."

She makes her way downward into another hall leading ahead

to an intersection. She had been trying to make systematic runs through each branch she could find, hoping to cover everything, but at this point, it was difficult to be sure.

"I always hated scouting, but Thaelyn says it's a necessary step if you ever want to learn what's out there. Even the best may not come home the first day with newsworthy results."

She continued forward, turning at the intersection, and running up to the next one, pausing to decide which way to go, and then running to the next corner, all the while trying to remember where she had been so she could take another direction if need be.

As she approaches another intersection, she slows to inspect the latest choices, and then she hears something. She halts and listens intently.

"Footsteps," she mumbles silently.

She pulls back from the intersection and dowses her light, then peers around again to see if anything shows in the distance. The sounds were approaching from one side of the intersection, echoing through the corridor. It sounded like multiple bodies moving along. She studied the hallway leading off into the blackness until a light appeared around a distant corner, and turned in her direction.

"It's them, but are they coming in or going out?"

She examined the nearby walls for their texture and reimagined her shape to match a mound of slime stuck to one side. She then slid her way around the corner into view of the squad so she could watch them.

The team of four squad members marched through the tunnel using the lights on their helmets to illuminate the way. They approached the intersection, passing right by Kaliya on the wall, and turned along the path Kaliya used on her way in.

She continued to watch them stroll by, completely unaware of her presence, until they had moved away to the next intersection and turned again. She reshaped herself back to normal and lit her path again with the glowing aura.

"They look like they're coming in, going back the way I came, so this other way might be interesting to follow."

She carefully ran to the next corner and peeked around to see what was there. The passage simply continued, so she proceeded along to the next one. She followed a series of narrow corridors around two more corners until she arrived in a large room with the moldering remains of some ancient equipment that looked like it might have once been part of an early sewage processing facility. On the opposite side of the room was a hole with a curious glow emanating through it. She approached cautiously, and dimming her aura for safety.

She crept along the side of the wall and peered into the hole. It was elongated and large enough for her to walk through comfortably. The glow seemed to be reflecting through from further along. The sides appeared neatly cut, as if only recently carved out. She stepped inside and followed as it turned along a downward slant. The floor was composed of stepped gratings laid down to cross over support struts and hull layer segments. She could tell she was close to the outer shell.

In her projected form, she could not properly perceive the force of gravity while walking through this artificial tunnel. She noticed handrails bolted onto the sides, with more support grates and stairs to cross the spaces between the existing hull materials. She wondered where the gravitation originated within the city, and if she had passed beneath that layer by now.

"What do you do if there is zero gravity?" she muses silently. "I guess we'll find out."

And yet, in this form, she could apparently walk along normally in whatever orientation she might perceive is normal for the surroundings. It was a matter of her mental perception directing her.

Partway through, the stairs transitioned to a ladder, which might suggest an alternate orientation for the continued passage. She proceeded until she arrived at the end of the tunnel to find a small, enclosed room. The light came from a brightly glowing circle of fixtures inside. She peeked around to see it was an airlock, and it appeared to be attached to the outside of the hull.

"Interesting, this makes me wonder about the outer environment."

She climbed inside and studied the surroundings.

"If I'm in an airlock, they must've landed on the outer shell and essentially walked in, maybe using magnetic boots or something. Hmm, this should be fun to see."

There were no windows, only a control panel with a set of buttons. She examined it and selected one to open an adjacent door which stood upright in relation to the hull surface.

"I need to remember this to bring others here. I'll probably be calling for help with this."

She passed through and found another control panel to close the door behind her, and finally a panel for an external door, which had a window in it to see outside. She peered through before proceeding.

The sight through the window was of a brightly glowing sea of light and energy, which seemed to stretch into infinity. She recognized it, as she had passed through here once before.

"The Astral Sea," she gasps. "I came through here once when I was practicing that first time to borrow Ayene's memory to see if I could follow it to a new location. It took me to the Spire on Cynosure. And to think, here I am again, and to see this…"

She could see the immediate area outside seemed clear of anyone. She didn't technically need to cycle the airlock, as she could simply fold herself to the outside surface, but she remembered the open door leading back to the inner compartment.

"I don't want anyone to get any ideas about this," she muses. "I'd better leave it like I found it."

She hits the button to close it, and then folds herself outside onto the outer hull.

She was now standing on the surface of the outer shell of Sigil. The structure was vast, reaching around a broad curve away from her. From her perspective, she could see the greater part of the torus shape stretching off in the distance. It was huge, where the diameter was easily that of the cross-section of a large metropolis. She had never seen such a sight so perfectly shaped and yet so large.

As she turned around to scan the area, she noticed a shuttle transport latched onto the side using magnetic grapplers. Through the windows, she could see it appeared to be empty, so she approached it.

The shuttle was typical of many Suuden-Aryku transports. She peered through the windows cautiously, in case there was anyone onboard, but it was indeed empty. The crew must've fully debarked to enter the structure.

She next tried looking around her in the sky overhead, to see if anything stood out against the glowing heavens. She saw a dot hovering in the distance which seemed out of place for the area.

"I'll bet that's it. This should be fun. I don't think I've ever tried anything like this before."

She altered her form to her bird shape in preparation for her travel. This was due to carrying her shard-com, and she needed to include the holster. She then set her sights determinedly on the dot, folding across the long distance to what she thought to be the side of the ship. She had to keep her focus constant to drive herself across the extended reach.

As she made her approach, she was better able to direct her landing, settling on a convenient surface of a large military cruiser. Around her, she saw broad stretches of hull section panels, several point-weapon mounts, and in the distance to the rear along the sides were the engine nacelles. Finally, studded along the sides of the ship, she could see arrays of windows. She folded herself over to one to take a closer look.

"Here we have our chance," she considers. "But how do we approach it? I need a body. For now, let's just see what's inside."

She steps up to the edge of the window and peeks inside. It was a crewman quarters, currently empty. She places her focus onto the floor and folds inside the room.

The room was a basic design for a military crew cabin. A bed, a dresser, a closet, a chair and a desk with a data terminal, probably for personal use to keep in touch with family and maybe for entertainment, and a door leading into what appeared to be a washroom.

"Do I take my own Suuden'kai costume?" she wonders in her thoughts. "And take a chance these people aren't so familiar with each other that they don't notice I'm not part of the crew? I may have to, there's no other way, at least until something better comes along."

She reimagines her shape and assumes her Suuden'kai disguise. She makes a quick survey of her image to make sure it's complete, and then steps over to the door, pressing the button to open it and glancing outside.

The corridor was currently empty. It gave the impression of a crew segment, and they were all out on their duty shifts. She walks outside, making sure she put on the appropriate face, and closed the door behind her. She then studied the hall in both directions, trying to decide which way to go, so she turns to the right and starts walking.

She continues along to an intersection where she found a door to a lift. She presses the call button and waits for it to arrive. When she steps inside, she studies the control panel to select her destination.

"What are my objectives here..." she mumbles to herself. "One is to see if they're on the active or passive mode of those chips. This especially means the bridge crew. But I also need an excuse for it in case they ask questions as to why I'm visiting. Either that, or a really good disguise and a place to sit."

She stares at the panel, contemplating her next move. But she also recalls the discussion with Thaelyn and Aerlie back in the WIC building.

"And then we somehow need to divert them away from this place. So, do I use my love and kisses approach again? I need to test the water first."

She studies the control panel with the destination options.

"Something noncritical, low security..."

She decides to hit the button for the medical ward.

The lift begins to move. Its progress through the shaft network is brisk, and a moment later the door opens. A new corridor leads off ahead of her, with the door to the medical ward on her right. She steps up to enter inside.

The Ward was a well-appointed medical facility, with several examination beds lined up next to workstations and analysis equipment. Robotic arms in the ceiling carried platforms of scanners, and the monitors all stood ready to display the diagnostic details of any new patients to be examined. There were several medical technicians and interns attending to their desks, some of which were conducting reviews of personnel records while others cataloged their inventory stores and made requisitions for resupply.

Kaliya paused a moment to conjure up a viable reason for her visit. An initial thought comes to mind, and she prepares to casually stroll inside. But she quickly halts as another thought follows closely behind.

She directed herself to bring out her shard-com, where she placed it into record mode. Her team had been trying to make it a habit of recording their actions for later review, especially if they shared any important dialog with anyone. And she was expecting this occasion to carry some curious subject matter.

She puts the unit back into her pocket, and now she strolls into the room to one of the stations being attended by an intern. The intern notices her uniform, which holds the rank of a Lieutenant, and stands up to greet her.

"Lieutenant," he salutes. "What do you require?"

"I need a medical scanner. I am conducting a study of a local anomaly."

"A medical scanner?" he turns to a cabinet where they kept some of their equipment.

He opens the door and pulls out a scanner from their stores, handing it over to her.

"Do you require any assistance?" he asks. "What anomaly is it you are studying?"

Kaliya pauses to examine the device in her hands as a delay tactic, while still struggling to refine her reasoning. Then a cute idea flashes into her. She raises her brow as she begins her play.

"I am trying to conduct some research, but it comes in multiple forms. As for this," she flashes at the scanner, "there is an unusual energy emission in this space. It just barely registers on the analyzer. I am attempting to refine the calibration, but the ship's scanners do not appear to be configured for this purpose. I am therefore conducting a smaller scale study to test a theory. And I hope to begin by analyzing biorhythmic emissions."

"Biorhythmic? Is this emission organic in nature?"

"This is the only viable theory I have on hand, as the other scans made by previous expeditions seem to have come up empty. Therefore, in the absence of anything recognizable, I must fall back to the only thing left in my arsenal of research…my imagination."

"Oh. Well, I suppose that might be reasonable. But what do you think this energy anomaly is?"

"Most people describe it as abnormal energy, but I am sure there must be a rational definition to it, do you think?"

"Yes! I have often wondered about this. When I hear people describe something as abnormal, I must ask myself if any of them are trying to define it, or simply passing it by."

"Indeed. But this is only one aspect of my study. The other is this space itself. Have you ever paused to look out a window? The sights are rather unique, to say the least."

"I have, and this is another thing…abnormal space, as they are calling it."

"Yes, how convenient. They do not bother trying to give it a more appropriate name, so it is simply…abnormal. But I had a thought come to me recently, and if I'm right, this could blow the horns off our science factions back home."

"Really! What is your thesis?"

"Let us take the concept of jumping through space. When we engage the nether-space drives, we are essentially opening a dimensional rift from point to point, bypassing the physical distance in real space by coursing our way through what is sometimes referred to as hyperspace, or simply nether-space, as we like to call it back home, right?"

"Yes Ma'am."

"But the science factions back home always tell us how nether-space itself is not a valid destination endpoint. Therefore, people sometimes make the statement, perhaps in jest, or perhaps as a caution, of getting lost in nether-space, or some other anomaly that is otherwise undesirable. However, what is this out here, if not something we can otherwise measure by our traditional methods…

meaning to say that three-dimensional space we are so familiar with. I ask this based on my experience from a previous assignment I was at once where we found a completely new universe, which itself would blow the factions out of the sky."

"A new universe!" he blasts. "I do not recall hearing of that."

"No, of course not, as the Marshal seems to have neglected to release this to the public. For that matter, he seems to have neglected even to share it with the rest of our military," she shrugs. "Instead, he classified it...it never happened. And here we are now in THIS space, which I am quite sure he knows what it is...after all, he told us to come out here and do something...but he simply allows us to call it abnormal?"

"Whoa!" he yelps, and quickly clutches at his interface. "Is this to say he has no desire to inform us of where we actually are?"

"One would think, if his purpose is to provide advanced wisdom to us, THIS would be a prime example. After all, we are supposed to be helping him with his problems. Would it not be necessary to tell us where we are going along the way? We certainly are not in any form of space OUR science can define. In fact, for some strange reason, our science back home seems determined to DENY nether-space as a valid endpoint, even WITH the Marshal presumably offering so much wisdom. But if to look out that window, I think we proved that wrong. That out there is four-dimensional space, outside any recognizable three-dimensional universe. And I believe I can demonstrate this, if only in theory, if you look closely and see huge bubble-like objects out there. Those are the membranes of universes, much like ours, but as seen from the outside."

At this moment, the discussion had caught the attention of several others in the room, including the chief med-tech. They all began to gather around and listen in.

"But why would he tell us to go places," the med-tech asks, "like this abnormal space, and not inform us of where we are?"

"You might also ask why that other universe and not tell anyone. I was once part of a highly classified operation on that world. It was a mining base pulling up a very unusual mineral, which coincidentally echoed a trace signature of this same abnormal energy. Along the way, we were told to send this to a processor, which used proprietary tech to refine this material into what I can only describe to be a kind of extract of that same abnormal energy. This clearly tells me he KNOWS what it is, but does not tell US anything about it, as we had no definition of what we were doing, OR why we were doing it. But one thing I can say about it, which was also very highly classified, is it was destructive enough to blow apart a full star system."

"In all the nether-space!" shouts a female intern. "Why would he want that?"

"Your guess is as good as mine, as he doesn't seem to like to explain himself. Even the HC has been overheard to say the Marshal tends to keep a lot of private details to himself. BUT…private detail or otherwise, you might think, if he wants US to do anything for him, it would be a very kind courtesy of him to tell us if we are producing star-destroying explosives. That might be nice to know, so we might understand just how critical the operation actually is."

"Yes! I would agree."

"Um, Lieutenant," the med-tech wonders. "If all of this is so highly classified, why are you telling us?"

"Why, Med-tech? For the precise reason he classifies everything, and thereby preventing us to know what we're doing for him in our… voluntary…service to aid him. There is a recent development back in CC, where some of us who are starting to question that being who does not like to be questioned, and why he places everything into such categories of high security that no one in our military, or anyone back home, is ever intended to know anything, like this guy here," she points at the intern at the desk.

"But could there be a rational explanation for it?"

"Maybe, but is HIDING such a world-sensation event like the discovery of a new universe something to classify simply for the discovery? I think not. We describe the Marshal as a benefactor, but he doesn't seem to be benefiting us with a lot of things we might otherwise find useful to know, or even necessary to know, if we are to serve HIM for all his problems. And this is after ten millennia of waiting for his old promises of great wisdom. But then, I guess a lot of us stopped counting when the stories just kept on repeating until our horns sagged down to our ankles."

"I may need to agree with this," the female nods. "I felt this way on a few occasions."

"Now, here we are, in what I can only describe to be that one place our science denies even to exist. And even the Marshal, who clearly knows it is out here AND is a viable destination to travel to, is also omitting an explanation. Further, if he knows what this abnormal energy is, but doesn't tell any of us, and yet he can create such a device that could easily represent a weapon, this represents the foundation of a picture some of us SHOULD be questioning, and ESPECIALLY if he likes to classify so many things to prevent any of us knowing about it. After all, are we his minions to serve as trained animals, or are we people who willingly offered ourselves to his aid?"

"Right! I agree. This is rational. We offered ourselves willingly, so we should be deserving of a few explanations on occasion."

"Perhaps, but unfortunately, this is also untrue."

"Untrue?"

"Yes. Along with the highly classified nature of that mining base, located in the highly classified discovery of that new universe, the base commander, who happened to be a fleet commander in our space navy on reserve duty at the time, was taking up what Central once advertised as a very important role in...serving...our most revered benefactor. But his service was...questionable...to say the least."

"How so, questionable?" the med-tech asks.

"This is also classified, and likely to cover up what we did there. The planet was fully populated by a native society when they first found it. The population was described to be sympathetic, or maybe owned by these insurgents of his. Therefore, it would be highly unlikely we could mine anything there without interference."

"Yes, that would be a problem."

"Until our space navy was called in to blast it to nether-space."

"What?! Aargh..." he grunts as he takes a feedback hit.

"And it was likely on the active mode of their chips, as I think they would quickly realize a preindustrial society is actually NO real threat to us…or to him."

"Preindustrial?" he whimpers. "But to blast them? I mean…well, preindustrial… They would not be a threat on the ground, in orbit, or anything else. In fact, why not simply go to some other world? Is this mineral so important, as well as limited, to just this one planet?"

"I might say, if it was found on one, it might be found elsewhere, if you look hard enough. It radiated with this trace energy, so it might be a product of that space, meaning a space WITH this abnormal energy present. But because he did not teach OUR people how to harvest it, which might also involve teaching us what this abnormal energy is and how it works, he needed local labor. So our mining crew was ordered to enslave the one surviving city as our workforce. And THAT was also so heavily classified, Central barely even knew we existed to send food on occasion."

"Incredible! Yes, that would be a very criminal action, and on multiple levels."

"But which one, Med-tech…the aspect of blasting the world down to one surviving city, and then enslaving what remained, or the aspect of placing our otherwise willing workforce, who is serving our most illustrious benefactor no one chooses to question, on the active mode of their chips, thereby treating them as trained animals to do as we are told and NOT ask questions at all, just to get the job done."

"Aargh!" he clutches at his interface again for another feedback.

The rest of the medical staff also grabbed their heads for similar reactions.

Kaliya watched, and while she felt a mild sense of mischief for her statements, she also felt sympathy for their suffering. Unfortunately, these statements had to be revealed to these people, who did not otherwise hold enough ambition to seek their own answers. And they all had chips installed, which was a complication she could not bypass.

"And according to this commander," she continues. "This was not the first time he saw such as this."

"There was more?"

"He confided in me, as he was also quite tired of what he called inconsistencies in the Marshal's instructions, that he was once in charge of a task force in our space navy. And during his tour of duty, his task force was sent out on numerous campaigns to fight those insurgents. Unfortunately, this is where his other experiences come into play. His full crew was placed on active each time, and then told to blast entire planets, many of which apparently did not fight back, or represent anything that even knew what hit them. And these are supposed to be people of such a highly developed potential as to kick Sargeras in the tail one time."

The med-tech gaped at her for the scandalous accusation, as did the rest of the medical staff.

"Um, Lieutenant," the intern at the desk wonders. "Can we offer any rational explanation for this observation, to say nothing of the reasoning for blasting whole planets?"

"He was given reasons for it, but they did not make a lot of proper sense in the end. Not for what he could recall of his observations once he came off active. Then the case was closed, everything was classified, buried, and no one allowed to speak of it. However, I think I CAN offer a direction for you to consider, and it is right outside the window. Abnormal space…as well as abnormal energy. Think about this for a moment. The Marshal clearly knows what all this is, but he is not telling us, and I think this would be important to know if it relates to his insurgents and their technological capabilities. If he expects us to go to war with something, I will surely hope he would explain…exactly…what it is we are going to war with. Would you agree?"

"Yes, I think this is an obvious direction to take."

"Good. But he not only forgot to teach us about this abnormal energy, even after ordering us to make a weapon out of it, he also forgot to help us understand what our science, which he is supposed to be uplifting back home, is unable to define as we look outside the window. This goes a little beyond simple negligence. This is an outright denial to inform."

"I would agree," the female nods. "This is more like cheating us out of something we ought to know."

"And then we have all those so-called insurgents back home in our home galaxy, where we were sent out, in active mode, to destroy whole planets filled with what could easily be unrelated populations, because we do NOT have this abnormal energy in our universe. So, I will put this to you for consideration. If HE, as well as whatever society he came from, knows, perhaps also uses, maybe even depends upon, this abnormal energy, why would they come into our space where we have none? You need a jump drive for that, for one thing. And if they can JUMP into our space, and if they really wanted Sargeras, they should have no trouble finding us to jump right on top of us and finish it properly, especially if such a society is capable of building star-destroying bombs, and might otherwise make their home in FOUR-dimensional space, where we can't even track them. What do you think?"

Now, the whole room erupts with shrieks, followed by groans and whimpers, as every member of the staff doubles over from feedbacks.

Kaliya continues, "Now ask yourselves about our most illustrious benefactor. If he brought us out here to find anything relating to not only his insurgents, but ALSO this place where the rest of Sargeras's people are found, they cannot be native to a universe like ours. This places them just a little bit outside our normal capacity to fight. And yet, wow, did our military do a tail-spanking job with everything back home. Now, how do you feel about all those highly classified… things…he never intended us to know about? And this naturally brings us full circle to his original promises…which we are STILL waiting for. Well, some of us are tired of the wait. Especially as we find ourselves in such places, and doing such things, that really do need an explanation, here and now. But he's not doing it."

"Yes, Lieutenant," the med-tech responds feebly. "I think I would need to agree, as painful as it is to admit to it. But we should probably report this to someone, just to let them know to keep a watch on it, if nothing else."

"Yes, but the Council is not likely going to help," she reflects conspicuously. "After all, they are responsible for basically handing over our military to his exclusive authority. If you recall, we did not HAVE a military before he came along. So, everything we represent here is entirely his work. One might even say he owns us, especially if you consider those chips the Council mandated once, and each of us takes so consistently."

"Consistently!" the female scorns. "Yes, I will say consistently. I did not want mine, but it was pushed at me regardless."

"The same for each of us, I think," the intern at the desk agrees.

Kaliya continues, "So I am going to say the Council took this great wisdom he offered and ran away with it. No one has seen them since the day they went into deliberation, and I hear the doors are locked and visitors kept out. Not even the normal duty of government affairs is being processed, at least not BY the government. A few secretaries, maybe, but not the Council members."

"That does not sound at all good for our government leaders," the med-tech considers.

"No, it does not. Call it greed, call it gluttony, call it negligence, but do not call it responsibility to the people, as the PEOPLE certainly do NOT need the secrets of the universe. But we do need a lot of other things closer to home."

"Then it needs to go up to the HC," the female suggests.

"But intern, here we have another problem. He also has a chip."

"What?!" she shouts. "Aargh!" she screams, then follows with a whimper as she tries to continue. "The HC has a chip? But he is the HC! He, of all people, should NOT have one of those."

"Perhaps. But it would seem, especially if you apparently do not know of it, this must be another of the Marshal's highly classified secrets. I know the people inside Central Command know this, but they are physically present in the room to see it. Worse, he is most often on active, thank you Marshal Darumon, and has been most of his professional career. NOW…who do you think owns our military, and what are WE in his eyes, if not trained animals expected to jump when he calls for it. And next is this thing outside."

"What about it, do you think?" she trembles.

"The HC is apparently fighting his chips. Although, for some nether-wild reason I can't quite fathom, he hasn't put it together yet to order his chip turned off. His loyalty to the cause must be very high, but this is probably due to his military discipline, I think. Still, he hates the thing, but HE has not taken the hint to correct it, as only the Marshal seems to hold that level of authority, and he must have a difficult time making his own choices."

"If his chip is turned on," the med-tech muses. "It could be he is unable to make that decision on his own as effectively."

"Yes, but it is also said he is avoiding his maintenance, thereby his chip seems to be weakening. Maybe he might one day succeed."

"That may be true, but at a risk, I would say. If his chip is so past due on its maintenance, it could fall out of sync with his neural patterns, and this could cause injury."

"Then I hope he makes that choice sooner, rather than later. Meanwhile, he recently ordered this new survey pattern, and my understanding here is HE did this, not the Marshal, who is apparently telling us to break and enter into someone's home and stick our horns in places we might not otherwise be welcome. My interpretation is to finally assess what sort of people we have inside HERE, to understand what we might one day find ourselves on active and blasting to nether-space, but to avoid it this time."

"To catch him at his own game, you think?"

"Oh, I am sure of that one. The HC must be coming to a few of his own conclusions, based on some of these same inconsistencies, and also from such people as that fleet commander and his experiences. Maybe also if you consider who must own that thing, where we are, and what they might truly be capable of that the Marshal has so far not fully informed us about."

"And that…alleged…rift thing we are supposed to be looking for," the female notes timidly.

"Alleged…" Kaliya raises her brow. "Whether or not there is actually anything to look for, it has been described as a detention, or even a prison center. So, here we are with a being of unknown and questionable intentions, telling us to blast worlds apart, which I think should be illegal, to say the least, and also to enslave innocent populations, which is certainly illegal, at least according to OUR laws…who knows about his. We illegally steal native resources from those nearly dead populations, and then build super weapons out of it. Then, he refuses to teach us anything, even if it represents a critical detail to explain what he has us doing, and after offering so many grand promises to uplift our society, and furthermore places people on the active mode of our own form of slave device to perform deeds we might not otherwise agree with. And he classifies everything he does to cover his tail so we cannot even research it without breaking a few security codes. Now, he is telling us to find and release someone from a prison? You might want to consider turning off that Suppressor chip, so you can laugh at the idea."

The staff members all glance around at each other in hesitation and fear.

"So far…" Kaliya continues. "We are simply playing the tourist, and this seems to have quieted the situation. Maybe our first arrival, using military troops, violated or disturbed something in there. Insurgents or otherwise, we did violate their home by cutting a hole in it, and they probably know this, if there is no other obvious way in…at least not that we are aware of, or that the Marshal informed us about."

"This is true," the med-tech nods. "And it holds merit for our observations since then."

"But the Marshal seems very determined to get what he wants, especially if he is so content to use coercive methods to meet his needs. Even if…and at this moment, it is a big if…he is holding legitimate direction, such that we who never held any true militaristic background may not recognize, it is still reasonable to interpret a valid target when we see one. A preindustrial society is not a valid target…not for us, and certainly not for him. If all you need is a preindustrial society to throw out Sargeras, they are NOT who they claim themselves to be. This might also equate to that empty promise of great wisdom…there is none. But clearly, they had to come from somewhere, and if he knows how to do all this, it has to be something well above preindustrial, but not within the knowledge base of our people, and I feel it must involve what we see outside."

"All right, so we make our assessment of that society and compare with what we must assume to be a representative example to his form."

"Good. If only we had this opportunity before, but our people were on active back then. However, this brings us to the next point. That interference. He doesn't seem to like people interfering with his wants. Just look at that mining base and the world he blasted to steal their minerals. That is your example. Now apply that here. What if those people, who might take exception of us going military on them again, should try to interfere? What will he require of us, and will it involve blasting anything while on active if we should hold any objections to it?"

"I understand your point."

"But more than this," Kaliya concludes. "I feel we should share these perspectives with others. He is known to classify everything he does, with the apparent intention of hiding his actions…actions that are clearly questionable. You asked why I'm talking about it? Because he denies anyone to talk around here. Therefore, he gets away with murder, in a literal sense of it, for all his secrets."

"That is not good."

"And even if HE might know what he is doing, and even if HE might hold a reason to do it, do WE want to be responsible for destroying worlds along the way for his empty promises of something he won't even explain if we see it out a window? We should hold ourselves to higher standards than that. If there is great wisdom out there, it would be far more appealing to simply go out and find it ourselves. The challenge to overcome the discovery is much more fulfilling."

"Those are very inspiring words, Lieutenant. Well spoken."

"Indeed, Med-tech, I was raised in a family of scientific background. It is our job to ask questions, AND to share the details of what we learn."

She now turns and leaves the room. If these seeds of malcontent held any value, she hoped they might spread to others.

<hr>

"Your Lordship," Kailen announces. "We have a new delivery of chips from our spy-cams, one from the control center, and a very interesting recording of the Commander in his private office."

"Which of these do you wish to begin with, in this case?"

"Let's take the activity in Sigil first. Apparently, Central has received an order to step up their operations in the city, making short incursions and using more deployments."

"Indeed, then I suppose I must afford Aerlie a good call, as this was one of her suggestions. But are we speaking of using greater force, or simply more covert actions?"

"So far, it appears covert, but if the Marshal is getting anxious, I wouldn't put it past him to take it even further, all things considered. We still have that one occasion of a hint to seek ways to optimize their efforts."

"Yes. And the Commander was apparently seeking a comparison of the population inside that city in relation to his own. I am curious as to his direction."

"Well, I think I have an answer for you, if you're really so interested," he grins.

Thaelyn studied his quirky expression, and rolled his eyes towards the General.

"We do not...yet...have him on our list. Is that correct, General?"

"Not as yet," he smiles. "He has been keeping a low profile in this regard."

"Yes...so it would seem. Very well, Commander, what do we have on Geilv this time?"

"Lieutenant Lapäli and I reviewed the video a couple of times just to be sure we understood how to interpret it. I also referred to Ankhia for a few points to see if she might have some perspectives to offer, at least from the medical side of it."

"The medical side?"

"He looks like he's still struggling with his chips, and our observations force us to ask an interesting question. How effective are they, in his case?"

"This is an interesting quandary. What is the impetus for this question? Is he showing some capacity we might not otherwise expect? That is, considering the description of how these chips are intended to behave."

"I think so. First, he appears very mature, as an elder member, and by this, I mean one-fifty plus."

"But we are speaking in terms of centuries again, so this equates to something like fifteen millennia and above, correct?"

"Yes, and this would place him before the arrival of Sargeras. He was carrying on a private conversation with himself in his office, which allowed us to study his manners. Ankhia suggested this habit of talking to himself might have developed as a defensive means to overcome the inhibiting effect of his chips, particularly the authority chip. He was also demonstrating himself to be rather lucid, maybe not to the point of carrying on such free thought as one of us, but more so than you might expect of someone under the active mode of that chip, at least by the way it was described."

"And what is Ankhia's interpretation of this?"

"She is asking about the age of those chips, and what effect they might have by this time. It comes two-fold. One being the question of whatever form of maintenance they keep on those chips. Everything has a lifespan of some sort, so could his chips be so old that their effectiveness has weakened over time."

"How curious! Yes, this would be a noteworthy mention. And at his age, I can see where this is going, if he got those chips at an early moment in his career. Perhaps they have simply worn out and he has a greater capacity unto himself as a result."

"But not perfect, as his speech patterns still seem to show a control effect."

"Very well, but this is a step forward for us. What else?"

"His age, and his duration under the effect, might have also allowed him to develop a type of resistance to it, perhaps even an adaptation. Ankhia tells me that neural tissue can be dynamic on occasion, especially in the event of damaged or restricted areas, where the surrounding regions might try rewiring themselves to bypass the affected area to overcome the restriction. Could it be his constant struggles have allowed him to reroute some of his capacity around it by now? Ten millennia is certainly enough time for something to occur."

"Powers be blessed if he is able to do this. Then he might have made an adjustment of a sort, especially for the long duration and perhaps his constant resistive efforts. This might represent a form of unconscious therapeutic rehabilitation, especially if to consider how often he was placed under this control influence. I wonder if the Marshal ever took notice of it, or if he even considers this as a potential concern."

"If we judge by Geilv's current condition, either he's kept it hidden, or the Marshal just assumes his toy soldiers are behaving as good little minions."

"Most interesting..."

"One other thing that comes to mind is Kaliya's people have reported once or twice that he IS known to be skipping his maintenance intentionally. This represents a form of defiance, so we might wish to add this to the list if the chip is simply failing by now."

"Indeed, he must be a determined man. But then, if he is so determined to defy the chip, why not simply give the order to disable or remove it completely?"

"Unknown, unless he doesn't hold the keys for it."

"Wonderful. Very well, this is one more aspect to consider. Now, as for these private musings."

"First, he seems to spend a lot of time in his private office. The videos show him sharing conversations with the Marshal on the com-links, and these usually translate to orders given to the others in the control center. But this last one had the Marshal once again disgruntled by the lack of progress in the city. He even made mention of feeling the loss of his elves who could've infiltrated the area under a cloak or simply not stand out as much."

"Indeed, so this might represent a potential use for them, if we had not otherwise taken them away."

"Now, if we reflect on that one occasion where he ordered that survey of the local population, I think I have a follow-up to his thoughts on the matter, and this also seems to carry through from the Morndindor incident."

"Which means our work there is carrying a lasting impression. Good."

"It would also seem your conversation with him as they were pulling out from their operations here also left a lasting impression. He was starting to remember portions of it."

"Indeed! I am actually very pleased to hear this. But how does it play a role?"

"He was apparently mulling over certain aspects of these details. This included Commander Kriv'tik's message of Morndindor, and I must assume some earlier conversations they shared on those other worlds he blasted. He briefly reflected on Ytani and seemed upset that the Marshal didn't disclose the details of that weapon until after it became a critical concern, and further to wonder why it was needed in the first place."

"This is certainly a fair topic of consideration."

"We keep hearing him use the expression, 'containment procedures,' in his statements. This must be a key element the Marshal used as an excuse to blast everything. But then he started to associate a few of these points and came to a number of shocking conclusions…pun intended," he grins.

"Shocking? For him… He still has a Suppressor chip in active play, correct?"

"Oh yes, and we watched as he took a number of feedback hits, some of them severe."

"And therefore your pun, I suppose," he smirks. "Gracious, I hope he does not take injury from it."

"First, he questioned the need to blast entire worlds that did not apparently show the capacity to fight back. He compared this with Kriv'tik's experiences of his earlier missions, and then Morndindor, and also Therinë. He seemed to be trying to rationalize this in relation to them being described as belonging to the Marshal's opponents, and finally reflecting on you."

"Me? Personally, or figuratively?"

"Both, actually, like with your army during the war campaign here. Yours was the only force that actively fought back, and you won, if only due to the fact you used what he describes as Abnormal Energy…your magic, I suppose. The others didn't apparently demonstrate this, and those worlds local to Azgarén wouldn't have it in the first place."

"Powers above, the man must be truly struggling at this moment. What else did he say?"

"The Marshal was afraid of your opponent forces, and ran away. This represents a threatening potential well above the otherwise inferior forces of these worlds they assaulted before. He began to put together that the Marshal was surprised at your arrival, after ten millennia of fighting someone who ought to know of Azgarén by this time. BUT…" he waves a finger for emphasis. "You apparently played the role that you didn't know the Marshal or Sargeras directly, and this gave the impression of yours being an unknown NEW encounter with the Azgarén military."

"Indeed I did…" he smiles mischievously. "And so, it played out as I hoped it would."

"For instance, one aspect is the Marshal did not expect to see such as you come out of Tae'Eladar after his little incursion. Meaning either you would not normally belong there, or the timing simply had you present in order to respond. Either way, the Marshal did not seem to expect repercussions, or not those of your caliber. Therefore, the timing may have backfired on him, if he was expecting more of those inferior societies to play with, like those here on Therinë, or elsewhere."

"Ah, so the Maker's little plan is bearing fruit?" he grins.

"You apparently knew them by name, but NOT by reference

as some outcast government body. And after all this time fighting something, this might suggest, whoever his real enemies are, it is NOT what he was fighting all this time, as now here YOU are, representing a new element that likely never knew HE was out there."

"Nicely done, my Lord," the General smiles. "That should put a fine question in his mind."

"So, he started asking who those other worlds belonged to," Kailen continues. "And why the Marshal wanted them blasted, if they could not possibly hold any true relation to you. Then he recalled your statement of a lawful government body apparently protecting such worlds, but rather than punish his people directly, you let them go. This seems to be confusing him, but you clearly demonstrated the capacity to act. So, he's worried right now about the next time."

"The next time," Thaelyn muses. "Perhaps meaning to say Sigil?"

"Yes. He remembered your warnings, and now he's afraid of what sort of repercussions might come out of Sigil and the trouble they're making there. He finally started calling himself a criminal for blasting innocent and otherwise defenseless worlds that shouldn't have been targets to begin with."

"Gods above," the General relents. "I actually feel pity for the poor man."

"Yes, General," Thaelyn asserts. "And I must also wonder where this could lead. If he is placing so much effort into piecing these components together, would he choose to take any form of action to protect himself and his military, and possibly also turn against the Marshal for these criminal acts? He very nearly did so at the loss of Morndindor if you recall. This carries the potential for its own form of response, which could complicate things for us."

"Personally," Kailen reflects. "I'm wondering about his request to that ship out there to put together a survey of the local population. What sort of report do you think they'll return?"

"If they do not otherwise understand how to interpret this abnormal energy, they might simply judge it at face value, which will likely appear as an early to middle Industrial Age environment, depending on how deep they go and how they interpret the sorts of devices they see. Some elements might appear very strange, as they do use a few forms of arcanic technology, and I am aware many of the people do not carry weapons of the sort you would identify as technological. They might carry staffs and blades, however, and this could step back the interpretation a bit."

"Wonderful, but do they use magic at all?"

"There are some who are well-versed in it, others with rudimentary skills, but it is not as homogenous as on Tae'Eladar. We also have a number of people with other, even stranger talents, better explained with your metaphysics. And likely, they will see devices of an unknown design and with no recognizable theory of operation."

"That should be fun to catalog, especially the metaphysical aspect. They never did like that subject. So, I wonder what the end result will be and how he might react to it."

"I must agree here," the General submits. "In addition, I feel that at some moment, we might have to contact him in order to bring the situation into our favor. He may see Sigil as another of the same, and conclude the Marshal takes pleasure in the destruction of random targets, perhaps to say random inferior targets."

"This is a good point, General," Thaelyn admits. "Therefore, we will observe and look for an opening, although how we will approach it may remain a mystery for now. He is very close to the Marshal, and we do not wish to imperil him for his own awareness."

✦ ✦ ◆ ✦ ✦

"Now listen, Marelle; no crazy maneuvering, no wild stunts, and no sudden starts or stops. Just take off, make a smooth ascent, once around Selûne, and back to base. Understood?"

"Oh, you're no fun! But all right, on this one occasion, I'll try to behave myself."

"This is only a prototype, so we're still trying to work out a few of the bugs."

"Thanks, do any of those bugs bite?"

"So far, it looks good in the lab, which is to say the drone we sent up last month came back in one piece."

"Oh, that sounds encouraging," she smirks. "But that was by remote control, right?"

"Yes, and it only made a few circles in the sky above. This one uses a larger version of the same drive system, but under manual control."

"And those controls are now the same as what we use in the simulator…good. So, we take it slow and easy until I get a feel for it, then make a quick run and back again."

"Correct… Good luck to you, Lieutenant."

Marelle was visiting the BRC on Tae'Eladar, where they've been making steady progress developing some of the new hybrid technology between the Tae'Eladaran scientists and the Daanen-Aryku engineers. A new experimental craft had been designed with a new drive system based in part on the Daanen-Aryku spatial-inversion drive and the Tae'Eladaran transport sphere, giving a very unique result which now needed testing.

Marelle was called in as their test pilot. She had just been briefed on the new system, and given careful instructions to make a simple run outside the planetary sphere, followed by a single loop around the local moon, and back again.

She climbed into the pilot's seat of the prototype craft and made herself comfortable, strapping in for safety. She carried a portal rune with her for emergency recall, should anything go wrong with the craft, and she was dressed in a sealed pressure suit and helmet, in case of the loss of atmosphere inside the cabin. She also wore a special form of virtual gloves to interact with the holographic fly-by-wire controls. These would allow her to control the flight characteristics of guidance and thrust, as well as a set of conjuring orbs for weapons, but that feature was not enabled yet.

She closes the hatch and seals the compartment, powers up the craft and makes ready for her run. She calls in to signal her condition.

"Lieutenant Carronel to base, ready on deck."

"Acknowledged, Lieutenant, your telemetry looks good. You are clear for departure."

"Understood. Lifting off."

She applies a gentle upward stroke on her lifting control, located on her left hand next to the throttle. It was a small cross-shaped sensor pad used for vertical takeoff and landing, as well as a horizontal strafing action. As she gradually runs a finger up the strip, the ship hums softly. A barely perceptible wave action ripples outward from above along an invisible bubble surrounding the ship. The space above the ship was being sucked into a compression field and drawn along the contours of the bubble downward, lifting the bubble and its contents at the same time. She studied the action carefully, along with her status readouts on a projected heads-up display in front of her. She continued the upward motion until she was at a comfortable height above the ground.

"Lift-off appears successful, all indicators are good," she announces.

"Our telemetry confirms your condition. Proceed forward slowly."

She now moves her left hand to the throttle strip, which was essentially a straight line. She starts at the base and very slowly runs upward, and the ship begins moving. Her right hand hovered over a circular directional control, which would alter her course in much the same way as a traditional flight stick. For now, she kept herself centered.

She gradually moved across the field, increasing velocity carefully, and practicing a few turns, but keeping her flight level. She increased the throttle a little more to pick up speed, now travelling at a moderate rate relative to light aircraft, again making practice turns and circling around the base.

"Base, the controls seem responsive and accurate," she reports.

"Excellent, Lieutenant, your telemetry is still good. We advise gaining altitude for a high-speed run."

"Understood."

She gradually runs up the throttle and angles up on the flight path, now picking up speed and slicing through the atmosphere. Unlike in her simulator, there was no wind outside, as the surrounding environment was being cut away by the inversion bubble, pierced through, pulled around, and closed up behind. She was not a physical object moving through physical space. Space was moving around the bubble, and she was just a massless passenger inside.

She made another series of cautious maneuvers, turning, diving, and climbing. The controls responded nicely. She reflected on her experience in the flight simulator. The feeling was very similar to the computer-generated scenario, and the controls were everything she thought they should be.

"Base, this stage appears nominal," she declares. "The controls are working according to expectations, scaling with my speed factor, and the ship is responding with high precision. I am now awaiting permission for the next stage."

"Acknowledged, our readings are good here. You may proceed on your run, Lieutenant. Keep a close eye on your gauges, and good luck."

A broad smile wrapped around her face as she hit the throttle, running it up midway and beyond, and angling skyward.

The ship accelerated rapidly past supersonic velocities, as measured by an outside observer, then to hypersonic. The surrounding scenery flashed by the windows. Distant cloud formations in the sky fell beneath her like rocks in a pond. The world below shrank, and the land features blurred into a generic smear of terrestrial shapes.

As she penetrated the upper atmospheric layers, she hit a scaling control alongside her throttle to bump her speed factor to the next increment. This control represented a multiplier for the scaling factor, from standard combat velocity and planetary travel to something more approximating orbital velocity and basic space travel. The directional controls also had to scale, so her turns wouldn't rip the ship apart with hairpin maneuvers at extreme speed.

"The multiplier control seems functional according to specs," she notes on the com-link.

"Affirmative, Lieutenant. I'm showing a change from mag-0 to mag-1. You should be good to go for orbital insertion."

The change in multiplier upward reset her throttle to the lower end, so she again ran a finger up the throttle, but only slightly in this case, as the multiplier was exponential in scale. This was enough to achieve orbital velocity. She glanced briefly out the side window at the world below, observing how smoothly it slid away behind her. She turned to follow an orbital curve, giving herself a chance to test this new condition.

"Keep in mind, Lieutenant," the voice calls on the com-link. "The faster you go, the farther ahead you need to watch for any hazards. Use your nav scanner for this."

"Understood. The scanner has scaled to the new mag level, so I'm showing a compressed view of my flight path."

She studied the HUD in front of her, which displayed a three-dimensional tactical representation of her local space. It updated continually from her scanners, giving her details of any other objects around her. She began another series of movements to test her controls.

She first tried a roll maneuver, which was a two-fingered action, keeping one centered and the other moving sideways. If to use only one, it would instead result in a sharp turn. The maneuver reoriented the ship relative to the surrounding area. Then she pulled into a slanted upturn by moving her finger into the upper right quadrant, next to turn the other way, followed by diving maneuvers of a similar sort, circling her finger around the grid to test all quadrants.

"My directional controls are still showing accurate movement," she affirms. "All scaled to mag-1."

"Excellent."

Now she feels more confident. She takes it up again, this time orienting on the moon Selûne, aiming just off to one side to make a pass around it, and she increases thrust again, paying as much attention to her HUD as she was outside the window.

The view now changes as the increased power causes a more noticeable ripple effect around the bubble. The image was still recognizable dead ahead of her, but along the sides it seemed elongated. She had to focus on her HUD if she wanted to understand the nature of her immediate surroundings. The power multiplication to the engines was still sub-light at this setting, but it was enough for the test run. She only needed a small fraction of lightspeed to reach the moon in a timely manner.

The moon loomed ahead of her, and was growing rapidly, while Tae'Eladar fell behind, even though she didn't dare take her eyes off her HUD to watch it. She was moving at phenomenal speeds now, no longer measured in relation to sonic or even orbital velocities. The distance from Tae'Eladar to its moon was measured in hundreds of thousands of miles, and she was crossing that distance in seconds.

She wanted to comment on the extraordinary sight, but she could not afford the luxury of taking her mind away from her work. This was a frighteningly quick rate of travel. Even though she had some fun with this in the simulator, now it was real. As she neared the moon, she slowed her passage and brought the ship around the back side of it, seeing the moon rotate below as the local universe seemed to spin on its axis, quickly to reveal Tae'Eladar popping into view at distance on the other side.

"Unbelievable!" she mutters breathlessly.

"Easy does it, Lieutenant; try not to plow any new holes in the planet."

"Yes Sir, but the sight is amazing. And this little ship is remarkable."

"I can appreciate what you mean. Our people worked hard enough on it. I'm pleased to hear we got it right."

"All systems still appear functioning at nominal levels, I'm coming in."

She increases the throttle again, taking great care not to overrun her mark, and keeping her pace steady as the planet below comes back into range. She returns to the orbital speed setting and orients to a gentle downward angle for reentry. And as she makes her way down through the layers, she resets the multiplier for atmospheric travel.

"Setting to mag-0..." she declares as she hits the switch.

The controls alter their scaling factor, and the throttle resets to its uppermost setting as it descends from the higher scale. This causes the ship to automatically decelerate from the lower end of mag-1 to the upper end of mag-0, chaining from one to the other, and thereby reducing speed for travel within the atmosphere again.

She watches the nav markers on her HUD for the base locator beacon and follows it back to her starting point, slowing to a crawl as she makes her final approach, lining up with a landing pad and bringing down her gear, then settling into position vertically with her landing control. Once safely back on the ground, she lets out a sigh of relief as she powers down and removes her helmet.

✦

"My Lord, I'm back," Kaliya announces as she returns to the WIC building.

"Ah, good, that took a while, but did you find anything out there?"

"I did, and I learned a few things which could be useful. I also did something, um, naughty," she smiles bashfully as she rolls her eyes.

"Oh dear Powers, what is it this time?"

"First, I found the exit point leading outside Sigil. That place is amazing as seen from the outside. I was standing on the outer surface and could look back to see the whole toroid. It's massive!"

"It must have been an impressive sight. Perhaps, at some moment, you could share your memories on this."

"Oh yes, I'd be happy to, maybe even to take pictures. But anyway, the Suuden-Aryku cut a hole and attached an airlock to it. I was able to find my way out onto the surface where I saw a shuttle belonging to a recent scouting patrol that came inside, and I also found their ship, which was actually quite distant from me, but I was still able to fold over to it."

"Good. And once inside, how did you proceed?"

"I took my Suuden'kai disguise and wandered around a bit. No one really took notice that I wasn't a regular part of the crew, so I'm guessing they either don't pay as close attention to that, or the crew rotates so often that it doesn't matter. My first stop was the medical ward."

"Oh? And why did you choose that?"

"I was trying to consider my approach, and a low security location might make a good entry point. I could test the waters there, and maybe even tickle their soft underbelly a little."

"Oh dear…" he moans. "General, she is tickling their underbellies now."

"Good gods," he winces. "This young lady is a bold one."

"Hey," Kaliya retorts wittily. "We have objectives, right? And I considered I needed an excuse to visit the bridge so I could check the reactions of the crew for their chips. For that matter, just about any place might do, but the bridge would be an important example. But the medical ward might also offer a cute place to deliver some local gossip, just in case those poor soldier boys don't watch the nightly news as often."

"And is this where you begin tickling their underbellies?" Thaelyn muses cautiously.

"I recalled our discussion about dropping hints of what they're doing, and the trouble they're getting into, and I figured the medical ward, which was essentially a noncritical part of the ship, and likely filled with people who might be a little more open to casual conversation, would make a good starting place."

"Most interesting, and it does offer a good point. And so, would this be part of that naughty bit you mentioned?"

"Maybe…" she looks away innocently. "I came up with a great idea, and the purpose is to break those people away from their clear dependency on their most beloved benefactor who can do no wrong… even though they have absolutely NO idea what he's actually doing."

"Uh huh…"

"Therefore, I chose to stop by a desk to ask a local intern for a medical scanner."

"A medical scanner. Do you actually know how to use one of those?"

"Well, when I was little, I used to visit Ankhia in the Ward back home. We would talk, and she might show me some of the really fun gadgets she used."

"Oh, yes...gadgets. I like that term, so scientific," he chuckles. "So, why would you need one of those on this occasion?"

"An excuse to start a little conversation. I'm making a study of something those dull-horned galoots are simply passing by without asking about it. It's called...Abnormal Energy..." she flutters her fingers theatrically.

"Powers help us, she is doing what Darumon himself would not."

"Not completely, but at least in theory. And then, that space out there, they also call it abnormal...space, in this case. Which means they have NO idea where they are, or what relation it has to our science back home, which flat-out denies it even exists as a valid destination endpoint...and yet, here we are."

"Oh! Truly! And how does this unfold? They do not recognize the existence of that very same nether-space they speak of so often?"

"No, they do not, as nether-space is more often a fictional void you want to stay out of, not venture into and learn something. And I'm wondering who invented THAT idea."

"Uh huh, and this is starting to point a finger now. How did you approach it?"

Kaliya pulls out her shard-com and sets it on the table.

"I recorded the conversation for our records in case you would like to review it. Here is how it goes, generally speaking. It began with this one intern, but quickly drew a crowd, including the med-tech and others. They are completely unaware of Morndindor, or that other universe they discovered, which means not even the remainder of the military knows they discovered a new universe, to say nothing of the people. Therefore, I claimed I once served there briefly under the base commander, but without an actual name."

"I see...clever."

"The idea here is to unveil some of those highly classified details the Marshal is keeping away from people, and MAKE them ask those questions he does not want them asking...if only privately. First, if you only look out a window, you'll see something that is NOT recognized as our classic interpretation of three-dimensional space. So what else can it be. And since we already have that unpublished sensation of a new universe, this means we are breaking our scientific perspectives back home. Therefore, if you look into that sky, you might see the bubbles of those same universes, but here seen from outside in the higher realms of four-dimensional space, that same location our science refuses to acknowledge, just as it once denied other universes. Thank you, Marshal Darumon, who once promised us so much wisdom, to bring us into places we cannot define, and NOT explaining what it is."

"Ouch!" Kailen winces. "Yeah, that might go over really well with someone."

"He promises us his wisdom, but then we have that mining base. During my tour, which was also highly classified, we discovered this new universe, and in that universe, was this abnormal energy. The mining base was hauling up a mineral which held a trace amount of it, and the Marshal, with his processor, and what was obviously a proprietary form of tech, was refining it into a super explosive substance. This is a clear indication he KNOWS what abnormal energy is, but so unfortunately is not sharing this with the rest of us, even though he has us building a super weapon out of it."

"And that's another ouch."

"I also explained that planet…a population said to be in league with his insurgents, but blasted to nether-space down to one city, which we then enslaved, because WE are not allowed to know how to harvest this material, therefore we need local labor. But how do you justify doing this to something that is also preindustrial, and could not possibly qualify as anything relating to an opponent to anyone but themselves."

"And another ouch…this is building a nice picture, but a dangerous one."

"This is also hitting some of their chips for the feedback by now. Then, we follow with Kriv'tik and his task force, and placed on active to keep them from realizing what they're doing, or objecting to it."

"Oops!"

"Then back around to where we are now…or where THEY are. They are in a space our science refuses to acknowledge, even

WITH that superior alien mind that once promised to uplift us, but is not. We are travelling to places with this abnormal energy that the Marshal clearly knows how to use, especially if he can build super weapons out of it. Therefore, it must represent a resource to him, and maybe all of his society. Perhaps it could also be a demand for their form of tech. But we do not have this back home. So who were we fighting in a space without the tech they need to fight with?"

"Ooh! That one will hurt."

"As such, they must be unrelated, and especially if you factor in the chips on active so WE can't question it. Then to classify it to cover it up, for whatever reason, and actively denying people to talk about it."

"Cu'Nar's grace, Kaliya..." he frowns.

"Finally, to see where we are now. We are looking for this prison rift...emphasis on PRISON...for a guy who seems to be doing a lot of illegal stuff everywhere else, and he wants to release more of the same, perhaps? And further, in a space that we cannot, and for that matter DO not even recognize exists, filled with all this abnormal energy we know nothing about, and that he won't explain to us. And then, this thing out there with people inside who make this their home...and we're supposed to fight that? If this is where they come from, we can't even track them, much less prevent them from jumping into our home FROM that space to hit Sargeras directly."

"Great gods," the General grimaces. "If this does not leave a few fears in them."

"Therefore, all or most of Darumon's stories, fables, and promises are brought into question, and placing him in doubt for his integrity. At the very least, he is telling us to do things without explaining what, where, how or why, even if we can see it outside a window. Then he classifies it so we cannot discover it by any other means. And we are expected to offer ourselves as his willing compatriots, when in fact he uses us in active mode simply to get the job done, and our opinions do not matter. As such, beware of this next one, because anyone who can build that thing is not preindustrial. And if they use this abnormal energy that can build star-destroying bombs, you probably don't want to see what else it can do. This is clearly not a science we possess, but HE does."

"Kaliya…" Thaelyn muses. "That could easily frighten them into mutiny with just the one statement. What sort of reaction did they have?"

"Oh, well," she waves it off nonchalantly. "For one thing, to report it to an authority figure. So I had to explain their gluttonous Council hasn't been seen since they got this famous promise, then locked the doors so they don't even perform their standard duties, much less anything else. And they handed over our planetary military, with all of us force-fed these chips, to the Marshal to have his way with it… including the HC, which they were rather surprised to hear about."

"None of them knew the HC was under active?" Kailen wonders.

"They didn't even know he had a chip in the first place! After all, he's the HC, and presumably immune to it."

"Cu'Nar's pity!" he blasts. "So, what are we saying here? That these people are so ignorant as to the condition of their own superiors?"

"I find this very disturbing," Thaelyn admits. "Commander Kriv'tik knew of it, but then perhaps his close association granted him this privilege. The officers within Central Command proper seem to know, but this could simply be due to proximity. Maybe it is largely restricted to those who are close enough to see it, or high enough to be granted privilege to know of it, but the younger or lower ranking officers are not so fortunate."

"Maybe so," Kaliya shrugs. "Or maybe they don't speak about it, maybe to save face for who they THINK is running the military, because in their minds, it is not the Marshal. They are voluntarily offering aid to him, not his trained animals with programmable chips."

"That is simply wonderful…" the General moans.

"Anyway, the only authority here is the one who likes putting people on active if they ask too many questions or file too many complaints."

"Powers help us…yes," Thaelyn accedes. "General, I think you are right. This would certainly frighten them."

Kaliya concludes, "I would encourage you to listen to this recording for the intimate details of how it came out. In the end, we are going to monitor it closely with this new survey of Sigil, along with a comparison with Darumon and what he represents, to find a little evidence, then to watch for his response, if they continue to make trouble for us. And also, I added a touch of the Measure of Balance with a final word that we need to show higher standards for ourselves, and seek our own wisdom, not take someone's promises, whether real or imagined. As the search for knowledge, in itself, is worthy."

"Ah, do we have a little of Lord Oghma speaking here?" he smiles.

"Hey, I'm a paladin, so I need to learn to preach a little. And also, we are going to share this with others to further break his control of information, at least on the ship. This level of control, and revolving around so many questionable deeds, MUST be questioned, regardless of his highly classified security demands. We don't want to be responsible for so much destruction, even though we already are."

"Great cu'Nar, Kaliya!" Kailen groans. "Are YOU trying to start a revolution?"

"Indeed, Kaliya," Thaelyn admits. "You would make an especially dangerous insurgent by yourself. This is a strong mention to raise suspicions, and possibly to start another mutiny."

"I suppose this has to be our direction in the end," she shrugs. "So, I'm simply following the teachings of Oghma to educate them with details they were not privy to before, and then to…inspire them…to think and rationalize the logical conclusions."

"Oh! Falling back on THAT now, are we? General? This might make a noteworthy addition to the list."

"Oh dear, and another one," he shakes his head.

"Uh oh…" Kaliya covers her eyes and ducks away. "But I stand by it. This IS his teaching. At the very least, I hope to open their eyes to pay closer attention to their orders and to realize where they're coming from, if not the guy they're supposed to be coming from. If this revolves around making people do things, regardless of their personal opinions on the matter, they need to know who is giving the order and that there is no one else acting as an integrity check on him. This tends to fall in line with what we said on Morndindor, that if the people don't like what he's telling them to do, he has other ways of telling them to do it."

"Gods above, Kaliya," the General wheezes. "You are becoming a strong deliberator. If this does not impose some sort of reaction, I cannot see what would."

"Yes..." Thaelyn nods. "You are correct. And I must say it was well played. You opened up a series of clear statements, forced the notion of integrity checking, exposed a number of intelligence failures, and all this without actually inciting a reprisal. This follows nicely for your actions on Morndindor, and I might further suggest this would not filter back up to the Marshal, at least not as eagerly, if he is suspected of wrongdoing where the application of these chips is concerned. This might instead cause them to hold back, if for no other reason than the suggestion of activating the chips simply to quell their objections."

"Absolutely!" the General agrees. "And with no other authority figure to question him, not their High Commander or even their Council, this might raise a few thoughts of an internal conspiracy. Where might this take us, I wonder?"

"It would certainly raise a few thoughts of a rebellion," Kailen notes. "Large or small, I can't see how anyone would stand for this."

"They very nearly weren't standing for it after I finished," Kaliya asserts. "And not simply for the scandals, but all the feedbacks they were taking," she smirks.

"Oh, and is that face of yours suggesting some small amount of pleasure?"

"I did feel for them, but at the same time, I suppose rubbing their faces in the fact that the view outside isn't just good for a tourist photo. Regardless of the Marshal promising us anything, we should still try to figure out a few things for ourselves. We are still scientists, aren't we?"

"Possibly, although seeing them in this state makes you wonder."

"I simply hope we do not invoke the Marshal to take corrective action," Thaelyn muses. "And neither Commander Geilv, according to our recent observations of his manners."

"Did he do something?" Kaliya asks.

"He did. Your brother just finished a careful review of the most recent spy video. Geilv is apparently pushing his limits beyond those chips to make associations of the Marshal's so-called opponents in comparison to the technologically backwards and otherwise innocent worlds they destroyed, including Morndindor and this one. He was comparing his memories of Kriv'tik's statements, our actions here during the war, and my unexpected arrival on the scene. I was apparently not expected to exist at all, believing Tae'Eladar to be just another inferior world to play with. But then to have me show up due to those orcs, and later with Darumon running away from it, claiming I was his true enemy, when in fact I did not seem to recognize HIM. This now raises questions in Geilv's mind of what they were actually doing out there on his behalf."

"Yikes! Well, we should bring these two sides together somehow. That'll fix things up nicely."

"Indeed! And he now considers himself a criminal for these actions and is worried over the repercussions of what course they might take with Sigil."

"Oops! Well, if any of these statements on that ship filter up to him, hopefully that one about the active mode will hold enough value to keep it quiet. But if he's thinking of going against the Marshal for his criminal actions, we need to make our move first."

"Yes, we do, but so far it is problematic to decide how to go about this without endangering him in the Marshal's eyes as someone going against his will."

"Cu'Nar's pity, that's a bad place to be. Well, as for that ship, I would recommend assigning a few of my people to watch things. I repeated some portions of this message with several others throughout the ship, just to make sure it got spread around, in case these people don't like to make casual gossip. Although, that Med-tech commented on my final statement about inspiring people, and he seemed to like it. He even complemented me. So, I simply returned that I came from a family of scientific interest whose job it is to do so."

"Boom!" Kailen mumbles. "There you go, baby sister."

"I'm fairly certain they're all under the passive mode of the chips, and this allowed them to interrogate the situation, maybe even to wonder about the reasons for these actions. But to ensure it stays under control, we need people on the inside."

"Agreed, see to it," Thaelyn affirms. "Try to maintain a level of containment to just these ships. We will work on the rest separately. We should also place additional focus on Geilv and how he behaves when that survey result comes in."

In the Bahlaie Research Center, Petrith was in consultation with Chief Technician Lapäli about some of his recent work inside Central Command and their future plans for the media network.

"So far," he explains. "I've released a number of incremental software patches to reconfigure their security system. I'm actually installing some of the same types of algorithms we used in ours, like those we had on Ruuki uy'Daan."

"Like the one you hacked into once upon a time?" she grins.

"Well, um..." he chuckles. "Yeah, but it would seem ours were more progressive. These people must feel very comfortable in their position of authority. I guess after so long under those Suppressor chips, no one has any ambition to do anything nasty. So, they lost all interest in securing themselves on any level beyond the basics because it doesn't seem necessary for them to bother. There's no one offering any kind of real threat."

"Yet... So, what does this actually mean? Because at this point it sounds more like you're helping them."

"In a way, I suppose I am. But ultimately, it belongs to the military, not Darumon. He's going to find his terminal doing strange things soon," he snickers. "Also, I need these protocols because we're planning on interfacing with the media streams one day, and we all know how the Marshal likes to play his little propaganda campaigns. So, we're just providing a few interfaces to ensure things go the way he would otherwise want them to…sort of."

"Sort of…" she sighs. "And this is where I come in, I suppose, to help design some of these interfaces."

They begin reviewing a series of design specs Petrith brought with him on the existing network protocols and server configurations.

"All right, if you or Kaliya can bring back any examples of their interface kits, we'll take a look at it. We'll need these inside their media networks, as well as routers in their military servers, so we can imitate these press releases they tend to make."

"And I'm also thinking of a covert interface inside Lieutenant Ti'van's new security agency. She needs access to this information without anyone being able to track her. We also need the ability to funnel our data back here."

"And how do you plan on doing that?"

"With a mini version of the Harvester… We want to see if we can import a unit into the basement of her office building. This will give us the ability to use our magic in that place, and some of our native technology, like the shard-coms. Then, we just link their native data networks to a secure server in her office, and she can send vid-mails and other stuff to us directly."

"You don't ask for much, do you…" she grins. "But you do have a point. We have the designs in a prototype stage. We still need to refine it, and the Professor is working on the storage units, trying to optimize them for size and efficiency. But these systems are power hungry. How much power delivery do you have over there? Or maybe it would be better to simply install a mini fusion reactor as well," she giggles.

"I don't know, but we'll work on it and see what we can accomplish. I doubt they have the space for a reactor, so what if we used several rows of those fuel cells linked in series?"

"Maybe. I'll check and see how much we can get out of it for a small Harvester unit."

The Chief glances over the plans they were studying together and ponders the future direction of these projects.

"Petrith, I don't know where you're going with all this, but in the end, you'll be a hacker spy of the worst kind."

"I'm actually thinking of making a profession in software security systems."

"Really! Well, that would certainly be a productive use of your talents. And speaking of talents and our new technology, I need Kaliya to make a visit to help me test a few prototype weapons we're putting together."

"What kind are those? As if she needs another one to play with. Have you seen that vicious blade thing she carries?"

"Yes, I did. It's enough to scare me into submission just looking at it. No, these are rifles, based on the pulse plasma design, but also incorporating a stun weapon and an EMP disruptor."

"An EMP...what do you plan on hitting with that?"

"That one and the plasma blaster will ultimately translate into designs to be used on the combat vessels. But we need to get the mechanics of it working first, and for this we need someone of sufficient proficiency in mage craft to operate them, which means Kaliya so far."

"What Circle do you need for it?"

"The current designs require a Seventh Circle proficiency level."

"That'll keep it out of a lot of hands, I think."

"Well, they are military, and designed only for our people, not the enemy."

"I doubt the enemy would know what to do with it even if they did get their hands on one, unless they also knew how to wield magic."

"It may be possible that one day we could run into something like that," the Chief infers. "Not here with the Suuden-Aryku, but in case we should ever go forward with future explorations and discover something. That's why we're putting in some security."

"Security? What kind?"

"This actually falls in line with your profession. Each weapon will be coded to one primary user. If anyone else gets their hands on it, it'll lock up tight."

"Nice, unless you have someone like me who gets a thrill out of breaking locks," he laughs.

"Don't even think about it, Mister Girhani," she jeers.

<hr>

The streets of Sigil, which normally would be a bustle of casual activity, were being punctuated by the occasional shouts and cries of citizens sighting Suuden-Aryku intruders. The occurrences were happening all over the city, no longer in a few isolated locations.

The Suuden-Aryku scouting patrols were making short appearances from any sewer exit they could find, mapping more of the underground labyrinth, and on occasion, cutting holes between segments if no direct paths were found. The outside of Sigil now had several entry points being cut into it to gain greater access from multiple directions.

Two new ships had been brought in, frigates in this case, to join the cruiser as an escort. They supplied additional troops and support equipment for the extended effort.

Kaliya had shared her memory image of the outside of Sigil to allow other members of her team to follow her and begin interacting with the ship crews, trying to raise awareness of the past actions of the military and the fault of the chips in the hands of one who might not be following the rules. Furthermore, to explain the illegality of violating what had to be private property, despite the Marshal's claims. And also how the Marshal was leading them to places and into deeds without adequate explanation, which under these conditions might be warranted by now.

Onboard each of the ships, members of her team had infiltrated their crew complement and were passing new gossip and rumors of worlds being destroyed and civilizations bombed into extinction. The images were derived from Commander Kriv'tik's experiences, as well as generalizations of Morndindor and Therinë, but without mentioning names.

These were building on the original suggestions Kaliya gave during her first visit, and her scandalous suggestions. They were intended to supplement the idea that their fight against these insurgents is not meeting up to the expectations of who or what these insurgents ought to be, especially if to consider where they are now and what relevance it might have for a society that might make this place their natural home. But the statements were tempered that if to argue, they might find themselves placed under the active mode of the chip simply to enforce their compliance.

Kaliya also reported back to the dabuses inside Sigil to relay a message that efforts were underway to redirect the Suuden-Aryku, and to offer restraint in future responses, despite the tactics being used by the soldiers.

"If the Lady can hold back from dispatching any more of their teams," she notes to a meeting in the WIC building. "We could save lives while I work on those crewmembers."

"But..." Thaelyn advises. "We are assuming they do not come too close to the portal rift in the meantime."

"Right. I met with Cardinal Nemelle up there, Aelwyn's friend from the Guild of Sensations. I paired up with her to act as an interpreter to help me communicate. Our instructions are that the Lady will monitor the situation from her personal chambers, and only respond if the situation demands it."

"Excellent. And it would seem you are forming a few meaningful connections along the way. Nicely done. And perhaps this will offer us a small reprieve. Then, we simply need to find a way to disarm the situation with those ships altogether."

"Yeah. We're working it through, and so far, it's looking good. I've been in consultation with the ship's captain as an advisor, and he's putting in some extra time on that survey report, hoping to verify whether or not these people might actually represent a valid target relating to these opponents the Marshal speaks of. So far, however, the results aren't looking good for it," she smiles. "We may have them concluding before long that this is a false report."

"And then what? What sort of reaction do you think they will have?"

"Our aim is to have them rebel against these orders, claiming the Marshal may have made either an error in his interpretation of who owns this thing, or that he's targeting yet another innocent population for whatever reason. Either way, I need to be present to nail it home to ensure we get our results while keeping it under control."

"You are turning out to be quite the gifted young officer, Kaliya," he nods. "Either that, or a devious little rabblerouser with a penchant for corruptive mischief," he chuckles. "But you are also causing me to ask myself if we should modify your last merit badge to include pips denoting a rank ascension."

"Oh dear cu'Nar, please!" she moans and shakes her head feebly.

"And now, on the other side, we have Geilv and his concerns."

"Yeah, he seems to be waiting on this report before taking any new action. But he seems hesitant to do anything at all, by this time. We also have the ARC, and if that prophecy holds any relevance, it must carry an important role, so Ayene is making another trip out there today..."

✦✦✦

In the city of Capitol Prime, Ayene was making another visit to the research center after a week of absence. She needed to spread these out so as not to appear too hasty in her approach. Besides, Azina was a working girl, and Ayene didn't want to occupy too much of her time, thereby potentially causing trouble with her employer. She also needed to give the appearance of having her own work to do.

"Is Intern Nur'ten available?" she asks as she approaches the front desk in the lab department.

"I will call her for you," responds the desk clerk. "One moment..."

The clerk engages her intercom to call Azina forward. A moment later, the girl arrives. When she sees Ayene standing there, she felt a quiet sense of elation to meet her friend again, but she had to temper it with an outward façade of coolness until they could find a private room to talk.

The two of them moved away to a meeting room which was currently unoccupied, where they sat down for a friendly little chat.

"All right you!" Azina blasts. "You left me tied up in knots that last time! I hope you can help settle some of it now."

"Wow, Azina, are you having another of those mood swings?"

"I've been pulling my horns out ever since your last visit. According to you, Central is subject to these chips, which are subject to the Marshal whenever he might have an interest in using them. Even the High Commander, the one who is supposed to be in charge, but if he's got one on active, this just makes him a servant under someone else, and it doesn't look like the Council, in this case."

"All right, and did you try checking the DataNet like I asked?"

"Yes, I did a little research on it to look up those reports you mentioned. I found the part of the last time the Council was ever seen in public, the elections that never changed anything, and the families all behind some kind of military security protocol, but it wouldn't let me see it on my terminal."

"You need to access it from Central Command directly to unlock that one."

"That's what I thought, but this is a serious situation if the Council is actually missing. What did you find when you went inside the Grand Hall? I'm assuming you DID go in there..." she glares sternly at Ayene.

"Fair enough... I'll tell you what I didn't find, and it's what was supposed to be in there all this time."

"Meaning they're gone. So the question is, where are they?"

"Did you share any of this with the Director?"

"Yeah, we had a nice little talk, and he's just as upset. But Ayene, he reminded me that we're supposed to be scientists here, so we don't want to go around with a lot of crazy ideas without having some evidence in our hands to support them. The Council could still be out there, just not where they're supposed to be, and the rest could have other answers…not nice ones, but still…"

"All right, one could argue this," she relents. "Although it still represents a conspiracy of a sort, as we were never told about any of it."

"You're right, of course. And then there were those regulators you say you arrested, as well as the Internal Secretary. I didn't find any mention of this on the DataNet, or anywhere else in the media. Was it published at all?"

"No, this represents a sensation we don't want to let out yet, the same as what we found inside the Grand Hall. If there is a larger force at work here, we don't want to make waves that could turn against us with that military controlled by your chips."

"Oh wonderful! Ayene, that just means we created a monster and now it's haunting us. But what about you? If you're military, who do you actually work for if you're working AGAINST the Marshal at this point? You mentioned researching those families with such like tax returns and other government level documentation. But according to my research, you would need a government level passcode to access that information. So, this naturally raises the question of who you really are. If you're only a Lieutenant in the military, Ghantil and I have doubts you would hold this level of access."

"Did you give him my name during this time?"

"No, only that you were military, and the rank as a reference."

"All right, this is reasonable. And thank you for being discreet. I suppose this is a valid question, but my position is very sensitive right now. So, for the moment, I have to decline to answer that. Instead, maybe we could change the subject to something softer this time."

"Something softer…like what?"

"We speak of wild theories and conspiracies, and you, as a scientist, prefer to have evidence in your hands to prove this or that. But unfortunately, in a well-played conspiracy, you might not find it unless someone makes a serious mistake to reveal something critical. I suppose it could also follow that after a long time playing it out, a build-up of smaller details might begin to surface. But unless you're looking very closely at it, you might miss it…perhaps, for instance, if your horns have begun to sag so low that you no longer bother to ask questions."

"Uh oh…here we go again. What did we miss this time?"

"Let's carry ourselves back to the beginning. When Darumon and Sargeras first arrived, they made promises of sharing this great wisdom in trade for our service to aid in their fight against those who stole away his possessions and position of power. Do you remember this?"

"Yes, I know the story, but is that the real story? I can't even be sure if I should trust this much anymore, even though this was the original story from way back."

"This much I think you can depend on for what they said. But the events that followed are what are coming into question. You know about the Council, you know about the military where these chips are concerned and the potential they carry, and you know about the media. Now, let's move forward."

"Speaking of those chips, I did a little research on them."

"Oh? What kind?"

"I suppose it goes without saying, we're the ones who originally invented them, with the Marshal's help of course. Ghantil suggested I look for any old records relating to the justification for those chips, since they were originally a controversial product."

"That doesn't surprise me. So, what did you find?"

"The authority chips came about when the Marshal started calling for our enhanced military. This was supposed to help us fight against these insurgents that were now making advances on us. I actually found an old publication to justify the research. Can you believe it? Someone stuck it away in a clipboard file, along with some of the rebuttals, and finally the decision to classify the research so people would stop arguing about it."

"Really!" she chuckles ironically. "So, I guess someone still had their horns turned the right way."

"Yeah. The report said the Marshal claimed we don't apparently know how to fight true wars, being such a…sophisticated and well-cultured…society of scientists and scholars. Therefore, we needed a boost to our effectiveness, and this called for the chip to be applied as a training aid. Can you believe that! A training aid!"

"That's a good one, I'll admit. It makes me wonder why we still need this training aid after ten millennia of fighting so many insurgents so successfully."

"Yeah," she giggles. "It must've worked wonders on all those dull-horned recruits of scientists and scholars."

"Amazing…" she shakes her head. "But this reminds me of a colleague of mine and the troubles she is having with that same military that STILL doesn't seem to know how to fight a true war."

"How do you mean?"

"She's working another investigation, and so far, the military servicemen she has been interviewing seem to believe all you need to do is stand on the street and fire a pulse rifle, and ba-bam, your enemy falls flat on their tails while you take no hits whatsoever. Our superior tech is so overwhelmingly potent, we are invincible to anything, even a simple knife stuck in our bellies. And this has nothing to do with the seeds so far, and whatever washroom accident we might take that could kill us."

"Oops! Then I guess those training aids need improvement."

"Oh, please, as if they were not bad enough," she chuckles.

"Right, so Ayene, what's going on here? What was this other part you say we apparently missed out on?"

"First, I will take it apart to examine the pieces, and then reassemble them in a new way. I'll leave it to you, the scientist, to come to your own conclusions, rather than try filling your head with more conspiracy theories."

"All right, I'm listening."

"Just like you have this Project that's trying to discover something new on the Tav'ageen Anomaly, it stands to reason there are other things out there that should come into question over the course of this long period of time. Let's go back ten millennia. The Marshal comes in and tells us his story. The first thing he does is realize we have this terrible thing we're calling the Tav'ageen Anomaly, so naturally he offers to help."

"And this ultimately results in the chips."

"Ultimately, yes, but not immediately. First it resulted in the seeds. His initial response was this need to evacuate our home to find any and all new worlds to colonize, and use the seeds as a means to enable this, at least in the beginning, due to the panic that was occurring about the Anomaly."

"Right, and here is your earlier statement about all our old tech we forgot about, and how his alien mind should've given us the chips first, if this was really the solution to it."

"Good. So, the sequence goes as the seeds, the insurgents, the military and their chips, and then the Suppressor chips to finalize a solution for the Anomaly, at least until something opened up for us."

"Yes, so far, I'm with you. And we also have this pollution along the way from that dirty industry."

"Right. Now, one could say if these Suppressor chips are so effective, we technically don't need to fear the Anomaly, and therefore, we don't need to run away from our native home. We could just stay right here. You said it yourself; this Project is hoping to understand if the cause is still present, or if it simply died off after a while. So, why are we still using the seeds?"

"I know I said this before. This is where we have this pollution, meaning we effectively did this to ourselves."

"Yes, we did, but was it necessary?"

"And again, here is your statement about the rush job for the military, therefore the industry. And this naturally leads to the question of why no one remembered the eco-friendly stuff to replace it after a while."

"Good, you remember. We need to bring this into conversation again for our reference. We poisoned our home for him, and no one apparently thought about the repercussions of it, perhaps because no one cared enough about it, especially if we were supposed to be evacuating anyway. I could even quote another legal infraction relating to this: Article Twenty-Three, the Environmental Preservation Act of 6210. It makes all that stuff illegal to have at all. Those industries should either be shut down, or forced to upgrade to cleaner tech, along with fines and punishment for the damage already done. And who do you think ordered it in the first place? And then, why didn't they review it after the initial emergency was over?"

"Wow, that's bad."

"So here we are, still at home, with no REAL need to vacate, and using these seeds to survive in a place that doesn't need to be so polluted. Now let's talk about the Tav'ageen Anomaly for a moment."

"The Anomaly?" Azina muses keenly. "Do you people actually have something on this?"

"I have a few very curious points to share. First is to ask why we are listening to an alien being that is described as a military advisor, but giving out medical advice. What does he actually know about anything where OUR species is concerned, medically speaking?"

"Um…"

Azina frowns sternly at the ludicrous suggestion. On the surface, it simply doesn't make sense that someone of this job description would qualify for anything else. And worse being alien to this world.

"Could it be he has some kind of degree in medicine from somewhere?" she asks timidly.

"All right, let's consider this briefly. We'll say he holds some special degree in, say, exobiology, which at this point is the only thing I can suggest for him, unless we say he spent a long time in one of our native medical schools."

"Yeah, right, and I think I can see where this is going already. This still wouldn't necessarily qualify him. So, what if he simply worked alongside a team of our own people and offered whatever knowledge he did have?"

"This might be the only remaining solution for us. But next, we have to ask this question. Our own science has never been able to identify it, but the Marshal, with all his great…military…wisdom offering his aid to our medical research, was able to figure it out, even though he didn't apparently help US understand the discovery hardly at all."

"Yeah, and this is one of the controversies the Director has always been upset over."

"Yeah, you speak about evidence," she chuckles. "And this makes us ask about his first official reaction to the Tav'ageen Anomaly. If he came here to help us overcome our native troubles so we could help him with his, even to offer us something he called his great wisdom, his first reaction to seeing the Anomaly was to say: RUN! It's an alien!" she waves her hands theatrically.

Azina couldn't help but burst into laughter at the display. Although the cause wasn't necessarily a humorous situation, the presentation was hilarious.

"Yeah, all right, that is a little ridiculous for someone who is supposed to be in possession of great wisdom, military or otherwise."

"Then, as the result, he helps us design, or maybe I should say redesign those seeds, since they were originally an old tech that was brought back into play."

"Right, and this is another issue Ghantil is unhappy about. He apparently wanted us off this planet for some reason. Even to the point that he rushed these seeds at us, when a more reasonable solution was possible."

"Hmm, this is how he sees it?" Ayene considers. "Interesting. But then, we have these insurgents. He develops our military, including the chips, and essentially takes us to war. So, given the technological design of those things, I suppose we have to give him, and whoever worked alongside him, the credit for their advanced design. This follows with the Suppressor chips, which at this point is more of an afterthought, since NOW we find ourselves forced to stay at home. So, why did he want us to leave in the first place? He forced us to use these seeds as part of the plan, then later gave us the chips, but forgot to tell us to STOP using the seeds, as the chips effectively removed the imperative threat of the Anomaly, so now we can take our time with it. And this doesn't cover the industry and its pollution yet."

"Not yet? Why not yet? I mean, sure, we should've converted to an eco-friendlier tech somewhere along the way, but..."

"Yeah. This alien being from a superior technological society tells us to use the dirtiest tech we have on record as a rush job to build our military. But after ten millennia of fruitless efforts to clear the path, he neglects to remind us of our own superior tech to clean it up."

"Uh oh…HE forgot to remind us…the one who pushed it on us to begin with. We're not speaking of the Council here. And this represents another of those dull-horned things we apparently missed. I'm really starting to hate this. What have we become, Ayene? A rush job is one thing. Ten millennia of not cleaning it up with our native eco-friendly tech is another. But to have HIM not remind us, is a bit naughty on his part."

"And this is someone we're supposed to be expecting the secrets of the universe from."

"Yeah!" she snaps. "Now that's not a nice thing for him to do to us. And he essentially forced us to keep these seeds as the result."

"And filled us with so many stories of how…any day now…we'll fulfill our purpose. So, it just continues along with fables, but no results."

Azina frowned at the idea, but by this time it made sense. They were being led along without a final destination.

Ayene continues, "Now, there is a direction to this, if you're clever enough to see it, and evacuating the planet wasn't it. Let's continue for a moment. Now we have the Suppressor chips, and things settle for us here at home, but we still have those insurgents out there. I find it interesting you did that research on those military chips, too. So, let's involve that."

"Oh dear…all right, what do you think about this?"

"We're not a military society. I think it's just not in our blood. We can train for it, I suppose, but it's not a primal instinct for us. Just like I said about my associate, our people have no idea what fighting is actually about. If we were to place our people face-to-face with real combatants…veterans who make it a living to fight…we wouldn't last long enough to realize how easy it is to die."

"Especially if you factor in those seeds."

"Oh yes, if our enemy were to learn of this…" she rolls her eyes. "This could be the reason he invented those chips as what he calls training aids. But let's give our people the benefit of a doubt for a moment. After a while, people can learn almost anything. Therefore, do we actually still need those chips after ten millennia of combat experience? I might be willing to accept it in the very beginning, but not after some period of time when we got some real experience in it."

"Right, I think I might agree."

"Especially if you consider such people as the HC... He's been using this since the early days, and I'm fairly sure he was a veteran soldier even before that. We may not have had any wars, but he was serving long enough to know a few things. Then, why is he on active so often, even now?"

"That doesn't make any sense. Not to me, and I doubt it would make sense to anyone else, especially inside the military."

"He's not on the front lines. He spends most of his time in his office, as far as I know. So, it doesn't make sense he should even need it. But ALL our military is using them. And it doesn't seem to hold any relation to training. Half of them don't even go out on missions, so why do they need them in the first place. As for the rest, well, I think ten millennia of warfare should teach us how to train by more conventional means. This brings us back to the question of why we still have them. But we know the Marshal uses them on any occasion where he wants our people to go out there and do something, regardless of how many times they've been out there previously."

"This sounds like what you were talking about last time. He just wants them to go out and do something without arguing it."

"And you would be surprised at what he's actually doing with them. But this is another story so far. Let me continue with this one for now."

"Wow, Ayene, you're starting to scare me."

"We'll turn back to the beginning again, now focusing on these insurgents. According to our records, we've been very successful at holding them back, with or without these training aids. Our military files tell us most of our battles were very clean and efficient. There were apparently some that cost us, but ultimately, we won every battle."

"Really! So I guess those training aids really did help after all!" she giggles.

"So it would seem, but there is a catch here. Again, we're not naturally militaristic. Training aids or not, we don't conduct warfare as a natural habit. The whole idea of it just doesn't appeal to our senses. And here we are going up against his insurgents for an extended period of time doing something we're not made to do naturally. And we're winning?"

Azina gazed at Ayene perplexedly for the suggestion.

"Could it be his superior military wisdom playing a role for us?"

"All right, let's say he gave us a little of that. He did apparently help us build up a big military. He is also said to come from a superior society with superior technology. And if they were so successful at ousting Sargeras, they must apparently hold some superior military prowess to overcome whatever he had previously that kept him in power. And again…we're winning against that?"

"Uh oh…this is showing up a problem."

"Ten millennia and no losses on our side…" Ayene muses. "Wow, those training aids must be simply miraculous!" she grins.

"Yeah. So, how do you figure this? Because I think you're teasing me now."

"Either they're not so superior, or not so militaristically proficient. In either case, they don't stand up to the descriptions the Marshal gave us. And we need training aids to fight that? How unfortunate for our side that we're so inept, we can't swat a bug without hurting ourselves."

"But Ayene, um…" she flusters. "First, let's try to analyze. Like Ghantil said, we're supposed to be scientists, right? So, let's see if we can find a reasonable answer to this."

"All right, we'll start again at ten millennia ago. He comes here, and the first thing he does is tell us to run away from something no one can identify, but it's apparently killing our people and causing a panic. He tells us to use the world's least desirable tech as a tool for our survival in places we might not otherwise want to live, all because this thing no one can identify is nesting in our native home and we can't get rid of it. But oh no, here come the insurgents. Now we're stuck here."

"Um, are you actually trying to analyze, or simply rehashing?"

"Wait till I finish. Now he builds up our military to fight all these awful insurgents, where our militarily inept society can never lose a fight against a superior force. He demands we use mind-altering chips to program our people to kill on sight with no questions asked. It doesn't technically matter who we point our guns at. With the chips turned on, we're shooting them anyway."

"Uh oh…" she moans.

"This story persists, and for no logical reason, as we, who are NOT military minded enough to know the difference, are winning battles we should not otherwise win."

"Oops!"

"Then, he gives us the Suppressor chips, and everything quiets down at home. But we're never told to abandon the seeds, and his dirty industry simply reinforces the idea on us. He conveniently forgets to remind us of our own technologically advanced eco-friendly tech, and stupid us, we stop asking questions at about this time. And coincidentally, he also forbids us to research a countermeasure to the seeds. Do you see a picture developing here, Azina?"

"Huh? Wait! Dammit, yes…those seeds! Now I'm starting to see something. He pushed them at us for some kind of reason. We're told to leave home for this emergency, using the seeds as our escape ticket. But then, suddenly, we CANNOT leave home, meaning we're now stuck here, WITH his dirty industry, and WITH his seeds to cover for it!"

"There you go," Ayene smiles. "We have more than enough tech to build in just about any environment we might choose to inhabit, including space. Why do I need this bug on my back to live somewhere that will probably involve a sealed habitation module anyway? Like I said before, am I supposed to run tail-naked in the grass and live in trees?"

"Right! I'm sorry, Ayene. Dull-horned is right. In all the nether-space, we really did sink low, didn't we!"

"And here is the clincher. It was the first thing this alien lifeform ordered us to use because of another alien lifeform he claimed was infesting our world."

Azina gawked at Ayene for the suggestion. Her voice left her, and she simply wheezed unintelligibly.

"As for these insurgents," Ayene continues. "If they really are his former people, we should be dead by now. Why would they waste their time trying to occupy some far distant world as a military outpost if they could jump right on top of us and blast us out of existence? That is, of course, if they really wanted HIM out of the picture. But each of those battles took place somewhere else…lots of them. Where exactly are these people coming from, and why do they apparently own so many locations? We have just one world to ourselves, and we can't even get away to colonize a simple moon."

"Wow…"

"And in ten millennia, they have neither won a battle, nor taken the hint and left us alone. They're simply…out there…and we're always being called to battle for something…and NEVER allowed to leave home for anything else."

Azina gaped at the list of accusations. She closed her eyes and shook her head morosely.

"Furthermore," Ayene adds. "This also defies the notion of them overthrowing any sort of leader and keeping it that way if the Marshal had to come all the way over here to find help from non-militants to take his fight back to those people who are worse fighters than we are."

"Now there's a paradox!"

"And therefore the question, what are we REALLY doing out there if those insurgents are so impotent. Further, that we need training aids, even after ten millennia of persistent successes. By the sound of it, my great grandmother could fight them from a hospital bed," she laughs.

Azina shares the moment with a hearty chuckle, but soon returns to the discussion.

"All right, so what I'm getting out of this is these insurgents don't meet up to our expectations of a dangerous enemy, not when compared to what the Marshal told us about them. Also, he apparently forced these seeds at us for some reason, claiming it to be his first and foremost answer to this awful alien infestation we were panicking over."

"This is a good start."

"Then came the Suppressor chips to settle the panic, but the seeds were still in production, and those insurgents were making trouble for us, so we couldn't fulfill the promise of moving off-world. But no one bothered to tell us to forget the idea, so we're still applying the seeds until the pollution levels got so bad, it was no longer a simple issue of preparing to move off-world. We needed them here now."

"Good, Azina."

"And all of us were made to think this was the plan, even after ten millennia of waiting. In all the nether-space, Ayene, suddenly I don't like the sound of that number."

"Neither do I, and until recently, I was a part of it, just like you. Then, I had my eyes opened to it, and I'm thoroughly disgusted by the notion. But my education included a number of additional pieces, and the picture gets even worse. We know what the Tav'ageen Anomaly is. We know what these seeds do. And we know who the Marshal is in reality. And none of this is what HE told us."

"Oh wow…and are you actually going to tell me, or are you going to play more games on me?"

"I'm not here to play games on you, Azina. I'm looking for allies."

"Allies! But I'm a medical intern, not a soldier!"

"First, you're a citizen of this world, and whatever happens in this world is as much your concern as it is a soldier's, regardless of your occupation. You have one of those seeds stuck to your back no less than any other."

"All right, you got me."

"Next, and perhaps more importantly, you're someone who is known to have worked on his death toys, Azina. That's what those things were that you invented for him. I know precisely what they were used for, and trust me, you wouldn't like it."

"Death toys..." she grimaces.

"This is what we call them back home. I learned of them from people who discovered when, where, and how he used them, but not any of OUR people, because ours might actually hold objection to it. And this makes you an accessory. He used them in a weaponized form. Technically speaking, we need to shut this down. Therefore, we need people inside this building, and you very conveniently made yourself apparent to me on that first day."

"But I thought you asked me to be your friend," she frowns.

"I did, and I mean it. But friend, or ally, it's all the same. We are fighting a common enemy, you for your reason, me for mine. But I'm a soldier in a fight for the survival of our world. That means my friends, whoever, whatever, and wherever they are, must be made soldiers right alongside me. The fact that you mentioned this Project of yours only added to the flavor of it, as you're clearly opposing the Council with your own little play of intrigue."

"So, you're not actually a part of it? But I thought you said..."

"No, Azina, I didn't specifically say I was, but I'll admit I did play a little game to get more information. If you're doing something we could find useful, I needed to know. Sorry, but it was necessary."

"Well, you could've told me earlier."

"I had to test you first. There are too many dull-horns in this world. Trying to educate them is a job in itself," she chuckles. "But my job is very sensitive. The Marshal has a full naval fleet of people he could order to blast us down here with the flip of a switch. And if he doesn't like how we seem to be behaving, he could do just that."

This sent Azina nearly into shock. Her gaze went completely blank, and she sat there motionless for many moments until she could regain her composure.

"How we behave..." she gulps.

She pauses to glance towards the door and a window looking out into the hallway, but their conversation was private and not attracting any outside interest.

"All right, Ayene," she murmurs softly. "I need to ask you a few questions, and I'll ask you to give me some kind of answer before I lose my horns. Who are you and who do you work for? Because I don't think it's the military, and it sure isn't the Marshal, at this point."

With this, Ayene pulls out her trans-com and once again brings up her ID badge. She flashes it at the girl.

"Azgarén Central Intelligence... And before you ask what it is, we're a top-level security agency focusing on internal security and planetary defense against all forms of conspiracy, espionage, corruption, and terrorism. We're a new agency with the authority to arrest anyone we point a finger at, including the Council. But in the absence of a Council, it's the Marshal. However, we can't take action against him until the military is disarmed. And this is what we're doing right now, trying to disarm all the little games he installed while our dull-horned society had its back turned."

"So, this bit about great wisdom was a lie, I guess."

"His kind doesn't give gifts, Azina. We're better described as minions, not anything his kind holds with high enough esteem to offer anything of benefit. We serve him, not the other way."

"Then who is he?"

"Before we go any deeper, I would like to bring your Director into it. As the administrator of this facility, we need his cooperation in our battle against Darumon. You have been supplying him with a lot of toys. It's time to put an end to this. This includes not only those special inventions, but the chips, as well as these seeds."

"Oops... Um, just for the sake of asking, how do you mean that? You mentioned shutting us down."

"I don't mean this in the context of bringing your fabulous business enterprise down. Rather, it's what you're doing for HIM. As far as Darumon is concerned, it's all business as usual. If he tells you to do something, you simply reply, 'Yes Marshal, anything you say, Marshal.' Then you come to me for the real instructions."

"This sounds very serious, but it also makes me ask if you can actually hold this level of authority. Not that I want to get in trouble for asking, but I think I should."

"I understand, Azina. So far, we have C.P. Security on our side. Therefore, we have the legal authority to take action for as long as we can provide our evidence to justify the cause. We're conducting a lot of investigations right now, so we're still collecting a lot of our own evidence, as well as people along the way."

"All right. But what about the military, and the HC if he's on active?"

"We're working several projects at once right now, and he's one of them, but it has to be very discreet since he's directly under the thumb of the Marshal. As for everything else, we need to stall for time."

"Why is that?"

"For the REAL insurgents to arrive, Azina. He and Sargeras are in hiding from some ancient enemies, not former loyalists. So, if you really want to see authority, it's a foreign military body Darumon started a war with recently, along with beings that might seem godlike as compared to us, coming to finish a job that began an eternity ago."

"Oh dear…"

"The two of them are all that remains of their former society. The rest were destroyed long ago for a variety of crimes. These two hid during this time, but Darumon was recently discovered trying to make a sneak revenge attack. Now they're coming for him. Meanwhile, my department is in contact with them. A military body is assembling right now and making plans for a covert operation. But he and Sargeras are considered a flight risk. So they have to do to him as he did to so many others, sneak up and hit him from behind."

"Wow. All right, so what do you want me to do right now?"

<hr>

"Ghantil?" Azina calls tenuously through the door. "I need to talk to you about something very important."

Azina had finished her conversation with Ayene, and the two of them parted ways to give the beleaguered girl a moment of rest and time to speak to the Director.

"Yes, Azina," he answers as he looks up at her from his desk. "You seem very distressed, are you alright?"

"Far from it, Ghantil, and I need your help on something very serious."

She sits down on the other side of his desk and leans over for a close private chat.

"Ghantil," she begins. "I've been given instructions to talk to you. We need to make an appointment for a meeting with a…um… very determined government level security officer."

The Director perked up instantly at the suggestion.

"When you say government level security…what do you mean, Azina? Did something bad happen?"

"Easy does it, Ghantil, it's not about the Project…well, not really."

"Azina, saying not really isn't the same as saying it's not. Who is this person and why are they here?"

"Um, maybe I should approach it softly. Will you let me?"

"Azina…" he moans. "All right, if you think it's best."

"This relates to that military officer I spoke of last time. You remember her? All those things we were talking about with the Council, the media, and so on."

"Right. So, is this person the same one?"

"Yes, she's apparently an officer in a top-secret security agency that seems to rise above just about everything else, including the Council. And her horns are twisted up real tight right now."

"About what? And how does this relate to the Project."

"Technically, she doesn't care about the Project, other than to say, we're peeved about the Council NOT allowing us to research something, so we're doing it anyway," she giggles softly.

"Uh…how am I supposed to interpret that statement?"

"We're rebellious. But in a good way."

"I can't very easily see how being rebellious is good."

"It's to say, the Council doesn't tell us to solve problems, because these problems are something they don't want people sticking their horns into to solve. THAT is how you describe being rebellious as good. They're corrupt. They WANT us to have those problems, not solve them."

"Oh! Is that what it is," he huffs. "Well, in that case…"

"Aside from that, she regards the Council to be operating illegally on multiple counts. As for the Anomaly, she seems to know something about it. Therefore, whatever WE are doing, it's probably moot."

"That's…very interesting. All right, so why is she here?"

"I just finished a long and very difficult debate with her, so let me try to summarize it. We started talking about things like the seeds and the chips, and the Tav'ageen Anomaly. We also spoke of the Marshal, this long ten millennia fight against his insurgents, and a few other things."

"All right, so where do we begin? And how does this actually relate to a security officer or the Project…or anything else for that matter?"

"Let me carry this through sequentially, and then you'll see it. Let's talk about the seeds. I'll preface this with your statements of how the Marshal seemed to want us off this planet. Do you recall this?"

"Yes, I know I've said this many times in the past."

"Good. So, in the beginning, they were supposed to help us leave home to find new worlds, but then the insurgents got in the way and we're still here."

"Right."

"The Suppressor chips were a secondary solution to resolve the panic, and they seemed to work so well that we didn't feel as much pressure to want to leave any more."

"Not as much pressure?"

"The urgency of it, due to the panic frightening us."

"Oh. Well, yes, I suppose you're right."

"But no one told us to stop using the seeds. So the message was, once these insurgents are out of the way, we're going again. Then we have the pollution, and the seeds are needed even here. And even after ten millennia, no one reminded us of all the eco-friendly tech we own to replace the dirty stuff we were using, assuming we're actually going to be staying home long enough for it to matter. Not even the guy who told us to use it in the first place."

"Not even the guy…"

"The Marshal. He pushed it at us and forgot to remind us, after those first few decades or centuries, that we have the means to clean house. So we can blame HIM, not the Council, for the failure. He with all his alien super-genius wisdom."

"Uh oh… I know the pollution has long been one of the things I've argued during this time. But who would ever listen to someone like me?" he chuckles weakly. "The situation was held in a state of flux for so long that people stopped asking about it."

"Yeah, this is a common problem for us. We stopped asking about a lot of things."

"So, is this part of your argument now?"

"I think it has to be," she shrugs. "Ghantil, we missed a bunch of clues piling up on us, and never put them together. Mostly, we look to someone else, like the Council, to take care of things. The way she talks about it, we worship them like a god entity. But they're gone. She said she did go inside, and it was apparently empty."

"Really. But did she offer any arguments as to why, other than this theory of them being lost somewhere?"

"Oh, Ghantil, just you wait until I'm finished. Your horns will be hanging as low as mine soon. So, we have the Anomaly panicking everyone so badly that they take the seeds. Here is where we apparently forgot all the rest of our technology to colonize things like moons, inhospitable worlds, space, and so on, which has nothing to do with the seeds. The panic disregarded all that and took the seeds anyway. Especially as no one ever used it to begin with. We don't have any colonies or anything to teach the people we actually DO have colonization tech. And a simple military outpost doesn't count, as it's not PEOPLE using it. It's military, and probably classified, or at least not as highly advertised."

The Director glared at her for the obvious insinuation. He huffed silently and glanced out the window.

"So, we conveniently take the first thing someone pushes at us as the ONLY way to leave home."

"But in the end," she continues. "These insurgents keep us from leaving, so now we have the chips, and yet we're still taking the seeds. And HERE is the one to kick you in the tail. Those insurgents don't seem to know when to stop. This effectively means, we're pinned down. But the battles are always…out there. Not here in our own backyard. If they really wanted Sargeras out of the picture, they shouldn't be leading us on so many wild chases across the galaxy. Their target is right here in the city," she points out the window.

He reflexively follows her gaze out the window again.

"And so, we're stuck here," she declares. "And at this moment, it needs to suggest we're stuck here NOT because of insurgents who never stop. And NOT because they can't find him to target him directly. Now we need to look at the other side of it. Not only did someone forget to tell us to stop the seeds, but they never once allowed us to research a way to remove them. So, this suggests it was intended as a permanent application, not temporary. Then we have that oh-so-inconvenient pollution out there. Therefore, whatever the reason, it was the SEEDS he wanted us to have, not any promise of leaving home. Everything else is just a story."

The Director gazed at her and frowned, then leaned back in his chair to consider this notion.

"And furthermore," Azina continues. "You ask about my reasoning for dull-horns not asking questions? Yes, ten millennia of children's stories convincing us we're going to leave, just as soon as those insurgents are out of the way. But we're still here, and still taking his seeds, still with that pollution, and STILL listening to those children's stories, despite the fact we don't need any of it."

"In all the nether-space…" he moans. "But why?"

"Apparently, they hold some meaning, and at this moment, I'm guessing it's not the advertised one."

"What?" he shouts. "But why would he even suggest this if it wasn't to leave home and colonize anything?"

"I might instead ask you this, Ghantil. You who likes evidence. When did HE ever give out any? We have here a military man giving out medical advice for an alien…to him…species he should not hold any medical knowledge over…unless we're missing a secret medical school program he attended. He also told us the Anomaly was an alien infestation of something our science could never identify. But

HE is an alien. So, what is alien to him that HE can identify but we can't, unless he put it there."

"In all the nether-space, Azina," he wheezes. "That would probably make more sense than anything else at this moment. And his solutions for it...let's see. He forces these seeds on us for some unknown reason, and then the chips as a more appropriate solution to absolve the panic and find peace from it. So, it was the seeds he actually wanted, and the chips were secondary. Then the Anomaly vanished. And we're prevented from researching anything on our own to further understand or correct it."

"Now you're getting it."

"But Azina, did he put it there, or was it there to begin with and he simply used it as an excuse? This brings me back to our old science faction. Do you recall the stories I told you?"

"Yeah, you said Elder Nazég was coming up with some interesting theories on it, but no one believed him."

"His faction was never very popular with the Council, Azina. And when he left, they further downplayed him to discredit his faction as so much nonsense."

"That probably didn't help matters for anyone trying to further research it to find the answers."

"No it didn't, and thus the Project. And then we have the Marshal. He was especially vocal in declaring him a traitor, and this would even further degrade his integrity. It's no wonder we're not allowed any further research on it. If we did, we might actually learn something and realize the Marshal is the one at fault, not Elder Nazég or anyone else."

"What did he call it again...a Prodigy Gift?"

"Yes, and it was occurring in our society even before the Marshal arrived. So, are we saying he made a secret arrival to invoke this on us to start the Anomaly, then an official arrival to offer his solution, or was it there for some other reason and he simply used our panic to his advantage?"

"That's a good one. And no one was able to understand it, except for this one faction."

"And so convenient, too," he huffs. "Even today, we can't research anything, including any statistical results to learn if it's still out there."

"But Ghantil, this leads me to the next point. Elder Nazég left us. The stories say some huge alien ship arrived and carried him away, along with a lot of others, right?"

"Right, and the Marshal claimed this to be his insurgents, and Elder Nazég joined with them for some reason."

"And here is where my second point comes in. There might not be any insurgents in the first place."

"No? All right, how do you explain this one?"

"Let's first make an assumption. If he's lying about so many other things, let's include this as well. Then, who was in that ship? The thing was said to be huge, so that demands some serious tech and resources to build, right? And all it did was take this one man, along with a large portion of his science faction, away from someone who might be doing something bad to the rest of us. And this one man might be the only one to recognize what it was and identify it for us."

The Director gazed at the girl for a long moment as the association made the connection.

"They were rescuing him…" he muses distantly. "While the rest of us were poisoned with the pollution and disfigured by the seeds. And had he remained, he might pose a threat to whatever ulterior motives the Marshal has, and this might translate to a need to remove him from the equation so the Marshal could have his way unimpeded. Dammit, Azina, that also makes sense, but I have to admit, it's also highly conditional. Can we validate this somehow?"

"Let me finish and you tell me. She said that after living so long under such mundane conditions, people become desensitized and stop asking questions. Not even after so many clues start to build up, which might paint a picture no one pays attention to."

"All right, you have a point. So, in all this time, the clues are out there, but we never tried bringing them together. I might also suggest he's keeping them hidden behind his censorship practices, too."

"Probably. Now let's talk about his insurgents. The Marshal is supposedly from a superior society of superior technology. The whole premise of him offering anything to us would suggest he has something to offer. But what about the rest of his people, the ones he and Sargeras ran away from as part of this alleged insurgency that overthrew him and kicked him out? If we assume for a moment that he had a military or security body serving him and keeping him in power, these others had to be even tougher in order to throw Sargeras out in the first place. How does this sound so far?"

"It makes sense. Well, wait, let me see for a moment. Yes, it could be a hostile body overthrowing a friendly one. But it could also be that same security force turning around on him."

"Yes, you have a point. But now, look at us. You remember what I said about that report I found on the chips, right?"

"You mean the one about training aids?"

"Yeah, here we are, a non-military society that needed training aids to fight in any way, going up against a society of clearly veteran military status and with superior technology on their side, and for ten millennia we won every battle."

Now the Director furrows his brow at the insane concept of this imbalance of power.

"Do we have a viable explanation for this?" he intones cautiously.

"Viable, not really, unless you suggest they're worse at fighting than we are. And then, we're still using those training aid chips even after all these victories. When do you think we'll ever STOP using them, Ghantil? The Marshal seems to like them…a lot."

"All right, just for the sake of argument, why would you put it into such terms?"

"With the flip of a switch, he gets a military that serves on demand without question. It doesn't matter who is on the other side. If he's not pleased about who they are or what they're doing… boom. Including us down here."

"Dammit!" he whispers urgently. "This does indeed represent an ulterior motive. But then, why? What did we ever do to him that he might do this to us? We offered him our help, a sanctuary from his enemies…"

"Ghantil," she asserts. "It's not about that. He lied to us. He's not hiding from former loyalists. He's hiding from a rival faction Sargeras and his kind got into trouble with once. Their entire society was described as criminals, and now they're destroyed, which means these two are sole survivor fugitives. Now he's out for revenge, and using us as a minion species to do his work. This is what that woman told me. And that rival faction recently discovered him, and is now making a covert advance to sneak up on him like he's done to a lot of others."

"Only recently discovered? What about those insurgents we were fighting for ten millennia?"

"I don't know, but he had a programmable military, so the targets could be anything at this point. This could also associate with the criminal aspect if he does this for a living."

"I'm not so sure if I like that suggestion. All right, I need to ask this question, as there is something seriously wrong with this scenario. Why is she HERE and talking to YOU, or even me, if she wants to make a meeting?"

"Oh yes. You'll love this part. Because the Marshal is using US to make what she called death toys, and she wants to shut it down. We became an accessory to weaponizing all our tech. This makes us no less murderers than he appears to be. Is that a good enough reason?"

"Oh no…" he moans and covers his face.

"He controls our military, and he apparently removed our government once all his mandates were in place. Then he replaced it with his agents, and essentially doesn't tell us to do anything unless he wants it for himself, like those inventions we spoke of so often."

"Dammit!" he curses silently. "But how do we fight something like this, especially our own military?"

"I don't know the answer to that, but maybe she does."

"Who is she, by the way? You mentioned military and something else, what was it?"

"Her name is Lieutenant Ayene Ti'van. She once served C.P. Security, and then went full military with some special project for the Marshal…a mining base, of all things. Now she's working as part of a new high-level anti-conspiracy, anti-terrorist security agency called Azgarén Central Intelligence."

"Huh?" he winces. "I never heard of that one."

"She admits it's new, top-secret, and keeping a very low profile due to the Marshal, but apparently working alongside C.P. Security arresting people related to him. She would arrest the Council too if we had one."

"This sounds like a covert operation to me…a very deep one, especially if you consider the aspect of the Marshal and what is essentially HIS military. But while I would not wish to argue, if we're speaking of a new government agency, who authorized it if there's no Council serving us."

"Yeah, that might be a good one to ask. But she flashed a very official-looking badge at me, and I think you need something like security codes to make those, don't you?"

"I don't personally know what you need for it, but I'm of the opinion a lot of things can be falsified if you have the right talent."

"Talent, like a hacker? Hmm…all right, I can't argue this, but wouldn't you also need the incentive to actually WANT to hack something? This would be a criminal thing, wouldn't it?"

"Yes, it would."

"And a criminal thing might be founded in a desire to achieve something…maybe something personal, right?"

"Probably…"

"Like greed, lust, love of power and authority…emotional things, right?" she raises her brow inquisitively.

"Uh huh…and I think I can see your direction here. With these chips installed, who in our society would have that. I am aware, since the application of the Suppressor chips, most of that faded in the early days. All right, wait. Let's check something here…"

The Director turns to his data terminal and pulls up a special app. Azina watches curiously to see what he's doing. She observes him as he enters a password, and the screen displays a new page with the Central Command logo.

"Ghantil, isn't that the military network?" she asks tenderly.

"You didn't see this, Azina. In my position, I've managed to gain a few privileges, and this is one. I have private access to their personnel files. This isn't normally something we should have here."

"It isn't?" she mocks. "Oh wow, what a surprise! So, not only are we performing illegal research on the Tav'ageen Anomaly, but you also have a backdoor to their server!" she chuckles faintly.

He punches in a search for the name, which brings up a military record. He studies it carefully, furrowing his brow as he scans the data.

"All right, Azina, we already have something strange here. You said C.P. Security, and I see this listed here, where she was apparently assigned to administration and city security."

"Yes, she admitted this to me as part of our talks. Then she went full military four centuries ago at this mining base."

"Four centuries?"

"Yeah, the same as these other things we keep talking about… like the Spores. It seems a little too coincidental if you ask me."

"All right, I suppose I can't argue that. But there's no record of that here."

"No? But she told me it was."

"What were they mining, did she say?"

"It was…oh! Wait! I remember something now. She said this mining base was producing something special for the Marshal, and our tech didn't know how to handle it. He didn't give any explanations, just orders to do it, and to send it to a processor. And also, I think she mentioned they were working under the threat of those chips being turned on."

"That might give an explanation, just by itself. He was doing something he didn't want anyone to know about, or even to question. This record might itself be falsified that she was never there…more of his censorship, maybe. But it also says she died some time ago."

"Huh? Let me see that thing…"

Azina leans forward as the Director turns the monitor around. There, she studied the military summary page, which includes a profile photo of Ayene.

"That's her," she points at the picture. "So, whatever this thing says, it's wrong."

"All right, if we involve the covert aspect and being outside the Marshal's military, and now you say she's working with this new security outfit that is essentially opposing him… Azina, this reeks of something. This might suggest something happened at that mining base to expose his operation, and either she, or someone else, falsified her death to remove her from his supervision."

"In all the nether-space, Ghantil," she shudders. "And she has emotion, too. So, whatever happened, they disabled her chip before putting her into this new service."

"That represents a form of defiance against the Marshal and his solutions to the Anomaly, and probably no different from our Project, for this point. It's no wonder she isn't opposed to it. She might actually favor it."

"She said when she discovered me that I apparently showed signs of the chip disabled, like word contractions. It's probably a habit I didn't realize I was playing. But this opened a door for her to investigate, as she wanted to find a way into our operations here anyway. She also said she knows something about the Anomaly, as well as the seeds."

"Really! This is interesting. Then, I can't see any other way around this but to meet with her and hope she can answer some of these questions. If any of this is true, like the military, these so-called death toys, and who knows what else, we can't simply ignore it. But let's hope she can provide a little evidence along the way."

✦✦✦✦✦

"Your Lordship, I have a report," Ayene announces as she arrives back in the WIC building.

"Yes, Lieutenant, what do we have today?"

"I've just returned from my most recent meeting with Azina. We're up to the point where we need to take it higher."

"Good, but exactly what does this involve so far?"

"So far, I've explained these issues in a mostly indirect manner, not involving specific people or places…other than the Marshal, that is. We spoke of the seeds becoming a permanent feature when they were only intended to be temporary to evacuate the planet, and also unnecessary if we have other techs to do the same job. The chips, which were much more effective at stopping the panic, were also a secondary solution given only after we found ourselves stuck at home for all his insurgents, and consequently infected by the seeds. Then these insurgents, a superior form of life, and us, who do not apparently know how to fight at all, are winning every battle. She also pointed out a curious little fact she dug up in their archives."

"Oh? And what was that?"

"You're going to love this one. Those Council-mandated authority override chips were originally justified as training aids for our young military to learn to fight with."

Thaelyn glared at her for the absurd rationalization. He raised his brow and began laughing impulsively.

"Indeed!" he chortles. "That is nearly worthy of a mark on our list, if not for the source. So, why does your military still need these training aids after so many victories?"

"This is a good question, but he sure does like having them."

"Yes, he does, so it seems."

"I finally had to admit who I actually work for, meaning our new ACI, and drop hints that Darumon and Sargeras aren't who they say they are, along with their alleged insurgents…but again without dropping any actual names. I felt I needed her to know these aren't simple conspiracy theories, but rather we know something about them that the rest of the world does not."

"Very well, this is reasonable, I suppose. At some moment, they will need to learn. Where do we stand at this time?"

"I asked her to relay this to her Director and arrange for us to make a meeting. The Marshal has been using them for his death toys, which she didn't seem at all happy about, and we need to shut this down, but quietly."

"Good, then our next encounter will need to cement this together."

"I would like to ask Kaliya to join me as a representative of the real insurgents, and together we'll tell them the story of what's really happening out there."

"Agreed, and then we will see what other opportunities we have in front of us."

"My Lord," Kaliya offers. "This could open up a possibility for us. If we look at this most recent prophecy, she said something about ambitious minds, so we must be using them for something important. We're talking about home-grown scientists with all the evidence we need to explain some of the other prophecies she gave us."

"Yes! You are right. Perhaps this is one valuable example. We can now begin to explore the evidence relating to her earlier prophecies, like your evolution as a species and Darumon's potential influence. Then we could present this to the people once we have the freedom to do so."

"And for this, we'll need to see if the Director has any friends or colleagues in other fields…those who are similarly ambitious to see something new in the world."

"Good, but we still need to keep this under our control. We will need to refer back to that news media of theirs and see how we can present this in such ways as it will not attract Darumon's attention… or at least not any we would wish to avoid."

"If we release anything at all," Ayene muses. "It would need to follow his usual censorship methods, which means it can't be a direct reference. This doesn't give us much room in which to work productively…unless…" she begins forming a curious grin. "Oh, I know. What about entertainment, maybe also advertising. I doubt either of those would represent something the regulators would bother with. My mother could be useful in this regard. She and my father both work in civilian industry, local to C.P. She works in an advertising department, so if I could make contact with her, she might hold enough influence to pass a quiet word around to publish a new advertising campaign, maybe by using imagery that contains some of our new suggestive notions."

"Good gracious, Lieutenant," the General chuckles. "And here I thought Kaliya was bad for her mischievous guile."

"I'm taking lessons from her," she smiles. "So, I guess it's rubbing off by now."

"These are all good ideas," Thaelyn affirms. "But Ayene, this will place a fair amount of additional pressure on you for the complexity of your workload. I think it would be prudent to recommend you bring in additional aid to assist you. Since we are now speaking of fields of expertise we do not have in our immediate capacity, you should seek out those amongst our civilian population that can provide this for you. I suspect we will be collecting a fair number of people of varying professional capacities to provide for all these venues we are creating."

"Ambitious minds with muted voice, a minor song is played," Kaliya notes quietly. "Cu'Nar's pity, she's a clever one. She's driving every little aspect of it. A careful chase will turn His eyes, in the Forgotten One's parade."

"Indeed, Kaliya, and this seems to be exemplifying our role in a much larger game. Ayene, when would you wish to proceed to our next step?"

"My understanding is Likha is close to finishing her initial phase of the experiment with the seed in maybe one or two weeks, depending on how quickly the Spore progresses through the thing. I would like to make my next visit before that time."

"Is there some reason for the timing?"

"I want to be the first recipient," she sighs gently and looks down at the table. "And I suppose I want to get this out of the way before that happens. I'll need to spend a lot of time here during the procedure, and I don't really know what to expect at the end of it."

"I think I understand, Lieutenant. You are feeling uncertain, perhaps even a bit afraid."

"Yes."

"The procedure, when we first used it on Tyanna, was nerve-racking for all of us here, especially Kaliya and her friends who were watching her so closely. But she got through it, and we feel this should proceed in a similar fashion. Still, if it bothers you so, you must understand you are not alone."

"Thank you. Um, if you don't need me for anything else today, I think I would like to spend some time in B.T."

"Very well, Lieutenant, you may go."

Ayene makes a professional bow and leaves the room. She proceeds outside and across the plaza to the city hub, and then across to Tae'Eladar. It was midday, and she was uncertain which way to go first. She desired to take a nice walk along the avenues, to breathe the fresh air and sniff the flowers in their planters on the sidewalks. She longed for this, as it was so peaceful to her. Back home, the city was all concrete and metal, and the air was so polluted, it smelled of smoke and noxious gases, not that she could smell this in her projected form, but the memory was there.

She left the gateway hub and began strolling northward along the streets, checking the local shops, and greeting people as they passed by. The people of Capitol Prime often did not give such friendly addresses, instead keeping mostly to their personal concerns. But the people here all tended to smile, and even though she was essentially an alien visitor, these people were remarkably xenophilic, and welcomed her.

She watched as horse-drawn wagons passed by in the streets. It seemed so pastoral, such a simple way of life, and she reflected on her home, where the streets were lined with rails of lights and illuminated guide markers for the hover-enabled traffic to glide along. And then there were the elevated lanes, and the skywalks between some of the taller buildings. It was organized chaos as compared to this.

She continued working her way along to the northern part of the city, unconsciously directing herself to one district she was previously afraid to enter, but today she pressed herself to make the effort. She eventually arrived in the Grove District, a quaint village-like setting of shops and homes, small shrines and temples, and a lot of foliage.

The centerpiece of the district was the city's dryad grove, the home of Shescellaie, the queen of the dryads, and her six daughters, as part of the grove setting. The district surrounded it in a circle, where the buildings were partially fashioned out of the local trees and shrubbery. The entire district was organic. The air was cool and moist, and fragrant from the innumerable flowering shrubs. The people who lived here were mostly elves of various races, although predominantly wood elves.

She arrived at the square where the dryad grove was found. She hesitated as she stood there gazing at it. The mother tree was taller than most of the local buildings and capped with a huge domelike canopy of lush foliage. The six daughter trees surrounded it in a circle, resembling smaller versions of the mother, with narrower canopies and neatly tucked underneath the mother, as if taking shelter by it.

She reflected briefly on the druidic ritual Thaelyn made on Morndindor, and the sheer power of the storm he brought down. The tree he planted there was a mere sapling compared to this, but she understood, if given time, it would grow, and that place would one day resemble something like this.

A local druid attending the shrine noticed her standing in the square in a state of wonderment. She walked over to greet her.

"Is there something I can help you with?" she asks. "Would you like to visit the tree today?"

"I don't know what to do. I'm not even sure if I have the courage to approach it."

"There is nothing to be afraid of. And I'm sure the spirit would be pleased for your visit."

"But I'm not one of you. I'm very different."

"It does not matter. You are a creature of nature, the same as any other. Whether you are tall or short, of blue skin, or any other color, we are all the same in the eyes of the Great Mother."

"But I'm not even from this world," she begs.

"And that makes you different? We have Daanen-Aryku who have visited the tree before, and they are also not from this world. In fact, they are the same as you… Well, except for this growth you carry," she notes gently.

"Yes, and this growth makes me ugly."

"The spirit does not judge you by such measure. You are still a living body, a creation of the natural design, and she would desire to meet you by no less."

"But I don't know how."

"Then come forward and I will show you. It is very easy."

"Yeah, that's what they all say," she chuckles weakly.

The druid leads Ayene to the edge of a broad circle. The grove was enclosed in a short wooden fence wrapped in vines. To one side was a small market stand. The druid pauses to explain the setting.

"If you wish to simply visit the tree, you may do so as you desire. Many people also give an offering, which is purchased at this stand here," she directs to the small vendor. "It is not required, of course, but this is how some, especially us elves, pay our respects to the spirit."

Ayene examined the market stall, studying some of the pre-made offerings, which involved small trays of woven twigs, laden with items resembling seeds, leaves and fruit.

"This tree is a sacred object, as I understand it, so is this offering like a holy rite?"

"It is simply a gift to the spirits of the grove. They draw empowerment from it, like many spirits with their offerings."

"Well, this is obviously my first time, so I think I'd like to make a good first impression."

She follows the druid to the stand and purchases one of the trays. As a displaced Suuden'kai, a foreign resident from a society that enjoyed an entirely electronic economy, the local use of physical currency was alien to her. But she had been receiving payment during her service to Thaelyn, and so she had an opportunity to save up a fair amount of money by this time. And she had a habit of being very thrifty in her expenditures.

The druid assisted with the offering, and instructed her on how to make the traditional approach by walking along the path into the circle. As Ayene made her entrance past the fence, she felt a sudden rush of warmth flow into her. She instantly clung to herself, wrapping both arms around and hunching over. Her knees crossed, and she instinctively tucked her tail in.

"Ooh!" she croons with a slight tremble. "What's happening?"

"You feel the power of the spirit entering into you."

"Yeah, something sure got in here. I'm tingling from horn to hoof…everything."

"If this is your first time, likely you are unaccustomed to it. How do you feel?"

"I'm not quite sure how to describe it. It's not unpleasant, just surprising. I step inside here and bam, it's like my whole body just came alive with something."

"I wonder, this entity you have on your body. I have heard of it. Could it be causing a reaction?"

"I wouldn't know how to answer that, but I'm feeling this everywhere, inside and out, and it's still going."

"Do you feel as if it could be harmful? The flow of the life-giving energies should not be hurtful to anyone. But if this entity is of some odd design, I wonder if it might be conflicting."

"Let's keep going, while I'm still standing upright. I want to do this."

"Very well, come forward to this first line. There we shall kneel as our first gesture."

She leads Ayene forward to a marker in the path, and they kneel, setting the tray on the ground temporarily. The druid directs Ayene to form up a gesture with her hands of a triangle between her index fingers and thumbs, curling the rest of the fingers in, and lifting it in front of the heart, the mouth, and the forehead, then waving it away over the head. She picks up the tray and they continue to the next mark.

Ayene is still clutching at herself. She is beginning to worry if the seed entity actually is reacting to the spiritual energies in the ground. The majesty of the tree was simply too beautiful to suggest it was wrong for her to try this, but considering what she had learned about the seed entity possibly being some form of parasite to serve Sargeras, she asked herself if it might not like the idea, if only on some instinctive level.

They reached the next mark and kneeled again. The druid placed the offering on a small altar and again made her series of gestures, which Ayene tried to mimic, but the tingling sensations were growing into a trembling.

"This isn't getting any better," Ayene admits. "It seems to be getting stronger."

"Then I suspect this thing clinging to you is reacting to the energies here. Perhaps there is some essence within that does not care for the type of energies the nature spirits produce."

"That actually makes sense to me. I'm no expert, but His Lordship and some of his people have suggested it to contain something that could serve Sargeras, and that means I'm polluted with it."

"I cannot speak assuredly on such matters, as I am not as well versed in the Primordials and their nature. But of the few stories I do have, I might suggest it could be an issue of the difference in their polarity and ours."

Ayene felt a shudder, and it caused her to topple over. She catches herself with one hand while still wrapping the other around her midsection. The druid noticed this immediately.

"I think we should help you out of here if it is becoming so difficult for you."

"My legs are feeling weak."

The druid calls up several others from the shrine to help. They rush into the circle just as Ayene falls further to the ground, now resting on her elbow and twitching. She looked up one more time at the mother tree, and then she noticed something moving.

The trunk of the tree had begun deforming on one side, as if something were emerging outwards from it. Ayene stared at it in wonder, unsure what to expect until she saw what appeared to be a face peering out from the side of the tree.

"In all the nether-space, what is that?" she wheezes.

The druid's attention is pulled to the sight as the face emerges more fully, forming a head. The material of the tree was spawning an independent form. The head further extended on a neck, and then a graceful feminine torso, followed by arms, which reached out and laid on the sides of the tree for support. A leg formed and stepped out, settling on the ground, and drawing the rest forward as the remainder of the body pulled itself into the open space.

The figure now stood autonomously from the mother tree. The body was covered with patches of leaves and vines, and its head blossomed with a rich mane of leafy foliage which rippled and waved in rhythmic patterns. The sight of it halted the druids in their tracks and they all dropped to the ground in reverent kneels. Ayene gazed at it, but otherwise couldn't move.

"This is Shescellaie," the druid finally responds. "She is the queen mother of the grove."

Shescellaie's movement flowed like a gentle breeze. She stepped forward and raised her hands to the surrounding daughter trees. Soon, the whole grove came alive, as additional bodies emerged.

The scene inside the circle had been drawing attention from passing shoppers and local residents. Ayene had mostly collapsed to the ground by now, and the twitching steadily increased. The sight of Shescellaie arriving in view drew even more murmurs, but when the six daughters began to emerge, the entire square erupted in oohs and ahs.

Ayene gazed around the scene as the younger spirits came into view. They appeared similar to the mother, but more like adolescent children in size and general appearance. They all converged in the center with the druids.

Shescellaie touched the heads of each of the druids as she made her approach to Ayene, and the daughters formed a circle around the stricken woman. Ayene now felt her body convulsing, and this time it was well-defined to be coming from the seed entity. The parasitic lifeform was having spasms, and it could be seen flexing beneath her clothing.

"It doesn't like this!" she declares nervously. "It's fighting back!"

"I suspect Shescellaie has something in mind. Try to hold on."

The spirit mother knelt down just within arm's reach of the bewildered girl, along with her daughters. Each of the younger spirits extended their hands over Ayene's body while Shescellaie reached out one of hers to pass across it. She begins speaking in words Ayene does not understand, but her voice resonated with a tranquil harmony.

"She says you are poisoned," the druid relates. "This thing brings pain to your spirit."

"I don't doubt it," Ayene mutters faintly. "And not only that."

Shescellaie announces a command to her daughters through a rhythmic pattern of rustling within her leafy mane. The circle of girls begins to coordinate their energies as they lean over Ayene. The unfortunate woman was jerking side-to-side from the reactions of the seed entity. Then, as the girls applied their skills, Ayene took notice of a swarm of small glowing entities descending from the upper branches of the tree. The druids all look up at the sight.

"In the name of the Forest Queen," utters the head druid. "I've never seen anything like this before."

A spiraling torrent of pixies from the boughs of the mother tree began circling around above Ayene as the child spirits infused her with a soothing aura. Her body began to glow ever so softly, and the twitching gradually subsided. Slowly, Ayene was relaxing, and she rolled onto her back, gazing upward into the whirling mass of pixies, while the child spirits continued their work. Her eyes lost their focus as she descended into a euphoric trance.

The scene around the square was packed by now with people watching the incredible ritual taking place. It was unusual to see even one dryad emerge outside their tree, and even more extraordinary to see all seven of them. But to see them perform a service like this was especially remarkable. Several of the spectators brought out primitive camera devices to photograph the sight, and a few journalists had gathered to oversee the event for the local newspaper.

The druids all gazed in awe as Shescellaie and her daughters attended to the strange entity and its reactions. After several moments, the child spirits pulled back, and the swirling pixies dispersed back into the tree. Ayene simply laid there appearing delirious.

The head druid cautiously leans in to check on her.

"Um…" she begins uncertainly. "How do you feel now?"

Ayene was initially unable to respond, but as she came back

around, she began forming a broad grin across her face. Her eyes still seemed unfocused and staring into the distance.

"Sparkly…" she croons dreamily.

The druids all turned to glare at each other for the curious response.

"Uh, can you hear me?" the druid tries again.

"That was better than Pinkweed."

"Pinkweed? What's that?"

"It's, um… Oh, wait, you're not supposed to know about that."

Now Ayene begins giggling mindlessly, as the druids again turn to each other and shake their heads amusedly. Ayene's voice escalates as she continues her incoherent laughter. After several moments, she begins to come back under control.

"That was really nice of her," she coos. "But what did she do? This thing feels like it fell asleep or something."

"Let me ask. Hold on."

The druid now turns to Shescellaie and speaks in the ancient language the dryads tend to use. As Shescellaie gives her answer, the druid relates it to Ayene.

"She tells me this thing does not resemble a natural form of life, which I think I can understand, based on what I've heard about it."

"Yeah, this much she has on the mark. It's a product of our science, and not a nice one at that."

"And then, she tells me it does not harmonize with our native energies. Therefore, the reaction, I suppose."

"Are we speaking of those polarities again?"

"I think it goes deeper than that. This is a very different example that is simply not compatible with the flows or the essences of our native gods."

"You know, that might hold a special relevance. It was made to serve a Primordial, not your Estelar."

"Perhaps so, and therefore it was reacting as the essence is incompatible. But anyway, she says she was able to place it into a dormant condition, so your idea of putting it to sleep is very close. But this is not a permanent effect. Once it wakes up, it will go again."

"All right, I should probably get out of this circle before that happens."

Ayene raises herself up to a seated position as she tries to shake off the last of the delirium. She gazes around the plaza at all the people.

"Oh great," she moans. "The last thing I wanted was to cause a scene."

"Don't worry about it. It's not your fault, and I'm sure we could not have anticipated this."

"Maybe..." she mutters as she tries rising to her feet.

The druids move in to help her, as Shescellaie and her daughters all step away. Ayene glances around at the group of odd creatures.

"They all look like half plant, half people."

"In a very real sense of it, they are. They are an element of our ancient home world which we brought with us as our ancestors came here to this one."

"You must have some fascinating forms of life over there. Maybe one day I can learn more about it. But only AFTER I get rid of this little bug."

"I have heard about the plight of the Daanen-Aryku and theirs. Is yours the same?"

"Similar, but not the same. We have people studying it right now for a solution, hoping to modify the methods they used on the Daanen'kai example, and apply it to us. Very soon now, I hope to take this and finally be free from it, assuming all goes well."

"You sound uncertain."

"I'm scared. It's experimental. And even though the other one worked, I'm nervous to try it, but I must. I want this thing off of me."

"I understand. Then I wish you well, and I will offer a prayer to the Forest Queen to watch over you, Child. Perhaps, when it is done, you can return back to us."

"Yes, I would like that, and hopefully next time not be the center of attention," she smiles gently.

"Do not worry about that."

The druid leads Ayene out of the circle, parting a way through the gathering. Ayene casts a glance back at the dryads, who were still standing by, observing her departure.

"Can you give them my special thanks."

"Of course, but I suspect they already know."

"Maybe, but I feel I should at least make the effort. Perhaps, next time I visit, I can make a double dose of that offering to pay them back for it."

The two of them giggle at the thought, as they make their way over to a bench, where Ayene can sit down to recover.

Chapter 5

SUMMIT TALK

"Commander!" charges an urgent voice on the com-link. "Are you having as many difficulties on your terminal lately as I am?"

"Excuse me, Marshal? What do you mean?"

"Every hour, on the hour, I have to enter a new password to unlock my terminal as part of some new security software update. It's driving me mad! Why must I suffer such things?!" he rages.

"Yes, I am aware of a new software upgrade. It is part of the new revision procedure we are undergoing due to Ytani and the potential threat he poses. I was briefed on this recently. We believe he likely carried away a number of critical security codes when he stole the Ghan'aju, and it became necessary for a total revamp of our protocols to prevent him access to our networks."

"And does this mean that every time I get busy with some important work on my terminal, I must be interrupted every hour to input a new password? And not simply that, but the manner in which they make me decipher it is unnerving, to say the least!"

"I am not the one in charge of that operation, but my information tells me he sided with some very resourceful allies, especially if you consider the deception he made on Morndindor. Therefore, we cannot take anything for granted. Until this crisis is resolved, we must simply tolerate the inconveniences."

"Aargh!" he screams and ends the link.

Commander Geilv studied the monitor on his local terminal and reflected on the Marshal's statement.

"This is curious. Why his terminal and not mine?"

But with no other option available to resolve this quandary, he simply went back to work.

✦✦✦

"What do we have, Likha?" Ankhia asks as she enters the medical ward.

"It's dead, right on cue, more or less…a little bit less than more, it seems."

"Did we give it too much? Not that I'm against it, but we were trying to calibrate for a month, like we did the last one."

"Yes, but it seems this one went down slightly faster. I'm speculating right now that it might be related to the overall biomass. This one didn't seem quite as robust as the Ruuki uy'Daan specimen, and I'm asking myself if this is due to that one being designed to debilitate whereas this is to enhance. Therefore, this one might be a little more optimized while the other one was simply a hack to make life difficult."

"That's a very interesting thought. All right, what do we have for the final readings?"

Likha and Ankhia were meeting in the lab to review the data on the seed entity that was used on their test platform. The entity had just given out, and Ankhia was notified to make an inspection. Likha gave her a data pad with the final bio-monitor readings while the two of them studied the experiment in the specimen tank.

"Good," Ankhia considers. "This looks mostly as I expected."

"The only thing now is to remove the remains, I guess," Likha suggests as she gazes longingly at her favorite replicant doll.

"Yes, and I suppose we should get to it soon, in case we need to recycle Banni for something else later."

"Poor little Banni, he has such a rough life."

"He's a tough little guy, he can handle it. He's given us some good results."

"So, the next step would be to report this to the Commander, and then call a volunteer."

"That's right, here we go again."

Ankhia picks up a trans-com and makes a call to Kailen at the WIC building.

"This is Commander Nazég."

"Kailen, it's me. I'm at the lab and we have a result with Banni. We seem good to go for the next step."

"How do the readings look to you?"

"As expected for our example, with the exception that it seemed to fail at a slightly shorter interval than the other one. Likha thinks it could be a design difference between the two, but nothing that would otherwise alter our results. I can't think of anything else to do now but to call for a volunteer."

"Understood, and we actually have one already. Lieutenant Ti'van has put in a request to be the first one."

"That poor girl, she's been through a lot. All right, if she feels up to it… One way or another, we'll need to process everyone. This design isn't quite the same as the previous one, so I am going to insist that she camp out on an examination bed until further notice."

"Well, I don't know if she would want to make any sleepovers in the med-lab, but she seems to understand the need to keep herself available."

"Good, I'm not going through another situation like with Tyanna. Tell her to meet me here at her earliest convenience."

"Will do…"

Kailen closes the link on his side and turns to look at Thaelyn, who was sitting at the table across from him. Kaliya was also sitting at the table as part of a recent briefing. They all looked down to the other end at Ayene, also present in the briefing, and suddenly showing extreme distress.

"Ayene," Thaelyn begins softly. "How do you feel at this moment?"

"Scared," she replies with a tremor in her voice.

"We have experience with this from the past, although this design, as the Med-tech said, is slightly different. Still, if it worked in her lab study, it should work in a similar way in actual practice."

"Yes, I know. I remember all the briefings, but this doesn't change anything for me."

She glanced around the table at the faces of the other officers. Her eyes were welling up, and her lip trembled.

"Your Lordship, before I do this, I want to make that one last meeting with Azina. I need to finish what I started."

"This is not the end, Ayene. We will get through this."

"All right, I'll try to settle myself, at least for now. This thing took almost a month, but that's a month of struggle for me. Allow me to make this one last effort before I go in. It'll be one less thing for me to worry about. And as I said before, I would like Kaliya to go along with me. She may need to go in sometime while I'm occupied, so we should introduce her now while we have the chance."

"Naturally, and as she is technically your superior officer in this matter, this would make a good showing. Kaliya, if you would be so kind."

"Absolutely," she responds.

"Find yourself a chair in the other room and try to relax. We will wait for your return."

Ayene excuses herself from the meeting, and along with Kaliya, retires to the room they often used to conduct their projection. They took up their seating and tried to relax. Kaliya was able to project fairly easily, and took up her classic Suuden'kai image, but the effort took extra-long on this occasion for Ayene due to her tension. When she was finally able to release herself, the two of them folded to Azgarén, and Ayene led them into the research center. She waved politely at the girl behind the front desk, and they continued on to the lift to ride it up to the third floor.

"We have a special passphrase we use when I call her into our meetings," Ayene mentions privately. "You'll need to pay attention to it in case you need to use it later. I'll counsel you on it if you need it again."

"What rank do you recommend I use here?"

"Your normal rank should do fine. We shouldn't need you to play something fancy. In fact, your existing rank is perfect for the occasion, as it represents who you are in reality, and we'll need to demonstrate this."

Azina was at her usual station processing orders when the call came in. She pulled herself away from her work to walk up to the front desk, there to find Ayene. The occasion didn't fall on the expected interval, or the time of day, and this occurrence left her feeling uncertain as now Kaliya was entered into the mix.

"Um, yes, Lieutenant," she emits tenderly while glancing at Kaliya. "Can I help you?"

"Yes, I have an urgent need to meet with you about matters of research."

Azina glanced briskly at Kaliya again as a visual cue for her involvement. Ayene expected this might raise a question, so she tried to settle it casually.

"Yes," she offers. "This is my immediate CO. She is here to assist in our meeting."

"Assist in our meeting... I see. This is new. Well, we should convene in the meeting room down the hall. Follow me please."

Azina led them down the hall to the usual room where she and Ayene held their gatherings. When they arrived in the room, they closed the door and sat down.

"Um, Ayene," Azina mumbles cautiously. "Who is she?"

"This is Captain Kaliya Nazég, and she represents my current CO."

"Oh, and um...I should probably ask...why is she here?"

"Just as I said...to assist with our meeting. Azina, relax, she's a friend."

"So, she's also involved in this special project of yours?"

"We're involved in a number of projects together. She has hers, I have mine. This is actually that one associate I mentioned before."

"Ah, I see. You people sound busy. All right, so I'm guessing you're here in reference to that meeting with the Director, right?"

"That's right. My apologies for the impromptu scheduling, but we have a series of objectives coming due, and I need to get this out of the way."

"And Captain, can I ask where all this will ultimately lead us? I'm a little worried for what Ayene said the last time we met."

"We're here to tell a story, Intern," Kaliya soothes. "And after that, we need to recruit your aid to bring down Creation's Most Wanted."

"Huh? Creation? What do you involve when you use the word Creation?"

"Everything that ever existed, past, present, and future… And right now, it's sitting right here in Capitol Prime."

"And I thought I was worried before this. Well, it goes without saying that we both have a lot of questions to ask, the Director most of all. Right now, my horns are feeling a bit soft, so if you'll go easy on me, hopefully we can get through this."

"We'll try, but what we have to say isn't nice, so be warned that your horns may fall off one or more times along the way."

"Well, then maybe I should run to the lab and pick up a tube of our patented horn restoration glue. I've been dying to try it," she grins shyly.

"Wow, an actual attempt at humor," Kaliya smiles. "And in a world full of people without a clue!"

"Yeah, a few of us have been conducting experiments to discover what this is. If I may, one thing we're wondering about is what your opinion is on our research project on the Tav'ageen Anomaly. It would seem you're not against it, but Ayene didn't say much more about it. The Director is a little nervous since this is a pet project of his and he feels it's very important."

"I would tend to agree with him, and more so if he might actually have the possibility to learn something. The chips were stated to be temporary, but with your little nondisclosure clause in there, it would seem someone very conveniently overrode that statement. So, as far as I'm concerned, you have a strong plus in your favor for assertiveness. Our society is supposed to be pursuing ALL forms of knowledge, last time I checked our Charter of Laws for its…spirit of the words," she smirks cutely.

"Really! Wow, he'll be happy to hear that."

"Technically speaking, Ayene and I couldn't care less about what you research, so long as it doesn't translate to more of Darumon's death toys. In fact, we have a few of our own pet projects to suggest to you, which we also feel are important."

"Wait a minute, you're her CO, but on a first-name basis?"

"We're friends back home in our service, so yes. This sort of thing can occur on occasion, regardless of any rank association."

"Should I be jealous now?"

"Only if you want to be…" Kaliya smiles. "We have a group back home we belong to."

"Yeah, now I am jealous. I wish I had a group."

"You could join ours, it's open membership. Although, we are rather far away from here to be very convenient."

"Figures… Well, follow me and we'll go upstairs to see the Director."

She stands up and leads the group out of the room and down another hall, working their way to the lift and up to the fifth floor, where they follow the halls to the Director's office.

"Ghantil, I need you for a moment," Azina announces as she peeks into the room.

"Come in, Azina."

The girl steps inside, followed by Kaliya and Ayene, and then closes the door behind them. The Director looked up at the two officers entering the room. He took notice of Ayene, recalling her face from the military profile he reviewed once with Azina, but obviously Kaliya was new. He then turned to Azina.

"And who do we have here?" he asks cautiously.

"Ghantil, this is her," Azina explains. "And her CO, um…sorry, Captain, uh…"

"I'm Captain Kaliya Nazég," she responds. "Good greetings to you, Director," she offers with a modest bow.

Azina directs the group to take up seating and join the Director at the desk.

"Nazég?" he perks up. "That name holds a special meaning in some circles, do you know that?"

"Yes, I suppose it does at that. But then, I think it largely depends on who you talk to."

"Yes, this much is true. By the uniform, you look like you belong to Central Command, the same as the Lieutenant here."

"These are disguises we're using right now to allay any outward curiosity by those we do not necessarily want to take special notice of us."

"Uh huh… So, instead of dressing as ordinary citizens, you dress as military officers who would probably draw more attention than the ordinary citizen."

"Well," she chuckles. "Yes, you have a point. But let me ask you this. If I were to step in here wearing my beachwear skimpies, would you think so highly of me for any manner of important business?"

"Um, all right, I suppose you do have a point."

"Good, therefore the uniforms. They might draw attention, but the attention, in this case, is to convey an air of authority, and in this business, if you want anything done, those first impressions count."

"Got it. So, you don't necessarily want to draw attention, but you DO want to draw respect for a certain position of authority. How interesting. I'm also noticing you seem to have a curious manner of speech. You don't talk like any military officer I've ever met before, and you also seem to have a slight accent of some kind, am I right?"

"I never thought of that before," she grins. "But perhaps I may. Wouldn't that be an interesting turn, if one of you thinks I speak differently."

"One of us?" he raises his brow. "It's also clear you seem to have emotions. And you, Lieutenant, may I ask your name?"

"My name is Lieutenant Ayene Ti'van, formerly of Central

Command, and until recently with my new service under the Captain, formerly in the service of Fleet Commander Lajivi Kriv'tik."

"I see…" he considers deeply. "This is an interesting selection of words, since Azina and I were trying to interpret a few things about you from our last conversation. All right, before we begin, I suspect this conversation will involve a lot of details, and for the controversial nature of the statements you made when speaking with Azina, I'm sure I'll want to take a few notes. Would you mind?"

"Go ahead, Director," Kaliya states calmly. "My suggestion is simply to use a trans-com in record mode and chronicle the whole thing. That's what we're doing for a lot of our activities back home."

"You're chronicling them?"

"Absolutely! Unlike Central and the Marshal, who would rather hide everything behind their security codes no one is allowed to peek under, we are recording our progress to peek under them and open up all his little secrets. I'm sure he would absolutely love to see the results, once we're ready to publish them," she smirks.

"Oh dear. Yes, you do seem to have emotions, and not nice ones at that," he smiles.

"Simply put, it's important for us to keep a record of our activities, both for future analysis as well as historical recordkeeping. We are moving through a very important moment in our history, Director. Our people need to know about it, so we don't find ourselves in the same bucket of nether-bilge again."

"Wow, Captain," Azina croons. "You don't play around with words, do you?"

"Not when there's work to be done. It goes with the rank. We're in a closed room, speaking privately, and we need to be on the level here. So, I figure if you're going to break the ice, hit it hard."

"Really!" she smiles tenderly. "Now that's the kind of attitude that gets things done. Why can't we see more of that happening around here?"

"That's what we're here to talk about."

"All right then," the Director relents. "If you'll give me just a moment…"

"Ayene, do you have yours? We might as well make our own, while we're at it."

"Yes Ma'am!" she replies eagerly.

"Are you now taking lessons from Marelle with that attitude?" she smirks.

Ayene flashes a wink at Kaliya as she and the Director each take out their trans-coms and place them in record mode on the desk. The Director then begins the session with a brief introduction.

"This is Director Ghantil Bak'vayn of the ARC, here in a private meeting with two military officers. The first one identifies herself as Captain Kaliya Nazég. Although she wears the uniform of Central Command, she tells me this is simply a type of disguise she is using to avert any unusual attention to her true character…whatever that is. The other one is Lieutenant Ayene Ti'van. She states she is formerly of Central Command, and according to their records, she is currently listed as deceased, which is a very unusual statement from our own military authority, when clearly, she is not. The two of them have come forward to offer inside information as to what sounds like a series of activities, many of which are stated to be highly controversial and perhaps conspiratorial relating to the Council and the Marshal."

He now offers a pause before beginning his interview in earnest.

"Lieutenant Ti'van," he resumes. "I would like to begin with you. I have a number of questions to ask relating to the statements you gave to the Intern here during your private conversations together. Among these, she says you informed her of a number of what we might describe as conspiratorial statements concerning the An'gamu seeds, the Tav'ageen Suppressor chips, and the Marshal and his long battle against these insurgents. Then we have the media streams apparently being influenced by hidden agents who were censoring the flow of information, mandated by the Council, and manipulated by the Marshal and his military. Finally is the Council itself, which you say is completely absent at this time, with the reasons hidden behind a lot of fraud and high security classifications, and this hints at a form of deception, to say nothing of an attempt to take over our government. Are these statements indeed made by you?"

"Yes, they are, Director," she responds calmly.

"All right, this represents a lot to go over, and most of it very unpleasant. My own opinions on the matter notwithstanding, I need to take this objectively."

"Of course, and I appreciate your professionalism."

"Thank you. The first thing I want to ask is who you actually work for, because your military record says you last worked as part of C.P. Security in administration and law enforcement."

"This is curious. Do you actually have access to those records here?"

"I have what we'll describe as confidential and private access to their personnel files, but I can't say anything more than that."

"How interesting," she smiles. "I wonder what the HC would say to that. Well, in answer to your question, yes, I did work for C.P. Security as my first job until I was transferred to Central Command about four centuries ago as part of a top-secret project the Marshal ordered."

"Top-secret… Would this explain why your military record doesn't show it, maybe because it was covered up for the security rating?"

"Quite likely. The project didn't officially exist, the same as the world we were working on. And neither did that other universe the Marshal brought us into."

The Director instantly fell back into his chair and wheezed, while Azina nearly fell out of hers and gasped.

"Another universe?!" she yelps. "We actually found another universe out there?"

"Yeah," Ayene admits. "But the Marshal apparently forgot to tell the science community, and for that matter, the remainder of our military…those who weren't actually sent there for any kind of exploration. But I'm sure they would've loved to hear about this one."

"Well, there goes that censorship. This is a good example of it."

"Actually," Kaliya muses humorously. "I believe he only promised you the secrets of THIS universe, not the others out there."

"Oh, thank you, Captain!"

"As for who I work for now…" Ayene once again turns to her trans-com for her ID. "It's called Azgarén Central intelligence. We're a top-level internal security agency."

"All right," the Director responds gently. "But I've never heard of this one before, so what is it you're supposed to be doing?"

"I could answer this in different ways, depending on how we wish to approach it. For instance, one could say our history represents a very sheltered example, Director. We don't have any enemies to speak of, so we don't have anything to defend ourselves against. No espionage, no international intrigue, no rivalries. We have a single world government, and all our people are united into one body, so we basically have nothing except the occasional traffic law to contend with. In other words, if something bad comes our way, we have no way to deal with it. We might not even notice it, because we're simply not looking."

"I see."

"Ours is a new government body designed explicitly to contend with those aspects of conduct that might disrupt our way of life. This involves preserving the custom of law and civil order, but not necessarily on the common civilian level. We have C.P. Security for that, and other similar agencies. But no one should be immune to the laws we place on ourselves, not the people, not the military, not even the Council that everyone around here seems so complacent to believe is doing as they're supposed to be doing. There are no official agencies to govern the government…no checks and balances."

"As I try to reflect on this, I think I can see your point, but also, it never seemed necessary before now. We have the Charter of Laws which is supposed to be universal, and the Council, above all others, is expected to follow this."

"Expected, yes, but this is our error. It is an assumption, nothing more. To say it never seemed necessary is because everyone is of the opinion the Council can do no wrong, and the people simply bow down to them as if they were a god entity. Therefore, no one ever bothered to check to see if they WERE doing no wrong, and they probably could not do anything about it, even if they did. Well, here we are…finally."

"All right, finally. But who installed you if you say the Council is apparently missing?"

"Yes, this does take us into a kind of gray area. It might also represent that alternate approach to our explanation. If we say the Council IS doing wrong, why would they hire someone like us with the power to take them down. Then, regardless of right or wrong, if the Council carries this image of a god entity, why would they hire anyone who might challenge that image. Either way, the Council would probably NOT want something like us because we would then hold the power to question theirs."

"That's a very interesting perspective. And this would further suggest they do behave like a god entity."

"Therefore, since we believe we are effectively without a proper government, we generally authorized ourselves. You might say we're an insurgency force taking back our government for the people."

The Director glared disbelievingly at Ayene for the openly ironic circumstance of that statement. As for Azina, she gaped at it briskly, and then broke out in hysterical laughter. Her insane cackling echoed around the room and bounced off the walls. She doubled over in her chair and drew the attention of everyone in the room, finally falling onto the floor, still bellowing her mad riot.

The Director lifted up from his chair to peer over the edge of the desk at the girl rolling around on the floor.

"Um, Azina, are you alright down there?"

"That's the most hilarious thing I ever heard in my life!" she crows. "Beware the insurgents! They're our own people!"

She continues her maniacal laughter, now drawing the Director and the others into it until she can finally regain control of herself and return to her seat.

"That would certainly twist a few horns," the Director offers as he pulls himself together. "So then, this is to say you apparently feel yourselves in such a strong position that you are attempting your own form of takeover. But I should think you still need some kind of authoritative power to conduct anything, right?"

"Yes, we do," Ayene admits. "On our side of it, we have my former Commander from the mining base offering his military background into the equation, and he is serving as the agency Director."

"And again, this time for the recording, who are we speaking of here?"

"Fleet Commander Lajivi Kriv'tik, who happens to be an honored and well-respected member of our military, but who was also at that mining base, and like the rest of us, is currently listed as dead."

"Another one? All right, and I'll admit this does offer a significant level of authority into things."

"We also have C.P. Security backing us up. I pulled a few strings with my former boss, who wasn't too hard to convince, since he hates the Marshal anyway, and I explained who we are on the other side of this equation, and he followed me. We began with a few items on our list that were easy to prove, like those regulators, and this got a hoof in the door. Then we found an agent in the Council Grand Hall, in the Public Relations office, who was a middleman to a secretary in the Marshal's office feeding his lies to us."

"And this would tie him into it."

"Also, the Internal Secretary confessed to us the elections have been rigged for as long as the Marshal has been offering his promises to us. Combine all this and you have, at the very least, a corrupt Council for refusing to abide by our election standards, and the Marshal, who represents a foreign body, taking control of OUR military and OUR governmental functions. He should not have any true authority at all, but he took it from the Council, who should not have the authority to give it to him in the first place."

"Wow," Azina coos. "That puts someone in a lot of trouble."

"Yes," the Director admits. "And this does indeed offer us a few very viable reasons for our own form of insurgency to take back control. And in the absence of that same Council, corrupted or not, it would likely have to be done independently. But can you do this with only a simple security office?"

"That's what she is for," Ayene thumbs at Kaliya. "She's the military body to back us up on the other side of things."

"Alone, or with an actual military behind her? With respect, the rank of Captain is a bit far from a full military. And if she's only wearing that uniform as a type of costume, who does she actually work for?"

"Let's come to me in a moment, Director," Kaliya infers.

"All right, then back to you, Lieutenant. Let's move forward. You say the Council is actually missing. Can you explain what you know of this?"

Ayene brings her trans-com back into play. She turns it around on the desk so she can call up her photo library for a pictorial review.

"These images I have here were taken recently inside the Council Grand Hall, after I forced entrance through their locked doors. They represent the inner chamber. It looks like a scene of utter devastation after almost ten millennia of decay and abandonment. You would think, Council or no Council, at the very least, a building maintenance worker would go inside to check the light bulbs, to say nothing of the roof collapsing."

She turns it back around for both the Director and Azina to lean in and check the array of photos. The two of them scrolled through the assortment of scenes, moaning and gasping over the clutter of debris and decaying furniture.

"In all the nether-space," Azina laments. "This place is supposed to be legendary for the architectural glamor and prestige, but look at it! It's almost destroyed!"

The Director simply gazed at the images and shook his head.

"This goes beyond any kind of conspiracy that they're missing. This is an intentional cover-up of their complete absence. You're right, Lieutenant, you would think a building inspector would go in once in a while, at least!"

"I called in Captain Bein'talan at the East City Center Precinct for this point," Ayene submits. "Together, we're going to cover this up on our own until a decision can be made on it. The Marshal is guilty for a lot of things, and this is comparatively minor at the moment."

"Minor?!" he blurts. "The absence of our planetary government and the condition of this building is minor?"

"By comparison to who he is and everything else he has done, or could do…along with his REAL reason for being here. Yes."

"All right," he sighs tensely. "Then, let's see if we can clear up the rest of it. Where would you like to begin?"

"There are multiple beginning points here, Director," Kaliya suggests. "And some of them not even ours. So, let's start with Ayene."

The Director nods and he leans on the desk attentively.

Ayene begins her review, "My story follows after the mention in your controversial access to Central's personnel files," she smirks. "Four centuries ago, I was stationed at a mining outpost on a world we called Morndindor. The world was originally populated by a local society who called themselves dwarves. This was a secret operation for the Marshal to haul up a local mineral which was unknown to our science. The natives held the knowledge to mine and process this metal, so we chose to use that rather than our own methods. Although technically, it could also be said that the Marshal did not WANT to teach us how to do it, as to do so would also be to teach us a series of other lessons he seems avoidant to teach at all. Well, so much for all his promises," she shrugs.

"Yeah," Azina moans. "That sort of diminishes the expectations a bit."

"But the Marshal doesn't go in and simply ask for something, and neither does he negotiate. His ambitions do not seem to care for other people's opinions. After all, he owns a military governed by your top-secret Council-mandated authority control chips. So, he blasted the majority of them, down to the last surviving city, and then had us enslave what remained using coercive methods to produce mining teams to do our work."

"In all the nether-space!" Azina shrieks.

"We were using a type of psychoactive narcotic produced by some alien variety of fungus, which I suspect was one of his death toys he had you research for him. This placed them in a catatonic state and extremely susceptive to suggestion. This means, we give an instruction, and they literally work themselves to death for it. And since this narcotic also carried heavy metals, this is exactly what they did."

Azina screams at this mention and clamps her hands around her horns.

"I'm sorry, Azina. But we warned you downstairs."

"Yes…" she pants. "And I think I remember that research project. I wasn't a part of it, but I know someone who explained it to me. We were told to research that thing for any possible pharmaceutical uses, but it was cancelled early."

"You probably only needed to research it enough to learn how to grow the stuff. It required a special environmentally sealed chamber to create the alien conditions it needed to thrive."

"So, he used us for only that part he actually needed from us. How typical!"

"My personal duties weren't really anything elaborate. I managed the base facilities, including the reactor, a conveyor, crew assignments, and supply deliveries. On occasion, I led retrieval operations to the local mine to pick up the metal and bring it back, then to forward it to a processor that apparently used a proprietary method the Marshal assembled. He had a civilian crew operating it, with barely enough training to know which buttons to push."

"Just how is he able to get anything done if no one knows how to do anything?"

"He's good at that," Kaliya offers. "He only gives enough information to do the immediate job, but nothing beyond that. So, one hand literally doesn't know what the other hand is doing in this world."

"Incredible…and I thought our problems here were bad."

"He also installed someone to manage his operation locally," Ayene continues. "His name was Ytani, although I don't know the family name. We never used that."

"I'm tempted to ask why, but I'm not sure if I want to know the answer."

"We never knew it, to be precise. He was a young boy when we started, and this is all we had at the time."

"Wait a minute!" she screeches. "A young boy? First, what was a young boy doing in a military outpost, and second, why was HE in charge?"

"This was a very curious aspect of our mission. He was given a special assignment because the Marshal explained he had a unique Gift which allowed him to interact with the locals on their level to perform this coercive storytelling he was handing out as to why they had to send up mining teams and local minerals from inside the city. These people live underground, and he played a trick on them to make them think there was this big nasty war going on outside. So, they had to barricade themselves inside, which isolated them so he could essentially have his way with them."

"Oh, how wonderful… So, it's not only the Marshal we have to worry about."

"The trouble is he was given a number of special privileges, one of these being a complete wave of the Council mandates for the seed and the Suppressor chip. We learned his chip was actually removed as part of his assignment."

"Removed? Why, do we know?"

"We do, but largely it represented a luxury on his part."

"Oh, I'm sure of that! So, he was essentially unmodified."

"And it went straight to his head. He developed a psychosis after a while, including a deep revulsion of those who WERE modified. As he grew up, his manners became offensive, abusive, and vulgar. He was constantly insulting our base staff for our seeds and chips. And then there were his sexual cravings."

"Uh oh, how old was he?"

"He started at seven decades. In those days, like with any child, he was tolerable. But as he matured, his cravings grew, and he started to ask for our female staff members to service him."

"And again!" she shrieks. "In all the nether-space, are you a brothel now?"

"It sure seemed that way."

"Lieutenant," the Director interjects. "Isn't there any form of law in that military of yours, or at least some kind of protocol to restrict people to a certain level of professionalism?"

"Amongst our own, yes. But he considered himself like a favorite child in the eyes of the Marshal. And he used this as part of his coercive methods to force our hands, meaning to threaten us with the authority chips. If we didn't obey, he would call his Big Daddy and have them turned on so we couldn't complain any more. The Commander hated the idea, as he DID have his turned on during many of his official missions in the naval fleet, and he hated every moment of it."

"What did he do during those missions?"

"He was ordered to fight the Marshal's insurgents by destroying whole planetary populations without the possibility to ask why. And these are societies who apparently never saw it coming, but were described as some kind of insurgent contamination by the Marshal."

This stifled both the Director and Azina, and they both reeled back from the blatant assertion.

"This is what your chips have done to our military, Director," Ayene continues. "Mandated by the Council on the excuse that they're training aids for people who don't know how to fight."

"I am suddenly very, very sorry we ever listened to him in the first place."

"Technically speaking, Director," Kaliya asserts. "It may not have made any difference. One way or another, I suspect he would have his way. He's not the sort of person to take no for an answer. He's a powerful being with some potent abilities, most of which we probably have no true defense against."

"And so," Ayene continues. "Ytani developed this mania, believing himself to be as a god for this Gift of his, able to control this pet population, and us for his threats of the chips. Along the way, he took up a weight training hobby, and if you know where the Alpha Male syndrome can lead, this will explain the rest."

"Yes! I do know about that one."

"He became violent, now abusing our female staff members

during his sexual encounters, and we suffered many injuries and three fatalities when he apparently deliberately cut the seed entity."

"What?!" he shouts. "That madman! And for what purpose?"

"Just to be in control of people's lives."

"And what about your military command? Don't they even pay attention to THIS much?"

"This is where we have one of our misfortunes with the Marshal's custom military protocols. The Commander was forced to give excuses for everything. And when he tried filing complaints, they were rejected by someone in an authority position, which at this point had to be the Marshal. He wanted his metal at all costs, it would seem."

"Unbelievable!"

"However, the Commander was secretly hoping SOMEONE in Central Command would have the horns to question it after a while, for all the lame excuses being handed back. Unfortunately, no one did. They were all of the opinion that 'the other guy' doing the work actually knew what he was doing."

"Oh, wonderful! Is that with or without the chip on active?"

"Without, in this case."

"I swear!" he growls.

"It got so bad after a while; the Commander was contemplating a form of rebellion. Azina, do you recall my visit for those diagnostic probes?"

"Yes, actually," she nods.

"We were planning on deprograming our chips so we could have the freedom to take our own justice, and later abandon the base, effectively going AWOL."

"That's bad."

"And we were right on the edge of mutiny when her people showed up," she thumbs at Kaliya.

"I see..." the Director admits. "And I wouldn't blame you for this point. Would this happen to have any relation to your military record listing you as dead?"

"It would, along with the rest of our base staff. We had to simulate the destruction of that base."

"All right, so let's see about touching on this. What happened?"

"Her military team raided the outpost, captured it, and took us as prisoners of war, at least until they had time to interrogate us and learn what was happening back home."

"Um, Lieutenant, I am having a little trouble with your statement. Are these people at war with us? And if so, why are the two of you now working together…or, actually, wait…would this have anything to do with this insurgency of yours?"

"Yes. But it actually runs a little deeper than that, so let's take this piece-by-piece. Once we understood the real story, we joined them and offered our service to their cause. This would be the end of my personal story, other than for my work since then, and now the beginning of hers."

"Ah, good, so then we should jump over to you, Captain. What do you have to say for yourself?"

"My story is complicated," Kaliya begins. "So, I'll give you fair warning, you're going to lose your horns in a big way."

"All right, I'll take that under consideration."

"Just as Ayene said, our team was working a covert operation to assault her mining base. We arrived on that world with the intention of discovering and shutting down his operation. We knew what he was making, even if she did not. The Marshal, whom I prefer to describe simply as Darumon, apparently didn't explain to them what they were mining, what they were producing from it, or why. But we knew, as we had information from an outside source."

"All right, wait a moment. A couple of questions. Why do you prefer not to call him by his title?"

"First, he does not deserve it. He's a criminal, not a military officer. And we also have information that his kind doesn't tend to use titles in the first place. For him, it's a disguise, much like my uniform, just to draw attention. And you people apparently fell for it. Although, we can also say you would have no idea, one way or another. He could call himself Darumon the Flower Salesman, and you would probably buy that one also, but you might not put him in charge of your military along the way."

"Uh huh, and I think I can see where this is going already. Next is you mention an outside source. I feel I should ask about this. Who or what is this outside source?"

"People who know what this stuff is and what it can do, and also relating to those teachings Darumon chooses not to share with anyone around here. This is a substance known only to a select few, and they don't commonly share this information because it generally frightens them for its destructive potential. The metal they were mining is one thing, and you need to be a native to really understand it. But what HE was making is another thing entirely, and this runs on a scale bigger than all of us. One could say he holds good reason not to tell us, but on the other side of it, if you actually did know, it would send those horns of yours into orbit."

"Very well, I believe I understand the reference, and it does sound like it carries some subversive undertones for his project. But as for these select few, are we speaking of the Marshal and his kind, or is there someone else out there. Because my impression here is you are not working for HIM, therefore it must be someone else."

"You are correct, Director. We are his famous enemy."

"Oops!" Azina yips. "That sounds like trouble, right there! Maybe I shouldn't have laughed at that insurgency thing a while ago."

"There are other societies out there, Director, some of them very advanced. We are in another universe, and those who are native to that space would know their native minerals. This one is called adamantium. It represents a metal with properties that make it superior to the finest steel. It can be further augmented to include additional qualities that our science would never be able to define by common means, because this other universe has properties we don't otherwise see here in our own."

"This would make for a truly fascinating study," he admits, "if we should ever have the opportunity for it. Do you understand any part of it, Captain?"

"Yes, actually, as I've spent a number of years there in intense study with one of those native societies, and I've progressed rather far in it by now."

"I see. And so, he's producing some kind of superior metal, but for what purpose?"

"Unfortunately, this metal is a rare find, so it's rather valuable. But he doesn't care about that. He's squandering it only to refine this unique property out of it that would allow you to augment it with something new. It's a trace energy signature which is absorbed by the mineral over time from the ambient space. Our science would be absolutely clueless on how to access this directly. Central often refers to it simply as Abnormal Energy, as it doesn't fit any existing scientific profile. Therefore, using this metal, harvested by the local workforce, is a patchwork effort for him to get what he wants."

"Really! So, it's not this super metal he wants, but something inside, and probably using vast amounts of it for the trace elements in order to procure anything useful out of it."

"Exactly. And when refined using his proprietary methods, he was producing a material which we might describe as a form of concentrated extract, and it is extremely volatile and highly explosive, on a scale even gods would be afraid of."

"That's a curious suggestion, Captain," he chuckles. "But I'm sure you realize we're not a religious society here, so can you put this into terms that a scientist like me could identify with."

"Not religious..." she smiles. "Yes, but you certainly do treat the Council that way."

"Well, alright, I might agree. But we are speaking of the worship of a mystical deity, not a body of people with a superiority complex."

"Indeed!" she broadens her smile to a grin. "All right, try this one, Director. As we took possession of that base, we also took possession of his processor and the depot where he was storing the material. The processor was located on a moon in a star system called Madzurki, which we suspect is located somewhere in this galaxy, and far from here. The depot was on a moon in a star system called Ooduan, and probably located even farther away."

"This already sounds bad."

"I'm sure it's for safety reasons. We made a special play, a bit like a theatrical play, to dispose of his mining base and his weapon, and we used Ytani's name as the culprit to defer attention away from us or the base staff. The Marshal has become famous for his use of deception, misdirection, propaganda, and other tricks to fool people into doing what he wants, so we're playing it back at him now."

"This sounds like what Ayene told me earlier," Azina relents. "His children's stories, as she called them."

"Right, and so we want him to think there is a new threat out there, while we sneak up on him from behind. In his current condition, with your military under his control, he is very dangerous, and we need to disarm some of that in order to weaken him."

"Yes, I can see your point," the Director nods.

"One part of this was his weapon. We used a conveyor method, directed at a distant galactic cluster, with a super-massive gravastar inside, and disposed of most of his weapon…all except for one unit."

"Um, one moment…" the Director interjects. "How did you manage to aim this conveyor of yours? Because, as I understand it, we don't even have proper indexing coordinates within our own neighboring galaxy. And then you say all except one unit? How big were these units, and why this one?"

"We are working alongside a society of beings who are much higher than ours. So, religion or no, if a god society can cover a full universe in relation to us, and perhaps more than one, you might want to rethink your earlier statement, as it's no longer mysticism. In fact, you have one of them living in that eyesore of a monolith downtown."

"Uh oh… All right, got it."

"Ouch," Azina winces. "That one bites."

"Our form of life is young by comparison," Kaliya notes. "And I might also say a little arrogant to think nothing else can be higher than that. I can't be sure where we get this idea, but perhaps in the absence of SEEING anything higher…that ever-desirable empirical evidence of existence…we choose instead to refute the whole idea."

"Yes, I suppose we must admit to this," the Director accedes.

"We might also wish to blame Saakerav for this point," Ayene adds. "After all, HE is apparently the one to redirect us on this path, and essentially outlawing religion in any form."

"Perhaps."

"Therefore," Kaliya continues. "The conveyor was provided by them using their own means and coordinate cataloging. We just dropped the stuff inside and poof, there it goes."

"Interesting," the Director nods. "This certainly seems convenient."

"It's nice to have friends in high places," Ayene smiles.

"As for the weapon itself," Kaliya resumes. "They were packaged in cubical containers, big enough to fill your arms, and suspended in a neutral-buoyancy gel to protect the contents. We took photos of everything along the way to document it."

"Wow, Captain," Azina croons. "You people are thorough."

"This was a rare, perhaps once in an eternity chance to see this stuff, so we wanted keepsakes. It's known to us by the name of Arcanicium, but some societies call it the Agent of Unmaking."

"Um, yeah...suddenly I'm not so sure if I want to know what that means."

"You're not the only one. We left this one unit behind so we could detonate it locally as a message to Darumon. He would know by the size of the blast cloud that ONLY one unit was responsible, and this would put the question in his mind of where the rest of it went, with Ytani being the only possibility."

"Oops! And that sounds really bad, especially for all that psychosis you mentioned."

"Right, and then our final play with the base, just before we presumably blew it up. This left Central Command with a few very deep worries. We had him steal a star cruiser along the way, which we needed for a mineral survey, and left the impression that he found new friends out there."

"He stole a star cruiser?" the Director inquires curiously. "How do you mean?"

"We were making it seem the mining operation was thinning

out and we needed to find new deposits, so we requisitioned a survey ship. Central complied, as expected, and I led an assault team up there to take it."

"You assaulted a star cruiser?" Azina yelps.

"It was a science ship in this case," Ayene notes. "Not quite as full military as some of the others. So, this young velvet-horn was able to take it fairly easily," she smirks.

"Oh really! And she's your CO?"

"That's right! And I'm learning everything she knows."

Ayene and Kaliya shared a brief laugh before Kaliya continued.

"Actually, as we were preparing our assault, I learned during a stall tactic interaction one of my teammates had with the Captain that he also had misgivings with the Marshal. So, we simply used this to win them over and confiscate the ship. He basically surrendered to me."

"In all the nether-space," Azina wheezes. "Do we actually have so many conspirators among us here?"

"It would seem there are more than just you people who don't like the way he's running things, and giving out so little detail for them to analyze. Once we had this, we made our theatrical play for him on the com-links to destroy the base with an uprising of their former slaves. We later disassembled the structures and removed them, so no one could find any evidence."

"Wow, now there's a complicated operation. So, we have Ayene and her people, listed as dead, Central apparently thinks they lost a star cruiser, and the Marshal lost his weapon to a psychopath."

"I'm still curious as to how potent this weapon actually is," the Director wonders. "Especially if you're using such a term as to frighten gods."

"Yeah, this one's nasty," Kaliya offers. "That one unit we left behind created a blast sphere that took out the entire Ooduan star system."

This left both the Director and Azina gasping. They glanced at each other gaping at the absurdity of the statement.

"Central sent a scout ship out there to investigate," she continues. "We have spies on the inside to inform us of what they're doing.

The ship laid a number of beacon probes using a conveyor launch system, hoping to measure the size of the blast cloud. The result was measured as a blast radius of two and a half lightyears. Now, Director, how do you feel about a religion? Because this one is certainly worth praying to something."

"Yes! I think I might actually agree with that."

"Not to mention, those I spoke of who call it the Agent of Unmaking, the ones we're working with who might span one or more universes, they actually are gods. So, religion or no, you might still want to consider praying to them. These are the Marshal's REAL opponents, and what Sargeras and his kind were once upon a time."

"Uh oh!" Azina whines boldly.

The Director stared at Kaliya for a long moment. He then glanced at Azina before responding.

"All right," he hesitates. "I'll admit, this might offer a definition for that conveyor, if they cover so much by now that they can point something somewhere…anywhere they need to dispose of a weapon like this. But I might still desire a little clarification as to how we define a god in this case."

"I could answer that in a couple of ways," Kaliya offers. "And some of it would be very ironic for people like us."

"How is that?"

"Let's say you have a civilization…young, impressionable, and just starting out. They don't know how things really work out there, so they invent a religion, maybe spiritualist, or perhaps with actual god images doing the work behind the scenes. This is our idea of mysticism. Then, as they grow and evolve as a society, with such as science and technology, they start to learn how those mysteries work, and it doesn't seem so mystical anymore."

"Right."

"So they begin to shirk the idea of mysticism, perhaps even to ridicule it as so much nonsense…until one day they evolve up the ladder so high that they become their own god image, able to do all those things they once thought were the realm of those older, nonsensical gods they threw out the window. They came full circle."

"Oops!" Azina yips. "I think I can see where that goes."

"Yes," the Director muses deeply. "That might be ironic for people like us who tend to dismiss such things so casually. And yet, here we are, in an even worse ironic situation, giving ourselves up to one, and asking for the secrets of the universe from him. Ugh."

"Yes. And THAT one bites even harder."

"But the time frame for all this might be truly eternal," Kaliya admits. "As the evolutionary process does take a long time, and I think this much you CAN attest to."

"Yes, I suppose I can," the Director agrees.

"On the scale of eons, Director, which might be older than life on our planet, maybe even older than some universes."

"Incredible…" he moans.

"As for the rest," Kaliya continues. "Let's come back to it in a moment, as it follows with another part of the story."

"All right, fair enough," the Director agrees. "But this story is becoming complicated, like you said. I'm glad we set up the recorders to capture it."

"Absolutely!"

"So, are we still with you and yours, Captain?"

"And what about Ytani in all this," Azina asks briskly.

"He's dead now…justice served," Kaliya affirms. "We sent him for a little ride with his pet superweapon at Ooduan."

"In all the nether-space! Did you actually need to blow him up on a stellar scale?"

"Well, he thought he was a god, so I sent him off with a Big Bang."

"Oh please!" she giggles.

"I cannot believe…" the Director chuckles and covers his eyes. "Is this how you people behave in your military?"

"Actually, yes," Kaliya smiles. "We believe in a good laugh here and there. It's good for morale. We still get the work done, but the culture of these people is quite different compared to what you have here. Such that they might even ridicule people like YOU, that you believe in so many things that can NOT be done."

"Oh! Now there's an irony. Is there a reason for this?"

"Yes, the stuff you'll find in that other universe, which we know nothing about here. They were using that to solve their problems long before they ever began to study what WE think is so necessary to solve things, and moving farther and faster than we in the same time."

"Oh dear…"

"And in the case of this one society, they also DO have a religion, following the teachings of those beings you refuse to acknowledge, and learning things you would similarly refuse to accept here."

"Oh please…"

"So it works both ways, Director."

"All right, I yield. But at the same time, as I look at you, you look rather young to be leading any kind of military force. Just how old are you if you don't mind me asking?"

"Four centuries, Director," she states calmly.

"Only four centuries and you're a military Captain?"

"My circumstances are a bit unusual, to be sure. I was pushed hard and at a young age. I'm a survivor of a long series of attacks, along with my people, all because of a difference of opinion with a godlike figure who believes he can have anything he wants."

"A godlike figure… And at this moment, who are we speaking of?"

"Darumon, in this case. If you thought he came from a highly sophisticated society, you're only scratching the surface. They have a history behind them…they, and those others out there, which predates us by an extreme measure of time."

"Extreme. Yes, I can see where this could lead us…at least in theory."

"Yeah, here is where our science fails us. We are limited to a three-dimensional universe. They don't live in this space anymore, having already moved on to higher dimensions, which by the way our science seems iron-horn determined to deny…nether-space, that fictional place we do NOT believe exists."

"Uh oh…"

"And this coincidentally makes a few of us wonder who keeps

pounding this into our heads, if not those people who once invented the idea. After all, when we use a jump drive, we are passing through it each time."

"And another uh oh…a bigger one."

"They are also evolved beyond the need for a corporeal body, using the natural elements you would find in those extradimensional domains. As such, things like mortality, disease, and other physical limitations we might normally suffer, which could be in part due to the decay of what we call primal matter and energy, no longer affect them. This grants them true immortality, and as such, they have the freedom to allow their minds to grow exponentially. With this, they can literally alter the fabric of space just by thinking about it. And this Abnormal Energy we haven't a clue over is the reason why. They live off this stuff, and it is abnormal for us NOT to have it here."

"Oh dear…" Azina moans. "So, our science fails because we're missing something critical here to study?"

"That…" Ayene mentions. "And also someone pounding so much nonsense into our heads to deny us asking about it in the first place. Especially after we travel to such like other universes, where we can see it right in front of our faces, but he refuses to tell us what it is."

"Yeah," Kaliya affirms. "Younger beings, like ourselves, can also learn how to use it, with a bit of training and conditioning. We can't claim ourselves to be anything on the scale of gods, but it's a start. With what I've learned as part of my studies, I could blow the lid off any science faction you offer your dedication to here. But to do this, I need to be inside a universe where this energy is found…or maybe have some way to carry a charge with me. We call these energies the dynamistic flows. It's basically an extradimensional form of substance with qualities that resemble both matter and energy, but nothing our classic physical sciences can define with simple numbers."

"Why not simple numbers?" the Director wonders.

"Because it's powered by the mind, not physics. The equations involved are more like conceptual perceptions, not empirical evaluations."

"In all the nether-space," he perks up. "Now THAT speaks to me."

"Now, moving forward, if we reflect on these insurgents, and if we say they really are out there trying to fight your military, I think not only would you lose the battle, but you might also lose the entire planet right out from under your hooves. THAT is how powerful they are. And they wouldn't waste their time with random outposts. They probably wouldn't even waste their time entering this dimensional plane. These beings typically live outside planes like this. So, all they need to do is look down on us from a higher dimension, and bam, no more planet, no more star system, and whatever else they might include as OUR contamination effect. And we would be the ones who never knew what hit them."

The Director's face went blank. He simply hung there wheezing. Azina was emitting faint whimpers as she tried to envision the scenario.

"Please tell me you're exaggerating at least some small part of that," she begs.

"Sorry, Azina, but I'm not. These beings are true gods, not some mystical thing you only pretend exists. You don't need to be religious to believe in them. They are eons old, and with the power of their minds, they could cause a planet like this to simply cease to exist. You wouldn't even have a dust cloud left over."

"Oh no… But you said you're working with them, right? Does this mean you're trying NOT to make this happen?"

"In essence, it's not necessarily you who needs to worry here. They're not unreasonable people, and they actually hold policies to preserve life. They take a parental role with people like us, teaching, advising, but only enough to encourage us to grow. They do NOT promise the secrets of anything, as we are expected to learn this on our own. But where Darumon and Sargeras are concerned, this is another thing. So, here goes the next part of the story."

Kaliya pauses to collect her thoughts as she prepares to continue her lecture.

"Sargeras is a member of an older, now defunct society of gods, we think a kind of precursor race that came before the present-day example. Here's how the story goes. Once upon a time, there was a race of these godlike beings called Primordials. This references Sargeras and his kind as interpreted by these others we call the Estelar. The word is likely a concept term to indicate 'That Which Came Before', as opposed to an actual race name."

"Interesting," the Director muses. "Is this to say they do not actually know their race name?"

"I don't know the precise answer to that, but their form of language is entirely telepathic, and conceptual in nature."

"Telepathic? Interesting."

"It could also be said how they simply don't care...they hated them so much. I've heard this term is used in a derogatory fashion, to give you an idea. Darumon, for his part, is simply a servant creature under him, not quite as godly, but close to it."

"And apparently very dangerous, for all the trouble he's making."

"This much is certain. We learned some of these details from the Estelar and their agents. But this isn't a simple race we're talking about. The Estelar are a gigantic society of beings collected from all across Creation, meaning all the universes out there that ever produced any form of life that might ultimately evolve to a godlike scale, and they united as a single body to govern the rest of it."

"Wow! So, how would this rate someone like Sargeras and the Marshal?"

"As foolhardy underdogs simply to think they could take anything away from them," she chuckles ironically. "They were a dying precursor race that was apparently on its way out by the time the first members of the Estelar rose up. It would seem gods are NOT eternal. Time can play on them even with immortality on their side, as the monotony of existence can eventually cause one or another to simply want to find peace and a final close."

"Incredible! Now there is a concept!"

"But Ghantil," Azina notes. "This does bring that term 'god' down a little more to our level of people just living lives, even if those lives extend across a time scale we probably couldn't measure by our standards."

"It does. So, the mysticism aspect is largely rhetorical, maybe also misjudged due to our prejudices for the term."

"Yeah," Kaliya nods. "This will sure twist the horns, and this might not even be the first time. It could be a cyclic thing of multiple ups and downs of societies. But the Estelar are apparently taking a different approach to it. Whereas the Primordials were an exclusive club, the Estelar survive by admitting younger societies, once they evolve highly enough, to join them. In this way, we think they could perpetuate their culture even if the older societies decide it's time enough."

"That would be a truly fascinating case study."

"Anyway, at some moment, these two societies came into contact. Some have suggested the Estelar held a deep loathing for the Primordials, perhaps from an earlier experience or a memory of some sort."

"How come, do we know?"

"In a general sense, we believe so. The Primordials were known to commit atrocities on younger lifeforms, using them as a form of expendable entertainment, and the Estelar may hold a memory of this from somewhere. And since they hold a philosophical belief called the Measure of Balance, which is to preserve life and give it a chance to evolve, this was offensive."

"Yes, I think I can see this now."

"It is therefore believed the Estelar literally hunted the Primordials into extinction for their crimes. And here we come back to Sargeras."

"Uh huh. And how do we explain his continued existence, in this case?"

"For this, we need to go back in time by a measure they describe as an epoch."

"Are we able to quantify that term?" the Director asks.

"There are scholars amongst some of the associated societies who study this, and this is best described on the order of a billion years."

"A billion! Are you sure of that?"

"Yeah, and this goes a bit beyond some of us to conceive of easily. But for these other societies, many of whom are described as Celestials, which is an intermediate form between such like us and the Estelar themselves, this is how they describe it. And many of them are also immortal by now."

"I swear!" Azina moans. "It makes us look so small by comparison."

"I know. And as I said, the Estelar are thought to be eons old by now. So, if there was ever a society you could call gods, this is the one."

"I see," the Director muses. "And by this definition, I don't think I could argue with you. Just to imagine the volume of knowledge they might have accumulated in that time, to say nothing of the evolutionary advantage."

"They exist mostly as potent minds, with their bodies existing as gossamer shapes composed of this substance we generally describe as ethereal in nature. And again, from what I've learned, those minds can literally bend space to their will."

"Yes, and this would also thoroughly refute the Marshal's insurgents. If one of those were to take offence at us for any reason, I think we would be in a lot of trouble."

"This also reflects on the dynamistic flows, which they use as a type of support layer, much like we have our native environment here."

"Really! So, um…they evolved into this, I suppose?"

"Yeah, part of a trade-off into godhood."

"And they can also use this layer as a type of utility to bend that space. But you know, this reminds me of some of the ideas that went around in the old science faction my mentor was once a part of."

"Oh? And which one was that?"

"Well, it's no longer supported by the Council, and was never very highly regarded to begin with, but it was founded on such concepts as metaphysics and paranormal studies."

This time, the tables are suddenly turned as Ayene gazed at the Director for his statement, and then turned to Kaliya, who was stunned by it.

"Kaliya, did you hear that?" she smiles.

"You remembered..." she croons softly. "Cu'Nar be blessed, you still remember it?"

The Director halted at the strange reference.

"Cu'Nar? What is that?"

"Director, you mentioned at the beginning that my name holds meaning in certain circles. Well, Director, my father is Velen."

Now his jaw drops, as well as Azina's. They both drew in droning gasps at hearing the legendary name, although the name held multiple interpretations at this point.

"Elder Velen Nazég?" he whispers. "Formerly of the Council? The one who left us all those millennia ago?"

"Yes!" she asserts sternly. "No thanks to your tail-yanking Council for all their support...may they rest in pieces. And then your beloved 'benefactor' and his chip-controlled military, hunting us like animals simply for his personal pleasures."

"I... Uh... But...please, don't direct your ire at me. Our movement had to go underground after that time. In fact, this Project of ours, to study the Tav'ageen Anomaly, is actually an attempt to continue trying to learn from it."

"Yes, of course," she closes her eyes and turns away. "You're not to blame. It's those people who are MIA from the Grand Hall, for whatever good they ever did to society. I can't hold anything against you, Director, but there are a lot of others who hold a considerable amount of guilt, and the Council is one of them. Fortunately, or maybe unfortunately, they no longer exist. So, they got whatever was coming to them for trusting an alien creature with his own motives."

"Yes, so it would seem."

"All right, back to the story. An epoch ago, by these measurements, the Estelar found the last pocket of these Primordials and saw they were again conducting a series of atrocities on what we often refer to as the Child Races, meaning to say people on our scale. Each Primordial had a sandbox world with a pet species they were playing with. But for them, life is a game of sport, and living creatures like us are toys. They were seen using them in a contest of battle to the death, where the loser society was wiped from existence and that god would create a replacement for the next game."

"In all the nether-space!" he screeches. "No wonder he seems to be behaving so abusively with us. What did these others do about it?"

"Initially, in fairness, I suppose, they gave an ultimatum to stop. But the Primordials refused. They apparently describe themselves as an overseer society, not underlings to anyone else. They are elitist, supremacist, and very domineering. As such, there was a battle… one final battle to finish them off. We call it the Celestial War, although I might also suggest this is the FINAL Celestial War out of many. The Primordials were finally destroyed. Some survivors were captured and imprisoned, but one apparently evaded capture and went into hiding. This was Sargeras, along with Darumon."

"And I suppose this leads us to the modern day, correct? Are they coming out, maybe with that weapon to take revenge or something? With a bomb that can take out a full star system, I think that would make a very fine weapon to use against gods."

"It would, and even worse. If detonated inside that energy layer, it would create a chain reaction to ignite the whole thing, and this is now on the scale of a universe, perhaps more, if you go outside. And he had over seventeen hundred units in that depot of his, enough for a large-scale multiple deployment tactic."

"Ugh…" he grimaces and turns away. "So, where does this leave us? What are these others planning for him?"

"We must first understand, the Estelar hold a very different perspective on life and living things. They feel life needs to be protected, nurtured, and allowed to grow, occasionally testing it to ensure its integrity so it can survive, and maybe one day, with a little luck, it too can become as gods. This is the Measure of Balance in a nutshell. The Primordials simply hate this concept. We have a spy recording of Darumon once where he was overheard to say his kind chose to dictate life according to their own values, at least up to the point where they don't want any competition."

"Oh, really? So, we might be allowed to evolve, but only until he says that's enough? How nice of him."

"This would answer the one about his promises, too," Azina adds. "We're not allowed to research anything unless HE wants it. Beyond that, we're just tools."

"And worse," Kaliya asserts. "We have another, more recent spy recording, where we are described as already very mature, such that we might be borderline of Sargeras's tolerance level."

"Oh! Thank you!" she yelps.

"The Measure of Balance," Kaliya continues, "is divided by the influence of positive and negative polarity, where each side has a different perspective of how to proceed. Life must therefore follow a path somewhere between. This is how the Estelar manage the great Seas of Creation, as they call them, meaning the full breadth of everything out there."

"I'm trying to imagine the implications of those words, Captain," Azina ponders dreamily. "It sounds so high, and so surreal."

"This is the realm of gods, Azina. So, for people like us, yeah, it could be. If only we could ever realize we can actually escape from our three-dimensional home...and like we said earlier, using our jump drives, we already have this ability, but not the horns to try it."

"Oh, we could do this even now?"

"We sure could. Unfortunately, the Marshal forgot to inform his people that's where they are right now chasing his insurgents," she smirks cutely.

Azina glared at her, as did the Director.

"You know, Captain," she mumbles. "I think you like tormenting people."

"Yes, especially when they fail to pursue new forms of science as our Charter tells them to do...according to the spirit of the words."

"Oh! Thank you so much."

"The fact is, Central has a bunch of ships out there trying to investigate something, but your dear benefactor forgot to tell them they just broke another of your scientific principles."

"Uh huh! Thank you!" she screeches. "So not only did we find another universe, which would be the sensation of the millennium, but we also disproved the age-long myth about nether-space!"

"Yeah, it hurts, doesn't it? And no doubt some of this was due to those same people who keep discouraging us against such nonsensical things as metaphysics and other tripe. After all, it's not measured in numbers," she grins.

"Yeah, and thanks for the rub."

"Anyway, by doing so, we would place ourselves into an environment where we would need to evolve into a new form simply to interpret where we are and how to use it. This is the Celestial form. Then, much later, we could jump to the next higher one, and this is where we lose what's left of our original, now vestigial corporeal bodies and become fully ethereal. Here is where we would join the Estelar. So, Director, evolution might begin in a three-dimensional space, but it doesn't end here. We are simply Children stuck in our cribs."

"Yeah, and that would be enough to cause a few horns to fly," he accedes.

"But now, as for us…here is our next entry point to the story."

"Another entry point," the Director muses. "And another aspect to make the story even more complex. All right, go on."

"Yeah, we've been living this for a number of years now, and it's no easier for us to keep it all organized. We'll begin this one with my father, and the arrival of Sargeras and Darumon here on Azgarén. As we learned from Commander Kriv'tik, Ayene's former commander from the mining base, you people apparently took notice of a rather large ship that came out of nowhere and picked us up, right?" she grins.

"Yes, actually," he chuckles. "And to say large is a bit of an understatement."

"Yeah, I know the feeling. Just to imagine the amount of materials and labor to build it, the inherent cost, and then to simply hand it over to us without obligation, is in itself enough to rip your horns off."

"Handing it over to you? I can barely even imagine something like that. And it caused quite a sensation, as I recall. The Marshal claimed it belonged to his insurgents, and your father was joining sides with them. And this made him go on a long pursuit, claiming you were stirring up everything else out there."

"Yeah, well, we didn't stir up anything until we met with these others, but that was much later. For eight millennia, your military would come out of nowhere and hit us, but only enough to bump us to a new world. We were then allowed a few centuries to settle, build new homes, and repopulate for all our losses, then you came again, and the process repeats. In other words, for someone who wanted us dead, he spent eight millennia just toying with us, but never actually killing us."

"Very interesting, and also very disturbing."

"And this is likely also using your famous training aid chips on active."

"Uh huh, very nice. Another example of someone who never saw it coming?"

"Never saw it coming, and with no way to fight back. Not that it would've resulted in anything, for how Darumon built up your military. So instead, we lost countless people along the way."

"Awful..." he shakes his head.

"We went through many generations...successive generations as we took hits, major losses, then major baby booms to replenish our numbers, then more losses, and so on. My father and mother are the only two people who are original to Azgarén. The rest are at least several generations away, and with virtually no ancestors to recall where they came from. Azgarén is nearly a fable to us by now."

"I am truly very sorry for this, Captain. I wish there were some way to express it beyond words."

"Oh, I'll give you a few things to help express it, just as soon as we're finished here," she grins mischievously.

"Ghantil," Azina mumbles. "You probably should keep your mouth shut. This girl looks devious."

"Yes, I see that now," he frowns uncertainly. "And you say your father is still alive?"

"Barely..." Kaliya nods. "Despite Darumon and his media reports about finishing him, he's still standing. But the long journey and all the hits, the death tolls, and the associated strain, took its toll on him. He's alive, but not in the best of health these days. Still, he tries his best to lead us. But he's not a fighter...he never was. He's a pacifist, like so many others around here, and maybe more than some, as it really offends him to fight something. But he was pushed into a situation of war where we never really had a chance. Anyway, we're not even in this universe anymore, so count that as another lie Darumon gave you. He pushed us ahead of him as he was making his drive for his real enemies."

"OH!" he blurts. "Really! So, he pushed you to a new universe along with our military, but like everything else, forgot to tell us about the discovery."

"We became an excuse, a figurehead for your falsified news media, where your military would hear of a...scouting report..." she flutters her fingers for emphasis, "...discovering my father, but before your shiny new military on training aids could mount a proper assault, we apparently escaped. I guess your training aids didn't teach you anything about stealth."

"I swear..." he moans.

"From our side, you arrived out of nowhere and only took a few potshots at us, sometimes with orbital bombardment, sometimes a ground invasion. And typically as terrorist actions, hitting non-military targets, but never the one thing you had to hit if you wanted us to stop running."

"Oh, well, that's certainly convenient!" Azina shouts.

"This frightened the horns off a thoroughly shellshocked civilian body, causing us to run away each time. We had no idea what these seeds were, or the fact you had chips in your brains. To us, you were cold-blooded murderous mutated beasts. We regarded our wonderful civilization to be dead because of you taking up with Sargeras and his promises. I might further say, we had no real idea of why he came here to begin with. So, on our side of it, we simply figured you were out to kill US for not joining with YOU."

"Uh huh," the Director mourns. "And this is so heartening to listen to now. Especially as I look outside this window at the pollution, and further that towering monstrosity in the middle of the city."

"Um, Captain," Azina mentions. "Speaking of mutations, meaning the seeds… In all of this, it sounds to me like you were never present when we had these going around, so why do you look like you have one?"

"It's more of my disguise. At four centuries, I would be expected to have one."

"Right, that's what I figured."

"We were probably no better at realizing a military objective than you, with or without training aids. So we never put it together that there could be some other reason for it, other than to simply terrorize us. We would run, find peace for a couple of centuries, but then… mysteriously…you arrive and hit us again. It didn't seem rational for you to find us at all, but here you are."

"Interesting…" the Director muses.

"Meanwhile, outside our knowing, this…discovery…of my father in his hidden hideout, introduced you to a new cluster of stars and their associated planets. So, here comes your fleet, saying, 'Oh look at all the newly contaminated worlds those nasty insurgents are occupying. Time for a little housecleaning…' This is where people like Commander Kriv'tik and their associated task forces in active mode come in for their target practice. And this is your fight against insurgents."

Azina let out a morbid wail and covered her face, while the Director closed his eyes and hung his head.

"What have we done…" Azina sobs.

"I am becoming seriously outraged by what he has done to us," the Director spurns. "You mentioned horns going into orbit? Well, mine are ready for lift-off."

"And we haven't even heard about those death toys of his yet."

"Easy does it, Azina," Kaliya soothes. "It's not over, and it also gets worse from here. Then one day, we're desperate to get away from you. We could never figure out how you always found us, so this one time, we made a wild jump to escape."

"A wild jump!" the Director shouts. "That's a very dangerous maneuver if I understand it correctly. What happened?"

"Oh, it was remarkable!" Kaliya rejoices. "Just ask my brother, our current HC. He was present at the time. We arrived, most amazingly, in an alternate universe, and so conveniently located near a star system with a habitable world. What do you think the chances of that could be? Azina, maybe you could try crunching a few numbers just to twist your horns a bit for the probability factor."

"Thank you, no," she relents. "My horns are already twisted up enough."

"I don't believe..." the Director blurts. "Wait, that statement rings with something, but it also contradicts the notion of a wild jump. You should be lucky to be alive, let alone near anything at all."

"That's what we figured," Kaliya affirms. "But we were tired and desperate, so we just counted ourselves very lucky."

"Amazing."

"But luck wasn't what played the role for us. We didn't know this at the time, but we had a spy with us relaying our position to your military every time we landed. So, it was never any mystery to Darumon where we were. He knew, probably because he sent us there explicitly."

"Oh wonderful. So, his chase, and searching for so long, wasn't a chase at all."

"No, more like him driving us in front of him as he had his fun. Now, this world we landed on had a native species on it. They were primitive, tribal, and rather brutish, but we tried to make peace with them, and took up a small space to ourselves for a single city, hoping this time we got away. We lived there for fourteen centuries and called this world Ruuki uy'Daan. And at this same time, we started calling ourselves Daanen-Aryku."

"People in exile, in a land of exile..." the Director mumbles. "How lovely..."

"Here is where the story starts getting weird. This is the beginning of a sequence of events that will eventually bring us back home, not that any of us ever actually expected to come back."

"And what is this about?"

"In the late years of our stay there, a child was born. At about half a century, she is discovered to be displaying the signs of what my father called the Prodigy Gift."

The Director instantly perked up and lurched forward.

"A Prodigy Gift!" he blasts. "You found another one? This alone defies the Marshal's statements that it's something manifesting itself in our native environment. What happened with her?"

"Easy now, this didn't go very well in the beginning. First, my mother is a psychologist, and she was working in our university at the time. She took it upon herself to study this thing, as best she could. She was formulating a few very interesting theories about this, perhaps combined with our studies of this local society and some of the strange mysticism they practiced. But at this moment, I will caution everyone here to use the word mysticism very gently, because there's more to it than you think, as we found out later. This also involves that energy layer."

"So, they were using it also?"

"In a more primitive manner, yes, and this would easily relate to what we might call magic. If a person is properly trained in it, they can literally alter the environment around them, maybe not on the scale of those gods, but it would sure twist a person's horns to see it in action. Unfortunately, it involves this energy layer, and we were no better at understanding it than any of you might be. Our narrowmindedness for empirical study simply didn't allow us to consider the prospect of magic in any form, even though this would likely be right up our alley for my father's science faction."

"That seems a bit ironic," Azina notes impishly. "You are THE people who would study this, and you still couldn't figure it out."

"Oh, Azina, if only you could've seen it. In those days, it was a hopeless mystery. Our schools were simply too restrictive. Everything had to be in numbers, all of it empirical study, just like back home. And our devices simply couldn't measure it."

"This sounds like another failure of our science," the Director muses. "Or maybe our entire culture. If we demand everything to be so empirical, and measured in such precisely defined terms, when in fact it uses a completely different principle, we might be sorely lacking the capacity to understand it at all."

"Exactly. The people I'm working for now have academy and university courses that are designed specifically for this. They might have the classic physical sciences, but this other study falls on a completely different side of the coin, complete with a native form of interpretation which is entirely conceptual."

"Incredible!" the Director gasps. "So, this is to say these people study this as a full academic curriculum?"

"It's a way of life for them. And they can make a form of technology out of it, as well."

"Oh, if we could learn any part of this…" he croons. "It could turn a few heads in our favor to reignite the old factional studies."

"I have some friends who are doing exactly this right now, so hold onto your horns a bit longer, Director. By the way, since we're here, I don't know if you people had this back in the day, but we have this thing we affectionately refer to as the riddle of metaphysics. Director, do you know this term?"

"The riddle of metaphysics? Hmm…" he muddles the thought a moment. "I don't think I recall that particular statement. What is it about?"

"It might have come later as we were travelling, maybe even on Ruuki uy'Daan when we had time to relax and study these orcs, as they were called. In comes in two parts, the first of which is a theorem, and the other is an axiom."

"This is interesting."

"Interesting, yes, but my father, for all his struggles, had a tough time ever trying to prove anything. The idea sounded great, in theory, but I think all that empirical study locked us in a closet. This is why our younger generation so often calls it a riddle, because it never made sense, even though this is supposed to be our faction. It seems to run backwards to common logic. I, on the other hand, finally proved it."

"YOU did? How? But wait…first, what are these components?"

"All right, the theorem. Perception enables recognition, existence demands definition, and from this, substance becomes our reality."

"Yeah, backwards is right," Azina giggles. "Don't you need something to exist BEFORE you attempt to define it?"

"But it does offer a curious twist to the theories," the Director suggests. "This might then reflect on the power of the mind, as she was describing earlier."

Kaliya continues, "Next, the axiom. We say, in a metaphysical reality, nothing unknown exists. It only exists after it is known."

"Ugh…" Azina grabs her horns and ducks away.

The Director's gaze drifts off as he tries to pull together elements from the conversation they've had so far.

"Yes, the mind…" he mumbles. "If we say it can alter the substance of reality, you will first need to understand what you're doing with it in order to create that alteration."

"Nicely done, Director," Kaliya smiles. "And this is the power of a god. It is also the power of magic, and invoked by the dynamistic flows. But an especially potent mind might be able to perform some of this even outside the flows, within reason. Maybe if to carry a charge with them."

"And how did you manage to prove this?"

"First, I had to take up studies with those people who teach it in a formal classroom. And Director, they're nowhere near our level of scientific esteem. Yet they already have devices and abilities we worked hundreds of millennia to achieve."

"You've got to be kidding me!" he blasts.

Kaliya simply shakes her head as she continues.

"Once we found ourselves among them, which I'll come to in a moment, I lost my horns on so many occasions, you wouldn't believe it. Just like all the rest, I was raised with our classic empirical studies. Right now, we're living among people who would be best described as Early Industrial for their level of physical sciences. Animals pulling wheeled carts, simple mechanical machines, and manual labor. They are only now entering the Age of Electricity, and yet with their magical studies…the other side of that coin I mentioned…

they have what they call portals, which are essentially conveyors, but using this energy and the power of the mind to open a hole in space for personal transport. And this done within their hands, not using machines."

The Director gawked at her for the outlandish suggestions.

"And THEN..." Kaliya continues assertively. "Using this technology they invented, they can create a device like our conveyors, but in THEIR case, this is used as a form of public transportation."

"Public transportation conveyors?" Azina shouts.

"Also, they don't use flying vehicles, but they do have animal mounts that can fly, and again using magic to zip them along at supersonic speed."

"Supersonic animals!" she screeches.

"They are extremely progressive. They would put us to shame for the rate at which they develop. They are highly environmentally conscious, so rather than the expected primitive forms of energy production, like natural organic fuels, they skipped a few steps to use fuel cells with a renewable hydrogen input based on a direct conversion of these energies into the unit."

"But that...uh, that..." Azina flusters.

"That would account as perpetual energy production," the Director concludes. "And that beats us, for all we have."

"In all the nether-space!" Azina screams. "And WE don't have this here!"

"Worse is the Marshal was promising us some of his great wisdom," he moans. "I think this would qualify as part of that, if his kind knows anything about it."

"I could offer a comment on that," Kaliya notes. "Although the meaning is subjective. As part of that same spy recording of us being mature as a society, he was groaning about the loss of his weapon. He commented on possibly teaching us how to do this ourselves, which means to mine the metal and to keep it local, but he later changed his mind, saying we're already too high. And while he didn't necessarily seem fully opposed to the idea, where I suspect we might hold increased value with it, on the other side is 'he', possibly meaning Sargeras, might regard this as too much. We think he was actually protecting us for this part, but likely to mean his investment for what value we hold for him."

"Interesting. While I suppose I might be thankful for the protection aspect, I think it is very bitter for the reasoning."

"And finally," Kaliya smirks. "Back to these people. If the rest wasn't bad enough, they recently invented a communication device, mostly due to this war we're forced into now, using concepts that go way over our heads…and theirs too, actually," she giggles. "But these people, with their close association to the Estelar and the Celestial races, have a few shortcuts available. This thing can communicate FROM anywhere TO anywhere, and I do mean anywhere, even other universes."

"But that shouldn't even be possible! At least, not without something like entanglement theory."

"This new tech might use something similar, but applied in a really nether-wild manner. It blew the horns off our Chief Tech back home so badly; she might not ever find them again. So, once we get our immediate business out of the way, we hope to bring some of this home for the rest of you to lose your horns over. There's no sense in us being the only ones," she chuckles.

"Thank you, I think."

"Now, back to the story. I believe we were on Ruuki uy'Daan."

"Yes, and this thing you call magic, and um…your mother… oh, and that Prodigy Child. I'm especially anxious to hear about that one."

"Good, and thanks. So, we have this Prodigy Child, but we didn't get very far with the study before we came under attack again."

"Oh great! Now what?"

"Him…as usual. You people probably didn't know this, but Darumon can alter his form. He's what we call a shapeshifter. He can change his shape to impersonate any other creature he chooses. This is how he was spying on us, by impersonating one of my father's advisors during our full journey."

"And here we go again with another uh oh…" Azina moans.

"This would account as one of his near-godlike abilities. My people also witnessed him folding space during our play with the mining base. This is the ability to transport oneself, by the sheer power of the mind, through a private spatial rift."

"Astonishing!" the Director mumbles.

"That would take some serious brain power," Azina adds.

"Absolutely!" Kaliya affirms. "But it's also extremely dangerous, as it opens up a huge volley of possibilities for him to come and go sight-unseen, and to impersonate anyone, anywhere, at any time, and without restrictions. This suddenly allows us to speculate on a lot of things. For instance, how your military found us, while he, on the other side, still appears to be chasing us. He simply passes from one side to the other to manipulate the whole scene."

"Yes, and I can see your point," the Director concedes. "And this is one more reason to raise my ire. He fabricates these stories of the pursuit, and keeps up this image for so many millennia, while at the same time causing chaos for you and yours with our mutated military frightening the horns off of you."

"Right. Here we return to that wild jump. Apparently, it wasn't so wild. He was probably acting as our navigator, and took us to a world he previously had contact with. They belonged to him."

"Wonderful..." he sighs. "So much for your beyond-astronomical probability of finding a new world."

"We believe he took offence that we had yet another of these children showing up, because almost as soon as we were starting to learn something, he ordered those natives to attack us."

"Um, hold on. Took offence...to yet another?"

"Yeah, remember how his kind doesn't like little things growing up too high."

"Oh, but of course!" he shouts and tosses his hands up. "How could I possibly miss that. And by your reference, this must also apply to the Tav'ageen Anomaly, as well as the Scare."

"And here we go with his seeds and chips," Azina moans. "Therefore, all his promises which never panned out, and the perpetual storytelling to keep us in our place."

"But this DOES imply he arrived earlier, if those original children died of anything."

"Meaning what…he killed them? Oh no…" she ducks her head.

"And therefore, his solution was a cover-up."

"Yes, Ghantil, a cover-up! Like Ayene said once, with nondisclosure clauses to prevent any statistical reporting, so we just keep on doing it."

"So complete…" he huffs. "But it does leave one lingering question… What is it in reality?"

"Let me come to that in a moment," Kaliya assures. "The attack, on this occasion, was vicious and devastating. Only a fraction of us actually reached the ship, out of a fairly robust city. We believe he tampered with our alarms, which were supposed to tell our people to run and keep running. And then we found saboteurs inside tampering with our nav and drive systems. This was yet another minion species he found recently and used in his games. Although, I think I may also add, HE might have done some of it himself, since he was clearly still present, and likely better qualified. But this caused us to divert to another world where he and your military were waiting for us."

"It sounds like he's finally putting an end to this chase."

"Yes, this was our impression as well. Also, during our escape, one of your wonderful death toys came into play, those rocket-propelled seeds. He equipped the natives to hit us from behind as a mere terrorist device."

Azina screamed abruptly at the thought of their innovative technological wonder being used as a terrorist device. She grabbed her horns as she let out her boisterous shriek, then slid her hands around to hide her face and shook fiercely.

The Director closed his eyes and shuddered.

"How intolerable," he moans tensely. "He used them on fleeing refugees during a horrific blindsided attack."

"We crashed on this new world, called Therinë," Kaliya continues. "This killed even more people, and what was left of us found ourselves in a fight for our lives. But he never had any immediate intentions to kill us. He was taking it slow, three and a half centuries worth."

"That fiend!" he scorns. "If there was ever a time when I looked up to him and his promises, I would rip my own horns out for the fallacy!"

"I don't blame you, Director. This would be enough to tear up even the most diehard believer. So, we have this new world, which was another of his works of art, once fully populated, but now blasted down to the last few cities. It had three native races on it, all stolen from yet another world where they were a happy little civilization together, at least until he came along one day and said, 'Hey everyone, I found a new world to colonize. Follow me!' And so, now we have the resulting civilization on that world, which was so inconveniently abundant by this time, that he had to prune it down a bit."

"In all the… I mean, seriously… I swear!" he shouts and grabs his horns.

"There was no way for them to find this world on their own, and they carried a history of someone coming out of nowhere with a suggestion to use a strange, and literally alien, rift device that brought them to Therinë. And this could not be native to that world. It used a form of technology only something like an Estelar, or maybe a Primordial would know about."

"Really! So convenient. But why populate a world only to blast it? More tools to exploit?"

"Yeah, expendable minions. He likes to simplify things, and big populations aren't simple."

"Ours is a big population," Azina mutters timidly.

"Yeah," Ayene offers. "But we also hold special value to him… Unfortunately."

"Un-fortunately?"

"Yeah, un-fortunately…where his personal needs are concerned. So, we're still alive for it."

"Thanks. That made my day," she huffs ironically.

"This is where he found those saboteurs," Kaliya continues. "He twisted one of these races to worship Sargeras as a god figure, and used them plus these natives from Ruuki uy'Daan, which he imported through mini conveyor units to Therinë, to harass everyone else."

"Mini conveyor units?" the Director considers. "Would this be another of his custom projects?"

"Probably, and likely through someone with an engineering background, rather than medical. But we also believe he applied a little custom engineering, Primordial style, to make them work. They're simply tiny, single-man size with matching fusion reactors."

"Yes, that would be a nice technological feat. So we need to know who did that."

"This is actually interesting to me," Azina muses. "Three races on one world? How did that happen? Where did they come from that you have three independent races living together?"

"This comes from the next world on our list," Kaliya affirms. "It became something of a gathering point for multiple societies migrating there from different source worlds. We think some of them had help, maybe from the Estelar. We're also aware Darumon must've been involved once to drop a bunch of his orc minions on it from Ruuki uy'Daan, just to make trouble."

"Well, that was nice of him. How much trouble did THEY cause?"

"They never made peace with anyone, but the other races, at this moment in time, at least held enough cohesion to keep them back. That is, until he sent a more recent incursion to stir things up, and here we have our war. But let me come to that in a moment. We're still on Therinë. Darumon was impersonating one of the locals at this point, having left us after the crash, and now acting as the governor of this one city, filling their heads with nearly as much fluff as he's been giving all of you."

"Very nice," the Director huffs. "What sort of tech level are we speaking of here?"

"Preindustrial, and also a bit superstitious, which he simply made worse. He had them believing this one race he turned was invoking a type of plague on them, possibly by using magical means, and they interpreted this as a type of curse. It appeared as a disease that would hit suddenly and kill them at a certain late moment in their lives."

"Well, that sounds convenient!" Azina blurts. "What did he do to create this?"

"You don't want to know, Azina, because it involves your Belvik Spores."

Azina's face sank quickly, and her voice left her. She gazed at Kaliya longingly, hoping she didn't hear what she thought she heard, and finally turned away.

"And I used the word parasites," she mumbles with a tremor. "Oh, how shameful. All right, what did he do?"

"This was a clever one, but also a truly sinister one. He first invoked this panic over a plague, but locked the people inside their city walls due to the idea of this horrible war outside, a little like Ytani on Morndindor."

"And this sounds remarkably like what he did to us," the Director considers, "with the Tav'ageen Anomaly and his insurgents."

"Yeah, this seems to be carrying a common theme here. Fear tactics, and then coercion. Then he made a complete mess of their native education system, so the people had no memory of their history or past relations with their former friends and allies. And he also fouled up their local religion, replacing it with his."

"It sounds like he made thorough work of the place."

"He was stationed there approximately four centuries, so he certainly had time for it."

"The same as those Spore deliveries," Azina recalls.

"The priests in his temple held an annual service for their children at roughly the age of puberty to conduct a kind of rite of passage to protect them from this awful plague curse. They would receive what they called a blessing from their gods, which in this case were entirely false, and this was supposed to protect them from harm. Unfortunately, it didn't apparently work. They died anyway, but the people were made to be too stupid to realize the failure of their false gods, being told to bow down to them, much like you and your Council, believing they were infallible."

"Um, I have a bad feeling about where this is going now."

"You're right, Azina, it was actually your Spores. They were inserted in these children during this so-called blessing, and set to tick off after several decades."

"Oh no… And in children!" she shrieks. "Isn't anything sacred to him!"

She once again wails boisterously and covers her face. She doubles over in her lap and screams, stomping her hooves and wrenching from side to side.

Kaliya and Ayene both felt for the girl, but there was simply no other way to present these horrors. So, they waited for her to recover enough to continue, with Ayene reaching over to wrap an arm around the girl's shoulders.

"We are speaking of a race called humans here," Kaliya resumes. "Their lifespans are well less than a century. Normally, you might say around six or seven decades on average, although on this next world, where they originally came from, it's going a bit longer by now."

"That's not much of a lifespan," Azina mumbles. "What's the childhood range, in this case?"

"They might describe themselves to be adult as early as seventeen in some cases, but physically, I would say more like twenty."

"That's actually a large portion of their lifespan just to grow to maturity, if the full amount is six or seven decades."

"It's actually far more common than what we have," Ayene admits. "Some people call ours ridiculously long."

"Oh, really!"

"Yeah, and these are people who might otherwise be immortal."

"Oops… So, an immortal being is calling us ridiculously long-lived?"

"The term MIGHT be subjective, but only for some very specific cases, and we're not one of those. Not for how old our civilization is. A Celestial society, maybe, if we say a young, entry-level example. But these run for a MUCH longer time than ours. Instead, they say ours should be perhaps one-tenth, at most, what it actually is, based on us being a mammalian species with puberty occurring at almost our first centennial. Most species of this sort fall into certain patterns, and ours is very exceptional. So, there's something very strange with us that we grow to adulthood in two centuries and have a hundred times that number to play with later."

"Uh huh…and instead, it should be twenty centuries, not two hundred?"

"Every society we've met among these people tends to have similar proportions, give or take, but never like ours. Infant to adulthood is roughly one-fifth to one-sixth their full lifespan, with puberty perhaps midway through childhood."

"Interesting."

"I wonder how this compares to some of the animal species we have here," the Director considers. "I am aware this caused a few controversies in our history, as we tried to understand our origins. We do have an exceptionally long lifespan as compared to everything else here. So, this would make a good study for comparison."

"We can give you a few ideas on this already," Ayene offers. "And it relates to that statement I just made. And you might not like the result. But let's finish this part first."

"Now," Kaliya continues. "The siege of that world went on for four centuries. Darumon was using it as a staging post with his military to plan an assault on his old enemies, the Estelar, which would likely involve that weapon he was making. The Estelar didn't even know he existed, believing the Primordials were destroyed an eternity ago. So, this would've been a surprise hit out of nowhere, and if using that weapon, it would've amounted to a cataclysm on a scale even they couldn't measure."

"And given what you said earlier about this chain reaction," the Director muses. "I can understand that. This would represent another terrorist action, to say the least."

"He's basically alone, so he doesn't have too many options. Your military, even with their training chips, probably wouldn't amount to much against the Estelar. Not even to any of THEIR servant races."

"Granted."

"One of his objectives was apparently to find that old prison and see about releasing the other surviving Primordials. So, he's got some of your ships out there making trouble in a large city structure the

Estelar own, and he's looking for the prison portal gate, which in this case is a conveyor-like rift aperture."

"Oh, great! So, he wants to bring the rest of them out here? No thank you!"

"I have some of my people out there already, dressed up just like me and impersonating crewmembers, and hoping to stir things up a little. We're playing it a bit like our operations here, by dropping hints to turn people's horns around and start asking questions. Maybe we can start another mutiny, but we want them out of there."

"That's a very compassionate strategy, Captain. I wish you well."

"It's either that, or I storm the place. But if I storm it, thereby capturing it, we're worried if Darumon would simply send more. So, whatever method we use, he needs to be deterred from trying again."

"Absolutely."

"Now, from here, the story takes a few very interesting turns, so try to pay attention. This is hard even for those of us who have been living it," she chuckles.

"Very well, go ahead."

"Returning back to Therinë, Darumon used a team of those Ruuki uy'Daan orcs to make a hidden incursion of this next world I mentioned, which was one step closer to his goal. He's looking for that old rift of his, the one he used to steal the local populations. But he doesn't dare show his own face again…for safety reasons, I'm sure."

"Yes, I think I can understand this much."

"But he was there once before, right?" Azina wonders.

"For that early invasion and to pull out those people…yeah, but this was also apparently a hidden scouting run, likely a necessary one to see what's out there, and therefore a calculated risk for him."

"Ah, alright."

"This rift leads back to where it all began, and therefore these Estelar that started it. It's the reason your ships are out there right now. He sent some kind of beacon probe through for them to follow. This place is a region we call the Outer Planes, and it represents a space combining multiple mini universes grouped together as their local homes."

"That is a truly fascinating concept," the Director muses. "Did they make them this way, or did it come like that?"

"I can't be precisely sure, but I am aware they have the ability to create dimensional pockets, like that prison. So, I suppose they made at least some of these as their personal homes after settling the area."

"Amazing. Settling an area on a scale like this."

"But here is where Darumon ran into trouble. Those orcs he sent made some noise along the way and drew attention."

"Oops…" Azina yips. "Here we go!"

"This is where they incited an uprising of the existing population Darumon dropped in their backyard once…ten millennia ago…" she glares at the two of them.

"And another oops! A big oops!"

"Yes," the Director groans. "He became active on multiple fronts, and not all of them ours."

"Now…" Kaliya continues. "These orcs don't socialize very well. They apparently worshipped him like a god, and like him, they were arrogant and violent. They got into a fight over there, and this attracted the attention of the leader of that world. And this is one person you do not want to lock horns with. He's a Celestial. But here I need to make a careful delineation."

"A delineation? But even with a delineation, if he is a Celestial, and you used this term before, that would place him rather high on the ladder, correct?"

"Yeah. We use two terms here: Natural and hybrid. The natural ones are like those we spoke of earlier. A species, maybe like ours, but after tens, or maybe hundreds of millions of years of evolution, which would normally dwarf where we are now, assuming our lifespans were anything normal, and ascending to that intermediate form, where we now take up residence outside our original home universe."

"Uh huh, and this seems like an extraordinary achievement, in itself."

"It would be."

"It also reflects on the Marshal and whatever he might describe himself to be, if not something similar, and where this places us in comparison, had we any real clue as to these definitions to begin with."

"Indeed! But then the other side. From time to time, and usually only in special cases, one or another of the Estelar might create a hybrid form, with one side being Estelar and the other being one of the Child Races. This is sometimes used to act as an intermediary between the two, especially if you intend to carry a close relation, like what they have there."

"Ah! This is an interesting one. So, these people hold this close relation, and through this hybrid Celestial, they are able to interact on some level?"

"Yes. The Estelar, as part of their Measure of Balance, hold a very strict set of rules that say a Child society must grow and evolve at their own rate, and NOT be given the secrets of the universe, as Darumon was promising, as it could corrupt and destroy their culture, maybe even their civilization."

"I see. So, Darumon should never have offered this to us, and I guess, for our part, we should never have accepted it...or at least our Council."

"Right, the Council's gluttony was their undoing. And so, we have Lord Thaelyn, King of this world we call Tae'Eladar."

"Did I say oops?" Azina mutters nervously. "I think I need a bigger word. He's a king of a full world?"

"Yeah, one he united in much the same way as our famous King Saakerav. It was once a bunch of national entities and feuding kingdoms, city-states, and whatever, then he comes along and teaches them better manners."

"Wow! Hey, I like that story."

"Yeah," Ayene notes. "We seem to romanticize a story like this one. And here is a real example of it, right in front of us."

"Yes, but..." the Director hesitates. "Is this supposed to be part of his...interaction? It sounds like he basically conquered the place."

"Technically," Kaliya resumes. "We can say you are partially right."

"I might also say," Ayene adds. "No less than Saakerav himself.

After all, we should probably ask if all those nations HE 'conquered' actually asked for it, or did he simply come in and say, 'Welcome to MY new nation, like it or not'..."

"Yes, I suppose this is fair to ask," the Director concedes.

Kaliya continues, "Thaelyn and his wife, Lady Aerlie, are both Celestials, and they were both essentially installed there for this purpose. They used political methods whenever possible, but not everybody saw things the same way. So HERE is where he conquered the rest to demonstrate this is how things are going to be from now on, and if you don't like it, we'll just wait for your children to be born and teach them instead."

"Oh...dear..." Azina emits sluggishly.

"I may be exaggerating this a little, but it's the idea behind it. He's really a great guy, but he's also determined. Celestials, much like Darumon, do not take no for an answer. And like I said, he was installed there...by a member of the Estelar. So, if a god tells you this is how it's going to be, you can argue, but where an immortal being is concerned, that argument isn't likely to hold up for long."

"He could simply outlast you, by the sound of it," the Director surmises.

"He can, and I believe he did in some cases. In others, it required force. So, we have Tae'Eladar, which is a type of garden world being cultured by this one member of the Estelar. The original species she put there was intended to serve a role. The others who immigrated later simply added more flavor to it. But segregating themselves, and engaging in internal conflicts? Uh-uh. This isn't what she wanted. They were intended to unite in peace and move forward as a collected body...personal ambitions notwithstanding."

"Wow, alright, that says something about these Estelar, I suppose."

"At least this one, who seems to have a special direction for us... ALL of us, including you, by the way."

"Us? Here?" he raises his brow. "Um...I, uh..."

"Allow me to continue, as it would seem our discovery of Azina over here was not accidental. It was predicted."

"Why do I feel my horns tingling?" she mumbles.

"Probably because your observational skills are improving," Ayene smirks.

"Oh thanks, Ayene! I think..."

"Thaelyn and Aerlie have a curious history," Kaliya continues. "As a Celestial, he comes from a much higher form of life, but he took up residency on Tae'Eladar, a world normally occupied by what they call Primes, meaning again people like us...mortal beings, corporeal life. This was because he had this crazy idea one time to come down and straighten those people out."

"A crazy idea..."

"Tae'Eladar was once a dead world in a deep ice age. Again, we think it measured an epoch ago, and we also believe it was a survivor of the old Celestial War. Maybe it was held by one of those Primordials at one time, but it's hard to say. Then, one day, something like thirty to thirty-five millennia ago, this one member of the Estelar we call Maker Kuroku came along and decided to do something about it. She apparently called in a society of beings called the Sarrukh, who we think are probably something on the scale of Celestials, since they can apparently speak the language."

"Do they use some form of common language in this case?" the Director asks.

"It would seem so. I believe this is a common interface the Estelar use with all the Celestial societies. They came in and literally refurbished a dead and thoroughly frozen world into a fresh new environment, and then seeded it with new life."

"Oh, this sounds wonderful," Azina croons. "But that would require some serious tech, I think."

"Yeah, no doubt. Then, somewhere along the way, we have these others migrating to Tae'Eladar, including a race we call elves, also some dwarves, which by the way came from Morndindor, then one called halflings, and finally gnomes. And they all took up space alongside the original ones, which were the humans."

"And here is where they probably segregated into nations," the Director conjectures. "At least until he came along."

"Yeah. He seeks to identify and exploit the strongest values in each person, and then direct them to the greatest common good. Some races have specializations, so if you combine this with others of a different sort, you can create a very robust unity of skill sets."

"Indeed, I think you would!"

"Over the course of his tenure, he built a global kingdom, and the people tend to look up to him as a father figure, almost to the point of worshiping him as a messiah."

"If he is literally half god," the Director submits. "By that definition you gave earlier, I think I can understand this fairly easily. This sounds like a very deep level of devotion."

"While this is true, it is not simply that he's half god. It also involves his teachings, his manners, the culturing he gave them along the way, and so on. Theirs is a VERY unique society by now, and entirely polarized on the positive side of the Measure of Balance, to match his nature. So, there's no crime, no war, no hardship, just pure progress."

"In all the nether-space, and all this without chips to govern anything, as ironic as that might sound."

"Yeah," she chuckles. "They owe everything they have to him, and he brought the teachings of the Estelar with him, although he is delivering this in very carefully graduated doses. So, these people have the unique opportunity to interact with their gods on a level almost like next-door neighbors."

"Incredible, and you said they were only Industrial Age?"

"As for the physical sciences, yes. But it won't stay there for long, I think. These people move fast, especially as compared to us. Their shorter lifespans demand much faster progress."

"But still, that would make an incredible sociological study."

"Well, if you play your cards right, you might have a chance to meet them, because he's coming here to remove Sargeras and Darumon," she grins.

The Director halts as he gazes into her smug expression of confidence.

"Um... Well, alright, I suppose if YOU have access to HIM, the reverse is also possible. Further, if you have access to HERE, this also associates. But his people are only Industrial Age. Do they have anything like space travel, along with those supersonic flying animals?"

"I don't think those animals are trained for space flight, but we are sharing a few things for the purpose of coming here. He has to measure himself carefully for what is necessary in this war, as opposed to his obligations to his people and their natural development."

"Ah, but of course. So, he might be making an allowance for this, maybe for his military, but the rest cannot know of it?"

"Right. It's a delicate juggling act. As of right now, they're testing a few prototypes that we might use later on."

"What sort of prototypes?"

"Single-man combat ships. Nothing too big so far, as they don't have a big dirty industry on their world to do anything more elaborate," she smiles.

"Yes, thank you, Captain," he chuckles. "But are we speaking of space combat, or planetary? A single-man ship isn't much to speak of."

"That's highly dependent on the tech you have to work with. We're developing a hybrid form with their arcanic technology, which uses the flows. This means, a single-man craft, maybe on the scale of a heavy fighter or small corvette class, by our standards, using spatial inverters and jump drives."

"What?!" he yelps. "Spatial inversion and jump drives! At only Early Industrial?"

"They already had some of the preliminary tech. Those portals use dimensional rifts, like our conveyors. Boom. Translate that into a ship and you have a jump drive. Those flying animals use what they call transport spheres, which is like a junior version of a spatial inversion bubble. Boom, upgrade that to a star drive. The transition barely broke a sweat for these people. But our poor Chief Technician will need therapy before this is over, along with several tubes of Azina's horn restoration glue."

The Director glares at the young intern across the table as she appears to be in shock.

"These people are as determined as he is to do a job," Kaliya continues. "And their tech level won't stop them. They have a very elaborate education system, and the full society, for whatever tech level they have, are virtually super geniuses for the amount of education they cram into their short lives. I know, as I had to go through some of this. It nearly fried my brain; it was so fast."

"How do they do this? Are we speaking of more of this magic of theirs?"

"It comes in many forms, including potions and elixirs, which might make use of native herbs that again absorb these energies for additional effects. And they use this one to accelerate brain function, so you get a ten-fold increase in your education speed. And they educate on the scale of years, not centuries like us."

"Amazing. This could explain a few things. And worse, regardless of their tech level, they could outpace us even for what they do have."

"So, when Thaelyn first arrived on Therinë, it was the result of those orcs and the war they started over on Tae'Eladar. Those orcs crossed a line with a number of unforgivable atrocities, including cannibalism of his people, which he simply could not forgive. So, he finally had to finish them, for all their long history of noncooperation."

"I suppose that follows naturally, and I can't say I would blame him. Cannibalism? This is an ugly thing."

"Darumon must've taught those orcs to use a form of magic to open portals, and used this as transport from Therinë to Tae'Eladar for their invasion. So, Thaelyn simply followed them back, as they were now running from him back to our side. This is how he found Therinë."

"Ugh…" he groans and clutches his horns. "Now there is a concept. Interplanetary travel without the need of traditional space flight. Just use conveyors."

"Not simply interplanetary, as Tae'Eladar is in yet another universe."

"That's even worse!"

"Then, on Therinë, he found the rest of us. Once he arrived, he was able to make an index for his own portals. So, this represents the first official off-planet excursion for his people. At least as far as exploration for the purpose of expanding their knowledge. They apparently had a moment in their history of discovering another local world, but the circumstances there were not quite the same as this."

"Interesting. That's a fascinating way to travel. What did they think of it if this was their first official effort?"

"They adjusted to it fairly quickly. The only true surprise were the stars in the sky."

"Um, stars in the sky? Are we speaking of such like constellations, or…?"

"Stars of any kind. They don't have any back home. And you can give thanks to that old Celestial War and those last few Primordials that didn't go down quietly. They dropped one of those universe-killing bombs in there hoping to kill the Estelar who were attacking them. Now, the entire universe, what's left of it, is a nebulous storm, where space was ripped apart at the quantum level."

"I don't believe this!" Azina shrieks. "Just how can anyone cause so much damage if they can't win a fight?"

"These people apparently felt they held more right to rule than anyone else. They are your worst example of bigots and sore losers."

"Really!"

"The Estelar built a massive, and I'm talking about a massive shell around the entire star system to protect it from the outer environment, and apparently relocated five other worlds in there with us, arranging them into two orbital rings of three planets each. Don't ask me how, but it had to be a good trick."

"A shell enclosure on the scale of a star system?" the Director intones cautiously. "And the Marshal complains about a little outpost here and there we need to destroy using people on training aids."

"Yeah, it's a bit laughable. So, here we have Thaelyn, trying to figure out what he's looking at for all the trouble Darumon made on Therinë. First, he finds people who shouldn't otherwise be there, as they matched the various races back on Tae'Eladar. Then he had us and all our troubles. Worse are more orcs, and THIS time with a name associated as to who they work for."

"This sounds like another oops moment," Azina muses.

"Right. It was always a mystery to them how orcs arrived on Tae'Eladar. They just weren't sophisticated enough to do it themselves. But the name being used here is Sargeras, not Darumon."

"Why is that?" the Director asks.

"We didn't have Darumon's name for some reason. When we spoke of things, it was always, 'Sargeras this, Sargeras that.' Some of us think that since Darumon was riding along with us, he was downplaying his own name as a form of misdirection for all our woes. This could then work to his benefit to deal so much havoc behind our backs…as if it actually mattered."

"Yeah, it sounds like he didn't need any special help for it."

"But now, Thaelyn had arrived. He is a smart military strategist, but he chose to keep a very low profile in the face of a lot of unknowns. We had orcs on one side, Darumon's pet saboteur race on another side, and your military, led by Commander Geilv, on a third side."

"Commander Geilv was present over there?"

"Yeah, they had a lovely planetary HQ over there while they wrecked the place, and he was apparently stationed there, along with Darumon at his post."

"Just wonderful!"

"Don't ever believe what you see on the nightly news," Azina moans.

"We had Sargeras's name associated with our chase," Kaliya recalls. "But no one remembered Darumon, except for my father… just barely. We had that governor of the human city, but he wasn't behaving as a man in a world under siege. You know, like someone who actually cared enough to go out there and fight. In fact, he took offence to Thaelyn's unwelcome intrusion to HIS private vacation spot."

"Oh, I am so terribly sorry to hear that," the Director satirizes. "A world destroyed, lives ruined, and he doesn't like a fighting force that actually fights. You said this was actually Darumon in disguise, right?"

"Now you're catching on. So, naturally, this is HIS game and Thaelyn was not only unwelcome, but apparently unexpected.

Darumon probably thought he could have his way with Tae'Eladar just like everything else out there. And here we come to our catch. Maker Kuroku."

"Uh oh..." Azina mutters.

"Now, I need to assemble a few pieces here to build a picture. Try to follow along. We have our ship arriving here and handed over to us so we can escape. What none of you apparently know about, which doesn't really surprise me, is there were beings on that ship delivering it to us."

"That makes perfect sense to me," the Director notes. "Unless you want to say it was on autopilot and just happened to make a wrong turn into our upper atmosphere."

"Yes, well..." she giggles. "These were strange. We call them the cu'Nar."

"Wait, you used that word once before. And this is a strange reference...they who follow?"

"I think the name is an interpretation of our interaction with them, as they who were...following...Sargeras."

"Interesting."

"Furthermore, in our time out there, we developed a kind of admiration for them, and their name worked its way into our language as a quasi-religious form of reverence for their help. They would occasionally make returns to deliver messages to my father, which we very often interpreted as a form of prophetic wisdom for how it played out."

"This is also very interesting. Is this how they normally communicate?"

"They're telepathic, this much I know, and their language is conceptual, not verbal. As for how they usually do it, this is probably subjective, as they had a special case with us."

"All right, but then, who are these people?"

"Yeah...people...and we might use the term VERY loosely. They're a strange form of incorporeal life composed entirely of energy. Thaelyn's people would call them elementals, or in this case Positive Primes, as they are composed of positive energy. And they're not native to any universe we might normally visit. Neither are they known to travel outside their native homes to places like this. And NEITHER are they known to interact with corporeal creatures like us. But here we are."

"Uh huh…and this naturally causes me to ask…WHY?"

"We think they delivered that ship on behalf of Maker Kuroku, because she apparently knows of us. These beings seem to work for her. They were also apparently acting as spies and messengers to tell us NOT to listen to what Darumon says. But your Council…" she rolls her eyes.

"Uh oh, again…" Azina yips.

"Yes, indeed!" the Director blasts. "So, we got a warning to turn away, but THEY ignored it?"

"My father tried to pass it along," Kaliya affirms. "But he also had instructions to run away and bring as many people with him as possible. We suspect the Council was already too drunk on the idea of great wisdom, and they didn't like my father that much to begin with."

"Yes, and even now, our faction is outlawed. And here we have you and your ship. And this naturally follows with the Marshal, his claims, the chase, and so on."

"But along the way, they also tried explaining who and what Sargeras really was. They used a term we didn't fully understand, describing him as part of a dead race, but with the word Titan. As I said, they use a form of conceptual telepathic communication, which requires a lot of careful interpretation, and this of course tested us to understand anything at all."

"I'm tempted to ask why this one word, because it sounds like they were trying to emphasize something."

"They were, because on that fated day, when we were ready to meet with Thaelyn, HE recognized it."

"And that's a big uh oh!" Azina whines.

"A fated day?" the Director wonders cautiously.

"We were being watched, and we were expected to arrive on

Therinë…WITH our message by the cu'Nar, for HIM to realize who Sargeras actually is, so he could help us bring our fight back home."

"Uh oh…"

"Hey!" Azina complains. "That's my line."

"Sorry, Azina," he smiles tenderly. "But it just seemed so appropriate."

"The Estelar like to play their own games on occasion," Kaliya continues. "And the Maker is a special case here. But unlike the Primordials and theirs, the Estelar usually hold a special purpose, and it often involves solving a problem. But they also have this rule of promoting a growth experience along the way, as part of the Measure of Balance."

"That sounds like a complex game of maneuvering."

"Indeed! And we think she knows who Sargeras is, and she wants him."

"And that's a scary uh oh!" Azina yelps.

"On this occasion, Azina," the Director intones uncertainly. "I'll have to agree with you. So much for the Marshal and all his stories of insurgents, and his fake news of how we're holding them back."

"The Maker seems to be managing a series of events," Kaliya asserts. "There's another individual working for her with the name of Adalon. She's a prophetess with an interesting history behind her. She wrote a number of prophecies relating to Tae'Eladar, beginning with Thaelyn's arrival, progressing to Aerlie's arrival, and everything they would do along the way to build that world. It's like a history of the world before it ever occurred."

"That sounds almost mythical for the level of accuracy," the Director relents. "But at the same time, if some aspects of it are being managed, could it be true prophecy, or simply planning ahead?"

"I would probably say there is some amount of prophecy involved, but it must also be very carefully researched to plan corollary events. The prophecies are extremely cryptic. She doesn't want anyone, and likely Thaelyn or Aerlie themselves, to realize what's coming until it actually happens. It seems intended to hide the details until a specific moment occurs where some critical piece of otherwise private knowledge becomes available to someone, somewhere, just when we need it.”

“That’s…ugh…” he grabs his horns and ducks away.

“Yeah, I’m with you on that much,” she smiles. “And here we come to her final chapter in her second book, which seems to be the culmination of the Maker’s work on Tae’Eladar. She knows our history here on Azgarén. She was watching Sargeras and Darumon this whole time and waiting for them to come out of hiding.”

“And here’s another uh oh!” Azina moans.

“She also knew about that one Prodigy Child.”

“And ANOTHER uh oh!” Azina shouts.

“SHE knew about it?” the Director asks hesitantly. “Just for the sake of asking, why would it concern her?”

“Because, Director,” Kaliya explains. “Our history, with our ridiculously long lifespans that can’t be natural, and the whole reason my father was trying to teach us about metaphysics, is due to something he likely discovered about our species at one time, but that someone else didn’t want us to know about.”

“Oh dear…” Azina whines. “Another scary uh oh!”

“You seem to like those suddenly,” Ayene muses coyly.

“Yeah, well, someone needs to do it,” she smiles timidly.

“I’m, uh…not sure if I want to ask this,” the Director flusters. “But go ahead and tell me. I’ll just have to make up a new order for Azina’s horn glue later.”

“I should start marketing that stuff,” Azina notes. “If this gets out on the streets, I could be rich!”

“All right,” Kaliya smiles. “Let’s visit the Prodigy Child first. After the attack on Ruuki uy’Daan, the few people who were still alive arrived on Therinë. She was lucky to be a part of that, but the traumas shook her badly for the horror of the assault, and worse for what was waiting for us on the other side.”

“Poor girl,” the Director mourns. “That’s not a good way to grow up.”

“Whatever she had before this was gone by now. The traumas simply took it away. Then Thaelyn arrives, meets with her, and he applies some of his special Celestial-style therapy and counseling to rehabilitate her."

"He can do that?"

"He can do a lot of things. And it worked! His Celestial teachings, which did so much good on Tae'Eladar, opened her eyes to a lot of things she blocked out or simply rejected before this."

"That sounds very effective. Those teachings of his must be miraculous, for all they apparently did on that world of his."

"Oh yes! But then, as she was undergoing part of this therapy, she had what we might say was a little accident. She experienced another of these episodes you call the Tav'ageen Anomaly."

"Ah! All right, now we're getting somewhere. Can you tell us what happened? Because if she's having this on a completely different world, two worlds by now, it can't be anything the Marshal was claiming."

"Yeah, but in order for you to thoroughly understand what it is, you need to be half-god just to give it a name."

"UH…OH!" Azina groans. "That says something right there. It's no wonder we can't figure it out."

Kaliya explains, "It's not a ghost, it's not some alien thing, it's not a disease, it's YOU, your mind projecting your spirit essence outside your body into physical space as a detached entity. And furthermore, we, as a species, should not be in possession of it. A Celestial race, maybe. Simple little us…uh-uh."

"As a species?!" the Director shouts.

"And we all got the chips," Azina grumbles. "A Council mandate for everyone at four decades, with no exceptions."

"Yes! A Council mandate for something the Marshal told us ghost stories over!"

"And Ghantil," Azina whimpers. "This simply brings us back to those early children, and what she said about him not wanting us to grow up so high."

"Right, so HERE we have the cover-up. But this still doesn't explain the seeds or his excuses to leave home. If his only interest were to cover this up, he should've gone straight for the chips."

"This is where it goes even deeper," Kaliya responds. "First, he was here unofficially long before he ever showed his face officially. He knows us better than we know ourselves…because he made us."

This statement stifled the Director, and it again sent Azina into shock. She tried screaming, but her voice barely even squeaked.

Kaliya continues, "According to Adalon's book, which at this moment has to be copied from notes left behind by the Maker, she apparently saw him arriving on our world and modifying our Eracyodine ancestors to create a new sentient species…us. Our full history is likely falsified to cover up for his involvement. This would explain why our evolution never made sense. We started out as an herbivorous prey species. This variety doesn't usually grow up and take over worlds. It would also explain our ridiculously long lifespans. He's immortal, and we're half Darumon. So, we're half an almost godlike creature, and with skills to show for it. Young or not as a civilization, we can actually compete for the Celestial status simply for our hybridized nature. But he doesn't like it. We're intended to be his minions, not genetic works of art."

"I simply…cannot…" he wheezes as he closes his eyes and shakes his head.

"And ironically, my father's faction is THE faction to teach us what this is. So your supremely arrogant dull-horned Council can kiss my crinkled tail for their treatment of our faction. WE are the ones to talk to if you want to learn anything."

"All right, Captain, I don't think I would argue with that…not personally."

"The Prodigy Gift, as my father calls it, which was thought to be such a rare thing, is said to be a latent ability, and likely only now showing itself. I would expect those children were simply forerunners. We, as adults, are likely too deeply entrenched in our empirical brainwashing to discover it…that and our prejudice, as you called it, for anything mystical. And this could be why your Project hasn't returned any viable results. We simply refuse to believe in it."

"Really! Is that the reason!"

"It's not impossible. Just look at Ayene here. We found her at

Morndindor. She tells us she DID have that Tav'ageen thing as a girl, then you stuck a chip in her brain and that was the end of it. But later, after we pulled it out and started teaching her, she eventually got it back."

"I would love to see your methods so we could try this here."

"I can share a few ideas with you, but you'll need to let go of your empirical school lessons to do it."

"All right, I'll make a note of this."

"Meanwhile, the Maker, through Adalon's books, and then Adalon herself with her more recent prophecies, tell us of Darumon and Sargeras arriving here, my father leaving, the chase, and eventually our arrival on Therinë, where we would meet with Thaelyn."

"This again sounds like that engineering aspect, but some of it might also need a bit of future sight, just to see where you're going with it."

"Maybe so. The Maker engineered Tae'Eladar, and so, if this is leading us to where we are now, THEY are the answer to OUR problems."

"Industrial Age people?" he smiles timidly.

"Exactly...and the last thing Darumon would ever expect to arrive on his doorstep, especially if they don't have space tech OR a jump index to Azgarén."

"She's got that one right," Azina notes. "He'd never see this one coming. All they need is a conveyor method. And if it goes on a personal scale, they could arrive in any corner or dark alley they choose."

"So, here we recap and push forward," Kaliya continues. "Thaelyn arrives on Therinë, and along the way, he uncovers all these games, including your death toys. And this marks Darumon as conducting a lot of really nasty crimes."

"Um, wait," Azina interjects. "You mentioned the Spores and the rocket seeds, but what about the Kajik'tav Serum? It was ordered at the end of that period."

"Oh yes, that..." Kaliya rolls her eyes. "Yeah, he had something special in mind for that one. But before you lose your horns again, we managed to catch it before it went critical."

"Thank you! Finally!" Azina sighs in relief.

"During this time, Thaelyn was sending spies into the city to investigate why their governor wasn't playing nice. Darumon was becoming more and more agitated at Thaelyn's interference in his plans, so he tried to assassinate him…twice."

"Oh, twice? That's nice! If at first you don't succeed…"

"Yeah, overdo it…" Kaliya chuckles. "The first one was a simple assassin. But you can't simply sneak up on a Celestial to plant a knife in his back. So, Darumon had one of his local agents, who was the Dean of an academy studying their magic, try something outrageously nasty. It was a process that could potentially bring a lot of bad repercussions, but I think I'll leave the details out, as it would take too much explaining for now. Just trust me, you wouldn't want to see the results. We have some video of the scene as he played it out."

"Maybe you could explain it more later and let us see it?"

"Sure, maybe later after we settle ourselves a bit. Anyway, the students were getting nervous and starting to protest the research going on in preparation of this event. Well, as you might expect, here comes Uncle Darumon with his feel-good medicine to make it all better. Just drink a little of this, and then go sit in the basement for a while, and everything will go back to normal."

"Oh wonderful!" she shouts. "The whole vial? Do you know what that stuff does in overdose form?"

"Yeah, our local med-tech explained it to us. And these humans are smaller than we are for their body mass, so that just makes things worse."

"Ugh! So, this is what happens if you don't agree with his methods, I suppose."

"That, or else his chips," the Director adds.

"Anyway," Kaliya continues. "He chases Darumon away with the threat of the Estelar arriving to investigate these lost people who should otherwise be on Tae'Eladar, and this frightens the horns off Darumon this time. According to Commander Kriv'tik, Darumon's special staging operations on that world were cancelled for completely innocent reasons, NOT his long-time enemies chasing him away. We also see where your famous Ileani Ur'paran quoted in your fake news where, 'Velen the Traitor was finally killed on the far side of YOUR galaxy...', when in fact he was on Therinë during this time."

"Yes, I like that one," Azina muses. "More joy with the Marshal's censorship."

"Now, the two of them are considered a flight risk, so the Estelar are keeping out for now until we make our arrival to distract him. Until then, we need to unravel all his games here. This is where you people apparently come in."

"With his death toys?"

"Not simply his death toys, Azina," Ayene suggests. "You can do some research for us to find the answers to things he was denying us before now."

"Oh! NOW we're allowed to research something?"

"That's right!" Kaliya asserts. "Although technically, I would say you should be doing this anyway. But according to Ayene here, you people need special permission from your god entity Council to do anything at all. So much for a bunch of scientists seeking ALL forms of wisdom."

"Uh huh, and thank you yet again. But I have to admit, you're right."

"I might also add another thing," the Director interjects. "And this tends to be rather unfortunate for some of the factions and their associated labs."

"What's that?" Kaliya wonders.

"While ours might be a bit more profitable than some, as we also develop and market a considerable product line for our inventions, many others do not have as much of a commercial enterprise, and therefore they are more dependent on the grant money to research anything at all."

"And is this why no one ever gets anything done?" Ayene asks.

"Quite often. The situation seems engineered around providing this grant money as the primary means to conduct any research.

And I am now interpreting this as yet another control mechanism to govern what, if anything, we are ever allowed to research. Beyond that, they barely have enough trickling in to keep the staff fed."

"Well now, that certainly sounds efficient!"

"And so typical!" Kaliya shakes her head. "But now, we have something else we need to discuss along the way. There are a few things you need to know, and this applies to every citizen here equally. First, stop allowing your horns to fly off every time you hear something that defies your empirical sciences. The Seas of Creation are a strange place, and we're a very young society that apparently doesn't know half of what's out there. We might understand the physical sciences, but this is only one side of the coin. The other side, unfortunately, is in another universe."

"All right, I suppose this is reasonable," the Director nods.

"I lost my horns so many times those first few days and weeks watching Thaelyn and all his craziness, I eventually had to grow a new set that was much more durable. Then I took up lessons in his schools. Now I'm able to set some of those same standards for others to follow. And this is exactly what I'm doing. Director, I am that Prodigy Child from Ruuki uy'Daan, and I am literally writing the book on how it works. And it's not just this projection skill."

"It's not?"

"Not nearly. Did you know my father once trained in telepathy?"

"I, um…believe I heard something about this once."

"Well, much like the projection skill, we have this one also. I'm training an army of people with these skills. We're using Celestials as our teachers for those skill grades, and Thaelyn's academies for the rest."

"An army? How many are we speaking of?"

"Thousands so far, with more to come, I think."

"Thousands! In all the nether-space, that will turn a few heads."

"And we're only beginning. Once we return, I expect to recruit more from our population here. We need to set a new standard, and Director, THIS one must be THE standard. And I'll explain why."

She pauses as she collects her thoughts for this part. This would represent her sales pitch for her new movement.

"Among other things," she begins. "Ayene once demonstrated what we think to be a form of precognition, the ability to perceive of future events. This occurred during my impending raid on the mining base. She could see us coming, even though her empirical mind didn't allow her to realize I was standing right behind her."

"That was a day I won't soon forget," Ayene muses. "She and her team snuck into my bedroom under one of their magical invisibility cloaks. They popped into view and hit me before I could even focus my eyes on them."

"Ouch!" Azina yips.

"But it's alright. One of these days, I'll be in those same classes, and we'll see if she can do this a second time," she smirks.

Kaliya continues, "Next, I have another friend who demonstrated a form of clairvoyance."

"He's the one who was peeking in on you in the shower, right?" Ayene grins.

"Oh no, here we go again."

"The shower?" Azina raises her brow.

"Yeah," Ayene smirks. "Her boyfriend, as it turns out. Clairvoyance is the ability to project one's inner vision to other locations, like familiar places or people. He was apparently having dreams where he could see her during her various activities. One time, he was watching her in the shower, studying her brand of soap. That's all, just the soap, not her naked body."

"In all the nether-space! There goes any hope I ever had for romance!"

"And how old is he?" the Director winces.

"Old enough to be interested in something other than soap!" Ayene chuckles.

"Poor Petrith," Kaliya shakes her head. "He'll never live that one down. And finally, I can also manifest objects into physical space, just by thinking of it. And THAT is a godlike power above most others. Just ask a Celestial."

"You can manifest an object?" the Director perks up.

"The riddle of metaphysics, the mind can do it if you can define it clearly enough to make it real. And I've done it. I just haven't told my father yet because he needs to stay out of our military affairs. We think Darumon might try using HIS skills to steal secrets from us, if he should ever get curious."

"Oh great, he might do THAT, as well?"

"Yeah, so we don't want to give him any ideas. Anyway, these are all Celestial grade skills of various levels. The projection skill, which the Celestial societies describe as metaphysical manifestation, is regarded as an advanced quality. The rest are quite commonplace for most of them. And while this might be fine for Celestials, who are exponentially older than we are as societies, what this means for us is dire."

"I'm getting a few ideas already, especially peeking in on people in their showers," he smiles. "But this could also be used for security violations and other things."

"Exactly. Ytani was one of these, and this is why he went tail-crazy with the idea of godhood. We need to prevent this, and to do this, we need people who understand what it is to educate the rest. We also need regulation and new laws to govern it, as well as technology to help monitor it. And THEN, we need to revamp our entire culture to teach our young society what it means to BE a Celestial."

"To BE one?"

"Ayene's earlier statement. Un-fortunately...we ARE a young Celestial society, but culturally, we have no idea what that means. We could possibly say those cu'Nar evacuated us in front of the danger of Sargeras and Darumon, and also to deliver the message to Thaelyn and his people. However, I would also like to see it as a form of pilgrimage to seek higher wisdom, in our case to learn who and what we truly are, and what we need to do about it."

"A pilgrimage... Interesting. And a little poetic, also."

"My father once thought the Prodigy Gift could be a sign of a form of transcendence to something higher. Well, he didn't even get it halfway. We're already there. We believe Darumon is our biological father, along with those early Eracyodines. We're basically crossbreeds, and this is what we mean by a hybrid. In addition, and although this might sound a bit naughty, we've been inbreeding as half-brothers and half-sisters, which probably refined it further. And NOW, it's going critical."

"In all the nether-space, that sounds serious. And you know, that would make sense to me, from the biological side."

"This means we're a society of people with nearly godlike skills and absolutely no idea what they are or how to use them. And worse, we absolutely reject the notion of mysticism, supernatural anything, and of course, metaphysics. And yet, strangely, if we look at that Scare you had once, even though we're a society of empirical minds, we're apparently still frightened by ghost stories."

"You got that much right."

"But here we have one of our biggest problems. We did not evolve into this condition; it was simply given to us. Had we evolved into it, we would be MUCH more mature in our culture, and not nearly as naïve. That god society come full circle. Just look at the mess we're in right now, as a bunch of dull-horns who stopped asking questions, and simply listened to whatever someone flashes in front of their face. It's disgraceful. Worse, Darumon never bothered to teach us anything, and instead he hid it."

"Yes, I understand, and I would choose to hold each of us responsible for our part in it."

"These Gifts are inside of us, like it or not. And so, we MUST, like it or not, evolve to meet this demand. The trouble is, who do you turn to for something like this? The Council? They're no better than anyone else, and worse than most, as they outright rejected my father's faction. HIS faction is the ONLY one to teach this. A Celestial society lives by these principles. The physical sciences become mundane after a while."

"Oh wow," Azina moans. "That would put something into perspective, although I can't say what."

"I'm able to read minds, project my thoughts to others, and

communicate this way. Azina asked about my…costume," she glances at her body. "I'm projected right now, and this image is my mind creating a shape to mimic the rest of you. I had never been to Azgarén before I met Ayene, but her memories of the place gave me access."

"Unbelievable!" the Director wheezes. "So, you borrowed her memories, and from this, you were able to transport yourself here?"

"My projection, yes. My body…well, both of us actually…they're on Therinë. That's another universe in case you forgot."

"In all the… You're able to project an image from all the way over there?"

"It's powerful! We can move by thought and take alternate shapes. But in order to teach and condition our public, you need someone to set the standards. That's what I'm doing now with my new military unit. I'm a paladin, a type of holy warrior WITH a religion giving myself to a member of the Estelar called Lord Oghma. A paladin is a highly regarded station of knighthood, one that sets standards for others to follow. Our society of people who don't believe in gods is going to have to learn who those gods actually are, and start listening to them because THEY must now become our teachers. Only they can teach us who and what we really are, and guide us as we continue our evolution."

"That sounds serious, but do you think you can actually do this? We're speaking of a full world here, roughly four billion people."

"It's a demand, not a desire. Just imagine that full world of people like Ytani. You don't need to go any further than that. This will be the end of us. Once you start turning off those chips, boom, there you are."

"Oops!" Azina yips. "She's got a point!"

"Yes, she does," the Director admits. "And I can already think of a few things. Not simply security violations, but also theft and fraud, and who knows what else, especially if you can impersonate someone else, like the Marshal has been doing to us."

"Ayene's ACI is one part of it, to secure our tails," Kaliya notes. "My part is the regulatory body, and it has to be government level. We're an elite force training everything Thaelyn can throw at us, and it's quite a list so far, many parts having nothing to do with a military aspect, and including our full set of native skills. There simply is no other authority on the subject, and we're trained by people who ought to know."

"All right, I suppose I can't argue this, especially if you already have experience in it. This simply exemplifies the insurgency idea. Regardless of where the Council is, it looks like they're being put out of work. But this does bring me to one important question, and that is how you intend to apply this? Do you intend to create a new government body out of this unit of yours?"

"For the moment, I can't be exactly sure how it will develop. First, we need to get Darumon out of here. After that, I think it'll take time to undo his work with the chips, the seeds, and such. But I suppose mine could simply be an office, a branch of authority. It needs enough leverage to set laws and principles, assist in the development of teaching new cultural mannerisms and ethics, technology standards, and other things to keep us safe. I should also inform you that technically, as a soldier in Thaelyn's military, I'm a citizen of his world, not yours anymore, as is my full unit. Many of our people are switching over by now since he offers so much as part of his kingdom. So, how we work that aspect of it, I don't know yet. We may need to join in some form of exchange or partnership until our people can find stability."

"Good. This sounds reasonable. So, it would seem we have a considerable amount of work ahead of us once we're finished with the Marshal and Sargeras."

"Right. But now, about them. Here we have one last topic, and one more atrocity I need to tell you about, so I'll give you one last opportunity to lose your horns. Those seeds..."

"Uh oh..." Azina moans.

"You had to get one more in there, didn't you," Ayene muses.

"It's to make up for that one Ghantil took away," she smiles.

Azina and the Director exchange a quick laugh at the idea, while Kaliya and Ayene smile amiably.

Kaliya continues, "Sargeras was said to have arrived in a sickly condition at first. My father recalled this, and Commander Kriv'tik also confirmed it for us. We believe we know why, and it once again relates to the dynamistic flows. He doesn't have any."

"OOPS!" Azina blasts.

"Yeah, oops. A lifeform like his would indeed be VERY strange for our medical science to understand, and I doubt you could replace that which you don't even know about. But Darumon, that's another story. According to the Commander, Darumon asked you to build that horrible thing in the middle of town that sticks out like a sore thumb. Here, he put his master to rest and recover from what we have to assume to be a deep dormant condition after he left home and came here. It's the only way he could survive in this universe without the flows. We believe that when you started seeing those first Prodigy Children; Darumon, who had to be watching, decided to take personal charge of things in order to...correct it."

"And here we are with him showing up with all his ghost stories."

"And if he's the one responsible for killing them," the Director scorns. "That's an indication of how desperate he was to cover it up."

"Worse," Kaliya notes. "You apparently had a lot of random deaths until those seeds and chips were fully installed. Well, the chips were his solution to disable the Gift, but the SEEDS were his primary interest to serve his master."

Both the Director and Azina grimaced at the suggestion. They glared at Kaliya, and then each other, and finally turned to their bodies with a renewed sense of revulsion.

"How so?" the Director asks tensely.

"First, a little lesson in the dynamistic flows. The flows are organic in nature, produced by lifeforms on another dimensional level. These creatures are often described as Arcanids, and life like ours shares a kind of symbiotic relationship with them. Our bodies produce a form of bio energy, often in surplus, and it radiates outward. These creatures are extradimensional, and they might cluster around bodies, like our world or our universe, soaking up this energy and emitting the flows."

"All right, this is interesting so far."

"Think of it like the relationship between plants and animals where the oxygen in our air is concerned."

"Got it. This is a good example."

"Now, the Estelar are beings of a truly different sort, having evolved into those places where this becomes their natural environment. We might also suggest any similar creature of that level of evolutionary design would be the same, including the Primordials. Darumon, being a servant creature, is probably of a lesser design, maybe part corporeal and part ethereal. We might actually associate him with an upper range Celestial for this much. So he might be able to exist in either domain."

"All right, I'm still with you."

"Next, we need to touch on how beings like us might interact with beings like those, for instance during the act of worship. Unlike simply bowing down in front of a statue, thinking you're doing something for your god, there's a special practice involved here. When we offer worship to our chosen god, in our case the Estelar, we donate some of our energies into them through a directed link. This takes the form of thoughts, emotions, and meditation, the application of mental energies sent up to him. These beings are mostly mental energy by now, so a donation of this sort can actually empower them."

"You know, from the biological side of it, this would be a truly fascinating study."

"I'm sure it would, but don't expect any of them to hold still while you try to dissect them," she chuckles.

"Yeah, that might be a problem."

"But now, we need to pull this together. Here is where it gets bad. In the absence of the flows, the spiritual energy of a corporeal lifeform can serve as a substitute. Therefore, your panic and all those random deaths…at least until the seeds arrived."

"Oh no…we became food for him?" he grimaces.

"The process described to us is what we might call a vampiric action, to suck out the life energy, leaving behind a husk like what you found."

"That would certainly qualify for an alien attack," Azina muses softly. "But we're speaking of Darumon here, not some parasite... although he sure is behaving like a parasite in this case."

"Yes, he is!" the Director affirms. "And that is perhaps the most disturbing part of all."

"Our Med-tech back home," Kaliya continues, "was trying to analyze those seeds of yours with our med-lab's genetic sequencer, and she found some really weird alien code in there that nearly blew out the scanner. This has to be Darumon and something custom-made for Sargeras, and likely to create a kind of aura effect, with your four billion population generating a cumulative layer for Sargeras to tap into, maybe like the flows, but as an artificial field."

"Uh huh...this is what I was thinking of just now. And the panic pushed them at us over any and all other forms of rational thought."

"Therefore, we can say he fabricated the Scare, gave you all his ghost stories, and forced you to forget all your other technologies for colonizing space, especially as you never did any colonizing anyway...which might again be him keeping you at home. After all, he certainly wouldn't want you running off all over the place."

"Oh, of course not!"

"Then his insurgents as a roadblock, denying you any further thoughts on the subject, and therefore justifying this continued storytelling that everything will be just fine once we clear the way... if and when we ever actually do. Then the industry and its pollution to keep up the image of pushing these seeds at you before you get any funny ideas that you are in fact NOT going anywhere. So, he covered his tail quite nicely here."

"He sure did, and he destroyed our lives and our home in the process."

"It's not the first time. He's probably been interfering with our history off and on many times, some of it to falsify our records."

"Like our evolution?"

"Yes, and we also think he was impersonating King Saakerav. So that romance is likely another propaganda campaign to convince us to follow his ideas."

"Him? How do you figure this?"

"Much like with Tae'Eladar and Maker Kuroku, he wanted us all in one basket, not making random wars with ourselves. We're easier to, um, domesticate that way."

"I don't think I like the way you used the word domesticate," Azina whines.

"Sorry, but this is how it appears to us, at this point. He unites everyone into one nation, and creates this fanciful story that he did such a wonderful thing for us, which I must admit he did, regardless of his personal motivations. Then, he directed us into this new society of non-violent pursuits, like science and scholarly teachings, which also tends to reinforce the idea of easy domestication."

"Dammit..." Azina mumbles softly.

"And now I hear you're using the name again for a space dock up there...more of his grand crusade for a great cause."

"Oh please," the Director moans. "Did you have to remind us of that? This certainly does fit the pattern."

"But now, Director, if there ever could be a silver lining here, it's Thaelyn. He's been rescuing people across each world Darumon devastated. On Therinë, that human city was leveled by Darumon as he pulled out and ordered a combination of bombardment and a group of dwarven miners he had working locally, equipped with plasma mortars from your military, to go in and blast everything."

"Ugh! That monster can't even run away without causing trouble!"

"We evacuated the city, because we saw it coming, and we captured those dwarves and treated their illness from that narcotic. Here is where we first learned of Morndindor, but it was out of our reach at that moment. Thaelyn then united those people together and rebuilt the city."

"He rebuilt it? That must've cost him a bit."

"It all came out of war and disaster relief funds, I think. He has a rather robust economy back home."

"While that's great, wouldn't this be reserved for his own people?"

"It doesn't matter, at this time. And he doesn't hold back. He made this promise once he learned of Darumon and speculated he might do something like this."

"Unbelievable! Then he must be quite wealthy to afford this for complete strangers, regardless of the fact they originally came from his world. This has to count as an independent society by now, wouldn't it?"

"It would, at least up until that moment when they joined into his kingdom out of thanks. But it's not that he's so wealthy, this is just who and what he is as a Celestial. They take a parental role with people like us. And his whole society follows this same philosophy. You should've seen the volunteer help he recruited."

"A parental role…" he sighs. "This would probably put people like us to shame after a while, especially if we must now consider ourselves to be on such a level, or at least a younger form of it. That society you mentioned coming full circle, as surely by now, we would qualify for some of this."

"Indeed, we would! And then he found his way to Ruuki uy'Daan, with my help in projected form. I brought some custom portal tech with me to establish an index, and this brought him across."

"Incredible! So, now you are planet-hopping using portals rather than any form of conventional space travel. We're clearly speaking to the wrong people where those two creatures are concerned. Secrets of the universe, my crinkled tail! And here is this Thaelyn of yours and his people, who are not even Space Age, and they've crossed two new worlds by now?"

"Three if you count Morndindor. When Darumon left, he did so thinking we would be stuck there. But Thaelyn loves a good challenge," she forms a devilish grin.

"Yes, he must," the Director smiles. "Especially if he has someone like you in his service."

"Hey, I'm not that bad!"

"Oh?" Ayene muses wittily. "How many marks did he give you so far on that list of his?"

"Um, we don't want to go into that right now," she smiles sweetly.

The two of them share a laugh, drawing the others in as well.

"You know," the Director mumbles to himself. "I have to wonder sometimes. Is it the females of our species, or simply youth? Or could it be a combination?"

They shared another quick round of laughter as they returned to the conversation.

"On Ruuki uy'Daan," Kaliya continues. "Thaelyn chose to finally spare the remaining orcs, who were down in their numbers massively by now, having been spent on Therinë so badly. I made some special efforts at diplomacy using my projection skill to simulate an image that fit with their native spiritualist culture and convinced them their 'god' was bad and he used them for his games."

"How interesting…and you would describe this as a form of diplomacy?"

"This is essentially how it played out. The natives there would consider the actions of those on Tae'Eladar to be offensive, so we decided to give them a chance. But they were still hostile, and I had to preserve lives on all sides, including some refugees still living on Ruuki uy'Daan who got left behind. Therefore, I went in, did a little creative storytelling to explain things, but using imagery in such a way that didn't necessarily spoil their culture with a lot of weirdness."

"And she won a special merit badge for it," Ayene notes. "Two of them, if I recall, one for charity and another custom-made for her unique skills and diplomatic action."

"Really!" the Director raises his brow. "And at only four centuries. You must hold a special gift, and not relating to this Prodigy business."

"I need to credit Thaelyn and his teachings," Kaliya offers. "At least in part. My traumas before this caused me to seriously hate orcs. Then HE came into it and turned my horns around so severely that I felt I needed to start over. After this, we found those mini conveyors, and one of them pointed us at Morndindor. And on Morndindor, we found her people," she thumbs at Ayene.

"Did they have a conveyor in their base? I believe we usually use those in cases like this."

"They did, but we didn't want to use it as it opened up inside Central Command. So, we took it OUR way. We taught her the skill, learned where Azgarén was from her memories, and now we're projecting a large number of people over here to conduct spy operations, among other things."

"Amazing. This would represent a story to teach many generations."

"It's not finished yet. We still have Darumon and Sargeras."

"If you're both projected right now, is there anything you can demonstrate to us about it? I'd truly love to see it in action."

"Oh, sure! Ayene, should we show them?"

"Absolutely!" she chirps. "After that last bombshell you dropped, we need to test Azina's new horns."

"Hey!" Azina protests. "I just got those!"

The two of them rise from their chairs and Kaliya directs Ayene to go first to give a quick run of her projected shapes. She steps away into the room and prepares for her performance. At first, she alters her image to her squirrel form, then the hawk.

The Director and Azina gaze in awe and hesitation at the display, until Ayene transforms into the tiger image, which caused both of them to recoil back suddenly. She then decides to try a few non-animal shapes, first transforming into a drinking cup, and then a chair, imitating the Director's office furniture. She finally returns to her natural form to judge their reactions.

"So…" Azina muses hesitantly. "If I come in here one day and want to sit down, do I have to worry about you attacking me now?" she smiles timidly.

"Attacking? No," she smirks. "Carrying you off to unknown destinations? Maybe…"

"I'm trying to imagine you as a drinking cup on someone's desk," the Director emits. "Talk about a security violation, and no one would ever know of it."

"I've used a variety of shapes in my service so far," Kaliya recalls. "And fooled a lot of people along the way."

Kaliya now takes the opportunity to transform back to her normal image as a Daanen'kai officer. This naturally excluded the seed entity disguise and restored her glowing eyes. She also changed her clothing to her Order uniform.

"This is the real me now," she infers. "I'm a military Captain in Thaelyn's service, which we call the Order of Tyr, in honor of his father, and this is an order of knighthood under a king."

"Knighthood…" he mutters. "That takes us back a bit. But, um, why do your eyes seem to be glowing?"

"This is another thing from the Maker."

"Ooh, sparkly," Azina croons.

"She apparently instructed the cu'Nar to share a little of their positive energy with us, claiming it was a form of cleansing. Thaelyn has suggested this could be interpreted as the Maker holding such a deep loathing for the Primordials that she wants all trace of them burned away, including in us. This infusion carries a visible effect, being the eyes, and aligns us on the Estelar side, as the two seem to be incompatible. And this is further evidence of the Maker attempting to assist us in becoming Celestials."

"She is TRYING to convert us into Celestials?"

"The Estelar don't throw things away, and she probably wants to steal us away from Darumon's side."

"Uh huh…alright, I won't argue that point. So, is this to say she would require this of all of us?"

"I'm going to make a guess and say yes, eventually, if her goal is to include everyone. But you only need it once, and it perpetuates through the generations. It becomes a part of you after that."

"Well, I can't say how I feel on this right now, but maybe with a little more study, and time to settle into it, I may hold a different opinion. But now what. Is this basically the end of the story and we're at the present time?"

"I think so. We are making our plans gradually. Adalon still has a few tricks waiting for us in her prophecies, but we won't know what they are until the right moment comes around to clue us in. She promises to be more generous in these coming elements, since we'll need to know how this is going to play out in the end. Until then, we're going on what we do know, and stepping our way through a process to disassemble his control mechanism. For instance, you should discontinue these chips. Start releasing people from their grip by disabling them, and either give excuses or tell them to keep it secret."

"All right," the Director accedes. "I can make a unilateral decision for those chips here in our own facility, but I'll need to pull some heavy authority to take control of the rest of the medical industry, to say nothing of anything beyond that. We also need to attend to his death toy manufacturing. Maybe I can call around to see who else ever did any work for him and pass the word."

"Ghantil," Azina offers. "What about the seeds? We should stop making and distributing those. We need to cut that part off…not that it'll matter much with so many people infested with them already."

"Yes, I'll give the word on our side. We're the primary manufacture and distribution point, so I think we can make this happen fairly easily."

"Speaking of those seeds," Ayene mentions. "We're working on some of our own research. We believe we have a solution to remove them, but it needs testing. I'm going in very soon to undergo the procedure."

"Wait! You are?" Azina yips.

"Someone needs to be first, and I want this thing off me. Then, once we have a final result of our progress, we'll share it with you for your own study and application to our people here. But we have a little stumbling point, and that is the Marshal taking notice of his pets shedding off their life support parasite. If we use this on our people, we'll need a really special excuse for it. Either that, or simply hide them somewhere, but that might be problematic. Nevertheless, it would work to our favor if we could remove a few plugs from his life support machine."

"I agree," the Director relents. "And I'll consider this once you get your results. But those seeds are not designed to be removed. What's your procedure look like?"

"We're using Azina's pet Belvik Spores to do what the originals did to those people on Therinë."

"Really! That's a novel approach."

"It worked on her rifle-propelled seed missiles."

"What?" Azina blurts.

"Yeah, Azina…" Kaliya notes. "We used one of your death toys to kill another one, so maybe you can take a little solace from that."

"All right, I can do that. And maybe I can do a little of my own research on the subject."

"I would also have you do some research on our behalf. We need to find the evidence he's been hiding on our true evolution. If we can collect this while he's not looking, we can demonstrate it to the people, but only in such a way that he doesn't get any ideas that we're misbehaving."

"And how do we do that?" the Director asks.

"Ayene and I have a number of ideas going around to create our own propaganda campaign. We'll use Ytani's image as a threat to Darumon with his weapon and Ytani's fetishes, just to see how Darumon likes having things turned around on him, and then subversive methods to get the word out for everything else."

"We're also working on the military," Ayene adds. "Like those ships out by the city of Sigil, which is where that prison portal is located. We're not entirely sure how this will turn out yet, but we're dropping hints that the chips are being misused by the Marshal to have his own way of things, regardless of who is on the other side."

"That'll sure turn someone's horns," Azina notes. "And what about Central?"

"Central already got the message when her team impersonated our former base staff. We made that elaborate play on the com-links to the people in the control center, and they took it rather hard. In fact…" she chuckles. "Poor Captain Ta'yeen had an episode where he collapsed from all his feedback hits."

"We also have Commander Geilv," Kaliya submits. "Our observations show him struggling against his chips, even in active mode. Do these things have any kind of a lifespan, like for wear and tear?"

"Technically, yes," the Director responds. "Most often, we have people come in for recalibrations as part of a maintenance procedure. Why, do you think he's not doing it?"

"Yes! We have statements that he stopped going in a long time ago as a silent form of protest for being on active most of his life. Right now, he's showing an unexpectedly lucid mind for being on active, at least as it's described to us by Commander Kriv'tik. He's questioning himself, the Marshal, and many of the experiences he's had, like from Therinë and other things. He looks almost like he's ready to rip that piece of junk out of his head sometimes, but he's definitely showing a level of control over it."

"Then he could be seriously out of alignment, which could be good and bad in various ways. It might allow him greater flexibility over his thoughts, due to the control mechanism being out of sync, but it could also cause injury if he doesn't correct it. Do you think you can convince him to simply disable it? That would be my suggestion for all of them, actually."

"We'll work on it, but the Marshal cannot know of it, this much is certain."

"Yes, I agree."

Chapter 6

INSURGENCY

"You know, my Lord," the General observes. "As I review these scouting reports, among other things, I am noticing their timing of day and night is considerably off from our own."

"Yes, not every world is made the same, General."

"I recall this from our history lesson back home," Kailen offers. "Azgarén has an especially long cycle. We use the term rhenuud to describe it. For us, it's the same idea as a day-night cycle for you, but in our case much longer."

"This will take some getting used to, I would think," the General considers.

"The extended duration may demand some consideration," Thaelyn suggests. "But I think it should not be too difficult. Depending on where you might find yourself on Tae'Eladar, you might also find longer or shorter cycles in different seasons and at different latitudes. But we still have our traditional clocks, and we will follow that which is natural for us, just as they do on Azgarén."

"Very good, my Lord," he nods. "But anyway, so far, we have nothing of extraordinary import for a landing site. Nevertheless, I would imagine we might need to take some of it underground. After all, we would not wish to stand out too much."

"Indeed, and I would further wish to keep it within some reasonable proximity to our mark. I hold the opinion that we will be engaging in some manner of confrontation, although how this will appear is still a mystery. I can only hope those last few prophecies reveal themselves soon to give us our clues. Until then, we might wish to consider one or another of these valleys near their capital city, perhaps on the opposite side of these lines of hills."

Thaelyn, the General, and the other officers, were in their usual meeting in the WIC building, this time reviewing a number of reports, a series of photos, and several maps they obtained from the local shopping venues in Capitol Prime as part of Ayene's infiltration efforts with her new agency. They were examining the geography of the region hoping to locate a convenient arrival zone for their official military incursion.

"But if this is the case," the General considers. "Any arrival we make, or any amount of digging-in, will likely make a lot of noise, to say nothing of raising a lot of dust."

"This is true, but here we might be able to devise a clever plan, if we are correct with this last prophecy and how it may provide us with some valuable sympathizers. If they can offer some amount of cover, we could disguise it as something else."

"Ah! Yes, my Lord, and then we might have enough freedom to take our time with it. Then, perhaps if to build some sort of staging area, but it would need to incorporate some of our new technology, especially the new Harvester device, and somehow infuse the area with an arcanic layer for our people to tap into."

"This should be fun," Kailen chuckles. "To see you bringing your magic to a world of people who would otherwise describe it as mysticism. Oh, I simply must see the look on their faces."

"Yes, Commander," Thaelyn muses humorously. "As would I… It would certainly make a fine and thoroughly unexpected turn… hmm…" he halts his thoughts briefly. "Yes, an unexpected turn. This could be rather interesting."

"My Lord?" the General inquires.

"He would never expect such as magic in a world like this. If we were to create a staging post in his backyard, much like he was doing here on Therinë, while turning his eyes elsewhere with our games, therefore playing his own intrigue against him, this would surely turn his ire. But at the same time, if he is not expecting us to possess this Harvester technology, he would never expect us to stand up to the same prestige in our battle readiness using magic as we did before. He would therefore consider himself to be in a stronger position for his forces. This could work to our favor, if only we can determine how we might advance on him."

"Do we have him come to us, or do we go to him, in this case. We want to keep it on our terms, as you know. But I somehow doubt the Harvester would offer us so much reach that it could spread all the way to their city to find him. In this case, it might prove better if he came out, or else to move our staging post closer to him."

"Yes, and let us not forget, we also have Sargeras, who is inside that one building. From our observations, and through Kaliya's people conducting their occasional interviews, we have determined he does not apparently come outside for any reason. This leaves us to either storm the building, or try to draw him out with a lure of some sort."

"Storming the building would place us square in the middle of that city, and I dread to think of the collateral damage it might invoke."

"Indeed, and I would not wish to give him such opportunity to hide behind it, either. So we need to draw him out to an unpopulated area, like this valley again. But this represents a paradox unless those last quatrains tell us something. We may need to place this element on hold until we can see that key event occur."

"This also reminds me of his tendency to use bombardment," Kailen notes. "If you set yourselves out in the open, you'll make a good target, once he knows you're out there."

"Then we will need to ensure ourselves against his military before that happens. This much we can be certain of."

"I wonder if Kaliya could use her love and kisses approach on a battle cruiser," he chuckles.

"Be careful of what you ask for, Commander," Thaelyn advises lightheartedly. "I think we still have a long way to go."

Kaliya and Ayene were arriving back in the strategy room after returning to their bodies from their visit to Azgarén. They had just finished the meeting with the Director and Azina, and passed along a series of instructions and ideas.

"My Lord," Kaliya announces. "We're back."

They take up seating at the table and join the group.

"Very good, do you have anything special to report on your meeting?"

"I have a recording to file with Commander Nazég here," Ayene pulls out her trans-com. "Beyond that, it was a long and difficult story to tell."

"We have a few interesting notes up front," Kaliya offers. "Apparently, that Director of theirs is a hidden member of father's old science faction."

"What?" Kailen yelps. "They still exist, after all this time?"

"Not openly, but yes. The movement went underground after we left and when Darumon turned everyone's horns down at it. But this is part of the reason for his secret project to study the Tav'ageen Anomaly. They're still asking questions and hoping to learn something. Unfortunately, the lack of any new statistical data, due to the stifling rules they had, prevented much of their progress."

"And how did he respond to our side of it?"

"Once he and Azina picked up their horns…several times…they were predictably outraged at the Marshal for everything we had to say about him. Now he's giving instructions to his full medical staff to disable their chips and discontinue their production, along with the seeds and the military chips."

"This is good," Thaelyn notes. "But let us consider these cranial interfaces, where you have a status indicator as to their operating condition. On casual observation, one can tell if it is active or not."

"Right. He says his team developed a way to reprogram the interface to disable the chips while at the same time still show an active condition."

"Very clever."

"Who is it we are speaking of, in this case?" Kailen asks. "We have that intern, but I mean the Director here."

"His name is Director Ghantil Bak'vayn," Kaliya responds. "He's the lead administrator of the ARC. So, if you have any need to interact with anyone in the future, he is an important figure in the field. He apparently has a number of close contacts in other areas, and he's going to pull some of them together soon for a confidential symposium to bring them in on this conspiracy. Then, he'll have them gather up some of their best researchers and look for our evidence on the Eracyodines, and provide it to us once we can establish our hidden propaganda network."

"Very nicely done, Kaliya," Thaelyn smiles. "I suspect this represents an important component in our insurrection. From here, we can perhaps discover a few additional secrets, and begin releasing these people from their intellectual prisons."

"We also shared the idea we have on the solution to the seeds, so they're anxious to see our results. Azina will also conduct a little of her own research on the idea."

"And so…" Kailen notes. "This generally brings us back to the Spores and the Naarg uy'Sodrad with Ankhia."

"Yes," Ayene responds uncertainly. "And that means me going in for it…and I'm feeling nervous all over again."

"Ayene," Thaelyn soothes. "Do you feel perhaps you would rather wait, maybe to ask someone else to go first? Someone will need to be first, so it stands to reason that first time will be nerve-wracking, and not only for you."

"No, I want this, and at this point, I think it doesn't really matter who goes first. Like you said, someone has to do it, so why not me, as opposed to another. I wouldn't ask someone to take this before me. To me, this sounds like a weakness on my part that I'm too afraid to take that critical step, and I don't want that image. But I just have this creeping feeling like something bad is waiting for me."

Kaliya perked up at the mention and briskly leaned forward on the table.

"A creeping feeling?" she wonders. "Ayene, how do you feel right now? Explain it to me."

"Huh? Why?"

"A creeping feeling...more of that precognition, perhaps? This is what you were doing on Morndindor, remember?"

"Oh! Right. Wow, so I'm doing it again?"

"Maybe. My Lord, how do you feel on this?"

"It is certainly worth investigating," he admits. "If she is experiencing such a strong sensation at this time, and she has past experience where it held relevance to an actual event that was imminent to occur, then we should see about exploring it."

"Good...so, um, how do you suggest we do this? You have a similar form of Sight, so how do you do it?"

"This is a sensation that in some ways resembles a distant object clouded in fog, where you need to focus on it carefully in order to interpret the outline of the imagery. Here, we have such like a memory, as opposed to a physical object, so you should allow yourself to relax into it and direct your attention to the meaning of it."

"All right, Ayene, he's the expert. Give it a try."

Ayene nods and tries to settle herself into this uneasy sensation. She takes a deep breath and leans back in her chair, calming herself with a light form of meditation to open her mind and direct her thoughts at this hidden feeling.

She convinces herself that this must represent a future event, and likely at a moment during, or perhaps toward the end of the procedure with the treatment of the Spore. She tries to imagine the passage of time moving forward to reveal that approximate moment, and therefore the cause of this nervousness. As she drives her thoughts forward, she begins to see a vision appearing.

"I'm alone in a room," she murmurs distantly. "I feel bad...maybe sick...ill in some frightening way."

She continues to ponder the images as the others watch and wait.

"I try to stand up. I call for help. But then...I'm not sure. Maybe I fall down."

She opens her eyes and returns to the group.

"I can't see anything else right away. It seems to be limited to this."

"All right," Thaelyn considers. "Let us try to interpret this. First, I would suggest you are an important member of our team, for all you are currently involved in. So, I think if we were to experience anything critical, Adalon, at the very least, might warn us about it to see if we could take any avoiding action. In the absence of that, I am going to speculate that whatever it is we are looking at can be corrected."

"Well, all right, I'm all for that idea."

"My first suggestion here is that you might be looking at the moment of the seed entity collapsing, like it did with Kaliya's mother. She experienced a rather frightening neural shock reaction which caused her to collapse to the floor in a deep state of delirium. But she recovered, and without any significant medical aid, as she was on Ruuki uy'Daan at the time in the care of Sulíma and Túfula."

"And neither of them are med-techs. So, if they could do it, I suppose that means it wasn't necessarily life-threatening."

"However, since you seem to cut out at this moment, I am going to suggest you spend your final stage of treatment inside the Naarg uy'Sodrad. It could be you experience nothing more than another of the same, or perhaps you fall unconscious as the result. Your seed is a different design than the Ruuki uy'Daan specimen, so the result might be more severe in your case. Therefore, we should not take chances."

"All right, I'll agree to this."

"I would further recommend you take time on occasion to reflect on this vision, maybe to refine it as we get closer to the moment. And inform the Med-tech about what you see, so she can keep a close watch on you."

"Absolutely. Then, I guess there's nothing else for me but to get on with it."

"Indeed. Just keep in mind, Ayene, we are a family together. We will stand by you."

"And then maybe I could visit that dryad grove without this horrible bug coming alive and nearly jumping off of me."

"Ah yes, I read about that in the local papers. Between you and Marelle, we are certainly keeping our people entertained," he chuckles softly.

"Thank you!" she smirks. "At least I didn't get on the front page with my nude streaking incident on Ruuki uy'Daan."

"You know," Kaliya offers. "This reminds me a little of our conversation with the Director. We were talking about the Maker, this blessing of the cu'Nar, and then the Estelar and the Celestial races being generally incompatible with the old Primordials."

"Indeed," Thaelyn nods. "And this could offer a form of evidence if the seed reacted so badly with the dryad energies."

"It was so amazing to see," Ayene croons. "She and all her daughter entities came out of their trees and surrounded me, then hit me with something so powerful…" she reflects dreamily. "I was simply in a daze afterwards. It was better than this stuff we call Pinkweed back home."

"Oh? And what is that? Or do I dare ask, if this is something I should not otherwise know about," he glares at her suspiciously.

"Yeah, one of those. It's a nonaddictive hallucinogenic compound. Back in my university days, I was part of a social group, and we, um, well, experimented a little. It's our way of trying to overcome that horrible Suppressor chip without getting hit by feedbacks. In a world without emotion, you long for a little…relaxation."

"I believe I understand. Even in our world, at least at one time, although it is illegal for us now, we had a few of our own substances."

"This one here isn't explicitly illegal…controlled perhaps, and designated for medical use, but still, it's not something you talk about much, either."

She smiles as she gets up from the chair. She makes one last look around the table at the supportive faces of her friends and fellow officers, and then turns to leave the building.

She uses the local gateway node and arrives in the village setting outside the Naarg uy'Sodrad. The quaint little fledgling town had been steadily developing since the end of the war, with the construction of workshops and market squares, new homes and industry, and several entertainment venues.

A large educational complex marked the backdrop of the village. It was a series of buildings that combined a junior school for the next wave of young children, although the children would not be ready for many years, as well as the foundations for a senior class facility, and a university for those of the older generation. This latter portion was currently the only one in attendance with students composed of the young people rescued from Ruuki uy'Daan.

She makes her way around to the Naarg uy'Sodrad, the great hulk that remained of the Daanen-Aryku's former ship that brought them to this place and was now half-buried after its violent crash-landing. But rather than going in the front door, she instead chose to use a tunnel that led into the hillside where they had a vehicle hanger. This represented a back door, and hopefully bypassing most of the local residents who did not otherwise know about the Suuden-Aryku refugees in Thaelyn's keep. From there, she meandered through to the medical ward to meet with Likha.

"Ayene!" the young resident calls out to her. "I was afraid you might have turned tail on us and run off."

"Hold that thought a bit longer, Likha. It might still come."

"Ayene, please relax. Kailen called just a moment ago and told me about your troubles. We'll take good care of you, and watch you every step of the way."

"All right, so what do you need me to do here?"

"It's really very simple…"

"Do you know how many times I've heard that statement lately?" she chuckles.

"Yes, well, I suppose it goes with the territory," she giggles softly. "Anyway, I just need to give you a hypo-spray, and then we watch and wait."

"Fine, where do you want to put it?"

"Let me take a quick look and see what we have to work with. Please remove your shirt for me."

Ayene unbuttons her uniform jacket and removes it, followed by her shirt, revealing the entity on her back, and the tendrils wrapping along her sides as it penetrated her body to interact with the various internal organs. Likha studied her from different angles to examine the arrangement, and selected a convenient location on her natural skin near the entity. She brings up a hypo-spray and makes ready to administer the contents.

"All right, you'll feel a little sting, but then I'm sure you know the feeling if you've ever visited a medical ward before."

"Yes, on numerous occasions."

Likha presses the device against Ayene's skin and hits a button to inject a portion of the vial's contents into her body. She then moved to a second location to finish it, distributing the contents for better coverage.

"There," she asserts. "Now, we will want you to make regular return visits for a monitoring scan during the first couple of weeks. The final week will be the hardest, as we need to watch you for any signs of the entity failing, so we can catch you before you fall down and hurt yourself."

"I think falling down and hurting myself is the last thing to worry about, Likha."

"Ayene, please, try to hold positive thoughts. Moping around isn't any healthier than simply being sick."

"All right, I'll try," she attempts a smile.

✦ ✦ ✦ ✦ ✦ ✦ ✦

"What is our actual purpose here?" asks one Suuden'kai crewman. "We are sent to locate an ancient rift, but how does this relate to anything else about the Marshal and his insurgents?"

"You mean, relative to these rumors going around?" rebuts a second crewman. "I cannot think of a proper explanation other than we might be in error here."

"Error?!" she groans. "We are inside nether-space! That alone might suggest these insurgents are something other than we were informed about from all this long engagement."

"Well, yes, this much I would need to agree upon. If we were fighting something in our home galaxy, now to find ourselves here, it might lead one to wonder how that first part relates to the rest. Further is all this abnormal energy around us that is said to be as much a resource to them, and also the Marshal, but our science has no idea what it is, and he never explained it to us."

"Is this in addition to his promises of great wisdom?" interjects a third crewman. "This would surely count as a form of wisdom, and like I am hearing going around, we can almost see it right outside the window. And he expects us to perform a service when we do not even hold enough informational detail about what we are doing to guarantee a result?"

"It makes you wonder about all those old promises. In this length of time, I think it is reasonable he should have informed us of something, and done so even before we arrived here, if only to prepare us for the clear and obvious violation of the long-standing scientific theories back home saying it does not exist."

"Yes! This much I would surely agree with. And then, like her..." he thumbs at the first crewman, "...what are we expected to do with that city structure out there. I am becoming very anxious to hear about that survey report, once it is finished. I would like to know what those people look like."

A group of Suuden-Aryku crewman on the ship named the Tul'ryk is in conversation during a break in the local cafeteria. The rumors started by Kaliya have been spreading, and further embellished by her teammates who were continuing to broadcast them in the hopes of eventually starting a form of mutiny that would turn against the Marshal and his objectives where the city of Sigil was concerned.

"Last I heard," the first crewman explains. "The report was not fully assembled, but so far it does not appear to meet with my expectations for our mission declaration."

"What do you mean?"

"First, we are told this structure is owned by the Marshal's opponents, but it seems to be inhabited by beings of a lesser technological grade."

"What about that authority being…and those municipal workers that can levitate. They must belong to something higher."

"Yes, but some of the others who are speculating on this are saying they do not constitute the full population. In fact, they only represent a tiny portion of that population. So, unless we say those beings use others of a lesser technological capacity as their citizens for some reason, they cannot be those same opponents the Marshal was speaking of, if only because they do not appear military in nature. Best case, they are a managerial body, maybe supervisory. And that is not a military force, neither would it constitute anything that could throw out a former leader."

"Could they be a replacement body?" the third one muses. "It has been a while. Maybe this is a new governing body, and the insurgent force moved on."

"While that is surely a valid argument, it only exasperates the situation. We are NOT in a recognizable universe, like our own. If these people can come and go to places like this, they are clearly not limited to a space like ours. This would naturally elevate them to something far above the earlier depictions of what these insurgents were supposed to be."

"I might even go one step further," the second crewman asserts. "If they hold the capacity to do something we otherwise never considered possible, by coming here at all, to say nothing of moving on from here, they are clearly well above us, and I might find it very hard to imagine us countering any military body they did have."

"Yes, this would involve a level of technology we would be very unfamiliar with, especially if it involves this abnormal energy people are talking about now."

"And this further complicates the situation. First, by saying whatever tech they do have might be very dangerous, and this is compounded by the Marshal coming from what is most often described as a superior race. Second, if our home universe does NOT have this energy, either they should not be there to begin with, if we were so successful in all our engagements, or else they should be wiser and bring some of this energy with them to use their superior tech against us from the start. And in ten millennia, someone should have learned a lesson."

"Wow, you are right. And this then suggests whatever it was we were fighting; it was not the same…or else these people were using a lot of decoys."

"If they wanted Sargeras so badly, I doubt they would have us chasing so many decoys all over our home galaxy. They should know where we live, especially if you consider the Marshal's vehement claim of that ship taking away Former Elder Nazég. That one DID come to our home world."

"Oops! That means trouble, and from the stories of that thing, it did represent something much more on the scale of this thing outside here."

"But then," the third member asserts. "Is this to say, based on the early surveys, that this is yet another decoy, or something unrelated?"

"One thing I think I would admit to is I would find it extremely difficult to accept them to be his people unless we are missing something very important here. Um…"

"What?" he wonders.

"Well, if we are speaking of populating something with something else, could it be like populating a habitat with a secondary species?"

"Interesting. But then why. Is this some sort of zoo? And then, to say we are here looking for something as important as this rift device. Why put that in a zoo, as if to say this place is a tourist attraction, not a home for residents."

The first crewman considers the prospect, and then emits a gentle laugh, just before taking a feedback hit.

"Carefully, Ensign," he cautions.

"That one was worth it. He has us investigating a tourist center for something like a prison rift. Are these loyalists on display as exotic attractions?"

Now the third crewman erupts in a minor chuckle, before taking his own hit.

"Yes, good point," he nods. "So this does not make sense. Then, secondary or otherwise, if these are not his people, he aimed us at something that does not fit the description. And if they are his people, they do not represent anything to overthrow him."

"And this is where some of those other stories might come in," the second member advises. "Recall what that other officer said. Those task forces were sent out on active. Here, we are not. The difference? This time we can analyze what we see, rather than simply blasting it because we are blinded by those control chips."

"I do not like the sound of that," the Ensign admits. "Whatever they were, it no longer matters. Just kill it. But if these people are capable of travelling through hyperspace as a common feature, those worlds should not even be involved, as they clearly do not live in places like that…or at least not without this abnormal energy being present. And not when you look outside here. THIS is where they live."

"That is a very dangerous suggestion, Ensign," the third member suggests. "And it brings us back to the beginning with our ultimate purpose here."

"Yes, and if we should question the Marshal's opinions on this matter, he could do the same to us. And this simply compounds the notion of the error, or whatever the cause may be overall, but unfortunately it also brings one to suggest this point is irrelevant."

"Who was that fleet commander, by the way?" he asks. "The one said to be leading that task force. I think I would like names and better-founded references before coming to any sort of conclusion. This almost sounds like someone is attempting to start a rebellion with controversial statements and unfounded accusations."

"Perhaps," the Ensign relents cautiously. "Except for the fact that, once again, if you look outside…" she thumbs over her shoulder figuratively.

"Yes, other than for that. But the two could be unrelated subjects."

"Fine, maybe they could be. But I also heard it said even the High Commander has the chip, and the Marshal often keeps him on active. I have been inside Central Command and seen him, and he does appear to behave as someone on active much of the time."

"All right, this, in itself, is bad. If he actually has a chip, this means he is subject to another authority. And if he is further on active, it only exacerbates the notion of that authority demanding compliance to these directives."

"It does. The HC is supposed to be the top man in our military. But if he is governed by the chip, who is he serving if not the Marshal?"

"It was once said our military is not OUR military," the second one adds. "As we never had one before this. It was the Marshal who essentially built our current military body for the purpose of fighting his insurgents. Otherwise, we, as a society of scientists, really have no idea how to fight wars. We are too docile."

"I am trying to reflect on our history," the third one ponders. "And I find I must concur. He did apply himself to modify our old Sentinels' service."

"Therefore, regardless of who owns this structure, he wants what he wants, and our opinions probably do not matter."

"All right, but what about this. That rift… Regardless of who owns or populates this structure, our objective is to find that rift because it presumably holds access to this prison where Sargeras's people are being held. This authority being may simply be the one guarding it, and this population could be whatever he, she, or it decides to include as local inhabitants, be it a zoo, or simply a habitat for secondary, maybe also harmless beings. Could we suggest them to appear this way as a safety precaution that might not interfere with the prison access?"

"You know," the Ensign asserts. "This brings up an interesting question, while we are here. Who would place access, whether by means of a rift or simply a facility proper, inside the bounds of a bustling city like this?"

"Um…" he considers briefly. "Well, we might have such as local security offices and their detention centers. But are you speaking of that, or a high-level facility?"

"My impression here would be more of a high-level facility."

"I doubt we have anything like that in active service back home," the second one reflects. "I think we do not have much in the way of crime on that scale, if only due to the Suppressor chips curtailing those ambitions."

"Yes, you may have a point, so we might need to consider from a historical perspective."

"All right, from a historical perspective, I would likely say no. Such a facility would more likely be remote, first to reduce or prevent the interactions of the local populace with the secure nature of the facility, maybe also to prevent escapees from so quickly running off into a crowd and getting lost. And also, I might think it would affect property values, if in a city where people would not care to have something like this in their backyard."

"Yes, these are my thoughts, as well. This structure appears much more like a city, not a utility feature for something like a prison center, despite the fact we are speaking of a rift as access. Therefore, that authority being might populate it with whatever is suitable as a civilian population."

"A habitat for any random species?" the third one considers. "But this would then bring us back to the beginning. If Sargeras was indeed sent packing by someone, and all we see left of that someone is this one authority figure, plus a lot of unexpected inhabitants, then that someone must be located somewhere else. Perhaps they have moved on by now."

"All right," she replies. "This may be all we have left to work with. Even though it does not make matters any more polite for the other aspects we have in front of us, like where we are, and what this thing represents in relation to us."

"And this does again demand us to consider those task forces on active," the second member reflects. "Whether or not you want to claim someone simply making noise, if you look at that thing out there, also to compare with Elder Nazég's ship, and further to say they DO clearly know where we live, we might have to admit that sending us all over the galaxy might seem like a waste of time, and especially for this long duration. For one thing, if these insurgents are as advanced as this thing suggests, with or without abnormal energy, they should have won a few battles. But our history says they did not. And worse is they, for all their superior wisdom, never improved their score. And we surely cannot be THAT good, not if we come from a society that does not even hold a strong militaristic background to begin with."

"Possibly," the third member muses.

"Next is this… We had to come all the way out here to find this thing. If these beings, who should know where we live, are watching us, especially if they are so capable of travelling in ways our science generally does not understand, this is bad for where they could be right now and what they are doing. Maybe sending us all over the galaxy WAS a decoy job…to use up our local resources."

"Oops, good point, and we probably did use a lot in this time."

"And did we accomplish anything? Are they dead? Did they take the hint and give up? What is THEIR purpose in all this? If they wanted Sargeras out, he is out. Done deal, go home, because we have not come any closer to returning him home in all this ten millennia, which is a long time for any of us, including the Marshal, who must KNOW where he once lived to find his way back to it, and thus to finally arrive here."

"Uh oh…there is a failure of logic in that statement."

"Yes!" the Ensign nods. "Especially if we won every battle along the way. What was standing in OUR way to arrive here earlier?"

"If this is where the prison is found," the second member continues. "It must also relate to where they once lived, and the people who took over. But this is NOT anyplace the Marshal ever described to us previously. And yet, here we are, looking for something he describes as a prison rift. Well, if his kind makes their homes in places like this, maybe also to use this abnormal energy along the way, and he has us killing everything in sight in our native galaxy, which does NOT have this energy, and this energy could actually be a requirement for them, could it be like you just mentioned, that we were fighting something else, not his people, AND on active so we could not argue with it. And now…we are looking for a prison. A prison…for criminals who do bad things."

"Oh wow," the Ensign moans. "That does paint a very controversial picture. Making noise or otherwise, we need to be sure of this."

"Yes," the third member nods. "I suppose I would need to agree. If they live in a place like this, and maybe do these 'bad things' on those who live in such other places…maybe to say looking down on them from out here, what does this say about them?"

"Absolutely. If you live in such an extravagant place as this, everything else might be considered beneath you by now."

"Ugh…" he groans. "I think I do not like that depiction, as it now gives credence to the idea with a form of prejudice."

"And good enough reason to lock someone up."

"All right. But even with this in mind, we have no true evidence of this structure belonging to the Marshal's enemies, only his word. And his word is what we are bringing into question here, if only because this structure does not represent itself as whatever he once explained of these insurgents. We have one lone individual in there that MAY be a part of it, and a lot of lesser examples that can NOT be a part of it."

"His word…" the Ensign huffs. "Is this related to that same 'word' of his promise of wisdom we are still waiting for, and that 'word' that he is even a Marshal of any kind?"

"Uh oh…"

"She is right," the second member asserts. "Virtually everything was on his word alone. And we call ourselves a society who so often demands evidence."

"You have a very valid point. Maybe someone should have asked for his credentials."

"And so, here we are. If the owners of this structure are paying any attention, we are likely being watched. So far, cutting holes in the shell of this thing and sending armed soldiers in, if only to browse the local shopping venues, might not be quite enough to retaliate against. But if the Marshal…and his chips…should take a different approach…"

"Yes! I will agree with you and the Ensign for this point. We should pay attention to that. Anyone capable of building that thing would be able to swat us like bugs out here."

"Indeed. And it stands to reason that if this authority figure belongs to any manner of society of a similar nature, regardless of whatever is populating that structure, we have certainly made our presence known to them. Especially if you consider they put out wanted posters for us to their citizens. This marks us as hostile invaders. And surely, that one individual should have communications access to others of a similar nature, and THEY are probably on the outside."

"Uh huh… But wait, let me ask this quickly, simply for debate. As for evidence. We were told to seek out this structure, and even given a description of what it looks like. Would this not represent some form of evidence of recognition for a target to pursue?"

"I suppose, you do have a point," he accedes. "So let us try it this way. Say I am a traveler, and one day I pass by a city that, oh, appears like Capitol Prime. I then return home and call up my friends and say to them, let us all go raid that city I passed by earlier that looks like Capitol Prime. Is this, therefore, evidence that I am entitled to something from it simply because I happened to pass by it one day and it appeared ripe for plundering?"

"All right, this is viable, and well stated. So, this city, and for that matter, anything else out there he might have once happened to pass by, could become a target for whatever…brazen…ambitions he might hold for it."

"And us on chips to do the work."

"And all this eventually boils down to one thing," the Ensign concludes. "Whatever he did in our local galaxy, now he is doing out here. Ownership or otherwise, if the Marshal, along with his chips and his brazen ambitions, should choose to take more assertive action, what might be the repercussions for it? Because THIS time, we are likely dealing with people who CAN fight back."

+·+·✦·+·+

Director Bak'vayn was assembling a conference with a large number of individuals, including other prominent leaders in the sciences, and the administrators of many other medical and research centers. This was to gain control of the various departments, and to bring together enough resources to pursue the study of their controversial history and evolutionary origin.

The meeting was urgently requested with extreme secrecy, to keep it under wraps so that none of the Marshal's assigns might hear of it, assuming they were even paying attention. Not even the media was permitted, as they often took an interest in the gathering of such people, hoping to learn of some new discovery or research project that might be newsworthy, or simply anything new to talk about.

"I wish to call this meeting to order," he announces to the room. "First, you must all recognize this meeting involves some highly sensitive information. Within the science community, we might not normally have anything like a security ranking system. But on this one occasion, I am going to demand we create one for ourselves, as this meeting involves details of such critical importance, it could cause not only scandals, but also panic, and possibly threaten the lives of our people."

"Director!" urges one member. "This sounds extremely serious. Can you explain the meaning of it?"

"Professor, you and I have known each other for a long time. You know I am not one to jump to conclusions, and I would hope my professional esteem is enough to grant me the confidence amongst my peers to listen to me during this time when I must explain to you a series of reports I have recently come into possession of. But before we begin, I would request a verbal agreement with you to these terms. First, it is to be classified and contained to only those who participate in this meeting. From there, it may be divested to your immediate officers and research teams, but only if they are deemed trustworthy and necessary to assist in our needs. It is NOT to be revealed to the public or to the media, or any other party or authority outside our circle. Do you agree?"

"Um, Director," she hesitates. "Please, one question before we respond. Where did this information come from? Did it come from the Council, or perhaps the Marshal?"

"No."

The Professor glared at him for the curt response. She then turned to examine several of the other faces in the gathering, before returning to his stoic posture.

"Uh, can you tell us where it did come from?"

"The source is third-party, and generally opposed to the practices of both the Council and the Marshal, and whatever service they seem to be performing, no part of which has proven itself to be providing a positive return to our people during this time."

"No positive return?" she balks. "But what about..."

"What about what, Professor?" he interjects. "Let's analyze the situation briefly. Do we speak of the Council's long deliberation? Do we speak of the Marshal's famous promises of great wisdom? How long has it been that we have been waiting for all these promises? The answer is nearly ten millennia. That's a long time to wait for something, even a simple progress report, or any indication that they are, in fact, doing anything at all that is positive, AND designed to benefit our people. Professor, with respect to you and so many others out there, when I speak of a positive return, I speak of the expectancy of a viable result, and within a reasonable time frame that provides a useful outcome we can find tangible enough to employ to the greater benefit of our people before we all die of old age."

"Oh, wonderful," she tosses her hands up. "All right, I see it. You are tired of waiting for it."

"Not simply tired of waiting, but I have also become aware of a few things which brings the entire situation into question. For instance, we did not hire the Council to discover the secrets of the universe for us. That's what people like WE are here for. We are the scientists. We are the ones with the research teams and the laboratories. This is OUR job. THEIR job, by comparison, is managing our world population as a political authority. This includes such things as proposing new legislation, social services, resolution of civic or legal regulations...maybe also cleaning up all that pollution out there that shouldn't exist in the first place. You know, the stuff a government body should be doing so the people can live healthy, comfortable lives."

"Thank you, Director. That is a nice slap on the tail. And by this statement, you are saying they are not performing this service… the one we originally hired them to perform."

"Exactly, Professor. And it should not be just ME slapping people on the tail. We have had ten millennia of this. That's a lot of tails that had to be slapped to remind people we have real scientists, like you and me, who are supposed to be doing real research to find real solutions. But we stopped doing this once Dear Marshal Darumon came along and essentially told us to stop thinking with our own horns, and let the Council do it instead. And this also includes simply looking out the window at those skies overhead and asking when THAT will be corrected."

"Oh, is THAT how it goes now!" she huffs. "No wonder you called this meeting in private."

"Indeed. And I might also offer a side consideration. Our entire scientific community seems engineered solely for the purpose of researching things if, and only if, the Council provides a grant to do it with. Most of us do not have the internal financing to take our own initiative, and neither do we seem to have the horns to think of it either. We are entirely dependent on THEM telling us what to do, or not do."

"Uh huh. All right, I think I can see that one, as well."

"Furthermore, I might also say the Marshal is not here to provide this either. It should not be described as his job to give us the secrets of the universe. We gave ourselves to HIM, to serve HIS needs, as part of a bargain agreement."

"I suppose I might need to admit to this, with or without his promises, which is really supposed to be much more a form of payment for our service. But like you said, there should be time limits to see a return, and ten millennia is a rather extreme one to wait for something, especially if it also pollutes your home environment so much that your people can no longer live healthy lives in it."

"Correct. So, here we are. My apologies, but for this reason, it has to be this way. The Council is demonstrating an irresponsible, perhaps even negligent behavior, maybe in part as a form of gluttony over this deliberation, and the Marshal is not offering any solutions, either. Therefore, it comes to us. And this new information I received recently only makes matters worse."

"Can you at least give us a small hint on your direction, that you need this new security protocol?"

"I will give you a word. Corruption."

"Great. I was afraid of that. All right, I will agree to this, and I hope you can offer us a full explanation for the nature of this situation."

She turns to the rest of the assembly, as each member is queried and responds affirmatively to the demand.

"Very good, and thank you," the Director submits. "Now, as to the details of this conference... It has come to my attention that we have a sequence of events that have taken place behind our collective backs, and this has essentially endangered our population. I will cover each of these in their approximate order, at least in part as a means of keeping my own thoughts in line for the complexity of the circumstances. The sources for all this are a pair of military informants, one of whom is currently working for a new government-level security agency none of us has likely heard of previously. One primary reason for this secrecy is largely due to maintaining their internal security in the face of a corrupt entity that is in possession of a very powerful military body hanging over our heads."

"Director, this does indeed sound serious, as well as frightening. Who or what is this military body? Are we speaking perhaps of these insurgents the Marshal has been fighting for so long?"

"Unfortunately, no, as his...insurgents...have apparently never been able to find us again after they so visibly took away Elder Nazég in the skies right over our heads."

"Um..."

This blatant mention stunned many in the meeting, as it made an immediate connection with a clearly obvious detail most people did not associate with before now.

"Director," the Professor asks delicately. "Would this in some way relate to your earlier mention of something taking place behind our backs?"

"It would, and at the same time it also defines how adept our society of scientists are at thinking with their own horns to recall the occasion, then to ask WHY those...insurgents...are halfway across the galaxy from us now, rather than launching a direct assault on the one thing they are supposedly aiming at to begin with."

"Yes, I suppose this would stand out...for those with the horns to realize it."

"I could, however, point out one possible answer, if also an unfortunate one, which could excuse our lapse."

"All right, and what is that?"

"We are not a naturally militant society. Therefore, our horns aren't designed to think in such terms. However, if we should ever cross paths with someone who is in fact militant, and who does think in such terms, he could use our lack of proficiency to fool us into thinking something as nonsensical as this."

"Great! And by this, I simply must assume you mean the Marshal, as these are HIS insurgents we are speaking of."

"And he clearly knows military strategy. Just look at that military he created up there...over our heads."

"Uh oh... But Director! You cannot mean our own! He is supposed to be our benefactor. Why would he do this to us?"

"There is a reason why, as well as a reason how, in case you would like to know, and I might also suggest a secondary reason for how, which is rather shameful to include. But a benefactor, he is not, and likely never was."

"Oh dear. So, um...which one do you wish to start with?"

"Maybe if I hit you with that secondary one, first. We are a society of scientists that tend to demand empirical evidence for everything we lay claim over. But did we ever demand this from him? Did he ever deliver it? The simple answer is no. And here we are, ten millennia later, describing him as a benefactor, when nothing he ever did for us was beneficial."

"Oh no."

"This is further compounded by our…faith…in the Council. And I use this word in such context that we seem to treat them as a god entity. Once they give a commandment, we all follow. We do not ask for evidence from THEM, either, as we assume they know what they're talking about…as any god entity would. We are not permitted to worship a religion, but this seems to serve as our substitute."

"Wonderful!" she moans.

"And so, here we are. We have chips stuck in our heads, these seeds on our backs, this perpetual promise of leaving home with no actual conclusion, that pollution up there, and perpetual children's stories to keep us watching the local news for any new, and truly fascinating episodes of our daily drive to follow their wisdom, just as they want it. And just as those followers of a religion who never ask for evidence, we bought all of it."

"Is this how you see it?"

"Professor, again, just look outside. He ruined our home and our lives, and lied to us for everything else. And we listened. So much for being a society of scientists."

"All right, Director, you do not need to chew our tails so harshly."

"I think I actually do, because no one ELSE ever did anything during that full ten millennia either. Once again, we do not do anything UNLESS our god entity Council gives us express permission to do so. In the absence of that…" he shrugs. "And this is a long time to realize we are not receiving any true benefit out of him. Furthermore, to realize the clear situation around us, and not take at least minor corrective action before it became so critical, like the pollution up there."

"All right, granted."

"Now, on to the primary reasons. Let's cover the reason 'how' for a moment. Unknown to anyone, except possibly the ARC, he once pushed a mandate through the Council for a classified piece of technology we call a military authority override chip. It's a neural implant, much like the Tav'ageen Suppressor chip, and was mandated for every member of our military. According to some old archival files we found recently, it was originally justified by claiming it to be a training aid for our young military. The story goes that when his insurgents started making their advances on us, we had to push ourselves to build a military body to repel them."

"Yes, I recall this from our history."

"Good, but we aren't a society that really knows how to fight wars. We've become much too refined by now as scientists, scholars, and other people who prefer more intellectual pursuits. In fact, war doesn't appeal to us, and I personally doubt it ever did. Therefore, the Marshal saw fit to apply this training aid to help us rise to the occasion of fighting his insurgents, which by the way are composed of people of a similar technological level to his own, and this is supposed to be well above ours."

"Right."

"I might further suggest they know warfare better than we do, especially if they so successfully overthrew Sargeras in the first place."

"I suppose this follows naturally."

"But after nearly ten millennia, we're still using them. You might think our veteran military, after such a long series of engagements, not one of which we ever actually lost, might know a thing or two about fighting wars by now. So, why do we still need training aids? The reason is because they're not actually training aids at all."

"All right, then what are they if not training aids, because if we never lost a fight, um… or am I going to get my tail spanked again if they are halfway across the galaxy when they should be right on top of us."

"Yes, this becomes another of our failures, that we do not apparently know how to fight wars, even WITH training aids. First, surely Sargeras must have had something like a security force to keep him in power. So, whoever kicked him out would need to contend with that in some way. This means they should know how to fight. Unfortunately for us, with or without training aids, we seem to think we can simply go out, bang-bang, they're dead, and then come home. We do not seem to realize that people can, and probably should learn to improve upon themselves to turn this around. Not unless they are so miserably bad at warfare that a bunch of people who barely understand how to hold a gun can beat them every time."

"Yes, this does carry a certain level of fault in the logic."

"In reality, what these chips actually do is place a person into a mindless state of conformity. You give them a command, and they do it without question or concern for what it means. And the Marshal owns the control switch. Even High Commander Geilv has one, and I have recently been informed that his is in active mode most of the time. This means, our military is not OUR military."

This statement sent a wave of moans through the assembly, and several hushed whispers ushered up from the crowd.

"Director, this is inexcusable! But can we at least find a justifiable reason for it? It was originally stated he was fighting insurgents."

"Yes, but WE, Professor, volunteered ourselves to assist him, not give ourselves over as programmable toy soldiers he can call upon with the push of a button to destroy anything he points a finger at. Our military is supposed to be OUR military, not HIS military to have his way with. For instance, we all believed the HC was the top man in our military, and we all took it on faith he was in control. But he is not."

"Uh oh… And on faith again."

"Yes. It's a bit like taking it on faith the Marshal came here bearing gifts we never received, promises he never fulfilled, and a Council doing its job, when in fact it locked itself away doing… something…no one knows anything about, and cannot query about without a lot of rhetoric to wait for some other day, hoping they'll actually give an answer. We are not the ones responsible for building that military, Professor. He is. He took what we had before, which was a simple Sentinels' service, and altered it to suit his needs. He also demanded these chips from the Council, who gave them to him in exchange for his great promises they ran into hiding with. So, we cannot claim it to be our work, as we do not know how to fight wars. And certainly not against superior enemy forces we do not even have a full explanation for, as he did not apparently give us such detailed information to help us understand who they actually were."

"And so we basically gave him our military to do what he wants with it?"

"Essentially, yes. And the HC does not spend his time on the front line fighting those wars that he, at his elderly age, would require a chip in his head for any reason, training or otherwise. But he does have one, and it is in active mode. Therefore, he is NOT in control, as this subjugates him to another authority. And we were never told about it."

"Oh dear. I can feel my tail getting chewed again soon."

"Yes, I agree. I was there not long ago. Professor, before this day is out, your Suppressor chip will probably have you rolling on the floor. You, and everyone else here."

"Oh wonderful… All right, please continue."

"Now, let's take a brief walk along Memory Lane. The year is 9764.53. This is the year when the Marshal and Sargeras first came to us. We often refer to this time as the Arrival. Coincidentally, it is also the year when Council Elder Velen Nazég was excommunicated."

The mention of this name invoked several members to erupt with soft grumbles and defamatory statements. The Director knew this might occur, but he held himself firm against it, and kept his own opinions hidden for now. At this moment, it wasn't the mention of the name that was so important, it was more about the date. But he wanted to remind them of the name for later.

"I'm sure we all know the history of what happened, so let's try to contain ourselves. The Marshal comes to us with his personal problems and presents his offer of trade to our Council. They accept it, and this is followed by a sequence of events that ultimately leads up to where we are now. One of these involves the Tav'ageen Anomaly. He assists in some part of the original research, but only to conclude it's some kind of alien infestation and we need to run away to some other world to escape from it. What is worse, we are experiencing many random and inexplicable deaths which we associate with this same dilemma, and this is causing a global panic, so our people are becoming desperate. Due to this panic, he instructs us to revive an old and generally unwelcome technology, the An'gamu seeds, telling us we need this in order to escape to any potential world we can find, including those that are not entirely hospitable."

He pauses to give this a moment to sink in.

"One thing that strikes me in all this is that our technologically sophisticated society, one that is capable of building space stations, remote outposts, and other structures on just about anything we can find out there, seems to have forgotten, in all this panic, that we still have those technologies to do this same job, even without the seeds."

This revelation sent a wave of murmurs and whispers all across the room.

"Director!" the Professor shouts. "In all the nether-space, what are you actually trying to say here? That we so thoughtlessly missed our own capacity to colonize other worlds with preexisting technology, all due to this crazy panic?"

"Apparently so, if you look at the result. It's right there on your back."

"But... But wait! I got this because of all that pollution up there."

"Yes, and then we have that. That pollution, Professor, is also the result of this technologically superior alien mind telling us to use the most primitive and dirtiest technology we have on record to build his mind-controlled military...even though we have a number of highly sophisticated eco-friendly techs to do the same job with much less impact on the environment. And once again to reinforce the idea of these seeds, as neither HE, nor WE, ever returned to it to correct that scenario."

"What?! Aargh..." she screeches, but then recoils from a feedback hit.

"One moment," interjects another member. "As I recall it, the original claim was to use these to abandon this world due to the Anomaly. But this statement is suggesting either there was another reason, or we simply neglected to realize what we were doing at the time."

"Honestly," the Director accedes. "I could say you are right on both counts. Allow me to continue. First, relating to the preexisting colonization tech. You know, it occurs to me that unless you actively use a thing, you might not even pay attention that you have it in the first place. And we never actually colonized anything before this. So, who is to know what sort of tech we actually have unless you have a functioning example to look at?"

"Now wait a moment!" the Professor interjects. "Did you not just now mention such as space stations and outposts, and such?"

"I did. But a space station is not the same as a colony base. And an outpost is more likely military, or maybe a limited application for research. It is not the same as a civilian colony to spread our civilization to other worlds. And some or all of this might also be limited in the public eye as either restricted or classified."

"Right, I suppose that does follow naturally, if also unfortunately."

"Therefore, if you have a society in a panic, they will take whatever you push at them, assuming you build a reasonable enough picture as to why they need it. Then, as for the pollution, we were told to build up that military as an emergency procedure, and who cares for the environment since we're leaving anyway. And no one ever went back to review it, even after decades, then centuries, and finally millennia of STILL living here."

"Oh wonderful, there goes the tail-chewing again."

"Yeah, it hurts, doesn't it? I tried arguing some of this during my career, but to very little response from the rest of the community, as we were all led to believe in the Marshal and his promises. We had a constant barrage of news media stories telling us…any day now…we'll be going. It was a propaganda campaign to keep up the image until the people became so desensitized to it that they stopped paying attention."

"Yes, I am beginning to see the picture now. This would be shameful, and after so long a time, we had to wake up and do something about it."

"Anyway, next… Along the way, we start to see these insurgents appearing, and the Marshal naturally needs to build up our military force to protect us. I'll reiterate for a moment, we did not have a proper military before this, only a simple Sentinels' service, which is primarily a law enforcement and security body."

He pauses briefly to clear his throat and check their reactions.

"So he tells us to build this dirty industry, so we can build this big military, so we can go out there with our training aids to fight his technologically superior insurgent force that had to be powerful enough to knock Sargeras out of his seat, and chase him all the way over here to our front door. This brings up a couple of curious questions to the thinking mind. Unfortunately, we stopped thinking after a while, due largely to his media campaign, and simply took him at his word."

"Oh great..." the Professor moans. "Now what?"

"One of these is how these insurgents might know where to look if the Marshal and Sargeras are essentially in hiding. Here is where we need to reflect on that ship that took away Elder Nazég, which the Marshal so fervently described as his insurgent opponents arriving to carry him away. Recall for a moment, that thing just appeared out of nowhere in our skies, which clearly suggests they had a jump drive in there, to say the least. Now, if those insurgents know enough to find Azgarén so they can drop that thing in our stratosphere, why not a large assault force instead?"

This sent a new wave of hushed whispers and murmurs around the tables.

"The next one is this..." he continues. "Think of the reports of that ship. It was stated to be huge, bigger than anything we own, bigger perhaps than anything our engineering specs could even imagine building, and therefore it had to be very technologically advanced, to say nothing of what it might take to actually build it. If THESE are his insurgents, they must be remarkably advanced to build such a huge ship capable of carrying away so many civilian refugees, but incredibly inept at building anything of a military nature. And yet, if they were so successful at deposing Sargeras in the first place, I have to assume they were strong enough to do so, and likely still are. Therefore, we have two issues to ask about.

First, why direct our forces all across the galaxy with so many wild chases, when they should KNOW where we are, and should be able to launch directly on top of us."

"Yes, this would be a very good question to ask, especially if we suggest they had enough resources to build THAT thing, and also to call our attention to so many places across the galaxy."

"Indeed, very good, Professor. The second one is why bother carrying away an individual who was…and apparently still is…so undesirable due to his science faction, when they could've just as easily dropped that military body in our skies to remove that one reason why they are coming here in the first place."

"Huh?" the Professor blurts. "But that simply does not make sense. And what about the statement of HIM joining forces and directing some part of this?"

"Yes, this is also a very good one. They recruited a political official who is probably LESS military than the rest of us, to direct a military body that can never apparently win a fight, when those insurgents know where we live and should've dropped their military right on top of us from the beginning. Instead, he invokes us to chase all across the galaxy to every other star system out there that is NOT a viable target. How do you like that for people who need training aids to fight wars?"

"Ouch! That one hurt!"

"I know, and then we have so many people here vilifying him for his apparent deeds."

"Uh oh, I hear something in that statement."

"Right, and it involves all that propaganda we were made to listen to."

"Oh great."

"Alternatively, we should ask this. What if that ship did NOT belong to any insurgent force? Perhaps, if Elder Nazég was regarded as valuable for some reason, he was instead evacuated."

"Evacuated! By whom?"

"Clearly, by someone who saw more value in him than anyone among us here, including the Council, the Marshal, and many of you."

"Oops," she mumbles. "I feel yet another tail-chewing coming on."

He gazes at her and shrugs, while he pauses to let this simmer and observe the reactions of the other members. There were numerous whispers echoing across the room as the people tried to conjecture the reasoning behind this strange reference.

"We will return to this in a few moments," the Director offers. "It wasn't until after these insurgents are so vigorously invading our space that we find ourselves stifled for the original evacuation orders. So this superior alien mind, after everything else he told us to do, miraculously invents the Tav'ageen Suppressor chips, which seem to have solved all our problems of the Anomaly, to the point where we really don't need to evacuate at all anymore. Why should we? Have we suffered any more of those death syndromes since that time? The answer, so conveniently, is no. So, here is where I ask, why are we still mandated to apply the seeds?"

"Um, should I again suggest that pollution, despite the error of not reviewing it. Or are you going to smack me on the tail again?" she attempts a faint smile.

"Professor, I'm a married man, so I don't think I should answer that for fear of what my wife might say about it," he grins.

The Professor and the others stared at him for the clearly humorous comeback and his obvious expression, and several of them glanced at each other for the odd implications, especially that he didn't seem to take a feedback hit.

"But in answer to you," he continues. "Aside from the fact that we forgot to review that industry, it was mostly his continued pressuring us to think we're still going to evacuate, and all this was only temporary. Well, it's been almost ten millennia. How do we define the word temporary? Because I was always under the impression it measured a lot less than that."

"Yes, I think I might have to agree. And in fact, to be honest, I have also contemplated this, among other things."

"Good, and here is where we bring ourselves generally up to where we are now. It is largely due to these stories running persistently for so long that our population stopped asking these questions. We have gone from a society that once behaved with such scholarly and scientifically minded interests, to a society of nearly mindless animals following the herd right off a cliff, and all at the beck and call of an alien being telling us it's good for us. Well, my friends, this is where we need to turn our collective horns around and remember who we are. And he cannot know about it…not with that military of his hanging over our heads."

"Director, is this the underlying reason for your demand to keep this such a close secret? If he should learn that we're questioning his motives, he could turn on us?"

"Precisely, Professor, so pay close attention to what I have to say next."

The Director now takes a data tablet he was carrying and sets it on the podium. He turns his attention to a large monitor hanging on the wall behind him and links his tablet via a wireless network interface. He then selects the photo library in preparation to bring up a series of images.

"This segment of our discussion contains statements and images that will probably cause many of you to experience feedbacks. I am sorry for this, but unfortunately, it cannot be avoided. At the end of this meeting, I am going to give a series of instructions for you to follow, and I will explain why during this next segment."

He again pauses to study their reactions. The audience simply gazes up at him, with a few of them briefly glancing around to observe the other members.

"These two people I met with in my office informed me of a series of offences, both legal and moral, that places us in a position I doubt our society has ever experienced before. In fact, I doubt ANY society might have experienced something like this before. They have been conducting a series of investigations into the Council and the Marshal for a number of illegal ventures they have been conducting, and they made several shocking discoveries along the way. I will take these one at a time to demonstrate my point."

He takes a deep breath to collect himself before going into the next part.

"Approximately four centuries ago, one of these individuals started work as a military officer on a top-secret project for the Marshal. None of us were ever told about it. It was a mining operation. Now, a mining operation might not seem like much, unless you ask what it was they were mining. Unfortunately, our science doesn't have a definition for this mineral, as it was very, well, alien in composition, and found on an alien world. And if this is not enough for you, it was also found in an entirely new universe outside our own."

This revelation sent a rush of gasps and boisterous gossip through the gathering. The Director held his stand for several moments while the room echoed with urgent musings and anxious declarations over this clearly groundbreaking discovery.

"The trouble with this," he resumes. "Is neither he nor Central Command, which we can clearly say is under his direct control, had any intention to reveal this to us."

"Director!" shouts one of the members. "This is an outrage! The discovery of a new universe would be the sensation of the millennium! Why would he hold it back?"

"I suppose we could say the pure discovery might be a sensation, but it was not about that. First, this was a top-secret operation. Officially, it never happened. Second, it relates to WHY he was there, which officially never happened. It also relates to what he was making along the way, which officially never happened. Therefore, officially, it doesn't concern us."

"What?!"

"That's right. As far as the Marshal is concerned, our interests don't matter. All he really cares about are his own needs. This could also relate to the reason none of us have seen any significant new research grants or other studies granted to us by anyone. At the ARC, the only thing we ever got were a few private and very custom research projects from him at Central Command. And these were to provide some odd purpose no one ever explained to us. This was due to his needs, not ours."

"But wait, it should be the Council giving out grants, not him."

"Yes, the Council," argues another member. "But is that before or after their gluttony of that deliberation they locked themselves away with?"

"And what about the Marshal's promises of this wisdom he offered?" wonders yet another member. "We offered our aid against these insurgents, and this was supposed to be our return."

"Granted," the Director responds. "When I was speaking to these people, one of them posed a very interesting, if also unfortunate response. He offered the secrets of THIS universe, not any of the others out there."

"Oh! Thank…aargh!" he cringes from a feedback hit.

"Technically speaking, HE is actually in control of these matters, not the Council. The Council, as I said, is not even performing their official duties, and there is a reason for this, and it is not about locking themselves away to deliberate anything. As for those promises, they were all lies."

"Lies! Aargh," shrieks another member, as he, too, doubles over from a hit.

"Once again, this mineral he was pulling up was undefined by our science. The base crew was under orders to perform their service, with a hidden threat of their chips being turned on, forcing them to do it anyway if they should ever question it. The mineral represented a metal of a superior industrial potential relative to anything we know of presently, but this was not his primary interest. It was instead a trace energy signature found inside. Now, allow me to make a definition here. Central calls it Abnormal Energy, and this is the one and only term we are apparently allowed to use, as the Marshal, who clearly knows what it is, is not telling us. More of his false promises of great wisdom."

"Wonderful!" he moans.

"It was sent to a processor, using proprietary technology he designed, but never explained to any of us, to be refined into a kind of extract, which I suppose is the best way to describe it, for this trace energy element alone. This created a substance of extreme explosive capacity, on the scale where a simple handful of this material holds the potential to destroy a full star system, and again without definition or explanation."

The crowd made an urgent round of oohs and ahs, coupled with an overtone of moans.

"That represents a lot of backroom dealings," the Professor muses.

"I agree. Right now, on what I might assume to be the far side of this galaxy, are the remains of a star system once called Ooduan. In its place is a blast sphere approximately five lightyears across. This represents one unit of that material, and I'm told he created over seventeen hundred of them, out of a quota aimed at a full two thousand."

This now caused an even louder cry from the audience.

"Director," the Professor emits. "Why, in all the nether-space, would he want something like this? I mean…wow! He would not be able to use it unless he detonates it by remote signal, for the unimaginable potential it has to kill whoever put it there."

"That's right, but he did in fact have a use for it. However, this is not something he would ever tell US about. Our entire purpose is to do as he tells us, and mostly using whatever bare fragments of instruction he donates to the cause. He seldom gives explanations, or allows anyone outside the immediate loop to know anything about what any other loop is doing. He further classifies everything so that no one else CAN learn anything. Therefore, his manipulation of information is astonishing, and again evidence that he has no intention of giving us any gift of wisdom."

"All right, but if you know this much already, does this mean you know the rest? Because I recall you said this was top-secret, and none of us even knew he discovered a new universe."

"Discovering is probably not the right word for it. I suspect he knew of it even before this, and likely did not even need our help to travel there. His form of life clearly knows a few things we do not, and again, he is not telling us."

"Then this suggests he was holding back on us, even from the beginning."

"Oh yes, and much more. Just wait till I tell you what he has our military doing right now…and in places our science never acknowledged existed. Anyway, that mining base apparently came under attack by someone who discovered it and dealt with the obvious threat. The base crew was captured, interrogated, and found to be generally guiltless of any true wrongdoing, being mostly victims of the Marshal's abuse for these chips and other things, and the weapon he was making was removed and disposed of inside a gravastar."

"Wow! That is certainly a good way to dispose of something."

"These two people who came to my office recently were involved in this, one of them being a former member of that mining base, and the other being a military officer who conducted this raid. But for security reasons, I think I should avoid using names."

"Um, one question, if I may. Why were they in your office? No disrespect, Director, but I would not expect you to be a target for a military security leak."

"Yes, you have a point. The ARC became a target for their investigation and interaction due to the Marshal using us on multiple occasions to research and invent what they describe as death toys."

"Death toys! Aargh…" she screams and suffers another hit. "Dammit…" she mumbles.

"Sorry, Professor… Yes, they have information concerning where these things went, and that they were used as terrorist devices on foreign populations."

"Terrorist… Devices…" she winces painfully through additional feedback hits.

"These people are now part of this top-level security agency investigating any and all additional crimes he has been committing, one of which is the installation of regulators inside our media streams censoring and falsifying our news releases, which coincidentally includes his long-standing propaganda campaign of our imminent need to evacuate from that Tav'ageen thing we were all made to fear, therefore that military, the dirty industry, that pollution up there, and the lack of any corrective action to it."

This new sensation sent a rolling shockwave of feedback hits throughout the room. The result was a raucous series of grunts and groans, several yelps, and a number of muted whimpers. The Director studied the reaction, feeling a sense of pity for his fellow colleagues, but also a silent hint of mischievous delight for the display. He discreetly rolled his eyes away as he tried to stifle any improper reactions.

"Director…" the Professor wheezes. "Are you here to tell us what is happening, or are you trying to kill us?"

"Professor, I tried to warn you in the beginning about this."

"Yes, all right. So, what else has that…creature…done to us?"

"The rest of what I have to say is going to stun you, so with my deepest apologies, try to bear up to it. These people have also investigated the Council itself, as these regulators were stated to be mandated by them. This brought the Council under suspicion of wrongdoing. But as they tried to conduct this investigation, they ran up against the same wall as the rest of us whenever we might hope to hear something…anything…out of them for any kind of report, research grant, new discovery, or even a simple legislative act. It's always the same story. They're in deep deliberation over something no one knows anything about or can get any information on. Have any of you ever tried researching anything on the DataNet about them?"

"Personally, no," she offers. "I might use the network for other forms of research, like historical documents, science papers and such, but accessing the Council Information Center is a lesson in frustration, thank you very much."

"Yes, I've heard this from other people as well. And it's probably because there isn't any Council."

"What?! Aargh…" she clutches at her interface once again. "You did that on purpose," she whimpers.

"Sorry…" he smiles.

"Director, how is it you seem to be exhibiting emotion during this time?"

"My chip is turned off."

"But that would be a violation of the mandate, correct?"

"Technically, no… And even if it was, we're not following those anymore. The mandate mostly tells us to stick it in our children at four decades and maintain it for the duration of this imperative need relating to the Anomaly and the threat it poses. But that same mandate doesn't allow us to monitor the threat due to a nondisclosure clause that denies us to collect any statistical data, even to know if the threat still exists. Therefore, the mandate is generally telling us to stick it in there indefinitely, and for no verifiable reason, other than because someone told us it was good for us. And who do you think that someone was, Professor?"

"Dammit, Director, this is becoming unbearable."

"If I had a D-probe with me, I would gladly disable yours. This will be one of my instructions to all of you once we finish here, to go to your nearest medical clinic and have it turned off. We will be delivering a special programming patch to download into your D-probes to disable the chips while keeping the activity light on. This is to falsify an active mode of operation."

"Why to falsify it?"

"In case anyone should take notice of us doing what the Marshal doesn't want us to do…violate HIS mandate, because that's essentially what it is at this point. Every mandate he pushed through the Council was HIS desire, not theirs."

"Uh huh…"

"Now, back to the Council… Apparently, the Council Grand Hall is empty. Look at this."

He now pulls up his photo library, sending it through to the monitor on the wall. He begins displaying the various photos received from Ayene of the inside of the Council inner chamber.

"This is the inside of the Grand Hall, where the Council has spent the better part of these last ten millennia deliberating something."

The people in the room gasped at the disarray of materials and clutter in the room. They moaned and whispered over the decaying furniture and dilapidated condition of the walls and ceiling.

"The room you see in these images is the current state of the Grand Hall inner chamber where the Council is supposed to be conducting its work…whatever work it might actually be. But as you can see, it is in a near state of collapse, all because the Internal Secretary in charge of the building refused anyone access to it. Not even a simple building inspector was allowed inside to check the structural integrity of the walls. He locked the doors, and no one has ever seen anyone come or go in all this time. The story we all got on the outside was they're in deep deliberation on something, but never an explanation of what, or how long it might be to hear a result. Furthermore, we have come to understand, due to that man being arrested and interrogated by these people, that all the elections that have occurred during this full length of time have been rigged to keep this one Council in power, regardless of the people's votes."

"Oh no!" the Professor groans.

"The explanation was due to the Marshal granting some special privilege to deliberate some of this great wisdom he presumably granted them, and they had to literally lock themselves away, for security reasons, to decide how to use it. But this also reeks of conspiracy, as many of them should have died of old age by now. Also, if you should ever find the time to research the DataNet, check what it says about their immediate families. All of them are missing from view, and the reason is locked behind a high-level military grade security rating. These people I spoke with apparently researched this, having someone on the inside with sufficient credentials to access that file. Would you like to hear what it said?"

"Director, at this point I am not sure, but I suppose we must."

"Of course. And the question was also rhetorical, as you will need to know anyway. Somewhere near the beginning of the Tav'ageen Scare, when our people were starting to panic over these death syndromes, the Council was secretly removed from the Grand Hall by the military as part of a quarantine procedure to protect our government body from potential harm. So far, it sounds innocent enough, but we were never told of this, and personally, this doesn't sound like something that should be so heavily classified away from the public eye if it only relates to what is essentially a disease or infestation event. Why would they do this? Who are they hiding from? They were only returned to Azgarén for press releases and other public events, but then removed again and sequestered away, along with their immediate families, in some secret military outpost with the codename Site One-Alpha."

"Interesting."

"Then we have the Marshal and all his efforts to research the Tav'ageen Anomaly, coming up with such things as his claim that we need to run away from it using his seeds, then his claims of insurgents, and finally the Suppressor chips. The last time the Council was ever seen publicly was during a press release on Actana 32, 9765.31, for the new development of the Suppressor chips. After that, they presumably locked themselves away in the Grand Hall, and their families are still hidden as military security Class 3. And by the way, according to Central Command's security files, Site One-Alpha no longer exists, having been destroyed as the result of an early insurgency attack."

"Uh oh!"

"But the statement we are making is there are no insurgents. So, who destroyed that base? Furthermore, who removed the Council and their families from our view, and then locked the reasons behind a lot of rhetoric and military grade security? Was it High Commander Geilv, perhaps in a maneuver to protect them from something? At this point, probably not, as he was likely under the active mode of his chip and doing whatever the Marshal ordered. So, who does that leave?"

"But Director, wait a minute, what does this actually say about the Council, and also the Marshal? Because this now implies a government takeover."

"Yes, it does, Professor. It says he removed them from power once he got what he wanted out of them...control of our government and suppression of our people with all his mandates. And with a military under the influence of these chips, where at the press of a button he can order them to destroy any world he points a finger at. This means, we are in a lot of trouble down here."

"Oh great! But this naturally forces us to ask who he is if not who he claimed himself to be."

"Yes, that empirical evidence we forgot to ask for in the beginning, such as credentials. This could also answer why we have seen no new research grants, project assignments, discoveries, or anything else you might normally expect to see out of the Council. If the Council is absent entirely, and it is in fact the Marshal controlling things, he will not ask us to research anything unless it serves him personally…and he already got what he wanted out of us. The only thing we might see after that would involve those custom projects we got at the ARC, which resulted in these death toys he used on other populations. This might similarly reflect on any other tech labs and engineering shops he used for his games out there in such places as these other universes."

"Director, this is simply unacceptable! Is there no law to protect us in such cases?"

"It's funny you should mention that, Professor. That's what these two people in my office represent. A new government-level agency they created as…get this…an insurgency force to take back our government."

She glared at him for the obviously ironic suggestion, and compulsively tried laughing, but only to get hit by another feedback response. The sentiment was repeated with several others in the group.

"These people also revealed a few other things you need to know about."

"Director, I am not sure how much more of this I can take."

"Try to hold on a little longer, Professor. Some parts of it do improve on matters."

"All right, if you say so…"

"Everything we thought we knew about the Tav'ageen Anomaly is largely a lie. We believe the Marshal himself fabricated it, along with those deaths, essentially frightening us with his ghost stories to fool us into taking all his solutions, thereby pushing these seeds at us, and then his chips, none of which hold their advertised purpose."

"Wonderful. What purpose do they hold?"

"If you recall, when Sargeras first arrived, he appeared to be weak and in a medically unsound condition. The Marshal insisted he would attend to his needs, saying our medical technologies would not suffice. All he requested from us was a place for Sargeras to rest and recuperate, so we built that sanctuary structure in the middle of the city. And what a waste that was…"

"Um, right… So, what was the real reason behind all this?"

"Sargeras represents a form of life we have never encountered before, and likely would not know anything about to offer any form of medical support. So, it stands to reason the Marshal was probably right in this regard. But it runs deeper, as Sargeras is a form of life that requires not food and water, as we do, but an unusual form of energy input to rebuild himself."

"Energy? What kind of energy?"

"Abnormal energy…"

"Oh! Fabulous! That same one the Marshal forgot to teach us about?"

"And that he clearly knows how to use, such as for building superweapons."

"Yes, thank you."

"But…it does not seem to exist in our universe; therefore, this other one, and maybe more after that, which might represent a source for it. This might then give you an idea of where they originally came from, if he requires this for his support."

"Yes, it would. Therefore, if we are not supposed to know who or what they are, OR where they originally came from, that 'discovery' would not concern us. Wonderful."

"Now, this energy is described to us as an unusual form of organic energy, as what might emanate from certain kinds of living entities. The way it was described makes me think of the relationship between plants and animals for the air we breathe, and the oxygen content."

"Interesting, and I am sure the biology faction would find this a good study," she turns to find the representative, who nods in agreement.

"This military officer who visited us at the ARC knows what this is, as she apparently took some special lessons from a foreign society who held a much deeper level of knowledge. But here is where we will twist your horns again, as it relates to where it comes from originally, and this would again defy our science."

"Uh huh…should I scream now, or wait for the official zapping?"

The Director smiled as he prepared to respond.

"Right now, our military is out there as part of the Marshal's most recent campaign, investigating a peculiar city structure for this so-called prison thing he claimed Sargeras's loyalists were sent into. However, what he seems to have neglected to tell us is that it is located in that place our science factions seem eternally determined to reject, in theory and in practice, even though when we use jump drives to travel around the galaxy, we are travelling THROUGH that space as we pass from one side to the other…nether-space."

This sent another wave of gasps and shouts around the room, along with several grunts, as some of them took more hits.

"I know, for instance," he continues, "that we use this term for a number of expressions, but most of it as a fictitious space that is not supposed to represent anything real. But in fact, if you look out a window while travelling through a hyperspace conduit, you are looking at it right in front of you. Why, then, do our science divisions refuse to acknowledge this, when SEEING it would account for sufficient evidence of its existence?"

"Director, I think I cannot answer that."

"Well, maybe I can…someone is force-feeding us a negative attitude. And probably because they do not WANT us to know about it…much like not WANTING us to know about other universes, this Abnormal Energy, or anything else that doesn't concern us."

"Oh great!" she shouts. "Him again?"

"We believe he has been with us for much longer, and likely influencing our science along the way, with only what he wanted out of us as we evolved up to where we are now to meet his ultimate needs. Then, he came out…officially…with his stories, and his master, who was in this sickly condition, as both of them were in hiding for a long time from their real enemies."

"Real ones…" she muses. "Should I guess these were NOT the ones we were fighting with our training aids?"

"You most certainly can. And along the way, he gave us these solutions to our problems, but only after panicking us into actually taking them. And here we come back to the seeds, to which we were all very thoroughly disgusted by the implications. And I might also mention that pollution, which is intentional to keep up the incentive. So, this is fair warning, Professor."

"Got it."

"Again, I feel a need to apply a definition or two, in order to help demonstrate my meaning. Central, with this mission they are on right now, is passing through what some are calling Abnormal Space. This Abnormal Energy seems to originate from there, due to an indigenous lifeform that interacts in this symbiotic manner with other forms of life on our scale. So, if you thought it was abnormal for being in some other universe, it is worse than that, as it is actually extradimensional."

"Wow! Now THAT is a definition."

"Worse than that, it is not actually so abnormal, as we are the ones who are abnormal for NOT having it. Most everything else out there does."

"Uh oh…this doesn't sound good for us."

"Life can apparently evolve into those spaces from where we are now. We might start out as simple corporeal forms of life in a common three-dimensional universe like this. But if we are so fortunate to evolve upwards, one day to realize this four-dimensional space as a valid endpoint, we might find a continuation of our evolution unique to that space. This new direction can pass through one or more stages, first as an adaptation into that space, to cope with the unique features of simply being there, but later as a complete adaptation to make our permanent homes there, which would then require this Abnormal Energy as our support layer, rather than what we started out with in a place like this."

"In all the nether-space…and literally so. That would be a truly fascinating study."

"The qualities of such a being would likely fly completely outside our existing scientific models. But if that same being should try coming back to a place like this, especially in a universe without this energy, which these people are calling the dynamistic flows, he might appear as Sargeras did in those first days."

"Uh huh, this might make sense."

"I suppose, if you still have access to it, even in some other universe, it would not be as bad. But I would imagine such beings might find it either inconvenient, or simply beneath their desires to do so under normal conditions. I mean, after all, if your home is so far above everything else, why would you want to come all the way back down here for any reason?"

"Yes, I might agree."

"And so we have Sargeras, along with what is described to be his servant…Darumon. Not Marshal Darumon, simply Darumon, as they don't tend to use titles, so I hear."

"So he is not even military?"

"He is a servant creature to his master, who is part of one such society as this. Darumon might be more of an intermediate form that can still pass between sides."

"Yes, actually, I think I see your point. He seems much more capable. But, at the same time, he comes from somewhere like that, and then tells us to fight something that probably doesn't even exist in our universe. Then, he brings us to places we don't otherwise believe exist, and fails to explain what we're looking at right outside the window."

"I know. So much for his promises of great wisdom, when he does not even give us a practical lesson on what he wants us to do. Now, moving forward. The seeds hold a special purpose for Darumon. He used the Tav'ageen Anomaly as a fear tactic to frighten us into taking the one thing I think none of us would want…not unless our lives depended on it."

"Yes, and thank you for the pun."

"He apparently reworked the old study to incorporate something new, which I am going to have my people at the ARC try to investigate, if possible. But this new element is thought to serve as a kind of surrogate, to create an artificial layer of this energy for him, and with our full population serving as a type of life support machine."

"I swear!" she screams. "Are we now food for that creature, on top of everything else?"

"It would seem that way. This would explain Darumon's urgent rush to push his seeds at us, and further his superior wisdom telling us to pollute our world, thus further emphasizing the need for these seeds right here at home. Then we have his insurgents keeping us nice and cozy, and with no end to this war we can never lose. Likely also with our military on their training aids, so they have no idea what they're shooting at, because they can't analyze it beforehand."

"Thank you! That just made my day."

"Yes, and we call him a benefactor," he shakes his head. "This one officer is part of a military body involving the REAL opponents to Sargeras and the Marshal, or maybe I should simply call him Darumon by now. Old habits..." he shrugs. "And until recently, they didn't know Sargeras even existed. It would seem Darumon recently led a secret campaign to make a sneak attack on these people as revenge for some ancient war these two sides once held, and Sargeras's side lost the battle."

"Oh, how nice of him. What actually happened during this sneak attack?"

"He was discovered and chased away. The way the story goes is that mining base had a fleet commander running it. I'm told he was on reserve duty. He was once a part of Darumon's campaign to fight all these insurgents. But according to him, his entire task force crew was put on active and told to blow up any planet Darumon didn't like, simply as target practice for our military on its training aid chips."

"In all the nether-space, Director, what has that monster done?!"

"A lot of evil... These worlds were likely inhabited by societies of varying technological capacity, but none of them hostile to us, nor perhaps even knowing of our existence, and yet we destroyed them. So, our society is now responsible for a loss of life on a scale we will never be able to atone for, all due to the Council's lust for the secrets of the universe, and our passive nature of never asking the right questions or safeguarding ourselves against an alien menace. I am going to hold all of us responsible for at least some small part of this, as we could've just said no…not that it might have changed anything."

"Why do you say that? If we said no, he might not have control of our military right now, and we might not be absent a government."

"Maybe, but he is a very powerful creature with some extraordinary capabilities that we might find hard to defend against…even if we did still have Elder Nazég among us to explain what they are. This was his department, to explain such a creature as Sargeras and Darumon, and the qualities they might possess. So, the next time any of you moan over his nonconformist science faction, you might want to know, his ideas on the nature of the Tav'ageen Anomaly, among other things, were not only correct, but he didn't even meet up to the full specification of what it represented…as this represents one of those extraordinary qualities you might find in such beings not found in our meager three-dimensional universe."

"Whoa!" she screeches, and grabs her interface again.

"Such beings as those LIVE off the principles of metaphysics, leaving many of our conventional sciences behind by that time."

"In all the nether-space, is THAT what happens out there?"

"Yes, it would seem so. Moreover, they can qualify as gods by this time."

"Gods?" she wheezes. "But, um, we…"

"…Are not a religious society? Yes, but this is beside the point, and I might also suggest more of that propaganda we had thrown at us causing us to reject such fanciful notions, when in fact we DO seem to worship the Council as a god entity."

"Oh! Yes! That one sure yanks the tail."

"These beings might hold every…practical…definition of a god by the time they finish this sequence of evolution."

"So, such a thing might actually be true after all."

"But in part due to our LACK of support, we rejected this and other theories, even though the Charter of Laws tells us we should allow ALL forms of knowledge. It would seem someone isn't reading those lines fully."

"Yes, and I am sorry for my part in it."

"And this would account for the real reason of that ship. Someone out there was watching us during this time, knowing who Sargeras really is, and they evacuated Elder Nazég and his people in an attempt to preserve them."

"All right, but who was on that ship?"

"The ship likely came from another intermediate lifeform, but serving one of those opponent gods Sargeras and Darumon are hiding from. We have this long history of blasting something out there, then around four centuries ago, his top-secret mining base, along with a simultaneous operation on another world in that same universe as a jumping off point to attack his old rivals. But he jumped off into a world in yet another universe, just to twist your horns a little tighter..." he smiles.

"Yes, thank you, Director. You are clearly enjoying this."

"And on that world was a society owned by one of these other gods. And THIS one was the one watching him, so the entire world was a trap for him."

"Ouch! That does not sound good...for someone."

"These people did not know of Darumon or Sargeras, and the other god society largely did not know, except for this one, who has a personal interest."

"Um, Director, please. If these beings are described as gods, um, how could they not know of him?"

"A couple of reasons. Let me explain, and then you'll see."

"Uh huh, and how many more hits should I expect before then?" she curls a tiny smile.

He smiles back affectionately as he prepares to continue.

"According to these people, Sargeras is part of an ancient society of gods from some extreme moment in history. These two sides got into a fight over a number of atrocities Sargeras and his kind were playing on little things like us. The other side took deep offence to it and demanded them to stop, but they refused, and so we have a war occurring. These others apparently waged a campaign to completely exterminate Sargeras's society for their refusal to comply with any proper ethical standards. Darumon and his claims are for revenge, not justice."

"Nice. Revenge, as if to say they held some sort of right to do this. Wow, there goes my newfound appreciation for a god society."

"I know, it seems to defy what we might think a god is supposed to be. But they're still people, so it seems, and this group was very elitist. Sargeras is therefore a remnant of that war, having apparently run away from the battle while the others fell. Then he and Darumon went into hiding, and likely somewhere in close proximity to our world since we seem to have them here now."

"So far, this sounds very unfortunate for us, but at the same time, I might suggest it would be that way for anyone they found, if not us."

"You are probably very correct on that," he nods. "But in answer to your other question, how could the others not know…because they believed this full society to be extinct by now."

"Uh huh. Figures. And they clearly missed one."

"Yes, people are still people. And if you are clever enough, you can still find a way. I might further suggest the location of his hiding place…the LAST place you would expect to see a being who is dependent on these energies to go into hiding."

"Oh! But of course!"

"And likely with Darumon maintaining him during this time. But what comes next is a very disturbing story, and it represents some research I am going to assign in order for us to assist our new friends out there."

"Friends…these other gods, or these military people?"

"Both, really, but mostly the military force. This other god society is actually very friendly, if you fit within the parameters of their rules, and they often take up a parental role with societies like ours to help us grow and evolve on occasion."

"Really! So, we are talking to the wrong people about any form of wisdom?"

"Yes, but they do not give it out free for the taking. We need to emphasize the evolutionary aspect of it. We need to earn it when our people are ready to grow into that stage. They might simply culture us along the way."

"All right, I will not argue. I am not afraid of a little work…it keeps be busy."

"Good. This one individual who ordered that ship also seems to hold a personal interest in Sargeras. At this point, the others are being told to hold back, as Sargeras is likely watching for them, and could try escaping again if he sees trouble coming."

"That's nice to know. So, Darumon was trying to sneak up on them, and now they are returning the favor."

"That's right. This other society is described to be vast by now, and this might also explain the quantity of that weapon, to hit many locations at once, and likely with our military on the active mode of those chips to set things off."

"Like sacrifices?" she winces.

"I cannot be sure what he had in mind, but at this point, it could be anything. Anyway, this individual… She apparently observed as Darumon and Sargeras went into hiding, then one day Darumon comes out to make some trouble. But the trouble he is making on this occasion is to create a society of what they tend to call minions to serve him later on, once he finishes breeding and grooming them to serve his needs. And unfortunately, that minion society is us."

This statement sent another wave of gasps and moans through the audience, invoking many to whisper about the relationships to the previous statements made about him.

"According to their records," the Director continues. "Which represents a series of notes described as clues to these activities, they tell us she observed as Darumon intentionally invoked a sudden and rapid evolutionary alteration of the Eracyodine species into sentience. This might then explain our strange history, and also the reasons why our science always tended to hold so many controversial questions over the integrity of our findings. Darumon, as a lifeform on this scale, would be immortal, like those of the higher form. So, time is not a concern for him. Furthermore, he can apparently alter his form to impersonate other creatures, including us, which means he can come and go as he pleases, and along the way meddle with our internal affairs, thereby altering anything he doesn't want us to have or know about. And this would imply his involvement in our evolution as a society. He made us who we are today."

"This is intolerable, Director!" the Professor screams as she clamps a hand over her interface. "This ought to amount to a violation of some sort!"

"Oh, I'm sure it does, and so one of our objectives will be to find our evidence. He's probably not expecting us to go looking for it at this time, believing us to be so complacent, and without a Council to deliver research grants of any kind, that he shouldn't expect us to misbehave on this level. Our friends are suggesting we seek out the old studies and revive them while his back is turned. We'll give the results to them, rather than the media, as they're planning a clandestine form of propaganda to undermine his censorship machine with a little of our own, and in this way deliver the information to the people, but without directly pointing fingers at who is responsible. At least, not until perhaps we can contain things better."

"Really! That sounds interesting."

"At this time, I should also inform you of another part of this propaganda campaign they have in mind, which will play out as a form of threat to the Marshal to distract him with a false enemy. That mining base was operated by an individual named Ytani. But Ytani was a maniac. He was psychotic, deviant, depraved, and even murderous. He is dead now, as these people delivered justice on our behalf, but Central and the Marshal don't know this yet. Instead, they tell us they intend to use his image to threaten the Marshal with his psychopathic fetishes, which often involved sexual fantasies, and also the notion that Ytani stole that weapon the Marshal was building. So, if you should see this on the news broadcasts, try not to lose your horns over it."

"Oh, thank you."

"Now, back to our evolution. The biggest trouble we have with

Darumon is not only did he artificially evolve us to serve as a minion race, but he did it manually, using his own body."

"Ew! Please, do not tell me that! I hate him badly enough from everything else. I do not want to be related to him!"

"I know, but at the same time, we need to understand this, because it reflects on us in the modern day."

"Uh oh... How do you mean that?"

"One would be what these two people are fondly describing as our ridiculously long lifespans. Darumon, being an immortal creature, apparently passed a little of this on to us, so this is our inheritance."

"Really! This is interesting, and it might also answer a few of those old questions. All right, I will take this as a small consolation."

"Good. I suppose this is not too bad if you want to applaud him for something. But more importantly is the Tav'ageen Anomaly. While I'm sure he would come here eventually to take possession of his work for his revenge attack, his main purpose for being here NOW, whether necessary or not for his other motives, is this. We started showing up something he wanted to hide."

"Oops. Am I supposed to be afraid of this, or now that we know of it, should it be another consolation to discover it finally?"

"The answer to that is highly subjective, as the quality may hold a variety of interpretations. But this is the reason behind all his statements, fear tactics, and solutions, as they were an attempt to gain control of something he didn't want us to know about. A nearly godlike gift, and another part of our inheritance."

"Um, Director..." she mutters uncertainly. "Godlike? Like, on the scale of those others, and what Elder Nazég might otherwise be useful for?"

"Precisely, Professor. Unfortunately, our society, which cannot seem to wrap its horns around anything mystical, magical, supernatural, or religious, is simply not prepared for this. And this is with or without him manipulating our sciences, as well as our belief systems. He came here with his promises, frightened us with his ghost stories, pushed his solutions at us, including the Suppressor chips, which effectively disable the ability to discover or use this

Gift, and then filled our heads with everything else for his revenge attack. His stories of an alien thing we could never identify was actually HIM causing so much trouble for us, including the panic and all those deaths."

"I SWEAR!!" she bellows, stomping her hooves and pounding her fists on the table, before doubling over in her chair for the anticipated feedback to follow.

"Easy does it, Professor, let's try not to short out those last few synapses."

He pauses as the beleaguered woman pants after her last outburst. The rest of the room appeared in a similar state, though perhaps not as passionate as she clearly was. One of them reached over to place a hand on her shoulder to comfort her as she recovered.

The Director continues, "The death syndromes involved here were indeed alien, HIS form of alien, and not in a polite manner of speaking, regardless of the fact it was murder. And it once again reflects on his need to serve his master above all other things. And this, in an empty, or as these people call it, a barren fold, or universe, for that energy."

"A barren fold?"

"It is a term these beings apparently use. Even the terminology changes, when your base level standard elevates so high, the more complex terms become mundane."

"Wow, you must really need to go high for that."

"I might further recommend a few of us come to learn these terms, as we might find ourselves using them here on occasion. Anyway, these deaths were a unique form of attack called vampirism, to literally suck the living energy out of a body, then possibly to feed it into Sargeras as a revival technique until the seeds were in place."

The Professor grimaced, and reflexively grabbed her interface, but by this time, the chip was too badly drained to make another hit. However, most of the other people in the room did feel a minor one. The crowd once again ushered up a series of soft groans and cries for their feedback, as well as the simple revulsion of the idea.

"As for what the Anomaly is truly about, well, this is revolutionary from the scientific standpoint, but only for someone who studies metaphysics, like Elder Nazég," he smirks ironically. "None of the other sciences would benefit, as it would fall outside those empirical forms of study which we are so conditioned to believe in."

"I think I hear a suggestion in that statement," the Professor muses. "So conditioned…by him, no doubt, to prevent us from realizing anything else."

"These are my thoughts as well. And further compounded by the Council and the Marshal so heavily vilifying him to distract the idea even more. For instance, I am aware one of his studies involved telepathy. It was believed he was able to study this at one time, and learn how to use it. But how do you measure, as with numbers, a person reading another person's thoughts. Best case, you could measure brain activity, but this is not the same as these two people sharing a memory. And a skeptic could all too easily criticize the result."

"I suppose they could."

"No doubt, there are other mental abilities out there, and these beings, who have evolved out of their original corporeal bodies, are mostly mental energy by now. This might say something…for them. But what about us? Well, we are a hybrid of a being that is nearly godlike in his own way, and further inbred as half-siblings to possibly refine it further. Therefore, we now see something newly developing as the result. Those early children were simply the forerunners who likely found it by accident, at least until he came along to spoil it."

"That beast! And he did this to children!"

"The Anomaly, otherwise known as a Prodigy Gift, is a latent evolutionary ability to project one's mind outside their physical body. This represents those early examples of a ghostly image that seemed to resemble the child still lying in bed. Then, as I suspect is the case, after he saw this occurring on multiple occasions, he made his official appearance with all his ghost stories to frighten us into taking his solutions to cover it up."

"Oh how grand! So, we have a godlike ability, and no one bothered to tell us."

"Yes, but it actually runs a bit deeper than that. This one officer is assembling an official authority on the subject, and planning on establishing a government-level body to help regulate how this is applied. Professor, if we are born of a near-godlike entity, that means we are half god, or close to it, and I am speaking again on the level of that intermediate form of life out there."

"Oh please! Not that!"

"I know, this is our problem, we are not ready for it. For all the extreme evolution we should otherwise have, like those others who have long since escaped from their home universes, we truly have no idea what it is or how to be responsible for it. So, THEY must now be our teachers."

"Oh dear..."

"This also involves us learning what metaphysics is about, as THIS becomes the scientific standard for us on that level. Everything else may simply fall behind us."

"And that is a bigger oh dear! This could put some of us out of business! So, for all our horn-pulling about his faction, and our Council criticizing it, HE was actually on the leading edge, and we did not even realize it?"

"I doubt we COULD realize it, as we do not have this ambient energy layer in our local universe to play with. So, this represents a handicap."

"Wonderful. And further evidence of his meddling to prevent us to know anything, if he is taking us to places that DO have it, but neglects to explain it to us."

"Indeed. Also, as a society that does not hold a religion, we are going to have to come to terms with the fact that there actually are gods out there, and a species in this position would normally become their students and apprentices as the next ones to come up to that level."

"And yet another oh dear. Does this mean we need to start praying to something?"

"I wouldn't necessarily suggest a need to pray to something, although they do offer guidance as a form of exchange, and this idea of prayer is actually part of a form of trade with lifeforms on this scale."

"Really! Well, maybe this would not be so bad."

"Yes, listening to their advice and guidance would certainly be a good idea. But as I said before, these gods do NOT simply give out the secrets of the universe. They DO nurture and support younger societies to grow and learn at their natural rate, as they are supposed to be doing. The Council made a big mistake taking Darumon's promises."

"Yes, I suppose they did. And I would probably also criticize the rest of us for so eagerly waiting for this great gift of wisdom, and not demonstrating the horns to pick a few of our own topics in the absence of the Council doing their job on a timely basis."

"This also makes good sense. And here we come back to the beginning, where I mentioned how we look up to them as this god entity, with the sole authority to assign any work to us."

"I think we all became very conditioned to this over time. Government grants, the one thing we need to authorize that work. Our individual factions are not necessarily designed as profitable ventures to pay for our own. Not unless we invent something we can then market."

"I suppose it hits all of us, at this point, even the ARC, though we do have a robust industrial side to us, if only due to the fact we offer so many medical products. And this brings us reasonably up to date. It now becomes our responsibility to redeem ourselves for all our errors and shortfalls by taking up sides with these new friends, and ridding what they call Creation of this horrid creature and his master, who is probably many times worse, if not for the fact that he's most likely sleeping. There is a military body out there making a series of careful plans for a secret assault, but they need to clear a few objectives out of the way to protect us in the process. Meanwhile, we have a job to do, and that is to find the evidence Darumon has been hiding from us all this time, so the people will know the truth of our species."

"All right, Director, I must agree with this. So, we need to gather up our teams, while keeping it very quiet so no word leaks out to the wrong people. And then uncover what he has been trying to cover up for so long."

"Meanwhile, as of this moment, I am discontinuing the production and delivery of both the seeds and the chips. I am further giving orders to my full staff to disable theirs so we can be free from them, since they really serve no other purpose than what some describe as a restraining collar."

"Yes, Director, I would be very happy to be rid of that, more than anything else."

"They do seem to deny us the capacity to discover the Prodigy Gift, but if this is in fact something we want to have, then it's time for us to learn what it is. However, what I've learned about it so far leads me to realize it holds a serious potential for misuse. Part of our new responsibility must be to modify our underlying social culture to instill the appropriately high level of respect, so that we don't see such as security violations, and other criminal acts. This ability allows a person to project an image into any form they choose, then come and go without hardly a trace. This is a serious level of power, and it MUST be regulated."

"But how? I mean, do we even have any way of tracking it?"

"Not so far, but this becomes a part of our new direction with this new authority body. They will help us. But I feel it must again be emphasized, if we are to classify ourselves as a society of this level of esteem, we need to start behaving like one. That means we should never again allow ourselves to run and hide in a closet whenever some alien creature comes along with his ghost stories. We need to evolve, Professor. This is not an option."

✦✦✦✦✦

"Now, Kaliya," Chief Tech Lapäli informs. "These are still prototypes, but we need to test the functioning of the arcanic inductors. Each design uses glyph plates to calibrate the output result, but the final product will use a series of selectable ensorcelled crystal shards, which the Professor has devised as an alternative to the larger, more standardized plates used on their earlier devices."

"Such as on their gateway portals and other things they were using before."

"Right, those were mithril plates inscribed with arcane runic carvings, and part of their original technology when we first encountered them. But the Professor has had to refine the technology to make it more compact and versatile for our new projects, like the ships, the shard-coms, and now these weapons. It's smaller, more efficient on how it channels the flows, and offers a lot more versatility."

"They're making some fast progress."

"Yes, and we have people working around the clock on some of this. This reminds me, we need to redesign your armor now. The base design should still work, mostly, but the electronics will need to undergo an overhaul."

"Would this involve the need to start carrying my own arcanic charge?"

"Yes, that's one of the biggest changes. We're struggling to refine the storage packs with superconductive containment cells, and borrowing from something the Professor demonstrated to me which nearly made my horns fall off."

"Uh oh, what was that?" Kaliya chuckles softly.

"Apparently, in their history, they became aware of a practice to enchant containers, mostly bags at this point, with something I can only describe as spatial compression techniques to fit more into less space, while also reducing the overall weight of the item. We can associate this with our science, but they used their magic, and this was apparently discovered many centuries ago. The result, in the finest example he brought to me, is what he calls a Bag of Holding, and it seems almost bottomless."

"Ah, yes, we have those at the academy," she coughs modestly. "I actually own one."

"Oh!" the Chief yips. "Well, maybe you could show me where

I could buy one, because my handbag is a little on the overstuffed side right now for all my notes!"

Kaliya was visiting the Bahlaie testing center to try out their new weapon designs. She and Chief Technician Lapäli were out on the field with a table and some of their latest examples. On the testing range in front of them were a series of targets. There were standard training dummies, some mock vehicles, and a simple building structure.

Kaliya picks up the first weapon and examines it. It bore the general appearance of a rifle, with a downward grip on one side for the right hand, including a safety button that she would need to press to activate the weapon. Her left hand also had a grip with the trigger, and the rear of the unit was a shoulder rest. The unit also had a video targeting system with image-recognition and selection markers.

The unit was bulky, but it was only a prototype using a more primitive convention to establish the basic theory of operation. It had an elongated bubble-like chamber to the rear, conduits leading through a tetrahedral box set with runic glyph plates along slanted sides, and finally into a crystalline lens at the front.

"This one," the Chief declares jovially, "is what we're calling the Arcanic Blaster model. It's essentially a plasma rifle, a little of a cross between the standard rifle version we use, and that mortar design the Suuden-Aryku were using. It's designed for anti-personnel, anti-vehicle…I suppose anti-buildings, and anti-whatever else gets in your way. May the cu'Nar have mercy on us all," she chuckles weakly.

"Gracious, how do we use it?"

"The user needs to direct their mage focus to gather up arcanic energy into this part back here," she points to the rear housing. "You'll need to calibrate your thoughts to your intended target. It doesn't technically matter if it's stationary or beating a hot trail trying to escape from you, the bolt is virtually guaranteed to track and hit the target simply because you want it to."

"Like a thought-guided projectile."

"That's the beauty of magic, I guess. Depending on your target, for instance a person as compared to a building, you gather up as much as your perception demands for the task, and then let it go."

Kaliya hoists it up onto her shoulder and steps out onto the range. She picks her first target, one of the training dummies. She grips the weapon firmly and engages the video targeting system to test the target selection feature, then depressing the safety release as she finds her target and takes hold of the trigger side.

The Chief moves cautiously out of the way to what she deemed to be a comfortable distance…far to one side. Kaliya notices the action and glares at her uncertainly, then returns to her target.

She charges up the arcanic capacitor and the unit begins to glow softly. A subtle indicator beep rings out in ascending tones until it tops out at max, and the unit hums at the ready. She braces her footing and fires.

A shot rockets out from the weapon and streaks across to the target, exploding into it and thoroughly rending the dummy into a spray of charred splinters and burnt cloth. The post it was attached to was uprooted, and the entire cloud was now settling to the ground.

"Cu'Nar's Grace, Tanjhira!" she shouts. "I've never seen anything like that before!"

"Like I said, you need to calibrate your thoughts to the grade of your target. I think you may have used a little too much on that one," she grins.

"You think? Right, so clearly, we'll need to practice with these to get it right."

"Try the building next."

Kaliya takes aim at the wall of the small single-room masonry building. Once again, she charges up until the beeping settles to a ready condition. She fires off a blast that causes the entire wall to detonate in a shower of dust and debris, sending a portion of the roof flipping over the other side, and portions of the other walls to fracture and fall away.

"Very good," the Chief asserts. "I would say that's a successful test for that one. Let's try the EMP next."

Kaliya puts the weapon down on the table and picks up the next one, which very closely resembled the first one except for a different set of glyph plates in the conversion chamber.

"What are we aiming for, those vehicles?" she asks.

"Yes, they're not complete vehicles, but they're fitted with some sample electronics to simulate anything powered that might be affected by an EMP hit. If it works here, it should technically work on anything else that is vulnerable to EMP."

"All right, here we go."

Kaliya takes aim with the new weapon at one of the vehicles. As before, she charges up and fires. A radiant orb of electrical discharge, resembling something like ball lightning, flies out and strikes the vehicle, impacting in a visual display of static bolts rapidly spreading across the target.

The chief was monitoring a data terminal at a nearby station where the readings of the equipment were displaying a continuous status report. When the weapon hit, the entire display went black.

"Wow, that thing is dead!" she announces.

"Now what, test the third one?" Kaliya asks.

"Yes, go ahead. Take aim at that marked dummy off to the side there," she directs to a uniquely designed dummy with several monitors and simulated muscle fibers.

Using the last of the three rifles, Kaliya takes aim, charges, and fires at it, releasing what vaguely resembles a short bolt of electrical plasma at the target. It zipped across and struck the target, causing a spike on the meters showing a stream of data on the Chief's terminal. Tanjhira examines her results.

"I'm showing a systemic shock comparable to a disruptive bioelectric impulse. Very good, this resembles what I was hoping for, similar to an electrical stun weapon. That should do it. I think we're done for now."

Kaliya returns the weapon and joins with the Chief at her station.

"What about the final product, will it be the same?" she asks.

"The final product will combine some or all of these into one, but the blaster and EMP guns will also find applications in our combat vehicles."

"Tanjhira, if I were on the other side, should I be worried right now?"

"Probably…"

<hr />

Thaelyn and his officers were still in discussion about their ideas on how to approach Azgarén, along with Ayene who by now was a week into her procedure for the seed entity. Together, they were studying a series of charts and a terminal monitor with displays of the local geography.

"So far," Kailen asserts. "We've managed to make some fairly accurate counts of their forces at Central Command, which includes their air and ground vehicles."

"This is good," Thaelyn offers. "Even though we still do not have an accurate premise for our engagement, at the very least, we must consider a few contingencies. This would naturally involve disabling some or all of their mobile capacity in case Darumon should try using any of that against us. And the most critical is their air force, although much of it seems engineered as a civil security fleet."

"And then the ground units, but there don't seem to be too many of those, either. Most of it appears to be utility or basic transport. I guess no one ever got this close to strike in their backyard before."

"If he never had any true foes before this, and his only real enemy is the Estelar, and he would need a very different tactic with them anyway, then he must feel himself very secure for that point. This could be one of his reasons for clearing out the competition. He nestles himself neatly in his pet world without a care for anything else. Good, perhaps we can use this, but again it must be discreet, and likely hidden underground."

"If we are to build underground," the General muses. "This valley to the west might be a good choice. But once again, the dust we would raise would surely be noticeable."

"General," Ayene offers. "I think we could offer a cover for that if we're clever about it. The Director has a large number of people in his pocket from a variety of professional backgrounds. What if we simply ask for his support, along with maybe some of his colleagues, where they all chip in a little contribution to the protection of their world and their way of life, and we pool some resources for a construction project."

"A construction project? What sort, do you think?"

"Well, it's our world, after all, so I think a construction project based on our native needs wouldn't be so unusual. That valley represents a large open space, and depending on how big you need to go, we could describe it as something either commercial or industrial. Let me see…"

"Commercial…but in that valley?" Thaelyn wonders. "Are we speaking of a large shopping venue?"

"Well, no, I don't think that would go over very well in that area. We need to think of the zoning restrictions. This might draw some of the attention."

"Indeed, and this might also represent a rather odd configuration for any sort of native architecture. So, the explanation would need to be rather unique."

"But at the same time, it needs to defer attention as anything excessively strange. And then, being so close to C.P., it might also need to involve something of an educational or perhaps entertainment design, like a park, or a research facility with a public viewing center…" she ponders the idea briefly. "Oh! Hey, I have an idea. What if we say it's a new conservation center? Something like a zoo, with space for visitors to see the animals. It fits the idea, at least in principle, as we are actually trying to conserve something. And considering the local environment, it couldn't hurt."

"This is an interesting thought. But a conservation center to deliver a military force?"

"Well, it's just a cover story, you know. I doubt it'll look like one by the time we're finished, but how would anyone know before then."

"Perhaps."

"So, what are our parameters here? We need underground space as our staging area. But we also need space for utility, maybe storage, and probably some sort of control booth to coordinate our people, like the control center in Central Command, with communications and monitoring terminals. I would also suggest a few other amenities to make it comfortable for our people to come and go as we move around."

"This is getting complicated, Ayene," Kailen winces. "And how much would something like this cost?"

"The Director should be pulling together a lot of people right now, and many of them are likely to have their horns twisted up at the Marshal before long. So, in the absence of the Council doing their job, we have to rise to the occasion as our own insurgency force to protect our homes and our people. We also have a deep responsibility to uphold here. I told the Director that he needs to impress upon those people all of their combined failures and the collected result which brings us to where we are now. Not only for our failure to think with our own horns and protect ourselves against a creature like Darumon and his promises, but what we allowed him to do to us along the way."

"These are very good principles, Ayene," Thaelyn nods. "You are learning your lessons well."

"Something tells me, as we come out of it on the other side, there will be some important changes in our world. One of these might be our government, as this last one slipped the tip with their ambitions."

"Slipped the tip?" the General muses jovially.

Ayene giggles as she tries to explain.

"This is one of our many expressions, General. The tip of our horns, here at the end of the spiral," she points at hers as an example. "Slipping the tip is to go too far with something, usually something important or sensitive, and missing the target along the way."

"How curious," he grins. "You do indeed have such a generous culture, Lieutenant."

"Thank you..." she smiles. "We also need to realize the damage we caused, not only to individual people, like Elder Nazég, but all those worlds out there we blasted. I don't know if we'll ever be able to atone for that, but it becomes a part of our legacy. This needs to be made known, and our people need to hold themselves accountable, not necessarily as individuals, but as a race."

"Ayene," Thaelyn infers. "You are truly showing a fine quality of character. I think all your interactions with Kaliya, and maybe your other friends, is rubbing off on you."

"Well, yes, I suppose so. And Kaliya has me in the temple lately starting up my worship of Lord Oghma. If only my mother could see me now. If she thought I was something abnormal with my Prodigy Gift, she would probably lose her horns at this one. But I need to start turning my horns the right way if I should ever hope to get into your academy. Soon, this bug will be off my back, and hopefully not long after that, I can take that test."

"Yes, but we generally feel that you are what you are, so I think this is simply a deeply hidden part of you now coming to the surface."

They return briefly to their maps and charts to consider this new idea of a base.

"Then, if this is our goal," Thaelyn notes. "We need to lay out a design and what we are going to use it for. For instance, do we use it to launch out, or to draw in?"

"Your Lord… Oh blast!" Ayene slaps her forehead. "I did it again. My Lord…"

"Do not worry about it, Ayene," he smiles. "No matter how it is spoken, it is still an appropriate address."

"Ayene," Kailen comforts. "Our society hasn't served under a monarchial rule since our early history, so it is not unexpected. I suppose I'll have it worse than most when my day comes, as I've been addressing him that way for years now."

"Yes, but I need to condition myself," she admits. "Anyway, Kaliya's plans with the Tul'ryk are leading us in a certain direction. Combine that with Ytani and the trouble he's going to make one day, and I had a few additional ideas. For this, I think a certain secret agent may need to meet with Commander Geilv in his office about some of these recent activities, and how they're pointing at a national security issue."

"Is this part of your new play with these scandals and conspiracies?"

"It'll play into things on a certain level," she grins. "For instance, we want to lay a foundation to drive Geilv into a type of rebellion against the Marshal, at least insofar as to take charge of his own life, to say nothing of his own military. Kaliya and I were talking this past week about how we might play this through, but it has to come in pieces."

✦✦✦

"This is confusing," states one crewman. "We are no longer losing our squads to that authority figure, but we have lost several members to the local militia force."

"This is simply the result of that wanted poster," suggests a second crewman. "The local population is becoming hostile to our continued incursions. I would actually expect this by now."

"Yes, I suppose you have a point. We made forced entry, and we are apparently unwelcomed in their city."

"If you owned a city like this, and someone cut a hole in it, do you think you would thank them for it?"

"Well, no, but what confuses me is that authority figure has not been seen for a while."

"I think I can offer a suggestion to this," mentions an officer arriving at the table.

Kaliya was making a visit to the Tul'ryk to check on things and come forward with some additional details she felt were important to share at this point in time. The group at the table all stood and offered salutes.

"At ease, gentlemen," she offers. "This is a casual meeting."

"Yes, Lieutenant…"

They return to their seats and Kaliya settles in next to them.

"My personal opinions on the matter are as such," she begins. "Ever since the Captain ordered that survey, he has been under advisement by the First Officer, and me as well, to play it cautiously. To lose our teams wantonly is unwise. And it is clear that authority figure is a potent force."

"I agree, by the reports I heard. But why do we not see it anymore?"

"This survey order was accompanied by a proposal for a new tactic, which was to go in unarmed and appearing as tourists…in other words, harmless. I am aware the Captain received a suggestion from Central Command that there could be something like gun laws in there, and this could have sparked a quick response if we violated something."

"Really! This is new," the first crewman accedes.

"Yes, if you live inside a closed environment, it might make sense to avoid using the sort of heavy arms we tend to use. Therefore, we are not presenting ourselves in such an aggressive manner this time. Our first incursions made us appear as a foreign military force on their streets that was clearly searching for something in a determined manner. They might be very sensitive to this."

"I also recall someone mentioning our errant behavior, such that we might have been taking up the same as the Marshal has been described lately. Meaning to say, brazen and possibly arrogant, like as if we might hold impunity for our actions."

"All those early operations by the fleet? Yes, this is surely a bad form for us to display in someone else's home. Regardless of whether he explained to us any detail of what we were doing, or if those fleets went out on active and simply did not have the opportunity to analyze it, the outward display would not be a polite one. And it might even play a role on our own attitudes after a while if we thought what we did was appropriate."

"I think I would not want to be a part of that," the second crewman admits.

"True. And this could easily be regarded as hostile. But since taking this new tactic with the survey, and following this pattern to appear minimally hostile, perhaps we are presenting a new image as people who are genuinely interested in learning something about where we are."

"Learning something…" the first one muses distantly.

"This would also reflect on those rumors again," the second

crewman offers. "In relation to the authority chips, where we are not on active, so we have this opportunity to actually study something."

"Of course, but are we suggesting they know this, or is it coincidence?"

"I would find it unlikely they could know of the chips, but a friendly attitude is certainly more permissive than a hostile one."

"Yes, I suppose I must agree. But then, how do you explain that militia force attacking our people?"

"I have been paying attention to the details being collected in that survey," Kaliya responds. "It would seem this city contains a broad variety of lifeforms of many descriptions. One might say each segment has its own cultural appeal. It is likely the authority figure has a macro level of governing power, but the segments each have localized forms of security which are independent of that. And since the population seems to regard us as invaders anyway, it is probably inevitable for us to encounter one or another of those."

"Do you think that authority figure does not control them?"

"I think the answer to that depends on context. We are speaking of an alien society, so we cannot fully understand how to interpret what we see unless maybe we can go up to one and ask them. In the absence of that, one might analogize by asking if the Council gives independent instruction to C.P. Security on who to pull over each time they commit a violation. Another might be to say the authority being is only concerned for the safety of the city proper, and each culture has its own localized authority for civil affairs."

"Ah, maybe like mini nations? Interesting. But we are still considered as unwanted."

"And this still demands the question of our ultimate goal for the city," offers the second crewman. "I find it unlikely that this city could be the home of, or a possession of anyone or anything relating to Sargeras or the Marshal...especially, as she says, if it holds so many differing cultural zones. The Marshal never said anything about this."

"I must admit," the first one relents. "You are correct, but I am still waiting to hear about that Fleet Commander who is passing these stories of blasting whole worlds apart."

"I am also waiting for this," interjects a third crewman as he approaches the table and joins the group. "We have been listening to these rumors, and I will admit, they do raise some valid concerns over the use of the chips, to say nothing of him explaining anything he has led us into, including this space and what we can clearly see outside which defies our science back home. But to say the Marshal has actually done this in the past requires something more definitive than a seditious rumor."

"Ensign," Kaliya leans forward. "I am the one to speak to about this. Do you have something specific in mind for your evidence?"

"Lieutenant? You are the one? My apologies, but I did not mean to overstep my bounds."

"It is irrelevant," she waves it off. "If there is a question, it must be answered. But the missions in question were all classified by the Marshal, as are most things he tells people to do. For instance, I doubt there is a single scientific mind on Azgarén at this moment that is aware we discovered a new universe, as well as this outside. The Marshal simply did not allow us to reveal this. This would represent perhaps the sensation of the millennium for our science back home, maybe more than one by now, but no one is allowed to know of it."

"Why?"

"One answer could be we are on a classified mission, so the security concerns might get in the way. But technically speaking, why should we avoid speaking of a discovery like this, regardless of our mission. Each time we jump through nether-space, we can see this outside. But our science divisions back home persistently deny it exists, even though we can see it during those jumps. This, in itself, should be confusing after so long a time using jump drives."

"Yes! I would certainly agree with that. And now we have found a valid exit point into something we never thought was real. Regardless of the fact we are HERE with this special mission, this is still a discovery to tell someone about."

"But he does not allow it. So the reason of why might hold something of personal relevance, like as if he came from here."

"You think?"

"Well, if he knows what it is, and that it is valid, he surely knew we CAN come here. And if he knows of this city, and further to give such detailed descriptions of it to look for it, it must mean he knew of it beforehand. Now, we could say he only passed by one day and saw it, or he might know of it by other means. But this must involve something beyond simple guesswork."

"Yes, agreed."

"The other argument I have is this story of his insurgents. If they make their residence in a place like this, they must hold a much higher level of capacity than anything he ever let on before now. Also, we have this Abnormal Energy out there, and it seems to be everywhere, even in that new universe. If he refuses to explain it to us, it must also hold relevance. But it would seem, by his manners, even though we can see it, and at least partially detect it, he does not care to explain it to us. Why? One reason could be that mining base, with that unique mineral, which held a trace signature of it that he was refining into this condensed form that held such fantastic explosive potential. Whatever else it can do, if he knows how to make a weapon out of it, but does not tell us what we are doing on his behalf, this suggests a surreptitious act. And a surreptitious act like that, then leading to a place like this, which I must interpret to be his final objective, can only lead to a few conclusions, most of which are not nice."

"Yes, this might follow logically. You do not make an explosive unless you have in mind to use it."

"And it likely also involves this Abnormal Energy. Our home universe does not have this. Now, let us make a few assumptions here. He KNOWS how to use this, so we must then assume the rest of his people know how to use it, and likely make use of it for a variety of things. After all, we can make a bomb out of unstable atomic materials, but we can also make a variety of industrial applications out of it, even a few medical ones, and so on. So just because you can make a weapon out of something does not mean this is the ONLY thing you can do with it."

"Agreed."

"Then we have his claims of insurgents, in OUR universe, which is absent this energy. We were so very successful at fighting them in this time, you might think they are terrible at combat. All right, if we assume they were so terrible because they were missing their favorite tool to build stuff, this could account for something. But if they are so advanced as to build something like this outside, I think they are not as dull-horned as we were made to believe. If we say they use this Abnormal Energy as a tool, maybe a necessary tool in their form of technology, our universe would be a bad place to set up shop. Especially if they hope to launch a war effort against people like us. And this doesn't yet include the idea of them arriving from outside our universe right on top of us to hit us without warning."

"Of course, you are right."

"But in addition to this space out here, we also have that other universe. It should not be as much a concern at this time for the security rating, and yet it is being ignored, even covered up. It is as though it never happened. Is this due to that classified mining operation and his weapon? Well, if you do not want people to know you built a star-destroying bomb, I suppose this is good enough incentive to hide something. But hey, you do not NEED to tell them about that one planet. This is a whole universe!"

"Absolutely!"

"So the Marshal must have an ulterior motive here, and at least part of it does not involve telling us the intimate details of things that could clearly uplift our science...which was his original promise that got the whole thing started. And now he has us out here doing... something. If his insurgents, or whoever owns this thing, live out here, what were we doing back home, and to whom. I think this is a very valid question to ask, if these people hold the capacity to move through alternate universes and hyperspatial environments. Why would they waste their time setting up anything at all as an outpost in our space?"

"Yes, this is a good point. They could do it anywhere, and like you said, drop in on top of us without notice."

"And as I said previously, this Fleet Commander gives the statement his task force was put on active at the time. So he did not hold the capacity to study the situation to find his own answer."

"But Lieutenant, this now becomes the question. Who was he? Because all these statements are very scandalous. And while the arguments do hold a lot of merit, if taken in the right context, they could just as easily be a lot of rhetoric to stir up contention."

"They could," she nods. "But then I suppose you could say that for a lot of things, even WITH a name."

"Well, yes, I suppose you have a point."

Kaliya paused to conspicuously glance around the room, as if checking for anyone who could be eavesdropping, before answering the question. Of course, it did not actually matter if anyone was listening in. The more, the better, for this point. But she had to put on the display.

"We are speaking of Fleet Commander Lajivi Kriv'tik. He was on reserve duty at the time in that mining base."

"Kriv'tik!" the third crewman interjects. "Yes, I know him, at least by his reputation. He is one of our best officers."

"I met with him once as I was on a brief tour of duty. We got to talking one day about the Marshal and the fact that we discovered a new universe, and of course the scientific implications, and he told me the Marshal classifies virtually everything he does, to the point where one operation does not know what another one is doing out there."

"That sounds very severe."

"Not simply severe," the first crewman considers. "This could easily suggest he is undertaking a number of subversive operations, with each one being kept in the dark about everything else. What does Central know about this?"

"They barely knew that mining operation was out there," Kaliya responds calmly. "They knew only enough to manage the supply deliveries and the occasional crew replacement. Beyond that, it was simply mining something, and for some reason the Marshal desired."

"Wait. Mining something for some reason, but no explanations of what or why?"

"This is the story, as it was so heavily classified. Officially, it never happened. Then we have the Marshal, who barely gives enough instruction to do the job at hand. And this was the same for that Fleet Commander and his assignments for the Marshal to fight his insurgents. The Marshal apparently gave him a command to seek out a world said to be holding his insurgents, but the Commander was placed on active so he could not analyze what he found when he got there. His instruction was simply to destroy. Not a point hit of an outpost base, but a blanket effect of the full planetary surface, which was presumably fully inhabited by…something…that, according to his recollections afterwards, did not appear to know what hit it."

"Unbelievable! Aargh…" he shouts, but then clutches his interface for a hit.

"Yeah, I know what you mean. And this occurred multiple times, not only by him, but he knew of others at the time flying other task forces, and doing the same. He apparently shared a number of private conversations with them, suspecting foul play, and trying to find a little of his own confirmation. But with the worlds already destroyed, and orders to go home, what can he do."

"And let me guess," the third one offers. "All of it classified, such that no one knew what anyone else did out there."

"Precisely. Such as it was for virtually everything he did to us. I am also aware he and the HC were close friends, and shared some of these same stories."

"But if Geilv is aware of these, why does he not investigate them to verify their validity?"

"Other than the fact that he is also on active, and most of the time, I suspect the classified nature bypasses even him, as it is the Marshal classifying things, not the HC. I recall a conversation where he was overheard to say the Marshal keeps a lot of private details to himself. Well, if destroying worlds that didn't see it coming is a private detail, I think I would like to know who was on that world that can travel to hyperdimensional destinations, but not see US coming to blast an entire planet away."

"Yes! This is clearly irrational. Even if it was only a lonely outpost on someone else's home world, that one outpost should know something, or else have communication with someone who can retaliate."

"And especially after ten millennia of us doing it, you might think they would be on the lookout for it by now."

"Indeed! And have better defenses, or a ready response force."

"Even if we suggest there is a legitimate excuse," Kaliya offers. "The Marshal seems to have some very strict demands on our military. Whatever he describes as his insurgents becomes a target for us. But this does demand we ask why. Who are his insurgents in reality if we find ourselves out here now?"

"This does not sound good," the second crewman reflects. "Worlds that never see it coming, the lack of this Abnormal Energy which may be a requisite for their tech, and classifying everything so we cannot analyze it. Private detail? More like hidden motives, especially if you count that bomb of his."

"This reflects on that brazen attitude again," the first one accedes.

"Even worse," the third one adds. "This could be criminal. Especially if those worlds were unrelated. I think Kriv'tik would do his job if he thought it held merit. He would not just tuck his tail and run. This says his opinion was irrelevant."

"It does," the second one admits. "And likely the same for each of us if any would question that same merit. In fact, I am surprised WE are not on active right now."

"He probably figures we are too thoroughly domesticated by now," Kaliya smirks softly.

"Domesticated!"

"This is the only word I can think of to describe they who so blindly follow his direction, even to describe him as a benefactor, when none of this sounds beneficial."

"She is right," the first one submits solemnly. "It does not sound very professional for us who are not trying to analyze this, regardless of his classified restrictions. It has been going on for too long, with too many inconsistencies, and when you factor in where we are now, as she said a final objective, this should be the final yank of the tail to wake us up and see the equations do not balance."

"And if we DO try to realize those equations," the second one admits. "We will likely be placed on active, just like the others, to stave off our protests."

"Thank the Council and their grand reasoning for those chips," Kaliya adds. "They basically handed us over to an alien mind with ulterior motives, and with no recourse to object to it. Well, I hope they are enjoying their deliberation...it is taking long enough."

By this time, the conversation was drawing attention from others in the room, and a crowd was forming around the table.

"Lieutenant," interjects an arriving crewman. "What are we saying here, because if this is now involving the Council and their mandates..."

"It says they really like the idea of his promise of great wisdom. So much so that they apparently locked themselves inside their chambers while the rest of us suffer these outrages. These feedback hits, the seeds, our military and THEIR chips, and a lot of promises and backtalk of why we STILL live on a world we were supposed to be vacating a long time ago, but didn't. So we poisoned it instead."

"Um, that suddenly involves something not previously relating to the discussions here."

"Yes, but it probably SHOULD be involved, for anyone with half a horn to actually think of it. Because this also involves the Marshal and his influence to create it. Why do we have these seeds? Answer, we were told to run away from the Tav'ageen Anomaly using any means necessary, which coincidentally does not involve our preexisting colonization tech we forgot we had."

"Oops!" the third crewman notes. "She is right about that one."

"Why do we STILL have them? Answer, the pollution we poisoned our world with over the course of time we were waiting for the evacuation...and never once took the time to correct."

"Boom, another one," the first crewman rolls his eyes.

"Why do we have the Suppressor chips? Also because of the Tav'ageen Anomaly, and ALL of it said to be temporary. And how long ago was that? So, where is the Council to decide on correcting some or all of this, because it's been ten millennia. This is surely enough time to come to at least a few conclusions on something. And the Marshal just keeps sending us out to hit things that can't fight back, and with stories that, any day now, the rest will eventually come."

This new bombshell drew even more people around the room, and with even more feedback reactions.

"All right, Lieutenant," the arriving member resumes. "But, um, can you suggest something for the reason we are here looking for some sort of rift access to a prison thing? If these insurgents are not what he said they were, being those in our home galaxy, and then this here, and if so many of his stories are coming up questionable, why ARE we here?"

"If we are here looking for a prison thing, and if there really IS a prison thing to look for, it probably holds more of the same who like to make up fascinating tales and performing questionable acts. Or maybe worse. If nothing in our home galaxy was an insurgent, and we destroyed innocent worlds, he must like killing things that can't fight back. Especially if he can convince people like us to put mind-control chips in our brains and do things our better senses would say no to."

"That is bad!" the third member intones sternly.

"Also, I am aware of a world he was occupying during this past four centuries as part of a staging post operation said to be making ready to launch out against his insurgents. This mining base was coinciding with that to prepare this superweapon. Unfortunately, according to Kriv'tik, several years ago that other operation was cancelled. According to the scuttlebutt at Central, they said they had to pull out when those same insurgents arrived to investigate another devastated world. I wonder…first, why didn't we just blast THEM, like we did everything else, especially if we had such a big military build-up making ready to launch out anyway. That should've been easy."

"Yes, I suppose you do hold a point," the other crewman agrees.

"Next, this was in that same alternate universe. So this already makes you wonder who it was that frightened them so much… on THIS occasion…to make them run away. Now, the official story is they had to pull out to preserve their operational integrity, meaning to say, those insurgents were not supposed to know they were coming. All right, fine, in a time of war, a little stealth is a good thing. BUT…I am aware of a few people who were present, including Geilv to oversee the operation. And if you can pry their lips open wide enough for them to actually tell you something, some of them might say, those insurgents…or whoever it was that arrived… fought back, and won."

"Won?!" he shouts.

"And using Abnormal Energy as their weapon, and methods and tactics our technologically gifted society we think to be so invincible in battle, could not repel. And yet, here is the clincher for you. On the surface, based on tech we might otherwise recognize by our standards back home, they appeared rather primitive, surely well below us. However, using this Abnormal Energy, which our scans picked up in multiple areas and for multiple applications, they had a conveyor, flying animal mounts travelling supersonic, and some form of shield that seemed impervious to our weapons. Now, I ask you, who were we blasting all across our galaxy, because THAT could not be the same one."

The room erupted in oohs and ahs at the depiction, but no one could answer the question immediately, so Kaliya continued.

"The Captain is currently conducting this survey in there, and close to a final result. Some of it appears to be primitive, like an Industrial era format, with some elements we do not know how to interpret, which is probably more of this Abnormal Energy in play. But this again reflects on who we hit back home, and THEN to ask why we are here now. If they really CAN defeat us in a fair fight, despite the outward appearance of tech we can recognize, the Marshal clearly lied to us about the rest."

"This might follow logically," the second crewman nods. "And it might also suggest their outward appearance is irrelevant if part of it uses this other form of tech."

"In our home galaxy, either they were handicapped without this energy, and we hit people who could not fight back due to this reason…and this would represent taking an unfair advantage of people who were not a threat to us, or we hit unrelated innocents who were native to our own universe, and again who were not a threat to us. In either case, we killed people who were not likely a threat to us."

"You know, this does bring up a curious side note. In all our history of exploring our home galaxy, you might think we would remember who lives out there."

"Absolutely!" the fourth crewman exclaims. "And this might be a good cause to put someone on active, to negate the recognition."

"It would!" Kaliya affirms. "And here we are claiming them to be advancing on Sargeras, who SHOULD BE their primary target, not some random world as a remote outpost in a space they cannot function in properly."

"Ouch, Lieutenant!" he winces. "And now we are here, but for what purpose? To hit more innocent or unrelated people?"

"Or people who CAN fight back," the first crewman asserts. "If only we place ourselves on the streets with them. But then, for what purpose. We were looking for that prison rift."

"Yes, a prison rift. Prison, people! This is the word going around, and it makes sense now. Insurgents or otherwise, if the Marshal likes going around hitting things that can't fight back, and then pulls out when he finds something that can, this is your reason. Anyone relating to that should probably stay in that prison. And these might be more of the same who actually got caught."

"I think I might offer one more idea for your consideration," Kaliya muses openly. "Who actually owns that thing? The Marshal may have claimed it has a prison with Sargeras's loyalists inside, but are we saying this used to be HIS home? Those people in there don't look anything like either of those two we have back home. This naturally causes me to wonder if it is owned by someone else. If the Marshal likes going around blasting things, maybe someone took exception to it, and this belongs to them. And now he wants to break his buddies out to try again."

"Someone else…" the first crewman wonders. "Like another society? Something like…what…"

"A rival society, at this point," asserts the third crewman. "Either that, or a law enforcement body, if to have a prison."

"Certainly that much, rival or otherwise. And if that body may appear as primitive to us for their common tech, but uses this Abnormal Energy for everything else, it could not be anyone in our home galaxy, or universe for that matter, if this is native to some other place. And yet, like she said earlier, here we are in this space we never knew existed. You know, if anyone could travel up to a place like this, they should be able to travel anyplace else they desire. If only for the demand of this energy. This might speak to us for the targets the Marshal was hitting. That one world, where someone arrived and fought back… Yes! Law enforcement to investigate a destroyed world…more primitive people who could not fight back, and maybe hit by means they could not target if they could not reach that high."

"Yeah, bombardment, blasting from space, as with a task force on active, so THEY could not argue the point. Now here we are, an enclosed city that probably could not fight us outside here…and he was making a super bomb?"

"Oh no, did you really need to put it into such terms?"

"Well, it stands to reason, if you want to remove something big, and do so without any trace of something to analyze…"

"And that prison rift?"

"If it exists at all, he might try a prison break, and blast the rest to remove the evidence."

"Uh huh, I was afraid you might say something like that."

This final account incited an outpouring of cries and shouts, which was quickly muted by groans and whimpers due to the feedback hits. But the outrage was becoming clear that the Marshal was simply using them for his own goals and criminal lust. And the potential for yet another of the same, where this city was concerned, was becoming apparent.

"We need to take this to the Captain!" shouts one crewman. "He needs to be made aware of these statements."

"I think he has been keeping informed through the First Officer," submits another one. "At least partially… But this new survey holds the evidence, and we need to point out these details so he can make a decision on it."

"But then what? Commander Geilv will want to hear a report, and this will go back up to the Marshal, right?"

"Actually, no," Kaliya asserts. "My information tells me the HC ordered the survey, not the Marshal. I think he is trying to understand these same issues for his own information."

"While on active?"

"There are rumors going around Central right now of how he has not been performing his maintenance according to schedule. So, his authority chip might be out of sync, and therefore he is showing a higher level of lucidity than normal. We think he has been fighting this for a long time…his own form of protest against the Marshal and the chips."

"Incredible. Then this definitely needs to go to the Captain so we can decide how to proceed."

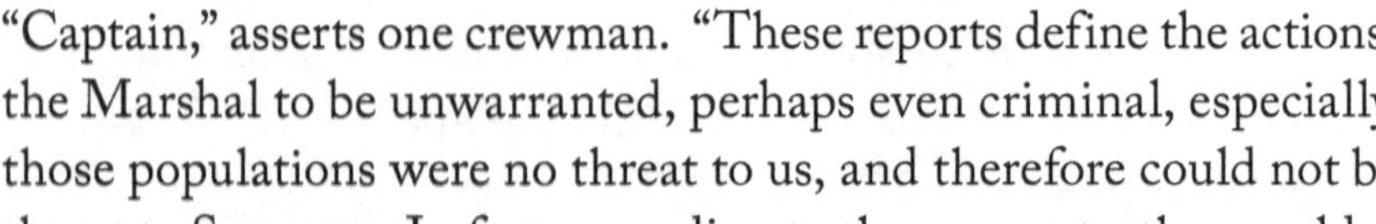

"Captain," asserts one crewman. "These reports define the actions of the Marshal to be unwarranted, perhaps even criminal, especially if those populations were no threat to us, and therefore could not be a threat to Sargeras. In fact, according to these reports, they could not even be spacefaring societies, and here we are in a space that simply cannot be related to anything back home, also with this Abnormal

Energy everywhere, which may further influence the equation, and further deny anything in our universe to be involved."

"Worse than that," offers another. "Even if they did represent these insurgents, and if those insurgents came from a place like this, which again involves this Abnormal Energy; our universe, if it is consistent that we do NOT have this, would be a bad place for them to set up an outpost of any kind, and for any reason. They would be at a severe disadvantage to do anything, and we wiped them anyway. This is not trying to reclaim stolen holdings. This is destroying something simply for sitting there. That should account as murder, regardless of who they were."

"And furthermore," argues yet another. "He is apparently known by a well-respected Fleet Commander that he covers up anything he does not want our people to know about. Even the HC is aware of this. He is also on active, but apparently fighting against it as a form of protest."

"Sir..." begins a female officer. "In this time, we discovered a new universe, as well as this space, both of which our science denies the possibility to exist, if only for our lack of insight to imagine such a thing. And then we have the Marshal, promising us great wisdom, but not allowing us to realize that which we already hold in our hands. It is right outside the window, but he does not even explain THAT to us. Instead, he tells us to destroy worlds that do not hold the capacity to fight back, and on the active mode of the chip, denying us the ability to verify his claims."

"And this is in addition to our forgetfulness of who might live there from all our previous surveys."

"Previous surveys?" the Captain wonders.

"Yes, the hundreds of millennia of space exploration we conveniently forgot about at the push of a button. And yet, on active, who cares by now, as we cannot remind ourselves under those conditions."

"Yes!" the female resumes. "And so, is this the mark of someone we would describe as a benefactor of any kind? Where is the evidence of his claims if we are not allowed to examine what we are doing?"

"This also follows with the mess we have back home," reflects another female crewman. "Our Council basically sold us out to him and vanished with this deliberation we know nothing about, while we poisoned our world with his pollution and refused to correct it during this time..."

"Wait a moment. Refused?" the Captain interjects. "How do you mean?"

"Meaning to say, we had the time and opportunity to realize the build-up long before it became critical, and we did nothing about it. We certainly have the tech for it, but did anyone, like the Council, or even the Marshal, who should be just as knowledgeable as anyone, give directions for it? Apparently not. And as someone who once took a few law courses at the U, this is a violation of environmental protection laws."

"Yes, I suppose it would be."

"Further, this naturally forced us to pollute ourselves with these seeds we probably do not need by now. We were all told this was temporary to leave home, but this was half an eternity ago. When do we finalize any of his promises, or should we simply give up on it by now? It sounds like a lot of backtalk and excuses."

"And his insurgents who were in our way during this time?"

"Sir, seriously. We travelled halfway across our galaxy chasing people who clearly know where we live, and have jump drives to reach it. Why are they going so far out of the way when their primary target is right in our backyard? Furthermore, if they can build THIS..." she points at the main viewscreen with the image of Sigil outside, "...I doubt anything we have back home could stand up to it."

"Wait...know where we live? How would you describe this, if only in argument?"

"Two words...Elder Nazég. He was taken away by someone the Marshal described as insurgents. Further, he was described as aiding them during this time. Either or both of these should point them at Azgarén. I mean, seriously, how many horns do you need to figure that one out?"

"Yes, you are correct."

"And this simply brings us to a final conclusion," the first one resumes. "He tells us there are supposed to be prisoners being held somewhere. Well, Captain, if the Marshal is acting with such criminal interests, I must ask myself who those others are he wants us to release from a prison."

"All right, everyone, hold!" the Captain raises a hand to pause the barrage of arguments. "In all the nether-space, let us try to bring a little order to this. I have been trying to follow the advice from my officers here during the course of this survey, and I must admit, according to our studies, these people do not represent the same level of society I would expect to find relating to the Marshal and his claims. In addition, the First Officer tells me there has been a considerable amount of debate where these claims are concerned. I would like to know where this is coming from before proceeding."

Kaliya realizes this is her turn. This is where she now needs to come forward with the next part of her plan to bring this under control. She steps out to present herself in front of the Captain, as well as the assembled group. She holds herself up proudly as she begins.

"Here, Sir."

"You, Lieutenant? You are one of those who have been advising me during this time."

"Yes Sir, but I am not actually a Lieutenant working for Central Command."

Kaliya now decides to reveal herself by changing her projected image to her natural Daanen'kai form, along with her Order uniform, but minus the glowing eyes. The resulting transformation sent the whole room into shock, with many of them stepping away from the surreal apparition.

She continues, "I am a military Captain working a covert operation to investigate the Marshal for all his...questionable...actions during this period of time. You people are splashing your hooves in a very bad place out there, and some of us back home, who are FINALLY putting these pieces together, are realizing what he's doing."

"What in all the nether-space did you just do," the Captain gushes as he gazes at her unaltered form.

"Captain, our people are conditioned to desire empirical evidence before we can accept anything as true…well, at least up to the point where we seem to be taking the Marshal at his word and no more," she smirks. "Therefore, if I am to explain anything to you, and do so without you simply laughing in my face for it…or at least trying to, if you consider that chip, I need to give you what you need to realize how much trouble you are in by assaulting that thing outside there," she turns to point at the main viewscreen with the image of Sigil on it.

"All right, you certainly got my attention, empirical evidence or otherwise. But can you tell me how you did it?"

"At this moment, we should keep it very simple. When you consider where we are, what is outside this ship, that thing over there and who likely owns it, and a number of other things our science back home is simply not prepared to handle, let's just say I was using a type of illusionary disguise to cover my body, which I turned off to reveal my true form. Is that sufficient?"

"Yes, it will do, but it must be a very advanced form of tech you are using."

"Oh, this one is special, I can assure you of that. I do not have that horrible seed thing, and neither do I have that chip. Our department chooses not to follow those awful mandates the Council pushed on so many others out there because we feel they were questionable, and very shortsighted from the very beginning."

"But then I need to ask, if you work for a secret agency, how did you get out here?"

"We have spies in a lot of places, Sir. And we do not stop at security roadblocks, especially his. And if you can use a disguise like this, it's as simple as walking through a door."

"That's a very dangerous situation, do you realize that?"

"Oh, I realize it more than you can imagine. It also requires a similarly extreme level of respect and responsibility. But we're trying to save a world, Captain, and this automatically negates any concerns for security, especially if it comes out of that creature."

"A world. Which one, in this case, because we had several of them flying around a moment ago."

"Our own, in this case. Azgarén."

"I see. Then, who are you if not a lieutenant working for Central?"

"With respect, as well as with apologies, I feel I must keep my personal identity out of it. The Marshal cannot know we exist, and we do not want a lot of random people walking around, possibly speaking things, if any of it could echo up to his office…willingly or otherwise. He is not who he once claimed himself to be, and we have friends out there making moves on him as we speak. He is a criminal on the run from people such as those who built this outside. And yes, they ARE a form of government body and law enforcement, and those in that prison ARE regarded as felons. Beyond that, I was never here, and not even Central is allowed to know about us."

"Central cannot know? I think I should ask why."

"At least in the present time. Captain Kan'vrij," she explains. "The Marshal owns our military, so technically it is not OUR military, especially if you consider these chips. The Council put an alien mind in charge of something that was very important to our people and our world, all on the promise of great wisdom, which we are still waiting for. And by the way, none of it with any of that much-desired empirical evidence our society so often craves."

"Yes, and thank you for the rub."

"Therefore, the LAST person we should be trusting is that one we were trusting. And Central works for him."

"This sounds serious, but can you at least explain a little of this to us so that WE might know of it? I think I can surely order the security of my crew here."

"I would not wish to deny the responsible nature of our military forces, assuming they can do their work without his famous…training aid…military chips," she smiles cutely. "So, perhaps, if these people here can keep the secret, we can give it a try."

"Training aids?"

"Yes, according to the ARC, they have some old data files where the authority chip was once described as a training aid. How do you like that, Captain?"

"Uh huh…nice."

"But naturally, we have our own security concerns, and HE is on the other side of it."

Kaliya now begins a classic pacing across the room.

"First and foremost, we do not want to be responsible for any more loss of innocent life, as it has been suggested so many times before. And I think it goes without saying, we do not want to be placed on active if the Marshal should decide to force the issue. This is his way of saying, do as you are told, and do not ask questions about it, as HE, being such a superior alien mind, is above ours. This already represents a supremacist attitude. This can also be associated, at least indirectly, if you look at his LACK of explanation for where we are, this Abnormal Energy, the discovery of that other universe, and other things, even though he once promised us great wisdom, but after ten millennia, we do not even have a progress report that someone really is deliberating anything on it."

"Uh oh…"

"It took us this long to piece together enough information, for all his roadblocks and security classifications, to finally assemble a few items of relevance. We need to reflect on our history for a moment. We have his insurgents popping up everywhere across our home galaxy. This was already strange, as they clearly knew where we were if he claimed Elder Nazég was being taken away by someone. This points to them knowing where we live, but I guess the news sensation of that ship didn't set the idea fully in our minds that if you have a ship in our skies, and that ship belongs to those insurgents, then those insurgents know where we live. So, we go chasing halfway across the galaxy for it instead."

"Yes, and that is another clever rub," he shakes his head. "But I cannot argue with you."

"Our people, for all our scientific prowess, are apparently not very keen on figuring out military strategies. And his storytelling is becoming famous in our eyes back in our office. And the fact that our people actually listen to it is also becoming famous for our society of scientists not using their horns to actually study something…at least not unless they gain special permission from the Council, along with their grant money, to do any actual work."

"Oh, is that how it works for those people? How unfortunate, especially with that Council stuck in this perpetual deliberation."

"Yeah," she shrugs. "But his policy to hide everything so deeply, coupled by all his toy soldiers on active doing the work, leaving little or no evidence behind to study, left us a bit stifled. We therefore began to infiltrate such things as Central Command's security systems to see if we could unbury what he clearly buried. Do you know what we found? Empty data files where once there was likely a project report by those fleet commanders after they returned home. He erased them."

"Oh, really! How nice of him to interfere with our recordkeeping."

"This further stifled us for our investigation, as clearly there is something wrong with this picture. But like so many others, we would much rather have evidence of wrongdoing, not the lack of evidence of what might seem so questionable. Then, many centuries ago, he apparently led our people into that new universe. The circumstances over how they found it were hidden, and no one back home was told about the discovery. This was not necessarily suggestive of wrongdoing, in and of itself…not the same as blasting worlds in active mode…but it did stand out."

"Would such a discovery like this need to be so heavily classified in the first place?" asks one female officer.

"Generally speaking, I would think not, regardless of the military nature of the investigation, as surely it would hold a significant number of civilian applications, and our science divisions back home would probably love the idea. But then, we discovered he was building that mining base. This too might hold an innocent purpose, if only he would tell us what we were mining and why. Then to send it to a processor to make something highly volatile, and again without explanation. This is now pointing to something subversive, but again very carefully covered up. And yet, it still did not provide us with enough to make a full assessment. We still have these insurgents, who did not apparently present themselves as such a threat potential… not to US, and surely not to HIM, that he would need a bomb of this sort. So, what is he doing with it?"

"And it was made out of this Abnormal Energy, correct?" asks a male crewman.

"It was, which was also unique in our minds, as this is the first time any of us have ever seen this stuff. So, clearly, he knows what it is, and in addition to everything else he seems to be hiding, this is now one part of it. NOW…we find ourselves out here, the last place I would expect any of us to discover, as it was so often denied back home even to exist. Four-dimensional space, that famous nether-space we so often talk about, but never believe in. And clearly, he knows about THIS too, but neglected to tell us about it, even after arriving here. So, as far as his promises are concerned, we regard this to be false, as THIS…" she waves at the viewscreen, "…is evidence enough that he has no intention of teaching us anything, even if it is pertinent to our work."

"Then what do we say about the Council and this alleged deliberation of theirs?" the Captain asks.

"Alleged is the only word that applies here, as they surely are not doing any of their normal work during this time, either. They locked themselves in their chamber and have not been seen since. And the evidence for THAT is actually quite easily accessible, if any of you would bother to check the Council Information Center on the DataNet. Do we have access to that here?"

"Um, sure. Comms, link us to the DataNet a moment. Bring it up on the screen here."

The officer at the communications station now links the network to a feed from the DataNet back home, tying it in to the main viewscreen and intercom system. Kaliya turns to face the screen as she begins to interact with the AI interface.

As with Ayene in those early days in Capitol Prime, a pleasant female voice came online with a standard greeting.

"Welcome, Citizen, to the Council Public Information Center. How can I help you?"

"Computer, inquiry…" Kaliya announces boldly. "Research for me the last known occasion of any active Council member being seen publicly for any reason, such as news events, public announcements, and other noteworthy moments."

The computer now pauses to conduct a careful search of the historical records, until it returns with a result.

"The results of the inquiry are displayed in the following table… The last recorded public event involving an active Council member occurred on Actana 32, 9765.31 CTD during a public news announcement. Do you wish to review the video?"

This result, if only for the date of the event, sent a wave of gasps and moans through the assembly of crewmen and officers.

"Negative," Kaliya responds. "But what was the subject matter of this news event?"

"The subject matter relating to the news event involved…the public announcement of the Tav'ageen Suppressor device."

"Thank you. Pause."

She now turns to the assembly.

"And that was the last…useful…purpose they served our people. After that, it becomes highly questionable as to what they have been doing since. Especially if you ask the next logical question that should come to mind."

"And what question would that be?" Captain Kan'vrij asks.

Kaliya turns back to the viewscreen with her next sensation.

"Computer, inquiry. Research for me the last known change of seat for any Council position. This includes elections, as well as for other causes."

Once again, the computer scanned the historical archives for the data. In several moments, it returned another result.

"The results of the inquiry are displayed in the following table… The last recorded change of occupancy within the Council occurred during the non-election period 9764.53 CTD with the removal of Council Elder Velen Nazég and the associated factional representation."

This result sent an even louder rumbling of moans and cries through the assembled crew, including the Captain, as many of them now experienced feedbacks.

"In all the nether-space," he shouts. "That takes us all the way back to the beginning! And what about things like elections and such since that time?"

"You might also want to ask about their ages," Kaliya responds. "As some of them were old-timers at the time. This now makes us wonder who is actually in there deliberating anything, if not the secrets of the universe…ours, or any other out there the Marshal never told us about."

"Yes! But does anyone else know about this?"

"Those in our office do, Central does not, and again due to the Marshal hovering over our shoulders, as HE is the one ultimately responsible here."

"Uh oh…that is now suggesting something."

"Captain, I am here to prevent you from starting something that could reflect back on our home world by beings that previously did not know Darumon or Sargeras even existed. But we must play a careful game of intrigue here until our side is ready. He has our full society by the tails due to all his devices and false promises. But he is also regarded as a very powerful being, capable of many things our science does not understand…not unless you involve Elder Nazég and his unappreciated faction, which might be the ONLY faction to explain where we are right now, OR such beings that might live here. Does this now build a new picture for you?"

"Incredible. And dammit, yes, it does. Whoever came for him took him away, because likely as anything, the Marshal would want him out of the way for everything else he did to us."

"Precisely. And as a side note, but very confidentially, this 'device' I am using for my disguise, is based on those same principles. Therefore, your horns would likely shoot right into nether-space if

I tried to explain it to you, and that's not too far away from us right now…" she smiles and glances at the viewscreen again.

"Thank you, Captain. And you sure do seem to be enjoying the moment."

"Yes, well, those chips are simply awful for this point. But anyway, those insurgents, if they were indeed insurgents, or anyone else, were not these people we were fighting during this time, as we have one additional piece that came up for us due to the Marshal's antics in recent times…a staging post world where he was hoping to finally launch out against his opponents."

"And what happened there?"

"Officially, the report says he pulled out due to someone arriving to investigate that world being out of contact, which is essentially to say, he blasted yet another world, and someone got curious after a while."

"Oh, how nice!"

"But, if you know of anyone who was present at the time, and on this occasion, there were those who were NOT on active, so they had time and opportunity to do a few scans and some study, even if they had no idea what they were looking at. But our office heard a few statements, which gave us a final important piece of the puzzle, and it again reflects on this Abnormal Energy. These new people used this as an alternative to our form of science and technology, and it seems to be as powerful, if not more so, than anything we could hope to understand."

"Oh dear!"

"I suppose we should qualify this with their experience levels, as this would surely require some form of study on their part."

"Yes, I suppose it might."

"Initially, the scans showed a society that was well beneath us in anything we could recognize, meaning the sort of tech we might use back home. But, using this Abnormal Energy, they had conveyors, supersonic flying animal mounts, and a shield projection that blows our tech to nether-space, as it was able to repel our famous pulse plasma fire. And they won their battles against our troops using simple swords and bows. So, this might give you an indication of what it can do, and at a much earlier moment in the tech tree. And this is what we were fighting before? If we don't have this back home, they cannot be the same people."

"No, it cannot be, if only for the fact we do not seem to have this energy. Did they have space flight?"

"No, they arrived using a form of conveyor tech. However, here is a good one for you. According to those we managed to make talk…you know, for all those security roadblocks, the Marshal didn't seem to regard them as a problem. Just more little people to push around, even after they started demonstrating this Abnormal Energy of theirs. So, clearly, he does not regard anything beneath HIM to be a bother if he has people like US to just blast things."

"Even WITH that energy?" infers a female officer.

"Yeah, as he surely knows what it is, so we might need to include this as a tech tree he might evaluate in addition to our own."

"Interesting."

"But strangely, he didn't order this initially. It wasn't until something occurred on that world that apparently announced who these people work for…being those opponents he seems to be hiding from. And then, he promptly turned tail and ran home. This now says, whoever his REAL opponents are, not only did he not recognize them when they first showed their faces, THEY did not seem to recognize HIM on their initial arrival. This now tells us the two sides were not expecting to see each other on that world."

"I swear!" the Captain spurns. "And that would suggest he is planning some form of sneak attack on them. And probably unprovoked."

"This allowed us to finally draw a few conclusions. One, his opponents use this Abnormal Energy as their form of technology, and this automatically excludes anything in our universe. So all THOSE stories are now rendered false. And this is aside from the fact of where we find ourselves right now. Second, he ran away from someone who clearly frightened him, even WITH our glorious military, and our long history of successfully blasting things, but could not blast this one. Now, could it be he simply did not want to try, or is there another reason. Something happened, and…suddenly…he wants to run away. He is hiding from someone, and did not what THEM to know he even exists."

"Uh huh, and this is pointing us in a very specific direction now."

"Yes, and it might also involve that prison thing. This is where our office had to go investigate. But Captain, you didn't hear this from me, as we have additional pieces of this puzzle that need to be carried out independently in order to preserve lives, whether here, in Central, or simply back home on Azgarén. Got it?"

"Yes Ma'am, what do you have in mind?"

"He and Sargeras are considered a flight risk, and if you think he did a lot of harm to us, we do not want him to escape to some other universe and do this to anyone else."

"I understand."

"Therefore, you need to play into his game, as if nothing happened out here. Same as those in Central once we can get THEM to turn it around. We are the ones doing the work, as we have the resources, as well as the hidden guise to do it with. He does not know of us, and WILL not until we are ready. We need to unravel his games and free our people. The seeds and chips are all his work to cage our population behind false premises. We believe nothing he told us is real, and this includes his insurgents, and even the reason behind the Tav'ageen Anomaly."

"Great! So he destroyed our local environment to force these seeds on us, and covered it with something relating to the Anomaly, which really equates to these chips that zap us on so many occasions."

"Yes. And if I may offer a suggestion, call your med-tech up here and order those things turned off. We need to start releasing our people from his control mechanism."

The Captain gazes at her a moment, then turns to view his people, who were all showing signs of distress by now. He then turns to his First Officer.

"Do it!" he orders. "Get the full team in motion and start processing our people. And call someone up here to do us."

"As for our plan," Kaliya resumes. "We have been playing a series of theatrical acts to dissuade him from moving forward, and using us as his strongarms to push people around. We already have contact with those on the other side. Some of these people here have questioned why the authority figure in there is no longer pursuing our efforts at invading the city. The reason? We know Geilv asked for this survey, and wisely he asked to make it seem passive. This is to try to understand who is inside there. Good. He is growing wise to the Marshal. As for our part, since you are no longer trying to stick your horns into places they do not belong, we passed a quiet word on their side to leave you be while you struggle to interpret the situation in there. There IS a prison rift, but it is also a high security thing guarded by that one who governs the place, and she does not allow ANYONE access to it."

"So those first occasions were mostly a security function?"

"They were watching and waiting, ever since that one world. So they were expecting you, and this is a priority. Since then, we were trying to work a solution to deter you, and by association the Marshal, to simply go away. He is not welcome here, therefore he should go home and crawl back under that rock until we're ready. Now that these people know he exists, they want him and Sargeras dead, just like the remainder of their race. This is who they are... destroyers of worlds, and full populations of...little things."

"In all the nether-space!" screeches a female officer. "And he made us do this back home with so many worlds? What have we done!"

"You unfortunately followed someone who offered you something you should never have accepted in the first place, the secrets of great wisdom our society is clearly not ready for. Not if you include Elder Nazég and what he tried to offer, which would also relate to this Abnormal Energy and this Abnormal Space, and whoever might live here. Though I think I should also note, he was clearly out of his element even to think of it, when no one else could envision such a thing."

"Maybe so. And worse for what the Marshal and the Council did to him."

"Right. And this is the price we paid. Now, we need to finish this, but in a very delicate manner. And as far as you people are concerned, I was never here, and you did not hear this."

She paces back across the room as she formulates her ideas.

"This is going to be your story for Central. And at this moment, it cannot include the Marshal. You are on this mission to investigate this city out here, but along the way you are listening to…someone… who is apparently fed up with all these inconsistencies and roadblocks, and the Marshal's lies and storytelling, which denies us to learn anything, even if it holds relevance to our missions, or simply to know what we are doing and why. Therefore, we have the gossip on this ship, which is generally an attempt to make you people start talking…carrying on actual conversations, which none of you seem interested in doing as a general practice, if we suggest the Marshal doesn't like people talking about anything…"

"Uh huh…" moans the female officer. "And she does have a point. Our single-mindedness of professionalism. We do not talk about anything, including the weather…not that it is anything interesting to speak of in the first place."

"Right. But NOW, you are being made to talk, because you have something you feel is simply necessary to talk about. After all, we're supposed to be a society of intellectuals…scientists…and this is what we do."

"Yes, and thank you for reminding us…by spanking our tails."

Kaliya can only shrug and smile gently.

"This is leading you to a series of conclusions, which will ultimately cause you to rebel against him. And here is where you will reveal pieces of it, delicately, to Central, next time they demand a report on your progress. But if any of this reaches the Marshal, he will not likely be happy about it, because I am already aware he has plans, at least in a preparatory stage, to optimize, as he likes to call it, your efforts out here, meaning to probably blast something new that is getting in your, or maybe HIS way of having what he wants. This is more of his supremacist attitude."

"Yes, and it figures!" the Captain relents. "But what do we do if he actually asks for this?"

"This depends on what he asks for, and represents a variable we cannot fully predict at this time. So we may need to play it by ear for now. We are aware he uses the ARC back home for a lot of custom research projects with sinister purposes, so we are watching for more of the same. Meanwhile, we have you here, as compared to Central back home. Each player can only be brought in by a certain amount. You, being all the way out here, can learn a little more, but those inside Central are right under his nose, which is a bad place to be."

"Right, I get it."

"We will have you delay any new reports until Central actually gets anxious to hear something. We will excuse this by saying you are trying to analyze this survey detail of yours. After all, those people in there are a little…strange. And if it involves this Abnormal Energy, some of you are becoming very curious as to what this actually is. Furthermore, we have someone, like a certain bright-minded young officer…" she smiles innocently, "who is going around suggesting this Abnormal Space out here is that mythical nether-space no one ever thought was real. In other words, we are going to start dropping hints of the Marshal's failure to teach us anything by rubbing a few noses in the view outside."

"You must hold a nasty streak of mischief in you, Captain," he attempts a smile.

"I guess it goes with the territory."

"But Captain, while I would not want to argue whatever authority you have, we are the same rank. And if I am to take orders from someone…"

"All right, how about Fleet Commander Lajivi Kriv'tik. Does that meet the need? He's working as part of our secret operation."

"It would! But I thought I heard he died in some sort of accident."

"Don't believe anything Central tells you, as it's all more fiction by the Marshal covering up his secrets. The mining base he was working at was presumably destroyed by an uprising of his slave population that was doing the actual mining of that strange mineral they found. The Marshal listened to our play on the com-links, and then wrote them off using whatever fanciful tales he could conjure up. Central does not know they are still alive and now working this new department, and it has to stay that way for now."

"I see, and this is painting a very unfortunate picture for so many of our elements."

"I would like to make another small side note here, while we're on the topic. He has to remain hidden, just like the rest of us, but he and Geilv were apparently close friends, and we injured that poor man with the loss of his long-time friend when we made our play. We'd like to patch this up, but it has to be delicate. So, somewhere along the way, if we can suggest something indirectly, we could leave a hint that he may NOT be dead. After all, he was a clever guy, and I find it unlikely he would so easily fall victim to something as obvious as whatever happened to that base…at least on the com-links."

"Uh huh… Did I mention a mischievous streak? I think you're worse than that. All right, got it. I will see if I can work something into it. But you should know, my acting skills are not especially high."

"Do the best you can, Captain. It is all we can ask for. And then, once we remove the Marshal, we will patch everything back to normal. This is our promise. Anyway, we need Central to rebel, especially the HC, but in such a way that THEY need to know what game to play on their side. And for this, we are planning a special meeting with the HC with new details for the game HE needs to play. And no doubt, his will be the worst of it, being directly under the Marshal as his favorite pet."

"I swear, how did you manage to plan all this! For that matter, why go through all this random gossip, when you could come right up to me with it?"

"This is an excellent question to ask. But it also reflects on that premise of us being intellectuals who should be trying to figure these things out anyway, but are not. Like this girl over here said…" she points at the female officer. "I almost had to literally slap you on the tail to remind you how to think, and also how to talk to each other, therefore bypassing the Marshal's security protocols and preferences to simply keep silent. This is not how you learn things."

"Got it, and you do hold a solid point. And I will thank you for this much."

"It goes along with some teachings we have recently been taking from the other side. They are sharing a little of THEIR wisdom with us, and some of it is simply to realize the secrets of the universe are out there, but we need to earn them."

"Absolutely!"

"Therefore, I needed to raise up suspicion and intrigue by making these people deduce some of their own conclusions based on the obvious clues we could bring together, as well as this hidden knowledge none of you were ever privy to, but now I am intentionally leaking. We need to break the Marshal's information block, and this means Person A needs to start talking to Person B and sharing some of those details that might be so questionable that the rest of us need to know about it. From there, once we hit a threshold level of awareness, then I could come forward and explain myself. It carries a little more weight to it that way."

"Very clever, young lady. Whoever taught you this game, taught you well."

Chapter 7

CONCEALED REPRISAL

"My Lord, I have some welcome news for you."

"Ah, Kaliya, welcome news is always, um…welcome," he chuckles. "What do we have this time?"

"Another mutiny…" she smiles innocently.

Thaelyn eyes her suspiciously before glancing at Kailen and the General.

"Kaliya," Kailen muses. "You're dangerous to have on a star cruiser."

"It must be that youthful zeal of hers," Thaelyn considers. "I have heard tales by old sailors where women on ships are concerned."

The group ushers up a bold laugh before Thaelyn continues.

"So, are we to say you were finally successful in turning those ships around for us?"

"Yes, I was," she affirms. "I joined with my teammates, as we were spreading our careful gossip, until finally I let go a few more pieces to cement it together. Eventually, we got a rally going and we took it to the Captain, where I laid it on him that I work as a secret agent for a clandestine department trying to put together the pieces that most everyone else missed, all because the Marshal doesn't seem to be living up to his promises, to say nothing of his statement of who he is supposed to be fighting, especially if you consider where they are located right now, which would deny most everything else he said about insurgents."

"Very good, this is reasonable so far."

"I felt it was necessary, at this point, to reveal my true image, but without the eyes on this occasion, and explain it as a form of disguise using principles that may be based on those abnormal things our science would otherwise lose its horns over. The 'empirical evidence' of seeing me changing shape, would be enough to shock them to realize I'm not just some girl with a wild story. And of course, we certainly wouldn't want them to lose their horns directly out there into nether-space," she giggles.

"Uh huh. General, what do you think of this? She is trying to prevent the random scattering of horns into the Seas of Creation now."

"Well, I must certainly applaud her for the cleanliness aspect," he grins.

Kaliya continues, "I also explained the deeper side of it, about our need to play our own game, and we all need to understand our roles. So we have him turning off their chips and going silent for a little while until Central gets antsy for a new report."

"Good! This should give them some relief, but where are they right now and what are they doing?"

"The Captain put their activities on standby while he considers how to present this to Central. I mentioned Geilv appears to be fighting his chips, so this should leave an opening for a sneaky little maneuver I hope to play on him next."

"Oh, that poor man…if only he knew," he grins.

"Yeah, we'll drop a few hints about what we're looking at in all this. This ought to cause Central to go a little tail-crazy once we play it out. And it should finally make them realize at least some part of what's going on out there."

"Very well, then I recommend following this through until we have a final result. If we can bring Commander Geilv to our side, this could then filter back down to the rest of it and disable their military threat."

"Yes, my Lord!"

"We also have a need to pass a message through to the Director at the ARC. We may need to call on him and his fellows to assist in a construction project."

"A construction project?"

"Yes, we have generally decided to make use of the valley to the west of the city as a local base of operations, although we are still somewhat undecided as to how this will ultimately play out. But we need to start making a few plans for it. Therefore, we are basing our motives on the assumption that we need at least a staging post of some sort, and a variety of support amenities to carry us as we move forward. And as a cover, Ayene suggested asking the Director to offer donations of funding and a local workforce to give it the appearance of a new conservation center."

"Well, as Relissa would say, that sounds just ducky," she grins. "But I would imagine he'll want to see some kind of design work so we can make some cost estimates."

"Of course, so we will have you make runs to-and-fro as we settle these details. Are you still projected? If so, you could make a quick visit to inform him, and maybe also have him coordinate through our local office."

"Absolutely."

Kaliya makes a quick bow and flashes out of sight. She arrives back in the city of Capitol Prime and chooses to take a cautious approach to the ARC by appearing in a hidden alcove outside, then to make her way in manually. Even though she gave instructions to the Director to bring his staff into the equation, she was unsure how much progress he had made, and didn't want to frighten anyone by popping directly into view. On her arrival, she also took her Suuden'kai disguise.

She enters through the front door and strolls up to the desk, where the secretary offers her traditional greeting.

"Welcome to the ARC, how may I help you?"

"My name is Captain Kaliya Nazég. Has the Director passed the word about our operations yet?"

"Actually, yes, Captain. He briefed our full staff on your activities. You're a part of that classified investigation, correct?"

"Yes, I am. I'm here to speak with him about a few things. Is he available?"

"Let me check."

She makes a quick call on her vid-com terminal to the Director's office to check on his status. After a brief moment, she returns to Kaliya.

"Yes, Captain, he's available and in his office. You should take the lift to the fifth floor. His office is just down the hall from there."

"Good, and thanks."

Kaliya turns and proceeds to the lift. She calls up a car and rides it to the fifth floor, where she continues down the hall to the Director's office.

As she arrives, she knocks on the door before peeking inside.

"Captain," he calls out. "Come in. How are you today?"

"Quite well, Director. I'm here with some new instructions for you. His Lordship would like to begin arranging a few projects with you and your associates. So far, we're still in the planning stage, but we need to establish a base of operations for his military to begin making their advance on Darumon and Sargeras."

"This sounds serious. How does he hope to accomplish this?"

"We are generally of the opinion that we need to catch them off-guard. If they should get any ideas of losing control here or of the Estelar making any advances in this direction, they might choose to run. And given Darumon's history of burning his bridges behind him, we don't want anything bad to happen down here."

"Yes! I would have to agree, based on what you've told me of his past activities. What about the military threat? Do we have any new information on that?"

"We've made some progress on that fleet out by Sigil. My team has been dropping hints and local gossip to disrupt their faith in the Marshal's honorable intentions, and we just recently invoked a minor form of rebellion amongst the crew. The Captain has given orders to disable their chips, to prevent the Marshal from getting any funny ideas with them, and so far, they're in a standby condition. Now it's just a matter of containing Commander Geilv and Central Command."

"Do you have any plans for that?"

"I do, but it has to be played out very carefully. He needs to come to a few of his own conclusions. We can't let him know we're here. He's right under the Marshal's gaze, and that's a delicate position to be in."

"Yes, it is. All right, and what is it you have in mind for us now?"

"We want to use this valley to the west of us. It's close by, so it's convenient, and it seems to have a lot of space out there. We need to begin with some kind of staging area to host our people, and a number of support areas for utility and staff member operations."

"Do we know how this will appear? If we're talking about a large construction project, we'll need plans in order to approve the zoning and construction permits. We'll also need to allocate funding."

"Where permits are concerned, this is a critical operation, so if we have any troubles with that, I'll have Ayene and a few of her people…massage…the situation in our favor," she smirks. "As for funding, although Thaelyn is willing to offer compensation, he is already thoroughly stretched across the three other worlds he is rehabilitating due to this war. So, we're hoping you can call for donations. After all, we're talking about saving a world here, and with all due respect, you people allowed Darumon in the front door, so it's at least as much your responsibility to kick him out again."

"Yes, I suppose you have a point. Then I will need to make a number of calls and see if I can drum up some support for this. I can also call in our people from the Project, and ask them to offer some volunteer labor. This will certainly help us to break ground. But we'll need to hammer out some plans for what it is we're building."

"Right, and for this, we're recommending you work with us through our local ACI office. Did Ayene give you the address?"

"Yes, and this is just one more fascinating piece of the puzzle. You established a government office, complete with government funding, and all without an actual government pushing the paperwork. How did you manage that?"

"We have a number of people working for us by now, some of them ours in projected form, and others who are local to the city. But when you can project an image of any kind into any office or position of authority you choose, many things become possible. It's as valuable for the utility as it is dangerous for the security violations. This is one of the reasons my new military authority will need to serve as a regulatory body."

"Yes! I would agree, but how do you regulate something like this?"

"We'll need to develop some new technologies, I'm sure. But we can come to that later. So far, I think time is on our side, as the people don't even know about it yet."

"Let's hope so. Now, back to this project, I recall you said you're trying to make a discreet entrance, so how do you expect to cover for this, as I would imagine it'll stand out to anyone who might take notice."

"It'll be described as a new conservation center, at least on the surface. But we're not simply talking about a surface feature. We'll need to bury half of it inside the mountain."

"Inside the mountain? Do you people actually build underground like this?"

"In this case, we'll need a hidden facility for our staging area. But not to worry, Director, as we have some people among us who are experts at carving out mountains."

"And how do you plan on importing them? If you need to arrive in physical form for this point, you'll need to come down from above, and that'll surely cause Central to take notice of any spaceships arriving."

"It would if we were using spaceships. But you forget, we have portals, and these can fit into some very small spaces. We just need a hole big enough for a person to walk through and there you have it."

"In all the nether-space, so you just pop through a hole in space and suddenly you have an instant workforce. This I need to see."

⋅ ⋅ ◆ ⋅ ⋅

"Commander, do we have any new reports regarding our search efforts?"

The raspy voice of the Marshal was making a call to Commander Geilv's office for the latest update. Geilv turned to his vid-com to answer the call, but his manners were hesitant to reveal all the details of the Tul'ryk's most recent activities in the city.

"The situation of the Tul'ryk is generally unchanged," he reports. "One of their recent reports described attacks by what they believe to be local security forces. They lost several men before retreating."

"Blast it, Commander. Those peasants are proving to be more difficult than expected, but we will not be so easily dissuaded. I had hoped we might have the opportunity to conduct our searches with much less interference, but I suppose the situation simply did not permit us the luxury. Therefore, in my spare time, I have considered a few options that will allow us to seek better results."

The Commander's face was flinching. It had become a regular feature on him since his private thoughts began taking shape for the statements made by Commander Kriv'tik on Morndindor, those of Thaelyn on Therinë, and the many curious and unsavory actions taken at earlier moments of his service to the Marshal. He listened to the statement, now secretly wondering what the Marshal had in mind this time. He didn't pay as close attention to this before, believing the Marshal knew what he was doing. But now, he was paying closer attention for his own judgment.

"What options?" he inquires cautiously.

"We simply need to, eh…pacify those citizens so that they do not take as much offence to our people wandering through the streets. They seem much too edgy, perhaps due to your troops appearing as foreigners. But surely, Commander, they must receive the occasional visitor passing along, albeit not necessarily dressed so formally in battle suits," he chuckles coarsely.

"Perhaps, but what about that authority figure?"

"Commander, we are here for a righteous cause, and that authority figure, as you so aptly describe it, is standing in our way. Surely, you can oppose a single creature with a little military might. And since there only seems to be one, it should not be too difficult. Then we should have more than enough freedom to conduct our searches without any further delay."

"Marshal, I feel I must remind you of Therinë, where we were discovered by…"

"Commander!" he interrupts. "I do not need you to remind me of that most unfortunate event. But I will remind you that it was not our immediate fault how those impudent orcs tripped over their own feet and drew that unwanted attention. If not for them, we would not have found ourselves in that situation to begin with. Everything was moving forward according to plan until that moment. But this one, Commander…this one will be kept under better control, I assure you. We will not depend on a group of bungling oafs to do our work. Instead, we will use our own professionals and the proper tools to get the job done according to our preferences. And if any of those peons get in our way, we will remind them of who they are."

"Yes, Marshal, as you say."

Geilv glared at the terminal, where the communication link was limited only to a voice interface, with no video. So, he could not see the Marshal, nor could the Marshal see Geilv's displeasure at the argument.

"Now," the Marshal continues. "I will be submitting these plans to the ARC for research and development, as usual. When they are ready, you will forward them to the Tul'ryk where they will be applied according to their directions. Understood?"

Commander Geilv's authority chip was only partially functional at this point, being so severely out of alignment that it was barely working at all. This allowed him to force his will to intervene with the control override and impose his own decision-making. But the Suppressor chip was still quite functional, and the feedback hits were continuing to inflict a visible twitching and jerking in his face. Nevertheless, he still needed to make an open show of compliance for appearances, even though he was not going to let this one pass without a personal review.

"Understood," he replies in his classic cool tone.

The link ends and the Commander scanned the room contemplating his next move. The trembling in his face was unnerving, as well as distracting, but he attempted to ignore it.

"Containment procedures…" he grumbles. "Peons? Is this what they are to you? I recall you used that word before with people who got in your way. What are you planning this time that you need to…remind…someone of something?"

He paused to consider the possibilities a moment.

"Submitting plans… What plans? To the ARC? It will be a day or two for them to receive and process them. I will need to wait before investigating. Until then…"

He rises from his chair and strides out of the office and down the hall. He works his way towards the control center. On his arrival, the resident officers all stand and offer salutes.

"Captain Ta'yeen," he issues. "Do we have that survey report from the Tul'ryk yet?"

"Not as yet, Commander," he replies. "But I think they said it should be ready very soon. Should I contact them for an update?"

"Affirmative, I want to speak to the Captain."

"Yes Sir."

He directs the comms officer to make the call.

On the Tul'ryk, the Captain was still contemplating his report to Central after a long period of deep consideration of Kaliya's last words. The congregation of crewmembers had returned to their posts by now, all of their expedition teams had been recalled, and the bridge crew was relaxing on standby.

"Captain," announces the comms officer. "Central is calling us. Do we respond?"

"Central? But of course," he muses distantly. "They probably want to hear about that survey by now. Here we go with it. But I wonder who is listening. Put it on speaker. We cannot keep them waiting."

The officer answers the call and places it on the bridge's open com-system.

"Central Command, this is Captain Kan'vrij of the Tul'ryk."

"This is Captain Ta'yeen at Central Command. What is your current status?"

"Our status is..." he mulls briskly, "...unchanged since our last communication. We have not lost any new teams, nor taken any further attacks."

"Acknowledged. Commander Geilv is present and desires to know if you have that survey report ready."

"Yes, Captain, we have concluded, to the best of our ability, a survey of as many of the areas as we can safely traverse under these conditions, and I have a report ready to turn in. Would you care to hear the highlights?"

Geilv steps in closer to the com-system to enter the conversation.

"This is Commander Geilv. I wish to hear what you have to report. First and foremost, how does this population appear for its technological capacity?"

"Commander, yes! The report we have been assembling is the best we can offer, due in part to the unusual features we are observing in there. But I think you might find it interesting. For instance, on the surface, as far as we are able to determine, based on recognizable forms of technology we are personally familiar with, the society inside this structure seems to represent the technological equivalent of a roughly midrange Industrial Age proficiency, if taken by the architectural designs of their structures and some of the equipment we were able to observe. Although I will also admit they seem to be in possession of devices of an unknown design and purpose. We are assuming this to represent some manner of custom technology that could be based on this Abnormal Energy we see everywhere around us."

"Understood. What about offensive and defensive capacity. For instance, those local militia forces, how did they appear?"

"Sir, these people only seem to use simple bladed weapons, and it gives the appearance of a mostly defensive design. We did not see anything that resembled guns or rifles. In fact, one of my officers here suggested they might limit themselves in this area due to being inside a closed environment, and such weapons could be dangerous to the structure. We observed knives of various designs, and that local militia attacked our people using swords, of all things."

"Swords? Then how would you describe them in relation to our level of development? By this description, they do not seem to meet our level of military standard, is this correct?"

"If to compare with our plasma rifles, or anything else, not in the least. Not unless you consider anything that might use that Abnormal Energy."

"Abnormal Energy... What about that authority being, and those municipal workers? How would you define them in relation to us?"

"Our observations of the municipal workers are that they seem entirely focused on their work and otherwise unarmed. We are uncertain how they maintain their levitation aspect, but they do not appear as a hostile force by themselves. As for the authority being, the descriptions are vague, as the teams were dispatched almost as soon as they spotted it. It also seemed to levitate, did not appear to be carrying anything representing a recognizable form of weapon, but whatever it did, it was fast and efficient. However, it stopped appearing once we took to this new pattern of scouting their local culture."

"Stopped appearing?"

"Yes, we are speculating that our new movements, being more casual and not as aggressively determined as we were in the beginning, may have given the impression that we are no longer demonstrating a hostile stance, as we were when we first arrived and began searching for something. Now, we appear more as a, uh...well, as I believe someone once said before, as a group of tourists on a sightseeing visit. This might have calmed their attitude towards us somewhat."

"Interesting. But this also suggests that if we should begin our search again, or take any other activities of an aggressive nature, it could return their attitudes back again. And yet, these people are no threat to us. Not unless we allow them to come within physical striking distance."

"Yes Sir, I suppose this is reasonable. And one of my officers here even went so far as to suggest we violated someone's personal property. How would you react if someone broke into your home and started looking through all your private belongings?"

"Understood."

The Captain listened to Geilv's attempt to analyze the report, and in the process realizing the level of control he seemed to be demonstrating. This caused him to recall Kaliya's statements about where this careful play had to be made. Now was the time for him to try his own tactics.

"But at the same time, I am asking myself how the Marshal could claim them to be anything in relation to himself, based on what we believe we understand of his own nature. They do not even look like the same race, for their physical features."

"Oh? How do they appear?"

"We have tallied up multiple distinct species of lifeforms in there. One of my officers even described it to appear almost like a zoo for how many seem to be cohabitating in there, possibly even with segregated habitation zones for their different cultures. I do not recall the Marshal mentioning anything like this, or even to hint at it."

"Interesting."

"But it does force me to ask how he can claim them to be relating to him, these insurgents, or anything else."

"Yes, these are my thoughts at this time, trying to compare the two."

"Only two, Sir? Are we speaking of this zoo in here, or the body as a whole. And then, what about all those worlds he had us attack during his campaign?"

Geilv suddenly jerked back at the blatant suggestion, as it was at least as much unexpected to pull in a detail not openly related to this mission.

"What do you mean?"

"Sir, I am aware we have ten millennia of blasting something out there all across our local galaxy. Call it outposts, call it worlds, whatever, but there were a lot of them, and I doubt any of it could be related to what is inside here. First, an Industrial Age body does not necessarily represent something capable of that level of space travel. Second, we are in a VERY different location, not our native universe."

"Agreed."

"In fact," he admits intrepidly. "My officers here have been trying, rather desperately I might add, to interpret something we are seeing right outside our window. You should see it, the view is wondrous, but entirely unlike anything our science back home might be prepared to admit to."

"Huh? Admit to?"

Now Captain Ta'yeen was leaning forward to listen more intently to the conversation.

"Captain," he interjects. "What do you mean? Are we speaking of that structure?"

"Well, naturally this structure would be a marvel of engineering, at least as compared to anything we could ever dream of in our wildest fantasies. Anyone who could build this would likely be entirely deserving to live out here in this extraordinary space."

"Um...yes. But then, what are you speaking of, in this case?"

"What I'm speaking of, Captain, is what the Marshal, for all his promises of uplifting our society with his fine wisdom, apparently neglected to inform us about when he first directed us out here. And this is naturally in relation to so many other things he promised, or otherwise told us about...or NOT told us about."

"Captain! Can you please put these into words that make sense?"

"Certainly, as my crew has been discussing this at length recently... one thing we do not seem to have a habit of doing within our military circles...discussing things the Marshal does not otherwise want us to discuss..."

"Uh oh..."

"Yes, and I think you can blame a few of our working conditions for that. A general air of NOT talking about things. Another general air of classifying things that are not our business to talk about... even if we are the ones who did it. Maybe also that chip that puts us into such a state that we cannot talk about things to begin with.

And then, if it involves anything he simply doesn't want to explain to us, with or without his great promises."

"And another uh oh… This is starting to look bad."

"Yes, it is, and especially for a society that so often prided itself on seeking wisdom…by researching things!"

"All right, Captain, your point is made. We slipped the tip on this one…rather badly, it would seem."

"Therefore, I'll give you two words that make sense. The first one is nether, the second one is space. Now put those together and this is where we find ourselves…but our science back home, for all his promises of teaching us anything, does not seem to believe this exists."

Now Captain Ta'yeen jerks back from the console, to meet with Geilv and several others by now who had turned to the attention of the statement coming over the comm channel. They all gazed at each other disbelievingly in silence.

Captain Kan'vrij continues on the speaker, "We are looking at what can only be described as true four-dimensional space. It sure isn't three-dimensional space, and nothing like what we have back home. And the place is saturated with this stuff we've been calling Abnormal Energy. We have come to a tentative conclusion that this energy forms a blanket layer out here, and likely native to this space."

"Native to it!" Captain Ta'yeen shouts.

"Yes! Try to imagine it, an extradimensional form of energy. Why, if a person or a society could ever learn how to use it, I can only imagine the possibilities. Too bad the Marshal forgot to tell us about that."

"Hold on, Captain, how do you mean that?"

"Captain Ta'yeen, he had us blasting everything in sight in our home galaxy, calling it an insurgent. Well, from our observations inside this city, at least half of their technology is likely based on this stuff, and it is NOT apparently found in our galaxy. Now, how do YOU explain THAT, Captain? And those insurgents seemed so determined to find Sargeras, when they ought to know where we live, if you consider that ship that came by for Elder Nazég. And these clearly extradimensional beings can't find him a second time to finish the job?"

This caused the officers inside the control booth to reel back, with some of them letting out soft yelps as the shock reaction invoked a minor feedback hit.

Captain Kan'vrij paused a moment before continuing his statement, which was part of his private musings on how he would present this.

"First, we have his stories of that ship belonging to his insurgents, taking away someone no one back home apparently cared for to begin with. But then, suddenly he is front page news as a terrorist we need to chase all over the galaxy to stop his insurgent buddies from hunting our most beloved benefactor. Unfortunately, it would not be until NOW, after breaking not one, but TWO of our deepest scientific principles, the first one being the discovery of a completely new universe, and then this here, when some of us who might actually still have our own minds to think, as opposed to being placed on active whenever the Marshal's tail itches, can study where we are and what we're doing. And none of it appears to relate to anything he told us about. If THESE people are his insurgents, or even if they are not, they probably have nothing to do with anything in our lonely little galaxy where they would likely be handicapped without their technology demands."

"Captain, where did all this come from so suddenly?"

"From someone amongst my crew who apparently held some experience during other tours of duty in places that were so heavily classified by our benefactor that the rest of us, who were promised so much wisdom, could not learn anything even if we begged him for it. And she tells me she, among others, are tired of listening to his false promises. Especially if he brought us to this place and forgot to tell us we broke one of our most famous scientific principles that nether-space is a myth."

"All right, wait. I need you to settle down a moment and just explain to us what happened out there."

"Of course, Captain, but first, where is the Marshal at this time?

Because I think he might hold an opinion of us learning something he refuses to teach us otherwise."

"Holds an opinion?"

"Yes! He apparently doesn't WANT us to know, that's the whole point. He lies!"

"Containment procedures…" Geilv grumbles tensely.

"Oh dear, not that again…" Captain Ta'yeen hesitates as he glances at Geilv for his growing distress. "Just give us what you have…calmly. The Marshal is in his office, as far as I know."

"Calmly," Captain Kan'vrij offers. "I don't think there is a way to do this calmly, Captain. But here it goes. First, he comes here with his stories of insurgents, and so many other things. During this exceedingly long period of time, he has us chasing all across the galaxy for people who clearly know where we live, if you look at that one ship, which by itself clearly resembled something maybe like this out here for the scale of it. That's a society well above us. Furthermore, it appeared out of nowhere, meaning it must have had a jump drive in it, and next is they clearly had an index right into our upper atmosphere. This can give you an idea of proximity to attack us right on our home soil. And apparently, for all the Marshal claimed about them, the rest of us very quickly forgot this little detail, causing us to go chasing all around the galaxy for them. How convenient. As if we needed that sort of exercise."

"Yes, I believe I see your point."

"Captain, it is not simply a point to make, it is a failure for all of us not to add these pieces together so much sooner and ask those questions we had to ask ten millennia ago."

"I did, once," Geilv groans. "And he argued that I needed to learn more, so he placed me on active."

"Yes, Commander, THAT is what happens when you ask questions of a supremacist alien mind that doesn't like being questioned."

"Supremacist?"

Geilv's face was twitching vigorously by now for his feedbacks. Captain Ta'yeen took quick notice of it, and placed his hand on Geilv's arm in a vain hope to comfort him.

Captain Kan'vrij continues, "Therefore, all those worlds he had us attack…while on active…was to keep us from asking those questions, and instead simply do the job of blasting whatever was down there. I had another of my officers remind me of our hundreds of millennia of space travel, suddenly forgotten at the push of a button, rather than to remind us of who else lives in our own galaxy. And so, we blast them as alien insurgents."

"Oh great," Captain Ta'yeen moans.

"Yes. He seems to like that, especially if they cannot fight back. I suppose it might also go along, if you stretch the definition a bit, of a being that lives in extradimensional space and likes to look down on everything else."

"You mean, prejudice?" he wonders.

"Peons, he calls them," Geilv mumbles. "This is one of his words he uses on those he does not care for."

"Oh great, Commander! That makes my day. So he tells us to blast anything we can get away with, and for what reason; his pleasures at seeing the mushroom clouds?"

"This is what he did on Therinë as he pulled out, devastated a city that was not a military target."

"Thank you."

"Next on the list," Captain Kan'vrij resumes. "Although we might not have the capacity to track his actions for all his overly classified secret campaigns, we should at least bring together the discovery of that new universe, which apparently someone found, but forgot to tell anyone else about, including many of us. More hidden movements he did not intend any of us to learn about? So the obvious question to ask here is, what relevance does this have to insurgents of any kind. He never said we had to travel to a new universe to find them. Next is apparently a highly secretive, highly questionable, and highly subversive mining operation in that universe."

"What?" Geilv yelps abruptly.

"Yes Sir, the one that was producing some sort of highly explosive substance out of something the Marshal never explained to us… Abnormal Energy."

"More of that Abnormal Energy?" Captain Ta'yeen wonders.

"And this clearly tells us he knows what it is, and it must be important…to him at least. But again, this is another universe, and something unknown in ours, which might raise a few NEW questions as to its relevance. So far, those insurgents are looking less and less likely to WANT to set up in our galaxy. And further is the Marshal, for all his promises, is looking less and less authentic for the result."

"He certainly is."

"However, this might still not be enough to piece together something we can definitively judge for its character. He likes keeping secrets, he does NOT like being questioned, he once promised us wisdom, but the obvious stuff we can see right outside the window is apparently not included in that statement. And after ten millennia, we are still waiting for any part of his earlier promises, while our world sinks into oblivion for the pollution, and we, with all these temporary seeds and chips, are still using them."

"Um, well, yes. I suppose I cannot argue."

"And there was one final piece this officer brought to us, if only because she, and apparently others, are breaking open a few of those classified secrets forcefully, when the rest of us seem so complacent to leave them be, and likely because our horns have been turned down so low, we don't care anymore…with respect, of course. A staging post world, where we apparently did find someone tough enough, maybe also determined enough, to fight back."

"Them?!" Geilv shouts.

"Yes Sir, this would probably hold relevance, if only as an example to evaluate. According to this officer, someone finally opened up enough to reveal something about people who did fight back… successfully, and again using this Abnormal Energy as part of their native tech, which apparently is as good, and perhaps even better than ours, regardless of what we might think to be their official tech level…according to whatever we can recognize by the standards we have back home…much like inside this city. This now suggests this energy represents a completely different form of technology, NOT relative to ours. If these insurgents, much like him, use this as their technology base, NOTHING in our galaxy qualifies as insurgents. Therefore, we have two possibilities available to us to speculate on."

"Two. All right, what are your opinions on this?"

"One, if they ARE his insurgents, then our galaxy, maybe our entire universe, if we do not have this energy, it would represent a handicap, and much of their tech might not even work. This places them at a disadvantage relative to us, making our attacks unfair against a handicapped opponent. This makes us murderers and cheats. And this does not yet include that ship and them knowing where we live."

"Murderers and cheats."

"However, I was thinking of this, and thought of a small condition. If they are so good at using this energy, maybe they have a way to import it. But this then negates them being so vulnerable, and therefore so easily defeated, if that one world is any example. More than likely, they would defeat us instead, and this refutes the apparent outcome we had."

"Yes, I see your point. We should not have been so successful."

"Alternatively, if they were NOT his insurgents, we killed innocent populations that had nothing to do with him at all. They were probably native to our galaxy, much like us. This also makes us murderers, as well as accessories to HIS crimes. In either case, this doesn't look good for why he keeps pointing his fingers at someone, and with us in active mode so that we do not argue the point, much less try to analyze things. And now we are here, where he tells us to look for people in a prison facility of some kind. I wonder, do these people put murderers in a prison like we do? And then, who is it that actually owns this thing out here? None of these people represent either Sargeras or the Marshal for their racial traits, not even that authority figure, from what we can tell."

"Meaning..." Captain Ta'yeen muses. "They are a completely unrelated body."

"Possibly. And likely some sort of law enforcement if they own a prison facility."

"Government..." Geilv moans. "Yes, he said they own everything, a governing authority. And the Marshal, he did not expect them on that world. It was a NEW discovery."

"New, Commander?" Captain Ta'yeen states. "Or simply unexpected if he didn't expect to see them THERE. This sounds like he was more likely trying to sneak up on someone. If these people are extradimensional, you might not expect to see one in a three-dimensional space like ours, or that one."

"Yes! This might be the reason. He did not expect it. He treated them like all the others, until that meeting. He learned something, what was it..." he ponders his memories of the old conversation. "Not expected to be there...not something that SHOULD be there."

"Uh huh, that might explain it. Someone was present that should not otherwise be present."

"Yes. Next, he orders us to pull out."

"Commander," Captain Kan'vrij offers. "If he is trying to sneak up on someone to gain access to a prison, and also built some sort of superweapon along the way, this suggests an attempt at a prison break, followed by that weapon to clean up. Suddenly, this does NOT sound like trying to liberate prisoners of an insurgency, but rather releasing criminals, and further destroying whatever remains, as opposed to him always claiming to return stolen holdings. These statements are backwards."

"Much like all his promises," Captain Ta'yeen huffs.

Geilv listened to this obvious discrepancy between these observations and the historical statements. He also reflected on his experiences from Therinë, as well as some of his recent conversations with Darumon.

"That weapon..." he mumbles. "Two and a half lightyear blast radius..."

"A what?!" Captain Kan'vrij blasts over the com-link. "Did you say it had a two and a half lightyear blast radius? In all the nether-space, Commander. That goes a little beyond a simple clean-up."

"Yes, and...wait. He said something. In this universe..."

"In this one...meaning back home, I suppose. Uh huh, and I can already see something here. Our local universe, and WITHOUT this Abnormal Energy. Did he say anything about that? Or should I simply guess your answer."

"Yes, Captain, I think you can guess it by now. He said it gets complicated."

"Oh, my goodness!" he gripes ironically. "For a society that loses its horns so badly, no doubt. All right, allow me to make a small assumption here. We are surrounded by this Abnormal Energy. And if this stuff is made from it, it reminds me of something like a fuse to an even bigger bomb. Let's see...how might this work. If we say this stuff is so potent, but stable under normal conditions, such that you can use it for a form of technology, and whatever else they use it for. Yes! Let's say you have a cloud, and we'll use something we're more familiar with, in our case. A flammable gas, perhaps. If you keep it under control, you can use it as a fuel source. But if you let it get out of control, and maybe also add a spark into it. Boom! And this place is saturated with it."

"Oh no..." Captain Ta'yeen moans. "And he apparently made a large quantity of those...fuses. So, if nether-space is actually a real destination, and likely another reason he did not bother to explain it to us, it means he would have us deliver these fuses to cover the whole thing. And anyone who lives out there..."

"Right! And likely a great many of them, at this point, especially if you involve any other universe this seeps into. Except for ours, of course!" he huffs.

"I swear!" he shouts. "Aargh!" he crumples over with a feedback hit.

Geilv continued to listen, mulling over the possibilities. The revelations were finally allowing the last few pieces to fall into place for his own speculation. This was accompanied by a strong feedback hit crinkling his cheek.

"Containment... Procedures..." he growls irritably.

Captain Ta'yeen was observing him, as has become a habit for him lately due to the obvious ticking reactions in Geilv's face. He steps forward.

"Commander, has the Marshal suggested something to you about this?"

"For the city structure?" he reflects. "Yes, he is submitting something to the ARC to soften their attitudes, as he calls it."

"Soften! Is this how he describes blasting things apart? I am now thinking of Morndindor. Was that also considered to be softening attitudes...a planet-wide bombardment campaign to destroy every last one of them?"

"And he used the word 'peons' in this statement, and reminding them of their place. Does that suggest anything to you, Captain?"

"Yes, actually! Prejudice, supremacism... It certainly fits the profile. And it suggests he does not actually care who they are if they are standing in his way of something."

"More containment procedures; just like on Therinë. People without the capacity to fight back. At least until that new arrival."

"And like what Kriv'tik mentioned to us?"

"And they warned us about this."

"Warned us! Who warned us?"

"Him...on Therinë..." he struggles through his flinching. "He was a part of it. They came, they found us...found the Marshal... but did not pursue. They told us to leave."

"Commander, who is it we are talking about here?"

"He described them as his opponents," he continues dreamily. "The real opponents... But they did not respond as if they knew who we were. It was a NEW encounter, and he caused it."

The Captain felt a cold spike run through him, even with his chip straining to contain it. He turned to examine the com-system, which was still on, relaying the conversation to the ship.

The Captain of the Tul'ryk listened in on the conversation occurring inside the control room. It started to reflect on the actions they were hoping to incite for their own form of revelation. He decided to prompt an association.

"Commander," he asserts. "Am I to assume, by your statements, that the Marshal, one time, actually met with someone he called his opponents, but they were NOT the same as what Commander Kriv'tik was sent to assault?"

Geilv was suddenly yanked out of his personal thoughts at the mention of the name.

"Kriv'tik…" he mumbles, as he reflects on the conversation apparently carrying details someone was prying out of secrecy. "He was sent on many missions, this is correct. He spoke of this, but was unsure how to quantify it."

"Because he was on active, right? Then, boom, dead world, go home, only to ask what he just did, but without any way to go back and check on it. Am I right?"

"Yes."

"How many times? And for how long? And who else besides him? And then, so long a time after, here we are, in a place the Marshal never explained we needed to travel to, and didn't even explain it to us after we arrived. I don't know about you, and I have nothing against our military as a body, or the people who work there, but as an officer who would like to know a few things on occasion relative to what I am expected to do, to say nothing of the freedom of thought to do it without a mind-control chip driving me, I think this military is a heavy yank of the tail."

The Commander gawked at the com-system as he reflected on his past interactions with his long-time friend. Then his face flinched sharply, and he let out a restrained grunt.

"He said to remember his words…" he muses distantly. "Lajivi…"

"Commander, what actually happened with his last command? According to the word I got as part of the military scuttlebutt, he was killed due to some kind of trap left behind by these insurgents… an exploding asteroid if you can believe it. Personally, I do not. I find it hard to imagine what he would be doing with an asteroid. But if these insurgents, and I will use the term loosely here, do not even know we exist, or at least did not until that one occasion of your new discovery, who or what is the Marshal telling us to destroy, and what happened to Kriv'tik, because this officer told me the death record was falsified."

"What? Argh…" he clutches at his interface.

"Commander!" shouts Captain Ta'yeen. "We need a med-tech up here."

"Negative!" Geilv countermands feebly. "Captain Kan'vrij, what else have you heard about Kriv'tik? Who is this officer informing you about him?"

"All I can say about it is she is a new assignment to our crew, a Lieutenant who claims she once served a brief tour of duty with him at a mining outpost."

"Morndindor?"

"I do not know the name, but she did reveal he was harvesting an unknown mineral for the Marshal, to be refined into a highly volatile substance, also without definition, and with no explanation of why, and using a proprietary form of technology, also without explanation. So far, regardless of the fact this stuff might not fit any of our science, if he is telling us to build something with such a highly destructive capacity, I think we are deserving to know what we are doing, if for no other reason than for safety's sake."

"Yes, I would agree. I also asked this question, at least privately, after we had an…incident out there."

"An incident. It figures. Does this relate to that blast cloud? And further is to ask who he really is fighting, if not who we are TOLD he is fighting, and neither that they are likely to take up residence in our galaxy, or even our universe. This also demands us to ask where HE came from, that he knows any or all of this to begin with. Then he offers these promises we wait an eternity for, and as we have already suggested, he seems to hold both supremacist as well as prejudicial attitudes for anything beneath him. That's not a benefactor. That's a liar, a cheat, and if he's blowing up whole worlds, a mass murderer."

"A murderer…yes, that world, Therinë, what we did there. And Morndindor."

"And our Council, who does not seem to be doing anything other than this highly publicized deliberation of theirs, gave him the keys to our military, with all our world-destroying fleets, and us on these chips. It makes you wonder where he might point his finger next, especially as we are now realizing who he really is."

"What? What do you mean by that, Captain?" he asks urgently.

"Commander, you seem cognizant enough to answer that one yourself, even WITH your chip on active...which, by the way, is another thing a lot of us did not know about."

Geilv glared at the com-station for the bold accusation, but rather than argue it, his ire suddenly spiked. He roared in outrage and clutched hard at his interface.

"All right," Captain Ta'yeen exclaims. "That does it. Ensign, get a med-tech up here. I'm not listening to this guy anymore until he settles down with a heavy sedative."

"Captain," the voice on the speaker emits. "You might want to give the order to start turning off those chips. I gave that order here once we came to our own senses."

"You disabled your chips?"

"Absolutely! I'm not a machine, I'm a person with a mind that prefers to think for itself, and decide what, if anything, is a valid target to shoot at. Furthermore, to actually talk about things, if they hold relevance to our people knowing anything about what we are sent to do out there. As we might want to maintain records of the things we destroy, and WHY we are destroying them. But the Marshal doesn't give us this luxury. Not when HE wants us to shoot at something. I will not be a party to that, Sir. I refuse to serve such a creature as that. I will instead take a lesson from Kriv'tik and rebel against it."

"Huh? Rebel? What do you mean? We heard his base come under attack and be destroyed."

"I don't know or care for what you heard. Any sane man would rebel against something like this, and likely make up any excuse he can to escape from that monster."

This statement called Geilv's attention to the com-system. He gazed at it in disbelief, and a tiny spark of hope shot through him at the possibility.

"He said to remember his words...and then nothing. But Ytani... and then Ooduan...and Madzurki... Wait, Madzurki, it came after all this, after the Marshal returned, after he discovered what Ytani did. AFTER that incident. Someone came back and blew it up."

"Commander," Captain Ta'yeen wonders. "A clean-up? To remove something, more of the Marshal's illegal efforts?"

"Maybe, but who? They used an atomic on it."

"Well, we do have atomics in our stockpiles. And I suppose if you are desperate enough to rebel against such as this, you might find a way to acquire one. And his rank might afford him a few of his own secret movements."

"Yes, it might. Lajivi, what did you do, or is it simply wishful thinking?"

"And aside from that," Captain Kan'vrij continues. "This officer also mentioned one other curious note. She said the Marshal originally claimed we needed these chips as training aids. Well, Sir, how long have you been serving the military? After all this time, do you think you still need a training aid to tell you how to do your job?"

The Commander paused to consider this notion, and it began to twist his face with rage. His flinching actions grew in intensity and his voice began to rumble within his throat. Captain Ta'yeen studied him and knew what was coming from his own experience.

"Sir, you need to calm yourself. Ensign…" he orders. "Where is that med-tech?"

"Tell him to bring a probe!" Geilv groans harshly. "No more of this! No more, for anyone!"

+ + ◆ + +

A new day was dawning on Therinë, and Kaliya and Kailen were reviewing the latest surveillance camera footage from inside Central Command.

"My Lord!" Kaliya announces from across the room. "We have something here from our last spy run with the cameras."

"What is it, Kaliya? Suddenly, I am sensing an increased state of tension in you."

"You seem to be paying closer attention to your psionics lately."

"Considering the little games you and Ayene have played on me, I think I need to be more attentive. What do you have?"

"We actually have two items to report. The first one comes from Geilv's office during a conversation with the Marshal. The Marshal looks like he's following through on his threat to make things easier. He's apparently submitting plans for something to the ARC…probably another of his death toys. This is supposed to be sent to those ships out there and applied according to his directions, and likely inside the city."

"Either he must be mad, or else desperate…or both. He must feel himself quite confident in that space, and right under the noses of his opponents."

"If it helps any, he used such words as 'peons' and reminding them of their place. Geilv was also apparently studying these words. He was concerned about the authority being, and he tried reminding Darumon of Therinë. So the Marshal simply said to apply a little assertive military authority if the Lady should show up. After all, there's only one of her."

"Great gods," the General blasts. "That WOULD be insane."

"His justification was, 'Don't worry about it. Our professional soldier boys would surely be more effective at their jobs than all those rabblerousing orcs that brought you into it.'"

"Indeed!" Thaelyn frowns. "Powers help us, from both sides of it. This is at least as much madness as it is desperation. Maybe Aerlie was right with that suggestion she had once. Very well, let us hope our friends are wise enough to catch this. Nevertheless, I will need you to go there and try to investigate. Warn them, at the very least, and if they have already received something, see what it is."

"All right, I'll get to it just after this. We also have a result with Geilv. I would like to inform you he has apparently…and finally… snapped."

"Snapped," he muses. "In a good way or a bad way?"

"For our purposes, I would say a good way. Our work on the Tul'ryk has paid off. Geilv called them up shortly after he finished with the Marshal. He wanted to check on that survey report. The

Captain reported what he found, but then the conversation started to take on elements of our gossip, and our theatrical play to turn him around, along with the rest of them. He played a very clever role, so we should offer a nice hand to him for his acting."

"Good for him. But I suspect you also held a role by offering him coaching," he raises his brow.

"Well, maybe a little. After all, he was still on his chip at the time I spoke to him, and he didn't have much time afterwards to practice."

"Uh huh…well, still, good work."

"Along the way, we made a minor repair to our play at Morndindor where his relationship with Kriv'tik is concerned, planting a subtle suggestion of a rebellion, rather than outright destruction."

"Ah, very nice to hear," he nods. "It may not be a full correction, but it is a step in the right direction."

"And one other thing I think I would like to point out. Our society of thinkers is remembering how to think."

"Oh, it is? Dare I ask in what manner if it is coming up at this time?"

"They started speaking of that bomb. This followed the suggestion of Morndindor. This was in relation to that prison, and blowing things up to cover for themselves. But then, Geilv recalled that blast radius, and Darumon's statement of it being only in 'this' universe," she gestures figuratively.

"I see. And how does this play into it?"

"Well, aside from losing their horns over the sheer size of the thing, Captain Kan'vrij took the initiative to speculate on what might happen out there in Abnormal Space, especially since it seems saturated with all that Abnormal Energy."

"Oh dear."

"Yeah, like a fuse to an even bigger bomb. But not to worry, as our local universe doesn't seem to have any of this stuff, so they should be safe over there," she smiles sweetly.

"Indeed, how fortunate for them. And the rest?"

"Boom! Along with any other universe it seeps into."

"Incredible!" the General muses. "Though I suppose it is not too much to speculate on, with the right incentive and a few corresponding details, I might say that is a fine assumption."

"Yes!" Thaelyn affirms. "And this would surely raise its own suspicion for Darumon's intentions."

"Anyway," Kaliya continues. "All this got Geilv boiling to the point where he finally had enough of that chip of his. Captain Ta'yeen took his own initiative when Geilv started blowing his top, and then Geilv ordered those probes to turn everything off, deactivating them all around."

"Excellent!" he nods. "This finally disarms that threat, at least up to the point where the Marshal no longer holds the control mechanism. But this leaves us with the Marshal and his latest death toy. He will want to see a result of some kind."

"My Lord," the General urges. "How do we respond to this without also breaking our silence? If he is preparing another of his little surprises, this time to be played on Sigil, not only might he cause a significant amount of harm, but he could bring the attention of the Estelar into it."

"Geilv was also asking about this thing," Kaliya notes. "I think he's going to investigate once the ARC presumably receives the plans. And this gives me an idea," she smirks.

"Oh dear..." Thaelyn moans. "What are you going to do to that poor man this time?"

"Actually, this falls in line with some of our other ideas, so it just creates a convenient niche. The trouble is I need to coach Azina on HER acting skills, and make sure she is the one to meet him."

Thaelyn glares at her and raises his brow, then passes his glance at Kailen, who was smiling gently.

"Yes..." he coughs subtly. "Very well then, as you were..."

"Yes, my Lord," she salutes and dashes off to the other room to project herself.

Thaelyn sighs as he turns to meet the General's eyes. The General was silently laughing at the curious turn of events.

"She is clearly very talented, and full of ideas."

"The inspiration of youth, General, and in her case, we can expect a long duration of it," he chuckles. "As for the Marshal, I would hope whatever it is he is planning to create will take some time to develop, and then deploy. And maybe, if we can catch it before it could possibly reach that far, we can intercept the final product. After that… Well, let us give Kaliya a chance to report back first."

In the ARC, business was usual, except for Azina who had just received a new delivery in the lab. She was now rushing into the Director's office carrying a holo-chip.

"Ghantil!" she urges. "We have a problem."

"What is it?" he asks cautiously as he spies the chip in her hand.

"We just got this in the lab today. It's another custom order from Central, and it's got the Marshal's signature on it, like all the rest."

"Wonderful, what does he want? Did you examine it?"

"Yes, first thing when it arrived. I needed to know what that fiend was asking for, so I plugged it in and studied the specs. He's calling for some sort of aerial dispenser unit with a cyanogenic compound inside. I can only guess why, but it can't be good."

"Dammit, what world population is he trying to kill this time. We need to stall him until we can relay this to our friends. If Central asks about it, tell them we're…oh, let's say we're retooling our production facility for, um, enhanced safety protocols, especially due to this involving a toxic substance. Meanwhile, I should call this into their office. I'm told they have agents in projected form that can make relays to and from, as strange as that sounds."

"That's good, but how long can we hold this? They won't wait forever, especially the Marshal. He'll get anxious after a while."

"I don't know, but we have to try."

Kaliya was just arriving on the third floor where the bio-labs were found. She strolled up to the desk to speak with the intern on the other side.

"Excuse me, I'm here to speak with Intern Nur'ten."

"Captain?" the woman responds. "Yes, I think she'll want to see you. We received something here in the lab, and I just saw Azina run up to the Director's office with it."

"All right, thanks."

Kaliya recalls the image of the Director's office and decides to fold her image directly up to it, rather than taking the more conventional means. Her projection flashes out of sight, much to the surprise of the people standing in the room. She arrives in the office near the door to find both the Director and Azina still in conversation. They each jumped at the sudden arrival of the spectral apparition.

"Captain!" Azina yips. "In all the nether-space, I don't know if I'm happy to see you, or frightened by it."

"It's alright," she comforts. "You'll get used to it in time…maybe. We saw something on our spy-cam inside Geilv's office relating to the Marshal submitting a new order. Did you receive anything?"

"Yes! Right here…" she holds up the holo-chip. "The Marshal is calling for some kind of aerial dispenser unit that delivers canisters of a cyanogenic compound. Do you know what he has in mind?"

"Yes, and he's absolutely mad if he thinks he can get away with it. He's hoping to assault Sigil now, and this is the last place he should be assaulting. What are you doing about it?"

"Clearly," the Director interjects. "We have no desire to fill this order, so we've decided to try to stall for time. For now, we're going to use a story of retooling our facility to provide better safety due to the nature of this chemical. But we can only take this course for a limited time before he starts demanding results."

"Right, then we'll need to prepare some sort of response to insure against more of the same. In the meantime, Geilv has finally cracked and disabled his chips. He's also becoming interested in what the Marshal has been up to, and we think he might want to come out here to investigate this recent order."

"Uh oh…" Azina moans. "What do we do about that?"

"That's another reason why I'm here. How good are your acting skills?"

"Um, nonexistent?" she smiles innocently.

"That's what I thought," Kaliya smirks. "And Director, what about you?"

"Marginally better, if only due to my experience in my professional career."

"All right, we're going to sit down and I'm going to give both of you a crash course in how we do things back home. We've got a series of plans in the works, and we're going to blend this in as a little piece of a much bigger puzzle. And it looks like the two of you just became volunteers."

+ + + ◆ + + +

It was later in the morning, although Azgarén time measured it quite differently for the long duration of their circadian cycle. Commander Geilv had decided to make his visit to the ARC to follow up on the Marshal's most recent special order. He was just leaving the building at Central Command and taking his personal shuttle off the base and along the highway to the city. He exits on one of the main avenues and makes his way to the ARC building, where he pulls in and parks in the visitors' lot outside.

His face was no longer twitching, due to the full disabling of his interface and the associated chips. But even though he was free of their effect, the memories of having the authority chip enabled for such a long period, and so often during his lifetime, left a lasting impression. Now he was angry…angry for all the things the Marshal has apparently done, angry for losing so many good people along the way, and angry that his people have been made to commit so many criminal acts under the direction of an alien villain and his control devices.

As he approaches the building, he stomps through the front entrance into the lobby and up to the desk. The clerk at the desk recognized him immediately, as he was a well-known figure. She felt a shiver at seeing him marching in with such a determined posture.

"High Commander Geilv?" she announces, trying to keep her cool. "It is not often we see you in here. Can I assist you?"

"I require a meeting with someone in the research segment of the laboratory."

"Do you have anyone in particular you require?"

"I am uncertain. Where should I present myself to inquire further?"

"You would most likely need to speak with one of our residents, or an intern on Level Three at the desk."

"Thank you..." he responds and moves away to the lift.

The clerk watches him for a moment, and then makes a quick call on her vid-com.

"Research Department..." answers the voice.

"High Commander Geilv has just arrived here in the lobby and is coming your way right now."

"Got it! We're supposed to let Azina take this. She has special instructions."

"All right, good luck."

They end the link as the Commander rides the lift to the third level. He exits and approaches the administration desk. The clerk looks up at him in an attempt to maintain a calm demeanor as she greets him.

"Welcome, High Commander. Can I assist you?"

"I require someone to discuss a research project recently delivered. Are you aware of this delivery?"

"I am aware of a delivery that came in this morning from Central. Is that the one?"

"Most likely. Who do I speak to about this project?"

"One moment and I will check who is currently working that department."

The clerk turns and leaves down the corridor past the offices to the workstation where Azina was sitting. She hurries up to the girl and leans on the desk.

"Azina!" she whispers urgently. "He's here! Commander Geilv is out there asking about that delivery we got this morning."

"Here we go..." she sighs deeply. "Let's hope I get this right.

I never took a theater class in school, so this should be interesting. Meanwhile, get the Director. He needs to be a part of this."

"All right…"

The two of them split up and Azina strolls out to the front desk.

"Commander Geilv," she announces evenly. "My name is Intern Nur'ten. What do you need?"

"I want to inquire about a delivery the Marshal submitted for special research."

"Oh… That…" she huffs. "Yes, we received it this morning, and already we had the ACI on our tails for it. What do you want to know about it?"

"The who?"

"The ACI…" she pauses to study him conspicuously. "Wait, are you saying you don't know? Oh, right…your chip," she glares at him disdainfully and turns away.

"What are you talking about?" he inquires concernedly.

"What am I talking about?" she retorts nonchalantly. "With whatever respect I can muster, I was born and raised in a world where I was told we have a beneficent Council serving all our needs, a powerful military protecting us from all these awful insurgents the Marshal dragged halfway across the galaxy with him, and people like you who are supposed to be in those positions of authority to know everything about everything. Then, once I graduated from medical school, I was so proud of myself, landing a job here in one of the most prestigious medical institutions we have in this world, hoping one day to be a part of some miraculous breakthrough that could improve the way of life for our people."

"Uh huh, and already I am sensing something out of you. You know, your attitude on these matters is not entirely unknown. I have heard of it elsewhere."

"So be it. However, not only do we NOT receive any miraculous research projects from that beneficent Council who is so devotedly serving all of our needs, and for that matter an alien super mind giving us the secrets of the universe to play with, but our military, who is supposed to be led by people who know everything about everything, is instead blowing up that other half of the galaxy and not even telling us about it! Now, would you like to know about my attitude on that? Because, at this point, with my torture device Suppressor chip turned off, I do actually have a few feelings now."

"Miss, I wish I could answer some part of that statement, but at this point, I have a few of my own, and very similar to yours."

"Uh huh. So it seems. And therefore, here I am, in this prestigious institution, filling custom orders, like this one, to be used by that… creature…for whatever diabolical plans he was churning up out there, while he made the rest of us think he was our friend and… benefactor. And now we have the ACI threatening to shut us down, virtually destroying that prestigious reputation we worked so hard for, and likely putting people like me out of a job, to say nothing of my career. And no thanks to people like you on the active mode of your chips doing all his dirty work…which, by the way, we knew nothing about until recently, and making US your accessories."

"Again, Miss, my apologies," he rebukes. "It was not my fault the Council mandated those chips, and I was put on the list to get one, whether I liked it or not. I did not want it, like most of us in that military he created for his diabolical deeds, as even WE were made to think he was a benefactor. And whether you might know of it or not, he had me on active most of my life, and likely because I DID try to question some of his diabolical deeds, and this was my punishment. Does that say anything to you?"

"Actually, according to some of the things the ACI told us recently, it does. This is how he likes his…pets…to behave. But all right, Commander, I will offer a minor apology for my outburst. But it hurts to think you spent so much of your life on such wasted efforts. I suppose this is what happens when you bow down and kiss the tail of that Council for all their god complex of power, and the rest of us simply assume they know what's best."

"Them?"

"Yes, them. They're the ones who let that creature, along with his diabolical schemes, in the door, and sold the rest of us out to him. And unfortunately for the rest of us, we seem to treat them like a god entity that can do no wrong, never to question them. Commander, we're a society of scientists, right? We don't take ANYTHING as fact unless it includes that ever-popular empirical evidence to back it up. So, where are the Marshal's credentials that he is, in fact, a marshal, or anything else he ever claimed to be? Did the Council ask for it? The way it sounds, they lost their horns after the words 'great wisdom' came out. Did anyone else ask for it? I doubt the rest of us were even paying attention, simply leaving it to that beneficent Council to make all our decisions for us. After all, they're a god entity. They can do no wrong, am I right?" she smirks cutely.

"I am getting an impression here that you do not care for them, and perhaps even know something about what they are doing...or not doing...out there."

"Yes. And what they are doing is NOT what they should be doing...for the beneficent service of our people. We don't need the secrets of the universe. We do need that pollution up there cleaned up. We do need new or improved legislative policies and social services. In all the nether-space, at the very least, we could use a little work to keep all our scientists on their payrolls."

"You are not getting this?"

"Commander, I've recently learned that virtually none of the major research labs have any serious work to do. The Council hasn't given out any grants or other directives since that deliberation started. And worse is we became so dependent on them to do this for us that none of us have the horns to pick our own topics, let alone the funding to supply it."

"That sounds bad. No wonder I have not heard of any new developments during this time."

"Yeah. But it's bad on both sides that we simply didn't take the initiative to stop depending on THEM to do it for us. Those of us here included, by the way. The ARC is a large corporation with plenty of funding to do research, but we were waiting for them to give us something instead."

"Yes, I see your point, and it sounds like you and the others fell into a rut of some kind."

"We did," she nods.

"But if you are saying the Council is neglecting its usual procedures…"

"The ACI tells us they disappeared inside their chambers and haven't been seen since. It can even be verified if you check the DataNet for the last time they were seen in public…for anything at all. And it was a very long time ago."

"I see. I tend not to use that service, but I will look into it sometime. But then, who is this ACI you mentioned?"

"They are the agency that should have been asking those questions way back in the beginning, when the Council felt it held the power to turn us over to an alien super brain without asking him why he has such a super brain we're all supposed to be listening to. Unfortunately, they only came out recently, NOW to ask those questions, and now demanding those answers the rest of us were supposed to be asking for during this entire length of time we were waiting for his great wisdom…which we never received."

She pauses to glance at a nearby terminal, pretending to pull up something relevant to the request.

"All right," she asserts. "Come with me and I'll take you to the lab where we can discuss this most recent atrocity."

"Atrocity? What do you mean?"

Azina turns and waves at him to follow her down the hallway. Geilv has no other recourse at this moment but to follow along as she brings them to the lab where she most often conducted the processing of new orders through their automated production line. She directs him to take a seat while she sits down at the terminal.

"Miss, um…" he peers down at her name tag. "Intern Nur'ten, right? Although I can clearly feel your ire at this situation, I will say again, I was fooled by him just as much as so many others. In my lifetime, I did have such desire to understand what he was doing, if only he did not place me on active to force my compliance to his… diabolical deeds."

"Yes, Commander, but the ACI isn't happy about a lot of things. Not with you and yours, and not with ours. Although we MAY be allowed to continue our service, I just hope this doesn't get out to ruin our reputation. But they are demanding those answers that someone, most likely the Marshal himself, and probably also the Council, have been hiding all this time. Now, let's see..." she begins calling up some records on her terminal.

"By the way," he interjects. "Just how is it you know mine was on active? Most of our own people did not apparently know of this, and I only had it turned off recently."

"The ACI is watching, and we were informed of this, as we are now under orders to cooperate closely with their efforts as they investigate a number of things relating to the Marshal, the Council with their god complex, and even your people for all you're apparently doing out there. And this is all being described as a planetary security operation, with people like them, and even you, being on the wrong side of it."

"Me?!" he rebukes boldly.

"Yes, you...unfortunately," she responds firmly. "We could maybe...just maybe...excuse it if the thing was turned on. But unless you can tell me you can somehow override that chip while it's controlling your thoughts..." she shrugs. "It's not made for that, Commander. I should know; we invented it...by order of the Marshal. Then mandated by the Council as training aids for our military that apparently doesn't know how to fight. And by the sound of it, it STILL doesn't."

"Wait a moment! Help me to understand that statement. Not that I would argue, not after a recent discussion we had over in Central, but for reference."

"Ah, would that discussion involve yet another classified excursion into places our science never heard about, no thanks to our most beloved benefactor and all his promises of great wisdom? Abnormal Space, such a fascinating term... I wonder what relation THAT has to all those insurgents running amok throughout our home galaxy."

The Commander reeled back at the statement, as it reflected precisely on the discussion he had with the Captain of the Tul'ryk not long before. This also represented the other side of something that was occurring to break open so many of the Marshal's classified secrets.

"All right, Commander," Azina continues. "Let me see if I can give you an example. One day, something like ten millennia ago, we all look up in the sky and say, 'Hey, look!'..." she gestures theatrically with her hands. "...'That's a really HUGE ship up there!' Then the Marshal says, 'Oh no! Insurgents! Quick, everyone! Let's chase them all the way to the other side of the galaxy before they have a chance to jump into our upper atmosphere again!'..."

She finishes with a bright, if also ironic smile at her portrayal.

The Commander was almost ready to laugh at the imagery, if it were not also a direct jab at his military station to figure it out on his own. As a result, all he could do was frown glumly at the depiction.

"As I said, I did ask once, but I was put on active for it."

"Yes, Commander, and I am sorry for that, but don't we have any OTHER people out there who could take notice of this? Furthermore, if the Marshal so desires to put people on active, couldn't someone rebel against it after a while and turn those guns the other way?"

"All right, you have a point."

"This is further compounded, it would seem, for those same ten millennia of chasing someone around the galaxy. Then, you apparently found another universe out there. What does that have to do with insurgents in OUR galaxy? And now this thing you call Abnormal Space. Um, excuse me..." she places a finger against her temple as if in deep thought. "Is that the same thing as nether-space? Oh wow, you just broke one of our most famous scientific principles. And not only did you, or maybe he, forget to tell us, but this only makes matters worse for anything in OUR galaxy."

"Yes, Miss Nur'ten, I would agree. But I will also have you know that after a while, and especially in more recent times, on the order of centuries by now, I have been trying to gather some of my own observations, even while I was on active, to try to determine some part of this."

"Even while on active? Ouch! I'll bet that would be hard on you. I'm sorry, Commander. But when you add up all these pieces, it makes you wonder where that famous pursuit of ALL knowledge went to. Our military is still made up of people from our civilization of scientists, so you might think at least a few of them would like to talk about things on occasion. But it seems the Marshal doesn't let you do this."

"Yes, so it would seem."

The Commander now found himself reflecting on more of his conversation with the Tul'ryk, and the statements of people being made to open up about these topics, who were previously denied the simple freedom of conversation to share details of their activities. This also reminded him of the Captain mentioning someone on his ship revealing clues of some kind. Something happened, and it turned them around. Now it is showing itself again, and turning more people around.

He glared at her as she continued punching in her request on the terminal, quietly reflecting on his conversation in the control booth with Captain Kan'vrij.

"Miss Nur'ten," he strains to keep his calm. "I cannot argue some of this, not after what we just went through back in Central. Is this to say there is a hidden authority body now investigating all this, perhaps including us, about our involvement with the Marshal and his actions?"

"In a word, yes. They are a new planetary security agency that apparently came into service recently, and they are iron-horned to get the answers the rest of us missed all this time. One thing they ordered us to do around here was to turn off our chips, which they believe to be for false circumstances."

"False circumstances? One moment, this is new to me. Why turn them off? As I recall, these are supposed to be the solution to the old Tav'ageen Anomaly, correct?"

"This is the old explanation, but when taken with some of these new details they have been uncovering, they believe it was all a lie. And we, for our part, had to agree with them, based on our own information, that this might hold relevance."

"How so?"

"The old Council mandate forced a nondisclosure clause to keep any new discoveries quiet. It was apparently intended to keep the public calm, and not stir up any new panics, as we had once before. Sounds innocent enough, right? Well, maybe not, as it also effectively denied the medical practice to monitor the situation, discoveries or otherwise, simply to see if the threat was still out there, such that, one day, we might realize when we can CANCEL the chips. After all, they're supposed to be temporary, not a permanent feature for the rest of our lives. Unfortunately, they became permanent because the Council didn't allow us any other recourse. And the ACI thinks this is suspicious, especially after ten millennia of listening to all those stories that…any day now…we are going to leave home and fulfill that old promise of escaping from it."

"Uh huh…figures. That does actually make sense. And it follows with his promises of great wisdom, which he never apparently followed through on."

"Ten millennia, Commander," she advises solemnly. "And not so much as a progress report. We don't even know WHAT they are deliberating, as they don't even give us this much. Then, you apparently find a new universe, as well as disprove the old belief that nether-space is a fictional void. Either or both of those would surely uplift our science, but according to the ACI, who apparently have spies watching multiple aspects of what he's doing out there, he doesn't even allow us to know where we're going or what we're doing once we arrive."

"Do you know if they have any of those spies on one of our ships currently out there in that nether-space?"

"My understanding is yes, as they need to know what he's doing. They are completely ignoring your protocols at this time because those things PREVENT any of us from knowing what's going on out there. And if the Marshal came here with ulterior motives, HIS security now becomes moot."

"I see."

"He has been demonstrating himself to hide every little detail of what he does, and many of them critical, then denying any of us to know about it. They're tired of it. We volunteered ourselves to assist him, not become his slaves using these chips. That was not the bargain, even if he DID offer the secrets of the universe to us. In fact, I know of one person who suggested he only offered the secrets of THIS universe, so those others must not be included," she giggles ironically.

The Commander studied her, and reflected on the statement. And although it did carry an ironic direction, it was a bitter pill if the Marshal indeed had no real intention of offering anything for all he demanded.

Azina continues, "So he comes here with his stories, his promises, and his alleged aid to solve such as the Tav'ageen Anomaly. But this super alien brain only tells us to run away using the one thing no one wanted to begin with…the seed. Not all our preexisting colonization tech, which most of us forgot about in the panic."

"Yes, I recall this, including the mention of all our preexisting technology to do the same work. In fact, I am aware we used that technology to build outposts and research stations on many occasions prior to this, and it always stood up to our expectations. Those seeds, as I recall, were not required, and certainly not desirable."

"But Commander, according to the agent we were speaking to once, if the PEOPLE are not the ones using it, how would THEY know we even have it. YOU, the military, were the ones establishing those outposts and stations. This is not the same as a civilian colonization effort to spread out to other worlds, as we never did that. Therefore, she said, WE, the people, probably never knew just how much tech we really had. There were no PUBLIC examples of it."

"Really! Is that how they see it?" he muses distantly. "Well, I suppose…yes, actually, as we never really did make any true efforts at colonizing other worlds before. But now, about this new project the Marshal ordered…and I would like to emphasize, before you start chewing on my tail again, it was HE who ordered it, not I."

"Yes, Commander, and I'm sorry for chewing on your tail. And we might expect as much, based on his past history. But this doesn't change the fact that it resembles another of what the ACI is calling his death toys."

"Death toys?!" he jerks forward. "What do you mean? What exactly is he calling for? And again, who exactly is this ACI you keep referring to?"

Azina pulls back from her terminal and turns to him, although taking a softer approach this time to go easy on the guy for all his own troubles. She glances out the front windows, which opened up to the hallway outside, and observes a row of people gathering to watch the spectacle. The Commander followed her eyes to see the arriving audience, and started to feel a little vulnerable for having so many people watching him.

"The ACI…" she begins. "Azgarén Central Intelligence. It's a new planetary security agency they recently established to investigate high-level conspiracy, corruption, and even terrorism, if you can believe it. The explanation is since the unification of the Old-World nations, we stopped thinking about any sort of internal disruption to our way of life, such as from espionage or international intrigue. And since we apparently never found anything else out there, certainly not in close enough proximity to us to be a bother, we never had to worry about any threats from outside. So, we sit here, nice and comfy, thinking ourselves to be safe from anything that could otherwise threaten our lovely society of intellectuals. We even stopped supporting any kind of full military, as it simply wasn't necessary."

"All right, I understand your point so far."

"However, while our collective backs were turned, we DID apparently have something hanging over us making trouble. But our complacency to think everything was so comfy denied us to realize it. At least, until recently. Therefore, for those who actually took notice, and who grew so fed up with the complacency aspect of it, with a corrupt government on one side, a mind-controlled military on another side, and an alien super brain with highly dubious ambitions on a third side, here comes the ACI…that one body who will now make us STOP feeling so complacent, open our eyes, look around,

ASK those questions we otherwise failed to ask, or were denied to ask, and find those answers that have been hidden from us."

"And the Council? Something like this might normally be commissioned by them, I would think, but if they are being described as corrupt…"

"Yes. The Council is one of those on their list, which might make you wonder who installed it, if not a Council with a god complex who might not WANT something like this in the first place."

"Oops, but that would sound like a revolutionary body."

"Maybe, but it's being led by a group of individuals taken from various security, and even a few military sources, who have finally had their fill of things. And they have been collecting support from more bodies along the way. By the sound of it, if you want to describe it as a revolutionary body, we NEED this, as our Council is not even performing its common government duties, which is THE reason we elected them in the first place. If you want to research the mysteries of the universe, WE, the science factions, with all our professional scientists and laboratories, are the ones who should be doing the research, not a bunch of suits in a government office."

"Uh huh…that would make sense, from a certain perspective."

"And made worse by giving our society over to that same alien super brain, including our military with those mind-control chips, which is surely NOT the sort of thing a governing body SHOULD do, planetary security or otherwise. So, they are being described as having sold us out for this great promise…whatever it is they did with it. Therefore, they're pointing fingers at the media, the Council, you people, and even the Marshal."

"The media too?"

"Yes, apparently they found regulators in there fabricating false stories for our society of people desiring to learn a few things."

"Um, but wait. I am actually aware of those people. But they were supposed to be in there to regulate any sensational news to keep a public calm after that Scare."

"That Scare was ten millennia ago, Commander, in case you forgot what day it is now. But yes, so it might have been stated.

And yet, this is not what they were doing. They were outright lying to us about anything newsworthy. If you don't want to start another panic, simply don't tell people any new ghost stories. But the news we were getting was more like, 'Love the Council, for it is deliberating the secrets of the universe, and any day now, we will be uplifted to something godlike.' Then, such as, 'Love our benefactor, the Marshal, for he is trying so very hard to fight back all those awful insurgents, so that…any day now…we can leave this world and that similarly awful Anomaly.' And then such as, 'Be sure you get your seed implant on time, for all that awful pollution up there, and don't forget, any day now, we'll all be leaving this world to find new frontiers to conquer'…and so on. Get the picture? It's all rubbish, and made worse by repeating that 'any day now' bit to reinforce the idea NOT to think with your own horns about how long this has been going on."

"Wow. I actually stopped watching the news half an eternity ago when all this got started, so I had no idea it was this bad. And once again, it figures, as it fits with so many other things now," he huffs. "All right, let us see about these…atrocities…as you called them."

"Yes, Commander, but you're not going to like it."

She returns back to the terminal and begins reading from the latest order.

"This recent order calls for a custom designed project resembling a type of aerial dispenser system to launch canisters at range. It looks a little like you're getting ready to bombard someone. The canisters, in this case, are supposed to contain a cyanogenic compound, which on detonation could kill hundreds, maybe even thousands of people each, depending on how densely populated the place is, and he's ordering thousands of these canisters. Now, Commander, would you like to know why we call this a death toy?"

"No thank you, I think I can see that part already. He has us investigating a strange city structure that is a fully enclosed toroidal body of gigantic proportions. We estimate it could contain maybe a few hundred thousand people inside."

"A toroidal shaped city?" she muses intriguingly. "That would certainly be a hot topic, if it were ever to find its way on the news waves, regulators or no. A bit like the Abnormal Space it's located in."

The Commander glared at her for the obvious insinuation.

"This ACI you speak of must have some very determined agents in it."

"Yes, Commander, this much you can be sure of. When you start playing with people on that scale, you should probably be very careful of the puddles you go splashing in."

"Yes, I might need to agree. And I suppose, since we are again speaking of those regulators, where are they right now, if this ACI is so upset over it?"

"Arrested, along with someone in the Grand Hall building who was acting as a middleman with the Marshal's office. They even admitted to these charges, thinking they had a right to it, based again on the Council's god complex, or maybe the Marshal and HIS god complex, where he should not really have any legal authority in OUR world to begin with. Are you familiar with, what was it…Article Nine, um, Section Fourteen of the Charter of Laws?"

"I am probably not as well-versed in the Articles as I should be, but if you are referring to those regulators, I suspect you are speaking about something relating to censorship, correct?"

"Yes, and it's illegal, Commander. However, there seems to be a glitch in that law."

"What?" he cocks his head and frowns. "What kind of glitch?"

"It basically says, blah-blah, reporting true and accurate information…to the best of their ability. We have to reflect on the famous 'spirit of the words' here. But if the Council, with its god complex, should impose a war declaration and override that ability, they can essentially take over, cheating the spirit of the words, which we are all made to believe in, much like a religion, even though we describe ourselves NOT to be religious. Then, suddenly they can take over and still be technically legal, even though the spirit would say they are not. This is called authoritarianism. And this is not the spirit we were made to believe in from our school lessons. We're supposed to be a free an open society, not ruled by a dictatorship."

"Oh, how convenient!" he shouts. "Now I see your point on the corruption aspect of things. They got their blessed promise of great wisdom and turned on the rest of us."

"Yes. We waited ten millennia for his promise of great wisdom. What we got were these horrible seeds, his similarly horrible torture device Suppressor chips, a horribly polluted world, and all sorts of promises of doing something which never came to pass. Finally, I guess someone got tired of waiting. Unfortunately, it was not those people who were supposed to be paying attention to begin with. Now, the ACI is arresting anyone who gets in THEIR way, much like the Marshal seems to be doing with all those who get in his. That's who the ACI is, Commander, people who don't take no for an answer, much like the Marshal doesn't like your military asking questions…therefore, boom, active mode."

"Oh great. And so now they are going to tear us apart for it. They, and whoever they can call to their side, which could result in a full revolution, by the sound of it."

"I don't know, but we got ourselves into a bad place when we accepted that offer."

"Where are they now with it? It sounds like they will be knocking on my door soon for all our involvement."

"Probably so. So far, we're under orders to cooperate with them as part of their investigations. We're reopening the research on the An'gamu seeds to see if the Marshal did anything strange to them to justify why he pushed them at us so hard."

"Pushed at us?"

"It was his first solution to that awful panic we suffered. Rather than give us the chip to solve it, he told us ghost stories to frighten us off the planet using the seeds, rather than our normal tech."

"Ah, but of course, and here we are with that again."

"It wasn't until after his insurgents locked us in place that he had us turn to the chips. BUT…even though we had an effective solution to stop the panic, his perpetual storytelling that, any day now, we're leaving home, caused us to forget all that dirty industry out there, and the fact that we had cleaner tech we could use to upgrade things, once it should've become clear we are taking forever to actually leave. And so here we are now, forced to take the seeds even though it was never necessary."

"Uh huh, and another point I once tried arguing, but it did not work."

"Yes, he doesn't seem to like people questioning his superior alien wisdom. We're also reopening the Tav'ageen studies to see how and why he was telling us so many ghost stories, and if there was in fact any real truth to it, because we're suspecting the whole thing was a hoax!"

"A hoax!" he shouts. "Dammit! I knew there had to be something about that. He came in so conveniently just when we needed answers."

"Yes, this is part of the reason for it, and I suspect you're not the only one to wonder about that little coincidence. I guess it also goes along with how his alien super brain told us to run away for fear of these OTHER aliens we could never identify. But, more importantly, can you tell me why he was calling for all his little death toys these past four centuries or so. Because the ACI tells us they have confidential information describing where some of it went. And it does not apparently involve insurgents."

The Commander glared at her as he pondered the question. These were some of the same topics he had previously considered privately in his office once.

"Four centuries…" he muses softly. "This coincides with Therinë. I must admit, I am aware of a number of orders he made, but I do not know what they were. In fact, I seem to recall these were all part of his classified directives, so I am wondering how this ACI got hold of the information in the first place."

"Commander, these people don't stop at someone's security roadblocks. The Marshal has apparently classified so many things, he's covering up everything he does so no one knows anything about what he's doing…anywhere. The ACI is tired of it. He is an alien being who came here asking for our help, but he doesn't tell us why he needs this or that. So, they will push their way through any door, including ours, yours, and even his, to get this information. They have come to realize lives have been destroyed because of him. You might as well describe yourselves as murderers, and this invalidates your security ratings. Possibly even your authority as a military body serving our planetary population."

"Murderers!" he wheezes.

This suggestion instantly hit a mark with Geilv, and he found himself reflecting back on his old conversations with Commander Kriv'tik regarding his early missions. His mind began reeling from this and his earlier conversation with the Captain of the Tul'ryk, and also Captain Ta'yeen in the control center.

"Containment procedures..." he mutters softly. "This is what he called them. He told us they were part of his opponent's sympathizers, and needed containment in order for us to conduct our operations."

He covers his face and leans to the side, turning away from the window.

Azina felt for him, but she also had a script to follow, at least in a general direction as she had to ad-lib most of it. She waited for him to regain his composure before continuing.

"I heard about some of that. But Commander, does the word 'containment' suddenly translate to wiping a full, or nearly full planetary population? I don't know who those people might have been, but I seriously doubt they had to die for it."

"Yes, you are right. And most of them did not have the technological capacity to oppose us to begin with."

"And you balk at the idea of being a murderer? Chips or no chips, why couldn't you figure out at least this much a long time ago? How many worlds does it take to understand they are not valid targets? In all the nether-space, they were right. It's shameful to be a part of our species with examples like this."

"Miss, can you perhaps try to see it from my perspective? I was on active most of the time! I was unable to question or analyze it!"

"Much like those who did the deed. Yes, Commander, I understand this part. But there has to be a limit, or at least a threshold, when you start piecing a few things together."

"Yes, I will agree, if only we had something to look at afterward to find those pieces."

"Great, it was so complete, you didn't even leave enough evidence to study it? Yeah, that sounds like him…cover it up, and deny us to know what he did. Furthermore, our society of scientists who deny the existence of anything we refuse to believe in unless we have that hard empirical evidence in our hands. So convenient. One might suggest it goes hand-in-hand with the pounding in our schools for the spirit of the words."

"Pounding? You mean, something intentional?"

"Well, it certainly does seem to lead in a direction that could bring us to where we are now. And this naturally brings us back to the ACI and their gripe over the Council. They would surely be the ones to regulate these things."

"Yes, they would."

"And this is only one gripe they have. Another would be relating to the Marshal. For instance, according to the ACI, the Council gave illegal authority over our military to an alien being that should not hold any authority of any kind in our world. This not only makes HIM illegal for holding it, but it also makes the Council illegal for doing it."

"Yes, this is bad. I was not actually aware of this ruling, at least not precisely. Everything came under that emergency war declaration you mentioned earlier. But I will also admit, it does make sense, and I personally disapproved of many things relating to how he managed it during this time."

"And this is why he kept you on active so often, to make sure you behaved yourself?"

"Behaved… Maybe. I was asking a lot of questions in the beginning, and I suppose he grew tired of it. He appointed me to this position, replacing the former HC, and saying he needed someone fresh that he could mold to the new image of a new military."

"Wow, so that's how it happened. Well, I'm sorry for you, Commander. As for the Council, the ACI recently investigated another curious finding. Did you know that every election since the Marshal arrived has been falsified to keep this one Council in power, despite the voter opinion?"

"Huh? Impossible! How did that happen?"

"That's what the ACI is asking. According to the Internal Secretary over at the Grand Hall, who was also recently arrested on conspiracy charges, he said the Marshal presumably granted them some special immunity, along with this great wisdom he kept promising us, so that they could stay in power until they finished deliberating it. Since then, they locked themselves inside the Grand Hall, and no one ever saw them again…no one, either coming or going through those doors. Half of them should be dead of old age by now, to say nothing of anything else."

The Commander gaped at her vacantly. He rolled his eyes at the increasing number of people outside the window, many of whom appeared to be studying him as if he were a specimen in a zoo exhibit.

"Has the ACI investigated this?" he asks timidly.

"They did, actually," she muses as she casually glances out the door to find the Director. "But before we go into that, you might want to ask about the rest of the Marshal's death toys. This is one of the things the ACI is especially upset over, and asking how many of you were on active while you applied these things, or if you were just too dull-horned to ask what's inside the box."

"All right, please," he begs. "As I said already, I WAS on active and therefore could NOT ask what was inside the box."

"But were YOU the one to deliver it, or simply sitting in your office? Someone has to receive it, someone has to deliver it, and probably also open the box to apply it."

"All right, granted. And so, your argument is probably where the weak link in the chain could have been that might actually report something."

"It's a good question to ask."

"Yes, and I suppose, chip or no chip, our people were so complacent that they simply took it for granted that it was a necessary component to fulfill his needs, like everything else."

"That's a little disconcerting. You know, much like with our god entity Council, we seem to worship HIM as a god entity. And the funny part is, once again, we're not a religious society."

"Funny, yes, in a morbid manner of speaking. So, what do we have on all this?"

"First of all, the ACI seems to know where some of it went, and they say this is due to some military informants that came forward."

"Military informants? Do we know who?"

"They don't apparently give out this information as part of their internal security to protect those involved."

"I see. All right, I suppose I can understand that part."

"Now, we have this most recent one, and the ACI revealed to us that you have ships out there investigating that large city structure, so this gives us an idea of where it might be going, and possibly also why."

"Yes, and clearly they are bypassing our security protocols to find these details."

"Yes, but when lives are at stake, neither you nor the Marshal are going to stop them. They apparently have agents all over the place, including inside Central and on your ships. They said they were just recently successful at…inspiring…that task force to discontinue their operations and turn off their chips so they won't be subject to the Marshal and his schemes anymore."

"So, this is what happened. Yes, the Captain told me about some officer informing him of a number of things, and this caused his full crew to essentially mutiny against the Marshal's plans for that city. All right, I will n-…not…" he furrows his brow as he begins to feel a strange new sensation. "Will not…won't… Interesting, I nearly forgot what that word was."

"Wow, that took a while," she giggles. "I was wondering when that might finally come out."

"Wondering?"

"You apparently disabled your Suppressor chip, and now this is coming back to you. Although in your case, being so long under the effect, it took a while. An agent came to us earlier today. She said they're watching you over there, being such a prominent figure in control of our military. You apparently finally had enough of your authority chip, and I guess you disabled both."

"Yes, I did, but how is it I am…I am…I'm…now starting to recall these old words?"

"The Suppressor chips play havoc with several things inside our brains. This is yet another issue with the ACI. They ordered all of us to turn ours off. This is part of their inquiry into why we were made to use them. Meanwhile, we're discovering we can use linguistic contractions again."

"Really. How long has it been since the last time I had that?" he smiles faintly. "Anyway, I suppose I will not argue with this ACI for their actions on the Tul'ryk. If not for them, I would probably have given the same orders. I had the Captain conduct a survey of that city, hoping to provide me with a comparison for analysis to see what the Marshal was pointing us at. I have been recalling a recent series of events, and asking a few of my own questions."

"And this is while you're still on active?"

"Yes, I have been avoiding my maintenance services in an attempt to weaken its effect. I hated that thing…and he kept me on it for so long."

"I'm sorry, Commander," she frowns.

"What else do you show for his custom orders?"

"You won't like it, so prepare yourself. From the technological side, he had us invent some fascinating tools, but when the ACI showed up and started talking to us, our marvels of engineering started taking on the appearance of terrorist devices."

"Terrorist devices?" he mutters hesitantly.

"One was a pharmaceutical called a Kajik'tav Serum. This stuff is so old, no one here even remembered what it was. So, I had to look it up in the old archives just to find out how to program our production line to formulate it again."

"Kajik'tav…" he muddles. "I seem to recall that name. Remind me, please. What is that?"

"It's a drug once used to treat a rare lung disorder, but it was discontinued back around the time we started converting to these seeds."

"Why?"

"The seeds seem to overcome the original condition, among other things, so the drug was no longer necessary."

"Interesting, but then why was it ordered?"

"Like a lot of things, we don't get explanations. He submits his orders, but never tells us why."

"This reminds me of a few other things, by the way."

"I don't doubt it. This one was a rush order for two hundred vials. It was packaged in two boxes, and it was a fairly recent order, just several years ago. So, whatever happened, it was fast."

"Several years ago, yes... I recall a rush order, and we received two crates from here. Kajik'tav...now I remember, it was on the labeling. And it went to him at his forward station. But this doesn't make sense. He was infiltrating a local city, apparently managing it somehow, although I don't know how, as they were a different species. So, if he called them his opponents, how would he be able to manage them...unless, yes, I recall now. I think he used coercive methods. But why would he want...?"

His eyes suddenly bulged as he makes the association.

"What does this stuff do?" he asks cautiously.

"Well, it treats this lung disorder, which is a condition where the capillaries can over-dilate, causing breathing difficulties."

"Ah yes, I remember now. I recall that condition from someone I once knew when I was a boy."

"Excuse me, you're old enough to remember those days?"

"Yes, I'm one hundred seventy-three now..." he sighs.

Geilv now finds himself reminiscing about his time in the service, and his face begins puckering from despair. His eyes become moist, and his voice starts trembling.

"I spent most of my life serving that creature. You cannot imagine what it feels like to hear your best friend tell you he was sent out on these extermination missions only to hit whole planets filled with people who never saw it coming."

"Commander, did it ever occur to you that ten millennia of fighting what he calls his technologically superior opponents…people who had to be on the same level as he is, if only to throw him out of his office, and yet they can't win a single fight against us?"

"This was one of the things I would occasionally question, only to be put back on active as he claimed I needed further conditioning."

"Oh! Conditioning, is it?" she blasts. "That's how he describes domesticating you as a simple piece of livestock?"

The Commander gazed at her longingly, as this one clearly stung him. He quickly covered his mouth and doubled over into his lap, and further covered his eyes as he wept softly.

Azina realized very quickly that she had gone too far, though it was unintentional as a reflex action. So she got up and crouched next to him. She wrapped her arms around him to offer comfort, and spoke softly in his ear.

"I'm sorry, Commander, that was uncalled for. Please forgive me. It was just a reaction to all these atrocities."

He nodded silently as he continued to cover his face.

"But just like you," she reflects. "You can't imagine how WE felt when they came to us, telling us about all our marvels of engineering for his Great Cause, and what he's actually doing with them. I screamed over most of it. This is the same one we've been calling our benefactor for so long, and waiting for his grand promises that would elevate us to a new level of…whatever. Then to hear he's been using us for whatever he really wanted, and lied about everything else. And we bought the whole story…ten millennia of it. So, we're all a bunch of domesticated animals…our full society. It hurts, as I for one thought I was better than that. And I'm sure you did too."

He again nodded silently while trying to stifle his sobbing. He lifted one hand to pat her on the shoulder.

Azina holds onto him for several moments longer as she contemplates how to finish this without causing even more pain. Finally, he pulls himself back up.

"That Serum," he mumbles softly. "What is the normal dose for it?"

"According to our records, for an adult, it should be no more than ten CCs, taken orally."

"And those vials, how much did they contain?"

"Forty CCs each, enough for four doses."

"And what if it was given as an overdose? Maybe also to a foreign species of lesser physical proportions than ours."

"Eek! In a case like that, you simply wouldn't want to know. From the specs I was reading, it could cause convulsive spasms leading to severe choking, and finally suffocation as the lungs might literally shrivel up."

The Commander grimaced at the depiction.

"Yes, that would certainly be a terrorist device if given to anyone. In fact, 'terrorist' isn't even enough. What else was there?"

Azina returned to her seat to continue the review. She glanced at the terminal, although she didn't actually need to pull up anything else as she had it all memorized by now.

"We are under advisement that a variant of the An'gamu Seed might be another example, as there is simply no proper explanation for a practical purpose for it."

"Why? What was the variant supposed to do?"

"It was an alteration of the existing seed, but replacing the augmentation code, which ours has, with debilitating code. It was then packaged in a remarkably advanced missile projectile made for a rifle launching system. Does this sound familiar to you?"

"A rifle?" he frowns. "How long ago was this?"

"About three and a half centuries ago."

"Three and a half centuries…let's see…" he mumbles to himself. "That puts us back, but that couldn't be…I don't recall receiving anything like this over there… No, wait. Oh no, he wouldn't do that…" his voice escalates. "And against those people?"

He finally recalls the moment of the Daanen-Aryku moving from Ruuki uy'Daan to Therinë. He now closes his eyes tightly and winces sharply. He covers his face again and ducks down, letting out a mournful wail.

"Rifles!" he whines. "Yes, I remember now. And we had to

give instructions on how to use them. But WHY?!" he screeches. "What did they ever do? They didn't even have a proper military!"

"Commander," Azina asserts. "If you have any information on what these things could've been used for, you need to report this to the ACI. They'll want to know."

"Oh, I'm sure of it," he groans. "And they might yet put me behind bars for it. Was there anything else?"

"Two things come to mind, actually. One of these occurred over the four centuries they say you were stationed somewhere. It was a regular annual shipment of dispenser nodes filled with a custom program of Belvik Spores."

"Belvik Spores?! Why that, of all things?"

"Yeah, this one hurts. The marvel of our medical science was apparently used to kill something. About four centuries ago, we received a sample of alien neural tissue, and we were told to prepare a Spore program to destroy it. It was to be packaged in these dispenser nodes, which have to be surgically implanted, and he also ordered a custom device to automatically implant the nodes."

"A device? What sort of device? What did it look like?"

"According to the specs we have in our files, it might appear as an awkward-looking neck brace, or maybe an oversized collar, so we're suggesting it might be placed around the neck, and likely held there while the device was activated."

"Around the neck? Four centuries..." he starts turning pale. "Yes, he was doing something over there in that city. Coercion? This is worse than coercion!" he frowns. "What was he doing over there?!" he screams and covers his face again.

Azina once again had to wait for him to recover from this most recent outbreak. She glanced out the window, which was now packed with eyes peering in to watch the scene.

"Commander, perhaps a mild sedative would help in this case."

"Negative, I don't want it. I'm as much a murderer as he is."

"Commander, didn't we just talk a moment ago about these chips?"

"Yes, and you chewed my tail thoroughly for my lack of integrity as an officer."

"That's actually beside the point right now. It's clear he used you like he did everyone else in our world, and probably still is. He forced his military chips on you, his Suppressor chips and seeds on all of us, and his lies for everything else, keeping us neatly bottled up behind his censorship campaign while he pranced around the galaxy blasting anything he found pleasure in destroying. So, your tail isn't the only one I want to chew on right now."

"So it would seem," he pulls himself up again while wiping his tears away. "You said there was one more?"

"Well, one more that stands out in recent history. I think it was closer to five centuries ago, by now."

"Five centuries… That puts us before my last duty post. What happened?"

"This was apparently the result of a military informant they spoke to once. We received a strange variety of fungus. It required some truly unique environmental conditions in order to thrive. Our instructions were to see if we could find any medicinal purpose for it, but the project was cancelled early after we only got so far as to figure out how to grow the stuff successfully."

"So far, it sounds interesting from the scientific standpoint, but how does this fit in with the rest?"

"This is where that informant came in. It produced a potent psychoactive agent that could put a person into a near-catatonic state, and likely with a hypnotic effect, making them very susceptive to suggestion. But it also carried heavy metals, so it would be poisonous after a while if ingested."

"Poisonous, but with a psychoactive agent…"

"Yes, and this informant told the ACI you were apparently using it in a top-secret mining outpost in that other universe you found once."

"Huh?!" he blasts.

"Huh for which part, the total sensation that we discovered a new universe, or the disgrace that you were drugging a local population for slave labor?"

"I believe we already covered the one about the universe. It's the mining base."

"Yeah. She said it was apparently being used as a coercive agent to drug the local mining teams to do your work for you. And so, Commander, do you think I have justifiable reason to be a little upset? He used us to make his death toys to kill people. As a medical professional, I am deeply offended by that. Not only that, but I actually helped develop a few of these things."

The Commander gawked at the young Intern, as this forced him once again to recall the conversation he had with the Captain of the Tul'ryk.

"Someone on his ship told him about this..." he whispers. "An agent of some kind? Wait, he said this officer had personal knowledge...something about once serving with Lajivi at that base! Of course! They must've served at Morndindor once! But that means this person must now be working for the ACI if they're an agent. What in all the nether-space is this ACI? Who is actually running it? It's not us, and it can't be the Council. Who creates something like this, and especially if they're able to break through so many security blocks?"

"Commander, all I can say is these people are determined to uncover the Marshal's secrets, and as I said, they don't take no for an answer. If they're breaking your security blocks, they probably have people who either know how those things were made, or they're simply hacking their way through them."

"Likely so."

"And they're asking the questions the rest of us should've been asking all this time, but unfortunately it took us this long for someone to actually realize it. They describe themselves as an anti-corruption and anti-terrorism secret intelligence agency, a kind of checks and balances to our god entity Council. So, it's no wonder the Council would never install anything like this. They like playing god. Why would they ever want someone to question them? This sounds like someone ELSE came in and set themselves up as a type of hidden watchdog agency, watching and waiting for them to splash in that one really nasty puddle to expose them. Well, it looks like they did, along with the Marshal."

Azina now passes off to the Director, who was waiting outside among the crowd for his cue. He steps forward inside the room to join the conversation.

"Commander Geilv, I'm Director Ghantil Bak'vayn. My apologies for interrupting this meeting, but it would seem we have a very serious situation here."

The Commander looks up at him uncertainly, and briskly passing between him and Azina, as well as the crowd of people outside.

"Um, yes…hello, Director. What are you going to lay on me now?"

"Commander, that creature who once came to us with so many delightful promises has instead taken control of our society and our world. And he did so through deceit and all his mandates through the old Council."

"Yes, I'm beginning to see this now. And I suppose you're going to accuse me of playing a role in it?"

"Not if you were in fact under the authoritative influence of that chip. This was clearly one of his toys he made us invent to take over our society. What we've been describing as OUR military is actually HIS toy for whatever games he's playing out there. If you date back that far, you surely must recall we had a Sentinels' service, and that was NOT a military body."

"Yes, I recall this," he nods. "And those were much better days for me."

"So be it, Commander. But apparently, he likes his minions, as these people describe us, as complacent followers who don't ask questions, and your statements relating to your chip seems to authenticate this. But Commander, there is something you don't seem to know about, and it relates to the Council. When was the last time you ever saw or heard anything from them?"

"Personally? I've been too wrapped up in his campaign against his insurgents to pay attention to our world politics."

"What about news reports, or anything you might know of within your military circles?"

"As I was saying to her, I stopped listening to the news media half an eternity ago when it came under his censorship rules. I didn't see a point to it after that. We knew more about what was out there than he let anyone else know about. As for what we have inside our military, well, we haven't dealt with them directly since they went inside their chambers for this long deliberation…which I'm wondering about now, especially after her mention of the DataNet."

"Yes, and if anyone else actually paid attention to it, I'm sure you wouldn't be the only one. The ACI has been pulling together a number of resources in order for them to conduct these investigations, and none of this has been made public so far. First, for similar reasons to that censorship campaign, but here for the legitimate need to keep the public in the dark over what could be a new panic-invoking sensation. And secondly, since the Marshal likes his minions to remain complacent, they're working to perpetuate this image as part of their security process. Do you understand the principle here, Commander?"

"Yes, but what is it you're trying to suggest to me here? Am I now supposed to keep all this bottled up due to this new security concern when we have a monster controlling us?"

"In a word, yes, and for a reason. The ACI knows who he is. They apparently made contact with someone once."

The Commander gaped at him for this unexpected revelation. He straightened his posture, but remained silent as he pondered this bizarre turn of events.

"What about the Council?" he wonders. "Are they aware of this?"

"Commander, with regrets, there is no Council."

"Huh?" he shouts. "What do you mean, no Council? Who's inside the Grand Hall right now?"

"It's empty, and not only that, but abandoned and in a near-state of collapse due to negligence. The ACI arrested the Internal Secretary while investigating the election fraud, and had to force their way through those locked doors to see what was inside. The place is a wreck, and it looks like no one has been in there since the last time anyone actually saw a Council member in public, which was last recorded in 9765.31 for the press release relating to the Tav'ageen Suppressor chip…the last thing the Marshal actually wanted out of them."

The Commander now went into shock. He was panting over this latest bombshell. He sat there motionless as the Director continued.

"The ACI has been keeping us informed as part of an inner circle of confidants they're creating…people in certain privileged positions that they need to contain, since the Marshal has been using us for his own purposes. Together, we're uncovering all the little tricks he's been playing on us. For instance, we believe the Tav'ageen Anomaly was actually HIM causing all those deaths as a fear tactic. This led us to take whatever solution his superior alien mind pushed at us, until we were fully infested with his seeds and chips. The ACI believes he holds ulterior motives with those."

"Ulterior motives!" he blasts and quickly examines his body.

"As for his insurgents, they're most likely fake, another part of his plan to push those seeds at us, as he told us we needed to run away from this infestation he claimed we had, but could never actually do it with those insurgents out there. This effectively keeps us at home, where he wanted us all along."

"And with all his pollution to reinforce the idea," Azina adds.

As the Commander listened, he once again found his mind drifting back to the conversation with the Tul'ryk, and this time even further with his old friend.

"Lajivi," he whispers mournfully. "You were right. They were never real. Abnormal Space, Abnormal Energy…some weird new form of technology, like what we saw in play on Therinë, and people who might actually be extradimensional, and who should clearly hold easy access to Azgarén for a direct assault on their primary target. In all the nether-space, how could we fall so low!" he ducks his head and covers his face.

"Commander," Azina soothes. "He clearly knows where to hit

us, and how, if he wants us to be his minions. His storytelling must be something of a fashion for him."

"Absolutely," the Director affirms. "So, try to pull yourself together, as you need to be a part of our solution, not falling apart on us. During this time, and further to reinforce the idea, as Azina said, we were never told to stop the seeds, even though it was perpetually claimed to be temporary. And this also extends to after we had the chips, which effectively negated the threat potential and the urgent need to evacuate. And finally, we were never given instructions to research a way to remove them. This automatically makes them a permanent feature."

"So," the Commander reflects. "He wanted us to have the seeds for a reason, and the rest was simply a cover story. Do we know the reason for all this?"

"We're currently trying to research this. We have a possible suggestion, but we need to find our evidence to demonstrate it."

"And what about the chips, he pushed those at us too. Do they actually serve a purpose, or are they simply another of his toys?"

"We think they might hold a purpose, but not the one he told us about, at least not precisely. Although, the feedback feature would certainly qualify for the toy aspect, and yet it might also serve a function, depending on how you look at it. I don't know if you recall, but the original studies of the Tav'ageen Anomaly were about a group of children that were found exhibiting a strange condition. The reason might be behind that, because since applying the chips, we haven't seen any more of those. I've been trying to collect some statistical data, but that old mandate denies us the opportunity due to a nondisclosure clause, and this is likely more of his censorship to keep it hidden."

"Meaning he knows something, but he's trying to hide it from us. And the chip may also cover it up."

"Yes," he sighs. "Now, I don't usually talk about this to anyone, but I'm secretly a part of a forbidden science faction that studies metaphysics. This faction once belonged to Former Elder Velen Nazég if you can recall him. But the Marshal once made a hard campaign to publicly debase him, and we think we know why. He was perhaps the one and only science faction to truly understand what the Anomaly was, and the Marshal would want him out of the way."

"Oh really!" he balks. "And this is why he made so many efforts to kill him, I suppose. But how do we explain that ship of theirs?"

"Someone helped him, but at the time, we had no idea of who it was. Then recently, the ACI came into knowledge that the Marshal is a type of creature that can alter his form, and in so doing, he can impersonate any other creature he desires. This would allow him to interfere with things, impersonating people to falsify just about anything, and for any reason. He can also apparently fold space with his mind. Just think of our conveyors and how they work. Now imagine a creature with such power that he can bend space for his own personal travel. So, Commander, if anyone or anything out there can be described as an opponent to this, we are speaking on the scale of gods, religion or not, and likely those same extradimensional beings, and our military would never be able to stand up to that."

"So much for his claims of insurgents, unless you can tell me we can kill gods now."

"Yes, this would certainly be a mythical achievement," he chuckles. "But it also means he can come and go anywhere, at any time, and impersonate anyone, which is extremely dangerous. This opens a lot of possibilities for where all your insurgency reports actually came from, among other things."

"Yes, it does…" he drifts off.

The Commander now begins reflecting on the long pursuit of Velen and his people, recalling the myriad of scouting reports, only to discover Velen evaded them before they could mount a proper attack.

"He must've known where they were, and it was all just a false front for us with his insurgent forces to chase. We get a report of a sighting, but how do you track something after a jump…" he halts abruptly as a flash enters his mind. "In all the nether-space, no… THAT must be the reason!" he shouts. "That monster! A wild jump? Oh, naturally, and we had the extraordinary luxury of a random probe following him into that new universe!"

"Um, Commander?" the Director wonders. "What do you mean?"

The Commander sighs as he tries to compose himself.

"This goes back several years to my last post on a world we called Therinë. Someone arrived and chased the Marshal away. He claimed them to be his opponents, but the meeting represented a new encounter, as they didn't show any recognition of us…after our ten millennia campaign. This one named Thaelyn contacted us on a lost trans-com, and basically chastised me for what we did there, along with, um…uh…" he hesitates and ducks his head.

The Director and Azina both knew where this was heading, as they already had the story from Kaliya and Ayene. But they had to follow a program here.

"Commander?" the Director probes gently.

"It was about Elder Nazég and his people…whatever is left of them by now. He criticized me for pursuing civilian refugees who made a desperate wild jump to escape from our…" he glances at Azina briefly, "…murderous rampage. This followed with asking how we could possibly find them…AGAIN…and now in a completely new universe."

"Interesting. Did you have some special clue for this much?"

"Oh, but of course we did," he mocks. "According to our scouting reports, it was an odd occasion of someone detecting some sort of tracking probe that so conveniently attached itself to them as they made their last escape. This allowed us to follow them…even though he argued that they should not have been a target in the first place, and certainly not after leaving our home universe."

"Uh huh…a tracking probe, that certainly sounds convenient."

"Yes, and I also recall something else. He shared a conversation with the Marshal during this time. A kind of farewell, but with several moments of taunting and more criticizing. Personally, I think he was trying to invoke a reaction."

"In all the nether-space," Azina gushes. "That would be a brazen attitude!"

"You're right," the Director grins. "This sounds like someone with more horns than any of us down here," he chuckles.

"Oh yes, he did have that!" Geilv attempts a soft smile.

"But a reaction? What kind, do you think?"

"It was apparently to reveal certain details he previously shared with me, but this time as a hidden move to make the Marshal admit to them…in front of us, those of us who were in the room at the time."

"Very interesting," he croons. "This fellow seems like a clever deliberator."

"Yes," he nods. "And this now makes me think that NEW discovery of a universe wasn't so new…not to him. That world was apparently seeded by him once, and so he was simply returning back to it now."

"Unbelievable!" he moans avidly. "And naturally, he tells you to blast it, or something, as more of his games, right?"

"Yes, containment procedures, this was his excuse."

"Great!" he tosses his hands up. "And this brings us to the next point. Commander, there is something you need to know, and this probably relates to his military chips he pushed at us, which is his way of saying, 'do as you're told, or else…'."

"Yes, and I especially enjoyed that 'or else' part," he huffs. "I had virtually no opportunity in my life to actually have a life."

"I'm sorry for that, Commander. But here we come full circle back to the Council. The ACI did some research on this and found you once used a secret location called Site One-Alpha as a quarantine base to hide the Council during the time of the Scare. Do you remember this?"

"Site One-Alpha…yes, I remember that name. It was an old research outpost we once had. It was repurposed for this emergency condition, and also classified behind a high-level security rating. So, whoever is inside this ACI, they're breaking a lot of codes."

"Yes, well, in this case, we should ask who those codes are actually supposed to be serving. You? The Council? The public? Or the Marshal and his designs…because if it involves him, they shouldn't be there to begin with. These were OUR people he was dealing with, representing OUR government body, and now they're gone…all of them. The ACI says they can't find any trace of the Council OR their immediate families, and they were all supposed to be hidden away inside Site One-Alpha during the Scare."

"But..." he muses faintly. "They were supposed to have been brought home."

"The records say the Council was returned home only for press releases, but then sent back to Site One-Alpha, at least until the Scare settled and they presumably came back for this deliberation. But the families are still missing, and still classified behind that same security wall. And Commander, in case you weren't aware, Site One-Alpha is gone, allegedly due to an insurgent attack. So, if the insurgents don't actually exist, what really happened to Site One-Alpha and those people who were probably still inside of it?"

This stifled the Commander, and he felt a morbid chill wrap around him. He leaned back and stared into space as he tried to recall the old memories of the occasion. The chill gained strength as the realization came into focus. He reached up and grabbed his horns as he let out a painful wail.

"That monster killed the Council?!" he shrieks. "And I can't even recall which of his infuriating insurgent attacks he could've used as his excuse, there were so many of them!"

"Oh, I'm sure of it," the Director relents. "But now, Commander, we're working in cooperation with the ACI to essentially create our own insurgency against what the Marshal did to us. They believe he removed our Council once he got what he wanted, which was control of our people through his mandates, and control of the military through those chips. The rest is just his way of having a little fun as he prepares for his grand plan."

"A grand plan?!" he snarls. "And what sort of grand plan does he have?"

"Before I answer that, Commander, you need to understand your role in it, and you DO have a role, or else he might be a little more assertive in his purging of innocent life...and right here at home. He wants us as his minion species, and he expects us to behave."

"Then how do we correct this if we have to behave as..." he glances briefly at Azina, "...as domesticated animals."

"As I said, the ACI apparently made contact with someone. We suspect this may be in relation to that Abnormal Space you found, and the implications of who might live out there, especially when you take all these other pieces…which are fairly recent pieces now being discovered…and tie them together."

"Yes, the Captain of that ship out there mentioned something, and between them and us in Central, we think they may be an unrelated body. And this also reminds me of what that Thaelyn said about a governing authority, and here with a prison the Marshal is looking for."

"Quite possibly. And I suppose, if you include him with all his stories of insurgents, sending our people across the galaxy and back again, destroying whatever he takes pleasure in, a prison is a good place to drop someone like this."

"Naturally. And this makes me think of Therinë again, where we met someone he claimed to be them, even if it did not have the reciprocal recognition on their side. Could they be the same people, and he is making another attempt?"

"That would be rather unwise, if he already opened the door once."

"It would, and further how he likes to put people down, calling them such names as peons who need to be reminded of their place."

"Yes, that would be a fine indication of how beneficent our benefactor truly is," he chuckles ironically.

"This could then explain their rapid response to our intrusion in that space. They might be watching us by now. And this would ultimately reflect on Thaelyn's final message to me. Don't do it again, or else…"

"Yeah, and here we have another 'or else' statement, but this time the Marshal is getting chewed for it, for all the good it actually does. As for watching, this could be our clue, and this second attempt could be a spur."

"Could this also be why that authority figure in there stopped appearing?" he wonders silently. "Someone made a deal to hold back while they worked on our people."

"If so, it would demonstrate a rather extreme sense of empathy for all we've done so far. These people are working to save our world. I can't be sure of all their inner workings, as this goes a little above me, but if the Marshal has any real enemies out there, they are the ones to talk to. For this, you should probably speak to one of the ACI's agents for more information."

"And hope they don't lock me away first."

"It may not go that far, not when you consider these chips. But Commander, you are in a precarious position, being right under the Marshal. You, of all people, are expected to behave precisely as he wants you to behave. If his manners are to remove people he doesn't otherwise see any value in keeping, you are at the top of the list, I think. So here is where you need to play your role very carefully, and let the others make their moves against him in secret."

"I see…" he nods solemnly. "So, I have to pretend everything is business as usual, even though I want to rip his throat out."

"Yes, and try to stifle your emotions, as you're not supposed to be disabling your chips, either."

"Right. Well, if he should ever ask about that, I'll just give him a little of my own authority. After all, as the HC, and after ten millennia of faithful service, why do I still need his training aid?"

"Perhaps, but try not to get him mad along the way."

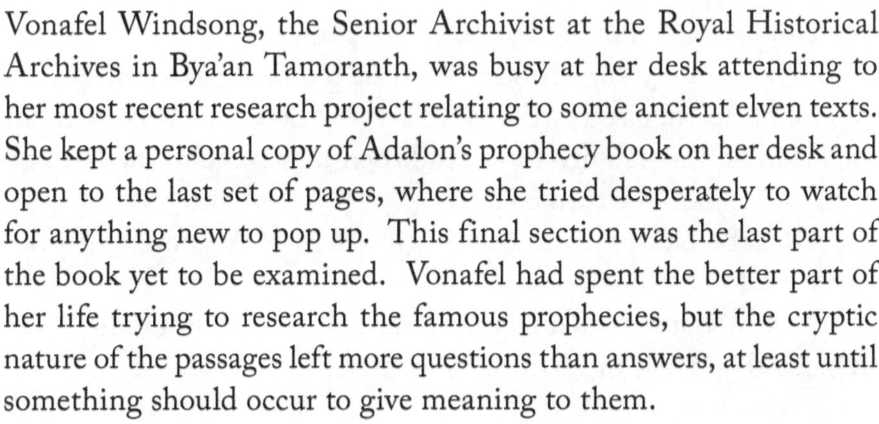

Vonafel Windsong, the Senior Archivist at the Royal Historical Archives in Bya'an Tamoranth, was busy at her desk attending to her most recent research project relating to some ancient elven texts. She kept a personal copy of Adalon's prophecy book on her desk and open to the last set of pages, where she tried desperately to watch for anything new to pop up. This final section was the last part of the book yet to be examined. Vonafel had spent the better part of her life trying to research the famous prophecies, but the cryptic nature of the passages left more questions than answers, at least until something should occur to give meaning to them.

These last several pages were even more difficult because they were hidden behind a veil of encryption to keep them from being discovered prematurely. It was believed they held something of a critical nature, and Adalon wasn't taking any chances at this point to let something slip before its time.

As she sat there with her attention carefully focused on her work, she caught a glimpse of something occurring out of the corner of her eye. Her tension in recent times where the prophecies were concerned made her take quick notice, and she jerked up from her work to study the book. Then, as her eyes came into focus on the second to the last page, she couldn't believe what she saw. The entire page, perhaps two-thirds of which was empty, had finished filling in. She stared at it in awe.

"Grace of the Seldarine!" she gasps. "Girls! Come in here, quick!"

From another room, her two closest assistants rushed in to join her, one of them being her granddaughter.

"Grandmother? What happened?" asks the girl. "Did we get another one?"

"Casarolyn! Come quick! You need to see this."

The three of them converged around the book and gazed into it.

"Gods above!" Casarolyn wheezes. "That's not just one. Where are we here?"

The other girl directs them with her fingers.

"I'm counting one…two…three…four of them! That's the whole rest of the page!"

"Not just that, but look at how they read."

They carefully run through each of the new passages, quietly mumbling to themselves the words, even though at this moment the meaning is still a mystery. And then they come to the last one in the set…and they turn cold.

"Gods be blessed," the second girl gasps. "I've never seen her do that before."

"Indeed, but if she's doing it, it must be serious. Grandmother, we need to get this to His Lordship…fast!"

"Yes, you're right," she affirms eagerly. "Fetch me a coach! I'm getting too old to simply run it anymore."

Vonafel packs up the book and holds it tight against her as she and the others hurry outside. The two girls flag down a passing coach, and they ride it to the local gateway hub, where they hire a private car as part of the routing through the interplanetary transit to Therinë.

Thaelyn and his officers were again in discussion of the plans for the military base they were hoping to plant on Azgarén. They still needed to decide on how it would appear so they could submit the plans to the Director at the ARC to pass along to his people for donations and volunteer help.

"The biggest issue is how to bring him outside," Kaliya notes. "I doubt you can just call him out, like as if you're going to host a barbeque or something."

"He never came outside during my lifetime," Ayene relents. "At least not that I ever knew of."

"Then we might be forced to enter that building to engage him," Thaelyn muses. "If Sargeras does not make a habit of going for a daily stroll, we can only hope to take him down while he is least expecting it. But this again runs the risk of him using some portion of the city either to empower him, or simply to devastate it if he will not let go politely."

"Do you actually expect him to do anything politely?" she smirks.

"Indeed, no. And therefore, all the more reason we must be sure of ourselves."

"He might also choose to run again," Kaliya admits. "But then, this reminds me of his energy supply. What if we cut it off to the point where he can't fight back as much?"

"For the quantity of people out there with those seeds, that would take time. But it does pose a possibility if we can recruit enough help through the ARC and their affiliates. And then we have Darumon. He is the most active. He needs to be contained somehow."

"We already have a partial success with their military. When

Geilv had his episode, he called for all their chips to be disabled. So, at least the Marshal's chip-controlled killing machines are gone."

"But this just leaves him alone without any recourse," Ayene suggests. "If he should start putting together any of these pieces, our trouble will be keeping him in one place and not making any more death toys, even without the ARC. Also, we don't want him going out with any new ideas for another public panic attack."

"If he does that," Thaelyn considers. "We might need to intervene, if only to save lives. We will not wait for our Harvester technology. We will simply rush him with what we have, and let the Chief Tech finish her work and come for us later. We cannot have him taking revenge on those people for simply choosing their own way."

"The next thing on my mind is this," Kaliya offers. "Once Ayene finishes her medical procedure, I want her back out there to rally up additional support for us. We need her and Petrith to work up a plan for how we'll use their media streams for our propaganda. I also want to organize a series of investigations of their industry to see what they're actually doing, and why they're using such dirty tech for it. Either we need to shut them down, or retool them to use cleaner tech."

"Shutting them down is my first thought," Ayene mentions. "Whatever it is, if the Marshal made it, we probably don't need it. I'm sure we must've had industry before this to produce whatever spaceships we had previously. This isn't our first time, you know."

"You have a point. First, let's see what they're doing, and try to follow the chain of production. But we'll probably need a lot of extra people working on this for us, so we'll have Kriv'tik help organize the excursions and sort out the details. By the way, how is he doing on his projection skills?"

"He keeps telling me how you can't teach an old bull new tricks," she giggles. "I just say, if he wants the world to be a better place, he needs to drop the bull so he can learn to fly like a bird and prowl like a cat. So far, he's still practicing his animal shapes."

"Yeah, this should be fun to watch," she grins and shakes her head. "But it'll be handy to have him present to take charge of a few of these operations. If we go into those industrial facilities, they might not want to simply shut down because we tell them it's bad for the environment."

"Yeah, that's what I'm thinking. We might need some muscle."

Vonafel and her two assistants were just arriving in the plaza outside. They made their exit from the gateway hub and were now marching across to the WIC building. As they made their way through the halls and up to the strategy room, Vonafel peeks inside.

"My Lord?" she calls out gingerly. "We need you...right now."

Thaelyn and the others turned to the address, but the tone of voice had them instantly concerned.

"Vonafel, what happened?" he responds gently. "It must be important if you have cohorts travelling along with you."

"Yes, this one is big."

The three women enter the room and approach the table. Thaelyn directs them into chairs to join the group. Vonafel sets her oversized book on the table as she sits down.

"What just happened over here?" she asks.

Thaelyn glances around the table, suddenly curious as to the meaning.

"Kaliya, do you know of anything special occurring today on Azgarén?"

"Not really," she ponders. "The Director is waiting for us with these plans. The Tul'ryk was on standby, last I heard. I, uh...well, wait a minute. Geilv was going to make a visit to the ARC, so maybe he did that today. But I would hardly think...unless..."

"You had special instructions for the Director and that Intern, did you not?"

"Yes, I did," she nods. "So I wonder if we got some sort of a result out of that. But then, what is Adalon talking about now?"

"Vonafel, what do you have?"

"The rest of the book just opened up...all at once, four new ones."

The full group gasped and exchanged astonished glances.

"Cu'Nar's pity!" Kaliya muses timidly. "Then I guess something big happened if that's really the one. I'll need to check on it."

"Perhaps in a moment," Thaelyn mutters. "Let us see what we have here so far. Vonafel, where are we in the book right now?"

"The first one fills in the gap between that one where Ayene met those new people, and an older one where Kaliya met with Adalon that day…the one where Darumon meets his match with silver wings."

"Very good, and how does this one read?"

Vonafel opens up her book to the final pages and begins reading the first of the new additions.

"A foreign shore does Children bear, of scholarly delight; drawn to play with swords of steel, an ancient game of plight."

"That has to be Azgarén," Kaliya muses. "They're all scientists and scholars over there."

"Yeah…" Ayene winces. "But playing with swords isn't my idea of fun…not with those seeds attached. That's the last thing they should be playing with."

"An ancient game of plight?" Kailen wonders. "Meaning to say they're placed into an unfortunate or undesirable situation for what… someone's amusement?"

"The Marshal has certainly done this often enough in the past," Thaelyn considers. "Very well, we will think on this and see if any clues make themselves apparent. If she gave us four of them, they must lead to something as a group. Vonafel, what is next? You said this preceded the one with Kaliya's meeting with Adalon?"

"Yes," she nods. "Let me refresh you on that quickly, since it falls in sequence here. The Forgotten One, whose guile intrigued, so many brought to mind; shall meet his match on field of play, with silver wings aligned."

"All right, we seem to be speaking of the final meeting here, and at this time, I believe Adalon herself will be playing a role."

"A field of play," Kaliya suggests. "A battlefield, for some kind of showdown."

"That game of plight, no doubt," Ayene offers. "And somehow involving those swords, with our people fighting something."

"You know," Kaliya muses. "This might reflect a bit on that earlier one of his children turning on him…maybe?"

"Wow, that would be a sight, and using swords?"

"I'm lost on this next one," Vonafel relents. "These represent the last three I think we have on the page. This also tends to finish the book, except for that last odd one, which still doesn't mean anything to me. And this just makes me wonder what I'm going to spend the rest of my years studying now, if this is finally finished," she giggles feebly.

"Not to worry, Vonafel," Thaelyn soothes. "We will think of something to keep you occupied."

"But, you know," Casarolyn mentions. "This will surely be something of a legacy for my grandmother to look back on. It also makes me wonder what I'll have for a career after she's finished."

"You'll probably be the one to tell of this legacy after I retire," Vonafel smiles. "So, here we go… Two lost souls will meet at last, the Master and His Slave; hidden tidings are revealed, where the Forgotten One is knave."

The gathering falls silent as they consider these words. They each look around the table to see if anyone has anything to say, but nothing immediate comes to mind.

"I might suggest the final line," Thaelyn asserts, "where the Forgotten One is knave, might again refer to Azgarén, and perhaps more specifically in or around their city where he plays so many of his games."

"Maybe so," Kaliya accedes. "A theater of operations. It's their capital city, where both he and Sargeras are holding up, so it makes sense. We have Central Command, the ARC, and whatever else in the local area he was using so often. But two lost souls meeting? Who are they supposed to be? The Master and his Slave… This couldn't be Sargeras and Darumon if they're already travelling together."

"Then we must have a new figure entering the scene, someone not seen for a long time, and telling a story of some kind…those hidden tidings being revealed. And it must also occur at roughly the same time as that game of plight. Before, during…or maybe after?"

"We have speculated in the past how the Maker may want a piece of this," the General offers.

"Yes, but she is a member of the Estelar, and I find it unlikely she would ever have been a slave of any kind…not to them, not the way they lorded themselves above everything else, and not the way the Estelar were hunting them for so long."

"Of course, it would seem backwards to think the Primordials might carry this."

"This may require us to wait and see…unless something else arrives before then. But so far, we have this game of plight, and what we must assume to be Adalon arriving on the scene. Then this other individual arrives and tells their story. Therefore, I might suggest it involves some old history."

Thaelyn pauses to consider this new thought.

"That would be a curious one…old history from a time most have forgotten by now."

He continues mulling the notion, when suddenly an idea flashes into his mind.

"Old history… An ancient game of plight… Ancient! Powers behold! A GAME!" he shouts.

Now they all turn to stare at him as he leans back in his chair.

"Yes!" he surmises excitedly. "This would certainly do it. We enact one of their famous games of plight. Two sides battling with swords, just like in the old days…gladiatorial combat. That would entice Sargeras out of hiding, most assuredly!"

"Oh dear," Kaliya moans. "But are we speaking of literally using swords and fighting?"

"I would not command an actual game of that sort…rather a mock contest. They would need to use actual weapons, but perhaps more like what we use in a sparring contest, and not sharpened. We simply play a role to draw and hold his attention. And I suspect those two lost souls represent something relating to our final move when we spring our trap. Vonafel, what else is there?"

"Here we have what I think is Kaliya mentioned again, for all her hard work," she smiles tenderly. "The Hooves of Storm will make their name, where Two become as One; the Ancient Ones will fall at last, by wings and riddles won."

"I sure hope so!" Kailen moans. "It would be about time for it, too."

"Huh?" Kaliya blurts unexpectedly. "There's another reference to those wings. So, that has to be Adalon making her move. And Ancient Ones, in plural, must mean the two of them together, Sargeras and Darumon. But riddles?"

"Could she be talking about these crazy prophecies?" Ayene wonders.

"Well, I suppose, but I can't believe she would mention her own prophecies in all this. Riddles…something we are discovering along the way."

"All of Darumon's little games, perhaps? Um…" she pauses in reflection.

"Wait…" she hesitates. "Riddles! I think I get it. Hooves of Storm…and our Gifts! Father and his science faction, the riddle of metaphysics; this is where it comes into actual play."

"Cu'Nar's eyes, Kaliya!" Kailen gasps. "You're going to pass him up!"

"You mean, I haven't already?" she smiles sweetly.

"Well, yes, but it sounds like you'll be setting a new standard here. And along the way, likely vindicate him and his faction."

"Indeed," Thaelyn offers. "I must agree. Here is where I think your Stormhooves come into official service. Congratulations, it would seem you are fated to make history."

"Oh please!" she flusters. "Being a hero where those orcs were concerned, or even with what we did on Morndindor, is one thing. But this would make me some kind of living legend! I didn't ever ask for that!"

"Ask for it or not, it would seem to be coming to you. But for now, you must still follow your course and not let this influence you. We do not know precisely how this will play out in the end, and every plan we make must proceed with all due diligence."

"Yeah, and put even MORE pressure on me!" she huffs amusedly.

"My Lord," the General interjects. "How do we interpret that Two becoming as One? This is a most curious one."

"Two…" Ayene ponders. "Could it be the same two as that master and slave? Do they join together or something? That doesn't actually sound very good to me, especially if one of them relates to either Darumon or Sargeras."

"Hidden tidings are revealed…" Kaliya reflects. "A history lesson? Maybe. But more likely, this is part of a confrontation. I think these two can't be related to Darumon or Sargeras. Not unless THEY join together, but in my mind, they already are. And I can't see why anyone else would join with them."

"We need to consider who is on the battlefield at this point," Kailen suggests. "If we're playing a game, Kaliya and her people might be out there in this mock battle scene with…someone, probably Geilv and his people on their side, playing the home team."

"Likely so, at this point," Thaelyn affirms. "And this is perhaps the reason why this revealed itself to us just now. He has just come over to our side. And this is a game we put on to bring Darumon and Sargeras out into the open. This also tells us how to finalize the plans for our base. We need an arena to host this game. Therefore, our staging area should be underground as a rally point to house and conceal our troops, and then a large open field as our staging area. We should also surround it in a wall to enclose it."

"Suddenly, this is getting scary," Kaliya emits warily.

"This is also where we should apply our new Harvester technology," Thaelyn declares. "We will need it in a confined area on that battlefield for our people to make use of during our play. We are not going to play this out as another of Darumon's easy targets, like he did his military and all those innocent worlds. Ours is a combat force to be reckoned with."

"But do we go all out with it on the first run? If our purpose is to entertain him, we want his attention on us before we pull whatever trap we hit him with. I'm recalling some of your field tactics, the lion, the bear, and the ram feints."

"Yes, you are right. Then we will make a series of…maybe…yes, acts. Oh yes…" he croons. "I like this now. Just like in the Days of

Old back home on Tae'Eladar. A tournament, complete with recital music and banners..." he smiles brightly.

"Wow! That actually sounds like fun...I think."

"We could bring out a line of our troops, and dress them in a common form of equipment, rather than our best. They will be our first procession. I think, if we are to make it interesting, we must allow him to believe his side holds a sturdy advantage due to what he should think to be our weakness of not having the flows with us. But THEN, we open the floodgates and enrich the field for our second act. This should turn his ire nicely enough. And this, my dear young lady, is where your Hooves of Storm will make their name."

"Whoops! There goes Azgarén!" she chuckles.

"But we still have that Two becoming as One out there," Ayene recalls. "What two are we speaking of? Does this involve another new arrival on the field? It sounds like it coincides with the Stormhooves. So, they're playing an act on the ground, but at this moment, I think we need to be ready for him when he sees his home team not doing as well. This is where we need to spring our trap, right?"

Kaliya listens to the suggestion and tries to puzzle out the meaning when a vague association comes to mind.

"Two becoming as One..." she recites distantly. "Two... As One... Coming together...maybe to say coming BACK together? Like in that other prophecy, the Divine Justice, One divided by Two...maybe?"

Thaelyn felt a sudden chill strike him. His face transitioned to dire distress, and he jerked around to glare at the young officer. His surprise was so severe, it could be felt empathically, and Kaliya felt it all the way across the table, as did the others in attendance.

"Uh oh... Cu'Nar's grace," she mutters. "You could put Aelwyn to competition with that one. What did I say?"

"Powers pay witness," he wheezes softly. "Could it be? She would know of it...yes, most certainly she would know of it!" his voice rises. "In fact, how could she miss it?!" he growls. "She was standing right next to us in the temple! That old soft-scale, what did she do up there!"

Thaelyn's voice begins to falter as his mood clearly changed. His stern gaze suddenly breaks, and he covers his mouth briefly as he seems to descend into melancholy.

"Father," he whispers silently. "What happened on that day?"

"My Lord, um…" the General inquires tenderly. "Can you help us understand your meaning?"

"General, with apologies, I am not permitted to answer you on this topic. But I need Aerlie. Please call her…now! She needs to be present for this one."

"Right away, my Lord."

The General calls up a page from outside in the hall and gives instructions for Aerlie to be summoned from Tae'Eladar.

Thaelyn buries his face in his hands and leans forward on the table. It was obvious he was deeply affected by this new revelation, but he did not speak again until Aerlie finally arrived in the room.

"Thaelyn, what happened?" she barks urgently. "I could feel your despair from the first moment I arrived through the gate."

He points at Vonafel's book.

"We have our final words," he issues delicately. "HE must return. I think he plays a role in the final chapter of this game."

"He?"

"Vonafel, recite those last lines for her."

Vonafel gazes at the two of them as she returns to her book, now relating the previous quatrains to Aerlie.

"Well, it certainly sounds promising," Aerlie considers. "And no wonder she kept them hidden from us. I would describe this as critical detail, and surely it would need to wait for the right moment. But Two becoming as One?"

"Kaliya," Thaelyn directs. "Your line again, from your cu'Nar."

"Yeah, this should be fun," she notes comically. "The cu'Nar spoke of the Divine Justice, One divided by Two."

Almost instantly, Aerlie broke with a sharp gasp. She jerked back and covered her mouth, no different from Thaelyn, and felt her own moment of discomfort. Just like before, the other members at the table could feel a subtle empathic release from her.

"You know," Kaliya muses ironically. "Between you and Aelwyn, I'm sure to develop a condition before long," she chuckles faintly. "Well, whatever it is, it must be very serious, as well as very private."

"Yeah," Vonafel notes. "More of that private knowledge."

"Yes," Aerlie affirms. "Especially this one. This is a secret we were made to keep once by Lord Torm. But Thaelyn, are you saying it was planned?"

"Aerlie," he responds softly. "When was the last time any of them bequeathed something like this to anyone? I cannot think of another occasion, and here we are with Adalon suggesting the Two become as One during this final play against Sargeras."

"Yes...and I suppose it does make sense, especially the way she seems to be directing things. Or perhaps, we should point a finger at the Maker for this much. She seems to be the ultimate instigator behind so many of our affairs. This would represent a final closure to an Age-long miscarriage of justice...and here we come full circle."

"Full circle, yes..." he nods. "As Adalon so often likes to say, the circle closes at last."

"So..." Kaliya wonders. "Does this mean we need to wait to see what it is?"

"With apologies, I think this one item, more than any other, will need to stay hidden to ensure we can catch them unaware. It is not by our choice, but that of Torm, maybe also Maker Kuroku, if she is involved. However, I would imagine, before that day is out, this will change."

"All right, so what's left? Vonafel?"

"Yes," she admits. "We have one more. But this one frightens me. She's never done this before. She's issuing a warning."

"A warning!" she emits grimly. "Uh oh...and if it comes from her, I think we need to pay attention."

Vonafel returns to her book, now referring to the final passage relating to this long sequence of events leading up to the final encounter. She reviews the last few lines again.

"The way she's wording this, it sounds like this last one is a continuation of a thought. We have the previous one, where she says the Hooves of Storm make their name, the Two become as One, those Ancient Ones going down, and then…" she clears her throat as she prepares to recite the last passage. "But warning comes into the mind, of they who would prevail; the Children are discreetly caged, collapse of thought assail."

"Uh oh…" Ayene moans. "That doesn't sound good…whatever it is."

"No, it does not," Thaelyn concedes. "But if she is giving it as a warning, perhaps there is a way to prevent it. This does indeed sound as if it follows the previous one. They who would prevail, meaning we who might win the day, and this follows the last act in the battle scene."

"She's using the term Children again," Vonafel asserts. "And this seems to be her reference to those people, as she's used this several times in this chapter."

"Indeed, but to say discreetly caged suggests they are bound by something we cannot so easily see."

"And that collapse of thought," Aerlie offers. "This suggests they fall victim to something relating to this cage. It assails them, like an attack."

"And it comes as an afterthought to either Darumon or Sargeras falling. Ayene, you were right when you said he does not let go of anything politely. This sounds like a feedback hit of some kind. Now, we simply need to understand what it is and find a way to prevent it."

"And I need to find myself a new job," Vonafel huffs.

"Oh Grandmother…" Casarolyn comforts. "Don't look at it that way. This is a crowning achievement for you. Your name will be all over this thing!"

"Yeah!" Aerlie teases. "And don't they keep you busy enough with anything else over there?"

"Yes, but Aerlie," she relents. "I spent all my life on this, and it leaves a little bit of an empty feeling that it's all done…well, except for that one last piece. And coincidentally, it still doesn't make sense, even with all the rest of it done now. So, I think she's going back to her old habits of leaving it with personal knowledge, or some as yet unknown event still to occur."

"Well, if it's an open passage, she might be doing just that. One final word before we close up," she smiles.

"Maybe so. All right, back to work for me."

"And Kaliya," Thaelyn resumes. "I need you to verify what happened over there before all this began. Make a tour of your objectives to see which one might have invoked this. But if we are right, and it is Commander Geilv, then we might have just found our best ally yet, as he will need to cooperate in this final play."

Chapter 8

SUBTERFUGE

"Our only remaining…immediate…concern now is Sigil," Kaliya considers. "We still have those ships out there. He hasn't actually recalled them yet, but we also know he's not going to make any new incursions. At least, not until the Marshal's new death toy is ready, and then we have a new problem. Geilv needs to at least pretend to obey."

"And for this," Thaelyn admits. "We need to make a decision on how to carry this such that Darumon will not desire to pursue it further. And the only way for us is to use a similar tactic as we did here on Therinë. We must call the Estelar into it."

"Figuratively or literally? For instance, are we going to make another show on their com-links?"

"It seemed to work nicely enough the first time, assuming they are voice-only. So, we must ensure this is the case. But the first stumbling point is to remove the existing crew. If your team is to go in and practice the sounds of an exploding ship, we do not necessarily want witnesses to it that need explanations. I think we will want to contain them separately and let Commander Kriv'tik handle that part for us."

"Fair enough. So, do we ask him to simply leave, and we take over, or do we make up a really good story to get the Captain to abandon ship? Personally, I don't think captains are best known for doing that," she giggles.

"Indeed, they are not," he smiles. "Therefore, we may need to bring about orders from a higher authority. But this leaves us with the question of how to approach that higher authority. Ayene has been working that office of hers with Petrith to, eh..." he coughs subtly, "...modify their internal security protocols. But I think I would like to keep her face in the background for the immediate term, as I feel we will have better use for her later. Therefore, we will need another agent, and preferably one he might not associate with anything else."

"That's easy, we have plenty of those. But now, how do we approach it. What will be our story?"

"Your roleplay with the ARC had the Director reveal the ACI as having a contact of some kind, and further that this contact allows access to Sigil to make arrangements of some sort. Therefore, we should use this, perhaps even to build on it. But I think, before Geilv would be willing to give up one of his ships, or even a full task force, he might want to see something, if only to convince him there are indeed other lifeforms out there of a substantial nature to represent a true opposing force. And at this point, we are speaking of something that might exist in extradimensional space. So, Kaliya, this is where you come in, but we need to invent a new image for you."

"Uh oh... Am I now playing a real god image, not just a stone giant?"

"Perhaps something of a slightly lower form, but certainly within that context," he grins. "They come in many sizes; you know."

✦✦◆✦✦

"All right, Petrith," Túfula asserts. "I have something inside my head. Let's see if you can see what it is."

"All right, relax," he states calmly.

Petrith, Túfula, and Sulíma were convening in the courtyard with

Relissa and the others. They were enjoying a pleasant afternoon and having a little fun playing with Petrith's new telepathic skills. On this occasion, Túfula and Sulíma were taking turns conjuring up thoughts for him to reveal. He extended his thoughts into Túfula's mind to see the girl's presentation. An image slowly emerged as she recalled a moment in her personal experience. Petrith studied it carefully, and a smile began to form.

"I see you and the gang at the old mining base when Kali first showed up as a bird, and poor little Suli fainting when it turned into Kali proper."

"Hey!" Sulíma protests. "You're not supposed to show him that! It puts me in a bad light."

"Well, it's better than the one YOU gave," Túfula retorts playfully. "He was blushing all over from it!"

"Yeah, but it was fun to watch!" she grins brightly. "Especially the bar of soap I put in my hand, just to make sure I had his attention," she giggles.

"Jiggers," Relissa moans. "Petrith, you need to take care of this girl quick-like to use up some of that energy."

"One of these days, she'll have her turn at it," he agrees cheerily.

"Promises, promises… That's all he does," Sulíma pouts.

"Well," Túfula admits. "He sure does seem to know how to get inside a person's head, even if he doesn't get into…um…anything else," she chuckles.

"Yeah, so at least I can pass all my dirty thoughts at him without anyone knowing."

"But Suli, leave a little bit for me and Kali."

"Hey, you can do it too, you know."

"Yeah, I suppose I could," she considers briskly. "But if we bombard him with too many at once, he might not get any work done."

"That depends on what kind of 'work' he's supposed to be doing," she smiles.

"Girls," Petrith argues. "There's only one of me here. At least allow me to take it in sequence."

"So, Relissa…" Túfula wonders. "How's your ranger training

coming along? I haven't seen that wolf this week. Are we done with that?"

"Aye, he and I had a good run together, but I can always call him back out for a bit of exercise. Now I'm moving into the next stage, which is coming up on my closing term. Next month I'll be practicing something new."

"And what's that?"

"Dire beasts…"

"What's a dire beast?" she asks hesitantly.

"Well, they're bigger animals, a little harder to tame at first, but they make great companions if you ever get in a pinch. But you have to start them out young."

"Oh. And so, you'll be parading around with one of those here soon?"

"At least for a wee bit till I finish the course."

"Remind me to stop making visits at that time."

✦✦✦✦✦

"Director, this is outrageous!" shouts the voice on the vid-com link. "The High Commander of Central Command admitting to the Marshal's activities, or at least that portion he was personally aware of, to say nothing of what the Marshal kept hidden even from him! How could we allow this to go so far, that's what I want to know! Unfortunately, like you said in that meeting, we're all to blame for it, at least in part. It's simply shameful."

"I know, Professor, it hits all of us in a sensitive place, and worse for the situation we're in right now because of it. But on the lighter side, at least that military threat is reasonably under control. He's disabled the chips by now, and I sent some of our people out there to assist in reprogramming the interfaces with the false active indicators in case the Marshal should take notice of anything."

Director Bak'vayn was in conversation with one of his colleagues on the matter of the High Commander coming forward with his revelations. He had been sharing these details privately with his closest friends who were part of his earlier symposium. By themselves, the accusations were bad enough, but having the High Commander come forward as he did, only served to reinforce the notion of Darumon's ill intents.

"I must agree, Director," she relents. "It's one less thing to worry about. But now we need to find a way out of it. What about these new friends of ours, what are they doing so far?"

"Last I heard, they need to divert the Marshal away from his most recent campaign, which is to assault a city complex belonging to his true opponents. He is apparently looking for a rift aperture leading to a type of prison which holds more of those like Sargeras. They need to chase him out of there and keep him away, while at the same time not revealing the fact that they are actually pursuing him here."

"That sounds like fun. Well, good luck to them."

"In the meantime, we have a set of plans we're working on for this construction project that will serve as their staging area. We have already broken ground on it, but additional aid is always welcome. I've been in conversation with several people so far to spread the news."

"I understand, Director. I'll tell our people to add into the pool. I only hope these friends can bring this to an end without destroying our world."

The link ends, and the Director ponders the growing concern of the Marshal's devious methods. He looks through his window at the cityscape standing out in the bold daylight, with the hazy sky overhead from the local pollution.

"So do I…" he muses silently.

♦

It had been several days, and Kaliya was meeting with Thaelyn in the WIC building in her projected form to prepare for a mission to interact with High Commander Geilv. Kailen was present, along with one of Kaliya's squad members, Navina Lar'akan.

"The first thing we must consider is how you will appear to

him," Thaelyn announces. "Your image cannot resemble anything he might otherwise be familiar with, assuming he has any personal knowledge of lifeforms outside of Azgarén. For this purpose, we must create something unique."

"What do you have in mind, then?" she asks. "We want it to appear like what might be expected out of that so-called Abnormal Space, so how abnormal are we going with it?"

"Let us begin with a blank slate. I will have you change your shape to a generic form to start us off."

Kaliya was in her usual self-image. She glances down at her body trying to visualize a shape to begin the process.

"Male or female? And um…" she clears her throat for emphasis, "…with or without clothing," she smiles timidly. "After all, my brother is here."

"Indeed," he grins. "So let us not shock him by observing just how fully mature his little sister has become. We will try to avoid a repeat of Ayene's exhibitionist spectacle on this occasion, and instead aim for something neutral. It does not need to be anatomically correct, rather like what you might find with a doll. Perhaps an androgynous form would suffice."

"Ah, got it."

She reimagines her shape into a featureless form somewhere between male and female in its general figure, and without clothing to give access to the body for further refinement.

"And here we go," she muses. "Almost like a living mannequin, except for it being a projection."

"Indeed, this is a rather curious perspective to work from."

Thaelyn now examines the figure to consider his modifications.

"First, we must consider what he would be most familiar with and remove that from the equation. Such features as horns, the tail, and hoofed feet, we will exclude this. Let us also consider the need for hair, as we are trying to depict a higher form of life, and often this feature might have evolved away by that time. So, we will leave you bald on this occasion. Lastly, your facial features and extremities should be altered, to represent a species evolved by different proportions."

"Dear cu'Nar, let's try not to frighten him too much."

"No, we will not, but we must represent a creature of a sort he might have offended from the space he trespassed into. We will keep your current height, simply to meet within reason face-to-face. Make your head smooth and let us reform your ears to small dome-like projections."

Kaliya complies and observes herself in a floor mirror they brought in earlier to assist in her reshaping process.

"Now, as for your face," he muses. "I think I would wish to keep the glowing eyes, as they already embody a curious trait. Then, if we draw from a common habit the Estelar might use with the Child Races, at least on those occasions when they manifest themselves in front of unfamiliar bodies, they might take the form of a smooth mask wrapping around their face. This represents a generic corporeal image."

"Interesting. How often do they do this?"

"Where the Child Races are concerned, it is very rare, but it does occur. If they represent a dedicated deity for a race, they might take a form that is most appealing to the senses, meaning an image that is similar to the Child Race itself. But since they do not hold a recognizable form by our standards, they often have to project this image as a telepathic overlay into the minds of the locals. However, there is a catch, and this catch might relate to the number of those who are present, and how homogenous they are."

"So, if speaking of ones and twos, they might take a native image. But if speaking of a larger crowd, maybe with many different races involved, it's something more generic?"

"That would be generally correct, and also depending on how skilled they are, which might relate to how many times they have done this before."

"That's a fascinating thought," Navina considers. "To say a god has experience that relates to a form of training to interact with others by projecting this avatar image into their minds based on a recognizable pattern."

"That's right," Kaliya muses. "And to think, we have this chance to actually learn something like this."

Kaliya returns to the mirror and studies herself again as she reshapes her face like a smooth porcelain costume ball mask, leaving holes for the eyes, nostrils, and mouth.

"Good, this should do nicely," Thaelyn observes. "Now, the greater part of your body will be covered in a gown, and this would conceal the remainder except for your hands and feet. Let us consider that next," he pauses in contemplation. "On this occasion, we will not use a traditional five-fingered appendage. Let us make them with four fingers, but not in the typical arrangement. What if we position two of them naturally and the other two in opposition like that of your thumb, but mirrored on both sides. It could perhaps represent a claw arrangement, but without the talons in this case."

She tries to imagine how this would appear, creating a very strange representation of two outward fingers and the equivalent of thumbs on both sides of her hands.

"Make them just a touch thicker," he motions, "and the thumbs longer to compensate for your reach."

She continues to alter her shape, with the digits becoming slightly chubbier and the thumbs extended to offer better interaction with the fingers."

"How am I going to use this if I should ever need to pick something up?" she asks wittily.

"I doubt you would have a need for this, if your only purpose is to talk, but in actuality I suppose one might answer this as to imagine the interaction of your first finger and normal thumb, but doubled... or perhaps if we consider the use of tongs or a grappling claw. I can only suggest you play with it if you desire."

Kaliya brought up her strangely deformed hand and tried moving her new fingers, using her best imagination as to how they ought to bend and flex, and trying to bring her fingertips together in pinching gestures.

"This will take some time," she giggles.

She tries reaching playfully at Navina, but the girl simply ducks away.

"Hey," she grins and swipes at it. "Don't bring your wicked-looking alien fingers at me!"

"All right, what's next?"

"Next should be your feet," Thaelyn continues. "If we are using a four-digit approach, the feet should mimic this. Bring a similar configuration to your feet, but in this case…hmm," he ponders briefly. "Yes, this should make an interesting display. Have your feet resting on the toes, rather than a pad or heel ball, as most of us use. The toes should angle downward and be thicker and shorter than what is on your hand. Imagine that of a flightless bird if it helps."

"All right," Kailen muses. "Let me see if I understand this correctly. We're using an evolved avian species as her god image now, right?"

"Well, it certainly holds the merit of never having been tried, at least not to my personal knowledge. But in actuality, there could potentially be one out there."

Kaliya winces at the thought, but looks down at her feet as she tries to create the image of an elevated four-toed foot, angled like that of a flightless bird, with two bulky toes in front and two on the sides turned slightly to the rear to offer balance.

"This is…very strange, my Lord," she admits. "About as alien as I think we could muster."

"Indeed, but it does offer us some good experience," he grins. "And I am sure we could afford even more if we desired. Now for the clothing… In this case, we should make it a flowing gown, perhaps with movement, as if being blown by a gentle wind. We want to present an astral image; therefore, the material should be as gossamer."

"This is going to require a lot of concentration on my part to animate."

"And we are not finished yet. We still have your voice," he chuckles.

"Oh, dear cu'Nar, what are you going to do with that now?"

She adorns herself in a shifting gown of translucent material, now directing part of her attention to the animation of movement.

"And finally," he offers with a broad smile. "We are going to try something a bit different for this appearance. I want you to become ghostly transparent."

"Now I'm supposed to do all this as a ghost?" she moans.

She gazes at herself in the mirror and reformulates this absurdly peculiar image as a spectral apparition.

"Let us take a pale blue-white hue," he suggests, "thus to match that glow in your eyes."

She again alters her form. She now represented a pale ethereal figure of otherworldly design, not one of specific suggestion to either male or female, and hidden behind a mask as the Lady of Sigil tended to use…minus the blades, of course.

"Very nice, Kaliya," Thaelyn admits. "I will have you practice this for a time to become familiar with it. Perhaps you would also like to play a little game with your friends at the guildhall. We can call it a test run, and a pleasant return for all the pranks they have played on me in recent times," he chuckles.

"Oh yeah, I'm sure they'll get a good laugh out of this one. But now, about the voice, what do you have in mind for that?"

"We are presenting an image of a manifestation here, on the level of a being that might naturally exist in this fashion."

"Perhaps like the Estelar, right?"

"In a manner of speaking. And so, the voice should seem similarly ethereal. Like a ghostly echo resonating around your words as you speak."

"Oh, this should be fun. All right, let's see what I can do."

"We must also consider what you will say, and the words you will use, which should be carefully chosen to depict the linguistic styling of a higher form of life attempting to communicate with a lesser one."

Kaliya gazed at him disbelievingly for a moment, and then turned back to her mirror. She attempted to envision her voice in a tone of ethereal resonance. She realized she would need to engage in some very carefully rehearsed acting to get this right, so she tried a few sample lines.

"I am that which comes from the mists of reflected enlightenment, the entanglement of thought and form casting its shadow upon Creation. And this is the strangest projection I think I could ever have attempted in my life!" she finishes with a bold laugh.

"Indeed, I would have to agree with you, Kaliya. And I think we have a fine example to work with. Next, we will need to coach you on some wording and terms we might use in the Outer Planar regions. Perhaps I can call Aelwyn to assist in this."

"My little sister," Kailen mutters as he watches the affair. "What has he done to you?"

"Kailen, how would you react if you saw one of these pop into your office?"

"I think I would be popping out through the nearest window," he chuckles boisterously.

"My Lord," Navina moans. "You want me to walk into Commander Geilv's office and introduce him to THAT?" she points at Kaliya's apparition.

Thaelyn simply smiles and shrugs, and then nods.

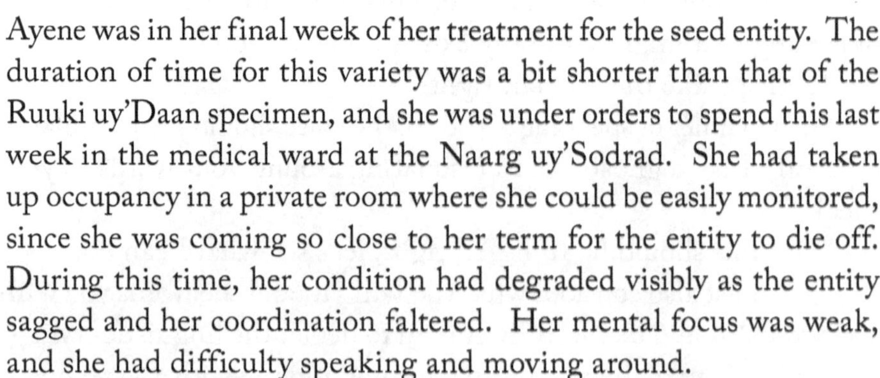

Ayene was in her final week of her treatment for the seed entity. The duration of time for this variety was a bit shorter than that of the Ruuki uy'Daan specimen, and she was under orders to spend this last week in the medical ward at the Naarg uy'Sodrad. She had taken up occupancy in a private room where she could be easily monitored, since she was coming so close to her term for the entity to die off. During this time, her condition had degraded visibly as the entity sagged and her coordination faltered. Her mental focus was weak, and she had difficulty speaking and moving around.

She arose from bed late today, feeling generally lethargic and nauseous. She did not feel at all like eating, instead fearing she was growing deathly ill. These last several days, she had been dwelling on her memories of the premonition she had that warned her of this occasion, and the moment felt as if it was now upon her. She pulled herself sluggishly from the bed to a desk on the other side of the room and engaged a vid-com.

"Medical Ward, Likha Vuurti here," sounds the voice on the monitor.

"Likha…" Ayene gasps breathlessly. "I…need…help…"

But before she could mutter another word, she slumps onto the table, and then falls to the floor unconscious.

"Ayene!" Likha shouts.

She closes the link and reopens a general intercom.

"Emergency call to patient room six, we need a gurney and life support monitors, now!"

Likha rushes out of her office grabbing a hypo-spray and a field kit with a set of emergency pharmaceuticals she had on hand for this occasion, and hurries down the hall to Ayene's room. Several other people also showed up, some with a gurney to carry the stricken woman to the medical ward, and others with medical scanners and life support equipment.

Ayene was lying on the floor when they arrived. The first group ran a quick scan to check her life signs. The readings were fluctuating rampantly. An oxygen mask was applied, and she was transferred onto a sheet laid out on the floor next to her. The sheet was then lifted onto the gurney, and she was transported back to the Ward. Likha followed while continuing to study the monitors.

"Someone call Ankhia!" she orders. "We need her in here. And send word to Rolsklinde and ask for Lady Aerlie."

The gurney was brought into the Ward and Ayene was transferred to one of the beds.

"I need a bio scan!" Likha shouts.

An intern starts programming a scan procedure on the automated arm over the bed. It comes to life and passes a wide beam along the woman's body. The image comes up on a monitor on the wall.

Another set of interns were removing Ayene's clothing to examine the entity. The sight of her body clearly reflected on their previous experience of the Daanen-Aryku patients, but those examples did not fall unconscious from the event.

Likha studied the scan results and a statistical readout of the bio functions.

"Her heart seems to be restoring to a natural rhythm, and her lungs are drawing oxygen. And I see her internal organs appear to be returning to their autonomous control."

She punches up a filter to scan the cranial activity and examines the results.

"Dammit, this one is a little tougher than the other kind. It took her into a mild coma. We need to stabilize her."

An intern brings out a hypo-spray from a cabinet and selects a series of vials, then begins applying dosages of mild steroids to control the swelling.

In the WIC building, a call comes in on Kailen's trans-com.

"This is Commander Nazég."

"Commander, we need you to call for Lady Aerlie to report to the medical ward at the Naarg uy'Sodrad immediately. Lieutenant Ti'van has collapsed."

"What's her condition?" he asks urgently.

"She was discovered in her room unconscious. I don't know the full details after that. But she's in the Ward right now."

"Understood, is Ankhia there?"

"She is on her way."

"Got it, I'll pass the word."

The link ends as he gets up from his desk and charges over to the main conference table.

"Your Lordship, Ayene has collapsed. They're calling for Lady Aerlie."

"General, send a page immediately," Thaelyn instructs as he gets up from his chair. "Commander, what is occurring right now?"

"She's in the medical ward. So far, they don't have a lot of information."

"Very well, let us adjourn our meeting for a time. I wish to attend to this matter, if only to offer support."

They hurriedly made their way out of the building and across to the gateway hub to find transit to the Naarg uy'Sodrad.

In the medical ward, Ankhia arrives and begins studying the bio-monitors and scan results.

"What's her status?" she asks.

"Life signs seem stable, within reason," Likha responds. "But she's on assisted respiration until we can stabilize her coma condition."

"What about her neural activity? Do we have any damage?"

"The scans show her activity to be in a state of flux, but I'm not showing any serious injury, at least not beyond that which you might expect for the entity dying and pulling away from her. Judging by the scans, I might suggest it was some form of shock that put her under."

"If that's all it is, then we're in good shape. Maybe this one just didn't want to let go as easily."

"Yeah, let's hope so."

"Once we get her stable, we'll work to remove the entity. I want to be ready as soon as Lady Aerlie arrives."

A page arrives in Bya'an Tamoranth and hurries through the temple to find Aerlie. He urgently informs her of the situation at the Naarg uy'Sodrad and the two of them rush out to the local gateway node, following the network through to Therinë and arriving at the Naarg uy'Sodrad to meet with Thaelyn and the other officers gathered in a waiting area.

"Where is she?" Aerlie asks.

"In the Ward there," he directs. "She is apparently in a coma, but I think they have managed by now to bring it under control."

"That sounds worse than the others. I hope this doesn't turn out to be commonplace with this variety."

"We will need to collect as much information as possible, and I would suggest forwarding this to the ARC for review and to see about refining the process. Perhaps we can find a way to prevent such a strong reflex reaction in future cases."

"Yes, I would agree. They should know this entity better than anyone, as well as these Spores. Surely, they can find a reasonable solution to it."

Aerlie pats him on the arm and enters the Ward to lend her assistance to the surgery procedure.

✦✦✦✦✦

Kaliya was giving a briefing on the athletic field outside the guildhall to a large body of her troops. They had gathered there as part of a new operation to investigate the dirty industry on Azgarén, and either attempt to shut it down or else give ultimatums to convert to cleaner technologies. But this operation would likely require squads of agents arriving at the various sites to make larger and more official-looking inspections. It might also involve multiple arrests if the owners were uncooperative.

"All right people, here's the plan," she begins. "At some moment, we will need to involve people in physical form to assist in these operations. But until we can hire and train them, or relocate some of our own to Azgarén proper, then we'll just need to work with the local security forces as best we can. Fortunately, the trans-coms do seem to work for us while in projected mode, as I guess comm signals are still comm signals."

She pauses to study them before moving to the next subject, which she reviews on a clipboard she was carrying.

"There is a statute known as Article Twenty-Three in the Charter of Laws we need to become familiar with, otherwise known as the Environmental Preservation Act of 6210. This statute says, in simplified terms, that any industrial activity which could result in some form of ecological damage, whether involving chemical, biological, or radioactive waste; noxious, suffocating, or climate-changing gasses; excessively acidic or alkaline substances, heavy metals, untreated sewage, or improperly handled refuse materials, must either conform to the laws by incorporating the appropriate decontamination technologies prescribed for the industry type, or be closed down, with fines and detention penalties to be determined dependent on the type and level of pollution being created. This is our mantra. We have Petrith inside Central Command feeding us details of what industries the Marshal created for his super military machine, and now we're going to conduct a series of inspections to see what they're making and what we can do to put an end to it."

She holds up the clipboard for display. It contained a stack of papers attached to it.

"These are the industries we're going to investigate so far. Commander Kriv'tik will coordinate from Ruuki uy'Daan, and once he perfects his projection skills, he'll make visits inside the ACI office in Capitol Prime. He will assign our objectives and collect the data, and our team leaders will deliver their squads to conduct the inspections. You will carry local trans-coms and use them as necessary to report your operating status to the ACI, or if necessary, call in the local security agencies if these people give you any trouble. Even though we aren't technically an officially authorized law enforcement agency, we ARE a liberation force, and this means if the Marshal made it, we're unmaking it."

She makes one more survey of the assembled troops before giving the final words.

"Not only do we want to know what they're doing, but also if they're working in conjunction with any other industries that might be affected. No doubt, this will be a large-scale operation, and a test of our team coordination and professionalism. So, let's get to it! I want everyone to get spooky and reconvene on Ruuki uy'Daan. We'll go from there."

Kaliya directs the assembly to return to their respective dorm rooms where they'll individually project and travel to Ruuki uy'Daan for their first assignments. Kaliya joins them as she takes up a chair in a conference room inside the guildhall, and projects her image to follow the rest.

On Ruuki uy'Daan, a large number of projected bodies were appearing in the street outside the Sentinels HQ building. Commander Kriv'tik was at his desk when one of his assistants informed him of the arrivals. He emerges outside to meet with them.

"Commander," Kaliya announces. "My troops are at your disposal for the duration of this operation. I'll tag along to supervise this first round, but I'll need to return to my other duties afterwards."

"Good enough, Captain," he nods. "Let's go inside and plot our first objectives."

Kaliya calls her team leaders to join her as she follows the Commander to his office. She sets down her clipboard on his desk and waits as he studies the list. He selects several entries and turns to his terminal to find their coordinates on a regional map.

"We'll begin with these," he directs to his terminal. "They appear to be raw materials processors. So, if we can either clean them up or shut them down, anything that follows the chain, which are most likely assembly plants, will eventually find themselves running out of input stock."

Kaliya directs her squad leaders to each take an assignment. Then the group offers a modest salute and leaves the building to rejoin their teams.

"This is it," she declares. "Let's show those people how we do business the right way."

✦✦✦

The day was long and the waiting room at the Naarg uy'Sodrad had filled up with additional people. Thaelyn, Kailen, and the General were still waiting patiently. Word had spread by this time to the guildhall, and this brought Relissa and Haran, along with Sulíma and Túfula. Kaliya had been on her assignment, but once she returned, she rushed over to join the rest, and together they tried to calm themselves with some simple conversation.

Aerlie and her medical team worked alongside Ankhia and hers in the surgery room to remove the seed entity from Ayene's body. As with the Ruuki uy'Daan specimen, the process was delicate, and it took time to ensure they got everything. At the end of the procedure, both Aerlie and Ankhia finally emerged through the doors to give their report.

"The surgery is finished," Aerlie declares. "She is currently resting, and I'm going to recommend she remain that way through the night. I placed a sleep chant on her that should keep her for now, and we'll wake her tomorrow to see how well she recovers. The coma condition was apparently only a reflex reaction of the seed entity reaching its critical failure. However, this does bring up a delicate worry where future treatments are concerned."

"And this will need to be forwarded to the ARC," Ankhia adds. "We've been collecting all our scans and medical analysis into a file for them to review. Hopefully, they can find a way to lessen the impact of this hit, otherwise they're going to have a lot of complications on their hands."

"Speaking of complications," Thaelyn offers. "This reminds me of Adalon's warning: The Children are discreetly bound. If this relates in any way to those seeds, there might be an even larger concern at play here. If this entity reacts so badly to its own failure, how might it react if the link it shares with Sargeras should fail?"

"Oh wonderful, Your Lordship! You just made what's left of my day. If these things are designed to feed into him, and share any kind of feedback link, and then you take him down, his death could send a feedback hit into anyone in possession of the seeds."

"This is a very serious dilemma, Thaelyn," Aerlie frowns. "We will need to get those people at the ARC working not only on a treatment for the removal procedure, but also some kind of general preventative for the public. Unless we can say they can remove all these seeds before we take down Sargeras, we could be looking at a global crisis."

"That monster," Kailen grumbles. "First, he makes us serve as his pets, and then he links us into this global battery pack to be short-circuited if his master dies. We were never intended to have our own lives."

"Take ease, Commander," Thaelyn soothes. "We will see to it as best we can. But Aerlie is right. We will need some sort of preventative solution on a global scale, as I doubt we will be able to process the full population within any reasonable time frame, and certainly not before Darumon takes notice. I would further recommend the medical staff be on a priority list to be processed first, as they represent the most critical emergency workers."

"I have to agree," Ankhia nods. "Without them, nothing else will get done at all. I would probably suggest law enforcement and other emergency services should come next, as we'll need some form of control mechanism to keep things orderly while we settle everything else."

"Very good," Thaelyn affirms. "Then we will deliver these notes to the Director at our next opportunity."

"One problem I can see already," Kailen ponders, "is how to explain these people showing up in public without their seeds. Someone will eventually take notice of these people walking around the streets. Wouldn't this filter up to the Marshal in time?"

"I suppose it would, but it is not practical to simply hide them, and neither to keep them locked in a room, as they must surely have lives to live. Therefore, I think it is time for the people of Azgarén to realize they are in fact NOT departing from their home anytime soon, and therefore the advertised purpose of these seeds is hereby rendered moot...other than for that industry and the pollution it creates. But let us not forget, they DO have other forms of technology at their disposal, and such a thing as...oh, perhaps a filter mask, might be a fair and reasonable alternative."

"And the Marshal?" he raises his brow.

"Clearly, we will need to find a convenient way to deliver this message. But he will simply need to accept the fact that his complacent little minions do in fact have minds of their own. He cannot possibly expect them to go on forever without taking notice of what he has NOT provided them with after all his promises. Combine this with a little of our own propaganda, and he will find himself losing control of his tidy little project."

"Children of Breed, slowly grown..." Kaliya muses distantly. "Leading to his demise."

"Indeed, this would represent a good example of that prophecy."

"In the meantime," Aerlie suggests. "There is nothing more we can do here until morning. Ankhia and her team will watch Ayene through the night, and we'll return tomorrow to check on her. But we might need to give her a few days to make a full recovery, as she'll likely be confused and disoriented after her ordeal."

"Very well, then I suppose we should return to tidy up the day's affairs, and then retire for the eve."

Outside of Capitol Prime, across a modest river in a valley beneath the rocky slopes of a range of mountains, the local vegetation and underbrush was being cleared away by an army of earthmovers and excavators. A large region was being carved out and leveled to make the foundation of the new base for Thaelyn's army. But to the local authorities, it was going to be a new conservation center.

A news team from the local media center in the city was visiting the site after hearing of the intense activity in the area. They approached a foreman in charge of the removal project as part of an investigative report.

"Excuse me," the reporter calls out. "I represent C.P. News, and we recently heard of this new construction project occurring out here. Can you explain the purpose of this effort and who authorized it?"

The foreman was one of the Director's volunteers from his Project. He was expecting the construction site to come under scrutiny at some moment, so he was already prepared for the occasion.

"Yes! This site will be the future home of a new conservation center. It is part of a collaborative effort resulting from a coalition of science departments meeting to discuss the growing magnitude of concern to the deteriorating environmental conditions and the resulting stress imposed on a number of endangered species."

"And who authorized this project? Was it the Council?"

"To my knowledge, the Council seems singularly focused on their deliberation. And personally, if they were to involve themselves on anything relating to the environment, I think it should first be the pollution, not the preservation of everything around us that's dying because of it."

"Well, yes, this would certainly follow more sensibly."

"Therefore, this out here is actually the result of a joint venture between several biological and zoological research institutes, along with the support from a number of others who are offering monetary contributions. And I might further say, this is despite the Council NOT taking a similar action."

"Not taking it…" she muses.

"Right. But I believe the one to make the initial proposal was Director Ghantil Bak'vayn at the Ark'ravan Research Center in Capitol Prime."

"I see. But why would the administrator of a medical research center apply himself to such concerns as zoological conservation?"

"Likely because he holds himself more responsible at preserving things than the Council seems to be doing, and he led the others into this agreement."

"Wow, you must hold a few opinions over the Council."

"Wouldn't you, if you simply look up into that sky overhead?"

"Well, yes, and I do, but unfortunately, I do not hold that level of clout to make this sort of movement."

"Maybe, as an individual. But every citizen is an individual in this world, and that pollution up there affects ALL of us. So, if you simply add all that up into a collected body, what do you have? Something that might hold more of an opinion on things than the Council seems to be demonstrating."

"Got it. So, the Council slipped the tip on this issue. Therefore, the rest of us should be taking the initiative in their stead."

"Exactly. And the ARC does hold a bit of clout, so they're using it. But you know, as for slipping the tip, I think it should be everyone's responsibility to do our part in protecting what is left of our world. Slipping the tip is to realize we're still living here, and no one apparently realized the bad weather in this time."

"Indeed, this is correct," she nods. "And I suppose I must agree with that perspective. It is simply that I would more likely expect a project like this to be the domain of those factions who specialize in this field, meaning to say the biology and zoology factions, not the medical faction."

"Maybe so, as for the research studies, but they are not the only people in this world who are watching things die. Instead, I would actually say that we should ALL be a part of the solution, regardless of any professional specialization. When I speak to people like you, you seem to think that only Person A should hold any level of authority over Principle X, and the rest of us should move along and find something else for ourselves. But if Person A has to wait an eternity for the Council to give a direct order to get involved in anything, Principle X goes unattended for that same eternity. And so, here we are."

"All right, please. Yes, I see your point, and I apologize. I recently had a rather disturbing experience back at our office, and it is still hanging off of my horns. So, no matter who was present at this meeting, we should all be contributing into the solution. And at this moment, it simply happened to be the people at the ARC to initiate things."

"Yes Ma'am. Even our own people are suffering for all the pollution, if not for these awful seeds on our backs. And one more reason the Council should be paying more attention to the cause, rather than the effect."

"Naturally, you are right."

"But now, if you want anything more, you should speak with the Director about the details. My team was simply employed to prepare the region for the construction crews to begin setting down the initial foundations."

"Of course," she nods politely. "And thank you. Then, I will visit the ARC and see what they have to say about it."

The reporter moves away, taking several long moments to examine the work, which was occurring across a wide swath from the mountainside up to the river. The area was teaming with work crews and equipment. It was an effort of unusual size and vigor, compared to how other projects tended to operate. Material was being collected and hauled away in large hover-trucks, and cleared areas were being packed down as a base for future buildings and other improvements, all the way up to the mountain, where a line of flagged markers had been posted for later development.

The reporter takes her team back to their news van and returns to the city, where they continued along until they arrived at the ARC building and parked in the visitor's lot. They reorganize themselves and walk inside the building.

"Welcome to the ARC, how may I assist you?" asks the desk clerk.

"I represent C.P. News. I desire to speak with Director Bak'vayn about a development project occurring in the Bintavyan Valley, across the river."

"I believe he is currently in his office. If you desire, I can call him to meet with you."

"Yes, thank you."

The clerk makes a call on her vid-com to the Director's office, informing him of the visitors. She then motions for the news crew to take a seat in the lobby while he makes his way downstairs. In several moments, he arrives through the lift.

"Director Bak'vayn," calls the reporter. "My name is Ileani Ur'paran and I represent C.P. News."

"Yes, I recognize you. You're a very well-known vid-com persona."

"Thank you. I would like to ask you several questions concerning the new construction project occurring in the Bintavyan Valley at this time. The foreman I spoke to said you might be helpful in this regard."

"Yes, of course..." he nods. "We expected someone would eventually take notice of the activity out there. I'm actually pleased to see it's you."

"Really! Well, I am flattered by your support."

"The project in question is the result of a recent symposium we conducted to discuss several aspects of our world's condition relative to our lack of attentiveness in modern times where our responsibility to the natural environment is concerned, among other things."

"Um, wait, please. Even though I already got my tail spanked by your foreman out there..."

"Oh, he did that? My goodness!" he subtly raises his brow.

"Yes, well, I suppose I had it coming. Old habits, I suppose, and unfortunate ones at that."

"Yes, I see that a lot these days."

"Anyway, I need to ask this as part of my profession. Two things. First, a symposium? Who was involved on this occasion? And second, you said a lack of attentiveness? How do you mean this?"

"Let's take the lack of attentiveness first. All you need to do is look outside the window and you have part of your answer. That pollution is the direct result of all that unfortunate industry we once built to serve our military needs due to that awful business with the Marshal's insurgents. Do you recall this?"

"Yes, I do."

"Unfortunately, in all this time, waiting for a final solution to those insurgents, that industry has been continuing to operate, continuing to pollute our environment, and even though we have long held many forms of cleaner technologies that are not as harmful to the environment, no one ever bothered to upgrade that industry when it became clear we were not evacuating our world, as the Marshal once claimed we must due to that old Tav'ageen thing. So here we are, in a heavily polluted environment, also with these seeds stuck to our backs, because it became necessary to use them right here at home, and our Council hasn't done anything about it…in ten millennia of waiting for that famous solution."

"Uh oh. Now I think I see where that guy out there has an issue with the Council. We were speaking of this, and slipping the tip on something that had to be obvious after a while. But what you are saying is it did not have to be this way from the beginning?"

"Yes, if only we could realize, at least within a reasonable time frame, where it was going. Next, we have the symposium. We gathered together the leaders of many prominent factions who all share one thing in common, and that is the living conditions under which we must suffer due to the overwhelming pollution levels hanging over our heads. And I will emphasize again, this was correctable, and long before it became a health hazard, if only someone, like the

Council, could pull themselves away from whatever it was they were doing, look outside and say, 'Hey, that doesn't look good up there….'"

"Naturally. But why was the media not invited to this symposium? I would think such a meeting as this would make a noteworthy news release."

"It might, but on this occasion, we had a number of topics which we felt were of great importance to discuss, and it had to be confidential, if only to be certain those parties with the true concern for our world were the ones actually making the decisions."

"Um, wait, relating to your earlier argument, would this now involve that Council who slipped the tip on things?" she raises her brow.

"Yes, as they might actually oppose our interests. After all, they're the ones who put that war proclamation out there, which effectively overrode the sensibility of our environmental protection laws, and then…slipped the tip…to go back and review it."

"But…but… Are you saying it might actually be intentional?"

"Let me answer that question with one of my own. When was the last time you saw them do anything at all, other than deliberate something that is technically nonessential to the survival of our world? We do not need the secrets of the universe revealed to us. We do, however, need clean air to breathe, safe living conditions, occasional new legislation and social policies for our world population, and other…political…things the Council was originally hired to perform. If anyone should be researching anything, it should be the researchers in all our otherwise empty laboratories. Now, what does that say for our most benevolent Council?"

Ileani stared blankly at him for the long list of accusations. This also invoked her to recall the recent fiasco at her office where those regulators were concerned, and their subsequent arrest. She then briefly glanced outside a nearby window, and then at her cameraman before returning to the Director.

"Suddenly, this sounds a little more serious than simply slipping the tip. This is pure negligence."

"Yes, that's one word for it," he admits. "And therefore, we felt it was paramount to maintain our secrecy, to ensure those people who are truly concerned over these things, as opposed to the miraculous secrets of the universe, to which, in all these ten millennia, we have not even seen a simple status report, come together and try to enact a real solution to a real problem."

"Got it. But the media? Are we also included in that statement?"

"Unfortunately, Miss Ur'paran, it had to be on this occasion. The privacy of the meeting had to consider anyone who might otherwise try to interfere with what we believed to be an important cause, and unfortunately, this also involves the media, as you would surely draw attention by those we were excluding."

"Uh oh…so you are interpreting us to be a loose wire, I suppose."

"Nothing personal to you, Miss Ur'paran, but yes. If all this outside was indeed intentional to pollute our world, and also our bodies, with something we might actually have the horns to correct one day, and after ten millennia of NOT realizing it, it makes you wonder… Did someone slip the tip, or did they do it intentionally. This now reflects upon the reasoning behind it, and all the storytelling we had to listen to along the way. And some of us are tired of it."

"Wonderful," she sighs.

"I think I should also point out another factor in the decision-making here," he asserts intrepidly.

"Oh? And what is that?"

"As for our symposium, and now that we have our agreement, thereby organizing ourselves to this cause, the situation may permit us to make a few allowances. We have a threshold of involvement by now, and I feel it might carry on its own from here."

"Good. So, maybe I will have something new to report on, finally."

"Oh yes, I hope to see a few things occurring to make life a little more interesting. But Miss Ur'paran, you might want to consider a few things about how our society seems to behave. And some of it is rather unfortunate."

"All right, what can you say about this?"

"Our society needs to remember we still have minds capable of thinking. And as a society that must take responsibility for what we do, thinking is the one thing we should be doing most of all. But apparently, we are not. We can say that industry was a rush job to solve an immediate problem, but in the years, decades, and even centuries following, once it became obvious that we are destroying our native environment and not actually leaving, as we were once promised, this is where we see one of our failures presenting itself. We expect someone ELSE to do the work, and the rest of us simply wait by the vid-com for that special report of something extraordinary occurring to brighten our day. But it never comes."

"Uh huh. And I think I am starting to see a direction here. And this is apparently reflecting on the negligent Council again with their iron-horned deliberation."

"Precisely. We look up to them to serve all our needs, make all our decisions, and provide all our research labs with their directions to do anything at all, as those labs do not seem to have the authority… maybe not even the horns…to choose their own topics."

"Really? In all the nether-space, no wonder life seems so dull around here!" she huffs.

"I would agree. We might see a few small projects requested by the military for one thing or another, but nothing like a new research grant for anything substantial. And I have a number of friends and associates in other departments who tell the same story. And then we have that occasional news broadcast, like yours, for instance, telling us everything is under control and not to concern ourselves with the weather outside. Because…any day now…it will all blow over, and we'll be on with this famous evacuation we were all promised. And such things as these seeds would FINALLY come off…even though that same negligent Council never gave us their authorization to research a removal procedure for it."

"What?!" she shouts. "Ow!" she clutches at her interface.

"And this is further compounded by those news feeds and THEIR storytelling claiming that same 'any day now' aspect of things on behalf of the Council, and also the Marshal, neither of whom wanted us to think anything different…due to those regulators you had in there feeding the rest of us their fantasies about our…continual emergency…to leave home, and therefore, don't bother thinking about anything else."

Ileani was stifled by this sudden depiction. The picture being painted here was bad enough by itself. But the involvement of the regulators and what they did in her newsroom only made it worse. She gaped at him with a rush of shock zipping through her, and this caused another feedback hit, forcing her to reach for her interface again.

"Now, Miss Ur'paran," the Director continues calmly. "Would you further like to know about that project in the valley? Because, for those of us who have grown tired of waiting for unfulfilled promises, we are beginning to realize we are sitting under a huge cloud of smog that isn't supposed to be there, and our negligent Council never once tried to do anything about it."

She again reflexively glanced out the window at the sky overhead as she considered her response, and then timidly peered over her shoulder to find her cameraman.

"Shut it down a moment," she waves at him and turns back to the Director. "How do you know about those regulators? They were operating under a secret authority, but then recently we came under investigation by some people…"

"The ACI…yes, I know. They arrested those people and probably put the rest of you under orders to keep it quiet…am I right?"

"You know of them? Personally, I never heard of this department before."

"Yes, they came in here as well. It's enough to unravel your horns. We're under orders right now to cooperate with them for a number of special investigations they're demanding, and all of it based on some custom orders the Marshal pushed through here at one time or another."

"Was this part of the Council issuing something new?"

"This relates to those special orders from the military, and all of it highly classified. So much so that it was buried so deeply, no one other than the Marshal really knew anything. And this includes those who may have handled the orders along the way."

"That sounds serious. But can we at least justify it with a valid reason?"

"The only reason would be personal to the Marshal, and no one else was involved. And for all the secrecy, plus the fact he intentionally buried it, means he does not CARE for our opinions."

"Oh no. But what about the Council. Surely, they ought to hold an opinion on some part of this, iron-horned deliberation or otherwise."

"The Council?" he huffs. "Miss Ur'paran, according to my own research, the last time they had an opinion on anything was the press release of the Suppressor chip. How old are you? Do you know when that was?"

"Me? Um…well, I am thirty-two, but in answer to when it was, I cannot recall precisely right now."

"9765.31 is the year. Now, how long ago was that, Miss Ur'paran? Long enough to make you wonder what they're doing in there, if not their jobs. Of course, this assumes you're actually paying attention to it, which it seems most of us are not. More of that censorship, no doubt, and the rest of us no longer thinking with our own horns."

"9765.31? In all the nether-space, that is a long time. But I always heard they were in deliberation over something relating to this great wisdom we were once promised."

"Yes, deliberating… If you were to ask their Public Information Center on the DataNet, it simply tells you they're in deliberation of something, but with no explanation of what it is, how long they've been doing it, how long to expect it to continue, or why. This is another of his unending promises. As a businessman, if I were given a proposition to trade my services for some form of payment, I would expect that payment within a reasonable amount of time to encourage me to continue my services. Wouldn't you?"

"Well, yes, I suppose I would. But are you suggesting he could be reneging on this promise?"

"Reneging? My opinions on the matter are very different, for this point. But regardless of this, waiting ten millennia for anything is unthinkable. We have not even received a partial payment in that time, to say nothing of the full amount. And yet we sacrificed a lot along the way," he directs outside the window. "This is yet another of our failures, to ask about this and either demand something to keep us on retainer, or give him the old hoof in the tail, along with his insurgents and all his superior advice."

"Yes, maybe..." she attempts a cautious smile.

"But now, try this one for your recently liberated journalist mind, Miss Ur'paran. We could claim he is simply preoccupied with those insurgents out there who can't take no for an answer. But did you ever consider that if those insurgents come from the same society as this being with so many promises of great wisdom, it stands to reason those insurgents must also hold great wisdom, which by definition should be well above ours. So, why is it they can't take no for an answer and keep trying to attack us without success?"

"I, um..." she puzzles.

"You don't need to answer that, and at this point, it might just cause another feedback in that torture device he forced on us. By the way, we're under orders to start disabling those..." he turns to the secretary behind him. "Get Azina down here with a D-probe."

"What?" Ileani objects. "But these are necessary...and mandated by the Council!"

"Yes, that same negligent Council who forgot about our pollution and all the eco-friendly tech we had, and coincidentally at around the same time as hearing the words 'great wisdom', and then after all this time, STILL forgot to tell that industry out there to clean it up. And then we have these...temporary...chips, along with the seeds. The mandate put a nondisclosure clause in there to deny any reporting on the Tav'ageen business. This prevents us from collecting any statistical data to see if it's still necessary, or if we can remove them by now. They simply told us to apply them 'until further notice,' but that notice never came."

"But does this not say it is still out there?"

"Miss Ur'paran, what did I just now say about thinking with

our own heads. We are a society that tends to demand empirical evidence to prove the existence of a thing. But neither the Council NOR the Marshal ever gave us any to prove the existence of that alien thing they pushed at us. And in the absence of the freedom to pursue any further study on the topic, the message is, 'Take this, because we say so.' And it stopped at that."

"Oh no…"

"After all," he continues. "How would THEY know, if not even WE know? WE are the medical faction. They're just a bunch of government suits in an office, not medical professionals in a laboratory, and certainly not all-seeing god entities to know the wisdom of the universe, with or without the Marshal's promises. Therefore, what it says is they don't care. We are the ones who are supposed to say if it's still out there, not the Council hiding in their chambers doing anything OTHER than paying attention to the world around them. This clause says we are not allowed to do our work, and likely due to similar reasons why you had people falsifying your news. Therefore, the ACI thinks the whole thing was a hoax."

"A hoax?! Argh…" she shouts and grabs her interface harder.

"The Marshal invented those things," he points at her interface. "Just like he invented the seeds he pushed at us with his promises of imminent departure from our ancestral home. But after ten millennia, we're still here, and yet no one told us to stop the seeds, either. And the Suppressor chip very conveniently negates the need for leaving home now. So, why do we need the seeds, and do we still need the chips after so long with no new cases being reported, nondisclosure clause or not. Some of us think the chip is no longer necessary, and the ACI is asking if it ever was."

"Then what was the Tav'ageen Anomaly in the first place? If they are claiming it to be a hoax, then what about that public scare we had once. It was historic!"

"Historic is one way to describe it. Another would be to say sensational. And for a public that most often listens to the news media sensationalizing such things, the panic was sure to spread exponentially. One might even describe it as a form of incentive, to invoke a particular form of response. Now, if you were someone hoping to cash in on a public scare in order to have your way with it, what would be the best way to accomplish this?"

Ileani halted her rebuttal and stared at the Director. The meaning carried a clear undertone, and it began to settle with some of the other mysteries circling around her mind.

"Are you saying he took advantage of it, or maybe even invoked it? But why?"

"These are the questions the ACI is investigating. They're ordering us to reopen the Tav'ageen study to find out. And since the Council isn't giving out any instructions one way or another, we're not going to share this with them for their lack of interest in doing their job, therefore our secret symposium. They haven't given out any new research projects since the Marshal went to war out there. And in fact, we only seem to THINK they are doing their job if only because we bow down to them like a god entity, and that god entity is ALWAYS doing its job, even if no one has seen them in ten millennia. So, for those of us who are realizing we still have horns to think with, we're starting a few of our own projects to see what he's going to war with, and using us to create what the ACI is calling his death toys."

"Death toys?" she wheezes.

Azina was just arriving on the lift and emerging into the lobby when she sees the Director and the beleaguered reporter.

"Are we chewing on someone else's tail today?" she smiles brightly.

Ileani glared at the perky young intern with her blatant emotional display.

"How many of you are doing this?" she whispers.

"Doing what? Realizing we're natural creatures with minds of our own, and feelings we want to experience without being zapped for it? You might be surprised. Now, hold still while I plug this in."

Azina connects the probe to Ileani's interface port and engages the reprogram feature.

"Ghantil, are you explaining anything so far?"

"I'm working up to it. So far, I'm still trying to disrupt her nearly religious faith in our All-Powerful godlike Council doing any kind of actual work, like everyone expects of it."

"Nearly religious, yeah, that's the funniest part. We, who are not supposed to have a religion at all. And the most unfortunate part is she's a reporter…the one person in the world who is supposed to go out there and investigate things. Well, would be, if not for those regulators keeping her chained up."

"Will the two of you please lighten up on me?" Ileani begs. "All my life, I wanted to serve a useful purpose to our community. I studied hard at the university and graduated with top honors in journalism. Then I went to work at CPComm thinking one day I might have a chance to report on all these great discoveries we were supposed to be making, but soon to realize I have regulators rewriting all my articles. It was perhaps the biggest disappointment in my life. I almost quit the position, asking myself if there was any real point to it."

"Sounds a little like my own story as a medical intern, and a few others I've spoken to."

"Yes, it does," the Director relents. "All right, Miss Ur'paran. My apologies, but like with so many others in our world, you grew up thinking there WILL be great discoveries coming one day… and then waiting one more day, then a year, then a century, then a millennium, and so on, but never once asking why it's taking so long."

"Actually, Director," she reflects. "I did ask…many times. But there was never any answer to it. As you said, that Public Information Center is a waste of taxpayer money, and no one in the right positions gives out anything useful."

"I fully agree. I have a number of close associates in top research positions for several of the factions out there, and they all hold similar opinions."

Azina finishes with the reprogramming function and disconnects the probe. She then moves to the cameraman to attend to his interface.

Ileani pauses a moment to realign her thoughts from the subtle twinge associated with the disabling effect. She takes a deep breath before continuing the debate.

"Now, what is this you said about working up to something?"

"All right, listen," he continues. "The ACI told us they have an interest in you for a project of theirs. This is the reason why I mentioned my pleasure at seeing you stop by. We might be working together sometime, so we should probably become familiar with each other. I don't know the full details of what they have in mind, but it sounds elaborate, and would serve as a counter play to what the Marshal has been doing to us."

"The Marshal! Are you saying he is cheating us or something?"

"Cheating isn't the word for it, Miss Ur'paran. He flat-out lied to us. Now, as I understand it, you're under orders by the ACI to keep your secrets. This is an issue of planetary security, which means our world and our people are in true danger, and not from any dull-horned insurgents who should be in possession of technology that could wipe us out of existence, but don't know how to use it. We're taking sides with the ACI, so that brings us into one pot together. Do you understand?"

"Yes, but it does not actually help me understand everything you are talking about. I still need to ask about the Council, as they should be doing something, at the very least, especially if this is an issue of planetary security."

"You would think so, but no one has seen or heard of them since they went into that deliberation. I learned a few things during this time, but I'm also under instruction by the ACI that we each need to play a very narrow role in case the Marshal gets curious about any of it. Therefore, I think it's best to let the ACI decide which pieces to reveal and which ones to keep hidden. The last thing we need right now is another public sensation leading to another public panic."

"Uh huh...so even without regulators, we still have regulators."

"But these are here for a legitimate reason. We need to allow the ACI to make these decisions, and then pipe them through our supposedly Council-censored media streams."

"Supposedly..." she muses. "All right, I think I am seeing something here. First, those regulators were arrested, but we need to play like they are still in effect?"

"Yes, he thinks they're still in place, because it's a part of his control mechanism, and we don't want to give the impression of anything changing."

"This sounds like a lot of tail-yanking, and I do not like my tail being yanked."

"I'm sure we all feel the same," he smirks. "But now, you want a story? Here it is. That project out there is a brand-new conservation center brimming with new technologies recently developed to help us preserve all the critically endangered species in this world due to this awful pollution we are so unfortunately plagued with as a result of our most benevolent efforts to aid those wonderful beings that came to us asking for our help. Got it so far?"

"Wow, and here I thought those regulators were bad," she emits a tender chuckle.

"Yes, well, I've been receiving a bit of coaching lately. Anyway, the Marshal is the true enemy, and he's far more dangerous than any insurgents. But until we can deal with that, we need to put on a show for him...exactly the way he expects it out of us."

"Got it. So, I need to play like those regulators are still in place, or else he gets angry and uses his superior wisdom and these death toys, as you call them, to wipe us out of existence, or something like that."

"That's right, Miss Ur'paran. Now you're catching on, and the ACI will fill you in on more of our plans when they're ready to bring you further inside."

"All right, I suppose I can play this game. But I do hope, at some moment, someone will tell me what is going on so I can deliver a real story just once in my lifetime."

"Miss Ur'paran, I think they might have something special in mind for you, so just be patient."

✦✦✦✦✦

In the days following Ayene's surgery, she made a steady recovery after her coma. Kaliya and her friends made visits to encourage her along, and Thaelyn and Aerlie, along with the other officers, all stopped by to help her reconnect with her lost memories and fill her in on the latest news.

As she began to realize where she was and the removal of her seed entity, she felt a flood of emotions race through her; at first elation, but also a breakdown from all her previous fears and worries. She studied herself carefully from all angles, expecting to see scars and damaged areas of skin. But the restorative process of the priests, combined with the techniques of the medical technicians, left her with smooth lines and soft curves. She was everything she hoped she could be, resembling how she once looked before receiving the seed implant.

Ankhia kept her under observation for nearly a week before releasing her back to duty. But Ayene was given instructions to take things slow until she could work her way back into her original routine. Her first objective was to visit the ARC to check in with Azina.

She had just arrived outside the ARC building and was entering the door when the clerk at the front desk noticed her.

"Lieutenant!" she calls anxiously. "You're back! We were worried about you. How do you feel?"

"I'm feeling much better now, thank you," Ayene replies. "It was touchy there for a while, but I got through it."

"We heard about what happened. Your Captain came in several days ago with the final report on your medical procedure. You fell into a coma? Wow, but I suppose that's still better than what happens with the reflex reaction that little bug has if you simply try cutting into it."

"Yeah, but now we need you to find a way to resolve this other reflex of the shock feedback. And it could apparently go even deeper than that, as we think it could relate to Sargeras. If we try taking him down, his death could feed back into the seeds and take us all with him."

"That sounds so much like what the Director has been talking about lately with the Marshal's death toys. I wonder if this was intentional, or simply coincidental."

"Who knows, at this point, but we need to break it."

"But now," the girl studies Ayene's image. "Are you still using your disguise?"

"Yes, for as long as I'm walking around outside."

"Well, you don't need it in here. Can you show us?"

"All right."

Ayene changes her shape to her new form, now without the seed entity. The difference in her appearance was significant, now a trim and slender young woman without the bulky mounds and ungainly growth from the entity wrapping around her body.

"Amazing..." the secretary croons. "I hope I can look as good when my turn comes. What about scarring?"

"None in my case, but then I had some special people working on me. Still, I'm sure you have a lot of professionals in here, so you should know what they're capable of."

"Yes, we do, and we're rather proud of our work. Well, you should go upstairs. I'm sure Azina will be waiting for you."

"All right," she smiles.

Ayene continues down the hall to the lift and proceeds up to the third floor where she approaches the desk in the lab department.

"Ayene!" shouts one of the clerks. "Where have you been all this time?"

"Wow, has everyone here really been so worried about me?"

"Of course we were! Here, let me call Azina for you. She hasn't come out of the lab since the day your Captain delivered the news. She's been pulling her horns out trying to find your answer to that feedback hit."

The intern calls the girl on the vid-com and a moment later Azina is seen dashing up to the counter.

"You had us worried to death, Ayene!" she yips. "When your Captain came in and said you were in bed recovering from a coma, I almost lost my horns...again!" she smiles timidly.

Azina studies Ayene's new form without the entity, pausing in amazement at the slim figure.

"Is this what you actually look like now?" she asks.

"Yes, it is. I had to study myself in the mirror for a while to get the new projection shape just right, but this is me now."

"Looks great… But now, we're conducting some research on this procedure you used. I did a number of tests in the lab during this time, and we found similar results where we could kill it without any major damage to the host. But like you, I suppose, this didn't include the reaction on the neural tissues. However, now that we have your data, I'm going to pull the original research files and see if I can decode the genomes that are responsible for this."

"According to our med-tech, she thinks there's some crazy alien genetic coding in there, so good luck trying to figure that out."

"We have some powerful technology here in our labs, so I'm confident we can handle it."

"Good, and once it's dead, you can apparently use standard surgical procedures to remove it, although it's a complex process."

"No doubt! This thing was designed to interact with all the major organs, including the brain," she sighs. "I hope this is the last time we ever bring up this horrid technology."

"You're not the only one to wish that. But we also have that link with Sargeras and this new fear of a feedback reaction if he goes down."

"Right, so our first objective will be to identify what's causing it, and then what we need to either bypass it, or maybe find a remedy to weaken it so it's not as severe."

"Good, you work on that. Meanwhile, I need to get back to my duties."

"Speaking of which," Azina recalls. "We had that reporter, Ileani Ur'paran, in here not long ago. The Director spoke with her a little to bring her into the circle a bit, but nothing outside the basics."

"I see. I'll need to meet with her sometime, but not yet. We're working to coordinate a few of our hidden projects with a press release to lay the foundation for a number of corrective movements the people are…suddenly…realizing they need to make," she grins.

"Suddenly?" she wonders inquisitively. "As if to say, after ten long millennia, we finally turned our horns around and realized something was wrong somewhere?"

"Well, better late than never, I suppose," she chuckles.

"Just what are you talking about!" the factory administrator argues. "We have special override authority to conduct our work here. This was granted to us by the Council on request of the Marshal due to this emergency condition relating to the ever-present situation of those insurgents out there threatening our home."

"Sir," the agent rebuts firmly. "First of all, in case you were not aware, those insurgents never once arrived close enough to Azgarén to become a threat of any kind. The military holds a record of being undefeated against the Marshal's terrible insurgents that so easily and efficiently overthrew him and Sargeras. This means, whatever force they used at that time has never once been used on us here, and this also brings up the question of how and why they even bother advancing on us if they represent such an inferior force in relation to our own. This further brings in doubt the Marshal's claims of who those insurgents truly are, if not this superior force that overthrew him in the first place."

"What? Are you saying he may have lied to us about them?"

"To answer that, let me point out a clear and obvious detail that a lot of people apparently missed. The ship that took away Former Elder Velen Nazég. It appeared right over our heads and inside our atmosphere. This says two things right off the top. They know where we live AND they have jump drives to reach us…right inside our atmosphere to launch a direct point-blank strike on what should be their primary target…Sargeras. Now, if THAT is his insurgents, as he so often claimed, why are we chasing THEM halfway across the galaxy and defeating them each time?"

"Um, right, I see your point. That does not necessarily make sense."

"Furthermore," the agent continues. "It is clearly obvious that his continual claim of this so-called emergency condition, which is so easily refuted by our undefeated rating in combat, is simply an attempt to perpetuate a scare tactic to keep this industry he demanded in operation. If there is no true reason to be so afraid of his insurgents, there can be no true reason for us to be on emergency alert, and certainly not for this length of time that it destroys our native home…which we are STILL living on. And should I again reiterate that time period for us to take notice?"

One of Kaliya's team leaders was in a hot debate with the most recent of her assignments to investigate the military industry the Marshal once ordered, which currently produces more pollution than anything else. She was in discussion of these issues with the factory administrator about the need to either reform their standards or be shut down completely.

"And what does the Council say about this? They are the ones who make the laws around here."

"Yes, the laws. Let's see if we can recall one of those. Are you familiar with Article Twenty-Three of the Charter of Laws?"

"Actually, yes, I am. That one is a well-known standard of industry waste management and emission regulation. But the emergency condition overrode that statute, again due to these insurgents."

"Very good, and during that initial moment when we had to respond to them, perhaps it was necessary. But unfortunately, Administrator, we failed miserably to take notice of something that was right under our noses, and again due to the Marshal and his scare tactics. As it became clear that we were so efficiently winning each and every battle, it should have become equally clear that the emergency condition had to be dismissed, and this industry either converted to a more ecologically friendly standard or discontinued altogether. Our military seems more than capable of disposing of the Marshal's otherwise impotent insurgent forces, but he refuses to acknowledge this, even though he is the one managing them. This tells us he holds a special interest in having this industry exactly as it is, and it has nothing to do with his insurgents or any emergency condition."

"It does not?" he muses.

"Well, if you consider he is supposed to be a super brain, he should realize after a while that same pollution up there and do something to aid in cleaning it up. After all, he IS our…benefactor, right?"

"Um…"

"We could similarly claim this of our most beneficent Council, whose primary concern should be the health and safety of our world population, not some mysterious, and entirely unnecessary secrets of the universe. We don't NEED those. But we DO need clean air. This now makes them negligent of our basic needs, to say nothing of the other political demands of their office. And I will emphasize the word 'negligent' here, as this is what they are, and likely also corrupt if they are placing more interest in a nonessential deliberation rather than their assigned duties as our elected government authority. Do you see a picture developing here?"

"I think I do."

"And as such, whatever mandates and other claims they might make, we are declaring them not only negligent, maybe also corrupt, but also incompetent to perform their assigned jobs."

"Uh oh…"

"This is made even worse when you consider the nearly ten millennia we had to endure this. It is appalling to think that no one ever tried to analyze this before. Now, look at us…" she points out a nearby window at the pollution outside. "THIS, Administrator, is the true crime here, and the Council has broken its own laws. They refuse to comment on it, they refuse to correct it, and since we have never lived up to the Marshal's once great promise of leaving this otherwise contaminated planet due to his claims of that old Tav'ageen phenomena, we are now suffering more from his pollution than anything else, and some of us are tired of it."

"But, if the Council…"

"Administrator," she asserts. "Our public seems to believe the Council is always right. We treat them as a god entity that can do no wrong. It is one thing to have an emergency, but after some amount of time, wiser minds need to realize a corrective effort to clean up after that emergency. Inaction, Administrator, to correct a thing should be as illegal as the wrongful deed itself. And not even the Council should be immune to this. And yet, their perpetual storytelling that…any day now…we're leaving home, so don't bother thinking with your own horns, let THEM do it instead…is a story to close our eyes to a greater truth. And that truth was all a lie, simply to lock us down and destroy our home."

"Oh no! All right, I see your point. But what does this actually say about the Council?"

"It says, if they cannot even come outside to smell the smog, they are no longer serving the best interests of the people, despite whatever it is they are supposed to be deliberating in there. The Internal Secretary of the Grand Hall keeps the door locked and refuses anyone access to speak to the Council on any matter of real government policy. So, we are declaring them ineffectual, and all their past mandates are hereby being rendered null and void. Only the Charter of Laws matters now."

"This is a very serious accusation, but do you actually hold that level of authority?"

"In the absence of them demonstrating their authority, the one we actually elected them to uphold, we, the people, are taking our own. We will become the new authority in this world, and choose a new government body to replace them. But in the interim, until that body can be arranged, we must do what they did not. And WE, good Sir, will expect results. No more empty promises. This is a revolution, Administrator, and we have the law enforcement agencies, as well as several prominent military officials backing us up."

"A revolution…" he wheezes. "But what about the Marshal? Surely, he might have something to say in his defense."

"The Marshal, and I use that word loosely, will need to pack his bags soon. He came here with promises, none of which have been fulfilled. Instead, he made us destroy our native home to the point where it became almost uninhabitable. His claims of the old Tav'ageen Anomaly are being brought into question, and it would seem the Council even went so far as to grant him official authority over our native military. Administrator, the Council should not hold the authority to grant someone, certainly not one without an official, and credible title, and especially not an alien creature, the power to hold ANY native government or military authority position. This further makes the Council an illegal body for doing so, and it makes HIM illegal for holding it."

"Uh oh… So, what does this mean for the Council, and also the Marshal?"

"Our agency is currently investigating both of them for crimes against our people and our world. We intend to push our way into the Council's chamber to get an answer once we finish collecting our data. I find it unlikely they have anywhere to run. But the Marshal is deemed a larger threat to us than a group of people who forgot what sunlight is about. Regardless of who he describes as his insurgents, it does seem he personally holds a considerable amount of technological wherewithal, and this could represent a danger to us if he should begin to realize we are dismantling his control machine. But if to take it out of his hands and put it back into ours, we can weaken his grip on our people and send him packing with a minimal amount of backlash."

"Backlash… Are you saying he might get angry and take some form of retaliatory action?"

"Excuse me, did you look outside recently. Backlash? That up there in the sky could be minor as compared to what he might be capable of if he loses control of things. And we can't take that chance, not until we remove some of the machinations he planted under our hooves while we were learning to breathe toxic fumes."

"All right, sorry for the lapse."

"Fine. But if his purpose in coming here was to fool us into giving our world over to his control, then yes. Our world is polluted with his industry, and our bodies are polluted with his inventions, and with no recognizable medical need, which naturally demands us to ask about their true purpose. He further denies us his promises as payment for our services, and instead feeds us lies and propaganda about insurgents we need to be afraid of but can never lose a battle against. Therefore, as a society, we need to realize his crimes and take our own retaliatory action."

"Yes Ma'am," he replies feebly. "I believe I see your perspective now, although it pains me to think about it."

"I understand, Administrator. Then let us work together on this rather than becoming enemies. My team is here to investigate your plant and see what it is he has you making, and where it is going. Then we must decide on what sort of reforms we can apply, or if we should simply bring it down due to the lack of any practical need to serve our people."

"But it does serve a need for the military, does it not?"

"This is one of our issues, because if the Marshal made it, we're asking what he's using it for if not a big, strong military to fight all those terrible, awful insurgents of his."

✦ ✦ ✦ ✦ ✦ ✦

Ayene was making a new visit to Azgarén in her projected form. On this occasion, she wanted to follow through on another aspect of her plans to bring additional support into the equation of their insurgency against the Marshal and his designs. But this visit also carried a personal overtone, as she was flying over the western suburb region of the city towards her family home.

She travelled over the rooftops in her bird form, but flying casually to give her time to think of how she would approach the situation. The first hurdle would be right at the front door. According to Central Command, she was listed as dead. But as part of her early infiltration of the military data networks, she and Petrith modified this with secret vid-mail notices to certain select family members to soften the blow by saying the various people recently listed as dead were in fact reassigned to something highly classified. It was not too far from the truth, and intended to ease the pain they would otherwise feel if they thought their loved ones were actually dead.

She arrived in the vicinity of the neighborhood where her family home was located. It was an average middle-income development of single-level homes closely packed together. The general scene of the area, at least as viewed from above, appeared peaceful and neighborly. Many of the yards were struggling in the harsh conditions, but the area was reasonably well-maintained.

She singled out her home and circled around before finally choosing to land on the ground out of view to one side. There were no pedestrians passing by, and no traffic as most of the people had already come home by this time after their work shifts. She expected her parents would be home, as well.

She reshaped herself to her standard Suuden'kai form, which included the seed entity and cranial interface. She stood there a few moments examining herself to ensure the shape was accurate, but at the same time she considered silently if she wanted to use the disguise at all, or simply walk in there in her true natural form.

"I'll probably have to show them…" she muses privately. "I'll need to if I'm to explain the Prodigy Gift. I also need to consider how to explain my death notice, the ACI, and everything else. All right, if we're going to cause their horns to shoot off, let's go full throttle on it. It's probably going to happen anyway."

She reimagines her shape to her new form, with no interface and no seed entity. She further changes her clothes to a fashionable white shirt, pale blue pants, and a matching split-tail coat.

She strutted briskly out onto the sidewalk in front of the house, taking care to avoid being sighted through the windows prematurely. From there, she strolled towards the driveway and along a walkway leading across to the front door.

She turns to examine the house. It was mostly as she remembered it from her last visit, but that was a long time ago. She stopped visiting when she was assigned to her post at the mining base on Morndindor four centuries prior. Time seemed to move so slowly for her kind, she thought. Her more recent interactions on Tae'Eladar and Therinë put a new meaning into the concept of rapid development. Here at her family home, the place she grew up and spent so much of her youth, it seemed like an icon lasting half an eternity. But this was common for them. They just keep maintaining it indefinitely.

She hesitantly approaches the door. The shrubs in the front yard looked arid, as if just barely holding on. The yard was sparsely landscaped, with a decorative rock covering and a variety of evergreen and flowering plants. She halted in her steps, and although she held confidence in what she knew, and this had to be presented, she found herself stalling for time before knocking. She reflected briefly on how she would open the conversation, and then reached for the call button. She could hear the faint ringing of the bell inside the house. Her mental simulation of nervousness heightened, but she had to contain it.

From inside the door, the sounds of hoof steps echoed, and the door latch turned. Ayene held her head low, waiting for the door to open. As it did, it revealed a youthful mature woman. Ayene looked up to see her mother.

The woman's reaction seemed delayed, as if held in suspension, unsure of what she was looking at, and disbelieving her eyes. She stared at what seemed like a surreal image of her daughter, but it could not be her daughter, not for the obvious lack of misshapen contours of the body. There was no seed entity, therefore Ayene appeared unreal as compared to the last time she was seen visiting. The moment broke suddenly with a yelp, and then a whimper as the woman clutched at her cranial unit.

Ayene watched and felt a moment of guilt for causing this reaction, but it was unavoidable, and quickly overridden by the declaration that this was only the beginning. The story she had to tell would likely cause more.

"Hello, Mother," Ayene announces calmly. "You should be more careful. You know how the chip reacts to these outbursts."

"Ayene? Is it actually you? But what happened to you? Just look at you."

"Yes," she glances down at herself. "I had a little work done on me recently."

"A little work? But it looks like you lost your seed implant. Did someone remove it?"

"Yes, actually. It's a revolutionary new procedure we just recently developed. I was very nervous to try it, but it worked."

"Incredible. Is this something the medical industry is bringing out to the public soon?"

"Hopefully. We have a few small kinks to work out as far as publicizing it, and of course there is the usual bureaucratic rigmarole to wade through."

"Yes, I suppose so. But next is that strange notice we received a while back. Ayene, what actually happened to you? First, you get a notice from Central Command that you were killed in an accident, but then we get another one, this one telling us about some highly classified project, and you were reassigned. I do not understand what those people are doing over there anymore."

"Well, we could argue about it out here, or maybe we could sit down, and I'll twist your horns with all the nasty little details."

"Oh, but of course, please excuse me…"

The woman stands aside and Ayene steps into the room.

It was a pleasantly decorated family room, with a sofa and two easy chairs circling a low table. Across the room was a large vid-com unit currently displaying a popular entertainment series, and Ayene's father was sitting in one of the chairs. He stood up in awe as he saw his daughter enter the room.

"Ayene!" he shouts. "In all the nether-space, am I pleased to see you again! We got a notice from those people, but…"

"Yes, Father, we just covered that over here."

Her father glares at Ayene, again for the obvious figure that seemed absent something important and commonplace in everyday life. He also took notice of the missing interface on her head.

"Ayene, what happened to you?" he asks tenuously. "Your seed implant, and the interface are both missing."

As Ayene's mother was sitting down, she jerked around at the mention to examine Ayene's head. She then directed a concerned glare at her husband.

"Yes, Father," Ayene responds casually. "It was decided I don't actually need any of that junk after all. It doesn't serve any true functional purpose."

"What?" he balks.

"Well, maybe I misstated it a little. I suppose we could say it does serve a purpose, just not the advertised one."

"Wait, what do you mean by that? Did the medical community make some new kind of decision on it?"

"Yes, I suppose you could say that. The ARC over there is especially upset. So much so, that they're discontinuing the product lines and turning off all the chips. And as Mother already commented, my seed is gone due to a new procedure we're developing to remove that as well. It feels great not to have that horrible little bug on my back anymore."

"I suppose it might, but the chip was another thing. Why are they discontinuing those? Because we were always told it was still necessary."

"Yes, the medical community is told to tell you this because the Council never told them to do otherwise. They don't even allow the medical community to conduct studies or collect any statistical feedback from any potential new cases to see if it's still out there, and this effectively denies any continued research to learn what's going on."

"It does? But why? I would think they would need this in order to realize it is still a problem."

"To realize it is…or maybe it is not. There are those who were questioning this, for the obvious LACK of feedback. No one has died from it since we all got the chips, way back in 9765 or so when they first came out. You do recall the history, right? In 9765.31, the Council announced the famous press release of the Suppressor chip…and this was the last time they did anything useful for our people…not that the chip was really useful to begin with."

"But of course it was useful. Just look at what it did for our people."

"Father, the chip did nothing for our people except leash them inside a restraining collar. The cause of the Tav'ageen Anomaly was not solved by the chip. The chip is not based on our famous empirical evidence of the existence of any alien thing. It's based on another alien thing claiming something, but without proof of existence, and then our gluttonous Council taking his simple word on the premise that they'll have the grand secrets of the universe as their reward for polluting us with all their garbage. And THAT, Father, is the truth of our history. Anything else relating to it was buried under a mountain of bureaucracy, and the real scientists out there denied any further review. In other words, it was a conspiracy."

"A conspiracy!"

"In fact, among all the parasite things bothering us right now, the worst of it is that seed thing they made us stick to our bodies, and then denied those same scientists the means to research a way out of it…another conspiracy."

"Aargh!" he screeches as he grabs his interface.

"And all of this due to that OTHER alien thing. You know, the one who calls himself a Marshal, but without any empirical evidence to show for it…like credentials."

"Oh great," he moans. "Then why…I mean, if the medical community says it is not a problem…um, but our med-tech always told us different."

"Father, before either of your horns goes flying off…at least completely," she smirks cutely. "Listen to me. The Council ordered a boilerplate statement to be issued irrespective of the truth or any proper medical advice, all because they want you to think what they tell you to think. They are behaving with a god complex, and your opinions don't matter."

"Then what is the chip doing if not solving the Tav'ageen thing? And, um…" he glances nervously at his wife.

"Yes, I think I know what you want to say. I suspect the two of you know something, and this is the reason why we have had so many troubles in our family since I was a little girl. I learned something recently that informed me of what the Tav'ageen Anomaly really is, and this answered that age-old question of Mother's strange behavior. Unfortunately, before now, there was no real answer to it because first, the Council is dead; second, the Marshal is a criminal; and third, we've all allowed our horns to be dragged so low, we don't even know what year it is."

Both of her parents glared at her, and then at each other, silently thinking she had lost her mind. Ayene gazed at them, wondering which would come forward first to inquire on any of this. Finally, it was her father to enter the debate again, but very tenderly.

"Ayene, what is all this you are talking about? Are you actually alright, or did something happen as part of that notice we received from Central Command?"

"As far as being alright, I am probably more…alright…than I've ever been in my life. Because now I know the truth of the world around me, and the answers to a lot of hidden conspiracies. And yes, this is because of something that happened to me that Central thinks I'm dead."

She leans back and crosses her arms with a confident smile on her face, waiting for her father to respond.

The man glared at her, along with Ayene's mother, and the obvious emotional display, which at this point should be expected if Ayene's chip was gone.

"All right, I am listening. Because, unless you are some kind of ghost, clearly they must be wrong."

"A ghost?" Ayene guffaws. "Oh please, Father, you don't really believe in such nonsense as that old thing. I mean, we're a society of scientists who demand the ever-famous empirical evidence, and who completely refuse to accept anything supernatural or mystical. After all, look at how badly the Council, and even the Marshal, for all his super alien genius, vilified poor Elder Nazég way back in the day when he was trying to explain these things to us." Now her expression turns more serious. "And no one listened."

"Uh oh."

"Yulin," Ayene's mother emits tenderly. "I think I hear a message in that."

"Yes, Lenya, and this might then relate to that…thing…that happened, where they think she is dead. If those scientists out there, who are not allowed any further review, did something outside the authority of whatever conspiracy was locking them down, this would reflect on that same Council, as well as the Marshal, who are the ones responsible. And this also means Central Command."

"Right!" Ayene perks up and leans forward again. "So listen carefully and pay attention. First, I don't work for them anymore. Four centuries ago, I was assigned to Central as part of a top-secret project the Marshal ordered. No one knew about it, and neither were they ever intended to know about it, all because the Marshal doesn't tell anyone, not even the HC, about most of what he's doing out there. He gives each person their independent instructions, just enough to do the job, and to be carried out in total secrecy relative to everyone else. And this is how he can get away with murder and no one knows about it."

"Really! Well, that does sound extremely villainous. But surely there must be someone, like the High Commander, who should be aware of these details, right? He is supposed to be the top man in there."

"Supposed to be, yes, but in actuality, he is not. It's the Marshal, an alien being given authority over OUR military body by a government that should not hold the authority to grant such a thing. In other words, the Council was illegal to do it, and he was illegal to take it."

"Illegal!" he shouts, and reaches for his interface again.

"Father, you should prepare yourself. You're going to get a lot of hits from his little torture device up there."

"A torture device…such an interesting term. All right, go on."

"My assignment involved activities most people were completely unaware of, including the HC, and again due to the Marshal keeping a lot of personal secrets, most of them very unsavory."

"Such as what?"

"All right, an example… We found a new universe out there. But did he tell our science community about it? No. Why? It doesn't concern them. In other words, what HE wants doesn't concern any of us, even if it represents some new and clearly fascinating piece of scientific discovery."

"Interesting. And this would certainly reflect back on all his promises of great wisdom. If he will not even allow anyone to report on a simple discovery, what does this have to say about his promises?"

"It says he never had any intention of giving us anything unless the result somehow serves his needs. But he knew what strings to pull with our Council, and most of us, so we invited him in and gave him the keys to our lives. It's really very shameful, especially that we let it go on for so long and never realized the clues to his mischief were right in front of us, but we never openly asked about it."

"Clues... What sort of clues are we speaking of? I hesitate to ask this, but I need the details of it to realize your direction."

"Then let me summarize this for you. They were building up over time, and perhaps gradually, that you might need to see it from a larger perspective, maybe also in hindsight, now that it's all there, rather than the piecemeal as they came along. One, he comes in with his ghost stories of these insurgents. Along the way, he offers to help with this Tav'ageen thing. Two, he tells us it's some alien thing and to run away, but without any of that empirical evidence to prove himself. Three, the Council takes this on his word...after all, he's an alien super brain. How could he be wrong, especially if he's offering the secrets of the universe as our reward for taking his word on anything. Do you see a pattern building here?"

"Yes, and it is not a nice one. He basically bribed the Council with that promise."

"This is further compounded by number Four...the panic, where we have his continued ghost stories, but this time with the 'evidence' of dead bodies turning up everywhere, and yet with NO evidence of how that really occurred. This leads our people to take his wonderful solution of the seeds, along with the idea to simply run away. Five, here come his insurgents, along with Six, Elder Nazég and that ship that carried him away. It was big, it was scary, and it jumped in right on top of us. So, here we have Seven... INSURGENTS!!" she screams and waves her hands theatrically. "And here we go chasing all across the galaxy for fantasy people who clearly know where we live AND have jump drives to reach us. But his ghost stories clouded our scientific minds of that empirical evidence of what once appeared right over our heads," she closes her eyes and shakes her head.

"In all the nether-space, Ayene," he moans. "That is a heavy yank of the tail...for anyone who ever had the horns to think of it."

"There must have been at least a few out there, but those ghost stories are simply awful. Eight, that industry and all the pollution, that no one ever thought about during this time to clean up, such that, Nine, it polluted our environment so badly that, Ten, we need those seeds right here at home. So, here we are, trapped on a polluted world with ghost stories STILL telling us...any day now...blah blah. And by the way, don't bother thinking with your own horns. After all, that's what the Council is supposed to be doing...but it isn't."

"I do not like that in the least," Lenya admits. "She has a point; this is certainly a conspiracy for all those statements."

"Yes," Yulin nods. "But it still does not answer the part of the Tav'ageen Anomaly, and what they were saying about it once."

Ayene continues, "I'm part of a new top-secret government security agency that's investigating all of this. He essentially fabricated the panic for the Tav'ageen thing, taking an existing dilemma, where such as Elder Nazég, among others, were trying to research it, but made it worse by hiding the evidence, and instead feeding us his ghost stories...the one thing we, as a society of scientists, should NOT be falling for. This was then compounded by all those deaths, which HE is responsible for, to further emphasize his ghost stories, and ba-boom. Here we have a sequence of events that leads us through the rest...and all of it fake."

"Then what was that original dilemma you mentioned."

"A new quality just developing in our species, but he doesn't want us to know about it. Therefore, the chips, to disable it. His kind are very supremacist, and don't like...little things...with fancy skills."

"A skill? Some kind of ghostlike thing?"

"Yeah, the one thing our nonreligious society of scientists, who wouldn't otherwise take a supernatural explanation, even if you put a gun to their head. So he uses his ghost stories instead, which effectively was a gun to our head for his solutions. And Elder Nazég, the one guy who might dare to use his horns outside the box of that empirical evidence the rest of us so often demanded, was trying to invent something new. But the Council didn't like the idea, and once the Marshal showed up, at least officially, there he goes."

"Officially… Which means he was here previously, as well as unofficially."

"Right."

"All right, go on, Ayene. You had some sort of mission once, right?"

"Yes. We were a mining operation on a world formerly populated by a native society that was generally well below us in their tech levels. However, this world had an important mineral the Marshal wanted at all costs, including that society that would probably not simply hand it over to us without a lot of effort. He doesn't negotiate for anything, not when he has a military like ours in his pocket. So, he ordered them to blast that world to oblivion, down to one surviving city, which he then ordered us to enslave using drugs to pull out mining teams."

Both of her parents were aghast at this depiction, causing them to clutch at their interfaces and gape at Ayene for the lengthy barrage of offences.

"And before either of you ask why I did it," she continues. "I wasn't actually part of the bombardment campaign, but our base staff was under the threat of one of his toys none of YOU were ever intended to know about, but that was pushed through the Council to serve our military. It was a type of mind-control chip to ensure we did as our master ordered."

"A what?" he blasts. "What kind of chip is that! Who made it?"

"He made it, of course, the same as the seeds and the Suppressor chip. These are all his inventions to control our people. The chip in question here is known as an authority override device to force a person into a mindless state of compliance to follow orders without question, and he used this a lot with our military…every time he wanted something dead."

"All his fantasy insurgents? But if those insurgents are simply a fantasy ghost story, who was he killing?"

"Anything and everything within our galaxy that represented target practice for our military to play with. The base commander was a former Fleet Commander in our navy. He was sent out on multiple missions in charge of a task force to hit the Marshal's so-called insurgents. Everyone was placed on the active mode of the chip and given one instruction…see planet, destroy planet. It didn't actually matter who it belonged to because they never saw it coming. We probably cleaned out most of the galaxy of anything that used to be alive out there, and this would make us the All-Time biggest murdering society in the history of the universe, all because we allowed an alien with big promises to simply take control, and no one questioned any part of what he did."

"Wonderful. So, why did he actually want this mineral, and at the cost of an innocent planetary population?"

"Again, he didn't tell us anything beyond what we needed to know to do our immediate job, and that was to force mining teams to do our work for us, and then to pick up the mineral and deliver it to a processor to refine into a substance he didn't explain to us, except to say…do not drop it! In other words, it was extremely volatile, and he was making a very large quantity of it."

"Interesting. And what world did he have in mind for this?"

"It wasn't any simple world. It was all those other universes out there where he had true enemies he wanted to take revenge on. But of course, he never explained this to any of us. You see, Sargeras and his kind once got into a war, and lost. Darumon is a servant being under him, and he wants to serve his master by taking revenge for all the others."

"Really! And how does this explosive material fit into it?"

"Within that other universe, and likely a lot of other places, except ours, is an energy layer Central is calling Abnormal Energy, for the lack of a proper scientific designation, as it doesn't fit any existing science we know of. This material, which is actually derived from it, if detonated in our universe…and again, we do NOT have this energy layer here…can create a huge, and I'm talking stellar-sized huge blast sphere. It was demonstrated once in a star system called Ooduan. One unit, as it was packaged in his storage depot, created a five-lightyear diameter hole in space."

"In all the nether-space! Ayene, please tell me you are exaggerating that number."

"No, I'm not. Central measured it to verify the blast zone. From Ground Zero to the outer edge was two and a half lightyears of total destruction. But take this into that other universe with this Abnormal Energy, and it starts a chain reaction to take the entire cloud, which likely spans the full universe. And this would effectively destroy everything, including all his real enemies, who are likely spread out across many universes by now, among other things."

"Unbelievable! But how is it you actually know this if he is keeping so many secrets?"

"Our base was attacked by someone a couple of years ago. It was a covert operation that took us by surprise. We were captured, interrogated, and then the REAL situation explained to us by those same people he wants dead. In this case, at the same time as we had our operation, he was conducting another operation on a world he was using as a military staging post in preparation to make a hard advance on his old enemies. But he made a mistake along the way by sending another minion species he acquired recently, which was even dumber than we are, and they made a bit of noise on this world he delivered them into. The people of that world went to war with this little invasion, drove them back to his staging post world, and along the way made a most shocking discovery. Darumon and Sargeras, both of whom belong to a dead society, are in fact still alive."

"A dead society? So, if I am following correctly, his insurgents are something completely unrelated, and his real enemies thought he was long dead. But now, what is this new part about?"

"Here is where our society of nonreligious scientists needs an education. Sargeras is a godlike being called a Primordial, as far as we understand the terminology. Darumon is a lesser godlike being and part of a servant race to the bigger ones. Their entire society was once found by another godlike society, and they got into trouble. These Primordials aren't nice people to little things like us. We're toys to them, to be raised like animals and spent as cheap entertainment. The others, called Estelar, hold a much more reverent perspective of life, and took instant offence at this, so they went to war to put an end to it. The Primordials were destroyed, or else imprisoned, but we think Sargeras and Darumon probably ran away and hid. Now, here they are, unfortunately for us."

"So it would seem."

"The Marshal was discovered on this other world, but they let him go at that moment due to our military with these chips making them potentially unpredictable. They had already destroyed most of that world, so these others wanted to save whatever was left of it."

"I can certainly understand that, for all the devastation he seems to be conducting out there. But ultimately, it does not necessarily help us here."

"It will. This is why I'm here now. I work for them."

"You do? Very well, but now can you explain the part about the Tav'ageen thing, and maybe these ghost stories and their resulting parasites."

"The Tav'ageen Anomaly, or rather the Scare, was a hoax, perpetrated by the Marshal to frighten us into taking the seeds... that gun to the head, as I'm sure no one would willingly take our society's least favorite invention."

"Absolutely."

"They are thought to supply an artificial replacement of this Abnormal Energy, which is found in so many other places, as a support input to Sargeras to sustain him. His form of life isn't like us, and this follows the same with the Estelar. They are extradimensional creatures who make their homes mostly in a space that is rich in this stuff...that same space our science absolutely denies existing at all, nether-space."

"Nether-space!" he reaches for his interface again.

"Yeah, and you can thank the Marshal for showing us how to reach it, when he absolutely DENIED our science to learn it exists."

"Oh, yes, and thank you, Ayene, for rubbing in that last hit."

"Sorry, Father, but you're not the only one. This becomes their native environment, like ours here in this material world."

"Ugh…all right, so it is drawing from us and feeding into him. I think I am thoroughly disgusted by that notion."

"Right. If in any other space, it might not be necessary, but here in our universe, where we do not have this native layer, he needs this as a substitute. Therefore, we have the Marshal frightening us with his ghost stories of the Tav'ageen thing, but NOT telling us to use the chips as his first choice. Instead…oh no!" she animates theatrically. "We need to run away, and use the seeds, not any normal colonization tech, to colonize anything we can find out there. And the dull-horned population, who never once actually colonized anything anyway, bought it, if only because no one apparently knows we DO have a wide assortment of colonization tech to play with. Just ask the military…but oh, wait, they tend to classify most of that," she shrugs ironically. "How do you like that for a society of intellectuals?"

"Yes! Thank you, Ayene. You said something about feedback hits. Well, this is a good cause for one. And clearly, you seem to be enjoying your newfound emotions."

"Oh yes! And I'm milking it for all I can get, almost thirteen centuries of it. Furthermore, I'm going to ask you to go back to your favorite med-tech and get your chips turned off as well. They're doing it to everyone, but we need to keep it quiet so far, so the Marshal doesn't get upset. He wants us to have this, after all."

"Uh huh."

"But Ayene," Lenya infers. "What about these chips? It disables something? Because if that old Scare was a hoax…um…" she glances at Yulin.

"Yes, Mother, this is the part that caused us so much pain, and I'm sorry. But unfortunately, you, like all the rest of those scientists listening to his ghost stories, fell for it. I suppose there was nothing else to do, but it really sticks a burr under the tail for the implications. For this part, we need to delve into another part of our history."

She leans back as she considers her next lecture.

"Apparently, our society has been under observation for some amount of time. And these others know something about him and his activities in our world, and it dates back a lot farther than his official arrival. Like I said, these beings are as gods to people like us, so such a thing as immortality is not outside of reality in their case. One of them knows Darumon and Sargeras, and we think this carries back to that old war. We believe she has something personal in this, because she has apparently been making a series of very secret plans to move against him, using these people from that other world as her strike force. She was also watching them during this time, especially Darumon as he made his first visit to our world…way back in the time of the Eracyodines."

"The what?" she gasps. "What do you mean by that?"

"HE is the real reason we exist. All that controversy over our evolution… There was no bizarre natural…whatever…event that changed them. They were artificially evolved by him to create a new sentient species he would come for later on. He made us."

"Oh no…" she moans.

"But there is a catch to this. He was in this universe, which is absent of that energy layer. Among other things, that stuff works like a super fix-it tool for them. It bends space and time to the will of the mind, just like you might expect for a godly power. In fact, if Elder Nazég were still among us, he could explain it to you with his otherwise unappreciated science faction. Too bad for us the Council chased him away."

"Oh, yes, so unfortunate."

"Yeah, with the Marshal claiming he was part of his opponents. But in our world, all the Marshal had was his bare hands…and I suppose a few other body parts…" she smirks with a brief downward glance, "…to make his work. So, as disgusting as it may sound, he's our father, biologically speaking."

This sent both her mother and father reeling. They each clutched at their chips and further grasped their horns and moaned.

"But on the bright side," Ayene continues cheerily. "We inherited some fabulous Gifts from him. As a near-god figure, we would be half of that, which makes us a form of hybridized species with some really unique talents…none of which he would want us to know about. One of these is our ridiculously long lifespans that seem to defy the evolution of anything else around here."

"Uh huh, so we have an answer to that one, finally."

"The other was his famous alien infestation he kept scaring us with. You see, as a society that is born and bred to shun such fanciful notions as magic and mysticism, we would automatically discredit anything that might fall into a category like Elder Nazég's faction of metaphysics. But strangely, we do still behave as frightened children who run and hide in a closet whenever we hear ghost stories. Go figure," she shrugs.

"Thank you, Ayene," Yulin relents sardonically. "I swear, you must really be enjoying your time without that chip."

"That, and also the seed. Father, Mother, I love both of you, and I'm sorry that I need to lay this on you. Yes, I do enjoy this, and I've even learned a few tricks to embellish things as part of my new job. Believe it or not, there is a substantial level of acting skill that has to go along with it."

"Acting skill. This is interesting. I never heard of a government security agency using an acting skill as part of their operations."

"Yeah, this is special. But the problem is, much like the other four billion people in our world, you listened to his stories more than you listened to your early schoolteachers giving lessons on how to think and rationalize the world around you. Assuming it didn't involve that famous spirit of the words they use to cover up the actual meanings."

"Oh great, something else? Well, yes, I suppose you are right."

"The Tav'ageen Anomaly is a latent ability only now coming to the surface in our otherwise inbred species. We are half-brothers and sisters, inbreeding his component, and no doubt this is emphasizing the half god aspect of it. Those first children were simply the beginning, but unfortunately for them, Darumon was watching and didn't like what he saw. So, boom, here we have the Tav'ageen Scare. Then boom, here comes the Marshal and all his superior wisdom to solve our problems. And as a godlike being that likes to use little things like us as toys, he certainly wouldn't want us to realize who we are and what sort of inherited Gifts we got from him."

"How nice of him. He gives it to us, and then he takes it away."

"Exactly. The Prodigy Gift, as Elder Nazég would describe it, is the ability to project a mental image outside the body into physical space. Those original children probably found it by accident. Then we have those crazy…alien…death syndromes. Our medical faction could never understand any part of this, but these people tell us it resembles a type of vampiric action to suck the life force out of a body, and this is how it appears afterwards."

"I am not so sure if I like the sound of that."

"And this is the fear factor behind those chips," Lenya muses. "That gun to the head, as she calls it. And it would certainly behave that way. And the perpetual ghost stories to maintain the image, plus the denial of the science factions to continue any form of study to correct it, along with that boilerplate message for the rest of us. Here, take this," she gestures figuratively. "Because it is the only thing we will ever offer to you."

"Exactly, Mother," Ayene nods. "And I'm sure you're not the only one, especially if we consider the parents of those original children, and anyone else out there who suffered. Here is where the Marshal tells us it's an alien parasite, which I suppose is true if you consider HE is an alien and behaving as a parasite."

"Oh yes, I like that one. And then we had that day…ugh…" she winces and turns away.

Yulin gazed at his dear wife as she shuddered from the old memory.

"Yes. I remember it too. Ayene, your poor mother over here…" he glances at the woman.

"She saw it once, didn't she. I'm willing to bet my left horn it scared hers right off."

"Yes, actually…both of us. She found it once, and then called my attention to it."

"Tuka, right? That imaginary friend I thought I had once, but it was actually me on the bed, asleep while my mind projected outwards into the room. It almost seems like a dream to me now. Some parts of it are lost in my memories, like how I came out and how I got back in. But this was ultimately the beginning of the end for whatever close relations we had, as you seemed to behave as if I was the alien thing."

"I am so terribly sorry, Ayene," Lenya mourns. "How could I possibly know?"

"It's alright, Mother, I'm not going to hold it against either of you. It was unfortunate, but let's see if we can heal those old wounds and start over, now that we know."

"But it all seems so monstrous!"

"Yes, it does," Yulin admits. "And the one person who might know anything was chased off as a traitor to the people."

"But Yulin," she begs. "Can we actually say we could ever possibly understand this, even with Elder Nazég's faction? If the Marshal was trying so hard to hide everything, do you actually think he would allow this to come out at all?"

"Lenya," he sighs feebly. "Probably not. In fact, if Elder Nazég had not run off, he might be one of those same statistics, especially if the Marshal was killing children to hide it. Do you think he would stop at a member of our Council?"

"He didn't stop at the rest of them," Ayene muses. "They're all presumed to be dead right now."

"Oh no! Do we know how...and why?"

"Within reason. The why is easy. He didn't need them anymore after he got all his mandates and control of our world. The last time anyone saw them was during the public release of the Suppressor chip... way back in the beginning. Then we have this eternal deliberation, and they are not seen since. Worse is that no one apparently takes notice...by any means, it would seem. For instance, the immediate family members also seem to be missing. And then, the elections during this full length of time were consistently picking the same people, even though, by now, half of them should be dead of old age."

"You must be...aargh!" he shouts and grabs his interface.

"Kidding you?" Ayene finishes with a subtle grin.

Yulin simply glared at her for the obvious rub.

"You just wait, young lady, until I get this thing turned off. Then we will see."

"Good enough. But if you check the DataNet for a few details, you can see it for yourself. Something the Marshal must've missed in all his cover-ups. We have all these ghost stories, and that long sequence of events leading up to the chips. Once he had this, the Council became expendable, as he now had full control of things using proxies who are replacing those components simulating any kind of actual government function. And by the way, this also includes inside the media stream, where he installed what was described as Council-mandated regulators censoring and falsifying our news broadcasts."

"Falsifying!" he blasts. "Great, there goes my last remaining interest in watching the vid-com."

"Easy does it, Father, we hope to change a few things. Meanwhile, unknown to anyone, he ordered the military to remove the Council from Azgarén during that panic as part of what they call a quarantine procedure to protect them. They were brought home for press releases, but then taken away again when not needed here. Then, once everyone had their seeds, and the new Suppressor chips were in production, this settled the panic. What came after was a fabulous invention of his superior mind and all his propaganda."

"Propaganda...hmm..."

"And all of this with the Council in this deep deliberation, so no one knows what happened, and couldn't pry them out if their life depended on it."

"So convenient... It is actually a very clever and intricate plan, if not also devious."

"Yes, it is, and I'm sure he worked hard on it. Again, if you check the DataNet, those family members are hidden behind a high-level military security code. There's no way of knowing if they're alive or dead, not unless you can break a few of those codes. And that quarantine site is gone, presumably destroyed by an insurgent attack. So, where do you think the Council and their families were if only a high-ranking military officer might actually hold the answer…either before or after he blasted that outpost? And likely in the active mode of his authority chip so he couldn't analyze what he was shooting at."

"But Ayene…" he wheezes. "What are we saying here? He killed them, and for what, just to take over our world?"

"Yes, precisely. We're his pets, so why do we need our own government when he only wants us as a form of life support for his master. He also needs us for those few technological devices we own, and which he probably helped us invent, that may be useful to free the remaining Primordials from their prison and destroy the Estelar. After that, we're just food."

"Incredible, and also horrifying. But now, what about you…your seed and your chip…"

Ayene gets up from her chair to prepare a little demonstration. She moves to the center of the room.

"First of all, I'm not corporeal at this moment. My body is on another planet, and this is a projection of my consciousness you are looking at. And I'm not limited to be myself in this form."

She now runs through her usual sequence of images, first a squirrel, and then the hawk. This sent waves of surprise through both her parents as they gazed in trepidation at the spectacle. She then takes her tiger form, followed by the tree and even a chair, before returning to herself. She finally returned to her seat to explain herself further.

"It's being described as the Prodigy Gift, which is a term first coined by Elder Nazég, who is still alive, by the way, and living in that other universe the Marshal chased him into," she smirks. "We believe he probably came into some form of understanding, maybe due to a personal experience, that we are more than simple beings made of flesh, unlike everything else around us. We're capable of a number of otherwise mythical mental powers, like telepathy and such, and this places us on a much higher level of evolutionary development, but without the actual evolution to earn these things naturally. Therefore, we're all complete dull-horns as to what it is or how to use it."

"Well, that is certainly nice to know," Yulin moans sarcastically.

"Is this to say you are learning of this now?" Lenya asks.

"I am," Ayene nods. "I'm still in my early lessons for some of it, but I'm proficient in the projection skill, and will soon be going into a new academy for even more study."

"An academy? Where?"

"On this other world where I'm living right now. They know what this is, and they can teach it. Our problem here is we're raised to measure everything in empirical numbers as part of our VERY material science. But this is NOT something you can measure in numbers. It's a power of the mind, and requires a lot of imagination to conceive of things you simply can't measure with empirical math. This is also where that acting skill comes in, as we might need to portray who-knows-what along the way. Oh, and that idea of magic is also real, but you need this energy layer to make it work. And much to our misfortune, we're born in a universe that doesn't have it."

"Oh, well, that is certainly unfortunate."

"Yeah, but I'll be learning a little bit of that too, one of these days."

"This would be amazing to see," Yulin remarks. "But it would also place these things well outside most of the other sciences."

"It would, although if we could evolve some of those, we could possibly create a hybridized form out of it."

"A hybridized form... Oh, that would be interesting to see."

"But now, Elder Nazég was carried away by agents relating to this opposing faction the Marshal is hiding from. This was to preserve him, not because he was joining anything. He actually had no idea who they were, except to say they were someone telling him to run away from Sargeras."

"Did he try telling this to anyone else, like the rest of the Council?"

"He did, but they ignored him, in part because they never really liked his faction to begin with, and in part because the promise of great wisdom sounded so much better."

"Oh, how wonderful!" he roars and clutches his interface again. "So here we are, with the Council murdered and the rest of us infected by all the Marshal's machinations."

"Yes. As for me, I'm now part of this new operation. It's basically an insurgency, a real one, but from the inside. He took away our government, so we're taking away his machines. We're conducting a lot of covert operations so far, like those regulators, and their associated contacts. We also pushed our way into the Grand Hall, but that place was a wreck. It looks like no one has opened those doors since 9765 when we last saw a Council member in public."

"Uh oh...what does it look like in there?"

"A complete ruin..." she shakes her head. "Dust and decay, crumbling walls and ceiling... It's amazing the place is still standing... what's left of it. We're also in the process of dismantling his dirty industry in the hopes we can reverse some of the damage he caused. But that's not going to be easy."

"I suppose we should all thank you for that. I wonder why no one ever tried doing this before. Whatever happened to the laws around here where pollution control is concerned?"

"It's funny you should mention that. All this began with a war declaration and emergency protocols to override those laws that were supposed to govern everything, and it never settled. And without a Council to review anything...assuming they might actually do so to begin with...the Marshal simply doesn't care, as it doesn't serve HIS needs. He wants us to keep those seeds, so he needs a reason to keep pushing them at us, and this was his imperative need due to these insurgents, coupled with this persistent threat of the Tav'ageen Anomaly that's supposedly still a danger to us, even though no one has died from it since we got the chips, and our...need...to evacuate at all costs, even though technically it doesn't matter anymore."

"Absolutely amazing," he sighs. "Yes, I can see your point, and further our shame for these clues you mentioned that no one seems to be paying attention to. Now I feel bad for my part in it."

"If it helps any, the people I'm working for right now have successfully created a solution to remove the seeds. They also removed our interfaces, and we're sharing our results with the ARC for further research and development as a general release. But we need to move cautiously because the Marshal is a dangerous element. We managed to turn the HC around, so he realizes all the crimes the Marshal made, but even without our military under his control, the Marshal is still dangerous."

"If he was the one responsible for all those Tav'ageen deaths," Lenya considers. "Then yes, I should think he is maniacal, to say the least."

"These people are making a careful covert move to catch both Darumon and Sargeras unaware. Along the way, they need to break all of his toys and bring us back to normal again. This is where we are now, and one of the reasons I'm here with you. I'm working for a government agency we created called Azgarén Central Intelligence. It's described as a planetary security agency that specializes in conspiracies and terrorism, among other things."

"This is interesting."

"We're looking for contacts we can use to bypass his usual control methods to broadcast a few things and undermine his authority. So far, we have Ileani Ur'paran inside C.P. News in mind. She'll be our release agent."

"Really! Yes, she would actually make a good choice. She seems quite popular, if only she would give us something useful to talk about."

"Yeah, I hear she's not happy about it either. But we can't make any direct statements, or else he might take notice and start asking questions, and we don't want that. We also have several science factions working on collecting data he must've hidden from us about our true history. We're going to use this by distributing it through venues he might not normally take notice of, like entertainment and advertising. Mother?" she grins. "This is your department, so if you know anyone in high places, we need to speak to them. And Father, you might know a few people who could be useful to help with one thing or another."

✦✦✦✦✦

Another week passed, and Kaliya had been in training for her anticipated meeting with Commander Geilv. She had been coached by both Thaelyn and Aelwyn on manners and etiquette, as most often applied by the Celestial races, to complete her presentation.

The research project demanded by the Marshal has been pending for nearly a month, and the ARC was still trying to delay it, hoping for some word to be delivered by either Ayene or Kaliya with new instructions. But before either of them could respond, they needed to have a plan relating to the Commander.

Kaliya was in her projected condition and receiving some last-minute advice for her mission. She was joined by Navina as her cohort ACI contact.

"No doubt this mission will involve some careful wording to reveal the details," Thaelyn remarks. "Fortunately, the stage is set with our other elements to build up a nice picture for ourselves. Our most immediate goal at this time is to establish a plan where those ships are concerned, but then we have our long-term goals. These may need to wait until later to finalize, but we should set the groundwork for them, at the very least."

"Got it," she affirms. "I just hope he takes to this new image as well as Relissa and the gang did over at the guildhall. That was fun."

"Yeah..." Navina chuckles. "I was there in the background watching, just to see their reactions. She had half the attendance bowing down and praying to her thinking they were being visited by a divine being of some sort."

"Yes, I heard of that one," he laughs. "It is not often when I can participate in such a game, but those rare moments are precious. Now, we must send you forward. Our scouts tell us he is currently in his office, which seems common enough. You have your script, so I hope to see you give us another of your fine performances."

"I just wish we could predict how they'll react," Kaliya notes. "The Commander will probably have a heart attack, but the Marshal is the bigger question. This game we're playing could turn in any direction, depending on how he ultimately responds to it."

"Yes, and we must be ready with just as many contingencies, not the least of which is to have your team ready to go on the offensive again."

"Right, well, here we go. Wish us luck."

Both Kaliya and Navina step away and recall the image of Central Command. On this occasion, they needed to make a more conventional approach, as Navina would represent an ACI agent and had to enter through the front door. Kaliya, on the other hand, folded her image behind the small spy camera that was located inside the ventilation duct in Geilv's office.

Navina arrived on Azgarén in a discreet location, and then strolled up to the lobby doors for the large military headquarters building. The lobby was well-appointed and professional for a military institution, including seating in a waiting area, some potted plants, several wall ornaments and recruitment posters, and of course the reception desk with the large Central Command emblem affixed to the wall behind it. She strutted up to the desk to present herself.

"Welcome, Citizen," the secretary offers. "Is there something I can do for you?"

"My name is Special Agent Navina Lar'akan..." she pulls out and flashes her ID badge. "I serve Azgarén Central Intelligence. I'm here on official business to meet with High Commander Geilv."

"The what?" she responds perplexedly. "Do you have an appointment?"

"Not precisely, but suffice it to say, he should be expecting me. It is my understanding he met with some of our other contacts in this time, so he should be at least partially aware of our operations."

"Suffice it to say..." she frowns. "And other contacts? Ma'am, this is Central Command. The only authority that is above us would be the Council itself. I do not know who this Azgarén Central Intelligence service is, but..."

"Then learn, young lady!" she asserts strongly. "I have had a horn-full of your military NOT speaking about the daily news around here. First, I'm a government secret service agent working for a planetary security agency with enough authority to haul away that very same Council who, by the way, is under investigation for a number of fraudulent activities."

"Fraudulent..." she mumbles softly.

"Right along with this place..." she waves a hand around the room, "...and all of YOUR fraudulent activities..."

"Us?"

"And I'm very nearly ready to haul those pretty little horns of yours downtown into my office. Your glorious military authority is currently under investigation for a number of illicit acts relating to the errant assault of foreign populations, the application of terrorist devices by our military agents, hidden research of dangerous materials and the improper handling of the result, the employment of radical agents and the subsequent loss of military personnel, as well as property, and finally the withholding of critical details relating to our planetary security from our government authority, to say nothing of the population. And this doesn't yet involve the discovery of extraordinary scientific anomalies that could lead to the prominent advancement of our civilization by a creature who once promised us precisely THAT sort of advancement in exchange for our services. Shall I go on?"

"Huh?" she gasps.

The laundry list of accusations had the secretary reeling in her chair. She gazed in astonishment at the young officer with the overly ambitious attitude and fierce approach.

"Now," Navina continues. "Call up the HC and tell him the ACI is here to meet with him immediately. I'm sure he'll know who we are, and likely run all the way downstairs for the mere pleasure of it."

"Ma'am, please," she begs. "All right, I will call him."

The secretary makes a frantic call on the vid-com to Geilv's office.

"This is Commander Geilv speaking..."

"Commander Geilv, this is the reception desk. There is a woman here from something she calls the ACI who wishes to meet with you immediately. And she doesn't sound like the sort of person you can say no to. Shall I send her up or will you come down here for it?"

"The ACI? Oh great, that's all I need today. Send her up here."

"Sir, if I may, who or what is this ACI, because after the blasting I just got down here and your apparent reaction, I am getting a little worried."

"They're a new government authority relating to planetary security, and apparently involved in a series of very delicate investigations relating to the Marshal, the Council, and even us. So, whatever she told you, keep it quiet."

"Uh oh... All right, Sir, but that list she gave me just now was frightening. Things like fraudulent and felonious activities, conspiracies..."

"Yes, and unfortunately, none of us was paying close enough attention to it for all the security covering it up. It would seem we got ourselves into a nasty situation where the Marshal is concerned, and our Council isn't doing the job we all thought it was supposed to be doing. But anyway, send her up. I'll try to take care of it from here."

"Yes Sir."

They end the link, and the young secretary returns to Navina.

"My apologies, Ma'am," the secretary offers politely. "It's just that your agency is so new to most of us."

"I know this, and I will apologize for the outburst, but if I could tell you how many times I've had to repeat those statements, and all for the purpose of enforcing some semblance of law around here, where so many of you place your unwavering faith in a body that supposedly can do no wrong."

"Yes, of course. My duties here are relatively simple, so a lot of this goes over my head anyway. But now, he is asking for you to meet with him in his office. Is that alright? Do you know where that is?"

"I'm sure I can find it. Thank you."

Navina pertly turns and marches towards the lift. She presses the call button and enters inside to ride it up.

She arrives on the executive floor where Geilv's personal office is found, along with a few other administrative offices. She navigates her way through the hallway to his door and knocks politely before peeking inside.

"High Commander Geilv?"

"Yes, please enter."

She enters fully inside and strolls up to the desk, where Geilv directs her into a chair.

"My name is Special Agent Navina Lar'akan," she again produces her ID badge. "And I work for the ACI. It is my understanding you have been in contact with a few of our other informants, for instance those at the ARC, in relation to some of our operations, correct?"

"Yes Ma'am, and before we begin, I would like to impress upon you that I am personally very upset and remorseful over the roles I may have played, as well as my officers, even though we might try to excuse ourselves due to the application of those chips. Although I must admit, this would seem like a very weak excuse."

"Agreed, Commander, but I understand those chips were a mandate by the Council, and at the time, we also had an emergency condition which did not seem avoidable."

"Yes Ma'am. So, how can I help you?"

"We find ourselves in a situation that needs to be handled very delicately. We have offended a society of beings of a supreme level of technological sophistication, to say nothing of their evolutionary station, and all due to the unfortunate circumstance of the Marshal directing us at his so-called insurgents which he once claimed to be his former loyalists. This is further complicated by the fact that we have apparently been discovered to be assaulting numerous unassociated worlds along the way, and these beings take particular offence at that for the simple loss of life."

"May I ask you a question about these beings? How and where did you first encounter them?"

"To begin with, technically speaking, you first encountered them on a world described as Therinë, it would seem. They remembered you as you made this new approach to this city structure they call Sigil. As for us, our department has been collecting information on these activities for a while now. We have been attempting to interview your military personnel, although very discreetly, to see about what sorts of activities have been occurring out there behind our backs. The Marshal has been making his promises to our people for far too long, and we are quite tired of waiting for it. We sacrificed much for his so-called Great Wisdom. Now we either want to see our results or see him removed."

"That might not be so easily accomplished, in my opinion."

"It simply needs a bit of finesse. And then, as we began to realize this new discovery of an alien super race, we started asking questions about their relationship. Clearly, if this is described to be his insurgents, they did not fit the previous descriptions for the result you found out there."

"I agree."

"We received one report of your operations on Therinë of how you suddenly had to pull out after encountering someone new on the scene. This caused us to ask who they were that they would frighten the Marshal so badly."

"Yes, I was asking that same question once, and that encounter was apparently a new discovery of some kind."

"Indeed, and this might refute some of his claims of all these insurgents coming at us. If we reflect on that ship that once came for Elder Nazég, where the Marshal so fervently declared it to be these insurgents, then it seems they clearly know where we live. Why then would the Marshal have us chasing all over the galaxy for something that has a jump drive and enough technology to build not only that ship, but also this city structure, to say nothing of whatever military applications they might own. Furthermore is to ask about the location…four-dimensional space. How interesting it is for him to lead us all the way out there when our science so often denied it exists, and he forgot to tell us otherwise."

"Yes, that might be funny, if it were not so disturbing for his promises."

"And so, we sent agents to your ships out there, infiltrating one as a resident officer who made a secret attempt at contacting the locals. The only trouble was to establish a common form of communication, so we had to employ one of our secret weapons."

"A secret weapon to communicate?" he raises his brow.

"Telepathy…"

"Telepathy!" he shouts.

"Yes, Commander, this is one of those things Elder Nazég was researching once upon a time, but apparently no one gave him enough credit to know what he was talking about. It would seem our species is capable of employing telepathic communication. Our department knows a few people who still study the old metaphysics faction, even though it was technically outlawed, no thanks to the Council. These hidden studies are hoping to unravel those old mysteries. In the meantime, some of us have refined Elder Nazég's study of telepathy to the point where it becomes a viable form of communication. And fortunately for us, it worked on this occasion."

"I don't believe it! So, it actually works? And what did you learn from it?"

"We learned who the Marshal truly is, for one thing, although surprisingly, these others who actually do regard him as an enemy, also thought he and Sargeras were both dead several eternities ago."

"Several?" he winces. "That figures, and this might also offer an explanation of that encounter on Therinë which seemed like a new discovery."

"Yes, it was, and they let you go because you had your chip turned on…you, and maybe some portion of our military, which could become unpredictable if they did attack. Otherwise, they probably would've smitten you and your military outpost to ashes."

"Great…but I suppose I'll take my blessings wherever I can get them right now."

"And this generally brings us to the point of the Marshal and his most recent designs on that city. We are aware of his new submission, and it's truly a sinister plot if he hopes to use it as we suspect. This, if nothing else, probably WILL bring the wrath of these gods down on our heads."

"I wish you didn't just put it into those terms."

"Perhaps, but this is essentially who they are in relation to people like us. In order to evolve up to the point where you live in extradimensional space, you have essentially evolved OUT of a material environment like ours. And the capabilities of such beings as these goes well beyond us. And many of them mental, by the way. This would be a perfect exercise for someone like Elder Nazég and his metaphysics faction."

"How nice to know…now."

"Yes, I might agree. Our society, at that time, probably wasn't ready for it…and maybe still isn't. But now, we need to take a few steps of our own to correct the situation, and for this we need to make one or two compromises in order to keep it under our control."

"All right, I'm listening. What do you have in mind?"

"These people regard Sargeras and Darumon, and I'll use his name rather than his title, as he likely doesn't officially have one, as an ancient enemy that shouldn't even be alive right now. But for this, I should bring in someone who can better explain it…my contact."

Navina now turns away from the desk to an open space in the room, which at this point faced the door and coincidentally the ventilation duct on the wall above. Kaliya had been hiding inside and waiting for her cue. Navina then brought a hand up to her temple, as if she were going into a slight meditative trance to conduct her telepathy. It was merely a show at this point, but she needed to act the role in order to summon the mind of her so-called Celestial contact.

Kaliya was waiting for this moment. Now she had to make her grand appearance. So, she began to fold her image into the room, taking an extended moment to form her image out of a cloudy haze before refining it into her new shape.

Commander Geilv studied Navina intently for her strange behavior. But as he began to take notice of this otherworldly ghostlike image forming out of thin air, he could feel his heart fluttering. He tenuously stood up and backed away at the surreal apparition.

As Kaliya's final image coalesced out of her haze, Navina stood up and bowed politely to the divine visitation. Geilv observed the clearly reverent gesture and suddenly felt weak in the knees, so he braced himself on his desk and made a desperate attempt to follow in kind.

"This individual," Navina begins, "is a representative of those people. Although they don't really have any special issue with us as a species, our unfortunate circumstance of falling victim to Darumon and his schemes, and thus leading to so many of our actions, has caused them to take special notice, and therefore concern for not only the hazard we represent under his control mechanisms, but also the endangerment we might face if we should ever discover the truth about him. Furthermore, as he and Sargeras are regarded as perhaps the worst criminal entities ever known, they find it necessary to take action. But along the way, we find ourselves with a stipulation."

She sits down again and waves for Geilv to return to his as well. Kaliya waited patiently for the room to settle before she went into her act.

"The Great Powers are most displeased," she intones in her ghostly ethereal voice. "As are their Children, the Celestial societies. Together, we once believed the Ancient Ones had been removed from the Seas of Creation; purged from the web of the Measure of Balance, such that all other forms would be free of their eternal malice."

"Do you have a name for your people?" Geilv asks timidly.

"The Celestial societies are many and carry many names. The Great Powers, however, are most often addressed as the Societies of the Estelar. To such Children as thee and thine, thy nascent breed would define them perhaps in such form as divine spirits, if thou wouldst hold such custom. But our interpretation places thy breed as one of scientific devotion. Therefore, we might employ such terms to define them as those societies that have matured to the highest pinnacle of their development, and over such a period of time as to become eternal."

"That does indeed sound like it could qualify for a god, religious or not."

"Indeed, and so it is. The Celestial societies are their closest Children, as we did once arrive within their nurturing glow, perhaps in time to join among them when we will make our final transcendence. All others are regarded as the Children of Creation to us. Thou dost have far to travel in thy present form."

"And that tends to put things in a very clear perspective for me. Thank you. But now, how about the Marshal and Sargeras, how do we define them?"

"This title thou dost give is unbefitting, as he is a servant to his

Power, and in our eyes no more than a keeper of younger breeds. The other is one we do describe as an Ancient One, as this is how we perceive them to be. To the Great Powers, they do declare them as Primordials, and in this way infer their nature as an ancient society of similarly timeless measure, but also in such form as to describe them diminutively for their behaviors."

"Diminutively? Interesting. But this sounds like another society of gods."

"This is true, but theirs is a malevolent one. Deep within the mists of time, the two once came upon each other, as the Great Powers did travel across the Folds of Creation in their search to learn its Ways. It is said the Ancient Ones did precede the Powers, a society of earlier dominion. But their time did exceed its maturity, and their society did fall into decline. This would then permit the rise of the first of the Estelar."

"Would permit?" the Commander wonders. "Was there something holding them back during this time?"

"Indeed. It is interpreted by many that the Ancient Ones did hold such prominence of spirit that they would deny any other society a similar esteem."

"Oh great," he groans. "So, this is where he gets it. The Marshal… um, Darumon has a tendency to use a number of derogatory terms on other races. Then, this is to say they wouldn't let anyone rise up that high, maybe as a form of opposition?"

"This is correct. And when the two did finally meet, we believe the Great Powers did hold memories of the malice once visited upon the Child societies, and they did find this offensive."

"And this simply means these others, the Primordials, have a history of this behavior. Well, there go the Marshal's stories."

"It does. When the Estelar did find themselves with such authority that they could now decree justice for these offences, they did engage in pursuit of the Ancient Ones to eradicate their malice from the Seas of Creation."

"Wow, that sounds serious."

"And so, it became. Across a time almost unmeasured, the

Ancient Ones did fall, and the Estelar did take their place, thus granting upon the Child Races their nurturing care and guidance according to their rule, which they decree as the Measure of Balance, where all existence must form a balance of equilibrium between the polarities of positivity and negativity. This rule must bring the harmony of life and the fulfillment of existence. It is a rule the Ancient Ones did once hold in great contempt."

"Just for the sake of asking, how do you mean this? Other than for the opposition aspect, that is."

"They once did believe they should hold absolute authority over life, that existence was only by their decree and according to their design. But they did not hold respect for life. They would instead treat this element as amusement in their eyes, and not to be granted the privilege of growth."

"None at all? That figures. This might also reflect on his promises to us, but with no tangible results."

"Persistently, the Great Powers did purge the Ancient Ones from existence, until the last of their kind would be found within a Fold far to the core of the realms, a Fold they once did own."

"A Fold. This is interesting. Is this to say a space, like a universe, and at this point, it might be on the other side of things from where these Estelar first began?"

"It would indeed. But this fold is a curious one, in the modern moment. Within this Fold is a domain where we interpret thy kind did once send an invasion of unwelcome Children to a home of special interest."

"I, uh..."

"Commander," Navina interjects. "Maybe I can help interpret this for you. In our time trying to learn a few things, we had an opportunity to realize a number of terms. This was further enhanced by a series of history lessons we've been taking since then. We are speaking of an invasion of some sort that occurred once upon a time to a world Darumon apparently visited as part of what we're interpreting, at least recently, as a scouting run to spy on his old rivals. But this world is also the same one he more recently invaded...again...which resulted in your unexpected arrival of people on Therinë. THAT universe is where the last of these encounters occurred. That's where we think those two originally came from."

"Oh! So that's it!" he shouts. "He's trying to go back home to hit those people who…stole…it away from him. Yes, now it makes sense. And likely using that star-destroying bomb to finish it off."

"Yes, and this would not make for a very happy return visit."

"Now wait. Let me think for a moment. This is likely something we had during that one conversation. He was speaking about that invasion of orcs. But, um… Oh, wait. There was a mention of an earlier invasion, where the Marshal dropped more of them over there once upon a time. And this new invasion simply stirred up the existing population. So, here come those people to finish it on our side. Yes, I'm sure this would be a surprise."

"Thusly," Kaliya continues. "Within this Fold, and once again, did they discover the Ancient Ones to be conducting their malice. But here they did find such aberrant deeds as to create life for the mere satisfaction of their pleasures, to be entered into a contest of sport. This sport would decree the very existence of the participants. Of they who failed, their existence would be made forfeit. Life held no value to them, as they could always create more."

"In all the nether-space, no wonder he seems to take so much pleasure out of destroying things."

"The Great Powers were no less appalled, and they did impose their decree to bring this practice to an end, but the Ancient Ones did refuse. This would bring upon them the final judgment of the Powers, as the Ancient Ones did once again violate the Measure of Balance. This principle must define all things within the Seas of Creation, where existence must be maintained in harmony with itself."

"Incredible! So, do these Estelar actually govern such a thing as pure Existence?"

"The Measure of Balance is as much a practice as it is a philosophy. All things must be made to balance. This may include such as material substance, as it would energy, that these may not fall too far to one side and cause the cohesion of Existence to fail. But life is also described as an essence in this equation, as there may be positive as well as negative forms. Both are necessary to develop and nurture such young breeds as thine own to ensure their integrity and perseverance. To bring this out of balance can deliver them into entropy."

"I don't think I would want to see that for our people. So, how can we prevent this? Should we now take up a religion?" he chuckles feebly.

"The direction of thy breed is thine own to choose, and within this Fold, the Great Powers do not travel, as it is absent the dynamistic flows. These flows are necessary for their sustainment, no different from thee and thine own environmental needs."

"Dynamistic flows..." he muses. "This is a curious term you use. Are we speaking of... Oh, wait, would this have anything to do with that Abnormal Energy we were detecting out there?"

"When thou dost speak of curious terms, it is thine own that is curious. The flows are quite commonplace throughout the great Seas of Creation. What is abnormal is to find a Fold without them, such as this one."

"I see, so I'm basically sticking my hoof in my mouth now. Then, our interpretation is actually backwards. And no thanks to the Marshal, I'm sure. But why don't we see it here if this is considered abnormal?"

"This is an interesting quandary, and the Great Powers do study this Fold for this reason. It is our belief that this Fold is simply too young to have yet developed the integration of the essences that create these flows."

"That's actually very interesting. All right, so back to Sargeras and the, um...well, Darumon. We have our ships out there right now. This brings me to an immediate thought. I, um...well, I suppose we owe you something for the damage we caused. Do you require anything of us to offer repairs?"

"Although She who governs the city has not specified any demands, I can refer to her this suggestion for consideration. However, I feel her manners are more preferential to use her own attendants, as they are better versed in the inherent methods."

"All right, but let me know if she wants anything. I don't want to make myself appear the worse for not holding up to my responsibilities."

"Thine offer is noble and shall be recorded in thy favor."

"Now, about Darumon and his latest death toy…"

"Indeed, this is a curious term. He searches for an ancient Door that leads to the prison where the Great Powers did once entomb the surviving Ancient Ones during these conflicts. But the Powers would never permit their release, therefore his advance must be restrained, and he must be deterred from any further attempts. But here is where we must make our stipulation. He did once flee from the ancient battle; he and his Power. And we fear he could do so again if we make our advance so prominently known. They must be contained until we can close their escape, and for this, we must distract their attention by sending others into this Fold to disturb them."

"But don't you think that might still be a bit risky if he should put it together by these other bodies showing up that you're coming for him?"

"His reach will be limited without thy support, and the manner of their approach will be sufficient to distract his mind as to the origin of their breed."

"Interesting. All right, so this means we need to tolerate him a bit longer, and hope he doesn't try any more of his games along the way."

"Indeed, and we will assist thee as we have opportunity. But thou must also realize the presentation may invoke sensation within thee and thine own. The Ancient Ones are potent and must not foresee our advance even within thine own mind."

"Oops, but then what about this interview? If he has his own form of telepathy, couldn't he just see this conversation and know something?"

"He could, and therefore we must make a careful calculation of the risk. Thou must not give him incentive to impose himself upon thee. Thou must shield thy mind to his thoughts and distract thyself with other directives."

"I might further suggest," Navina adds, "that you simply keep out of his line of sight. If he doesn't make too many personal visits, don't give him reason to unless it becomes absolutely necessary."

"Understood…" he nods.

"As for the vessels thou dost have in proximity of the city," Kaliya's apparition continues. "Thou must offer them as part of this compromise. The Ancient One must see their loss and know that he has been discovered yet again."

"Uh oh…and what about our people?"

"We shall preserve them, along with thy vessels, but a demonstration must be made within his eyes."

"A demonstration? How do you mean?"

"Commander," Navina offers. "What we're thinking of is to put on a show, maybe to play on that same scenario as what you had on Therinë, but do this on the com-link. If we use an audio-only link, without video, we can limit what the Marshal actually sees… or doesn't see…of our activities, but the sounds would surely be convincing. It is my understanding they could simulate the sounds of an attack, and this would surely convince the Marshal to crawl back into his hole for a while."

"Really. All right, but then what will actually happen to our people?"

"We shall deliver them unto a domain we possess," Kaliya emits in her ghostly resonance. "There they will be attended until the Ancient One is removed. But they must understand the nature of this demand and comply willingly, that we may reach our conclusion together. Then we must prepare ourselves, first with our Children who will make this disturbance, and then to our movement as his eyes are turned away from us."

"I believe I understand. And will you communicate with us directly, or through these people here?" he directs at Navina.

"We will pass our thoughts through them, and they will direct thee from that moment."

"All right, I will agree to this."

Kaliya now offers a modest but polite bow of the head before fading away.

Geilv felt a subtle release of his tension at the conclusion of this interaction, but only insofar as knowing he had a way to get through the most immediate situation. It still left a lot of outstanding questions.

"Some kind of disturbance in our local space?" he muses.

"Commander," Navina resumes. "At this point, I would probably suggest you not ask too many more questions, as holding too much knowledge can be harmful. I know this is frustrating, and it leaves a lot of unknowns, but we need to play this out as if we have no idea of what's coming for us, just in case he has some other form of sensation besides telepathy to detect something happening around him."

"That doesn't sound good, for any of us, really."

"I know, and this is one of the reasons we need to keep such a low profile. If he doesn't suspect anything unusual out of us, he'll have no reason to make his own investigations, and at this point, it could involve his ability to shapeshift, as they call it, to impersonate someone else."

"Shapeshifting…" he winces. "Yes, I recall the Director at the ARC mentioning this. Ugh, that alone is a very dangerous ability."

"It is, and at the same time, we also need to start feeding a few of our own clues to the public. But they need to be carefully worded to make it seem as if it is someone else, like some group or organization with an innocent point of origin, is doing the work, to defray the attention while at the same time informing the public if we have anything critical they need to know."

"You people," he chuckles softly. "Just where did you train for all this?"

"In truth, Commander," she smiles softly. "Some of us are making it up as we go along. This is a new crisis we find ourselves in, and it requires a new set of rules."

She gets up and offers a bow before turning to leave the room.

Chapter 9

BABY STEPS

"Those are some really long teeth," Sulíma whines.

"Those could pass all the way through a person's neck!" Túfula considers.

"And out the other side with room to spare," Petrith affirms.

"And there's no way you're getting me to pet it," Sulíma gripes.

Relissa was in her final term for her ranger training, and she had a new pet to play with.

"Easy now, peeps," she announces. "She's tame, like all the others, but you still need to show a little backbone."

"My backbone ran out the other side of the courtyard the moment you arrived. So, what did you call it again?"

"This is one of those dire beasts. It goes by the name of Smilodon, or more commonly as a saber-toothed tiger."

"A tiger... Is it anything like that thing Kali did back on Ruuki uy'Daan by Camp One that scared the horns off poor little Tana?"

"Actually no, that would be a normal tiger. This is a different variety."

"And this one is real," Petrith adds, "whereas that other one was just Kali playing games."

"Yeah, and this one really does look hungry," Túfula observes, "as compared to that wolf you had before."

"Well, you can bet they're fierce predators," Relissa admits. "Those teeth aren't just for decoration. These beauties are fast, strong, and deadly to anything that gets in their way."

"And you would use this for scouting?" Sulíma whimpers incredulously.

"Probably not so much, I'd use smaller critters for that. This little girl would be for protection and combat."

"And what if it gets hungry for those smaller critters you mentioned?"

"She wouldn't do anything nasty. They would be trained up as a set. She'd know better than that."

"But Relissa," Túfula complains. "How do you maintain discipline over something twice your size and maybe several times your physical strength?"

"It's all part of the training, for both of us. You'd raise it as a cub, while bonding with it along the way. If you have other critters, you involve them at a young age, and they all grow up together, a wee bit like a family."

"Yes, a wee bit, as you say, because this would be the weirdest family I could ever imagine."

"The nice thing about big critters like this is if you're out in the wild and don't have much to use for a shelter except maybe the clothes on your back and a campfire, you can snuggle up together and share body heat."

"Right, and this is where I think I'll stay away from the ranger profession. Under the circumstances, I'm worried about what else I'd be sharing with it."

"Oh, Túfu, it's not so bad. It can also hunt and bring back food and serve as a lookout for danger. A big girl like this can hit your opponents from the side while they've got their sights set on you. Having a companion like this can be a great help."

"If you say so…"

The animal seemed content to lay next to Relissa on the ground as they spoke, casually preening itself and letting off an occasional muffled growl. From time to time, it would look up to observe the passing of individuals through the courtyard. For such a large and clearly dangerous creature, it behaved more like a kitten. Relissa would periodically reach down to scratch it behind the ears, and it would lazily shake its head in response to the tender touch.

"Well, I don't want to seem like I'm trying to escape from this scene," Petrith offers. "But I need to head over to Rolsklinde to meet with Thaelyn about my latest assignment."

"Are you sure you don't want to take me with you?" Sulíma moans.

"Suli, you'll be fine, so long as you don't rub barbeque sauce all over your body."

"Gee, thanks."

He gets up and gingerly steps over to the big cat, feeling reasonably confident that they have spent enough time together that he could try making contact. He kneels down a short distance away and reaches slowly out with one hand. The animal watches him curiously as he extends his hand around one ear to offer a gentle scratch. The cat cocks its head to the side to give easier access.

Petrith peers back at the two girls, who were gawking at the audacity of his maneuver. He displays a careful smirk, and then pulls back, turns with a wave, and slowly walks away, secretly hoping to maintain his desperate attempt at calm while he casually retreated from the scene.

He made his way through to Rolsklinde and into the WIC building for his meeting with Thaelyn, where he takes up seating at the table.

"My Lord," he bows politely, and then sits down.

"Ah yes, Mister Girhani. We are moving forward with another of our objectives, this one is to begin interfacing ourselves with their local media stream. You and Ayene will make up an official team deployment to their CPComm media hub, where you will begin our work with that Miss Ur'paran. Ayene has already been briefed, so follow her lead."

"Excellent, but along the way, I had a recent thought come to me, and I was hoping I could present this to you for consideration of another part of this little game we're playing."

"A recent thought?" he muses tenderly.

"Yes, it's for a little trick I thought of that could be very useful for us in the later term."

"A little trick, hmm," he wonders uncertainly.

"And of course, naturally, I would want to bring it to your attention before taking any sort of action."

"Oh!" Kailen blurts. "Is this the same young man who once took it upon himself to hack his way into our old Security Council mainframe just to see if he could do it?"

Thaelyn studies the two of them, and then lays his head in his hand and sighs deeply.

"Dear Powers," he moans. "This generation will likely be the end of me in this world. Very well, Mister Girhani, what sort of idea for a little trick do you have?"

"All right, here it goes, let me know what you think. From what we have so far, we're planning on making some sort of incursion in their local space to offer a distraction. But I think we don't want this to be so completely covered up and hidden behind so much censorship, as everything else was. I don't necessarily mean to say we want to start a panic, but those people need to know there IS some kind of force out there making advances, and in so doing, break their idea of all their comfy security due to the Marshal and his superior mind creating a superior military to fight such a superior enemy force which represents where he originally came from."

"In other words, those superior insurgents he kept describing are finally learning how to fight a proper war."

"Something to that effect... So, what do we need to inform them that their local space is actually coming under attack? Or at the very least, that someone in the higher positions feels that it could be. We need an alert network."

"An alert network, such as sirens perhaps?"

"On Ruuki uy'Daan, and I suppose on most of the other worlds we settled on, we had raid sirens installed to tell our people when it was time to leave."

"Ah! Yes, I recall this now from your stories. This is interesting."

"If we were to install these around all the major cities and towns as a kind of global alert network, we could provide a way to inform the citizens of a serious threat, and with Ytani out there, this is surely justifiable."

"Yes, it is, and so this would serve to break their perceptions of their local security after all this time fighting something that never seemed to make a local approach."

"Simply to see them being installed would already invoke them to ask questions about their security, as they apparently never had this before. And we could use it later when we make our actual play, as we want all of them to pay attention to our little show, which will be fully publicized and documented by Miss Ur'paran. This means, whatever it is they're doing has to be cut short, and then they run to their shelters where they'll have vid-com monitors showing them the news report she is putting on."

"Indeed, this is very clever. And here is where we tell our story of the Marshal in his true form, and likely with a lot of misery along the way for the obvious implications, but we cannot avoid that aspect of it."

"Their news media already has a considerable amount of coverage, not simply in people's homes and many offices, like in lunchrooms and recreation centers, but I've noticed a few large public video boards in some of their executive plazas, shopping malls, and other places."

"For the people who happen to be walking by to take notice of… yes. Theirs is a very well-connected environment."

"We can also link with their trans-com network to send an alert signal redirecting them to our emergency broadcasts if they happen to be elsewhere and out of view of a vid-com."

"Good, and this will give us a considerable amount of coverage. And further relating to their trans-coms, where it does seem everyone around there has one in a back pocket, this could possibly afford us access to those who are inside vehicles and such, perhaps to inform them to pull off the road so as not to cause accidents."

"That's a very good thought," Kailen affirms. "Also, to make room for emergency vehicles that might need the right of way."

"Indeed," Thaelyn nods. "Most excellent, Mister Girhani. We shall add this to our list, and we should also give instructions to our friends that they must provide for the people on how to respond to this. Discipline will be necessary here to actually react to these alerts rather than to simply stand there gawking at the flashing lights."

+ + ◆ + +

"Ghantil, we have a visitor," Azina announces through the door of the Director's office.

"Yes, Azina, bring him in."

Azina was escorting Commander Geilv through the ARC to meet with Director Bak'vayn. They were just arriving at his door. As the two of them enter, the Director stands up to greet them.

"Yes, Commander, how can I help you today?"

"Director, it would seem we have some work ahead of us. I had a meeting with an agent from the ACI, along with a, um…a contact she has amongst these godlike beings."

"In all the nether-space, Commander, was this in your office?"

"Yes, it was, and I only just this morning managed to return the curl back into my horns from it," he chuckles cautiously.

"Really!" he smiles. "And what was said during this time?"

"We're apparently going to work a plan together with those ships we have out by that city structure to play a little game on the Marshal, or whatever he might call himself. After that, they need to make a series of careful plans on how to advance on him and Sargeras, as both of them are considered a flight risk if they see them coming directly. As such, we're going to be experiencing a series of localized incursions of some kind, which I suppose we'll need to make sure the Marshal pays very close attention to…to the point where he starts losing the curl in HIS horns…" he grins gently, "…and until they can make a final move on them as a set."

"This is very interesting, but it also sounds complicated. And what role do we play here?"

"I need a time estimate on what it might take for you to complete the Marshal's last request. We're going to let him think we're following through on it, but then he'll be discovered along the way, and this will turn him around to go into hiding again."

"Wow…" Azina croons. "That sounds like a sharp yank of the tail."

"It's the only way. We need to…sacrifice…those ships we have out there."

"Wait a minute…sacrifice?"

"On the surface, at least," he nods. "This is part of our show, at least on the com-links, and he'll need to be present to hear it."

"Uh oh… And then, who is making these incursions?"

"People he shouldn't be able to associate with anyone, but I'm not supposed to know any more than this for the security threat I represent, which is rather disconcerting but unavoidable for whatever godlike senses he might have to see through it."

"I'm sorry to hear that, Commander," the Director ushers. "That must be very hard for you, especially as a military leader who needs to be aware of so many things. All right, we did some preliminary estimates on this job, realizing the Marshal will eventually start asking about it. Based on the design work that came with the order, and the quantity of canisters he is asking for, we have totaled up between seven and nine months."

"Seven to nine… How do you figure this, just for my information in case he asks."

"The dispenser unit is a custom job and will need to be subcontracted out to an engineering firm. We've done this before with those rocket-propelled seeds, among other things. Between the design work and the fabrication, all of which is custom, we are expecting four to six months for the quantity ordered. The canisters, on the other hand, once we properly tool our production lines, should move quickly enough, but the quantity, even in our automated facility, would likely take three months to complete."

"And you're adding these two numbers back-to-back?"

"I feel this would be to our best service, at the moment. Due to the nature of this design, I will claim the need for the completion of a dispenser prototype before we can be sure of the specifications for the canisters and the performance values. After all, we need to do a little product testing and validation."

"Understood. And up until now, you've been claiming a maintenance refit to your facility as a delay tactic, if my understanding is correct."

"Yes, Commander, and personally, I feel I can make this claim with some reasonable justification, so he shouldn't have right to complain too much."

"Let's hope so. Thank you, Director."

The Commander turns and leaves the office. Ghantil and Azina stare at each other for a moment longer until he is down the hall and out of earshot.

"Ghantil," she whispers. "What was that?"

"He mentioned the ACI, so this must be the work of those people."

"Clearly, but I mean that godlike alien thing. Did they actually bring someone down here, or was this another of those projections?"

"At this point, I have no idea. But I will say that Captain Nazég seems to be a very talented young lady. So, if this was another of her projections, she must've taken a special course of some kind."

✦✦✦✦✦

Kaliya, Kailen, and Tyanna were convening for a pleasant afternoon break in a local outdoor café in the small village setting outside the Naarg uy'Sodrad. This was a casual family affair which, unfortunately, could not include her father, Velen, due to the secure nature of the subject matter they would likely be discussing. He, as well as the rest of the Daanen'kai Elder Council, had to be kept in the dark over just about everything concerning the war and Kaliya's efforts on Azgarén. However, Tyanna was involved, at least as far as to keep informed, though she could not share this with anyone.

"The work on that base in the valley seems to be coming along nicely, so far," Kaliya mentions.

"I recall that valley," Tyanna reminisces. "It was a peaceful setting. To think it will soon become a battlefield…" she sighs.

"It's necessary, Mother. I'm sorry if we're spoiling any memories, but we need a foothold, and that's our best choice."

"I understand. Further, it's disheartening to think of how they damaged our home with so much industry and pollution. It will take a long time to recover, and I'm sure much of the ecology may have already been lost."

"Yes, but I hear there are a number of conservation centers around the globe trying to maintain a lot of species."

"Inside closed habitats, yes, but the world is not a laboratory where you can simply adjust a thermostat and a few regulators, and everything is maintained for another day. We need the natural cycles to clean our air and refresh the environment. Otherwise, we may as well be living on a world with no environment at all."

"Once we achieve our more immediate goals," Kailen considers. "I think His Lordship will likely assist our people to repair the damage."

"Our people…" Kaliya reflects. "And to think, it was only a handful of years ago when we described ourselves as Daanen-Aryku and THEM as The Suuden-Aryku."

Tyanna smiled at the suggestion.

"Yes, you were born on a world so far away from our home, and so disconnected from our people, I am not surprised you might think of us as an entirely different species by now. But in truth, we are not. If it were not for all the hardships we suffered, we might not even call ourselves Daanen-Aryku."

"You know, my interaction with Ayene and the others we 'liberated,' as well as those on Azgarén, has brought home the notion that we and they are actually much more alike than we might have ever believed. If it weren't for the hardships THEY suffered during this time, we would be virtually indistinguishable."

"But it was impossible for us to know about this before now," Kailen relents. "Our perspectives were always oriented as us versus them. We saw them as monsters, so we gave ourselves a different name to create something new…and to distance ourselves from our ancestral origins. So, are we Daanen-Aryku, or are we simply a disconnected faction of Suuden-Aryku?"

"Kailen," Tyanna offers. "Your father and I are the last two survivors of our original excursion, and we are Suuden-Aryku. We freely admit to this, as it is all we can say for ourselves. Whatever Darumon did to the rest notwithstanding, we are all Suuden-Aryku, and we must hold onto this, as it is a part of us. The term Daanen-Aryku was bandied about during much of our journey, and many began to use it as a de facto term to distinguish us from the rest, mostly due to the others taking on this hideous form. But I think it didn't come into official play until after we arrived on Ruuki uy'Daan, and these two terms came into our language together."

"But now we're returning home," Kaliya admits. "The exile is almost over."

"Yes," Kailen wonders. "But can we still describe ourselves the same as those on Azgarén?"

"I think we will all be wiser for the wear," Tyanna proposes. "All of us, on both sides."

"Wiser for the wear," Kaliya muses. "We were called away for a reason, much like a pilgrimage, to seek wisdom. Father's faction was never appreciated back home, but the wisdom we found will completely turn that around…and more so, as we now need to realize a higher purpose for ourselves. The Prodigy Gift, or Gifts, if we take it in plural for everything combined. This changes things for us. And that…wisdom. We need this. But there is still one difference we should probably consider. In fairness to Kailen's statement, we have to remember the blessing of the cu'Nar."

"Yes, this is correct. The others will not see us as quite the same by now."

"But what about the Maker in all this," Kailen considers. "If she demanded this of us, what about the rest?"

"My guess is the same," Kaliya accedes. "And this would homogenize us as a species again."

"An elevated one, to be sure," Tyanna surmises.

"I think we were elevated to begin with," she chuckles. "But we will be more enlightened now. And so, we are Suuden-Aryku…with softly glowing eyes," she smirks.

"I never thought I would hear something like that," Kailen smiles. "But if the Maker actually called us away, were we ever truly exiles?"

"No, messengers at best…and on that pilgrimage to learn the truth. But it was a hard road to travel. Now we're coming home, and this time as insurgents!" she laughs.

"Yeah, and for all the rhetoric the Marshal was throwing out there, that's a true irony of fate."

✦✦✦✦✦✦✦

Ayene and Petrith had arrived outside the large communications headquarters known as Capitol Prime Communications. It was a global provider of news and entertainment, and a prominent feature within the city. They entered the lobby to be greeted by an array of monitors presenting a myriad of network programming examples, along with posters featuring the most popular films and new up-coming shows.

As with so many other locations they've been visiting lately, they strolled up to the reception desk, where the young secretary looks up at the two of them to offer her greeting. But on seeing Ayene's face again, she suddenly felt a cold shiver run through her.

"Welcome to CPComm, um…Agent Ti'van, right?"

Ayene was dressed in her ACI costume again, while Petrith was in a military uniform to represent an associated security officer.

"That's right. Relax, we're on the same side this time."

"Oh, good. After that last meeting, you caused the curl to fall out of my horns. What can I help you with today?"

"We need to meet with the administrator again, and this time also Miss Ileani Ur'paran. We are choosing her to participate in a special project as part of our operations. Can you see if she is available?"

"Sure, one moment…"

The girl first makes a call on her vid-com to Ileani's desk.

"This is Ileani…"

"Ileani, this is Teela at the front desk. That ACI agent is back and wants to speak to you. Are you available…I hope?"

"Uh oh…now who's tail is going to get cut off. All right, yes, I'll come out in a moment."

"All right, and she wants to meet with Mister Kan'tarru again, so grab him on your way through."

"All right, why not…two tails for the price of one…"

They end the link, and the young lady directs her guests to wait several moments until Ileani and the Administrator both arrive in the lobby.

"Agent Ti'van?" the man announces. "Is there something you need from us?"

"Ah, Administrator, and Miss Ur'paran, do we have a private room we could use? This is a confidential matter."

"Of course, please follow me."

He leads them deeper into the building to a conference room, where they take up seating around the table. Ayene waits for them to settle before she begins.

"As you know, our operations are investigating a number of criminal acts and conspiracies, and we have made several very disturbing discoveries along the way. While we would not normally wish to keep these from the public, as we do believe they have a right to know, at the same time we do not want to cause any large-scale sensations or other forms of public disturbance, or even a panic of any kind, like for instance what that old Tav'ageen thing did once."

"Um, Miss Ti'van," Ileani interjects tenderly. "I was just wondering something if I may. Not that I want to get myself or anyone else in trouble here, but I spoke with the Director of the ARC some time ago and he told me a few things. I'm wondering now where all this might ultimately take us, especially if you're talking about public panics on the scale of the old Tav'ageen Scare."

"Indeed, these revelations are not for the faint of heart. And as for where it's going, we are going to pull you into our circle a little tighter. As for you, Administrator, I want you to know this is a secret project we are engaging in to release certain elements, but very carefully. I hate to use the term to regulate, especially due to our most recent history, but we must regulate this tightly in order to contain the results. Our enemy here is the Marshal."

"The Marshal!" he blasts.

"This coincides with what the Director was saying," Ileani offers. "At least that small amount he actually shared with me."

"From this moment," Ayene continues. "I am going to pass some special reports to you, configured in such a way so as not to implicate any specific individuals that could later come under his scrutiny for retaliation. He came here with ulterior motives, and none of it being what he claimed. So, Administrator, I need your support to permit this, and Ileani, you'll be my top news reporter to actually broadcast this."

"Oh, so does this mean I can actually play like a real reporter now...sort of?" she grins gently.

"Sort of..." Ayene returns the sentiment. "You will need to coordinate with our office whenever we have anything special to release, and it'll come in small pieces, because we don't want too many big sensations all at once to draw his attention. But if taken all together, we are going to start painting a picture, and hopefully a few of those people out there will start taking notice and begin asking those questions they forgot to ask several millennia ago."

"Um, one more question..." Ileani wonders as she glances at Petrith. "What's his role in this, if the Marshal and his military were censoring us before?"

"HIS military is now back to being OUR military. The High Commander took the initiative, due largely to our covert efforts to help him make a few of his own connections, and now he is working for us. But each branch of this tree must carry its own weight, and his hangs right under the Marshal...unfortunately. Until we can further progress our efforts in other areas, some of which I simply cannot reveal at this time, we need to play a game in his eyes. Meanwhile, the Lieutenant here had a marvelous idea back at our office that we wanted to share with you for a new emergency alert network."

* * *

"Commander," announces the raspy voice of the Marshal on the com-link. "Do we have an update from the ARC yet on that last special order I submitted?"

"Actually yes, Marshal. I received a brief notice that they are beginning the design work, after having much of their facility closed due to a detailed maintenance procedure. They tell us the design and manufacture of the product should take upwards of seven months, largely for reasons of safety and product testing to ensure it meets with your specifications."

"Seven months, is it?" he muses. "Hmm, very well, I suppose we can wait for it. After all, that city isn't going anywhere, and perhaps if we pull out of it for a time, those people inside can relax a bit, at least until we make our return..." he chuckles grimly. "Keep me informed, Commander."

"Yes, Marshal."

The link ends, leaving Geilv sitting there glaring at the terminal.

"Until we make our return..." he grumbles. "Yes, Marshal, we will make a return...but I don't guarantee the results."

He ponders the situation of his conversation with Navina and her Celestial contact, further with the Director at the ARC, and then once again to reflect on his past conversations with others in the military. He turns again to the com-link and dials up a number.

"This is Captain Ta'yeen in Control..."

"Captain, this is Geilv. I want you to join with me in my office for a meeting."

"Yes Sir, I'm on my way."

They end the link and Geilv waits several moments until the door buzzer sounds. The Captain enters promptly thereafter.

"Commander?" he inquires. "What do you need?"

"Sit with me," he directs at a chair. "This is an informal meeting and entirely confidential."

"Yes Sir."

"And when I say confidential, I would further advise you not even think about it unless you can ensure your isolation from the Marshal and any thought tampering he might make."

"Thought tampering?"

"For lack of a better term, yes. It is believed he could be telepathic, so if he should ever get any ideas of anyone misbehaving, all he might need to do is zero in on your thoughts to see what you've been doing."

"In all the nether-space! That sounds awful, and even worse for the obvious security implications."

"I know. I'm probably in the worst position of all, being his favorite pet."

"Sir, is there anything we can do to safeguard ourselves? And where did you first hear of this?"

"I had a meeting recently with an agent from a new government security agency calling itself the ACI, Azgarén Central Intelligence. It's a new planetary security agency going around right now investigating the Marshal, the Council, and who knows what else, including us for all those things we did under those chips."

"Uh oh... But I've never heard of this one before. Where did they come from?"

"I can't be sure where they came from originally, but they apparently carry a lot of authority and they're backed by some big friends. But here is where I'm calling on you to help. I need you to be my backup. We have a plan, and I need someone to watch my tail in case the Marshal gets nervous. So, I'm going to give you a few details, just enough to bring you in on the most important objectives, and if anything should happen to me, I want you to finish it...whatever IT is by that time."

"Sir, I wish you wouldn't speak like that."

"I know, but I have to think of our entire world population at this point, so listen up. Where that strange city structure is concerned, this ACI agent brought in a contact she apparently has among a race that is associated with the owners of that thing."

"What?" he gasps. "Someone made contact?"

"It would seem so. This ACI must have been watching us for a long time, at least as far back as Therinë and that encounter we had there. Someone or something frightened the Marshal, and they started asking questions about who or what, then to see us here and planting agents inside those ships. This is why the Captain turned mutinous on us…or rather the Marshal."

"So, these agents are turning our people against the Marshal. This is the reason he had that informant telling him those things no one else was supposed to know about. But then, how do these people know if everything was classified?"

"They're breaking a lot of codes to get inside."

"Um, Commander, should I mention the security concerns again?"

"You can if you want, but at this point, these are the Marshal's, and I'm regarding them as forfeit anyway. Everything he ever did was for his own interests, not ours."

"Sir, what else did these ACI people say about him? Do we know anything about the real story behind him?"

"Oh yes…I got a full briefing out of this one calling itself a Celestial. These people are very literally like gods, so whatever it was the Marshal pointed us at, claiming them to be his insurgents, were simply any world he could find to take pleasure out of from its destruction."

The Captain winced at the idea, and then turned away in disgust.

"Apparently," Geilv continues, "and by her words, SEVERAL eternities ago, which tells me they must have been hiding for a much longer time than anything the Marshal ever claimed, Sargeras and his kind got into a fight with a rival body of gods. They lost. The reason being he and his kind were once found to be doing more of the same as what we're seeing now. We're regarded as toys to them, I suppose…a form of entertainment. They can apparently create life as easily as we can grow crops in a field. So, if a single stalk of grain out of a million holds no independent value, it is the same for us."

"Wow, thank you, Sir. That certainly makes my day."

"I know the feeling. But as for these others, it's just the opposite. They apparently do care for life, including all those worlds we blasted while on those chips."

"Oops."

"This naturally reminds me of Therinë and that conversation I had with Thaelyn. And then that city structure, where they seem to remember us. I'm guessing we have been observed during this time, so they were probably waiting for us out there."

"Sir, I feel a need to ask what they have in mind for us if we're being regarded as criminals."

"They know about the chips, and the Marshal's control methods. So, they will excuse us, if only we learn our lessons."

"Wow, this is enough to cause my horns to fall off and never return."

"Welcome to the club. My impression, after this conversation, is that Sargeras and Darumon are apparently all that's left of their kind. But it's enough to stir things up so much that these others… this government authority, or whatever we might call them…wants them, and they're willing to come all the way over here to get them. But here we have a problem."

"I'm afraid to ask what that is, especially if it goes on the scale of gods now."

"The Marshal is pushing his way into a truckload of trouble with that city. I'm actually surprised he would even dare, especially after Therinë."

"You're right. If they found him over there, why would he try again here?"

"As far as I understand it, he's in hiding, and I recall once a conversation I shared with him a while back, where he was speaking of a race of beings he apparently corrupted on Therinë to follow him. He was wishing he still had them, as they might not stand out as much, and therefore allowing him to move around easier."

"Oh great! Well excuse me for my oversized horns!"

"Yes, well…" he chuckles. "In the absence of that, here we

are. I'm also thinking of that weapon now, and this would likely make a good target for it…meaning these other gods as a revenge tactic. They apparently occupy many other universes out there, if my interpretation is correct, and given the number of units Kriv'tik was making at that mining operation, this would represent a terrorist plot to beat all other terrorist plots."

"Yes, it would."

"So, our plan is this, and you'll need to play a role, as it is likely you'll be present at the time, and my acting skills don't stand up to much."

"And you think mine do?" he grins shyly.

"At this point, we'll both need to work at it. Anyway, he needs to lose that fleet out there, and in such a way that he doesn't try going back. What this means is, they need to be discovered by his old enemies, much like we were on Therinë, but this time it comes back to us. Captain, do you recall my mention of the Marshal sending something to the ARC? The ACI is calling these things his death toys, and this wasn't the first one. He apparently used several of those on Therinë, and who knows what else."

"Death toys! Well, that goes nicely with things."

"This one is apparently to launch canisters of poison gas at range, probably to suffocate the population so we have easier access to do our work. How do you like that for someone who once promised us great wisdom?"

"Does that great wisdom include the legal infractions we're committing along the way, or does this…god…think himself to be above such things?"

"Yeah, you have a point. Anyway, this would surely invoke a response, if nothing else did, and here is where that contact came in with a solution. We need to put on a show up there on the com-links, as if the Tul'ryk is coming under heavy attack by something godly, ultimately to be destroyed, and in such way as to make it seem they know who it is…again."

"Whoops! All right, but this is a show, so what really happens to our ship?"

"We're going to lose it from the scanners, and these others are going to take it away somewhere, along with the crew, for safe keeping until this whole thing blows over. But the point here is to make the Marshal dig himself a new hole and bury himself in it. This should keep him quiet for a while until they make their next move."

"All right, got it, but then what is the next move?"

"We're going to start seeing someone making REAL incursions in our local space, and this is to draw his attention to prevent his escape should he see these other gods making a direct approach, thus allowing them to sneak up on him like he's apparently been trying to do to them."

"And who is it making these incursions? How do we recognize them?"

"I don't know, and I'm not permitted to know for that telepathy issue of his. So, whatever it is, we won't know until it hits and does whatever it does. I only hope no one gets hurt along the way."

◆ ◆ ◆◆◆ ◆ ◆

"All right, Ileani," Ayene concludes. "Do you have all that? It's quite a list, but we're following a kind of script here."

"Yes Ma'am. This could actually be fun after a while. What about the people who work there? What do you think they'll do about this?"

"Everyone is on our orders right now. For them, it's business as usual, unless of course things get a little out-of-hand and they can no longer do their work as effectively," she grins mischievously.

"Why do I get the impression you're already having fun?"

"Because I'm getting a little of my own payback against that thing who calls himself a Marshal."

Ayene and Petrith were just finishing up at the conference with Ileani and her administrator. The meeting breaks up with Ayene leading her team out of the building.

"We'll visit Geilv in a few days' time for that alert system," she remarks. "I don't want to push these things too close together. It might appear too coincidental, and for now we should keep the low profile just a bit longer."

They seek out a secluded area out of sight and fold away from the local area, returning home to report to Kaliya at the WIC building.

"…And so," Ayene relates. "Right now, Ileani is collecting a news team to go on-site, so we need to prepare our people on this side."

"Excellent," Kaliya affirms. "My Lord, if you'll excuse us for a while."

"I hesitate to see what sort of mischief you may be getting into," he asserts warily. "But whatever it is, make it noteworthy."

"Thanks, my Lord. We'll save a news copy for you to review later."

Kaliya now leads the troupe out of the building and across to Tae'Eladar, where she joins with a literal army of her teammates.

"All right, everybody, listen up," she calls to the assembly. "We have a job to do that will come in multiple parts, building up to an ultimate climax. We all have our roles assigned, as well as our theatrical props, so let's show these people how things get done."

The crowd lets out a loud whoop before returning to their respective rooms to project themselves. They then pass around a number of large signs on posts, as well as posters on ropes to hang around their necks, and vanish from the scene.

On Azgarén, Ileani was taking a hover news van along the highway to a large industrial park located outside the city. This represented the nearest example of the Marshal's dirty industry in proximity for easy access.

The news van was bristling with communications equipment to broadcast a live news report back to their home station for immediate delivery over the airwaves. They sped along the roadways as they hurried towards their destination, coming into view of the broad industrial park and all the factories that were so clearly spewing out their obnoxious plumes of smoke.

Kaliya and her people had been accumulating in the area and taking up disguises as a group of local citizens conducting a rally, complete with protest signs and banners. On her arrival, Ayene made contact with the local administrators, identifying herself as an ACI agent and giving instructions on how this game was going to be played. Their role was essentially to ignore the activities outside, thus leaving the acting to Kaliya's teammates.

When Ileani arrived on the scene, Kaliya's people were going into action, parading around in circles, holding up their signs, and chanting over the downfall of this horrible polluting industry. Ileani brought her team into position and called in to her home station.

"CPComm, I'm ready," she announces on her microphone.

"Stand by, Ileani… We're going live in three, two, one…"

On vid-coms worldwide, as well as public video boards, and even the DataNet as a priority news flash, heads were turning at the sudden presentation of the theme music and imagery of the CPComm logo, which was accompanied by the announcement of an important live news broadcast.

> *"This is Ileani Ur'paran for C.P. News, and I am currently live at the Tulara-Rashk Industrial Park, located north of the city of Capitol Prime.*
>
> *Outside here, we are currently observing a rally taking place involving what could number several hundreds of local citizens who appear to be protesting the industry that has been operating in this park for so long a time. According to the leaders of this rally, they identify themselves as an environmentalist group that has apparently had enough of the pollution this, and other similar industrial parks have been producing since the first days these facilities were built. With me now is one of those leaders to speak on behalf of the organization that is behind this protest."*

Ileani now turns her attention to a local member who was one of Kaliya's teammates.

> *"Sir, can you tell me why specifically you have chosen to make this protest, and why now, after this industry has been in operation for as long as any of us can remember?"*

"Yes, I can, Miss Ur'paran. Our organization has tried countless times to petition the Council to reconsider these industrial parks for the outrageous pollution they create, which is actually in direct violation of Article Twenty-Three of the Charter of Laws relating to pollution control and waste management. These centers were once created as part of the old emergency condition that was imposed on our world during the early moments of the insurgent attacks, and the imperative need to develop our military body in order to fight back as part of our promise to give aid to the Marshal and Sargeras. But in that time, we have seen great success in our efforts at suppressing those same insurgent forces, and we feel it is long past due for that emergency condition to be relaxed so we can return to a more natural way of life for our people.

Meanwhile, these industries have been destroying our natural environment, and since it would seem we are still bound to this one world, and never once attempted to move beyond to colonize any other destination, not even a simple moon, it becomes obvious to the thinking mind that we need to take better care of the one we have now, and which we have always called home."

"Sir, these industries have been here for a long time, and even though I recall from our history that emergency condition of the insurgents, why do you think no one has come to this conclusion prior to this?"

"I think no one came to this conclusion earlier largely because they always expected the Council to take care of it once this situation of the insurgents came under control. Unfortunately, those insurgents never stopped coming at us. But as it turns out, our military, which is being led by the Marshal himself, has done a very fine job at keeping us safe right here at home. So much so, that we have never had a recorded attack here in our own space. This, alone, represents a justifiable cause for us to realize our military body has effectively deterred those people from making any direct advances

on us, and for this, I think it becomes clear that the emergency conditions are no longer necessary as they stand. We might still be at war with them, but that war has always been, and still is, somewhere else."

"So, what you are saying is the Council should relax the emergency condition on the statement that we might never have been, and at this point no longer seem to be under any direct threat here at home, therefore we might afford ourselves to reconsider such things as this industry that was rushed into service, correct?"

"Correct, but not only that, as it is not simply the fact that it was rushed into service and maintained this way for the duration of this imminent threat of these insurgents. It is also the fact that after nearly TEN MILLENNIA, we have not once recalled that we have the technology in our hands, and always did, to build a much cleaner form of industry. Just look at so many other examples of industry around the world that conform to the legal codes. The only reason this specialized military industry does not is due to the fact that it WAS rushed into service nearly TEN MILLENNIA ago, and never once reexamined or revised to update it with more efficient technology after that initial imperative condition which prompted it in the first place."

"But what about the Council in this equation? Surely, they should know about this, especially if this is a violation of Article Twenty-Three of the Charter of Laws. I cannot believe they would violate their own laws, at least not outside a reasonable circumstance of a declaration of war and whatever immediate demands it might make."

"I would agree, but the Council, as we all know, has been thoroughly preoccupied during this time with this deliberation they have been making for so long. As I said, we tried countless times to get them to reconsider these actions, but to no avail. In fact, the only response we ever got out of the Grand Hall was that they were busy with their deliberations and would get back to us if and when they ever had an opinion on anything. Well, Miss Ur'paran, they must not have much of an opinion on the weather, because my information tells me they do not go outside very often."

"I see, and so we have you out here making a public demonstration on the matter, hoping to do what...raise public awareness in the absence of the Council taking their own actions?"

"Precisely! Our hope is to draw the people into this, in an effort to inform the Council that we are most displeased with their lack of concern for the more common matters regarding the management of our world affairs. I do not know what it is they are actually deliberating in there, but this behind me is an important real-world issue that needs to be addressed. Therefore, Miss Ur'paran, we want this resolved now, either to have it corrected or to see it shut down completely, and not just this one behind us, but all of them that serve the same function."

"But one moment here... This industry was built to serve our military body in order to fight those insurgents. How do we justify shutting it down completely while we are still essentially in a state of war?"

"Miss Ur'paran, I recall a few elements of our history. We have been travelling around the galaxy for a much longer period of time than the duration of this war, and long before the Marshal arrived. If we were able to build any kind of ships for space travel in that time, and without this emergency rush-order industry, I think we should not have any trouble maintaining things. In fact, I cannot even be sure what it is they are making in there, other than that smoke you see coming up. Over the course of time, we had a number of people visit inside there, for instance serving *as inspectors, auditors, and whatnot, and they told us it does not even look like it could be producing viable products!"*

"What?!" she shrieks. "Wait a moment, then what are they actually making in there if not viable products for our military?"

"Miss Ur'paran, this is a very good question, one that should probably be directed at the Council, as they are the ones to authorize it. As for myself, some of the information I received from our past interactions goes a little like this. It begins with a raw materials processor. This makes good sense as a starting point. Then, it chains to an assembly plant producing intermediate products. This also makes sense. But this now chains to ANOTHER assembly plant to apparently refine and remanufacture those products, as if to say they were not the right specs to begin with. Finally, this chains to one more, which seems to be a recycling facility to grind them up and send them back to the beginning, meaning to say the original raw materials processor. This simply does not make sense."

Ileani glared at him as he finished his statement. She rolled her eyes at the camera, and finally turned towards the factory complex.

"But… If they are not making viable products, or any products at all, and it has been ongoing for so long… Who is in charge here?"

"A few of our people have been asking those same questions, but the administration offices can only tell us they are under a number of military contracts, and all with strict nondisclosure clauses, meaning they cannot answer these questions. But again, my contacts, who were these inspectors, tell me this also seems to extend even to the other members within the chain. This means, each factory does not seem to know where their product is coming from or going to."

"But that would mean…um…"

"What it means is whoever originally set this up, did not place a great amount of careful thought into coordinating this chain of production. Nevertheless, it all falls into the hands of the military, which I suppose also means the Marshal, as he is the one to ask for it, and of course the Council again to approve it. Maybe he had special needs to fulfill to fight these insurgents, and some part of this might actually serve that function…or did at one time. But clearly, a lot of it does not make any sense for where it's going now, except out the smokestack. And again, for so long a time, when it should have become clear, after a while, that our emergency condition was unwarranted once we saw a viable result of our engagements out there."

"I see, and this does indeed represent a very serious matter. I will look forward to hearing any new results you may have as we move forward to understand how and why this is occurring at all."

Ileani now turns fully to the camera to finish up.

"C.P. News, as I stand here and look at this crowd of people, I cannot recall the last time, or ever for that matter, when we had a rally of any kind protesting something. Surely, this will catch the attention of the Council and press them to give some kind of response. I am sure I speak for many others where all I need to do is look at the sky over my head to see the results of this industry. And while I certainly would not want to argue the value of this industry as it provided for our military needs, I think I must admit that same job could probably have been done just as effectively if we used those same eco-friendly techs we use on everything else. This is Ileani Ur'paran for C.P. News, live on the scene."

As Ileani closed up the report, Kaliya and Ayene were standing just offside observing the scene. With those final closing words, they glanced at each other and around the area as they gave their new instructions to the army of people active on the field. Ileani marched up to the pair once the cameras were turned off. She gazed at them inquisitively as they wrapped up the demonstration and started dispersing the crowd. Kaliya then returned to the group with her final words.

"And so, it begins," she croons.

TO BE CONTINUED